Faded Rainbows

Psychospiritual Therapeutic Journeys

Marsha,
   Thank you for all your support
during my journey to bring this
book to fruition.
      Stay Vibrant!
            Shar

SHARON HUTSON CHESTON, ED.D.

iUniverse, Inc.
New York   Bloomington

D1207926

Faded Rainbows
Psychospiritual Therapeutic Journeys

iUniverse books may be ordered through booksellers or by contacting:

iUniverse
1663 Liberty Drive
Bloomington, IN 47403
www.iuniverse.com
1-800-Authors (1-800-288-4677)

ISBN: 978-0-595-53095-3 (pbk)
ISBN: 978-0-595-63152-0 (ebk)

Printed in the United States of America

Despite the human capacity to survive and adapt, traumatic experiences can alter people's psychological, biological, and social equilibrium to such a degree that the memory of one particular event comes to taint all other experiences, spoiling appreciation of the present. This tyranny of the past interferes with the ability to pay attention to both new and familiar situations. When people come to concentrate selectively on reminders of their past, life tends to become colorless, and contemporary experience ceases to be a teacher.

(van der Kolk, McFarlane, & Weisaeth, 2006)

Acknowledgements

I dedicate this book to all those who have taught me about therapy. Specifically, I wish to thank my:
Clients
Supervisees
Students
Colleagues

Chapter One
The Hospitality of Intake

> [Traumatic events] undermine the belief systems that give meaning to human experience. They violate the victim's faith in a natural or divine order and cast the victim into a state of existential crisis.
>
> (Judith Herman, 1992, p. 51)

Mary Elizabeth (Lisa) O'Hara

Being a mental health counselor is similar to being a firefighter. Some days, the task is to educate clients to recognize the warning signs that can save them from their pain and suffering, while other days the task is to attend to the five-alarm emotional fire that can lead to crippling trauma or even death. However, like most helpers, such as firefighters, we often neglect ourselves in service to helping others who are in crisis. In graduate school we are taught to bond with our clients by demonstrating essential relationship skills, such as empathy, faith in their ability to heal, and unconditional positive regard. However, one quality that's difficult to teach is the humility to know that we do not work alone and that, despite our graduate degrees, we are all wounded healers (Nouwen, 1979). Rather than being an impediment, the woundedness informs us,

1

keeps us honest, and brings us to our knees so that, ironically, we can be more effective.

As a mental health counselor for over 20 years, I have seen hundreds of clients who have been so damaged by life that their life essences seem to have drained out of them. They report walking through life feeling wounded, feeling half alive or, as one client put it, "half ghost". As you can imagine, the hours and hours of listening to others' problems often leave me feeling drained, half full of life, half ghost. To rejuvenate, I spend at least one week out of every year traveling by myself. During that time I speak few words, a relief from the deluge of words I experience every day. In the silence, I find myself again, reconnect with the holy, and refuel the half-empty tank.

One of my early traveling experiences that was particularly meaningful to me involved a two week trip driving throughout the western U.S. Beginning in Sioux City and driving a rental a car, I traveled through landscapes I had only previously seen in movies. My first stop, the Badlands, which really aren't Bad Lands, de-stressed my over-taxed brain. The Badlands are rugged, punctuated with delightful groundhog colonies. I was intrigued with the brave chubby little rodents who popped out of their holes in the middle of herds of grazing bison. Each bison weighs approximately 2000 pounds and I sat for an hour contemplating whether the bison hurt the groundhogs as they hauled their huge bodies around, stepping wherever they wanted, possibly even on a groundhog. I also wondered if the groundhogs in an indirect way harmed the bison. Do the bison step into the groundhogs' holes and break their legs?

These are the thoughts of a person in need of rest. The Badlands, Custer State Park, Mount Rushmore all satisfied my tourism need. However, when I arrived at the unfinished mountain-statue of Crazy Horse I felt inspired. I almost skipped it when I read that the monument was first begun in 1948 and was only 10% completed. I thought I'd come back later when there was more to see. Then the importance dawned, 55 years and only 10% finished? Why? So, I talked myself into seeing this marvel of human tenacity, a metaphor for my clients and for myself. For after all, when would I ever be out here again to see it? And even if I did return in 10 years, it may only be 12% completed.

Looking at Crazy Horse's face, part of his arm, and a mere outline of the horse's head carved into the mountain, I sensed the slow, persistent, daily movement of tons of earth. Inch by inch the mountain is being carved into a beautiful sculpture. This metaphor for how counseling works was the unconscious insight I sensed might be lurking beneath my mocking dismissal of the Crazy Horse sight as I had read in the brochure. Hour by hour, day by day, the client makes small changes chipping away at the mountain of pain that seems as insignificant as moving a teaspoon of earth, but in reality is change that reveals a work of art.

The insight was punctuated further as I perused the museum and heard the Native American's words, "Most humans think of themselves as a body with a spirit, but the truth is we are spirits with a body." I felt my spirit, in my body, and experienced the torrent of energy filling my half empty container. If the men and women working tirelessly on the monument, know that most of them will never see its completion, then I could work tirelessly for a few months knowing that I will never see the total completion of my clients' transformations. I silently uttered a prayer that God would grant me the tenacity to hang in there with my clients, as they tell their five-alarm fire stories and their minutia of movement that can be discouraging. I also prayed for the tools to intervene so I could be part of the transformation of their personal monument.

Leaving Crazy Horse and driving toward Yellowstone, I felt a light-headed, ethereal sense of self from the rejuvenation. A few teaspoons of change had shifted in me and the sky had a shifting, different look, too. Because of the flat terrain, I could see for miles, and as I drove toward my next destination I saw the dark roiling clouds signaling a summer storm. The sky was pea green around the enormous thunderclouds and, having lived in the Midwest for six years, I knew the signature of a possible tornado. However, from the manner in which the storm moved, I could also tell I was going to be driving parallel to its major threat. Still, the weather cell alternately shook my rental car with wind gusts, pummeled the earth with torrential rain, stopped, and allowed the sun to emerge.

I knew this was the perfect time to see a rainbow. I watched and waited as I drove, praying for that sign of hope, that covenant with humans that God made thousands of years ago. But, for me, no luck, no rainbow. The sky darkened again and more rain and wind buffeted my car, and again the sky lightened and I looked for the colorful bow. Still nothing. After two hours of driving in the rain, wind, and anticipation of a rainbow, I was exhausted. I needed to stop and get something to drink, preferably with some caffeine. The rain occluded my vision of the land ahead, so by the time I saw the small old fashioned gas station with a roadside diner, I almost missed the turn into the driveway. It was bustling with travelers, who had the same idea. The ambience was warm and upbeat inside, while the storm raged outside. I heard the waitress tell the patron in the booth next to me that a twister had been spotted 20 miles south. I smiled. All those years enduring the multiple tornado alerts had paid off. I knew the pea green sky held the possibility of a funnel. I was grateful to be inside and even though a tornado would not be stopped by a building, it's still an illusion of safety. (Thus, a second metaphor emerged on this trip. We often ignore or deny danger signs while intense trauma swirls around us.)

After filling my gas tank and my stomach with some homemade apple pie and black-tea, I was on the road again, trying to make Yellowstone by nightfall. The sky was much clearer, but many clouds remained and the rain lingered in the air. "Rainbows." I declared out loud. "I need a rainbow." Then slightly, shyly almost, the colors in the southwest sky began to take form. I could see the red shading to yellow and a bit of the blues, but it was faded as if it was trying to please me and just couldn't muster the energy to become vibrant. The storm's explosive violence had exhausted itself. I was disappointed and muttered, "story of my life, only a **faded** rainbow."

Instantly, I felt ashamed. Even during my personal crises and trials, my life has been meaningful and often produced undesired but necessary growth. Most of my clients think that because I have so much training and experience, I must have a near perfect life. I wish. Unfortunately, life doesn't give us a bonus because we have an education or a respected career. Life is just life. And counselors are no more impervious to the traumas, disappointments, and tragedies of life than anyone else. I'm grateful for one thing: I do have resources to deal with life's struggles. I don't use them perfectly, but I know what I must do for myself in order to continue the work with which I have been blessed. This type of vacation is one example of what I do for me, and this time it was working very well.

I got out of my car, stood by the side of the road with the wind and rain softly saying "goodbye", and watched the rainbow trying to form, as an apology for the tortuous storm. Alone, on the side of a rain-soaked two-lane road in the middle of nowhere, I realized the rainbow's message was not **about** me but **for** me. Its message held meaning for my clients' lives. They are often faded beings, who try their best to live with what they have been given, but storms keep pounding them and they quickly lose whatever vibrancy they muster between squalls. They lose heart and become discouraged, and when I sit with them, I can see them trying to form their rainbow of hope as they move their miniscule bits of earth to make beauty out of pain. Some days the bow becomes visible, but frequently it takes weeks and weeks to remove the dismal dirt of pain, which hides their true selves. With some clients I never see the colorful, vibrant bow; I only see the faded efforts of shimmerings, like this summer rainbow in Wyoming.

Wood Allen said, "If you are not failing every now and again, it's a sign that you're not doing anything innovative." I found my ideal career by failing.

I decided in college to major in K-12 education and become an elementary school teacher. I knew from the time I was 8 years old that I had the ability to take complicated information and break it down into manageable portions so others could understand it. I found myself tutoring my peers, and I enjoyed helping them. Perhaps it gave me a sense of power, at least that's what my first shrink said years ago. But 'helping' didn't feel like a power play, I felt I was contributing in a small way, assisting another kid so she could succeed. Those very early years I developed what one counseling theorist called "social interest", the need to contribute to the common good (Sweeney, 1998).

When I declared my elementary education major in college, I also chose to minor in psychology. At the time, I believed that the minor in psychology would give me insight into the psyches of the children I taught.

Graduating with honors led to an excellent opportunity to work in one of the best elementary schools in the state. I was thrilled about my first real job, with benefits! The school system assigned me to teach third grade, and I spent my entire summer creating lesson plans, devising teaching strategies, and designing my bulletin boards. I think I spent more money on supplies than I made. The first year went well. I loved the kids, and they said they loved me. I had good relationships with my fellow teachers and the principal, Ms. Smitts. Her evaluations of my teaching, based on in-class observations, were outstanding. However, she warned me about becoming too engaged in my students' personal lives. This puzzled me. I thought the more I knew about my students, the better equipped I was to teach them and understand them when they had difficulties. The students frequently confided in me about their home lives, and I honored their confidentiality. I flourished as a teacher and accepted the second year contract with enthusiasm.

The second year was equally exciting. I had positive relationships with all of my students. A couple of students were more difficult than others, but I was even able to bond with them. Half way through my second year, my principal decided to spend three hours in my classroom. She said she wanted to find out how I was creating such a great learning environment. She wanted to see what I was doing! I was thrilled with the compliment. However, after the observation, my principal looked puzzled. She slowly approached me as the children were exiting the classroom. Finally, we were alone and she said something to me I will never forget and something that forever changed the course of my life. She said, "Lisa, you're a great teacher, but you're not cut out to be an elementary school teacher." I was flabbergasted. "What?" I gasped. She tried to explain it several different ways, but I couldn't grapple with what she was telling me. I felt like a failure. I'm a good teacher, but I'm not cut out to be a teacher. What did that mean? Ms. Smitts tried to explain. "You get too involved with the students on a personal level, and while that meant the students love you and respect you, the involvement puts you in a position of being more of their counselor than their teacher." I was only 24 years old, and I believed I knew better. I once again received excellent end-of-the-year reviews and a third contract...but I was thrown into a funk. I was doing something that Ms. Smitts thought was incongruent with good teaching, yet she said I was an excellent teacher. I just didn't get it. So I did the mature thing, I pouted.

I had a difficult class in my third year of teaching. The students didn't get along with each other, and they didn't seem to want to learn. I was becoming discouraged and wondered if the students were more difficult or whether I was not on my game because of Ms. Smitts' comment the previous year. Blaming the third year experience on her comment helped me avoid culpability for my difficult year and let myself off the hook. Then one of my brightest students, Cheryl, started doing poorly in her studies. I contacted her parents, but they avoided revealing what was going on at home. I began to feel a little paranoid. Had Ms. Smitts talked to the parents and asked them not to share personal information with me? Would she do that? I withdrew at school and just spoke when spoken to. It was an infantile thing to do, but I was only 25 and I had been shaken at my core. If Ms. Smitts noticed my withdrawal, she didn't say anything, which added to the belief she was setting me up to learn how to be a teacher without becoming involved in my students' lives. I considered changing schools. Then, one day, Cheryl went into convulsions in the lunchroom. An ambulance was called, and they took Cheryl to the hospital. I wanted to accompany Cheryl to the hospital, but I didn't even suggest it. I knew what Ms. Smitts would have said.

That night, I debated about whether I should call Cheryl's parents. If this had happened in my first two years, I would have called her parents immediately, but now I was questioning myself everyday. I didn't know what to do. I decided to err on the side of being who I was instead of doing what I was told to do. I called. Cheryl's grandmother answered the phone and started crying as soon as I introduced myself. Through her tears, I heard her say

Cheryl was dying. My heart almost stopped; my head felt fuzzy. The words didn't make sense. Then her grandmother told me Cheryl had a congenital condition. The parents knew someday it would kill her. They had decided not to tell anyone so that Cheryl would not be treated differently. She said she didn't know what the condition was called, because it had a long medical name. I politely said all the kind and encouraging things. one says in a situation like this, hung up the phone, and vomited.

I felt sad, blindsided, enraged, and frustrated. I resented the family's decision to withhold information that affected **my** student. I was so self-absorbed about how I had been kept out of the loop concerning Cheryl's condition, that I forgot about Cheryl's parents' pain. I kept thinking that if I had known, I could have helped Cheryl more. I realized Ms. Smitts was correct. I was supposed to be a teacher, not the students' counselor. Who was I, that I should be privy to my students' personal information? Cheryl's parents had every right to withhold the information from me. I was not part of their family.

The next day, I went to school and Ms. Smitts was waiting for me. She told me Cheryl had died. I began to shake and cry uncontrollably. Mrs Smitts sent me home. In the midst of my despair, I called a counselor and entered therapy for the first time in my life. It was the best decision I ever made. For the next six months I unloaded my personal garbage, and the counselor became an important part of my life. I told her everything, EVERYTHING, and it felt so good to share my inner most self. Even though I was not Catholic, I believed that counseling must be like confession. I learned about myself and why I work the way I do. I learned to reel in my projections and to narrow my expectations of others. I left therapy knowing I was a good teacher, I had poor, but not inappropriate, boundaries with my students, and I could continue to be a teacher. However, I also knew I didn't have to be a teacher if I didn't want to be.

I met George during my six months in therapy, and we fell in love. The change in my life style began a process of desiring additional changes. I worked as a teacher for one final year during which George and I married, and then enrolled in my first master's level counseling classes. Two years later, I had my master's degree and was pregnant with our first child. Change was good. Life was good. I discovered that I fit in the counseling profession even better than I fit in the teaching profession. One day while stroking my pregnant belly, I realized that life is a series of stepping stones. You can't jump over critical ones in order to reach the next one. Each stone must be touched for learning to occur. I had to become a teacher in order to find my way to counseling. Through counseling I learned I wanted to further my education. Life is not an "is", life is a "becoming". Just as children step from one grade to another or one subject to another as they grow and develop new skills, so do we all move through life learning from each experience. Ms. Smitts was wise, and I had the chance to tell her before she died several years ago. Cheryl also taught me an important but painful lesson, but I never had the chance to say goodbye to her. Today, my spirit believes that she's aware of the role she played in helping me take the next step, as she took the next step to another life. That was over 25 years ago.

Casper Rheems (Caz)

The bell signals the arrival of my new client. I welcome Casper Rheems with a handshake and a smile, the signature of hospitality that I use to make clients feel welcomed. Clients are often anxious about beginning counseling with a stranger who expects them to unpack their deepest secrets, closeted fears, cherished misperceptions, worries that fetter them, and behaviors that defeat their dreams. A welcoming presence helps to sooth the jittery innards. I call this welcoming "counseling hospitality".

Casper immediately informs me that he prefers to be called Caz. He's 28 years old, Caucasian, never married, six foot six inches, and the facial expression of a 10 year old boy. His rosy cheeks, blue eyes, lack of facial hair, and a buzz cut add to the total gestalt of a giant little boy. Caz is dressed as if he were a 13 year old riding a skateboard, baggy shorts slung low on his hips with his underwear showing a bit, an extra large, colorful shirt, huge multi-colored athletic shoes, and a baseball cap. He shyly offers his limp, cold hand, and then hangs his head mumbling that his father drove him to the session. Caz asks how long the session will last so he can tell his father. I observe the incongruence in his size and his mannerisms. I reply that a first session is usually one and a half hours including paperwork, and subsequent sessions will be 50 minutes. He nods and opens the front door to my suite, goes to the end of the hall, opens the door to the second floor balcony, leans over, and yells the information to his father, who is waiting in the car. Not one of my clients has ever done **that** before, even my teenagers.

Caz was referred to me by his priest, Pastor Craig Morris, who left a message on my voicemail informing me that Caz' story is difficult and very complicated. He added, as an after thought, that the church is somewhat culpable in this case, so the Diocese will pay half of my fee and help Caz in any way possible because Caz is unemployed and has no financial resources. When Caz' father called to schedule the appointment, he volunteered to pay the other half of my fee. I was intrigued. How's Caz' church involved.

Caz completes the intake forms and signs the HIPAA regulations form. Included in the pile of forms are Authorizations for Disclosure of Confidential Information. The forms state that Caz is permitting me to talk his psychiatrist as well as Pastor Morris and the Diocese, if necessary. He doesn't ask any questions about why I want to talk to his priest and his psychiatrist. He simply signs the forms and looks at me expectantly. I tell him anyway. "Because the church is somehow involved in your situation and is paying for part of the session, I may need to talk with Pastor Craig if I have questions you can't answer. I also I want your permission to talk to your psychiatrist about your medications." Caz nods. Caz gives away his rights quickly. Of course, selfishly, this is easier for me. Sometimes clients ask a lot of questions before signing or resist signing the release forms because they want to be in control of the content of the therapy sessions and don't want me to have any alternative information or views of their situation. My paranoid clients usually jump out of their seats and run for the door when I pull out a release form. Not Caz, he simply nods and signs the releases.

I also check out Caz' alcohol and drug history (which is not impressive), the presence or absence of suicidal or homicidal ideation (which he reports as nil), and his medications (which he readily lists). Finally, I explain, as I do with all new clients, what counseling is and isn't, along with a brief synopsis of boundary setting (confidentiality, session times, lateness, cancellations, etc.). Caz sits quietly, nodding occasionally like he's been through all this before.

Caz
Reticence and Intrigue

I dread starting counseling again. I've been in and out of counseling and mental institutions since I was six and have seen all types of mental health people. No one helped. I guess most of them meant well, but they got tired of me and stopped caring. I'm sick and tired of others acting like they're interested at first and then withdrawing their support just as I need it. Screw 'em.

My father and Pastor Craig are insisting that I "do this for myself" and Dad set up the appointment with her. Others in my church have seen Lisa for counseling. They said she's compassionate and knowledgeable. They also told me she has faith in God. That's good. I'm trying to be positive, but I'm tired of this counseling crap. Entering her office feels like "here we go again". She seems friendly enough, but they all do at first. The question is will she have patience? Will she hear my story and not just be interested in the gory details? Will she be interested in ME? Will she know how to help me? Will she secretly laugh at my belief in God? My psychiatrist just nods when I speak of church and my faith. I think he's an agnostic or an atheist, so I pray for him. The counselor I saw when I was six used to say "That's nice." in a high pitched irritating voice when I would tell her how much I loved God. At first I liked what she said, but as I got older I realized "That's nice." was all she ever said and then she immediately changed the subject. My counselors at the inpatient settings didn't acknowledge or disapprove of my faith. They simply called my priest to handle the faith piece.

I hope, with Lisa, I will be able to talk about God and she won't say "That's nice." She has a kind face, and she dresses nice, more casual than most of my shrinks. She smiles as she introduces herself and asks questions. I feel she has a nice aura about her. I want to be able to read auras sometime in the future, but right now all I can do is get a feeling about the person. I sense she is a good person. We'll see.

She asks me why I've decided to come to counseling. Sure is a loaded question! I've been receiving mental health services since I was six. Where should I start? I was fired from five jobs in the last five years. I had sex with a church worker from the age of six through 16. My mom walked out on me, my brother, and father when I was five. I was kicked out of college with only a year to go. I'm seeing a psychiatrist I don't trust. I have no male friends, no girl friends, no money, and I can't sleep.

"Where should I start?" I ask Lisa. She responds with, "Wherever you want." Crap! That doesn't help. I hate when they do that, turn-it-back-to-me garbage. Maybe I should dump on her so she'll feel overwhelmed and drop me. So I say...

"I have been depressed most of my life. I don't sleep well. I don't feel like doing anything so I watch TV most of the day. I've been told I apologize for things that are not my fault. I can't stay focused on stuff. I also feel jittery and keyed up and even panicky at times. Sometimes I feel like every muscle in my body is a rock. I don't know what's wrong with me, and neither does anyone else. I never feel good. I can't imagine anyone thinking I'm worth their time. When I think about the things that have happened in my life, I get sick. I have a crappy life."

Lisa doesn't look overwhelmed. I've given that schpeel before, and I can tell when the counselor gets scared. The eyes dilate and glaze over. Lisa remains cool. Can she handle it? I continue...

"My mother told me I was "a difficult birth", as she put it. She thought I was deprived of oxygen because the cord was around my neck. No one's ever confirmed this and my mom lies, so I don't know if it's true. I do know I have a learning disability and ADHD (Attention Deficit-Hyperactivity Disorder). I've always been very artistic and not very good at math and science. When I was five, my mother said "I've had enough of these brats!" and packed her bag and left me and my four year old brother alone in the house. My father came home five hours later and found out his wife had walked out and left us kids alone. He was crazy with anger and said words that I didn't understand at the time. I thought he was pissed at me for causing Mom to leave us. I became so depressed that one day I talked Rom (that's my brother) into killing ourselves. I tried to hang both Rom and me, but I didn't know how to tie the knot right and we fell. Dad heard the crash and came running into our room. We were sitting on the floor crying with ropes and chairs all around. He cursed a lot, picked us up, and took us to a doctor.

That night I spent my first night in a psychiatric hospital. I turned six two days later. They said I was "profoundly depressed" and gave me some kind of drug. Don't remember the name. While I was there, they tested me for ADHD and learning disabilities and proclaimed I had both. I was given Ritalin and some information about how to learn my school work in a different way. I think I was there about a week, maybe two."

Lisa's still listening intently. She hasn't said anything except an "hmm", or "uh huh." Doesn't she need to take notes? Wait a minute; she's going to ask a question. I bet it's one of those questions that can't be answered, like "How does that make you feel?" I hate when they do that. She surprises me with "Why did you think that your mother left because of you?"

"I, I don't know exactly, but I remember my mother being really irritated with me when she would tell me to do two things, and I would get distracted between thing one and thing two. She'd yell and call me names I didn't understand. She said I didn't listen, and she said I was driving her crazy."

Lisa looks puzzled. I wonder if I said something wrong. She's following up with another question. "Do you think you were different than other five year olds in that respect, getting distracted like that?" Whew, that's an easy one. The answer is "Yes". Lisa asks, "How would you know you were different from other kids when you were just five years old?" I never thought about how I knew this. I just knew. She stumped me. I'll give her one thing; she listens and asks good questions. Silence. I'm trying to figure out how I knew I was driving mom crazy at five and that I was different from other kids my age. Images of my five year old existence are flashing through my head... "I KNOW!"

Lisa smiles, "Tell me."

"I know because Rom didn't drive mom crazy. He always did exactly what she and dad asked him to do. He never got into trouble for getting distracted or for not doing what he was told."

There, I did it! I figured it out. This counseling's better. More intriguing. Ok, bring on the other questions...I fold my arms and look at her. Lisa nods and says, "I'm impressed. You were able to reach back in time and figure something out very quickly. So here's another question for you. How do you know you were different from other five year olds -- rather than Rom was different from other four year olds?" I don't get her question. I must look confused because she asks it differently. "Caz, five year olds are usually a bit spacey when it comes to following directions. Yet, you seem to think that because you got lost between task number one and task number two, that you were an unusual child. Why? Because Rom didn't get lost? Perhaps it was Rom who was the unusual four year old child because he could follow instructions better than most five year olds."

I have to admit, she's got a point. I never thought about it like that. "Rom's really smart and he always made me look retarded. But I have a learning disability and ADHD, so doesn't that account for it?"

Lisa doesn't look convinced. She thinks before she speaks. "Well, you may have a learning disability and ADHD, but you were tested at a very difficult time in your life. Your mother had left, and you were depressed because you thought it was your fault. Perhaps all the trauma and stress affected the testing, perhaps not. Have you ever been retested?"

Whoa, she's right. I was never retested. My father and my teachers just assumed because I was tested, that was that. "So what do you suggest?"

"I'm not suggesting anything at the moment except you might want to rethink some of the assumptions you made as a five year old. Assumptions you still hold. Some of them may not be true. You may have been a perfectly normal five year old child who compared himself, and was compared by his parents, to a brother who was unusually cooperative as a four year old. You think you were not normal and you still think you're not normal. You may want to consider how that affects your view of yourself. You may also want to consider getting tested again, now that you're an adult."

I get it. "Yea, I never considered that." Lisa's picking up her calendar so I guess our session is over.

"Caz, how do you feel about working with me? Are you comfortable about the work we've done so far?"

"Yeah, I guess." I shrug. What am I doing? I want to scream 'YES', but all I say is, "I guess". Why don't I want her to know how I'm feeling? Geez, I'm so screwed up. Lisa is looking at me curiously. She's picking up my ambivalence.

"Are you sure? I can make a referral if you'd rather work with someone else. A man perhaps?"

I'm feeling panicky. Is she rejecting me? Was I not good enough? She thinks I might want someone else. I don't. I need to come clean or I might get myself referred/rejected. "I guess I'm comfortable with you, but I'm embarrassed about the rest of the story I have to tell you." We're both silent. Is Lisa letting me make the decision? "I guess I want another appointment."

Lisa softens her eyes. "I understand. We'll take it slow, and if you have difficulty sharing, please let me know so we can discuss it, ok?"

I nod. I feel the burn of tears starting. Why? Just because she's nice? I gotta get out of here...NOW! I quickly agree to another time, take the card Lisa wrote out, and leave. Whew! Made it without embarrassing myself. Dad's waiting in the car. He nods at me as I get in the car. "So how did it go?"

"Ok, I guess. I made another appointment."

"Good." He grunts.

Caz' Dichotomy

As first appointments go, that went pretty well. I'm struck by the dichotomy in Caz' persona. He's 28, but he looks like a ginormous kid, yet he talks like an educated man most of the time. I expected him to talk like a teenager or to slouch and shrug his shoulders like a teen. He did do some of that, but, in fact, he's very articulate and caught on quite quickly to questions. I could tell he's been in therapy before. He told his story as if he told it a dozen times. Yet, when I offered him a different way to look at something he considered it. I sense a lot of pain behind his eyes. They drooped slightly when he talked about his mother's leaving, and he swallowed hard, perhaps to control his emotion. I wonder why his mother left. Caz thinks it was something he did, but, according to Caz, his mother said "these brats", that includes both kids.

I have a sense there's a great deal of story-telling ahead. What I was able to obtain in this session are a list of symptoms, a brief synopsis of Caz' view of his mother's abandonment, and the subsequent events that led to Caz' first hospitalization and diagnosis.

Caz also looked ambivalent about being in counseling. I wonder what his previous experiences have been like. Because Caz is therapy savvy, I tried to ask questions that may not have been asked before. I wonder if he was relieved that I wasn't following the typical routine of an intake interview.

I couldn't tell if Caz had started bonding with me. He engaged at a couple of points but then seemed a bit reticent about making another appointment. Perhaps he's dreading telling the rest of the story, or perhaps he's had some experiences in counseling that were not helpful.

Caz
An introduction to Belle Surte

I expected Lisa to act like my other counselors. I could always get them to back off when I told the story of trying to hang my brother and myself when I was five. Sometimes I could see fear in their faces, and I'd increase the detail and see the fear turn to disgust. Sometimes I'd sense they didn't believe me. With Lisa, all I could see was acceptance. I'm surprised she picked up so quickly on the fact that I believed I caused Mom to leave because I was a ditsy kid. She offered me another way to see the situation that I hadn't considered before.

During the week, all I did was sleep, eat, and watch the Sci-Fi and Animal Planet channels. Dad's pissed, and Rom's ignoring me. I don't care if they're angry or ignoring me. It keeps the pressure off. But then I miss having a good relationship with them, and I feel guilty about not pulling my own weight around the house. Not guilty enough to do anything about it, though.

Today's my second appointment. During the second one, I usually go into lots of detail about my life, while acting detached. This usually gets me rejected at this point. Well, that's not fair. They really don't reject me, but I can tell they're overwhelmed and don't know what to say so they start with the "How does that make you feel?" routine. Or they say, "Could you say more about that?" The ones who really try hard to bond with me say something like "We'll get through this."

I don't know what I'll say to Lisa. Maybe I'll talk about the hospitalization and the months following Mom's leaving. I wonder if I should just jump into the relationship with Belle. Can Lisa handle this part of my story so soon? Can I? Would I be opening myself up too quickly? I don't have the energy today to talk about Belle so I'll stick with the hospitalization. Safer.

Dad drops me off and takes off for a cup of designer coffee. I wish we'd stopped beforehand. I could've used a double chai latte. That way I would have the cup to play with while talking. Takes the edge off. I feel the familiar emotion of being "left" as he drives away without a word. It pisses me off when he does that. I wonder if he's irritated because he has to drive me everywhere. I climb the steps and open the door and feel a little disappointed that Lisa isn't there to welcome me. There's no one in the waiting room, but I can hear two people talking in Lisa's office. I can't make out what they're saying because the voices are muffled. I wonder what they're talking about. Does everyone feel as screwed up as I do? The door opens, and I pretend to read a magazine as Lisa's client heads for the bathroom. Lisa waves me in and I feel another familiar emotion, dread. I really don't want to share the crap of my past, again. Yet, I'm intrigued by what questions she might ask.

Lisa asks me what I'd like to talk about. I start talking about the hospitalization experience. I'm bored reciting the feelings of being alone, locked up, monitored for suicide activity, etc. Lisa sits quietly, listening to my recitation. When I stop and take a breath, she leans forward and asks, "What meaning did you ascribe to the experience of being hospitalized?"

Where does she get this stuff? I could've told her that her next question should have been, "How did that make you feel?" I was prepared for that question, but what was this crap? Meaning? What the hell does she want? I look at her as if I don't understand. I know this look will force her to be more explicit. A great tactic to keep the counselor at bay. Lisa bites. She becomes more explicit. "Caz, you were six years old and your mother had just abandoned you and the family. You felt so depressed and guilty that you attempted a dual suicide with Rom. This landed you in the hospital which in some ways could be seen as another abandonment, this time by your father. What did this mean to you?"

"I dunno. Never thought about it before. But, it could mean I'm screwed up. I first chase my mom away, and then I can't even kill myself right, and then my father hospitalizes me so he doesn't have to deal with me."

"So you see yourself as screwed up, not as a child who has experienced a horrific event and reacts in such a way that baffles and scares adults?"

"No, I saw myself as damaged goods with no power over my life."

"Hmmm, I see it a little differently." She stops. What is she waiting for? Is she waiting for me to ask? Silence. She is! She is waiting for me to ask her how she sees it. Is this a game? I sit quietly, waiting her out. Damn, I'm too curious. Ok, I bite. "How do you see it?"

"I see a child who was faced with a situation that no child should have to navigate. You had several options as to how to act, and you chose the most extreme – suicide. Because you believed you chased your mother away, you didn't feel you deserved to live. Perhaps if you "brats" were dead, then your mother may return to your father. If you believed you had the power to chase your mom away (break up their marriage), then perhaps you had the power to bring her back, for your father. That means you thought you had great power, more than you should have had at six. So being hospitalized means what to you?"

"That the adults in my life were so scared of my power and determination that they had to strip me of my power by hospitalizing me, under the guise of protecting me?"

"Interesting. So the hospitalization meant what?" Lisa cocks her head to one side as she asks the question.

"They won and I lost." I responded quickly before thinking about my answer.

Lisa is quiet. and I'm struck with the implications. We sit quietly for a long time. Then I quietly reveal "By being hospitalized, I was told that I was only a kid, a kid with no rights. They took my freedom away and I relinquished my life. I never grew up."

Lisa nodded. "You assumed too much power as a kid – believing you had the power to send your mother away. They took the power back, but in doing so, they stripped you of **all** your power. Have you ever recouped any of your personal power?"

"No." I respond. "I still see myself as a little kid. I don't drive, I didn't graduate from college, I don't have a job, and I live at home. I never regained any power. I never grew up."

I'm exhausted. This insight seems big to me, and I can't wrap my mind around it enough to understand all its implications for my life. I look at the clock and see we have 30 minutes left. What am I going to talk about, now? I just wanna stop and think about this stuff for awhile. I pick at my fingernails, my shoes, and play with my shirt button. I look at the clock again, but Lisa doesn't follow my gaze. What to do? Can Lisa handle the next part? She's sitting expectantly but comfortably. She's letting me decide where to go next. I wonder if I sat for the next half of the session saying nothing, would she just sit and not talk? I'm so uncomfortable...OK, I give in. I launch into the next phase of my life.

"After my mom left and I got out of the hospital, I saw people looking at me. No matter where I went, I could see them nodding in my direction and whispering. I became shy and withdrew from everyone, especially adults. No matter where we went as a family, I felt people looking at us, especially me. Dad said I was imagining it, but I didn't think so. We went to church every Sunday, and some of the ladies paid a lot of attention to Rom and me. We were like little orphans, and everyone felt sorry for us. My dad got a lot of attention, too. I think the attention he received was aimed at hooking him up with another wife, but my dad didn't seem interested because he never dated after Mom left.

"I loved church and Sunday school because I thought maybe God loved me even if I was defective. At least that's what Jesus said in the Bible. Rom didn't much like Sunday school and church. He just went because Dad made us go. One day when I was at church, a lady named Belle sauntered over to my dad and asked if I could come to her house to play with some other boys from church. She said she had dogs and horses, too. I'd seen her at church serving on the altar with the pastor, so I knew she was important. She wasn't really pretty, but she was kinda nice looking. (Lisa is listening intently and nodding. Why do counselors always nod?) She was short and a little plump with strawberry blond hair and freckles that made her look younger than she was. As a little kid, I didn't know how old she was, but I now know she was about 40 back then. She said she loved boys and tried to help the boys who were having difficulty, especially those who didn't have mothers in their lives. She said she couldn't have children of her own, and her husband had died early in their marriage. He was a firefighter and was killed on the job. My dad agreed that both Rom and I could visit, but Belle said Rom was too young. She said she only takes the boys when they are over six. I was very excited about being chosen because it seemed that someone really wanted me. ME! Not Rom. Also, I was going to be playing with a lot of different kids and animals.

"I never had friends because I was so shy. I always felt there was something wrong with me and my mother left because I had problems following directions and learning. Having a learning disability and ADHD singles you out in school as needing special education and so other kids avoided me. I had a few friends who were also learning disabled or who had ADHD, but they didn't live close by. The thought of having a group of boys to play with and a woman who liked me was exciting, like I belonged somewhere.

"I didn't sleep the night before I went to Belle's house for the first time. I remember seeing the clock at 1, 3, 5, and 6. As I walked up the brick sidewalk to her house with Dad, I was so excited I almost peed my pants. She lived in a large two-story house with a huge attic. The main room was one humongous room with a kitchen and den and dining room all in one. I found out later it's called a "great room" and it really was! She also had a pool and a couple of ponies. She had lots of toys, televisions, computers, and sports equipment. I heard from a few of the boys that when I'm old enough, Belle would let me spend the night. Belle's boys ranged in age from six to fifteen.

"She had several rules. Everyone must play "nice" and she used her fingers to make quotation marks in the air when she said that." (I do the same thing to show Lisa what her gesture looked like.) "No bullying. No running around the pool. We had to eat what she made and not complain. We had to obey her. So far so good. I knew I could keep those rules. That first visit was sweet. I played there for five hours and then dad came and got me. She invited me back and called me a good boy. She ruffled my hair as she said it. This might sound corny, but it made me feel good all over when she said that. Kinda like when I call my dog a good girl and she wags her tail and her whole body follows."

Lisa and I both laugh at that statement, and she nodded like she understood what I was saying. I wonder if she has a dog.

"Over the next year, I visited a couple times a month but never stayed over night. She was a great cook and let us snack whenever we wanted. She also had a library of videos and video games that made the video stores look empty. Most of the videos I watched were Disney-like, but I never got tired of watching them. In the summer we swam in the pool. She had three dogs; I think they were all mutts. One dog I liked the best was Bessie. She looked like Lady in *Lady and the Tramp.* She followed me everywhere and would jump into my lap whenever I sat down. If dogs can love, then I think Bessie loved me.

"Belle also had two ponies. We were only allowed to ride them when she was around. She had lots of safety rules, but no one seemed to mind. I always waited for the next invitation. The year I turned nine, I was allowed to sleep over. Rom turned eight that year, but, for some reason, she never invited Rom to join the "Belle Club". Rom didn't seem to care and, to tell the truth, I was relieved to have this experience all to myself."

Lisa asked some questions to clarify my story. The second half of the session flew by. When I left after making a new appointment, Dad was waiting for me and this time he didn't ask me how the session went. We drove home in silence. My life is so lonely.

Lisa
Reflection on Caz' Session

Caz seems to be opening up. He didn't say this, but I felt like he was testing me to see if he wanted to work with me. He told today's story as if he had told it a lot, and he kept looking at me with a question on his face, almost as if he was assessing whether I was worthy to hear more. Caz doesn't seem to trust counselors, or anyone else, perhaps because he feels no one genuinely cares about him. His mother abandoned him, his father helped to hospitalize him, and people whispered around him. I need to find out more about this Belle person. She seems to have been the one bright spot in Caz' life as a child, yet I have a foreboding feeling the story is not going to turn out well. I think if Belle had been a positive part of Caz' life, then he would not be as damaged as he is.

I have had a lot of clients who were abused, neglected, or rejected as kids. These children develop symptoms that reflect the trauma they experience and usually involve depression, anxiety, recurrent nightmares, flashbacks, under achieving, distrust of others, chronic feelings of emptiness, low self esteem, inability to regulate their emotions, restlessness, poor concentration, irritability, difficulty sleeping or sometimes hypersomnia. Each victim has a personal constellation of several of the symptoms. While having some of these symptoms does not positively identify an abuse victim, most abuse victims have some or all of these symptoms. Caz has reported he feels like damaged goods, sleeps most of the time, has poor concentration, low self esteem, depression, anxiety, and is an under-achiever. Some of these symptoms could be the result of his ADHD and his mother's abandonment, but he could've also been abused. I need to listen for any sign of trauma. I've learned to let the story unfold as the client desires. To press the issue usually traumatizes the client further. Trusting Caz to reveal the story at his pace is the best choice.

Caz' relationships with his father and brother also need exploring. Caz has not revealed too much about them. There's so much I still don't know. According to Pastor Morris, the church played a role but how? I don't know, yet. Caz met Belle at church. Is that the connection? I don't know whether I should let Caz unfold his story fully before hearing from his pastor or whether I should call the pastor and get the story first. If I call first, then I have to be careful not to lead Caz into areas he's not ready to address. No, I'll give Caz the chance to tell his story before I talk to Pastor Morris.

Noelle Holly Kilpatrick

I don't wanna do this. I hate talkin' to people an' now I hafta talk to a shrink! I'm dreadin' it, but if I wanna keep ma'job I hafta go.

Lisa's New Client
Noelle

Noelle called three days ago to say she is being required by her employer to enter into counseling. She said little else except to confirm the time and location. She was direct and to the point, no chit chat, and no desire to tell me the presenting problem over the phone, the way many new clients do.

My morning routine at the office is to make a cup of tea after turning on the lights and getting set up for my first client. I'm ready. Standing inside my office door looking through the glass portion, tenderly sipping a cup of hot, hot green tea, I see a woman, whom I think is Noelle, walking down the hall toward my office. The carpet is institutional dark grey, the walls light grey and she looks like a phantom, a ghost, an apparition in her light blue/grey dress. Noelle is average height and very, very thin. I would guess she weighs less than 100 pounds. She has short, straight, light blond hair that almost looks white in the artificial light. Her hair color looks natural, not dyed. Her eyes are large, and as she approaches the door I can see they are the palest blue I've ever seen. Actually, they're more light grey than blue. Her skin is so pale it's almost iridescent pearl blue. If she wears a light blue or white dress she may not be seen at all. I wonder if her persona will match her physical appearance. There is usually some congruency.

"Hi, Noelle, I am Lisa." Pause. "Please come in." So far she hasn't said a word, just nodded.

"So, on the phone you said your employer has required you to come to counseling." I settle in for the initial session.

Noelle nods.

"Could you tell me a little about the reason you're here?"

"Yea."

"And that would be…?"

"I dunno know why I'm here 'cept ma boss sez I hafta do it."

"He didn't give you a reason?"

She shakes her head no.

"Tell me about your job."

"I'ma 'ssistant."

This is going to be a long hour! She doesn't want to be here, and says she doesn't know why she's here. Do I believe that?

"Assistant to whom."

"Ma boss."

Good grief! "Ok, and your boss does what?"

"He's in fi-nance." She says with a strong emphasis is on the **fi**.

"I see. What company do you and he work for?"

"He's th'owner."

"Ok. And you work as his assistant doing what?"

"Whatever he sez."

Holy cow. This is difficult. Will she do this the entire hour? Can I find a way to bond with her? Try a new tactic. "Could you list three or four things you do for your boss?"

"Yea."

I need to go back to Carl Rogers' listening lessons and ask only open-ended questions. "Please tell me what three or four things you do at work."

"Answer th'phone, type, an' file."

"So you do secretarial duties." Oops a closed question. I am going to get a "Yea."

"Yea."

"I assume you want to keep your job because you are here, in counseling. Can you tell me why you want to keep your job?"

"Pay's good. I'm alone in the office lots, so nobody bugs me. I don't wanna hafta to find 'nother job." Her face is blank, no emotion, and she speaks in a monotone voice.

"Those are all good reasons. How did you feel when your boss said you had to go to counseling?"

"Awful....Scared."

Aha! We have two feelings on the table, though they are a bit nebulous. "And did your boss tell you why you had to come here?" Thought I would try another closed question now that she has 'opened' a bit.

"He jist said I'm weird an' I need ta get ma'head shrunk."

Now we're getting somewhere. Where, I have no idea, but at least she didn't say "Yes" or "No".

"What do you think your boss means by 'weird'?"

"I'm sorta quiet. I jist do ma'work an' go home. He wants me to be more outgoin'."

"I see. Do you know what he means by outgoing?"

Noelle instantly scrunches up her face and bursts into tears. I had no clue that was going to happen. It's like a dam burst without even a crack appearing in the structure. I let her cry. She cries a lot and for a long time, and I let her. I just realize, she has yet to make eye contact. She has looked at everything in the room, 'cept me. Oh, no! Now I'm talking like her! I'll chalk it up to empathy. I'm sitting quietly not wanting to interrupt her too quickly. Her crying's beginning to subside.

"Noelle, I am glad you felt free to cry in here. Could you tell me what the tears were about?"

"No."

What!? She doesn't know or she doesn't want to tell me. I guess I'll ask. "Noelle, do you know why you were crying? And if so would you share that with me?" Darn I asked a closed question...here we go with a "yes" or "no"!

"No."

Sigh (internally). "Are you saying you don't know why you are crying?"

"No."

Oh, my! I got lost in the double negatives. I think that means she does know why she is crying. I need to ask this. "You know why you're crying, but you don't want to tell me?"

"Yep."

Ok. She may not come back but here goes. "Noelle, I really would like to help you, but I need a little more information from you than 'Yes' or 'No'. I need you to explain things to me. Things like… what happened just now when you cried, what your boss said to you, what you want to happen during our time together."

She takes a deep breath, speaks rapidly, all in one sentence. "Ma boss says I'm weird 'cause I don't have sex. He sent me here 'cause I don't talk at work, I jist do ma job, I won't entertain his outta town guests, I jist wanna be lef' alone, I wanna do ma job an' go home to ma' cat"

ALRIGHT! Where do I start? Summarize…that's it. "So you prefer to go to work, do your work, not interact (or interact as little as possible), get your pay check and go home. Did I get this right?"

"Yea….very gud."

"Thank you." (I think.) "But your boss wants more from you. He wants you to have sex with him and entertain his professional contacts when he asks you to?"

"Right."

"What did you say to him when he approached you about sex."

"I said, 'No thanks,' an' went back to work."

If this were any other client I would have laughed and congratulated her on her manner of handling a boss who's crossing the line, but I think Noelle would not see this as funny. "Did he continue to harass you?"

"He didn't her-ass me. He ast me polite-like ta'go out wiff him."

"Is he married?"

"No."

"So he's asking you out on a date."

"Yea."

"Is your dating him a requirement of your job?"

"No."

"So he's not pressuring you to go out with him or face losing your job?"

"No."

"What did you mean about the business associates who are from out of town, the ones he wants you to entertain. Do you believe he is asking you to have sex with his guests?"

"NO!!!"

"See, Noelle, I need a little more information from you so I don't go in one direction when the truth lies in another." Did I just sound too exasperated?

More tears…..lots more. She finally calms down. I sit back and remain quiet. I'm going to let her tell me what the tears are about.

She looks around, and pets her cloth purse that's sitting in her lap as if it's a cat. She's sitting with both feet flat on the floor with her hands on her purse. She does not look comfortable at all. She's sitting the way I was taught to sit 40+ years ago – the way a lady sits. Never cross your legs because someone could see up your skirt. Keep your knees together. Very prim and very appropriate. Closed, protective, wary. Wait she is going to say something.

"That's what ma boss sez."

"I'm sorry. What do you mean."

"He sez he needs more information from me so he knows what to do."

"I see."

"Can I leave now?"

"Sure."

"When can I come again? Nex' week?"

"Uh, sure, same time?"

"Ok. Can I take whatever paperwork you wan'me to complete wiff me so I can fill it out at work?

"Uh, sure, fine. Here's the file you need to complete, so I can enter you in my comp….

"Ok, Goodbye."

What just happened? She wants to come back??? Why? I don't even know if I have enough information to fill a paragraph of case notes. Well, I'll see if she returns. I'd love to know what's going on inside her head. Maybe someday she will let me in. Perhaps. On a scale of one to ten with one being she won't come back and work on her issues and 10 being she'll be back for sure, I give her a one or two. But I'm intrigued. Living and working in the Baltimore area most of my life, I've gotten used to the Baltimore accent, however, Noelle's was extremely pronounced. She never said, "Hon or zinc (for sink) or Balmer but she doesn't speak all the syllables or many final consonants. She reminds me of someone, but I can't put my pinky on it.

Noelle's Resistance

Leeza's very nice...an' patient. She didn't do what most people do ta'me, dismiss me. She would've gone on wiff the session if I hadn't walked out, eve'though I din't say much. I don't wannabe in counseling, but, if I've gotta, she'll be ok to talk to. Gerard sez I haf'ta talk to someone. So I am. I'm "fulfillin' his r'quiremen".

Caz' Abuse

This counseling relationship is not the same ole, same ole. Lisa listens, really listens. I don't feel judged by her. I wish she had been my mom. I bet she is or was a great mother. **She** wouldn't walk out on her kids. And I don't think she'll walk out on me. She takes what I say seriously and responds so that I don't feel ashamed. All week I've been planning how I will tell her the next part of the story, because it's difficult. The other stuff I've told a kazillion times, but this part of my life has never been fully told. I had a counselor when I was little, maybe 10 or 11, and I told her of Belle's and my relationship, but I don't think she believed me. I also told some of what happened to my psychiatrist, but he acted like he thought I was exaggerating or something. So I never told the whole story to anyone. I never thought anyone would believe me. Lisa might. She just might. Hope so.

As I sit in the chair I've been sitting in for the last sessions, it somehow feels uncomfortable, or maybe I'm uncomfortable. After a brief period of my rambling and chit-chat, I take the plunge. Here goes, this time off the high dive.

"One month after I turned nine, I got to stay overnight for the first time. I was so excited. I picked out my favorite pjs, the ones with basketballs on them, and packed my overnight bag. I also had a new swim suit. Walking up the brick sidewalk felt like going to school the first time. I was ready and excited to fit in with the older boys. Belle had assigned me to one of the bedrooms upstairs. She explained that when we turn nine, she gave us a bed and dresser that was ours to use until we were too big to come to her house. I thought, 'Too big to come to her house? How could that ever be? I was never going to be too big to have fun!' She walked me up the stairs and showed me a bedroom on the right that had four twin beds in it. My bed was near the window and had sports figures on the bedspread; a basketball player, a man playing hockey, a baseball player at bat, and a foot ball player running with the ball. I can see them clearly, colors and all. She then helped me get into my swim suit. She admired the suit as she helped me put it on and ever so slightly touched my penis as she helped. I was confused as to why, if I was now one of the older boys, I needed help putting on my swim suit. She had never helped me before. But, I must admit, I was happy for the extra attention she gave me and the kind, sweet way she helped me. She then tenderly took my hands in hers and said that I was a big boy now and big boys get to do things that little boys didn't get to do. I got excited at the prospect of even more fun in this wonderful house with my godbrothers. Bell insisted we call her Godmother and the other boys were all godbrothers. She then put both hands on my legs and ran her hands up to the edge of my bathing suit and then slipped her hands under my suit and squeezed my butt. I was surprised, but it felt good, and I thought 'This is different, but I like it. Maybe this is what Moms do to show they love you.'

"That night I got to watch videos that were off limits to the younger kids. The new videos had more violence and more dirty language. I acted like I was cool and knew all about that kind of stuff, even though I really didn't. Dad didn't let us watch mature movies. I was still watching Disney movies at nine years old. When bedtime came around we got into our pajamas and went to bed. After a little while, Belle came in and called one of my godbrothers out of the room. He came back an hour later. I wondered what lovely things he got to experience that I didn't."

Lisa's looking at me and I can see she's wondering what's going to happen next. I look down at my fingernails because this is a difficult part of the story for me to tell. Somehow looking somewhere else, and not at Lisa, is helping me to talk.

"The second visit starts out like the first. Belle takes me to my bedroom and begins helping me get into my swim suit. But before I can pull it up, she gently takes a hold of my penis and strokes it. I shudder, but it feels good. Belle says, 'You are a wonderful young man and I want to get to know you better. Is that ok?' I suddenly don't have any saliva and can't speak, so I nod. She then stands up and lifts up her skirt. She doesn't have underpants on and I can see the womanhood that some men obsess over. She asks me to touch it and I do. Then she takes my hand and guides it into the soft folds. She groans and tells me I'm really good at this so I wiggle my fingers and she arches her back, closes her eyes, and flutters her eyelids. She tells me that as I get older she will teach me how to put my penis in there. The words make me sick. Fingers are one thing but my penis! No way. She smiles as though she's reading my thoughts. She asks if I would like to put my fingers anywhere else, but I've had enough. I shake my head and she laughs and strokes my hair. "Maybe another time," she says. I nod again. Then comes **the statement**, the one that makes me realize there might be something wrong with what we're doing. She says there's secrecy surrounding our loving. 'We don't talk about any of this, ok?' I nod again, thinking, if I keep nodding my head will fall off. So this is what the older boys are doing when she calls them out of bed and into her room at night. I'm both scared and excited at the same time. My mother's not around, so I can't find out if this behavior is what all children do with their mothers. Somehow I don't think so, but I'm just nine. What do I know? Besides, I love being in Belle's house with the other guys. It's the only place I can be myself and have fun, so no matter what -- I **will** keep the secret because I don't want to stop coming here. I feel special in her house and I don't feel special anywhere else.

"I don't remember how many times Belle and I stroke each other before the first night when she calls me out of the bedroom. I'm almost 12. I'm really scared and yet excited. I'm not sure what to do, but I know she'll help me. So far, everything we've done was pleasurable, and I'm sure she'd never hurt me. I just don't want to embarrass myself so I keep promising myself I will do everything she tells me to do, so that I please her and don't look stupid. Belle starts very slowly undressing me from the waist down and she moves like a delicate moth, gently kissing me every part of my body. Then she opens her robe, and I see her completely naked for the first time. I start to get hard like I sometimes do in the middle of the night. I touch and kiss and insert my fingers everywhere, just like she gently instructs. It never occurs to me this is wrong because it feels good. When I'm hard enough, she lies on the bed and prompts me to climb on top of her and put my penis inside her. I'd sworn I never wanted to do this, but now I want to do this more than swim, ride the horses, play tennis, watch movies, or eat. I find myself intuitively knowing what I should do and when I'm unsure, Belle gently guides me. Over the next several weeks, I find my body parts can give her pleasure in the most unusual ways."

I look up again to check out how Lisa's taking this information. She looks sad and concerned. I had planned to talk about a lot of other things before I talked about sex with Belle, but somehow in this comfortable room with someone who doesn't interrupt me when I'm talking, things seem to tumble out easily. Lisa's very quiet for what seems a long time. Then she tilts her head the way she does when she is about to ask an important question and asks a question that totally rocks my world. "Caz, are you aware, when you told that last piece of your story with Belle, you switched from past tense to present tense?"

The room seems to become a tunnel and I'm flying backward, deeper into the tunnel. I didn't know I was telling the story as if it was happening, but now I do. Holy crap! I was reliving the story! In my past counseling experiences, I told parts of the story with detachment, as if it happened to someone else. This time, I felt like I was there, in those bedrooms. I'm quiet. I don't know what to think or say. I'd rehearsed answers to all the questions Lisa could have asked me about the event, but her question…it, it helps me understand the impact of the event. I had just re-lived my special time with Belle and…It felt really good. Yet, I'm embarrassed I told it with such detail. I hadn't intended to. I just got lost in the memory.

I'm sure Lisa has a lot more questions, but she doesn't ask any. Maybe I'm just doing a bang up job of sharing. So I start to share another part of the story, this time I will be aware of whether I am telling the story or reliving the story. However, Lisa stops me.

"Caz, you've just shared something very important. How are you feeling?" Ahhh! There's the "How are you feeling question?" However, somehow the question doesn't sound like a canned question. I believe she really wants to know. "I'm a bit shaken, but I'm ok. I feel like I want to tell you the rest, right now."

"Let's stop for now, because the session is almost over, and I want to make sure you're ok to leave here and go home."

"Lisa, I **am** ok. I just can't believe how the session flew. I have so much more to tell you."

"I know you have a lot more, but let's leave it for next time. Take a deep breath and collect your thoughts and feelings for now. Telling a story of that nature is very difficult and can stay with you after you leave here. Are you sure you're ok?"

I nod.

"Caz, I have to ask you a question that may upset you, but I am legally bound to ask, ok?"

"Yes."

"Has anyone reported Belle's activity to the Department of Children and Family Services? Mental health professionals are bound by law to report anyone who harms a child."

I'm annoyed at the question, but I realize she's just like all of us, bound by laws. My annoyance comes through in my answer. "Yes, she was reported. I'll tell you the rest of the story next time."

"I know you've given me permission to speak to Pastor Morris, but I want you to know I'll be contacting him this week about how the church is involved in this case."

"Fine. Whatever. In fact, I want you to talk to him. He'll have information I don't have."

"Are you still ok?"

I tell her I'm fine, and I confirm our next appointment and leave. Dad is reading the paper in the car, and when I walk out he does a double take. He asks what is wrong. "Nothing. Why?" Dad starts the car, but he continues to look at me. "I don't know," he says continuing to scrutinize me. "You just look flushed or strained or something."

"Dad, I'm fine. Drive."

Lisa
Reaction to Caz' Abuse Story

As Caz was telling his story I was struck with the horror of the story and the way Belle used tenderness, patience, and love to get what she wanted from the boys. No wonder Caz and the rest of the boys kept the secret. Why would they want anything to change? I'm amazed that this abusive conclave went on for so long without one of the boys blowing the whistle on Belle and her activities. I feel a bit nauseated. Why?

I've been listening to my clients' abuse stories for many years. Each situation has its own characters, themes, horrors, subtle messages to the victims, and long term effects. But bottom line the perpetrator uses his or her power to control, use, and abuse the victim. All this is done in service to the perpetrator's desires, wants, and ability to manipulate. Most abuse involves hurt, pain, and debasement, but in Caz' story the abuse was much more clever. Belle used love, kindness, and gifts to seduce the boys. The boys were set up to desire and please her, and they believed they were willing participants, so they would never have complained to someone else out of the fear that the fun and favors would stop. In most abuse cases, the child is a captive in the abuser's domain. He or she has no way to escape the abuse and dreads every day. In Belle's case, she held the children captive by creating a wonderful atmosphere. They didn't want it to end. So I guess, in some ways, the boys held themselves captive. I wonder if they feel guilt or shame for having gone along with the abuse. I haven't heard the rest of Caz' story, but this abuse was just as harmful as the wounding or punitive kind. I hope I can help Caz to understand the depth of the harm.

This woman was one of the cleverest abusers I've ever encountered. Part of me was in awe of her ability to set the abuse up in such an "amusement park" manner. The other part of me is enraged at the harm she did to Caz and the others. No wonder he appears to be a 10 year old boy in a man's body! He is developmentally arrested.

As I write my case notes, I'm increasingly surprised at the depth of anger I feel about the abuse. I have not felt this angry at an abuser in a long while. Perhaps I've become too complacent with hearing trauma stories, and this one's so different that it connected with a legitimate outrage that years of doing therapy has muted. Abuse destroys the human spirit. Why wouldn't I feel some outrage at a child being sexually abused? I wouldn't be human if I didn't have these feelings. However, had I become too clinically distant and therefore had not felt the burn of anger in a couple of years? Interestingly, Caz told the story without emotion. What's the extent of the damage this abuse has done? My hunch is Caz will see the situation with Belle as saving him from mediocrity, or worse from the abyss of non-existence. He felt special in her house. He felt accepted by her, unlike his mother who rejected him. Belle may have saved Caz from his own demise. She may have kept him alive to eventually work on the abandonment of his mother.

How do I explore the paradox in this situation? I wonder if he can get in touch with the anger that may be brewing under the surface and still see that Belle may have done him a favor.

The other difficult part of this story is the fact that this case involves a woman perpetrator and little boys as victims. In a book by Michael Lew called *Victims No Longer*, he explains that one of the problems with a female perpetrator and a male victim is that the culture sees this scenario as "the boy got lucky." The reality is male victims are as damaged by early sexual experiences as females are, and, further, they are less likely to tell someone about the abuse. If Caz believes he got lucky, then the work of helping Caz to feel irate at the situation will be very difficult. I also want to find out if Caz' father and brother know about the abuse. Finally, I need to know what the priest meant when he said the church is somewhat culpable in this case. I make a note to call Pastor Morris, and then think better of it. I call him immediately to set up an appointment.

Bally Ibutos, Jenkins, Sherwood, Coffey, Mars, Hawthorne

I met Bally two years ago when she was 39. At that time, she was drinking heavily and came to her first session inebriated. I was stunned by her beauty and appalled by her manner.

On an employment application, Bally could never pick a category for race or ethnicity. She will forever be checking "other". She has a mocha complexion with the exotic slanted eyes of Asian descent. Her eye color however is dark blue-green. Her hair color is black and straight, cascading to her shoulders. She is medium height, maybe five feet five inches and has a petite build. She was impeccably dressed in an expensive off-white suit with dark aqua blouse that reflected her eye color...and she was drunk. The alcohol seeped from her pores and filled the room. The stench made me gag. I asked her what she wanted to get out of counseling, and she responded that she needed to find out why she drank. It was 11 am and she was already so drunk that I wondered how she drove to my office and whether she had come from work. She had! She held a high level managerial job in a computer firm where she was a trainer. She claimed to be doing an excellent job, and no one in the company knows she's an alcoholic. "How could they not?" I asked myself. I explained to Bally that she needed to stop drinking first, and then we could discuss what life events trigger her to drink. She was not satisfied. She wanted to know **why** she drank, so she could decide to stop drinking. I again explained she was not available for that kind of counseling conversation until she was sober, which she clearly wasn't. Bally retorted that she **was** sober, but she had just one shot to steady her nerves, before coming to my office. She was arrogant. Her chin was held high and to the right in a defiant stance. Her eyes had turned to steel. I stood firm and said I couldn't see her if she was drunk. She huffed, said, "F you," and left. I didn't see her again until today.

Bally arrived on time, and this time she was not drunk. She was still strikingly beautiful and impeccably groomed. However, her eyes are filled with a sadness that had not been there two years ago. Perhaps the alcohol had numbed the pain? After exchanging pleasantries and completing the paperwork, I settled down to listen.

"First, I want to apologize for my behavior two years ago. You were right to refuse to work with me unless I was sober. After I left here, I blew you off as someone who didn't care. Two weeks later, my supervisor told me that he was going to fire me unless I stopped coming to work drunk. He said he'd pay for me to enter rehab and would give me flex time to attend AA meetings. I told him the same thing I told you…to f off. Well, I was fired. I continued to drink because this time I had a reason. I had just lost my job. My husband then kicked me out of my house and told me not to come back until I stopped drinking. I had hit bottom. So I went back to my boss, groveled, and asked for his support. He arranged for a 14 day inpatient stay. Well, that was a horrendous experience, but it worked. I was sober when I left, connected to AA, and had a sponsor. I have been working the program for the last two years and have remained sober. Unfortunately, my husband still didn't want me so we separated and the divorce was final a couple of months ago. Well, I'm still employed at my job, and they are pleased with my work. I'm returning here because all through my recovery over the last two years, I kept saying what a bitch you were because you wouldn't help me find out why I was drinking. The counselors and AA people kept telling me that you were right to focus on the behavior first. However, they also said it isn't important **why** I drink, it's the **fact** I drink that's important. Well, I disagree. I think I drink for a reason or reasons, I just don't know what the triggers are. I know how to control it, but I don't feel in control. I'm existing on pure willpower."

She pauses and looks to me for a response, so I tentatively offer, "That's quite a journey you've been on. I'd be glad to work with you, but I'm afraid if we start delving into the why of your drinking then you'll feel overwhelmed by the work and will relapse. What do you think about that?"

"Lisa, I won't kid you. After our last session two years ago, I didn't want to see you again."

"I'm not surprised, Bally. We didn't get off to a good start."

"Well, I asked my doctor, regular one, you know the 'primary care guy' for a referral after I left here, and he gave me your name. I couldn't believe it. You popped up again. I told him "over my dead, decaying body." Then I was talking to a friend, and she said she had the card of someone her mother had seen and liked. I told her I wasn't interested in seeing any shrink. Well, she still gave me the card and I didn't even look at it. I stuck it in a book. That was 18 months ago. A few days ago, I picked up the book again, and there was the card and it was yours. I felt like the therapy gods were beating me over the head, but I didn't think you'd be willing to see me."

"So are you afraid of therapy – finding out something you don't want to know about yourself, or are you just resistant to seeing **me**?"

"Both."

"Back to my original concern. What if you delve into why you drink, and you begin to feel a lot of stress and want to drink?"

"One of my sponsors asked the same thing. But I gotta do this. I feel like a hamster on a wheel. I don't know why I'm there, where I'm going, or how to get off."

"Tell me one more thing before we decide if we want to make a commitment to work together."

"Okay."

"Tell me what you are thinking or feeling when you feel the need to take that first drink." She hesitates and looks like she's going to argue or to tell me that she's already tried that approach and thinks better of it. She huffs and shifts in her chair.

"I think... well, I keep trying to meet other's expectations. It's too much for me. I feel pressure to conform and be perfect so others will approve of me, and I will fit in. Yet I resent that other's expect me to be perfect."

"So you just answered your own question as to why you drink. Do you have skills in place that keep you from drinking when those thoughts and feelings emerge?"

"Yes and they've worked for almost two years. I feel pretty confident I can remain sober. Well, it's a struggle, but I am doing it. You know the one-day-at-a-time thing."

"Then you want to find out what causes you to think and feel that others expect too much of you, that you need to be perfect and conform?"

"I guess. I don't know where I got these ideas. I grew up in a pretty normal family and had a regular childhood."

"What's normal?"

Another huff. "Shit, do you really want to know what 'normal' means or are you asking me to tell you what was normal about my childhood?"

"I am asking you to tell me about your childhood."

She shakes her head as if to say, "Why didn't you just ask?" But she continues. "Well, I'm lucky to have been born into a very racially diverse family. We had the best of what multicultural means. My maternal grandmother was Filipino, and my maternal grandfather was French. Well, they met before World War II in the Philippines and married. My paternal grandfather was African, and my paternal grandmother was Scandinavian. They met when my grandfather was touring Sweden in the late 1930s and married and immigrated about 1939. My father was an infant when they arrived. There's some indication that my Filipino grandmother was part Hawaiian, but that's speculation. My maternal grandparents had my mother in the Philippines and then immigrated to the U.S. in 1945, just as the war was ending. My mother was about two when they arrived. Well, both families lived in the same neighborhood in California. My maternal grandparents had three children. My mother was the first born and then there were two more girls (my aunts). My paternal grandparents had six children and my father was first born also. My mother is lighter skinned than my father, who more resembles his father. However, my mother's siblings look more like the Filipino side while my mother looks a little more European. My father and mother met when they were children and married when they were around 18. They had me a few years later, and then mom popped out two in a row. They didn't think they were going to be able to have children at first. Then I guess they couldn't stop. I'm the first born and my sister is two years younger, and my brother is four years younger. I think my brother and sister more resemble my father, but I resemble no one in the family. Genetics I guess. Well, when my parents would fight, my father would often accuse my mother of having a bastard child. I always assumed that was me because I didn't resemble anyone on either side of their families."

"What was that like for you? To hear that you were being considered a 'bastard child' by your own father?"

"I didn't pay much attention to him. He was a jerk, kinda paranoid, felt life owed him something. I guess because he looked more black, like his father, he was always expecting to be treated worse than other people. Well, he had more experience with prejudice than my mom did who look like a Filipino one minute and a European the next."

"But your father was also half Scandinavian right? Did I get this correct?"

"Yep. He had one eye that had a dark blue tint to it, and the other eye was brown with a green tint to it. He had darker skin, but he had some of my grandmother's features. He was a very handsome man. He still considered himself black though. He's half white and half black, but considers himself black. I never got that. Interesting? Huh?"

"Very. How do you see yourself, ethnically?"

"I am a Heinz 57 variety. I speak fluent Spanish from my mother and grandmother's influence. I speak and read French from my maternal grandfather's teaching. I don't speak any African dialect because my paternal grandfather and father refused to allow it to be spoken in our house. They said we are Americans, and we need to speak English. Both would get very upset when my mother and grandmother spoke Spanish or my grandfather spoke French. My Scandinavian grandmother spoke Swedish but only when her husband and my father were not around. So I grew up with English, Spanish, and French, but I can understand my Swedish grandmother."

"That's a lot."

"True, more than most. And the languages have helped my career."

"I bet. Quite an asset. So where did the message come from that you had to be perfect and please others?" Aha, the façade cracked. The almost-tears were sitting on her eyelids.

"I don't know."

I'm baffled. She is feeling something but doesn't have any idea where it came from. I let her sit with her tears. After a minute she takes one of her tissues, twists a corner into a small spiral, and dabs at the lower lids trying not to ruin her eye makeup. She looks at me expectantly. Guess it's my turn. "Do you have memories of your childhood?"

"No. It's as if I was beamed down from another planet. I don't have any memory before 12."

"I'm mindful of the time. How comfortable are you with our relationship this time around? Should we continue or would you like a referral."

"I'm ok with you. Let's meet for several sessions and see how it goes."

Just like a business woman, she takes control. We go on to discuss her need to attend her AA meetings and follow the program. We also discuss times and days and finally arrive at a time to get back together in a week and she leaves.

Reflecting on this encounter brought several questions to mind. I have had other clients with no memory of early childhood. Some just don't tune into the planet until they are about nine or ten. Some have not bothered to remember. Some have horrific childhood experiences. I'd place money on the latter, but I'll wait to see if she even returns next week before I place any bets at Atlantic City.

Bally's Arrogance

Back in my car and feeling very strange after the session, I turn on the motor and let it run for a few minutes. I like her a lot better now that I'm sober. I bet she's reserving her thoughts and feelings until I decide to return. Well, I don't blame her. I flipped her off and vanished from her office, and now I want to come back. I've told my ancestry story many times. People always want to know what kind of breed I am. I like shocking them with the story. Lisa, though, doesn't seem to be shocked at my variety of genetic material. She seemed more interested for different reasons. I wonder if she believed me when I said I didn't remember my childhood. I might be unusual, and maybe I challenge her perceptions about other ethnic groups. I might even teach her a lesson or two.

I really don't remember a lot about my childhood, but I know some of the things that happened because I have heard my family's stories. I wonder if I should share the stories or let her feel like she helped me to recoup some memories. Well, I'll give her another session or two to see if I'm impressed enough to stay in counseling.

Chapter Two
Exploration

**Memories of the traumatic event are immediate
and intense, experienced as if they were happening all over again in the present. Unlike normal,
narrative memories that shift, distort, and fade
over time, traumatic memories remain fixed.**
(Naparstek, 2004).

Caz' Time Warp

I felt unreal as I left Lisa's office. My father noticed something was
different about my demeanor. He couldn't put words to it, and I
couldn't either. I just felt like my head was full of cotton. I wanted
to finish the story, but I ran out of time. I felt like I had been talking
for 20 minutes when Lisa said the session was almost over. Wow,
kinda, like a time warp. Do, do, do, do, do, do, do, do, I am entering
the 'Twilight Zone'. I love that show. Sometimes I stay up all night
and watch the reruns.

My week was still the same, sleeping, eating, television
watching, dodging my father's and brother's disappointment and
anger. I did take the dog for a walk a couple of times and talked
to her. She listens as good as Lisa and she doesn't have to call and
report abuse!

My story with Belle is almost over. I want this session to be the end of the storytelling.

Caz
Teenage Experimentation or Abuse?

Lisa hasn't reached Pastor Craig. He's out of town at a national church meeting. I forgot to tell her. We had a supply pastor this week and she was great. The sermon was about the parable of a woman who lost her coin and searched for it all over the house. Somehow I thought this was relating to me...I lost a coin – my mother's love – and I have been searching for her ever since. I've never found her. I tell Lisa about the sermon and my connection to it, and she discusses it with me. She even referred me to another passage about a person who lost a pearl of great worth and searched the world over for it. I can see the yearning in me that my mother's leaving left. I continue my story about Belle. This time I purposely tell the story in the past tense.

"I don't remember when I knew this activity was not what other children experience. Every year a police officer came to our classroom and talked about predators who might touch us where we were uncomfortable, where our bathing suits covered. But I never thought this activity was about what Belle and I were doing. I never felt she was a predator. She loved me and I loved her, so I never thought the police officer was talking about me. When I got to junior high school and everyone was talking about sex and laughing, I was baffled. Didn't everyone have these experiences? I soon found out that I was special, and I also found out it was not usual behavior for young boys to be having sex with women. I guess I knew in my heart it was wrong, but I pushed it into a place where I didn't have to deal with it. I guess I kept quiet because I didn't want my time with Belle to stop. Then, I started looking at girls at school and picturing what it would be like to do to them what I did with Belle. I never did approach any girls in junior high. However, high school was a different story. At 14, I was an expert in sexual activity. I had experienced everything, and I started to see girls as much more desirable. I was not good-looking, and I was not an athlete, so girls were not attracted to me. But I was very attracted to them. I also started to see girls as more attractive than Belle who was now pushing fifty.

"By the time I was 15, she was requesting me less and less. Other, younger boys were being asked to go to her room. At first I was sad. Then I was hurt and jealous. But then, one day I was relieved. I was ready for girls my own age, and they were less experienced than I was. I was now going to be the teacher and they would be my students. My first conquest was a fairly unattractive girl named Jane, funny huh, "plain jane". I asked her out and slowly, ever so slowly, I seduced her. Belle taught me well. Jane was so sexually turned on by how I treated her, and so appreciative of my gentleness, she told other girls how good I was at "popping a cherry." And, for the first time, I became one of the most popular boys at school.

I knew the girls were just using me for experience. None of them were interested in a long-term relationship with an average-looking, non-athletic guy. I always had a date, but I also knew I would have to perform sexually by the end of the evening."

Lisa chews the inside of her cheek, something she does when she wants to ask a question. I stop talking.

"Caz, did you ever consider how Belle set you up to be used by others?"

"I never thought about it. I guess so. I saw it as… as…she taught me how to be significant in the world, when I was just average guy. I would never have had dates if I wasn't clever at sex. She taught me to be a man who could be an excellent stud to women. I sometimes considered that what she had done might be wrong, even though it felt good. Still I said nothing, and all the godsons said nothing. It was funny how we would see each other in school and simply nod. We never talked outside of Belle's house. There was a covert, unspoken rule that what we did at Belle's, stayed at Belle's."

"Interesting. Belle, in her inclusion of you in her sexual drama at her house, actually isolated you from the other boys outside of her house."

"Yeah, I guess. I never thought about it like that."

Talking about the details of myriad encounters with girls at school made me oblivious to the time. I've been talking non-stop for the 45 minutes. I worry that Lisa will see me as a pervert. However, Lisa had the look of compassion. She acknowledged again that Belle used her power to seduce me and taught me how to do the same to others. Lisa reiterates that what Belle did was more confusing because she was generous and kind to me. If she had been mean and hurtful, then I would've recognized sooner that what we were doing was wrong.

Belle was very clever in blending the fun things like pony rides with seduction. I guess she's right. Silence as both of us think. I whisper, "I think Belle's been arrested. I'm not positive, though." We made another appointment. Walking to the car, I feel the heaviness of emotion choking me and I begin to cry. Why didn't I cry in front of Lisa?

Different Presentations

Bally and Caz present with a multiplicity of problems. Bally has a pattern of unstable and intense relationships. She's impulsive and reactive. She's judgmental of others, and a bit paranoid. Bally's been difficult to bond with. She's resisted being in therapy, and her alcoholism makes her a high risk for therapy drop-out.

On the other hand, Caz is very cooperative and open. He presents differently from most abuse victims. He does not report the usual symptoms of PTSD because of the non-traumatizing atmosphere Belle set up. He has some symptoms, but they aren't obvious because of the love-abuse issue. However, he is functioning at a minimum level on his life-tasks and this may or may not be totally related to the abuse. I have to explore more thoroughly the symptoms Caz has and whether some symptoms predate the abuse by Belle and were triggered by his mother's abandonment.

Caz has become fixated at an early developmental stage. His 10 year old demeanor is astounding when coupled with a 6'6" body and an articulate man's vocabulary. However, some of the symptoms may be genetically part of Caz' psychological makeup. Depression and anxiety can gallop through families, and so I need to explore whether others in his family have suffered similar symptoms. As it stands, Caz reports depressed mood, lack of interest in most activities, hypersomnia, chronic fatigue, feelings of worthlessness, excessive guilt, and diminished ability to concentrate. He also reports anxiety and detachment from others. His trauma-related symptoms are not as clear. He feels helpless, and has recurrent memories, though I'm unsure whether they are intrusive or not. He has demonstrated physical reactions to telling his story. For example he plays with his shoelaces and avoids eye contact. He also switches to present tense as if he's currently experiencing the events at Belle's. How many of the above symptoms are indicative of depression, ADHD, his learning disability, his anxiety, or the abuse? At our next session I will ask Caz about his medications, again. He gave me a cursory overview in the first session, but it's time to get more detailed medical and medication histories.

Caz
Relief and a Plan

It's a relief to have the story of Belleland out in the open. Lisa's easy to talk to. Actually, I did most of the talking. I hope she didn't mind. My psychiatrist and previous counselors liked when I talked and talked and all they had to do was listen, but I also felt like I needed their input into my situation. I hope Lisa's more interactive with me than she was these last couple of weeks. I look forward to her questions. She makes me think and sort through things that have confused me for years. Both my psychiatrist and previous counselor focused on my mother's abandonment of the family, but that's all they knew. That's all I shared. Well, that's not totally true. I shared a little of my story about Belle with both of them, but they just listened. They never asked questions. I don't think they believed me. I'll see Lisa today and am really psyched, pun intended. I have dreams to explore and therapists like dreams.

I'm really tired this week and I'm having a lot of dreams that are disturbing. Maybe Lisa and I need to talk about something else this week. I'll share a dream or two, that'll take the pressure off.

Caz
Dreams Derail Session

A week has gone by and I'm seeing Caz today I still haven't heard from his pastor. I hope this week will be the charm, and we can connect.

Caz arrives five minutes late. He states he's excited about being here (10 year old boy is evident) and is sorry for the lateness (the man emerges). I smile and nod. (For after all, it's **his** session.) However, as I begin to pull my thoughts together concerning his medical history, Caz pulls out a small book and looks up sheepishly and smiles. "I keep a dream journal. I hope you don't mind, but my sleep has been filled with dreams this week."

I put my agenda on hold to listen to his nighttime adventures. I'm always happy when clients take responsibility for their therapy. (Hey, it makes my job easier. How self-serving is that attitude?) Many of them keep journals and dream journals are useful, especially when they're filled with unconscious information. Caz doesn't disappoint. He reports having two dreams, and introduces them by saying he has no idea what they mean.

> Dream #1: I'm working for a company that cleans out sewers. I go down into the sewer and find myself facing a sea of crap. I know I have to get down into the crap, but I don't want to. I almost quit the job, but then I decide to keep working even if it means getting dirty.

Caz is perplexed as to what the dream's about. We do some free association about what sewers, crap, and quitting mean to him. Caz is able to see that going through counseling means he'll have to sort through the 'crap' of his life. I accept his interpretation, but I feel there's more to his dream. The symbolism of descending into the sewer is like descending into the muck and mire of the unconscious. (Freud would have had a field day with that one!) Is his unconscious signaling to Caz that he has to be his own cleaning company that uncovers, sweeps, and removes the crap so that it can be dealt with in his conscious? The other area that intrigues me is Caz' desire to quit in the dream and then re-deciding to move forward. I'm sure, over the week, Caz has had approach-avoidance feelings about whether or not to continue in counseling. He intuitively knows that the process has already stirred up issues he would rather not deal with, like the abandonment of his mother, but he decides in the dream to keep going. I share some of my thoughts, and he looks at me and says, "I also had another dream." Clearly he isn't ready to go deeper with the interpretation.

> Dream #2: I have a friend in this dream who kills
> someone. The friend then asks me to bury the
> body. I didn't want to bury the body, but I do it
> for my friend. The friend is caught and sentenced
> to death and I watch as he dies. I have mixed
> feelings. I'm sad for my friend, but he deserved
> what he got. I feel guilty for covering up for him.

After some questions centering on what parts of this dream Caz believes applies to his current situation, Caz says he feels he has allowed other people to push him around and tell him what to do, even to the point of committing a crime (Is he referring to Belle?). I think his friend in the dream is Belle. She killed Caz' self and now she may be asking him to bury the body (burying the abuse with his silence). However, now that the truth is coming out, he's going to have to watch her die (arrested, tried, or jailed?). Once again, Caz shrugs his shoulders at my possible interpretations. He even sabotages his own ideas. It's too early in our relationship to dig into an important dream like this one. I accept Caz' interpretation, but I also see, once again, that Caz is dreaming about things under ground, darkness, death. Too soon, back off.

The dreams and discussion take 25 minutes of the session. I wonder if Caz is resisting getting into the "crap" of the abuse again. (Am I a skeptic or what?) But maybe I'm wrong, because Caz says he wishes his dreams hadn't taken so much of our time. Glancing at the clock, he reports he really wants to talk more about Belle. I sit back, and let him talk.

"I'm not sure whether I understand a lot about what happened last week when I was sharing my story of Belle, but I felt better after

I left your office. Like the world was being lifted off my shoulders. But I am also really tired this week.

"You know. I told my story to my psychiatrist when I was a pre-teen and to another counselor when I was a little kid, and they both listened but didn't say anything. I think I startled them with the information. Last week you listened, too, but you seemed to be interested in talking further about what happened. Am I correct? Do you think that by talking about this stuff, I can feel better?"

Ignoring his question, I respond a bit too abruptly. "They both reported Belle's activities to the Department of Children and Family Services, right?" I react too quickly here, because I feel the need to clarify what Caz was telling me. He told me in the previous session that Belle had been reported to the Department of Children and Family Services, but he didn't say who had reported her.

To my surprise, Caz replies, "No, I don't think either of them reported her because they didn't totally believe me. I sort of led them to believe that the time I spent with Belle was the only fun part of my life and I loved going to her house. I told them about the fondling but not about the actual sexual acts."

I pride myself on having a poker face, especially with clients, but I must have a look on my face that indicates I'm unhappy with the information that two mental health professionals saw Caz when he was a young child, knew about the abuse, and did not report their suspicions to the authorities.

"Did I do something wrong?" Caz asks.

Darn, he's internalized my reaction and is blaming himself. I knew I was too abrupt. Try again. "Caz, all mental health professionals have the legal responsibility to report any suspected sexual activity with a child, no matter what the child thinks about it." I then delicately ask Caz if the psychiatrist is the same person he's seeing now for medication. Caz looks forlorn "I don't want to get him in trouble." (lengthy silence). "I've been seeing him for the last 20 years."

Crud! Now I'm on a very slippery slope. I decide to go a different direction rather than make Caz feel guilty. The possibility that his psychiatrist and previous counselor didn't follow the reporting law could make him feel responsible for not being as explicit as he was with me. Perhaps I'm rescuing Caz from his dilemma but, hey, I can get a big rescue complex like the best of them. Again, I try something different. "I see you wrote on your intake sheet that you're taking 20 mg of Lexapro for depression, 150 mg of trazodone as a sleep aid, Klonopin (.25 mg prn), and BuSpar (15 mg three times a day) for anxiety." Caz nods. "That's quite a cocktail. How are they working for you?" He looks down at his shoes and plays with his shoelaces and says, "Ok I guess." I continue, "Does the Lexapro control your depression?" Caz shrugs "I guess".

"How about the Klonopin and BuSpar, do they control your anxiety?"

"Not really." he says.

"Are you satisfied with the medications you're taking?" Atta girl, go for the meds, not the ethics. Caz responds that he's still depressed and anxious and still not falling asleep until 3 a.m. This means he cannot get up in the morning, so he sleeps most of the day. His goes on to say that his father is **extremely** angry with him for staying up until 3 a.m. and not getting up until three in the afternoon. Hmmm now where to go? Am I being side tracked? To tell the truth, it's easier to talk about his meds and sleeping patterns than about possible ethics violations.

"Are you in bed and not falling asleep until three or are you staying up until three?" Caz stops and looks at his fingernails. "I don't go to bed because I can't fall asleep."

"So it's both." I say. Caz nods. I continue, feeling a little like the interrogation squad. "When do you take your trazodone?" Now I can see Caz crawling into his shell. The 10 year old is clearly present. "I take it around 1 a.m."

Here I go again, I'm going to sound parental, but I need the information, and Caz is not as forthcoming about his medication use as he was about his abuse. I wonder why. There is no way to ask this next question but straight up, therefore I gentle down my voice to make the question more palatable. "Why would you wait until 1:00 to take the trazodone?" Caz waits several minutes, still looking at his hands, playing with his cuticles. Finally he says, "I dunno."

I hate when clients do that! You know that they know, and they know that they know the information, but they don't share what they know! Ok, go easy with him, he's only 10 right now. "Are you aware the trazodone is being prescribed to help you sleep?"

Caz, "Yes."

Now I'm really confused, but I have a hunch I know what is going on. "Caz, are you avoiding sleep because of what happened at night at Belle's?" Caz nods and a tear falls on his hands, then another. He sighs deeply and looks up like a little boy who is confused as to why he's been bad. I need to shift my manner a bit. I'm still coming across too parental.

"I see. Well, how is staying up late helping you to avoid the thoughts of Belle?"

Caz says, "If I am not in bed, then I won't have the feelings of dread."

"Dread about what, Caz?" I ask gently. (However, I feel haughty because I know what he's going to say.) But I get slammed for my arrogance when he says, "That I may not be picked that night." Silence on both our parts.

Oh, no! The session is over. Darn, I wish I had more time. Ok, go for the easy fix for now.

"Caz, would you be willing to see another psychiatrist for a second opinion?" Caz looks relieved. He's off the hot seat,

His tone of voice changes and he sits up, "I would definitely be open to another opinion and would really like a Christian woman."

Aha, the adult persona returned.

Caz' Regret

I tried to control the direction of our session by working on my dreams. But now I regret it. My dreams were interesting, but not critical to the work we started last week. Lisa did have some interesting thoughts about my dreams, but I really like the fact that she lets me see the connections and doesn't tell me what my dreams mean. They are **my** dreams, after all.

The second part of the session we started talking about Belle, but then we ended up talking about my psychiatrist and counselor.

I know they should have reported what Belle was doing. I also know I feel somewhat responsible for their not seeing Belle as doing something wrong. I made light of it to them. I think Lisa would disagree and say they were the professionals and should have discussed the goings-on with my dad and the Department of Children and Family Services. This session wasn't as helpful as the first ones and I'm leaving the session with a heavy heart and the name of a new psychiatrist. My heavy heart is because I had to admit to Lisa that I'm avoiding going to sleep and am enjoying staying in bed all day. What's there for me to do all day anyway? I promise myself that I'll get back to Belle for our next session, if I'm up to it. Sigh.

Lisa
Disappointing Session with Caz

My work with Caz was not up to par today. I believe he was trying to avoid talking about the abuse by switching the topic to his dreams. So I went with the dreams. I didn't want to push him to stay with his abuse story because he seemed more fragile and less defended this week. Therefore, I let him drive the session as long as the discussion was helpful to him.

However, when he revealed that his previous mental health professionals didn't report the abuse, he put me in a dilemma about what to do with the information he gave me. At least I know Belle's not able to abuse anyone now. Or is she? I can't take the chance. A call to the Department of Children and Family Services or the police will give me the information I need. I don't think Caz is lying, but I have to make sure he's processing information correctly. He's too confused and too injured to see things clearly. In addition, I'm relying on his self-report with regard to the psychiatrist and therapist. Caz said he down-played the abuse. Did he share the abuse with them at all?

The call to DCFS is an eye-opener. The social worker tells me that in 1989, a woman who was seeing Caz for counseling reported the possibility of some sexual abuse of boys by Belle Surte. The person chose not to leave her name but asked the department to look into it. The social worker could not verify what type of professional had called in 1989. The report indicates that one visit was made to Belle's home. No evidence to substantiate the abuse was found, so there was no further follow up. The case was reopened this year when Pastor Craig Morris reported he had reason to suspect Belle of abusing multiple victims.

I inform the social worker that I'm working with one of the abuse victims and can substantiate Pastor Morris' concerns. She says the case was turned over to the police several weeks ago. I notice I'm breathing better with this news. When I ask her whether I'm mandated to report my client's previous therapists for their failure to report the abuse, the social worker stammers for a minute, spouting the law. I ask again, "If my client's mental health professionals knew about the abuse and did not report it, do I need to report that fact to their licensing boards?" She says she'll have to get back to me after she talks with her supervisor. My guess is I'll never hear from her again. These agencies are swamped. Ok, at least I'm on record about my concern. Unfortunately this doesn't let me entirely off the hook. I'll call the Board of Examiners of Psychiatrists because I know the psychiatrist's name, but I don't know the counselor's name so calling the Counseling Board would be a waste of time. Also, I can assume that the counselor was the anonymous tip, though I'll never know. The other alternative is for Caz to report his psychiatrist, but he's already so injured by the abuse that the act of reporting his psychiatrist before he's ready (If he ever is.) may be devastating to him. I realize the child abuse reporting laws are written to protect children, but the same law sometimes catches us in a double-bind when we're working with brittle victims. If I push him to report this possible infraction, Caz may crash or lose trust in me and refuse to return to therapy.

Caz Embraces his Sexual Abuse

I'm ready to talk about Belle again, no dream journal, no sidetracking. Lisa begins with a check-in about whether I've seen Dr. Jamison. I tell her I have an appointment next week. She seems pleased. Good. Lisa then approaches the subject of my previous psychiatrist and therapist. She acknowledges that memories about the sessions with the psychiatrist and counselor were those of a child. So the content of the sessions are foggy. She's right, I'm feeling somewhat responsible, but what I remember and what may be true could be different, because I was only a kid. I tell her I can't think about this now...I need to work on me. I say "If you have to report them then, go ahead. I don't remember the name of the counselor, so only my soon-to-be ex-psychiatrist is at risk." She looks a bit surprised but drops the subject, thank God.

Lisa asks how Belle was connected with my church. I ask her if she's talked with Pastor Craig, and Lisa says she hasn't. I thought Pastor Craig would tell her this information, but evidently it's up to me. For the first time I feel anger at Lisa. Why hasn't she followed through with Pastor Craig? Why is she pushing the reporting of my psychiatrist? That happened years ago! And in my sessions, I probably down played the incidents with Belle. Shit. This is getting too complicated. I need to focus. I take a deep breath and begin.

"Belle is a vocational deacon in the Episcopal Church and has been a deacon for over 30 years. When she was first ordained, she was assigned to another parish before ours, but she had helped out in our parish every now and then. She considered our parish her church home. Evidently, she was raised in our parish as a little girl and everyone loved her. When our previous pastor became ill, he requested she be reassigned to our parish. That was 10 or 11 years ago. Generally, deacons are moved after three to five years in a parish. However, the rector was a very good friend of hers. He buried her husband, Allan. Belle supported our pastor and his family as he was dying. She assumed most of his duties and kept the parish running smoothly through the long search for a new rector. No one would have believed what Belle was doing in her home. Even as a kid, I knew if I said anything about Belle's antics, no one would have believed me.

"When Pastor Craig arrived, he didn't have the same history with or attachment to Belle that our previous pastor had, so he was able to look at the deacon situation with a fresh pair of eyes. First he was surprised at how long Belle had been assigned to our parish. He also saw Belle violating small boundaries like spreading information about parishioners, and he asked her to cease gossiping. She became irate and told him that he didn't know the atmosphere at the parish. She insisted the parish was an 'open parish' in which we all know each other's problems and we pass information to each other for prayer purposes. Is she good or what!? (Lisa smiled. I'm glad I made her smile.) Pastor Craig didn't buy it and asked her to respect the boundaries he had established. She then began to spread rumors about Pastor Craig. I guess she wanted him to leave, but instead he saw this as a gauntlet challenge and asked the Bishop to reassign her to another parish. The Bishop was surprised by Pastor's request for Belle's reassignment. She had been the bulwark of the parish while the previous pastor was ill, and the Bishop thought she could be of great help to Craig during the transition, after which the Bishop was willing to reassign her. Once Pastor Craig insisted on her reassignment, the Bishop acted immediately. I learned most of this from Dad who was one of the church leaders. Dad never told me the details, but I frequently overheard some of his phone conversations.

"After she left the parish, one man named Bryce came forward and spoke to Pastor Craig about his experience with Belle. Bryce said he came forward because Pastor had shown great courage in standing up to Belle, and he felt he could say something now that he knew Pastor would believe him. I know Bryce. He's a couple years older than me, and he was in Belle's house through some of my most frequent encounters. He's married with two sons.

"Of course, when Belle was confronted with what Bryce said, she denied it all and called him 'mentally unbalanced'. The Bishop and Pastor didn't know what to do because it was Bryce's word against Belle's. I think they believed Bryce, but they needed more evidence. However, Pastor Craig didn't want a witch-hunt in the parish. He especially didn't want kids being coerced by their parents to come forward because of the possibility of a lawsuit against the diocese which could mean possible financial gain for the victims. I watched this all unfold and gained a great deal of respect for how Pastor Craig and the Bishop handled the problem. Recently, my father was elected to the vestry again and therefore knew a lot about Bryce's accusation. My father had to suspect I may have been involved, but if he did, he didn't ask me. Belle had been placed on suspension while the investigation continued, quietly. How this hasn't made the papers or the news, I don't know. Maybe with all the problems the Roman Catholic Church was having, this issue seemed too mild in comparison. Or maybe the church handled the problem with great care. I don't know what happened, but I do know I felt compelled to talk to Pastor Craig. I told him about my relationship with Belle and that I knew of a dozen others who had been involved as children. But I also told Pastor Craig that I loved Belle for all the wonderful times I had at her house. She made each of us feel special and she treated us with respect and kindness. Pastor Craig was shocked I felt this way.

"After I came forward, others did too. When the parish and the diocese realized the extent and impact of Belle's activities her deaconate was revoked or she was defrocked or something. I'm not sure what they call it. Over 100 boys had been a part of Belle's activities over her 20 years as a deacon. The police have begun to investigate and Bryce, who first came forward, has brought a civil lawsuit. I've been asked if I want to join the suit, but I don't know if I want to. I feel I have already betrayed Belle's trust in me, and I'm not sure I wanna go further and see her suffer more.

I look up and see Lisa sitting and staring incredulously at me. She doesn't know what to say. Clearly she had no idea of the extent of the problem. She only says, "Caz, I admire your loyalty and that you can forgive Belle, but she **did sexually abuse** you and the other boys."

I'm stunned. Abuse didn't seem to be the correct word, and yet I couldn't think of another one. So I ask what I think is a silly question, that turns out to be not so silly. "Why is what she did abusive?"

Lisa takes a deep breath, and I can tell she's choosing her words carefully. She says, "Because she had more power than you did. She used her power in the church to coax boys to her house and then used all of you for her own pleasure. The fact that you received gifts, swimming privileges, video evenings, and pony rides doesn't make what she did right or imply consent from you."

I frown like I don't understand and she continues. "It's sort of like prostitution. She gave you child currency (movies, ponies, swimming) in exchange for sex. Just because it felt good to you doesn't mean it was ok."

My head is beginning to ache. The realization that I have been brain-washed to believe what we did was ok was swirling around my head. If we had fun and enjoyed it then, it wasn't abuse. Was it? It was just, just a boundary issue. I want to keep talking and understand more about what this all means, but deep down inside I began to feel something shift. I begin to see the contradiction, and yet, I'm tenaciously holding on to my shreds of denial. I know I'm at a turning point and I JUST DON'T WANT TO TURN! My heart is screaming. I had been prostituted! My mind is saying, "But no money changed hands, and I never had sex with anyone other than Belle." Did I?

My brain is flooded with images. "OH MY GOD!" I scream, forgetting I'm in an office where clients are possibly waiting outside who could hear me. "I was her male prostitute! She shared me with her friends on occasion and she had us fondle and do oral sex on each other while she watched." My heart is pounding; my brain is turning to mush. I am confused. My house of cards is falling, and yet the cards are beginning to come together to make a new house. I have to let go of the fantasy of Belle and deal with the reality of what happened. But I don't want to. I want Belle, her love, her kindness, the fun we shared. I don't want this to turn into a horror. But it's turning into horror. I'm literally seeing red in front of my eyes. My entire being is shaken to the core. And yet, I'm just sitting there, stunned, quiet. My insides don't match my outside. Lisa's quiet. I'm quiet.

Lisa asks me if I'm ok and I say, "Yes" while screaming "NO" with every cell in my body. She asks me to take a couple deep breaths. I do. She lets me sit and internally process, but I can't make sense of all this. It was abuse! Not love. Lisa asks again if I'm ok. I say 'yes' and smile. I can't believe I mustered a smile. I nod when she confirms my appointment for next week. She asks if I need more time. She suggests that if I may need to regain my composure, I can sit in one of the other rooms for awhile. I again tell her I'm ok. I get up to walk and my legs are moving, but they feel like cement.

I begin shaking as I approached Dad's car and my father sees my unsteadiness as I get in the car. He reaches out to touch me, but I don't want to be touched. I shout, "Get away from me. I am dirty." My father looks hurt, but I can't comfort him. I'm too busy with my own pain. He starts the car, and takes me home and makes lunch as if nothing happened.

I can't eat. So, I do what I always do...I go to bed and hold my pillow. I cry, yell, curse, and then my body begins to heave. I have diarrhea, I vomit, I sweat, and begin to faint. My father hears a crash and runs upstairs. He finds me on the floor and starts to call 911, but I beg him not to call, so he hangs up. The room is a tunnel. My pillow feels hard and sharp. Nothing makes sense. By that time my brother runs up the stairs, I'm sitting on the floor like a floppy stuffed animal, legs outstretched, arms dangling at my side, head hanging down on my chest. I'm totally depleted. Both of them are giving me quizzical looks.

My father asks me if I'm alright. I nod. "I had a rough session and I felt sick." Dad looks compassionate, but Rom doesn't understand. I take a deep breath and retell the story I told Lisa, but I shortened it to a few minutes.

My brother says, "Unbelievable! And I was jealous because you got to go over there."

Dad and Rom join me on the floor. I cry and they hold me. Dad's stroking my head the way he used to do when I was a little boy and I had a fever. I feel a wet nose under my arm pushing me. Our Chocolate Lab, Cocoa, nudges her way into the middle of us and we hug her, too. We laugh through our tears at her need to be held too, just like one of the family. Maybe, I've just begun to heal, but I have a long way to go. I wonder if I'll ever be really whole. I want to call Lisa and tell her what impact our session had on me, but my dad says I should respect her privacy. So I don't call.

Lisa's Discussion with Craig

Should I have let Caz leave my office? His face was the color of raw snow peas. During the last five minutes of the session, he kept saying he was ok, but I had the feeling something was happening inside of him. He either wouldn't or couldn't share it with me at that moment. Perhaps he didn't even know what was happening. I'm grateful he has his father and brother at home, but I don't know if he'll confide in them. I'm debating whether to check on him or not. I don't want to increase his dependency on me, but, at the same time, if he's having difficulty, he needs to know he has options. New clients don't always know they can call for an additional appointment if they feel shaky after a very difficult session. I call Caz' home number. No answer.

A "free" hour during my day only means I don't have a client. The hour is hardly ever "free". There are always phone calls to make to insurance companies and prescribing physicians etc. Today I put in another call to Pastor Craig in hopes that his travels are over for awhile. My call is answered by his voicemail, again, and I leave a message, again, that sounds important, but give no hint of why I need to see him. He probably knows why I'm calling anyway. He calls back a couple of hours later when I have a 'free hour', and we agree to meet later this evening.

The old stone church is quaint and should feel safe. It doesn't. The access it provided Belle to contact innocent children, makes the church feel sinister to me. Maybe because it's 7:30 p.m. and I'm tired. I should have gone home and met Craig another time. However, I need to hear his take on the story. While I trust Caz' recount of Belle's history with the church, he's filtering his view of the situation through the loving experience he had with Belle. Caz was abused, yet never felt abused. He's just beginning to realize the damage he has suffered. However, Caz still feels badly about her pending legal problems. My hunch is Craig will be much less sympathetic of Belle's plight.

Craig is a slight man of average height with a receding hairline, which is receding too early for his age. He looks about 37 and his office is filled with "daddy" stuff. The handmade pictures, mugs, and handprints in plaster blobs all attest to the fact that he's a proud father of two children. Craig's greeting is warm, but he has the look of a man who has survived an atomic explosion and knows there's more nuclear fallout to occur.

Craig confirms what Caz told me about the number of children harmed, the manner in which he found out, the ridicule and rumors he's endured, and the support of the diocese. I learned Caz is a good historian. Then Craig speaks of his anger, and it's clear he's not come to grips with his own rage. I can't blame him. When I think of the abuse, I have difficulty seeing anything but fire engine red myself, and I haven't endured the personal attacks that he has. Craig's concerned about Caz centers around Caz' vulnerability, and he wonders out loud what the response will be when Caz finally understands what's happened to him. I ponder our most recent session and wonder if some of the enlightenment may have already begun.

I agree with Craig's assessment of how Belle's behavior affected Caz, and I have other concerns as well. Caz is a damaged person who may need years of therapy because of the abuse, but he also has a number of other disorders that may or may not be directly related to the abuse. My major concern is that Caz' coexisting disorders are probably interfacing with his trauma. For example, Caz reports he's depressed. Is this related only to Belle's abuse? Or does it precede the abuse? Could Caz become suicidal and would his father be alert to the possibility? Craig assures me that Caz' father, Stewart, is a kind man who's done his best for Caz and Rom. But, Craig believes that Stewart was unable to see what Belle was up to because he was enraged by his wife abandonment of the family, and he was further overwhelmed with raising two boys alone. Stewart was grateful for the respite care Belle provided by taking Caz to her home for weekends. Stewart blames himself for allowing Caz to be swept up in Belle's playground just so Stewart could get a break from parenting. His guilt overwhelms him at times. Craig has been helpful in these moments but Stewart refuses to see a counselor.

Craig suggests that Stewart should be given a place to vent his feelings and deal with his own issues so he can be more available to Caz. Stewart may not know that Caz has Posttraumatic Stress Disorder (PTSD) directly related to the abuse. He may not even know what that is, nor understand fully what Caz is currently going through. The symptoms of PTSD can include poor sleep patterns and lethargy. So can depression. While Craig is not a trained mental health professional, he has been ministering to several of his parishioners as they related their stories of Belle's abuse. He sees how damaged these boys and men are, and he seems to have a good relationship with Stewart. Craig agrees to meet with Stewart to explain what Caz and the other victims are experiencing. I agree with this being a positive first step and offer to make a referral if Craig feels Stewart needs more than pastoral support.

Because the abuse was perpetrated by a member of his congregation, Craig is knowledgeable concerning Belle's legal case. Twenty boys and men have come forward and the investigation is continuing.

"You mean Belle hasn't been arrested?!" I say incredulously.

Craig sadly shakes his head. "I think her arrest is imminent, but the police have been reticent to get involved with church business, and to be frank; I don't think they see Belle's activity as being 'real abuse' because many of the men and boys don't either. Craig explains that the two officers who interviewed him were very professional until one of them said flippantly, "I wish I had had a Belle in my life to introduce me to the art of sex." The officer winked.

Both of us sit quietly. "How do we make them understand the tragedy of this?" I ask.

Craig answers, "I'm not sure. How skilled are you at changing our world's cultural views?"

Touché. We part agreeing to make contact in a couple of weeks, after Craig has a chance to talk to Stewart. I introduce Craig to the release of confidential information form I use so we can talk openly with each other.

Drained of energy like a computer that's been disconnected from its power source too long, I walk to my car with Craig as an escort. I receive a warm handshake from a saddened priest who stumbled into the intimate muck and mire of his parishioners' lives. I stumble into that mire everyday with clients, but it's my job. I knew what I was getting into when I walked into my first masters-level counseling course. As he turns to walk away, I notice he's walking slightly hunched over.

Only two more days until the weekend, and I'm resolved to do something on Saturday that'll take me away from the pain

I hear all week. When I first started my master's degree, the faculty emphasized taking care of ourselves and leaving our clients' problems in the office. I remember wondering if I could turn off caring when I left the office and not think about clients when I wasn't with them. I thought if I failed at this new career it would be because I was unable to separate myself from my clients' problems once I closed the office door. For after all, my breaching of boundaries had occurred when I was a teacher.

The word 'failure' would loom over me when a faculty member would tell me I was over involved with a client. I didn't dare tell my supervisors that I thought about my clients in between sessions, let alone prayed for them. I knew what they would say. "You need better boundaries. You have a savior complex." However, I found I was wrong about my ability to establish and keep my personal boundaries. I became skilled at turning off my work clock and turning on my pleasure clock. In fact, I became irritated when clients would call me in between sessions with questions or information that could wait until I saw them again. My well-meaning faculty members and supervisors were also wrong. One cannot fake empathy or simply turn it off because it's time to go home. Some clients stay with you after the door is closed. I call this "break-through empathy". And to be honest, some of my best insights have occurred when I was not in the counseling room. It's as if my brain relaxes and the neurotransmitters allow an idea to break through the surface like a whale breaching the surface of the ocean.

From the moment I met Caz, I knew he was going to be a client who stayed with me between sessions, possibly invading my dreams and my prayer life. When Pastor Craig said that Caz' story was compelling, he was right. This young man has had a very difficult life, and he is only 28. He suffers from several mental disorders, and he's currently incapable of meeting life's simple demands, such as getting out of bed in the morning. In one of those moments when I was sitting still (which doesn't happen very often), I realized he's disabled, at least for the time being. I decided to shift from only working on his the problem areas to embracing his successes and using his strengths. I learned this technique from reading a book about Positive Psychology (Seligman, 2004). The theorist believes no matter what overwhelming issue a person is dealing with, there are strengths and positive areas that can be tapped and used to promote health. I have found this concept to be valid and helpful with clients. Refocusing on the positive often lifts a client's mood and calms the savage monster within. Little did I know, Caz was going to challenge my, and Seligman's, belief.

While waiting for my dinner to cook, I call again to check on Caz. No one answers the home phone and I don't leave a message because I can't say anything on an answering machine that Stewart and Rom might hear without breaking Caz' confidence.

Chapter Three
Deeper Explorations

Childhood feelings and conflicts emerge from the deep recesses of the unconscious: there is emotional regression. As patients once again experience these old emotions, they tend to attach them to the analyst. This process is called transference.

(Nye, 1986, p. 38)

Noelle
First Death Experiences

I'm surprised! Noelle shows up and is precisely on time again. She hands me the intake file, completed in very neat, perfect handwriting. However, she still hasn't made eye contact. She puts down her purse and is now concentrating on picking at the arm of the chair. Today she's wearing a light blue pantsuit, and she looks like the icebergs I saw in Alaska. The icebergs are light blue at the core because the ice is so dense they cannot reflect any color except blue. Noelle feels dense to me. She is tense, turtled-in, noninteractive, and shut down. She's, at the same time, both dense and faded. Noelle looks at me expectantly.

"Hi Noelle, how are you this week?

Shrug.

"I need to go over a few things before we begin. Okay?" She nods. I launch into my regular speech about confidentiality, insurance, what happens in the event of disclosure of child abuse, suicide or homicide ideation or intent, cancellation policy, substance abuse before a session, etc. She listens and then shrugs. I finish with, "I really want to assure you that, although your employer is insisting you come to counseling, I will not be able to acknowledge to him that you are a client and I will not speak to him about what you say in here. Do you have any questions?"

Noelle scowls and then shakes her head 'no'. All of this information is in the file I gave her last week to fill out and read, but I still go over the contents verbally because some clients, like Caz, don't read the information. They just sign where it's indicated.

"Ok. I'd like to get to know you a little bit better, May I ask some questions about your background?" She scowls again and looks up from under her eyelids and nods.

"Ok. Please tell me about your original nuclear family."

"Ma wha?"

"The family you grew up in. What was it like to be in your family?"

"Ok, I guess."

"Well, was it a warm? (she is shaking her head 'no'), caring? (she continues to shake her head), loving? (she stops sharking her head and shrugs her shoulders). Your family was sort of loving?"

Noelle presses her mouth into a line and her lips disappear. "They loved each other, but dey din't show it much."

"Would you feel comfortable in sharing your earliest memory?"

She doesn't ask what I mean, just launches into her first memory. "I wuz four an' in a church. Ma grandmother wuz up at the altar thing in a casket. I wuz scared, but ma'mom, she made me go up dere. She lifted me up so I can see Gran. I'm shakin'. I'm skeered to death. I start screamin' an' kickin' but, Mom, she holds on tight an' pushes my face into ma Gran's an' yells at me. 'Kiss her, kiss her goodbye.' An' I vomit into the casket. She's looks horrified an' drops me an' I land on Gran, but my legs, dey hit the edge of the coffin. I'm screamin' louder cuz now I'm hurt too, not jist scared. Everybody comes runnin'. Ma mom is sobbin' an' screamin'. "Git her outta here. She's ruined my mommy." Noelle looks up at me with the same straight line mouth and then, shrugs.

I honestly don't know what to say! For someone who hasn't said more than a couple of words, she came through with an intense memory. However, she told the story as if she were reciting her grocery list. I'm also aware that half way through the memory she shifted from past tense to present tense. I don't think it was because she doesn't know the difference.

"That was a horrible experience. "

"Yea, an' I can r'member it like it wuz today."

"Were you close to your Gran?"

Tears, lots of tears. Her voice shakes as she says. "Yeeaaa." Then the tears dry up as quickly as they start. She has an amazing ability to control her expression of feelings.

"What happened next?"

"Don't r'member nothin' afer dat."

"You don't remember the rest of the funeral or the burial or how your mother treated you later that day?

"No. I only r'member she wuz reeeel mad. She cried all the time an' slept a lot"

"Were you close to your mom?"

"I guess, but we weren't close after dat."

"What do you mean?" Gosh, we're really having a conversation!

"She stayed in bed lots, she didn't make us food. Dad did. He said Mom wuz sick. I thought I made her sick. But, I don't think dat now."

"What do you think?"

"I think Gran made her sick."

"I don't understand."

"Gran died of the bad kinda flu. Mom got it too."

"I see."

"Mom died two weeks later of 'nomonia."

I tried to remain very calm and not show the astonishment I feel, but this was getting to be quite a story. "Your mom died two weeks later?" I said incredulously.

"Yep."

"That's a lot of loss for a four year old to process."

She shrugs her right shoulder only.

"You don't think so?"

"I guess. Look I gotta run. I gotta lot of work ta'do. See you nex' week, same time?"

"Sure." And she's gone. I now realize Noelle is not able to tolerate much closeness or intensity with me and probably with most people. She seems to run or fade away. I notice she doesn't wear makeup which adds to the washed out look of her face. Her hair is cut blunt so she doesn't have to do anything to it except wash it. She doesn't want to be noticed. I'm sure her boss, who finds her attractive, scared her when he asked her out. She does everything she can not to draw attention to herself. In addition, her personality is blunted, almost like she didn't develop after a certain point in her life. She has expressed no emotion except she cries, but I'm not sure she knows why she is crying. When she's not crying, she has flat affect, is almost non-intractive in conversation, and has a grumpy look to her face. Darn, I wish I could remember who she reminds me of.

I look at the file she completed, and realize she was born on Christmas Eve 40 years ago. I guess that explains her name. Her middle name is Holly. In the space where it asks "What do you hope to get out of counseling?" Noelle Holly wrote, "Keep ma'job." Clear and to the point. I didn't expect anything else.

Noelle
I Can't Git Close

That wuz intense! I din't wanna go into ma past, but Lisa's too easy to talk to. I got caught up in her interest in ma story. I don't see the point. The pass is pass an' nothin' can change it, so why drag it up? I gotta watch how close I get to her, she's sneaky. Got me talkin' b'fore I know'd it. At least I don't hav'ta go back for 'nother whole week.

Lisa, Caz, and Frick and Frack

The week between the sessions with Caz flies by and although I call several times, there's never an answer. Caz does not call me either, therefore I see it as a sign he's all right after the last session.

I'm due to see him at 10:00 a.m. so I arrive at the office at 9:30 to prepare for my day. There's a note on the door saying the police stopped by to see me. I wonder if it's about Caz, and I begin to get concerned. At 9:55 the door bell rings to alert me that someone is entering the office. I turn the corner expecting to see Caz, but two police officers are standing in my waiting room. One is tall and lean with an angular face that hadn't experienced a smile in decades. The other one is short, pleasantly chunky with a "Peck's bad boy" smile. I immediately thought of Frick and Frack, though I have no idea where these names come from. I think the names mean that two people are closely aligned in some way. My mother used to use the names Frick and Frack in referring to me and my best friend, Bessie. We looked alike and acted alike. However, the two detectives are totally different on the outside, but they move in unison. They turn together to look at my art work, they nod together, and they even gesture the same way, therefore the names Frick and Frack stick. Detective Frick (tall and lean) says they want to talk to me about Caz and Belle. Because of client privilege, I can't tell them anything about Caz or Belle. I look blankly at Detective Frick. Therefore, Detective Frack thinks he'll have a go of it. "Doctor, we know you're seeing Casper Rheems for counseling concerning his allegations of sexual abuse by Belle Surte."

I'm astounded they know this, but that still doesn't absolve me of my ethical responsibility to protect my client's right to have our counseling sessions held confidential. I take a deep breath and begin, "First of all, detectives, I am not a doctor; I'm ABD, 'all-but-dissertation'. Second, I cannot even acknowledge whether a 'Casper Rheems' is seeing me. Third, you both know the law of confidentiality. I can only break confidentiality if one of my clients is a danger to himself or others or if my client gives me permission to talk with you. I have no one in my practice who is currently in such a danger. Detective Frack smiles and says, "Now, now little lady there's no reason to become upset. We've already talked to Mr. Rheems and he told us he was seeing you for counseling because of what happened between him and Ms. Belle Surte."

I can't believe it. Why didn't Caz call me to let me know he had spoken to the police **and** had given them my name **and** that they may be dropping by? Remember what I said about clients who call between sessions when they could wait? Caz shouldn't have waited. He put me in a difficult position with these men. Also, I have a hunch that Detective Frack is the one who said to Pastor Craig "I wish I had had a Belle in my life to introduce me to the art of sex." So, I immediately had a negative reaction to him. Wow, do I have to rein in my assumptions! Frack may not have said that and these men may not be the same detectives at all. Frick could have said it, though looking at him, I can't see him winking at anyone unless he was trying to remove an oak log from his eye with a gallon of Visine.

The door opens and Caz casually saunters into the office 10 minutes late. Well, so much for denying he's my client. Both detectives smirk at the irony. I groan, silently of course. Caz smiles, "Well, I see you three got connected." I put on my take-charge pinafore. "Detectives would you mind stepping into this office for a few minutes and can I get you some coffee?" Both detectives, in unison entered the empty office and declined coffee. "Caz, please come into my office for a few minutes."

To my surprise, Caz takes the lead. He explains that over the weekend the detectives spent time with him getting all the details of the 'experience'. He still is uncomfortable with the word 'abuse'. Caz apologizes for not calling me to let me know that the detectives may be trying to contact me. I nod. I explain to Caz about privilege and confidentiality. Caz looks unimpressed, "I would like the detectives to meet with us." "Really?" I say incredulously. "Yea," responded Caz. I invite the detectives to join us.

Ok, here I am, sitting in my counseling room with my client and Frick and Frack because my client desires it. Yipes. Detective

Frick starts, "We are trying to figure out if laws have been broken by these sexual encounters."

I have had it, "Experience? Sexual Encounters? Doesn't anyone see this as long term sexual abuse of multiple child victims?" Detective Frick continues, "We are having a difficult time finding men who were, to use your word, victims, and who feel they were abused. They are all stating that Belle is a wonderful person who doted on them and made them feel special."

I am so done; stick a candy thermometer in me. "Detectives, this is Caz' time, and we need to get started. But, before I let you go I wish to remind you that some of these 'men' were only 9 years old when the first sexual encounter took place. I don't care whether they enjoyed it or not, whether they loved Belle or not, whether they felt special or not. The act of a woman touching a boy inappropriately is against the law." Both detectives smile, look at each other, and say in unison, "You're right."

Frick continues. "We just needed to hear it from a professional."

I don't get it. I've dealt with myriad sexual abuse victims, and law enforcement officers never gave me the time of day. What is it about this case that they need a professional counselor to define the law for them? Were Frick and Frack setting me up to react? Well, they did a good job. My irate heart is pounding.

Detectives Frick and Frack rise, in unison of course, and Frick apologizes for interrupting our session with a very slight bow, which is duplicated by Frack, and they head for the door. Caz says, "I'm glad you were able to connect." With his hand on the door handle, Frick turns and explains that while the church is taking these actions extremely seriously, the males in the legal system are dragging their feet, even worse they are making jokes about Belle running a sex education facility. About 100 men and boys have been identified and have been interviewed. However, most of the men who have been abused are standing behind Belle and are not cooperating with the police. Twenty are cooperating but are downplaying the abuse and are reticent to testify. Only Bryce and Caz are agreeing to be witnesses. We're looking for confirmation that this is serious and that the men have been harmed by the activity, because most of them are not acknowledging that fact.

I am sorry, I still don't get it. This seems as crystal clear as a raindrop to me. Why is there such muddy water surrounding Belle's abuse of children. If she had been a man and the victims had been girls would this legal confusion and hesitation be happening? I doubt it. Is this a gender discrimination issue or reversal of cultural mores? I can think of this later, I need to deal with Caz.

Caz is smiling, really smiling. I don't think I've ever seen him smile broadly before. I ask him to explain why he told the detectives he's seeing me and he unveils the story of what happened when he left my office. He talks about his crying, physical illnesses, the group hug, etc.

"What was the outcome of my reaction?" Caz asks as if he is the therapist. "Well, I can see clearly now that Belle was an abuser. She used her home, pool, ponies, videos, gifts, etc. to get us to bed." Then his mood darkens and he says, "She didn't do these things for us because she loved us, though she said she did and I believed her because I was a little needy boy, she did them because **she** wanted us to perform sex acts **for her**. When I left here, I started to see this abuse for what it was and I felt duped, used, and betrayed. I had a lousy weekend, but my father and brother hung in there with me. On Sunday night, the detectives came by. I had spoken to them once before and told them I wouldn't testify against Belle because she always treated me with respect and love and I had fond memories of my time with her. On Sunday they came by again, and by then I was singing a different tune. I was feeling angry, and said I'd testify. They were intrigued with the flip-flop I had made and asked how this had happened and I said, "I got me the best little counselor in the world."

Caz is grinning from ear to ear. Is he kidding? We have a lot of work to do. Yes, the scales of having been brain-washed fell away from his eyes, but the hard work is still to be done. He looks so happy; I just can't bring myself to poke a hole in his balloon. Caz also reports seeing Dr. Jamison, and she left most of his medications alone for now. She did remove the Klonopin and increased his Lexapro. She also told Caz he could decrease the trazodone to 100 mg if he was groggy the next day. She affirmed he should take the tazodone by 10 p.m. All in all, I'm not completely satisfied with her decision, but Caz seems content and perhaps she wants to see what happens over the next month.

Caz' session is almost over. Between the detectives and the discussion about the medication issues, I feel we "lost" our time together. Caz stretches out his lengthy frame and covers the entire loveseat. He puts his head back and says, "I don't feel like working today. I'm tired of the emotional roller coaster. But, I do want you to know I was telling the truth when I said Belle invited a few of her friends over to have sex with us boys. She also watched us have sex with each other while she masturbated. I hadn't really forgotten about these incidents, but I did put them out of my mind because they didn't fit with the rest of the story for me. I realized over the weekend that if I acknowledge these activities then I also had to acknowledge that Belle was not interested in us as people, but in what we could do for her. My house of cards was built on **not** acknowledging what she was really about. That house of cards collapsed this week."

I smile for a change. "That's very insightful." Caz turns his head to look at me and he winks, "I thought so, too." The man Caz emerged. Until then I never saw Caz as the Casanova who, according to him, helped girls in high school to lose their virginity. I had a difficult time seeing this side of him, the teacher of young girls. I wonder if Caz can help me understand him as a whole, the kid of 10 **and** the slick 16 year old. I'm also concerned that Caz, by seducing the high school girls, may have abused them without knowing it was abuse, and worry what the revelation would do to him once he saw the pattern.

Caz
New Symptoms

Well, it's done. I agreed to testify with Bryce against Belle when her trial occurs. I don't know how many other men and boys will testify, but I hope there are more than just the two of us. I watched her arrest on the news. They're talking about her in words that just don't match how I remember her, but the words describe what I know she is. She looks awful. She is almost 60 now and she appears drawn, scared, and yet defiant, with her attorney at her side. The news was gentle with the church, though, and for that I'm grateful. The church didn't know about her activities and once the story came out, the church hierarchy acted immediately to assure she didn't have access to children or any other parishioners. I just wish I had stopped it years ago, but I really believe no one would have taken me seriously when I was young. Still, I should have tried. I feel relieved and yet guilty for not saying something years ago.

I'm tired and drained, and I sleep most of the week away. My father is fed up with me. I can tell he's trying to be patient, but, day after day, I stay in bed and don't get dressed. I'm not eating well. Each day I say to myself, "Today I'm going to get up and get dressed and do something, but each day I turn over and sleep. Six days have passed, and I have accomplished nothing.

I see Lisa today, and I'm ready to work again. I sort of blew off the session last week. I was too drained to work, so I was glad the detectives were there. It was interesting to see Lisa worked up over the sexual abuse. She was my advocate and the advocate of all those boys Belle harmed. The detectives really responded to her with respect, though I doubt she felt it at first. When I spoke to them on Sunday, they were very impressed with how she had helped me to see the abuse clearly. However, I think she was upset by their showing up on her door step unannounced. I probably should have called her and warned her that they were coming. I just didn't have the energy. I need to apologize, again, if I didn't last week.

Dad's ready to leave, and I'm not ready. He's angry at me again. I don't seem to be able to manage my life. I don't understand myself. I want to see Lisa, but I don't want to get up and get dressed so we can leave on time. Consequently, I'm always late and she doesn't or can't give me extra time if I show up late. If I value our time together, why don't I make the effort? Dad's clearly pissed with me, and asks if I took a shower and brushed my teeth. I didn't, but I say "yes". He tells me I stink. What's wrong with me? I have no energy but lots of anxiety.

Lisa's ready for me, as usual. I wish I could be more like her, organized, professional, and empathic. I bet she doesn't have trouble getting up in the morning. I bet she showers and brushes her teeth. I guess you have to care about yourself to want to do routine hygiene chores. I don't believe I am worth it, so why bother? Interesting, I wasn't like this in high school or college.

Lisa begins by asking me if anything's happened this week we should talk about. First, I apologize for not calling and warning her about the possibility that the detectives would call or show up. She explains that a call would have been welcomed and would have prepared her for their questions. I also tell her that ever since I agreed to testify in court, I've been jittery. She asks me when this event will happen and I tell her I don't know. She asks how I feel about testifying, and I tell her I'm scared poopless, but I want to talk about other things today because the trial's months away.

She indicates with a nod I should continue. I don't know how to tell her about my lack of energy and poor hygiene, so I sit for awhile trying to gather my nerve. Finally, I tell her that my father angrily accused me of not showering and brushing my teeth, and I'm hurt. She knows how to go to the heart of the matter. "Did you shower and brush your teeth?" I'm trapped. I value truthfulness, but I don't want to tell her I didn't bother to take care of myself before coming to see her. So I shrug. What a childish thing to do, but it's all I could think of. She knows I didn't shower or brush my teeth. Crap! However, she doesn't judge me, she looks concerned. "Caz, I need you to call Dr. Jamison and tell her that you're unable to take care of your own personal hygiene. I think she may want to adjust your medication." Of all the things that I thought she'd say, that was the last one I'd have thought of. All I say is, "OK". Lisa also explains that even though I signed a release for her to speak to Dr. Jamison, she wants my verbal permission to talk to Dr. J. I agree, perhaps she can explain this better than I ever could. What's wrong with me?

Lisa then asks me a question that I had asked myself most of my life. "Caz, I notice you have two ways of relating to me. Sometimes you act like you're 10, shy, scared, relinquishing your power to me, and sometimes you're like a man, funny, sure of yourself, flirtatious."

I know what she means, but I don't have a clue as to why sometimes I feel confident and adult and at other times I feel scared and child-like. "I feel that way too, but I don't know what it means."

With the issue named and defined, we agree to address this as it arises. We then spend the rest of the session talking about the positive things in my life. I really can't come up with any, so Lisa suggests a few. She asks about my church, my father who loves me, support from other family. I know she's trying to lift my mood and see the positives in my life, but I honestly don't see any. I see some areas that are not all that bad, but nothing in my life makes me look forward to getting up in the morning. Lisa then asks about my faith in God. She gets me there, but I tell her I even feel God's letting me down. My prayers are not being answered in any way that I can tell. I feel like shit. I wonder if I'm frustrating her.

Lisa and Helen
Consult about Caz

As I sit with Caz and watch him interact with me, I'm concerned that his mental health is deteriorating. While he feels good about having shared his Belle saga, he may also have faced the demons too quickly, too many dark secrets that he's kept buried for too long. When abused clients reach the point of full disclosure, it's not unusual for them to feel relief and also take a mental health slide backwards. Because Caz has little personal reserve, my fear is he will slide closer to psychosis if he becomes more depressed and anxious. Having recently confronted his abuse story, plus dreading the future of having to tell his story again, especially in open court, Caz could experience stress that may tip the scale for him in a negative way. He seems relieved to have the story out in the open, and yet seems more fragile than when he first walked into my office. I need Dr. Jamison to know the symptoms Caz is currently reporting, but I'm not sure he will tell her the entire truth. Caz tends to minimize his feelings and experiences.

Talking to a psychiatrist can sometimes be a delicate situation for non-medically trained professionals. We are not always treated as peers. However, Dr. Jamison is not only a good psychiatrist, she is also a kind and thoughtful person who appears eager to hear my viewpoint and respects my expertise. I call and leave a message for her to call me at home tonight. She usually calls back promptly. Several more clients arrive, talk about their issues, and leave. In between clients, I keep thinking about Caz. Long day. I need to go home and get some perspective. I can process better at home than at the office.

Home is my refuge. Most people decorate so everything looks like a *Better Homes and Gardens* magazine. However, I like comfort. Perhaps, because I deal with uncomfortable issues each day? Hmmm? I like pictures of my family, flowers, recliners, soft colors, and lots of books. Dinner's nothing special, just food to stop my stomach from gurgling. Somehow food doesn't hold much interest tonight. I continue to think of Caz's experience, of Bally as an enigma, and of Noelle's pale persona and dreadful childhood experiences. All these situations are extremely complicated. However, I'm the most concerned about Caz, today. His mental status may deteriorate before I see him in a week. Perhaps I should have insisted on seeing him again later in the week. I'll ask Dr. Jamison for her take on whether Caz should see me twice a week for awhile.

Dr. Jamison (Helen) calls. We always chat about personal stuff before we get down to business...keeps us bonded.

I tell her about the two sides of Caz, which I've seen and he acknowledges. However, he has no amnesia between his two personalities, so that rules out Dissociative Identity Disorder, which used to be called Multiple Personality Disorder (MPD). He still may qualify for Dissociative Disorder Not Otherwise Specified (NOS) which allows for two or more personality states with no amnesia. Caz acknowledges his little boy and the seductive man.

Helen is interested in Caz' reporting of new symptoms, and my observation, of the deterioration in his personal hygiene. With Helen I feel free to talk about medications so I ask about a low dose of Risperdal and she says it's probably a good idea considering the recent deterioration in his hygiene. However, Caz has no insurance, so she'll see what drug samples she has at the office. Helen agrees to fit Caz into her schedule within the next three days. I won't have to see him again this week unless he calls me.

Three days later Helen calls to inform me that I had been very wise to pick up on the hygiene issue. When she saw Caz, he acknowledged not taking care of himself and while this has been a mild on-going symptom, the severity has increased recently and is subsequent to his initial session with her.

For his next appointment Caz shows up ON TIME. He looks clean, neat, and much less tentative. He reports he saw Helen three days after our last session and she gave him some samples of Risperdal. He began taking the medication immediately and felt some energy return within 24 hours. In addition, he says he's looking forward to a social activity that his father and brother are organizing. I'm still uncomfortable about the amount of trazodone Caz is taking and how he misuses it, but I've learned over the years to let Helen manage the medications.

Even though Caz was upset when his father expressed anger at him for not showering or brushing his teeth, I'm grateful Stewart demonstrated his frustration. Because of Stewart's outburst, Caz brought the hygiene issue to counseling. He has frequently referred to his father's and brother's anger at him. He says they don't understand why he sleeps all day and does nothing around the house. Caz hasn't realized that he's his own self-defeating enemy. He's still not taking his trazodone until two or three in the morning and therefore he sleeps all day. In addition, he seems resistant to taking the trazodone earlier. Caz understands what he should do, but doesn't do it. I cannot tell if he's punishing himself, getting back at Stewart for not recognizing the signs of abuse earlier, or scared to go to bed. There also could be co-morbid personality traits that are interfering with his ability to demonstrate self-initiative. Caz doesn't seem to know why he is resisting being compliant with Stewart's requests. He states he loves his father, and his father has been patient with him during the crisis stage when he revealed the abuse. However, Caz thinks that Stewart is expecting, even demanding, immediate improvement. For example, Stewart became angry when he came home for lunch and found Caz still in bed. Caz tells the story as if he's indignant that his father should be angry at him. I ask Caz if he knows what his dad expects of him. Caz responds immediately as if he's reciting a list he's heard many, many times. "He wants me to take my medication when I'm supposed to, go to bed at a reasonable hour, get up in the morning, keep up my personal hygiene, work around the house, and take the dog for a walk." In response to my question, "What keeps you from doing these things?" Caz responds with another question, "What the hell is the purpose?"

I wanted to say, "For starters, it would keep your father off your back." What I did do was use a motivational interviewing technique (Miller & Rollnick, 2002) by beginning a discussion about living with other people, expectations about life, and honoring one's body, but nothing held weight with Caz. He demonstrated ambivalence with his current situation, but never got to a point of talking about changing. He says he knows other people do these things routinely, but he still won't follow through. I'm beginning to believe that he doesn't think he should have to do what others do every day because he's special. He's been abused. Talking with him is like trying to sculpt mayonnaise. Bottom-line, Caz says he has no motivation to change and no confidence in his ability to change.

Ok, now what? Shifting the focus to Caz' perceptions of the positive aspects in his life, I get stopped in my tracks. Caz makes sure the conversation goes nowhere, again. He sees nothing positive, only some areas that are neutral. Caz seems irritated at my raising the 'Pollyanna' issue again. Perhaps to a person who has been abandoned, abused, used, and rejected all his life, positive thoughts seem like aliens from another planet.

Following the discussions about medication, his conflict over his father's expectations, and positive features of his life, Caz boldly announces he wants to bring up another issue, one which "has been bugging me for some time". Caz begins, "I think I'm gay. I've experienced sex with mature women, high school and college girls, the godsons, and other men while in college. The sex I liked the best involved either the godsons or men. Yet, I dream of getting married and having children some day. I'm so freakin' confused. I don't know who I am."

I have been pondering how sexual intimacy with the other godsons impacted Caz' view of sex. Was it forced, uncomfortable, enjoyable? Caz seems to have enjoyed it more than straight sex but still holds an image of being married to a woman some day.

Caz goes on to say the sex between the godsons always happened when others were watching. I jump in with a hunch about how this affected his enjoyment. Sex with the godbrothers might have an added a sense of excitement or mortification because of the voyeur aspect, whereas, sex with Belle happened in private. Caz blows the observation off with a wave of his hand and "I don't know." I drop the topic, for now. Frustration is building inside of me. I can't seem to sculpt the mayo no matter how hard I try. So I go to my old stand-by, empathy. "I know the sexual abuse confused you, Caz. You've been through a lot. No one could fault you for being bewildered about who you are, what you prefer, and what you want to do with your life."

Identity concerns are additional pieces of a clinical presentation. He doesn't know what career he wants, what direction his life is going, what sexual orientation he prefers, etc. Many people who have been abused as young children suffer with their identity. The act of abuse causes distress and conflict at all levels of a person's personality and existence. This long journey of self-discovery is one only Caz can walk, and he doesn't have enough energy or sense of self to be able to discern who he is and what he wants from life, yet.

Caz simply responds with a nod and then recaps, in his typical 'poor, poor pitiful me' style, where his life is right now. "I am 28 years old. I let my driver's license lapse, and so I can't drive, I have no job let alone a career, no friends, and I'm dependent on my father and brother for all my needs. That's pretty pathetic."

"It feels hopeless at times," I reflect.

"Yeah."

"What career did you have in mind when you finished high school?"

Caz looks past me as if he is remembering/reliving a time long ago. "I finished high school, and decided I wanted to be a doctor. I applied for and was accepted at a small college out of state. I thought going away to school would be good for me, a fresh start. The first year my grades were ok, mostly 'Cs' with a few 'Bs'. They weren't going to get me into medical school, but they were decent grades for a freshman. In my sophomore year I was given a new advisor and I didn't trust her. She was very gruff and confrontational. I wanted her to take care of me in a soft way, like Belle did, but she was mean. She informed me my grades wouldn't be good enough to get into any medical school and further, because I missed so many classes due to oversleeping, no one would ever give me a letter of recommendation, and she would make sure of it. I was crushed, but I was determined to try, so I studied harder, and my grades improved to almost all 'Bs', but Dr. Creep told me I still couldn't get into a medical school because I was still sleeping too much, my grades still weren't acceptable, and I was crazy. She suggested I enter into counseling at the school's counseling center. I was trying to please her, so I agreed and she gave me the name of one of the counselors."

I heard myself sucking in air. I'm stunned. Does this man's story ever end? "What? She said that to you? That you were crazy?" Oops, I couldn't contain myself. (I talk to myself. "Reel in the reaction, Lisa.")

Caz nods excessively like a little boy does when he's exaggerating and wants someone to believe him. "She was awful to me!"

The little boy is very evident. The man would have said "Bitch!"

"What happened next?"

Caz continues. "Dr. Creep (by the way that's not her real name, I just call her that)..."

I figured that one out!

"... had given me the name of one of her friends at the counseling center. That woman, Dr. Reese, said if I wanted to be a serious candidate for any graduate school, then I'd have to provide her with my entire medical file so she could help me. I asked her why she needed my file and she said she thought something was wrong with me. I told her there wasn't nothin' wrong with me, and I wasn't crazy. I didn't like how she talked to me. I didn't think she had the right to ask for my files, but she kept insisting, saying they could help me at their medical facility better if they knew what my doctors had worked on in the past. Over and over again, I refused to sign the form she put in front of me. I refused for almost a year. Then in my junior year, Dr. Creep called me to her office and began hounding me for my files, too, so I caved in and I signed the release on the last day of classes allowing all my doctors, including my psychiatrist, to send my medical files, I started to feel the discouraged, depressed feeling again and my exams didn't go well and my grades fell to Cs and Ds."

Caz is whining in a little boy's voice. "A part of me didn't believe her and Dr. Reese when they said they really wanted to help me, but they smiled and said they did. I wanted to please them, but somewhere deep inside I knew Dr. Creep was up to no good. When I left for summer vacation, I was on probation because my grades had fallen, and I had a 1.9 average and needed a 2.0 to remain in good standing. When I got home, I told my father what happened. He was furious and told me to call all my doctors, including my psychiatrist, and tell them not to send the file because the school had no right to that information. So, I called all my doctors and rescinded the release forms. I also made an appointment with my psychiatrist because I needed a new prescription anyway. I told him what had happened at school, and he assured me if anyone at the school called and requested the files he would not release them, and he hand wrote a note in the file stating the content was not to be released unless I gave him permission in writing. I thought I had stopped them from getting my files. But, when I returned to school in the fall, Dr. CreepyShit …

I notice Caz changed her name to reflect even more dislike for his advisor. His verbiage is so immature, like he's ten again.

"….told me she had received a copy of my psychiatrist's file and that because of what was in the file the school would never recommend me for graduate school and I would be lucky to graduate. In fact, Dr. Creep said she and Dr. Reese would see to it that none of my teachers would be permitted to give me a reference because the school would not "endorse" me as a graduate. My dreams were dashed. I fell into a depression that first week of school and couldn't concentrate. I left school and went home. After crying for a couple of days, my father told me to call my psychiatrist and find out what had happened. I didn't want to. I just wanted to die. So Dad called him and asked him what happened. He said he would check into it. A few days later I called him again (because he never returns phone calls). His secretary told me Dr. Reese had called stating she wanted my records faxed. The secretary told me she refused to send the contents of the file because I had rescinded the original order to release the file. Later that day, Dr. Crete called back and screamed at her for refusing to fax my file. Bottom line, Dr. Crete had lied to me about the psychiatrist sending my file to her. She lied! Her lie had devastated me, causing me to feel depressed and drop out of school. I never went back. What could I do?"

I can't believe what I'm hearing from Caz. Is he lying or exaggerating to cover up the truth? What should I say? What I want to say is, "Get a good attorney and sue the school, and Dr. Crete and Dr. Reese." What I do say is, "So you were a victim once again."

Caz looks like the 10 year old, sad eyes, down turned mouth, fiddling with his shirt hem. Continuing to whine, Caz asks, "Why do these things keep happening to me? My brother was not abused, he went to college, and he graduated. What's wrong with me? Do I have SCREW ME written on my forehead?" Caz begins to cry, but continues to talk through the tears. "After I left the college, I tried working. I took several jobs, but I was fired each time because I was late for work. I couldn't concentrate at school, and my grades suffered. I couldn't concentrate at work either. In short, I screw things up every time. Now my father's frustrated with me because I don't get out of bed before noon and I often forget the stuff he wants me to do during the day. Will he fire me too?"

I think he's joking so I start to laugh but think better of it.

"I think I've improved because before taking the Risperdal, I slept all day, now I'm up by noon. I never did anything around the house, and now I am getting some things done. I think that's improvement, but he doesn't agree. For him it's all or nothing. If I do some chores, that's not improvement because I haven't completed **all** the chores. He treats me like I'm defective, like Creep did. I just feel like running away and being a homeless bum."

"Just like you felt when you ran away from college?"

Caz ignores my connecting the running away from college with his feeling of wanting to run away now. "Yeah, I think when all this first started and the abuse came out, Dad was understanding and supportive, but he sees me sleeping the day away as weakness or laziness. I try to explain I feel depressed and I can't get out of bed some days, but he doesn't think it's related to Belle's abuse because I've always been a kid who liked to sleep and couldn't get up in the morning. Dad tells a story of when I was nine. He woke me up for school and then went downstairs to make breakfast and to set out my Ritalin. When he didn't hear me moving around, he went back upstairs and found me sitting on a chair, holding a sock in one hand, and I was sound asleep. I think there's something wrong with me, I really do." His whining is grating on me.

"So this sleeping pattern, of not wanting or being able to go to sleep until the wee hours of the morning, and then not being able to get up in the morning is something that has plagued you since you were very young. And this has been a problem before Belle started abusing you but after your mother left?" How's that for a summarization!

All that summarizing work and Caz shrugs and says, "I guess, but the sexual abuse started when I was nine. I'm not sure about the time frame."

Caz was on Ritalin? I want more information. "Caz you said you were taking Ritalin when you were younger. How did that medication work for you?"

"It helped me focus better at school. I almost felt normal when I was on it. I took it all the way through elementary school and high school. The psychiatrist took me off of it when I went to college."

"Did you notice a difference when he took you off of it?"

"Yes, I slept more and couldn't get up in the morning, and I missed a lot of my morning classes."

"Why didn't you ask your psychiatrist to put you back on the Ritalin?"

"I don't know. I thought he knew what he was doing." Oh my, the whining!

Our time is up. Caz slowly pulls himself out to the chair as if he's 80 years old, and says he feels "bummed" about the session, feels he opened more cans of crap. I must admit I feel the same way. I'm overwhelmed with the succession of tragic incidences that have befallen this man. Did I make the correct choice by first dealing with the abuse? Should I have delved more into his history initially? But I wonder if Caz could have completed a thorough historical timeline. He has many overlapping issues and themes that run through his life. He doesn't see the patterns or acknowledge them. For him, the incidences are not connected. When I do offer insight into patterns, he dismisses them. He didn't dismiss my insights several weeks ago when he first started counseling. So he has changed now. He's dismissing any intervention I make. Sometimes the unfolding and acknowledging of the client's self-defeating patterns occur in the client's time and with the client's priorities.

For me, one important element of this session was learning how dependent and passive Caz has been and still is. He noticed the difference in his ability to focus when he was on Ritalin but never told his psychiatrist, or so he reports. As soon as I get home and have a salad (I wanted a burger and fries), I call Helen (again) and Craig for consultations.

Craig gets back to me first. He saw Stewart last week and was dismayed by the information Stewart shared. As a side note, he mentioned that Stewart eagerly signed the Release of Confidential Information form. Evidently, Stewart kept saying, as he was signing, "Whatever will help Caz."

They had discussed Caz' history of sleeping problems and lack of energy, and Stewart openly talked about the time when his wife left and how Caz thought he was the cause of her leaving. Stewart also expressed how responsible he still feels that he allowed Caz to go to Belle's. Craig tried to get Stewart to see one of my colleagues, but he refused. "We'll get through it." was Stewart's mantra. Stewart had not sought help for himself or the boys when his wife left, so all three men have been walking around wounded with their entrails dragging behind them. Each of them thinks he's responsible for her leaving. The abandonment was bad enough, but Stewart's wife never contacted him or the boys again, no Christmas presents, no birthday gifts, no cards. Stewart even called his wife's parents after she left, but they were unaware she had left her family, and they had no idea where she was. It was as if she dropped off the face of the earth.

Her complete disappearance and lack of any contact fueled the feelings of "I must have done something VERY wrong." in all three of the "men". Even Rom, who had not been abused and has the outward appearance of success, suffers from panic attacks that date back to when his mother left. He's never been treated either. The only family member to have sought psychiatric treatment and counseling over the years was Caz. Craig and I agreed that Caz seems to be carrying the burden of the entire family's heartbreak. Craig volunteers to touch base periodically with Stewart and to keep trying to get him and the family to see a mental health professional.

Right on the heels of Craig's call, Helen calls, and I tell her about Caz's history with a sleep disorder. She had known about the problem, but did not know it dated back to before the abuse started. She says she asked Caz to identify when he started having difficulties with hypersomnia and he told her "just recently". She says she's tried to get Caz to cut down on the trazodone and/or to take it earlier in the evening, but he has been unable or unwilling to do so. She believes Caz' relying on it, possibly abusing it. She's due to see Caz in a couple of weeks and will begin removing him from the trazodone and put him on another sleep aid. I also inform Helen that Caz was on Ritalin as a kid and teenager, and he reported it made him feel normal (whatever that is), but it was discontinued when he went to college. He noticed a major difference in his ability to wake up, focus, and get work done when he was on the medication. Helen is intrigued with this news, but she seems a bit annoyed at Caz for not sharing all this information when she took his medication history during their first session. She says she will look at his medications again and see if she could reintroduce the Ritalin or a similar one.

I'm bugging Helen about Caz too much, but she's not complaining. I am. My frustration with Caz is becoming irritation. He reveals new information each week that he hasn't shared with Helen or me. We both suspect he may not realize how all his history is connected to what he is feeling today. His disconnection from important information and lack of insight insinuate that he's not receiving the best integrative care from both of us. He's like Hansel who drops a variety of breadcrumbs on a path but doesn't see the connection...they are all bird food.

The final message on my voicemail is from the social worker at DCFS. She says since Belle has been arrested and charged, the department is no longer responsible for tracking the abuse. She suggests I contact the licensure boards for further information. That's a nice side-step she did. I don't blame her. DCFS may feel responsible that one of their workers visited Belle and dismissed the accusation when so much abuse was occurring. I need to think about calling the Psychiatry Board. I hate this part of my professional obligation.

Holy, loving God! This case is complicated, and the main characters seem to be determined to stay where they are in life. In Stewart's case that means don't rock the boat, I can't swim. In Caz' case it means I'm responsible for the family's pain, therefore I will carry the cross on my shoulders and because I'm burdened I can't or I won't take responsibility for my life, medications, hygiene, etc. In Rom's case, he just wants to be left alone and avoid the chaos. He seems to be doing better than Caz, but he has symptoms for which he never sought help. Panic attacks can be debilitating. I wonder how he copes.

Lisa's Tragedy

Thinking about my impending Caribbean vacation with two friends, my mind wanders to the sand and sun and the islands and then to bittersweet memories of family fun when the kids were little. Every year we took a vacation to a different island and each year we swore it was the best vacation ever. The kids grew up looking forward to that one week a year when the four of us left all of our stress and things-to-do lists behind and we played and reconnected.

We continued this tradition, even when Grace and Sam were in college. However, Grace died in a helicopter accident when she was doing an internship for our local television station. That year was the end of the family traditions and our lives as we knew them. The tragedy tore our family apart and nothing was ever the same.

Shortly after Grace's death Darryl and I divorced. We were one of those couples that added to the statistics that indicate marriages sometimes don't survive the loss of a child, even when the 'child' was an adult. Sam not only lost his sister, he lost his intact family. I suspect he was depressed, but he hid it from us.

After the divorce, Darryl ran away to California, took up surfing, and remarried. I stopped working on my dissertation. I lost the dedication that's necessary to achieve a doctorate. I had been pursuing my dream for four years and suddenly in 24 hours the dream seemed unimportant in the grand scheme of life. Six months later, Sam married suddenly and took a job working for the government that involved traveling around the world to dangerous locations. A part of me wonders if he had a death wish or at least wanted to flirt with the possibility that death could be an easy way out of the loss and pain. Currently he's in Afghanistan building schools. I seldom see him and when I do it's for a quick lunch. Suffering pain and loss cripples one's psychological resources, and, yet, the learning experience can't be compared to anything found in a course. Because of my loss and my pain, I can understand Caz and Noelle. I don't know specifically how they feel, but I can get close to understanding why they are experiencing the symptoms they have.

Bally is different. I have difficulty understanding her. My initial experience of Bally was to recoil. I felt relief when she walked out of my office two years ago. Then, she wanted to return and I was in a dilemma. I didn't want to see her again. I wanted to say, I had a full case load" and referred her. I suspect both of us would have been relieved.

But, now that she has reconnected with me, something inside of me says her addiction and arrogance are covering up a very dynamic person. She seems to have changed, and appears sincere in her sobriety. However, now that she's not drinking, she's even more haughty and self-centered. She's also very defended: one minute answering questions as if she's accommodating my need for information and the next acting as if she's engaged in the process. One interesting idiosyncrasy I picked up during our last meeting is that she starts a lot of her sentences with the word "Well". I wonder if the word has any significance for her or if it's just a habit.

While waiting for Bally to arrive, I'm looking through her intake form. Her first name really is Bally. I thought it might be a nickname. Her middle name is Ingrid. Sounds like her mother chose her first name and her Scandinavian/African father chose her second name. If I'm correct in my assumption, then Bally and I share a similar story.

My parents couldn't agree on lots of things including my name. My mother wanted to call me Mary after the Virgin Mary, and my father wanted me to be called Elizabeth after Elizabeth Barrett Browning. Therefore, my name is Mary Elizabeth and my mother called me Mary and Father called me Elizabeth.

One day when I was only five, I was watching television, and I heard the name Lisa. On the first day of kindergarten, when my teacher called. "Mary Elizabeth" from the roll, I answered "I'm Lisa, just plain Lisa."

From that moment on I established my own 'self'. I figured if my parents couldn't agree on my name, then I would find one I liked. Quite a decision for a five year old! My parents hated that story and my father continued to call me Elizabeth until he died. My mother tries harder to call me Lisa but she slips frequently into calling me Mary.

Verbal Sparring

Bally arrives in a bright pink dress and very high spike heels that lace up her legs. She looks like a runway model and she walks as if she's been trained to walk on a runway too. She sits and crosses her slender brown legs as if she's going to interview me. I feel drab and fat next to her. She looks at me expectantly.

"Bally, last week we ended with your telling me you had no memories before the age of 12. What do you think about that?

"It's normal for me." (Haughty)

"Do you wish you had more memory?"

"Well, it depends."

I wait for her to continue, but she doesn't so I wait. She looks at me as if I'm supposed to ask another question, but I wait her out.

Ok, three minutes is a long silence. Do I give in and ask another question, or do I continue to wait? I'm in a battle with her for power and I'm refusing to budge. She's refusing to budge. She just sits back and folds her arms. She's battling for supremacy! Wait, she's going to say something.

"What kind of crap are you pulling on me? You're supposed to ask another question, witch. That's why I walked out on you last time. You think you know everything, like you hold some god damn key to knowledge. What the f do you want from me?"

"Why are you angry? You said 'Depends.' And I'm waiting to hear what it depends on?"

"Well, why didn't you just say so? Why sit for all this frigging time waiting for me to say. 'It depends on whether the memories are good ones or not.'?"

"Because I don't have the ability to read your mind. I didn't know what your answer was going to be. How could I?"

"Well, you're supposed to be trained to know what I might say."

"Really?"

"Yes, really. Don't they train you to respond to someone who says, 'Depends'?"

"I've been trained **not** to put words into your mouth."

"Well, what else could the word 'depends' mean? Other than diapers?" She laughs out loud. I don't.

"You could've meant, 'It depends on whether the memories are about my mother.' She looks stunned that I could come up with an alternative. I feel like I'm in a dueling contest. Is she enjoying this? Is this the way she deals with other people? I'm taking a huge leap. If she runs, she runs.

"I'm interested in what just happened here."

"What do you mean?"

"In your business meetings, do you do this kind of verbal jousting?"

"What do you mean?"

Shit, she's now out foxing me and making me explain. She is gooooood! "Do you usually interact with people like you just did with me? Waiting them out, using anger to put people on the defensive, demanding they meet your expectations?"

"What the hell. I don't do that!"

"You just did. Instead of just talking about your lack of memories, we got into a dueling match. Who's going to out last whom? Who's right and who's wrong? Whether I was well trained? Seems like you used every defensive and offensive maneuver you know to avoid being more open and explicit."

She's quiet. I can't tell whether she's considering what I said, or she's rallying for another attack.

"What you just said. Is that ethical? To lay a client out like that?"

Yep, an attack! Parry and thrust. "What do you think is unethical about observing an interaction and asking you whether this is a normal way of communicating for you?"

"Well, I'm outta here! You're one crazy bitch." And she leaves by slamming my office door and then hitting the outside door with her fist as she opens it. What a huge amount of anger! Well, that's two times she's stormed out, and that will be the last time. Even if she returns, I'll set entirely new boundaries for her, if I take her back at all.

Bally Sabotages Herself

I can't stand that bitch. She's so superior and haughty and thinks she knows everything. I need a drink, but I won't to do that to myself, and I won't give her the satisfaction. A cappuccino's going to have to take the place of the booze. I find a coffee shop just around the corner from Lisa's office. I'm so pissed I bite the cashier's head off for giving me too much change back. Feels good to inflict some pain on someone else. I'm sure Lisa would have some wise-ass remark about that.

"Hi, Bally, still wasting your time being nasty?"

"Hi, Bernie, yes, why do you care?"

"I don't. I just wish you would get into therapy and deal with your rage and snooty attitude."

"Well, **you're** the cause of **this** rage. I just came from my therapist's office and we were talking about you and she churned up a lot of crap about how you treated me when you asked for a divorce after I had worked hard to get sober."

"Hey, babe, don't blame me for that. I was tired of the booze, the anger, the holier-than-thou attitude, your put-downs etc. YOU caused the break up. I just got the divorce. Did you tell your shrink that I'm husband number five? Bet you didn't. The sad part is you're one of the smartest, most attractive, exciting women I've ever met. But you spoil every conversation with your mind games. You wear people out Bally. Stay in therapy and get fixed."

"Great. Everyone's a shrink. Everyone seems to know more about me than I do. Get lost, Bernie."

"See what I mean? Good…..bye."

Why did I have to run into that bastard? I hate men. I think I'll become a lesbian. As I walk-run out of the coffee shop, I notice everyone's looking at me. I used to enjoy throwing tirades and having everyone look at me, but now I feel like crap. Everyone's judging me, staring at me, shaking their heads. Well, I'm done with therapy. I start my car and rip out of the parking lot. That's all I remember until I wake up in an ambulance.

"Wha' 'appened?"

"You hit another car. You're on your way to the hospital. Do you know your name?"

"Sure."

"Could you tell me?"

"Bally."

"And your last name?"

"Pissoff."

The EMT looks like he's going to pursue obtaining my information but thinks better of it. Probably he's going to let the hospital deal with me because I heard him say his shift is over in 15 minutes. No need to fight with a patient at this point. He stops asking questions and adjusts my IV.

Good, I don't want to be asked the typical questions. "Do you know your name? What year is it? Who's the president?" I can't believe this happened. Another car hit me and now I'm on the way to the hospital. Shit. Why don't people learn to drive?

The ambulance, with me in it, arrives at the hospital. There're so many people around me I can't keep track of them. Faces that's all. Most look serious. Questions, so many questions. They're going through my purse! Are they looking for drugs? What's going on? I'm scared and I feel dehumanized. They're cutting off my clothes. "Christ, do you know how much they cost?" They ignore me. They're x-raying my entire body right on the emergency room bed. The plates go right under the bed and they don't have to move me to take the x-rays. Cool. They're looking and poking every orifice. Am I hurt? Finally, one person talks to me.

"Who can we call for you? We went through your purse and car and only found your cell, home, and your business phones and there was no answer at either home or business."

"Dat's 'cause I'm 'ere you idiot." The person in green scrubs ignores my remark.

"Is there anyone we can call for you?"

"No, no one."

"How about another number at your place of work?"

"Sure, call ma boss, 410-555-6487."

"Okay." And the person dressed in green disappears. I'm strapped to a gurney with my head and neck taped into some kind of headrest. I can't see who's talking to me unless they stick their face in front of me.

I think the next person's a young man who's trying to help, but I can't tell. The voice is one of those that could be male or female. I can see the clock on the wall and hear the machines that are hooked up to my body. I don't feel that hurt, why the bother, why the fuss?

A police officer is now in front of me. "Ma'am, I have your address as 158 Caliber Road, Number 4, in Catonsville. Is that correct?"

"Yes."

"I have your telephone numbers for home and work. We are attempting to call your office. Who can we call in an emergency? A significant other? A friend?"

"No one." Didn't someone just ask me that?

"If you are released today, you won't be able to drive home. Your car's been towed. Who can pick you up?"

"No one." What's wrong? It hurts to talk.

"You don't have a friend or anyone who can come and get you?"

"No. I can't thin' of anyone." I spit out the words in anger, even though I'm feeling scared and lonely. I have no one to help me. No one who cares.

"Ok."

Now a doctor, who looks like he's 13, is in front of me. "Hi, I'm going to stitch you up and then we're going to run additional tests to see how badly you're hurt, Ok?"

"Do 'ou need a 'sponse to that question?"

"Excuse me?"

"Are 'ou askin' ma p'mission ta sew me up?"

"Yes, I guess." He looks confused by my question. Is everyone around here an idiot?

I can feel the needles going into my face and realize that my wounds are facial. Oh my god, my face, my face? "Ah 'eed to see a mirror!" I scream.

The doctor stops and leaves. Another person's now looking down at me. "Hi, I'm Dr. Sutton. Dr. Fields tells me you want to see the cuts on your face before we do the stitches."

"'at's wha' I said. Is dere a p'oblem?"

"No, but you could ask nicely."

Crap! Everyone's a therapist. "Ok, pleeeeeth. Ouch!"

The mirror immediately appears. My heart is pounding. My face has several cuts all over the left check and forehead. I'm hideous. "Oh ma Gawd! Ah'm a mons'er!"

"These look worse than they are. Most of them are superficial and should heal with a minimal of scarring. We have to stitch up just a couple of the deeper of ones. Your arm is broken, but I'm more concerned about your neck and head. We're going to run some tests."

"Ah wan' a 'lastic su'geon. No one in da E.R. ith goin' ta touch ma face. Ya un'erstan'! NO ONE! OW!"

Dr. Sutton backs off and nods.

As soon as he leaves, I sob. I don't care about my neck or head. I'm no longer the beautiful Bally who turns all the heads in a room. I'm now battle-scarred Bally and everyone will look at me in horror. As I sob, a nurse comes in and gives me something in my IV and I fall asleep.

When I wake up my face is stitched and bandaged. Damn. Well, I'm suing them for going against my orders to get a plastic surgeon. I can't speak clearly. I'm sore and fuzzy headed and I can't tell them now, but they will hear from my attorney....as soon as I hire one.

My eyes don't focus well. Another doctor is hovering, or maybe he/she is a physician's assistant, can't tell. The doctor-person is talking to me about the outcome of all the tests. There's some swelling of the brain but it's minimal. They are giving me something to reduce it. She/He is saying that they're keeping me overnight. If all goes well, then they will release me in the morning. I close my eyes and fall back asleep.

Noise shakes me awake. I have no idea how long I've been asleep. They're bringing another person into shock trauma and I hear all the sounds of the x-ray machine etc. that I had experienced 20 hours before. Twenty hours! Holy Crap! A nurse arrives to tell me that they are releasing me. She tells me to sign here, and here, and here and then helps me into a wheel chair and wheels me to a waiting cab. She gives me instructions about seeing my doctor and about how to treat the bandaged scars, neck brace, and cast. Only half of what she's saying sinks in. Luckily she gave me written instructions, too. The ride home is 15 minutes. As I open my door, I look at the hall mirror and am horrified at what I see. My entire left side of my face and head are bandaged. My eyes are sunken and my lips are cracked. I've never looked this ugly. I call my supervisor. I missed work yesterday and I'm now very late today. He answers on the second ring.

"Hi, Tim. Thish ish Bolly." I can hardly speak. The drugs, the bandages, the numbing agent keep me from being articulate.

"Hi Bally. Off the wagon, are we?"

"No!" Ouch that hurt.

"Right."

"Didn't the staff at shock trauma 'all ya?"

"Yes, they said you were in an accident and you were going to be ok. So you got drunk again and this time you were in an accident and not only hurt yourself but someone else, too. So what do you want?"

"Ah washn't dhunk."

"The doctor at shock trauma said you caused the accident. Do you expect me to believe you weren't drunk?"

"I washn't! Ouch."

"Yeah right. What do you want this time Bally?"

"I jis wanned ta tell ya Ah wash in an acciden' 'esterday, tha Ah spent all day and all nigh' in shock trauma. Dey sed I have a concussion. A cab jist bough me 'ome, but am too hur' ta come ta wor'. Ah need to take some shick leave."

"You are out of sick leave, Bally." He says with an exaggerated sigh.

"Well, then 'ill ya give me two 'eeks leave 'ithout pay?"

"Sure, it's called your being fired." Dial tone.

"Son of a bich! Ouch!"

Bally Returns

My goal today is to return all the phone calls from yesterday before I start seeing clients. It's 8:30 and I plan to make a few of them before my first client. Someone's hanging around my door. She has her back to me and when she turns around, I barely recognize Bally through the swelling and bandages.

"Bally, oh my heavens! What happened to you?"

Bally bursts into tears, leans her back against the wall, bends her knees, and slides to the floor crying hysterically. I quickly open my door and help her inside and into a chair. I only have 30 minutes before my first client arrives. I defensively over-explain this to Bally so she will know my time limit, but this time she doesn't argue, only nods.

"Bally, what happened after you left here yesterday?"

"Ah wen'... fir a capcino, wanted a drink.... ba settled fir tha coffee. I ran inta ma ex-'usban' at the café... an' he ga'e me a lot of crap. I got angry and storm'd out... of ta café, got inta ma car ta go ta work,... an' ran inta 'nother car. Ah thought it was deir fault, but the people at shock trauma say it was mine.... Two policema' at shock trauma... confirm'd tha witnesses sed Ah ran inta the other car... the other car was sittin' still waitin' fir a light ta change... Well, I don't r'membr... Was aful at shock trauma...Treated ma like a 'unk of meat,...not a person. Wen dis adolescen doctor sed he was goin' ta sew up ma face,.... Ah scream'd at 'im... Ah wanned a 'lastic surg'n...Dey put me out with drugs,... an' sew'd up ma face. A woke up lookin' like this... When they r'leased me,... Didn't have anyone to 'ick me up...took cab home at 5:00 a.m...fell asleep...woke up at 8. Well, (she takes a breath and closes her eyes as if she's in a lot of pain.) I call'd ma sup'visor ta let 'im know Ah was in an accident.... and need'd ta take some time off... Ee told me ee knew Ah was in an accident... Police call'd 'im as tha 'mergency contact... Ee thought Ah was in an accident b'cause I had been drinkin'...Fired me over the phone...Ne'er gave me a chance ta 'xplain... Ee said ee didn't b'lieve me.

Bally is sobbing and trying to talk through the sobs but can only get a few words out before the next sob breaks through. She finishes with, "Ah didn't know where else ta go....'cept here."

I had many thoughts and feelings running through my mind: Compassion, disbelief, amazement of the difference in this woman in 24 hours, confusion about part of her story. But, all I need to do is be with her. The time is running out before my first client arrives. I pick up my calendar to see if I have any time later today to see her and Bally growls through her tears... "Don't tell me (sob)...you're lookin' fir 'pointment time (sob)...fir nex' week!"

That did it! I'm going to take advantage of the fact that she can't easily come up with a rebuttal. "Bally I'm amazed at how you think you can read minds and always assume the worst about people. I just spent 20 minutes of my free time with you and now I'm looking for a time when I can fit you in TODAY and you snap at me! Even when people are trying to help you, you push them away with your assumptions and your anger."

She looks at me as if she were a small spoiled child who has thrown her last temper tantrum. I continue, "Would you like to come in at two or would you like a referral?" Bally looks defeated at last. She hangs her head, nods, and holds up her two fingers, indicating two o'clock. She struggles to get up out of the chair, as if she is in a lot of pain, physically and psychologically, she waves the appointment card and leaves. No word of thanks, but then I don't expect that of her.

Bally's Session

I have no one....I'm so alone...My ex-husband blew me off...my boss fired me...my therapist reamed me out... and I'm in pain. No one cares. I hate this world and the people in it. Well, I'm calling my boss and let him know what I think of him...after a nap. I can't keep my eyes open.

Five hours later I'm awake. I pull my hair in a ponytail, take a shower, and arrange for a rental a car. I call my insurance company to let them know about the accident, but they had already been called by the other person's insurance company. I start to explain to the claims adjuster, Ms. Firth, what I believe happened. She informs me that she needs to hear my side of the story and wants to tape the interview (I agree). I tell her what I remember, though I'm not sure I was able to speak clearly enough to get my point across. I tell her I thought **they** had hit **me**. Ms. Firth listens and records my version of the story without comment. I emphasize that I was NOT drinking and she kindly said, "I know, the hospital confirmed your blood work showed no alcohol in your blood." Thank God! I'm late to see Lisa! (not sure she's looking forward to seeing me).

Bally Demonstrates She Can Change

Bally is quite a bit more subdued, less tearful, quieter. She begins, "Than' ya for seein' me briefly dis mornin'." I nod. "Am confused 'bout how all this happened ta me. One minute I was in ma car an' the nex' I'm scarred fir life and getting my body scanned, ma face stitched up, ma clothes cut off, and ma personal b'longings searched."

"Must have felt dehumanizing."

"Xactly!"

"What will you do now?"

"Ah called ma insurance comp'ny, rented a car, and slept." She laughs a little. I'm unsure why she thinks that's funny.

"Good for you" I muster.

"Yeah an' ma 'surance company confirm'd I hadn't been drinkin'. Shock trauma 'ad drawn blood."

"Was there ever doubt that you were sober?"

"Ma boss thought so. I jist am glad dat dere is evidence ta back up ma story."

"I see."

"Am thinkin' 'bout callin' ma boss an' lettin' 'im know."

"How will you approach him?"

"Wha' do ya mean?"

"Well, sounds like he was very upset and jumped to the conclusion that you were drunk and had caused the accident due to being inebriated."

"Yea, he did! Tha jerk! Ouch."

"That's what I mean, Bally. I know you're angry at him and he may deserve your anger for not trusting you and jumping to the wrong conclusion about the drinking, but..."

"Damn straight!" (Bally sure got that one out clearly!)

"But I assume you want him to change his mind about firing you?"

"Hell, yea, Ee owes me."

"He does?"

"Sure, Ee fired me b'fore Ee 'eard the truth."

"You're right, but, you see, he was making his assumptions based on your past performance. You seem to forget that when you disappoint others, become enraged, drink, etc., then people come to expect that of you. It may not be fair, but it's normal to assume that past behavior is the best predictor of future behavior."

"So wha' are ya suggestin'? Tha' I kiss 'is ass?"

"No, I am wondering if you would like to try a different strategy."

"Well, wha' do ya suggest?"

"What I'm suggesting is to look at what you **don't** want to do."

"Huh?"

"Not getting angry at him, the way you are used to. Not going for his throat or paying him back for jumping to conclusions. Instead look at this from his perspective. He gave you a second chance, paid for your inpatient treatment, and hired you back after you completed the treatment. When he heard you were in an accident, he jumped to the conclusion that seemed reasonable to him."

"Well, Ee shouldn't 'ave done tha'. Ee doesn't 'ave a crys'al ball!"

"Exactly, he can't read minds!"

"Are ya sayin' tha' Ee did wha' Ah do?"

I remain silent letting this sink in.

"So, Lisa, wise one, wha' do ya think Ah should try? Kissing 'is right ass-cheek or 'is lef'?"

"How about understanding how he feels. You let him down in the past. He knows you're an alcoholic, and that you caused an accident...so wouldn't you jump to conclusions the way he did, if the tables were turned?"

She's quiet. "Ah can see that."

"Do you think if you started from that premise, you might understand why he acted the way he did? Then you could approach him with empathic understanding?

"Maybe."

"Then do you think he may be more apt to listen to what you are saying?"

"Maybe." And with that Bally picks up her phone, flips it open, presses a number and begins talking, "Ron, dis is Bally. A relize when ya heard Ah was in an accident, ya natur'ly assum'd tha' Ah 'ad caus'd tha accident by drinkin'. I don't blame ya fir that. I mess'd up a lot two years ago, but Ah 'ave not 'ad a drink in two years an' Ah was not drinkin' 'esterday. I 'ad blood drawn at shock trauma an' it proves Ah was not drinkin'. Ah would be glad ta r'lease the records ta ya if that 'ould help. Am askin' ya ta reconsider yur firin' of me. Ah can be at work t'morrow even though Am covered in bandages. If I don't 'ave any sick leave lef', then I'll be in, despite how Ah feel an' look. Thanks fir listenin' and thinkin' 'bout this. Bye."

Listening to Bally's skillful use of words, her clear, precise, to the point, business-like conversation, despite her difficulty speaking, I realize why she's good at her job and valuable to her boss despite her problems. Bally, snaps her cell phone closed and looks to me for approval. I nod. I'm impressed with how quickly she took our conversation and converted it into action. Maybe she **is** willing to learn.

"How do you feel about what you just did?"

"Ah feel good, but Ah felt like Ah was grovelin' an' Ah shouldn't haf ta grovel. Ah didn't do anythin' wrong."

"You feel that you are **totally** in the right and he is **totally** in the wrong? We've been over how he was wrong by jumping to conclusions. Where were you wrong?"

"With ma boss? Ee didn't give me a chance ta say much this mornin' b'fore 'Ee fired me, so Ah don't see how Ah was wrong." She's getting angry again, but she handled my challenge pretty well even though she didn't answer my question. At least she didn't scream at me or run away.

"How about how you were acting before the accident or after the accident?" Can she do any soul searching without putting the blame on others?

She ponders a long time. "After Ah lef' here, Ah went fir coffee an' Ah was really pissed at ya. Ah snapped at tha woman behin' the counter...gave me the wrong change. Then Ah ran inta my ex. Ee blamed me fir our marriage endin', told me Ah needed therapy, accused me of spoilin' every conversation with anger an' accuse' me of lyin' ta ya."

"How so?"

Oops she's caught. She looks at me out of the side of her eyes, which are blood shot from the accident.

"Ah've been married an' divorced five times. 'ernie was number five.

"I see."

"Wha'? No judgmen' tha way others do when dey find out Ah've been married five times? No diagnosis like chronic divorcitis?"

I had to smile at that one. "You expect me to judge you?"

"Yep."

"Well, I don't."

"Why not?"

"How could I help you if I judged you? I just want to understand you and help you to understand yourself. That way you can make healthier decisions and be happier."

"Boy ya're just filled with Pollyanna opt'mism, aren't ya? Well, have ya ever failed to help a client?"

"Interesting question. Do you think you might be the one I can't help?"

"Ah'm quite a challenge!"

I laugh and then get serious again. "I'm not perfect, Bally. All I can do is to provide you with a safe place to explore and understand yourself, try out different ways of being with yourself and others, and to give you the benefit of my knowledge and expertise. The rest is up to you."

Bally looks down at her hands, turning them over and over for quite awhile. "Do ya think Ah can do it?"

"If what I just saw today is an example of how you can make changes, then I would say 'yes' you can do this. But, you will have to stop getting angry every time you think I'm trying to hurt you, con you, or manipulate you. I don't do that. The world might, your family might have, you might trick yourself, but I'm a straight dealer. Therefore, if you can trust that I have your best interest at heart and not jump to conclusions and if you can stop believing you can read my mind, then I think we can do this, together."

Her cell phone rings and at first she ignores it until she sees the call's from her boss. She looks up at me and asks politely if she can take the call. I nod. I also pray that he's going to be generous.

Bally answers slowly and speaks as clearly as she can, "Hello. She listens to him for quite awhile and only punctuates his apparent discourse with "Ok... Righ'... Alrigh'... No problem... Ah understand... Fine... Ok."

Bally closes her phone slowly and looks up with tears in her eyes. "Ee apologized fir snappin' to tha conclusion that Ah had been drinkin'. When Ee heard Ah had a car accident, ee said that ee was so dis'ppointed that ee hadn't been able to save me from drinking, that ee got angry. Ee wants me ta take a week off with pay an' git better before Ah return to work." She tries to smile but winces in pain. I smile for her, asking "Would you like to come in twice this week or are you okay to wait a week?" Bally answered, "Ah can see ya again this week. Ah 'ave the week off, remember?" An appointment was made and Bally left. She seemed quieter and pensive.

Bally
Learning and Engaging

I can't believe my boss was generous. Lisa was right. I need to act like I understand him better and be more empathic toward him. I **know** these skills! I was taught them as negotiation skills at business school, but I only use them with business clients. Well, it's easy with my business clients, I have no emotional connection to them. It's business. I function better at work where I can stay in my head and play the business games.

I seem to get myself into more trouble when I'm in personal relationships. It's almost as if I'm two different people. I am competent, strong, knowledgeable, and I can close deals at work. I can problem-solve and negotiate anything, and clients ask for me specifically. In my personal life I'm defensive, angry, untrusting, irrational, crazy. I fall in love easily and can get men to fall in love with me. They feel they must have me all to themselves. Then once we're married, I become an angry, jealous, mean, nasty, critical bitch. Begrudgingly, thanks to Lisa, I can see how I might use my business skills to control outcomes that can work to my advantage in my personal life, too.

Lisa's Wary about Bally

I don't trust Bally. She's angry and hostile one minute and accommodating another. Which is the real Bally? Is she the person I saw today? The one who listens and considers other alternatives or the one who uses foul language to get what she wants? Does she enjoy manipulating others by using her different emotional states to control them and the outcome of conversations? I've seen these personality traits before in clients who have been raised in chaotic or abusive homes. Sometimes the personal outrage can emerge from parents who are ineffective, substance abusers, or absent.

I've even seen this type of manipulation and rage with clients who experienced natural disasters as children.

One young woman I worked with many years ago lived near the epicenter of an earthquake that had occurred in Mexico when she was 8. She was traumatized and blamed everyone in her family for not protecting her. She remembered running outside and lying on the rolling earth, trying to stop it from moving. Her parents stayed in the house cowering. She felt they did nothing to protect her and therefore she could not trust them. This feeling then generalized to not being able to trust authority. For days, her area experienced aftershocks and she kept trying to do something to protect herself and her three younger sisters while her parents just stopped what they were doing, held on to whatever was around, and waited out the aftershock tremor. She developed a personality style that was angry at everyone who wasn't pulling their weight and those who, she perceived, were not protecting her. Metaphorically, she looked for the next tremor or aftershock in every situation, and if one didn't occur, she created one to prove she was in charge and demanded people listen to her. Therapy with her was very difficult and while she made some progress, she was famous for not showing up for her appointments and trying to create a crisis, an emotional tremor that had to be fixed. When I reacted to her manipulation, she always upped the ante. When I didn't react, she upped the ante. When I confronted her, I was always the parent who was trying to get her to do something she felt wasn't in her best interest and sometimes she even said she felt like she was in danger when she came to see me every week because I "stirred things up" (more tremors). When I agreed to meet with her every other week, she would both cling to me emotionally and beg me not to abandon her because I was the best therapist in the world. Or she would blame me for trying to ignore her needs (like her parents did when they didn't try to stop the tremors by going outside and lying on the earth with her.) She had alienated everyone in her life and change for her was out of the question. It was too scary to let go of her need to control because "the big one" could occur at anytime and she had to be ready. Unlike Bally this young woman soothed with food. Bally soothes herself through the use of alcohol and anger.

With Bally, I see the same manipulative behavior. So far, I haven't experienced the splitting of good therapist/bad therapist like I did with my earthquake survivor. I just seem to be bad therapist or tolerated therapist at present. I also haven't heard about her early developmental years. So far Bally claims to have no memory of her childhood.

I'm not optimistic about being able to help Bally. Chances are I will be one therapist in a whole line of therapists who will be manipulated and dismissed. The therapeutic walk with Bally could be a very delicate one, supporting her while not supporting her self-defeating behavior, confronting her in a caring way while making sure she hears the important message in the confrontation, setting appropriate boundaries but not coming across as rigid and controlling.

On a positive note, Bally did hear me when I talked to her about how to speak her boss. At least she used the information to get what she wanted from her boss. She's smart, but is she able to be truly empathic with others? Can she recognize that others have feelings and needs that she should honor?

Bally has a number of important issues to deal with: substance abuse in remission (but tentative), explosive and manipulative behavior, narcissistic traits, recent divorce, recent auto accident, and difficulties at work. She's also confused about her childhood history and therefore, may be unsure of who she is.

Caz' View of Self
The Victim

I'm tired of being the object of other people's problems. My mother left us, and I felt and still feel that somehow I was responsible for her unhappiness. I was the child who was diagnosed with ADHD and had learning disabilities. I'm assuming she left because I was too difficult to handle. Belle picked up on my vulnerability and scooped me up, treated me like I was special, and then sexually abused and used me for several years. She made her sexual desires my problem. Dad's never gotten over my mother's leaving. He tried his best to be a good provider and an involved parent. But, he blames me for being a burden to him. NONE OF THIS IS MY FAULT! Why do I think it is?

Lisa's trying to help me see that I don't have to carry all this pain by myself, but I feel alone. I need a friend. That would help, but who'd want to be my friend? I'm so screwed up. I can't drive. I have no money to do things. I'd probably not show up for the social date because I'd sleep through it. I know everyone's trying to help me, and I know I should be helping myself, but I can't even wake up.

Dr. Jamison's changing my medication, **again**. This time it's a major change. I'm always scared to change anything in my life, and this scares me. She is weaning me off trazodone over the next three weeks. She prescribed Lunesta, a sleep aid, as a replacement. She's also putting me back on Ritalin. I thought that stuff was for kids, but she says it helps adults too. Do I dare hope?

I used to love coming here to see Lisa, but recently all I feel I've accomplished is to give her even more things to be concerned about. I felt like such a dufus sharing how I left college without fighting for my rights. Lisa's careful how she questions me. I don't think she wants to hurt my feelings and send me into a depression, but recently she's been zeroing in on my allowing others to put me in the victim role. She hasn't called it that, but I think that's what she's doing. She recapped the number of times I let someone hurt me without fighting back. I'll give her one thing, she has a good memory. Let's see, she said I took the blame for my mother's leaving. True. I was singled out by Belle (Rom wasn't invited) and when I felt it was wrong, I didn't say anything because I wanted to go to "BelleLand". True. I told Dr. Crete and Dr. Reese too much information and allowed them to browbeat me into giving my permission to release my medical records. True. I told the psychiatrist not to send the information, that was a good thing, but then Dr. Creep lied to me and I believed her, and instead of fighting her or reporting her, I left school and didn't return. True. I didn't tell Dr. Jamison about my history with some medications, and therefore she was working with partial information. All true. I'm a screw up. True.

Lisa'd be disappointed to hear me say all that. I hate myself for who I am and how my life's turned out. I think I'll tell her **that** next time and let her add **that** to my list of how I continue to victimize myself. Now I really can't sleep. I'm too worked up. I'm going to play computer games until 5 a.m., that'll really screw up my day tomorrow.

I didn't make 5 a.m., but I did see 2 a.m., and then I must've fallen asleep with the lap top on my bed and the control in my hand, because that's how I wake up. Dad's banging on the door telling me to get up for my appointment. I feel too groggy, but I slither out of bed and drag myself to the shower. At least I won't smell.

Lisa's her smiley, perky self. God, I hate how she can do that. I must look like I'm ready to kill grass because she asks me, "What's wrong?"

I scream at her, "I AM TIRED OF ALL THIS SHIT! I KNOW I'M A VICTIM. OK? I'VE REALLY TRIED TO CHANGE, BUT I KEEP GETTING VICTIMIZED. EVEN YOU'RE MAKING MONEY OFF ME AND MY MENTAL ILLNESSES. I HATE WHAT HAS HAPPENED TO ME AS A KID. I HATE BEING A VICTIM." I stop yelling. My breathing's heavy. Lisa's quiet. Is she hurt, angry, annoyed? Will she kick me out?

Lisa, once again, surprises me. She smiles! "Well, it is about time!"

"WHAT!?!" I scream at her.

"You're finally angry at the abuse you've been receiving. Let's start with your mother."

I can't sit still. As I pace, she's watching me. "My mother abandoned me. She didn't have the decency to call or write or even send a birthday card to me. She just left because she couldn't handle me, us, life. What the fuck do I know why she left? I was just a kid. How dare her! She selfishly left a huge hole in our lives. And who steps up to fill that hole? A middle-aged leech who pretends to love me all the while sucking the life out of me like a vampire, leaving me a cowardly, hurt, whining, sexually-charged maggot. My previous psychiatrist and counselor both knew about the abuse and never reported it. Dr. Crete was a busy-body bitch who not only wanted to know my deepest secrets but also wanted to know all about the abuse, so I told her. And she could have called the Department of Children and Family Services but she didn't.

My father and brother are pressuring me. I feel like a failure. Dr. Jamison is screwing around with my meds, and you're trying to get me to change when I can't."

I'm panting. I feel better, but exhausted. I just want to go to sleep for a month. Oh, no! What did I do to my relationship with Lisa!? I look at her, and she is still smiling. "Feel a little better?" she asks calmly. I smile too. "Yeah, I'm tired."

"Me, too." She says still smiling.

I feel terrible, I made her tired. "I'm sorry, very sorry. I didn't mean to pull you down with me."

"You didn't, Caz. Listening to this type of purging anger is part of my job some days. I'm glad you felt the freedom to erupt like that. I hope by letting out some of the pressure that's been building inside, you'll feel a little better. That's what therapy can do for you, give you a place to release the pent-up emotion that you can't release anywhere else.

She's right, of course. I could never have said that to my father or brother. "I just don't want to injure you or our relationship. And, please forgive me for saying the 'f' word.

She laughs! "I've heard it all before, Caz. These walls take a beating some days. But, Caz, you don't have to take care of me or worry about me. I entered this field knowing clients will say things that I normally don't hear at home. Just take care of yourself."

Long pause. "I don't know how to do that." I reply honestly. "I've been used by so many people that I think it's my job to be used. When I feel I've used someone else, like I just did, I don't think I have the right."

"Caz, you have the right to say what you think. Not all the time and not to everyone, that would be too hurtful to others...and maybe to you. You can say anything you want in here, but in the real world you have to monitor what you say and how you say it. However, you **do** have the right to stand up for your rights and express yourself appropriately."

"I don't even know how to do that. For example, yesterday I got up at 10, I cleaned the house, and made dinner. When my brother came home at 4:00 I was watching TV on the couch. He started to yell at me for lying around all day and doing nothing while he and

Dad worked to support me. He called me a freeloader and a lazy-good-for-nothing-freak. I was crushed. I just sat there and cried. He laughed at me and left the room. I cried for an hour, like my heart was breaking. But, I never told him I cleaned the house and had just sat down to take a break."

"You never defended yourself from the attack?"

"It never occurred to me to defend myself because I **am** a freeloader and I **do feel** like I am lazy and good-for-nothing."

"Wow. I guess every housewife and househusband must feel like that then."

"What do you mean?"

"Well, some family members stay home and take care of the house, do the shopping, take care of kids, if there are any. They seem to feel they're doing their part for the family. You put in six hours of work yesterday. Yet you feel you did nothing of value."

I consider this is new information. Why do I feel that if I do something for the family it's worthless? Why did I allow Rom to belittle me? Do I feel I deserve it? "You think I did a good thing, cleaning the house?"

"How did you feel about what you did?"

"I felt like it was about time."

"That didn't sound positive."

"It's how I felt. You want me to make up something else?"

Lisa ignores my question. "What did your father say when he got home?"

"His eyes lit up and he said something like how much he appreciated what I'd done and that he's proud of me because he didn't have to ask me to clean the house. He said I seemed to be getting better."

Lisa's picking up on something that I'm not. She's pensive and I can tell she's going to give me something to chew on. She does a little thing with her mouth when she is about to give me some ideas. She puckers her lips ever so softly and moves them to the side a bit. Here she goes..."You know Caz; it's interesting that you had two different reactions; one from your dad and one from your brother. Why did you choose to focus on what your brother said and not on what your father said? Obviously, your brother didn't notice the house had been cleaned, and your father did, so your brother's reaction was not accurate and your father's was 'right' (she makes quotes with her fingers). But, you just took your brother's statements to heart and didn't even tell me about your father's reaction until I asked. Why do you think that happened?"

See, I told you she was going to come up with a question I wouldn't know how to answer. I go back to my old standby. "I dunno."

"Have you trained yourself to hear only the negative things that are said to you? Do you only hear the rejection and you even amplify it? When people are kind and happy with you, do you dismiss or reject that feeling because you feel unworthy?"

She's right, but I've been doing this for a long time, and I don't know if I can change. "You're right, but there's more. I feel that when people are happy with what I've done, they expect me to continue to perform at that level. I know I can't always meet others' expectations, so I dismiss what they say as temporary because sooner or later they'll be displeased with me, again." I think I'm getting the hang of this therapy stuff, that's a good insight, if I do say so myself. But, I don't have to say anything, Lisa does.

"Caz, that was great!" Long Pause. "You do know that we're talking about your mother and Belle don't you?"

Stunned, scared, out of the blue, holy crap, this is tied to them? "Really?" I say hesitantly.

"Sure, you never felt that you could please your mother. I bet you tried hard but never felt you could make her happy. She left you and you said to yourself, 'See, I was right, I never was good enough for her to stay.' Then Belle came along and told you what a splendid young man you were and you wanted to buy it, but the price was dear. You always wondered if you were measuring up to her expectations and if you were worthy enough to be chosen over the other boys to pleasure her. You looked to her for affirmation and got it, but the affirmation also came with a price – sexual abuse. Then at 15 going on 16 you were rejected because you were too old. Can you see the link to how you feel about yourself and others today?"

"Sorta, but, I don't know if I can change."

"I know you can change."

"How do you know that?"

"Because you have good insight, and you've already begun changing. You're taking your medication, you're getting up in the morning, and you're trying to use your time more productively during the day."

I don't think these things are a big deal. Is she just trying to make me feel better? Should I say this or will I make her sad that she's worked hard and I don't feel that I've changed much? Lisa, "I don't think those things are such a big deal."

"I disagree; I think they're evidence of your willingness to change. You know what I would like you to talk about next week?" I shake my head 'no'. "I would like you to tell me about your faith in God and how that fits with what we have just been talking about."

"I would love to do that!"

"Great, but, would you try one more thing this week?" I nod, but I'm not sure I'm going to like this. "Would you try talking to yourself in positive ways this week?" I am not sure what she means so I look confused. That always gets her to explain more. "You're saying some horrible things to yourself and that's just reinforcing your negative self image. What if you said positive things to yourself instead?" I'm skeptical. "What if I don't believe them?"

"Well, you may not believe them at first, but after a while you'll start to feel like you believe them. OK? I'll see you next week."

I leave feeling good about the session. I might be changing a little. I've noticed my energy increasing, like I want to do something other than sit and watch TV or play video games. I'm really looking forward to next week's session. I love to talk about God.

Lisa
Caz and Faith

That session with Caz was interesting. I can see his strong dependent side that leads to his self-defeating beliefs. I also see he's transferring the dependency he had for his mother, and then for Belle, to me. He seems to want to please me. I ask him to be honest, but I can sometimes see him filtering his responses in order to please me, then, at other times, he speaks boldly. That outburst was great! He took a risk in expressing himself in an angry and vulnerable manner with me. Of course, then he apologized, but he was able to process the apology, too. And I didn't see the scared 10 year old persona or the 16 year old cocky persona. He seemed more real today.

Next week we'll talk about his faith. By his reaction, I think he expects to talk about his loving, caring, joyous relationship with God. We may, but I'm more interested in how he fits God into the equation of pleasing, rejecting, and judging. Does he walk on glass shards with God? Does he question, get angry, express his dissatisfaction to his creator? My hunch is (and I could be wrong) that he treats God the way he treats me. Angry one minute, apologetic the next, wants to connect and feel accepted but fears he will be rejected if he shows his real self.

I'm amazed how faith in God mirrors our relationships on earth. I've seldom seen a client who, in the end, hasn't benefited from exploring the relationship with the One that we believe created us and is in continual relationship with us. We often don't know how we should be in relationship to God, fearing that any anger, whining, sadness is somehow a demonstration of a lack of faith. There are many people out there who insist they have the one true way to relate to God. That may be true for them, but I've found that each person has his own way of loving and fearing the Holy. I believe no one is right or wrong in their faith search; they're just in that search.

I wonder how Caz will describe The Boss.

Noelle, the Murderer

"Hi, Noelle. Did you have a good week?"

"It was ok." She shrugs and walks past me.

"I'd like to continue with gathering some more information the way we did last week? I would like to know you better." Boom, she's up and running out of the office. Ok, that didn't go well. She's really scared. I guess I'll finish my case notes and take an early lunch. Ten maybe fifteen minutes go by, and I feel someone's watching me. I look up and Noelle is in the doorway looking down at the floor like she's been naughty. Before she could say anything, I jump in, "Noelle, I'm so sorry. I assumed that continuing to talk about your childhood was ok. I should have asked your permission."

Noelle sits down in "her" chair. She looks even paler than usual.

"Noelle are you ok?"

Noelle begins to explain, "It weren't your fault. I jist hav'a hard time tellin' my stories to other people. The more dey know the more in danger dey is in. It's dangerous to be 'round me. That's why I don't want a relationship with ma boss. He could git hurt. Trust me, you're in danger if I like you or care 'bout you."

"And that's why you leave abruptly during sessions? You're trying to keep me from getting hurt?"

"Yep."

"I don't understand. Could you explain it to me?"

Noelle, gets very still. Hands are in her lap, now. She's looking at the floor. "I'm warnin' you."

"Ok, I've been warned. Tell me what's going on anyway."

"I've the power to kill people." She whispers.

Question, question, I know I should ask a question, but I don't know which way to go. I could make her run again. I'm just going to reflect.

"That's a pretty powerful statement."

"It's true."

"You're saying that I'm in danger just because I know you?"

"No."

"Are you saying that you actually kill people?" I'm sure hoping this isn't true.

"No. Not personally."

"So what are you saying?"

"When I git close to people...they die."

"Like your Gran and your mother?"

"That's when it started, but I didn't know at the time it had started. I jist thought...people get old an' die. I wuz only four, so they were old ta'me."

"When did you put this together, that when you get close to someone or love someone, they die?"

"It wuz building all along, but really when I wuz 'bout 12."

"You know, Nicolle. I'm flattered that you're worried about me. It means you must be feeling more comfortable with me, and therefore the feeling has raised some concern for you. And so, tell me if I'm wrong, by running away, you're protecting me from yourself?"

"Yep. If I start ta like you alot. You'll die."

Wow, that's ominous! I don't believe it's true, but she does. What if by some weird twist of fate, I die while she's in treatment with me? The cycle would've just perpetuated itself and her belief would be even stronger. That's also why she won't get close to her boss! She's protecting him.

"There must be someone in your life that you care about and have known for awhile that hasn't died."

"Nope."

"Really?"

"Yep."

"Ok. Let me see if I understand this correctly, if I continue to see you, then you're saying that I'm taking my life in my hands."

"Yep."

"If I'm willing to take that risk, would you tell me your story?" There's a long pause. She's considering my question.

"I'm willin' to tell you ma story, but I can't care 'bout you. I hafta be business-like. Okay?"

"Fair enough. The issue is not that someone **knows** you or that **they** care about **you**. The deadly thing in your mind is if **you** care about **them**."

"I hav'ta think 'bout that one." She takes her time and thinks. She looks up and shrugs. I am not sure if she understands what I just said or she doesn't know if I'm correct. I clarify.

"Well, your boss obviously likes you and wants to take you out. He's been your boss for how long?"

"Four years."

"Ok, **he** cares about **you** and he has for awhile and he's still alive."

"So, Leeza, are you saying that maybe the death **only** occurs when I love others, not when they care 'bout me."

"Just asking."

"Hafta think 'bout that. I hafta go back over my life an' look at this.... pattern thing."

"I'd like to help you. May I?"

"You can try. But, I may run away."

"Fair enough."

Noelle sits quietly. Is she weighing her options? Is she ready to run? Her purse is in her hands again.

"After Mom died, ma brother died."

"How about telling me the story?"

She takes a big, deep breath. "After ma'mother died, Dad wuz fran'ic. He worked full time, helped us wiff homework, took us to sports, made sure we wuz clean an' fed. He kinda burned out, so he got us a nanny. Her name wuz Ginny. She wuz actually nicer to us than Mom wuz." She shrugs. "My brother wuz three years older an' I wuz now five. I loved him, idolized him, wanted to be like him. When I wus 'bout six, Billy wuz nine. He loved to ride his bike, swim, an' skateboard. He wuz very active an' fun to be 'round. One night I went to his room an' told him I loved him an' tried to kiss him an' he sez 'Eeewww' an' pushes me way. We both laughed."

Noelle is smiling very, very slightly at the memory an' switched to present tense again. "I go to his room the next morning to tell him that breakfast is ready an' he's cold, dead."

I'm quiet, real quiet. Actually, I'm holding my breath trying not to disturb her, lest she run. So far she's told all the stories as if she were explaining how to stir paint. I want to ask her why he died, but I need to let her decide what and when to share. She continues without prompting.

"The day b'fore, he fell off his skateboard an' hit his head. His friends said he got back up, rubbed the side of his head, an' laughed. A small blood vessel cracked open when he fell an' leaked into his head while he was asleep. It kilt him. Dat's what the autopsy showed."

I'm beginning to notice the subtle shifts in her otherwise rigid presentation. Noelle is looking a bit paler than usual but still no tears, just pain that's exhibited by small twitches around her lips.

"Leesa, I hav'ta go now. See ya nex' week."

"Okay, Noelle, be good to yourself."

Noelle's pain is so deep that she can only take a few minutes a week. She knows when she has had enough and runs. I wish she would just say, "I've had enough for day." Maybe we can work on this. She also needs space between sessions. Right now she's escaping the pain, but later I hope she'll use the full hour session to gain insight and the other 167 hours during the week to process information about each session and perhaps do some homework that will transfer the learning from the session to life.

As Noelle gets stronger I hope she will be able to tolerate more time and even want more time. Hopefully, she'll begin to feel, what other clients feel, that the session time flies by. This session, she lasted 30 minutes (only 20 if I take into account she was absent for 10 minutes due to her first flight), but it was tough for her to sit with her pain that long. Even though she does not emote very often, she feels the physical discomfort of her pain. She clutches her handbag or grits her teeth to endure each minute.

Noelle Resists Liking Lisa

Had a hard time t'day, sittin' wiff Leeza an' talkin' about ma early childhood an' the deaths that happened. Duz she really understan' how much danger she's in? I like her an' I'm tryin' to keep my feelin's from growin' for her. That's why I keep runnin' away from her. When she's nice to me an' tells me nice things 'bout myself, I begin to feel close to her, but I can't git close. I can't. She'll die! Does Leeza know I'm not tellin' her all the facts of the deaths? I wuz young, but I r'member evrythin', images, colors, feelin's. Somehow keepin' some information from her feels like I'm protectin' her. Does she know or suspect? I hope not or she might pry an' poke 'round too much. I gotta be **real** careful. I can't be responsible for another death.

Caz' Manipulation

Since Dr. Jamison changed my medication again, I feel better. Some of my sleeping all day may have been a hangover from the trazodone. Lunesta gives me a bit of a hangover, but it's not as bad. I'm still taking the Lunesta too late in the evening. Sometimes I don't take it until after midnight, and then I have trouble getting up the next morning. My dad, Dr. Jamison, and Lisa are all trying to convince me that I need to take Lunesta early. That way, I go to bed earlier, and I get up earlier. They all think I don't like going to bed because it reminds me of the abuse. I've agreed with them, but that's only part of it. To tell the truth, I don't like daytime. There's little for me to do except clean, cook, shop, and walk the dog. It's mindless twaddle. I would rather just sleep. Yet, when I'm 70, and look back on my life, I know I'll regret having slept most of my life away. I wonder if I should share that with Lisa. No. If she knows the truth, she's going to expect me to work on this issue by finding something for me to do during the day, like a job. I can't handle a job right now. It's better for all of them to think that my sleeping is related to the abuse, the depression, and the medication. I'm devious, but I just can't handle the pressure and expectations right now. It's better for them to think I'm trying and leave it at that. Some days I sleep all day, and some days I get up and work like a beaver building the Hoover Dam. That way, they all stay off my back. I hate manipulating, but it works.

Bally's Obsession with her Facial Scars

It's been three days since the accident and while the swelling's gone down a little, I'm becoming anxious about the scarring. Because my skin is darker than white people's skin, I tend to scar more. At least that's what a doctor said in the past when I had a mole removed from my thigh and it left a worse looking scar than the mole. I visited my general practitioner today. The docs at shock trauma recommended I check in with him. I dread going to doctors. I find them arrogant and aloof. My current doctor is no exception. He took one look at me and said, "What the hell did you do?" Why did he think that it was something **I did**? Well, it was, but why did he jump to the conclusion that I DID IT? It could've been someone else's mistake. Anyway, I told him about the accident and he shook his head. I felt myself boiling inside, but I tried to remain calm. Instead of giving him a piece of my mind, I gave him the finger when he wasn't looking. I told him about the doc at shock trauma, and how I asked for a plastic surgeon and they refused to accommodate me and gave me a sedative to make me sleep while they stitched me up. My doctor took off my bandages and looked closely at the stitched area. Then he said it was his opinion that a plastic surgeon did the work or someone very skilled. I don't know that I believe him. I think he was just placating me. I asked him how long it would take to fully heal, and he said I needed to be patient. What kind of answer was that? He told me he would refer me to a plastic surgeon if I wanted, because a plastic surgeon may be able to minimize the scaring. I took the referral he gave me, and I called the surgeon on my cell phone as I left his office. I have an appointment in a few days. The office seemed to accommodate me when I told them about the accident and how recent it was. The receptionist said the sooner the surgeon saw me, the better. What a royal pain the ass this is.

I'm seeing Lisa this afternoon. She seemed to be anxious to see me twice this week so I said ok. She probably needs the money.

Lisa's Kindness Rejected by Bally

Today is packed with more clients than I usually see in one day. I brace for a long day. One of the reasons I'm busier today is because I had to fit Bally in for a second appointment this week. I'm concerned about her emotional reaction to the accident and her facial scars. While she has her job back, she still could be fragile and may want to drink.

Bally is less swollen today and she seems to be walking with less difficulty. She doesn't smile when I greet her. She just hangs her head and walks into my office. She begins abruptly. "Well, you wanted this session so...go."

Whoa! She catches me off guard. I'm not sure what she means. When I asked her if she needed to see me twice this week, she said, "Yes". Now she's putting the decision on my shoulders. What's she implying? "Bally, I'm not sure I understand what you mean?"

"You wanted to see me two times this week. You were probably worried I might drink or something. You insisted that I see you twice this week."

"That's not how I remember the conversation. I asked you if you wanted another appointment this week or whether you wanted to wait a week. You answered that you wanted to see me again this week."

"That's what **you** wanted."

I think I'll call her bluff. "Would you like to skip this appointment then?"

She looks stunned and then quickly hides her reaction with an indifferent look. "I don't care."

"Then let me make another appointment for you next week." I pick up my calendar and find the page for Tuesday of the following week. "I can see you at noon, that would be your lunch hour because you will be back at work by then...or I could see you at seven that evening. I look up. Bally looks confused. She doesn't know what to do with this direct and honest communication.

"So you don't want to see me today. You would rather have the hour off for yourself than meet with me to help me through this crisis?"

Wow! She's unbelievable! I can see why she's such a good negotiator at work. She finds the weak spot and nails it. I keep repeating to myself, "I will not be manipulated, I will not be manipulated."

"Bally, I didn't say that. I said I was willing to see you again this week, that's why I made the appointment for today." (I am trying to keep my voice emotionless.) "You seem to think that this appointment is for me, but I don't need to see you unless you need to be here. The decision is yours." (Secretly I'm hoping she'll decide to see me next week and give me an hour break in the middle of this busy day, but I have to keep my feelings out of this.)

Right now, she doesn't have the upper hand and I can see she's uncomfortable. The confusion on her face speaks volumes. If she gives in and stays for the appointment, then she's admitting she'd like my help and she's more vulnerable. If she leaves then she's creating dominance over me and blows off the session, but she loses a session. She's in quite a stew, and I cut up the vegetables! But, she's very smart. If anyone can find a way out of this dilemma, she can.

"Well, since I'm already here, and we've already spent several minutes trying to negotiate this, I might as well stay. I can come up with something to talk about I'm sure."

She **is** good. I'll give her that. "Ok, what do you want to talk about?"

Bally gives me the run down on how she's doing physically. She has a plastic surgeon's appointment soon and that seems to create a feeling of optimism. She also tells me she wishes she were still drinking because it would help numb the pain. She's taking some non-narcotic pain pills, but they aren't eliminating the pain, therefore she's not sleeping well. She stops and fidgets with the strap of her purse, which is on her lap. She never put it down on the floor, another indication that she doesn't want to be here. I remain quiet. She's thinking.

"A couple of sessions ago, you...um...asked me about my childhood memories. Remember?"

"Yes."

"Well, um...I don't remember a lot."

"I know."

"I do have some flashes though. Are they significant? Flashes, I mean. If they aren't memories, just flashes of memory. Can you say whether they are real or significant?"

"I don't know. I guess I'd have to hear what these flashes are and together we could figure out if they're significant."

"Ok. Well, I remember one time when I was about three, maybe not even that old. I saw my father rubbing the leg of a woman, not my mother."

"Can you describe the scene a little more?"

"They're sitting on the couch talking and he's rubbing her leg, here." She indicates the thigh area.

"When you have that 'flash' what do you feel?"

"Sick to my stomach."

"Do you know who the woman is?"

"No, but, she's familiar to me, like I've seen her before."

"What interpretation do you assign to this flash?"

"That my father was unfaithful to my mother."

"Is that a current interpretation of the event or the three year old interpretation?"

"That's a current interpretation."

"What does the three year old think or feel or do?"

"The three year old feels confused and doesn't trust him, or her."

"Very nice Bally."

"Really?"

"Yes, really. What do you make of this?"

"A married man and another woman shouldn't be that close unless they're married. They shouldn't be doing that."

"Does this flash have meaning for you."

"Well, yea, I guess. Lack of trust in adults, people doing things they shouldn't.

"Anything else?"

"Yea, one more thing."

"What's that?"

"It's not real."

"What's not real?"

"The relationship. It's not a real one."

"What do you mean 'not real'?"

My three year old mind says, "They aren't married and not in love."

"Did they see you watching them?"

"I never thought about that, but yes, they knew I was there."

"What did the woman look like?"

"She was Asian looking, like my mom."

"Do you have any pictures of your extended family?"

"No, but, my mother does."

"Do you think you would recognize the woman if you saw her again?"

"Yes, I'd know her. I just can't place where I know her from."

"Do you feel like following up on this and finding out who she might be?"

"Not really."

"Why not?"

"I'm afraid."

"Afraid of....?"

Bally hangs her head and doesn't say anything. Perhaps I'm pushing her too hard to investigate this woman's identity. "You don't have to do anything about this flash if you don't want to. You can drop it."

"No. I don't want to drop it. I'm afraid, but I want to know. I've always wanted to know who she is, but I never asked."

"So what do you want to do?"

"I'm not sure. Can I think about it until next time?"

"Sure. Do you want to stop now? Or do you have another flash you want to talk about?"

"I have one other, do we have time?"

"Yes."

"I have a flash of memory that my father is standing in front of me and leaning over close to my face. He says, "You are very beautiful, Bally. You can have any man you want. But remember, all men want from women is sex. Don't give it away freely. Get something for yourself. Keep yourself perfect, not fat, don't let yourself go like some Asian women do.""

"How old do you think you were?"

"About seven. I know because I was wearing a plaid jumper that was my elementary school uniform."

"Anything else about the memory?"

"Dad smelled of booze."

"This seems like a memory, not just a flash."

"Yeah, I guess it does."

"What meaning does it have for you?"

"A woman's worth is only for sex, and I'm only worthwhile if I keep myself perfect."

"That's pretty profound considering you're sitting here with stitches in your face."

"Yes, it means because my face is damaged, my worth is also damaged. I'm damaged goods." She tears up and takes out a tissue, rolls the points, and dabs at the corners of her eyes.

"Do you believe you have always been damaged goods? Or is this a feeling based on the current accident?"

"I've always felt like damaged goods. But now it shows." She begins to cry softly and genuinely. No rolled up tissues. I let her cry until she stops. "I feel so sad."

"This is sad. A child feeling like damaged goods at only seven."

"Can I do anything about this feeling of damaged goods?" She asks.

"Yes, but first, you'll need to reject the messages you heard in childhood."

"You mean get them out of my head?"

"More like stop believing them as if they're gospel."

"How do I do that? They've been there for so long."

"Do you really believe that your worth is wrapped up in your looks?"

"Yes, I do. I don't think other people's worth is based on their looks, but I think mine is."

"So you're different from other people?"

"Sure, look at me. I don't look like anyone else in the world. I'm unique." Bally has a good point there.

"True. But, you have two arms, two legs, a head. We have more in common then we have differences."

"My flash of memory says I'm unique and because of that, I need to keep myself perfect because there is only one of me."

"Interesting you see it that way. As you were telling your story, I thought you father was speaking about all women not just about you. Am I wrong?"

"You may be correct, but I thought he was talking about only me."

"Does your sister have any similar encounters with your father?"

"We never talked about it." Long pause. "Maybe I should ask her."

"What would it mean to you if you found out that your father believed that every woman's worth was based on their looks, that he had made similar comments to your sister, mother, and others?"

"I'm not sure. I would definitely have to think about it."

"Here's another look at this. What if your father said something like that to your sister as well and she said, 'He's crazy. That's not true.' And she dismissed it."

"You mean I might have accepted what he said as gospel and she thought it was poppycock?"

"Right."

"I'll have to think about that, too." Bally is quiet again for a long time.

"Ok. Earlier in our session, I wrote down an appointment at 12 next Tuesday. Is that still ok with you?"

"Sure. Do I have time for one more question?"

"Yes."

"Do you feel good about yourself? I mean you're not a beautiful woman. You're kinda cute and all, but you're not stunning. No harm intended."

"None taken." Ouch.

"Even though you're attractive and cute, do you feel really good about who you are?"

"Yes." I fibbed a little.

"Why?"

"Because I'm a total person, intellect, feelings, behaviors, looks, spirit. It's the whole package that's important. And despite the fact that I might look **like** some other people, I am still unique."

"I guess but it still doesn't make sense to me. I am unique looking and I feel different. You aren't all that unique, and you still feel different."

"Ok, here is an example. Have you ever watched a strikingly beautiful man or woman on television who has looks, fame, money, etc. and then they get arrested for driving while intoxicated and the mug shot looks nothing like what they look like on television? It's as if you're seeing the real person in the mug shot, the one they look like when they are working around their house or when they are drunk. And they look like everyone else. The media image is simply a façade, the makeup, the hair, the suit. People can be beautiful on the outside, but if this doesn't match their insides then they're out of synch."

"I feel like that sometimes." Bally sits quietly for quite awhile. I could almost see the wheels turning in her head. "I gotta think about this. See ya' next week."

I noticed as Bally became more introspective, she let her diction slip. She wiped her eyes instead of dabbing them, like she usually does. Was she taking a risk at being more real? Well, for a session she didn't want, it was quite productive. I wonder if she had an unconscious sense that addressing memory flashes is where she needed to go today and she was resisting going there? One thing for sure, this job is seldom dull. That session was a very pleasant surprise, and I feel energized. Next!

Bally's Quest for Pictures

I feel strange after that session, and I want a drink to get rid of the feeling. I feel like a part of my world has been turned upside down. I thought my flashes of memory were of no consequence but just generated uncomfortable feelings. I didn't think they had any meaning that impacted my life now. I need to call my sponsor. The urge to drink is strong and drinking could dull these uncomfortable, confused thoughts and feelings. I don't want to drink, but I don't want to feel this way either. My hand is shaking as I dial. Damn I got her answering machine. "Hey Jen, this is Bally, I just had a session with my shrink and it stirred up a lot of crap for me. I feel like having a drink to calm down. Call me, PLEASE!"

No drinking, no sponsor to talk to. What am I going to do? I go into my fix-it mode. I call Mom. She's usually home and she is. "Hi Mom."

"Hello, Bally. How are you? I not heard from you in weeks and weeks."

"I know, Mom, I'm sorry."

"It's okay, I know you busy."

"Hey Mom, I gotta question for you."

"Okay, sweetheart."

"Do you have pictures, old ones, of our family when I was a baby and up to six years old?"

"I got lots pictures. Why?"

"Could I get some of them? Some copies?"

"Intressing. Your sister ask same ting."

"She did?"

"Yes. She want pictures too. I send her some."

"Do you have any extras or should I call her?"

"I have some extras, but she has many I give her. You call her and get some. Ok?"

"Ok. And Mom, are you ok?"

"I good Bally. Call soon again, ok?"

"Bye Mom."

Well, that's interesting. What does this all mean? I call my sister and she's not home either. I leave a message for her to call me. That should surprise her. I never call her. She always calls me.

Caz' Crisis with his Grandfather

Today was one of those days that I got up and worked around the house. I hauled mulch to the flower beds and planted the tomato and pepper plants along with the herbs Dad purchased. I'm thinking about the session coming up in a couple of days, and I'm looking forward to talking about God. The phone's ringing, and I ignore it. I'm filthy and don't want to stop the yard work and track dirt inside. Fifteen minutes later the phone rings again. Fifteen minutes after that the phone rings again. I give up and go inside to answer the phone, knowing that I'm tracking in dirt that will need to be cleaned up. I'm turning into a housewife!

"Hello?" I hear an older lady on the line and she's crying. "Grandma? Is that you?"

"Caz, your grandfather just had a severe stroke. The doctors don't think he's going to make it. Can you call your dad and brother and come as quickly as you can? I've been trying to reach you for the last hour." Great, now, I feel really bad. I thought her calls were nuisance sales calls.

"Grandma, I'll get a hold of Dad and Rom, and we'll be there as soon as we can. I'll call you when we're on our way, ok?"

"Hurry, honey, I don't think he has much time left and I know he'd like to say 'Goodbye.'"

I hang up and utter a prayer for Grandpa's soul. I call Dad. He's out of the office and his secretary says that a woman's been calling him for the last hour but wouldn't leave a message. Yipes, Grandma! I tell the secretary what's happened, and she launches into a professional rally around the office to find Dad. Then I call

Rom. He answers his phone with, "Have you been trying to reach me? I was in a meeting and I could hear my office phone ringing and ringing, but I couldn't leave the meeting." I tell him about Grandpa and he says he's on his way. I haven't felt this important in ages. I'm glad I wasn't sleeping when Grandma needed me. Feeling useful is energizing. Dad calls while I'm in the shower, but I had taken the phone in to the bathroom with me. Smart thinking! Dad's on his way home too. I finish getting ready and pack my bag, we'll probably be staying a couple of nights. Dad and Rom arrive within two minutes of each other and they each pack a bag. We're on our way in 30 minutes. I call Grandma and tell her we're leaving.

The two hour drive is a quiet one. I'm thinking about Grandpa and his life that's about to end. About half way there, I realize that it's my mother's father we're racing to see before he dies. Dad is just as upset about Grandpa's death as if he were his own father. Dad was always closer to them than his own parents, who died when I was a baby. Then, I wonder whether my mother knows her father's dying. Both Grandma and Grandpa said they didn't know where she was these 20 plus years. I always wondered if that was really true. They wouldn't lie, but I cannot grasp that she'd leave without telling them where she was going. Then again, why not? She left us and never told us. But, I was bad and that's why she left. Shit, I'm not supposed to say negative things. My grandparents are great people. This is not making sense to me. Sitting in the back, watching the countryside, I think about my grandparents' pain of having their only child leave her family, never to be heard from again. I feel sad for them.

Chapter Four
Patterns of Life

...the task is to provide honest acceptance and understanding during the clients' struggles toward a greater awareness of their inner experiencing and of the environmental influences that are affecting them.

(Nye, 1986, p. 104)

Noelle Reveals More Killings

Noelle sometimes spooks me with her admonishment, "If I get too close to you, you will DIE!!" On an intellectual level, I understand she's developed this defense mechanism to protect others from herself and possibly protect herself from feeling responsible for deaths. She also has had her early misperception, about causing others' deaths, reinforced each time someone dies. We all have basic misperceptions that we carry around with us. They are born in childhood and are reinforced by external events or can be reinforced by our internal talk to ourselves. If we really look at these misperceptions we usually feel chagrined that we were caught facilitating an erroneous belief. However, Noelle, **believes** she has this power, and she's scared and she hides constantly from others and life.

She had three deaths in three years as a small child. I wonder how many more stories she has to share. Well, here she comes, she looks like she has a bit more pluck in her walk. Or does she have new orthodics?

"Hi Noelle. How are you?"

"I'm ok. I'm dreadin' tellin' you more stories, though. It's kinda like they take on a life of their own an' I feel dirtied by sharing them."

"Dirtied?"

"Yea, I'm embarrassed that I kilt all those people."

She really believes that her love killed people. This misperception may be difficult to unravel. I hope I live long enough to help her or I will become one more of her "stories" or "evidence" that she has the power to kill.

"Well, let's throw caution to the wind and tell me more of how you developed this belief."

"Ya know, Lisa, you keep sayin' it's a b'lief. But, it isn't just a b'lief, it's a fac'. I wish you'd take it more seriously. I'm afraid for you."

"I appreciate that. I'll respect that this is more than a belief for you. Ok?"

"Ok."

"Where were we?"

"I have a confession."

"Ok."

"I tole those stories about my Gran, my mom, an' my brother briefly, but I do hafe full mem'ry of each death, even though I wuz young. Do ya wan'me ta go back an' tell you the whole story or should I go on?"

"Well, you've brought up a good point. Should I hear all the information quickly and then you can go back and fill in the details or should I hear each episode in full detail? What would be most comfortable for you?"

"I'd like ta tell ya all the stuff quick an' then go back an' tell you the details...if you're still alive."

Good grief! Talk about throwing ice water on someone's day! "Ok, that's fine."

"Aftar my brother died from that freak accident, my nanny died. She wuz hit by a drunk driver on New Year's Eve."

"When was that?"

"I wuz about seven or maybe eight."

"It was one or two years after your brother?"

"Yeah."

"Then Dad got hisself remarried. He married a lady (Sue) wiff one daughter (Carrie) who wuz 'bout my age. I hated her. She wuz a spoilt brat. Carrie got everthing she wanted. If she didn't, she threw a tantrum an' Sue'd give in. My dad an' Sue argued a lot about Carrie being spoilt. Sue treated me real good though an' I kinda think she liked havin' a less demandin' kid 'round who obeyed her.

"Sue got pregnan' right 'way an' Dad wuz thrilled. Me, too. She let me feel her belly evry day an' talk to the baby, but she lost it 'round four months. Then she got pregnant agin. Dad's op'mistic an' I'm happy. Carrie not so much. I rub Sue's belly an' talk an' sing to the baby boy, but he's born dead.

"Afta 'bout three (maybe four) years, Sue an' Carrie pack up one day an' leave. Dad wuz sad an' I tried to be good an' helpful to Dad. I'm too old to need a nanny any more 'cause I'm now 11, goin' on 12, goin' into Junior High School an' I feel big an' grown up. I cook an' clean an' hope that Dad won't need 'nother wife. Sorry, I can't do this anymore. I gotta run. See you nex' week."

Half-session

And she's gone, again. I've seen her for a month now and she has yet to stay for an entire 50 minute session. She seems to get overwhelmed with her emotions and that's her trigger or cue to flee. She did say however, that she'll return, so I guess she will do what she needs to do in each session. I wish I could find the words that would help to soothe her fears.

Noelle – The Alien

I jist can't take too much of Lisa's openness to hearin' my horrible stories. I worry I'll hurt her or even kill her if I get too involved. But, more than that, I get jittery inside, like I have bugs crawlin' inside ma skin, and I jist can't sit still an' tell her any more stuff. I'll go back 'cause I want to keep ma job, but I can't stay for long. I wonder if I'll ever be normal, like most people. I feel like an alien.

Lisa Changes Her Therapeutic Style with Noelle

I've been thinking about Noelle this week, and I realized she may be too anxious to stay in counseling and do the work that's required. If I move too quickly and push her too hard, she might run and never come back. I have to let go of my typical structured 50 minute therapeutic hour. She's not able to sustain that level of intensity each week. Therefore, I'll let go of my preconceived ideas of what a therapeutic hour is. I'll continue to let her decide when the session is over. I know she's coming to counseling just because her employer is demanding that she come, but sooner or later, she needs to make the decision for herself whether counseling can help her. Therefore, I'm going to back off and let her do what she needs to do in each session. And I won't feel guilty for collecting a fee for a half-session.

Bally's Homework

My sister calls back just like she always does. (She's the perfect one.) She was worried that something happened to Mom, but I assured her I had just talked with Mom and she's well. Carly, breathes a sigh of relief and I get down to business. Here goes.

"Carly, I've been in an accident. I didn't tell Mom, I don't want her to worry. Because of the accident, I decided to get some counseling. (I lied.) The counselor asked me about my childhood and I don't have many memories. I thought I might get some pictures that may stimulate some memory. Well, Mom has some, and she's sending what she has, but she said you had asked for the same thing a couple of weeks ago and she sent most of them to you. She said I should call you. Um, I want to know if you could copy them for me and then send them to me. I will pay whatever it costs.

Carly is quiet for a long time. "Hello?.... Carly, are you still there?"

"Bally, you were in an accident? Are you ok?"

"Sure. I'm banged up and bruised. I have some cuts and stuff, but I'll live."

"Were you drinking?"

"No, Carly. I haven't had a drink in almost two years."

"Just checking. Because I **was** drinking and got pulled over about a month ago and got arrested for driving under the influence. I have to go to counseling for the next six months, minimum. My psychologist asked me about my drinking and whether anyone in my family had a drinking problem. I mentioned you, and of course Dad, and I told him that I didn't have many memories either. I decided on my own to look at pictures, and I called Mom." There's a long pause while both of us let this sink in. "I'll be glad to send you the pictures. I think you might find them interesting."

"Did the pictures help you discover anything?"

"Yes."

I pause waiting for her to offer what she discovered, but she doesn't share anything.

"Bally, I think you should see the pictures and remember what you will and interpret what you see without my influencing you in any way."

"Ok. Now you've piqued my interest. Can you copy them and send them right away?"

"I'll do it this weekend."

"Overnight them ok? I will pay for everything."

"Ok. You sound like this is urgent."

"You know me. I am the impatient one in the family. Hey, have you heard from Atlee recently?"

"No. Have you?"

"No. I guess we have really scattered to three corners of the country. We were very close as kids. I wonder what happened. We're so disconnected now. By the way, how's the climate in Texas?"

"It's hot. It's always hot. The last time I heard from Atlee, he was in Seattle and loving it.

"Really? When was that?"

"It was in his Christmas card."

I didn't want to admit I hadn't gotten one from him or that I hadn't sent him one either. Carly is much better at keeping in touch than Atlee and I are.

"Do you have his number or email address?"

"No, I only have his address. Do you want it? If you do, I'll include it in the package I'm sending you."

"That would be great. How are your kids?"

"They're fine. I can't believe they're going to be teenagers already. Joe's aching to drive and loves high school."

"Really, it seems only yesterday that he was learning to ride a tricycle."

"I know. Bally, it's good to hear from you. Thanks for calling me, and I'm very glad you're in counseling. We all should be."

"Thanks, in advance, for sending me those pictures."

"You're welcome. And if you have any memories, would you share?"

"Uh, sure, in fact that's one of the reasons I called. I have a weird memory of Dad. He's standing in front of me and bent over close to my face. I can smell his breath and he's been drinking. He says, 'You are very beautiful, Bally. You can have any man you want. But remember, all men want from women is sex. Don't give it away freely. Get something for yourself. Keep yourself perfect, not fat, don't let yourself go like some Asian women do.' My question is this. Did Dad ever say something like that to you?"

"Never. He hardly ever talked to me. He'd never tell me I was beautiful and as far as the rest of the memory, I certainly think you are remembering something correctly. He would always say things like that to anyone who would listen. He never said it directly to me but I remember him saying, 'All men want from women is sex.' And I think I remember him saying that we shouldn't let ourselves go."

"What did you think about that?"

"I thought he was nuts. I dismissed it as his crazy view of the world. He was always focused on people's physical images. Is that helpful?"

"Very. Thanks. I gotta run."

"Ok. Call me when you get the pictures and have a chance to look at them.

"Ok, Bye."

Little Carly was stopped for drinking and driving? My little sister is drinking? She was always the perfect one in our family. I thought she was the healthiest of the bunch. She got married and had four kids right away, one set of twins. Her husband is very successful as a stock analyst. Very wealthy. And what's happened to Atlee? He married several years ago. I didn't go to the wedding. They had a child, a boy I think, and then he got divorced. The child should be 10 or 11. I can't remember his name. What's wrong with my family that we don't keep in touch and don't even know each other?

I wish I could ask Mom, but she seems fragile at almost 64. She's only 64? Why's she so meek, frail, and disconnected? She never talks to me on the phone for more than a minute or two and it's always superficial stuff, nothing important. I follow her lead and don't talk seriously either. I don't want to burden her. Why am I protecting her? Geez, this counseling stuff sure opens up a lot of crap. The interesting thing is I don't feel the need to drink. I'm on a mission. Right now I feel like a sleuth, and it's fun.

Caz' Grandfather's Death

Grandpa is barely conscious when we arrive, and Grandma's holding his hand. He's in and out of a coma and has tubes running all over the place. He gives me a little smile when I lean over to kiss his forehead. God, I love this man. He's always been so kind to me over the years and loved me unconditionally. He's a model train collector, and when we were little, his entire basement was filled with trains running over bridges, through tunnels, emptying milk cans, and herding cattle into a car. He, Rom, and I played trains together for hours.

Dad's weeping openly and that makes me choke up. I've only seen my dad cry one other time and that was when our Golden Retriever, Gillian, died. Rom's very quiet, but I can tell he's trying to hold in his emotion and is about to cry any minute. Grandpa lapses back into a coma again and we leave the room. The four of us stand in the hall of the hospital taking turns holding each other. No one mentions my mother. After a couple of hours, the intensive care nurse, Bev, tells us Grandpa's "slipping away". Back inside the room, we watch as the machines indicate that Grandpa is leaving us. We encircle his bed and then the machines fail to show any sign of life. It's over. Spontaneously, we start singing Grandpa's favorite hymn "Amazing Grace" and then we're silent, each of us caught up in our own thoughts. Grandpa's gone, and I wonder what he's experiencing right now. His pastor joins us minutes later and anoints my Grandpa's head and says a beautiful prayer. My insides ache. Why did he have to die now, just when I'm trying to get my life together?

The ride to my grandparents' house is only 10 minutes, but it feels like an hour. I ride with Dad and Rom drives Grandma in her car. Dad and I don't speak for fear one of us will break down.

The house feels cold and empty without him. Grandma immediately busies herself by making dinner (I guess that's what grandmas do when they have their family around). Dad tries to stop her. He insists we go out for dinner or order something in. Grandma will have nothing to do with that. Grandma is thawing something when some of her church friends stop by to bring food, a casserole, ugh. They knew Grandpa was in the hospital, but they hadn't heard he died. There were tears and questions and some laughter and they respectfully leave us with a ground beef casserole and an apple pie. While Grandma and Dad are getting dinner ready, Rom and I go into the basement for some beer. It's been years since we were in the basement and we're shocked to see the multilevel train display still set up. The tunnels, bridges, crossings are all in perfect condition. Grandpa must have continued to work on the trains even after we were grown. I put on Grandpa's hat and Rom starts the trains running. We just silently sit and watch for awhile honoring the exquisite work he put into the train garden and wondering what Grandma is going to do with it. Neither of us have kids and my mother was their only child. Grandma yells down to us that dinner's ready and Rom turns off the trains. I cannot bear to part with the hat, so I leave it on. Dinner is quiet. The only sound is the utensils moving across the plates.

Finally, Dad interrupts the silence. "I heard you running the trains. I didn't know that Grandpa still had the trains set up."

Grandma said he couldn't part with them. He used them to entertain the neighborhood children. Schools brought their classes over to see his trains and scout troops also visited. Suddenly, we hear a train whistle from the basement. All four of us look at each other. For a second, I think I'm the only one who heard the whistle, that I'm hallucinating. But, we all heard it. Dad says, "Rom did you turn the trains off?" Rom replies, "Yes." Grandma says, "You must have left one on." Rom says, "I am pretty sure I turned it all off." He looks to me for confirmation. I agree, "I thought you did, too." Dad slowly puts his napkin down and walks down the steps. He comes back, walking backwards up the steps. He looks like he has seen the rising of the Titanic. "The trains are all off." he says quietly. We all look at each other. Are we all crazy? In unison everyone turns and looks at the engineer's hat I have on my head. I snatch it off, but Grandma says, "No leave it on. I like it on you." She turns to Rom and Dad, "There are other hats down there if you both would like one. Both Rom and Dad jump up from the table and run downstairs like two little kids who were told there's ice cream in the basement freezer. Both return with two "Guest Engineer" hats that Grandpa always kept for people who came over to play trains with him. They brought one for Grandma too, and she laughs as she dons the hat. But, I have **his** hat, and I feel special wearing it. We finish dinner, clean up the kitchen, and then head for bed early. I feel a leaden tiredness of grief. I wonder if I'll sleep tonight because I forgot to bring my sleep medication.

I toss and turn for an hour before falling asleep. At 3:00 a.m. I awaken to the sound of a train whistle. At first, I'm disoriented, not sure where I am. Then I remember Grandpa's death and recognize the guest room in my grandparents' house. My first thought is Rom is playing a trick on me, but he's in the twin bed against the window. He turns over and looks at me with a questioning expression on his face. We both heard it. We open our door and tentatively walk out of our bedroom. Dad and Grandma are standing at the top of the stairs looking down. We must look funny standing at the top of the stairs in our pajamas, peering down over the railing at the first floor foyer. None of us wants to go downstairs, but all of us wants to know if Grandpa's ghost is in the house. Like little kids who are left home alone and "hear something" we slowly walk down the stairs, together. The basement lights are on, but the train set is not. There is hushed discussion about whether Dad and Rom left the lights on when they had gone downstairs to retrieve the hats, but none of us can remember. I'm the one who breaks the spooky mood and makes everyone laugh. "It doesn't matter whether the lights were left on or not." All three turn to look at me. "This is a great story for the eulogy." Everyone laughs. My comment broke the fear freeze. Dad goes downstairs and turns the lights out.

It's morning and no one has an appetite. We nibble at the English muffins Grandma had in her pantry and drink some hot chocolate. Then the four of us go to the funeral home to make arrangements. I don't know whether we all wanted to be part of the process or didn't want to be left home with a possible Grandpa-ghost. The funeral director is droning on and on and I'm bored. My mind wanders and I wish I could talk to Lisa. Holy Cow! I have a session with Lisa today. I look at my watch. I was supposed to be at her office 10 minutes ago. I excuse myself, walk outside with my cell phone, and call her office immediately. She answers. I explain what happened and launch into how sorry I am I forgot to call her. Most people would've been angry, but Lisa understands. She tells me to take care of myself and to be open to the experience. I wonder what she means by that, probably just some more 'therapist speak'.

Over the next three days we all are on automatic pilot as the preparations are made and the visitations occur. I smile and nod automatically when people I don't know talk to me about Grandpa. Many of Grandpa's friends tell me they remember me when I was "knee-high-to-a-grasshopper" as they crane their necks to look into my face. At dinner, we get giddy as we talk about the inane things people say at a wake. Like "Doesn't he look wonderful?" I wanted to scream, "HE'S DEAD!" But I just smiled and nodded. Then Dad suggests we take a chance and do something funny, something that Grandpa would have enjoyed. He says we should wear our train engineer's hats at the funeral to honor Grandpa's life and spirit.

Noelle
What is Past is Present

A week has lapsed and Noelle is again exactly on time. I wonder if she has a touch of compulsiveness or is she well organized and punctual. I make a note in her file to watch for other possible symptoms.

"Hi Noelle, how was your week?"

"Ok. I guess."

"What would you like to talk about this morning?"

"I'll start where I left off, ok?"

"Sure."

"I loved Junior High. Changin' classes an' havin' diff'rent teachers! Great! If you don't like one, you only hav'ta wait 50 minutes an' classes change. I fit in better there than in elementary school. My school had over 500 students. It wuz easy to hide in the crowd. Most of them were tryin' to outdo others...tryin' too hard ta be the most pop'lar. I hated that stuff an' I stuck to ma self. I babysat lots, 'specially for a family down our street, the Wallers. They were like the family I wanted and never got. They had a six year old boy, Jeremy, a four year old girl named Ruthie, and a baby boy, Calvin, who was 18 months old. I babysat after school an' on weekends when they needed me. One Saturday, the parents asked me to babysit for an evenin' while they went to the movies. They were goin' to see Star Wars, if I remember right. I fed the kids an' put them to bed an' watched TV. Mr. and Ms. Waller came home 'round 10:30 an' he walked me home. I remember wishing I belonged to their family as I went to sleep.

"The nex' mornin' I wake up hearin' my dad sayin' 'Oh, my Gawd, how could that happen?' I jist knew that somethin' was wrong at the Wallers. I don't know how I knew, but I did. I run down stairs and I'm breathing heavy-like 'cause I know somethin' awful happened. My father's sittin' at the kitchen table wiff Mr. Waller who's crying. As soon as I get to the kitchen door, Mr. Waller jumps up and runs to me and holds me tight, I can't breathe. I'm crying an' I don't even know what's wrong. Mr. Waller tries to speak but can't. My dad rescues him. 'Mr. Waller's little boy died in his sleep last night.' I'm cryin' now, but I still don't know which boy died. I ask 'Jeremy?' (thinking 'bout my brother and his accident years ago), but Mr. Waller shakes his head and whispers 'Calvin'.

"I kilt him, jist as sure as I'm standin' in my kitchen. I kilt him. I know when I love people, they die and I make a pact with ma'self, standin' there in ma'kitchen, that I will never get close to another person 'cause I kill people.

"Gotta go. See ya nex' week, same time?"

"Sure." And once again, she's left without my even being able to ask a question. What a horrible series of experiences she's had. I certainly understand how she came to the conclusion that she kills the people she loves. The coincidences are too many to ignore.

I'm struck how quickly she shifts between present and past tense. I notice she often starts out in the past tense and then she shifts into the present tense as the story becomes more intense, more personal, and more deadly. Most clients who do this show signs the material is becoming more difficult to endure. They get anxious, teary, and dazed. Their breathing changes, pupils dilate, and they perspire and sometimes tremble. Noelle tells stories as if she is reading the phonebook. Her words are filled with feeling, but her delivery is deadpan. Her emotions are as frozen as she looks and as the winter days into which she was born.

Tell my Story and Run

This is gettin' easier. I just tell a story and leave. I can handle this counselin' stuff. Gerard's glad I'm goin' and I'm not hurtin' nobody. So far.

Lisa
Noelle's session

It appears that Noelle has found a way to tell her story and not get involved. Over the week, I realize she engages in 'hit and run.' She arrives tells a horrible story and before I can explore the situation with her, she runs. That way she doesn't have to deal with the relationship of therapy. She probably feels she's preventing us from bonding and therefore saving my life.

Grandpa's Funeral and Jake

The engineer hats are a big hit at the funeral. Wearing them made people laugh. When my dad tells the story of hearing the train whistle as part of the eulogy, there isn't a dry eye in the church, half are laughing and half are crying. I keep looking at Grandma and wondering whether she's missing her daughter, but she never says a word.

There were a couple hundred people at the funeral and I felt overwhelmed by the names and faces. I'd never remember all of them, so I stopped trying. However, there was a man who kept to himself, never introduced himself to Grandma or us. He attended one of the evening wakes and the funeral. None of us knew who he was. We thought he must have known Grandpa from work or the model train club. When the man attended the burial, we all knew something strange was going on. Most people don't go to the burial unless they're family or very close friends. Grandma kept saying she didn't know him, but I wondered if she was too grief stricken to remember. The three days were a blur for all of us.

Then the man shows up at the house after the burial. As the crowd begins to diminish, he walks up to Grandma and says something. She grabs her chest like she's having a heart attack. Then she grabs him and hugs him and begins to cry. The crowd takes that as the cue to leave and within a few minutes, the five of us are alone. Grandma's still holding his hand. The man clears his throat and says words that I never thought I would hear. "My name is Jake and I'm your half brother." Dad's mouth literally falls open.

Jake spends the rest of the evening with us unfolding a story that could have been a made-for-television movie. Over 20 years ago, my mother went to the store one evening and was dragged from her car and gang raped. Dad was out of town on business. She kept it a secret from everyone and decided to forget about it and go on with life. Then she found out she was pregnant. She didn't know what to do. She thought because she hadn't reported the rape and hadn't told my dad, no one would believe she had been raped. From what Jake said, the rape must have been brutal. She spiraled into a depression and one day decided it would be best for everyone if she left our family and disappeared. Evidently, she felt an abortion was out of the question. She intended to have the baby and then give it up for adoption. She felt like damaged goods and believed no one would want to see her and her bastard child. Jake said she toyed with returning to my dad after she gave the baby up for adoption, justifying her absence by saying she had had a mental breakdown and had gotten better and wanted to come back home. However, six months after she gave birth, she found out she had AIDS. She lived for another year. In those days, having AIDS was a death sentence. She lived with Jake and his adoptive family for that year, and died a week before Jake turned one. She had confessed everything to Jake's adoptive parents and asked that Jake be told the truth when he was an adult. She even made a video tape in which she explained what Jake had just told us. When she disappeared, she knew she had hurt many people, including her parents, and wanted them to know what had really happened to her.

Grandma is the brave one to ask the question we all wanted to ask. "Do you have the tape with you, Jake?" Jake nods and asks, "Would you like to see it?" We all say 'Yes' in unison. We all gather around the television to watch a woman we hardly knew explain the story of her disappearance. She had pictures of Rom, Dad, and me and at the end she had Jake join her in the video. All I can think about is I need a session with Lisa, NOW!

Grandma and Dad are crying. Grandma has finally lost her daughter. All those years, she and Grandpa always believed that my mom would someday come home. Dad finally has closure, but, hearing the story seemed to awakened a longing in him. I've never seen my Dad cry like that. He wails like I did the day Rom told me I was a lazy good-for-nothing freak. I feel horrible for my dad. I think he held out hope that someday she would return, too. The story of my mother's rape and death is tragic. I feel stupid for crying just because my brother called me a name when all this tragedy brewed beneath the surface of our family.

Dad's crying softer now, and Grandma's holding his hand. She's still crying, too. Rom and I are sitting together on Grandma's couch, stunned by the information. Rom breaks the silence. "I always thought mom left us because I had done something wrong.

So after she left, I tried to be the perfect son, but the burden to be perfect has left me with feeling stressed-out and panicky. Sometimes I think I'm having a heart attack."

What? Am I hearing this correctly? I blurt, "I always thought mom left because I was such a difficult child with my ADHD and learning disabilities. I decided I couldn't be normal, so why try? As a result, I've been in difficult situations all my life."

Grandma reaches out to Rom and me and says, "I always thought your mom left because I hadn't taught her how to hang in there during the difficult times. I blamed myself, and so did your Grandpa. The fact she left you all and didn't come to us for help, told us that she was through with us too. We grieved the loss of our only child for over 20 years but always held out hope she would return."

Dad confesses, "I thought she left because of me. I wasn't the perfect husband and I often thought I wasn't as supportive of her as I could have been."

Silence. We all carried our own personal guilt and blame inside of us all those years, and we were all wrong! Jake gets up to leave. We were all so involved with our own loss and pain, that we hadn't bothered to get to know him. I jump up and hug him, and he begins to cry in my arms. The rest of the family gathers around us, and we have a group hug. And then I hear it again, but this time very faint. The whistle. Grandma doesn't hear it because she's blowing her nose. But, Rom and Dad hear it. Jake looks up when the whistle sounds and says, "I'll be damned, when you all told the story at the funeral, I thought it was joke." Dad laughs and shakes his head. "Nope, we just embellished a bit."

Jake touches my hat and says, "I wish I had known him." Grandma runs, really, **she runs** downstairs and gets the final "Guest" hat and gives it to Jake. He says he's very honored and he'll cherish it. We promise to be in touch and visit. I have another brother!

Caz
Life's Crossing

I must admit I was surprised when Caz didn't show for his appointment. He had been on time for the last couple of sessions. I had begun to run all kinds of possible scenarios through my head beginning with he forgot and ending with I said something that made him want to drop out of therapy. Yes, therapists can become a wee bit paranoid when clients don't show up for appointments. I was grateful he called me to let me know he's ok. We agreed on another appointment time.

We never talked about his grandfather, and therefore I don't have a context within which to understand what his death means to Caz. I only know that his grandparents disavowed knowing anything about their daughter's whereabouts and Caz believed them. I wonder if Caz' mother knew about her father's death and whether she had stayed away from this important event. Or whether she showed up and Caz saw her for the first time in over 20 years. Either way this experience may have a profound impact on him.

Caz sits in front of me with a big grin on his face and a train engineer's hat on his head. I can't read him. Of course I'm running more of my famous scenarios through my head. But, perhaps the best thing to do is just listen to him. As Caz masterfully unfolds the entire story, I'm amazed. I consider for a moment that he's telling me a whale of a tale just to tease me into believing him. Then I see what an impact this death, funeral, and discovery has had on him, and I am awed by the whole experience. Caz finishes telling the story and sits back. He cocks his head to one side and asks, "Do you believe that my grandfather was orchestrating the whistle?" I normally don't do the therapist technique that I use at this moment because it sounds phony. However, it seems appropriate here. "What do you believe Caz?"

Caz retorts, "Nice side-stepping, Ms. Therapist."

Oops, I'm caught. But, he takes my question seriously. "If I had been the only one who had heard it, I would think I was hearing things, that I wanted to believe my Grandpa was hanging around. But some of us heard it three times, so I think Grandpa was with

Mom and he was trying to get our attention, perhaps alerting us to the life crossing ahead of us."

Wow, that's a fabulous interpretation with a metaphor. "How has your grandpa's death and finding out the truth about your mother impacted you, brought you to a life crossing?"

Caz becomes silent for a few minutes then he looks up, "I don't know yet. I'm not avoiding your question." He says as he raises his hands in the air as if to stop me from chastising him for saying 'I don't know.' "I know all this has impacted me, but I just don't know how, not at this moment. I need time to think about this a lot more. It's taken me the entire session just to tell you the story. I need some time to um, think... feel ...pray. When I come next week, I want to process all this. Is that alright?"

"Caz, I think this is the perfect time to say 'I don't know.' This event is huge. It can be life-changing. It could be healing. It could hurt. Let's leave it at that for now. I'll see you next week."

Caz
Trial Preparation

I felt in charge during this session, and I think it's the first time I felt that way. Lisa just sat there and tried to contain her reactions, but she couldn't. Her eyes opened wider at times, she shook her head, she smiled, and she said "Unbelievable" a couple of times. Her question as to how it impacted me is a serious one. I may need to toss some old childhood messages in the garbage. I need help in how to do that. I also need to start working on my testimony for Belle's trial. The attorney wants to talk to me sometime in the next couple of weeks because the trial is a few weeks away. He said on the phone that several men and a few boys have come forward, but there are many, many more who don't want to get involved because they don't want to be seen by their families and business associates as victims. The D.A. said he's hoping that more men and boys will agree to testify.

One man, the attorney talked to, said everyone in his office is talking about the case and there are a lot of jokes going around that cause people to either laugh or become angry. He's trying to stay away from the office gossip. I'm glad I'm free of that baggage. I'm not looking forward to testifying, but I have a supportive family and church and I don't have business associates or children who'd look at me differently if they knew I'd been sexually abused.

Lisa
Caz' Experience

Clients who have experienced extreme trauma often experience a spiritual crisis also. A person's spiritual crisis can manifest itself as rejecting a faith or belief system or an increase in reliance on their beliefs. The belief in God or a higher power can become disabled or can become fraught with internal conflict. Doubts about self, others, and God can be punctuated with anger, guilt, and confusion. Trauma destroys the view we have of the way life should be. In Caz' case he has held onto his religion to survive. Thus, he was definitely more in-tuned with the possibility of a spiritual experience during the funeral and after. How will he internalize his experience?

Noelle
Calvin and Ms. Sprool

Noelle is as punctual as ever. I wonder where she will start this week. I wonder if she will let me ask questions about Calvin's death. Noelle is looking at me expectantly like I'm supposed to drive the therapeutic train again.

"Noelle. I wondered if I could ask you a few questions about Calvin's death."

"Sure."

"Did you blame yourself for his death, other than because you loved him?"

"You mean did I think I had done somthin' while I was babysittin' that may'of lead to his death?"

"Yes."

"I never tole nobody this, but I worried I made a mistake while I wuz babysittin', but the autopsy said he had a genetic defect. Something about a brain aneurism bursting. But, for about two weeks, I wuz scared. The family never ast me questions 'bout the night Calvin died an' the police, they wuz very nice to me. I had to tell dem everythin' we did from the time I started babysittin' to when the Wallers came home, but dey waited for the autopsy and stuff. I think the coroner said he died 'round five in the mornin'. So I worried I made a mistake, but I wasn't panicky 'cause he died seven hours after I lef'. I think the parents blamed themselves, though. Don't know fir sure."

Today, Noelle is a regular chatterbox! She stops and takes a breath and looks like she's deciding whether to continue. She thinks for several minutes and starts on another topic. Back to present tense!

"There's this one teacher I love, Mrs. Sprool, my English teacher. I have her for two years, seventh an' eighth grades. Then when I'm in ninth grade, she dies, chokes on a chicken bone in the caf'teria. It caught in her throat. I think before Calvin died, I knew if I love someone, then they died, but when Mrs. Sprool dies, I start to believe dat I actually kilt people with my love. The only 'ception is my Dad, so far. In high school, I begin to pull away from him, too. I stop hanging out wiff friends. It works. No one dies until I am 18."

"What happened at 18?"

"Time's up, gotta go. See ya nex' week."

And she gone!

Oops, no she's back. Poked her head in the door.

"You haven't ast me why my hair is white when I'm only 40."

"Should I ask now? You have more time in this session." (Thought I'd offer the opportunity, but I know she's done for the day.)

"No, jist thought you should notice an' ast nex' time. Bye."

Is Noelle now becoming more engaged? Am I grasping at straws? This is going really slowly, but Noelle needs to set the pace. I'm struck with how fast Caz was in telling me his story and how slow Noelle is in revealing hers. Interesting how different clients approach counseling in totally different ways. Caz would see me every day if he could, and I get the impression from Noelle that she would like to see me once a year, maybe to keep me alive longer!

Bally's Homework
Family Pictures

Carly, true to her word, copied the pictures and overnighted them to me, and they arrived just in time for me to go through them before I see Lisa. My hands tremble when I open the package. I'm not sure if I'm nervous about what I could find or if I'm excited to discover new things about my family. The first person I look for is the woman whose leg Dad was stroking. I have to get a magnifying glass to look closely. A lot of the pictures are small, old, and yellowed. I get about two-thirds of the way through and there she is in a picture with my mother and her family so I guess she's related to my Mom. She may be my aunt, but I don't remember her other than the memory flash. I call Mom. Gotta know.

"Hi Mom."

"Hi Bally. I just talked to you!"

"Yes you did. We talked about the family pictures."

"Oh, yes. We did. I send you some. Did you get them?"

"No Mom, I haven't received them yet.

"I send them two days ago."

"They'll arrive soon, don't worry. Listen, Mom, I have pictures from Carly and there are a few people I don't know. Would you help me?"

"I try."

"Well, there's a picture of your family. I can see you and grandma and gramps. There are two other people in the picture, but I don't think I know them. You are standing in front of our house on Heldam Street."

"Oh, yes that's one of the few pictures I have where my whole family is together. The other two people are my sisters. We saw them not very often. That picture was taken before they moved away."

"What were their names?"

"My first sister is 'Little' and my youngest sister is 'Sassy'."

"Sassy and Little?"

"That's right. Remember, in the Philippines we have fun names for each other. You ever hear my Mom call me Toto?"

"Sure. What does it mean?"

"I loved the movie Wizard of Oz and always wanted dog named Toto. So they called me Toto. My younger sister, she sass my parents when she was two so they call her Sassy and my older sister, she only four pounds when she born, so they call her Little One or Little for short."

As my mother was talking I realized she still talks as if English is not her first language. She still speaks like her parents did. But, my mother has lived in the U.S. for over 60 years. I wonder why she never learned to speak English correctly. Does she not hear us speaking correctly or is she holding on to her heritage or is she battling my father who refused to allow other languages in our house? What's with all the questions? I'm turning into a fricking shrink!

"Tell me about Little. I have a memory of her with Dad, but I didn't know who she was."

"Oh, yes. Little was your father's favorite. She was beautiful and she and your dad really liked each other. She very sexy and your dad liked sexy women. I often wondered why he marry me. I not sexy at all. I cute but not sexy."

"We all have our gifts, Mom. Maybe he saw you as a good mother to his children."

She's crying softly on the other end. I never heard my mother cry. "Thank you Bally. That was sweet of you. I love you. I gotta go. Bye. Call again."

"I will Mom. Bye." She definitely is not a person who likes to talk on the phone.

I look carefully through the rest of the pictures looking for more pictures of Little. I find two other pictures. In both she's standing beside my father and Dad is sideways hugging her. In one of the pictures, she's pregnant. And it looks like she had a baby about the same time my mother had me. I have a first cousin I never knew about! I wonder if Mom keeps up with her sisters. I wonder if they live here in the U.S. or in the Philippines. Maybe next year when I have some vacation saved up I'll go to the Philippines and track my ancestors on my mother's side.

I get out the magnifying glass and look at the two sisters again. The picture is too small to see them clearly. I'll take them to the photo shop around the corner and see if they can blow them up a bit.

The photo shop employee says the shop can enlarge the pictures, but I will lose some definition. She sends me to a computer photo shop across town. This store has the ability to enhance them to be near perfect, but I have to leave them for a couple of days. Darn. I was on a roll. Now I'm stopped in my investigation for a week. I hate waiting. I want them now! Maybe, I'll look at the other pictures very carefully because maybe some of them will need "enhancing", too.

Waiting also means, I won't have the pictures to take to counseling this week. I guess I'll have to wait until next week. I have never been, and I'm not now, a patient person.

Noelle's Thoughts about Dr. Brown

I wen' to a psychiatrist once several years ago when I wus depressed. He fell asleep in the middle of our sessions. I saw him for 'bout six months b'fore I finally realized he wasn't going to stay awake. The med'cine he gave me helped me feel less anxious and depressed, but I got nothin' out of dem sessions. I haven't told Leeza this. I don't know why. I thought I wuz boring, but Leeza duzn't think so. She seems 'ntrested. Wonder why Dr. Brown fell asleep an' Leeza doesn't? I r'member one time he snorted an' woke himself up. Didn't know what to say so I made an excuse and lef'. Maybe I should tell Leeza I take meds. I didn't put them on the sheet she gave me. I didn't put the Dr. Brown 'sperience on it neither. Maybe it's 'mportant for her to know.

I don't git why Leeza doesn't git angry when I don't stay for the whole session. Dr. Brown looked miffed, rolled his eyes, and shook his head. He'd say, "You aren't going to get better unless you stop running away from your problems and face them."

I would say, "I'm protecting you."

He would retort, "Horse shit. You're protecting yourself."

I would leave with my prescriptions...It's all I wanted from him anyway.

Bally
A Picture is Worth a Thousand Memories

Bally calls and leaves a message on my voicemail letting me know she was able to obtain pictures of her family. She seems excited. She couldn't wait to tell me about it until her session today. Interesting that she felt the need to call.

Photos help me to visually conceptualize a client's family. I have sometimes picked up important relationship issues in photos. For example, one family photo showed a family group containing a mother, father, two daughters, and two sons. They were lined up like a firing squad with their arms straight down beside their bodies and they were all smiling a plastic smile. From left to right, there was Mom, daughter, daughter, son, son, father. The son who was standing next to the father was the only person in the family not standing straight. He was leaning away from the father and almost touching his shoulder to his brother's. When I remarked about the son who was leaning, my client told me her brother hated her father, they never got along, and they still hate each other. I asked about the rest of the family and she casually remarked that everyone else walked the "straight and narrow road" set up by the father. She stated that Chad, the leaning son, always had an odd view of the family, especially the father. This led to a discussion about who was in an alliance with whom and how her dad was perceived by the others in the family as well as how Chad functioned or didn't function in the family's atmosphere. She said Chad was the "odd man out" and instantly produced another photo at Christmastime where every one was gathered around the tree in pajamas except Chad who was dressed and sitting in a chair off to the right almost out of the picture.

Looking at the pictures, my client was able to see how the family played out the alienation scenario unconsciously in photos. She remarked, "That's interesting! We never talked about Chad's isolation in the family. I think we all knew it, but we never mentioned it. It sure was evident though, wasn't it?"

Bally is walking down the hall with an envelope under her arm. I suppose those are the photos. She smiles at me! And waves! That's a change.

"Hi, I have some pictures to show you. I'll have a lot more next week and they'll be clearer than these because I'm having them digitally enhanced...." I'm sure she is having the best enhancement possible. She wants to continue talking at top speed, but I stop her.

"Bally, how are you doing? Your face seems to be healing well."

"Yes, I saw a plastic surgeon this week, and he confirmed my stitching was done by a plastic surgeon or a doctor who was very skilled in that area. Well, he gave me some ointment to put on the scars to minimize the scarring. I also feel better. Not as sore as I was. My back still hurts, but it's better."

"Nice to be out of pain?" Bally nods. "Now, what made you find these pictures?"

"Well, after I left here last week, I started thinking about the woman I saw with my father, you know the one whose leg he was rubbing? Well, I thought the place to start was with my mother. Mom was stunned I had called, not because I never call her, but because my sister had called her a few weeks ago and asked for the family pictures also."

"Really, why was that?"

"Well, Mom didn't know, but Mom said she sent most of the pictures to Carly. That's my sister. Anyway, Mom had a few left that were duplicates and offered to send them to me.. I then called Carly and told her that I would like copies of the pictures Mom had sent her. Well, Carly agreed to make copies at Wal-Mart for me, but she also wanted to know why I wanted copies. I told her I was in an accident and wanted to do some counseling and you wanted them. I guess I lied a little. Here's the kicker. Carly told me she had been pulled over for a DWI. My little sis! She never drank. I was the drunk in the family. Well, she's mandated for several months of counseling and her shrink (Um, no insult intended).

"None taken."

"...wanted to see some pictures of the family. How's that for odd coincidences?"

"That's a lot of coincidence."

"Yeah, that's what I thought, too. Well, as far as the woman is concerned, she is my aunt, my mother's sister. Here name is Little."

"Little?"

"Yes, the Filipinos have some weird customs about nicknames. Mom says everyone gets a nickname and it usually means something. For example, Little was only four pounds when she was born so they called her 'Little One' or 'Little' for short. I have a couple of pictures of her, but they are small and somewhat yellowed, but I dropped off pictures at a computer photo shop which will enlarge them and digitally enhance them so they'll be crystal clear. Here's a small one of Little, no pun intended."

Bally's speech is running a mile a minute! Is she excited or nervous?

I take the tiny picture in my hand, put my glasses on to examine it. (Isn't middle age great?) The first thing I notice is that her father has his arm around Little and not his wife. The next thing I notice is that Bally looks more like Little than her mother. Genes are funny, but it's worth noting. Third, Little is pregnant, maybe four to five months, and it's hard to tell whether Bally's mother is pregnant or not. The dress is a loose fitting one. Bally made no comment about how much she resembles her aunt or the fact that she's pregnant or the fact that her father is hugging Little and not her mother. Should I say something? I better not. Ask a question.

"Bally, I know this is a very small picture and perhaps it would be better to wait and see the enlarged version. But, do you see anything that stands out in your mind?"

"Yea. I noticed that Little is pregnant. That means that I have a cousin somewhere who is close in age. See the date on the back? That's when the picture was developed. I was born several months later. My mom is pregnant with me in this picture."

"Anything else?"

"I notice Dad has his arm around her and not my mom. That makes me uncomfortable, especially because of the flash I had."

"Anything else?"

"No, I'll be able to see more when the enlarged ones are done. I'll have those next week."

"That's a good idea."

The conversation then turns to Bally's family and how she's surprised they aren't close. She has memories of playing with them when they were younger, but now she doesn't even know where her brother and nephew live. She states she's interested in connecting with them. I hope she can be patient and obtain a lot more information before she proceeds. There could be traps she's unaware of.

After discussing the pictures, her family, and Bally's temptations to drink coupled with her ability to resist drinking; we made an appointment for next week.

Caz Improves
Now That's Eerie

This week I didn't sleep very well. Usually, I can't sleep because I'm depressed, but this week, I seem to be thinking a lot and feeling lots of things I don't understand. Also, I'm dreaming a lot and then when I wake up, I can't get back to sleep because the dreams are so real. Too much was running through my brain, I lost track and got confused, so I started a journal, even though I hate journaling. I was required to keep a journal in college and it was a horrible chore. I just made stuff up hoping no one would ever see it. Dr. Creep asked to see it though.

One funny thing happened this week. One morning around 7 a.m., I had a horrible dream about my mother. I couldn't go back to sleep, so I got up and fixed coffee. Around 7:15, my father and brother smelled coffee and wandered downstairs thinking they were having hallucinations like the train whistle, because Grandpa loved his coffee. When they saw the coffee pot was on, was dripping fresh brew, and no one else was in the kitchen they looked at each other in disbelief. Grandpa was making coffee! They never thought I was up! I came in the kitchen just in time to see their haunted looks and burst out laughing. When they realized I had started the coffee, they looked relieved and embarrassed. I said, "You look like you've seen a ghost! It was just me, unable to sleep past 7:00." My brother said, "Now, **that's** eerie!" I didn't take offense. I laughed too.

I arrive 15 minutes early for my session and the door is locked. I beat her to the office? After a couple of minutes, I see her get off the elevator carrying a bundle of books and magazines. She sees me and looks at her watch, as if thinking she is late. "Well, this is different!" she said. I smile and help her with the books while she unlocks the door.

Because I am on time, I have an entire 50 minutes! She looks at me expectantly, allowing me to take the lead. I open my notebook. "I want to talk about three things: my Grandpa and his death, my mother's saga and my interpretation of her disappearance, and my new brother." Lisa nods indicating I should start. "Grandpa was the best grandfather ever. He played trains with us, took us fishing, never played favorites, and always treated me with respect. I only saw him three or four times a year when I was little, but I looked forward to seeing him. He made me feel safe and valued. I don't know why his treatment of me has not taken the sting out of the other disappointments I have experienced.

"His death was a shock because it was very quick and none of us had time to grieve and prepare. That's the way he wanted it, I'm sure. Grandpa's death taught me I need to live now, because we don't know when we're going to die. Also, I want people to feel about me the way they talked about Grandpa at the wake and the funeral. The eerie whistle sounds like a childish spiritual need, but I think it was real and, I think Grandpa (reading from my notes, now) 'reached across the great film that separates us from heaven, nirvana, or whatever and got our attention. He was able to comfort us, make us laugh; and let us know he was with us. Perhaps he was telling us that Mom was with him, too. A train whistle can do two things. It can alert you of danger, and it can simply signal you're coming through. I think Grandpa was playfully alerting us that we are all at a crossroads, and we need to think before we make the next step.'" I look up from reading my journal.

Lisa is sitting quietly. I wonder if she is proud of me. I worked hard this week on this stuff. There is a little smile of joy on her face and for the first time I noticed how blue her eyes are. I think I never made sustained eye contact before. Her eyes draw you in and make you feel safe almost as if she is hugging you with her eyes. She says, "You really have done a lot of processing this week. Bottom line, you want to make a positive impact on other people the way your grandfather did. Do you know how you will accomplish this?"

"Nope, not yet. But, I'm looking at two things. First, I need to stop always thinking about myself and my problems and start thinking about others. I can start with my father, brother, grandma, and half-brother. But, I can also care and help others, even strangers. The second one is I need to think about a career in which I can make a difference. Getting up at seven and making coffee was a small thing but the three of us felt close and happy. I want more of that. I need your help in changing. It won't be easy. My bad habits are ingrained, and I've been self-involved for a long time."

Lisa nods, "Change is never easy. But, the more pleasant it is, the more reinforcing it is."

We discuss a few small changes I can make and this scares me, but I don't say anything to Lisa about my fear. I'm ready to move on to the next issue. I return to my notebook and read, "My mother, bless her soul, went through hell with the rape, a child, and AIDS, but she made one gigantic error. She didn't trust my father or her parents. She thought they would reject her or not believe her…or in her. If she had trusted my dad and stayed with us while she died, I might not have been as susceptible to Belle's wiles, and Jake would have grown up with us. Everything might have been different. I realize that I do what my mother does. I jump to conclusions and act on them without giving other people a chance."

Lisa looks confused. "Can you give me an example?"

"Sure, if I hadn't jumped to the conclusion I was the one who had driven Mom away, I might not have fallen for Belle's advances. I think we all make errors and assumptions, but we need to check them out. Rom does the same thing. He thought he drove Mom away so he's tried to be Mr. Perfect. Now he suffers from anxiety."

"Caz, before you go any further, I need to tell you that children jump to conclusions easily. They are great observers but very poor at interpreting what they have experienced. Children don't have the context within which to understand what's happening. So, don't beat yourself up. You were a child of SIX. Now today, you are 28 and you have the ability to decide whether to draw conclusions or get more information."

"Ok, I understand. But, I want to stop jumping to the conclusion that everyone hates me or is perturbed by my behavior. I have to trust my family even if I don't understand their actions sometimes. That means I have to tell the truth. Here goes. I have been keeping something from you. You think that I don't want to take my Lunesta and go to bed early because I don't want to be reminded of the abuse at night time. That's only part of it. The truth is I don't like daytime. There is very little for me to do except chores and it feels like a mindless, meaningless existence. I would rather just sleep my life away."

Lisa nodded, "I am glad you shared that."

"Finally, my new brother. I want to get to know him, but I'm having those thoughts in my head about 'Will he like me if he gets to know me?' or 'Is he a jerk and I haven't found out yet.' I think this has to do with taking risks and I don't do risks well. I need help in risking something and succeeding and risking something and failing and then being able to pick myself up and dust myself off and try again. What do you think?" Lisa and I discuss several incidents in my life where I let a failure define me and where I failed to celebrate my successes. Can I do this? Can I ever change?

Caz
Grandfather's Presence

Caz is processing his grandfather's death and the subsequent discoveries as if he is running a marathon, he's pacing himself, something he has never done before. His thinking is clearer on the new medication. However, the question is, is he strong enough to handle all these discoveries and changes in his life? What if he is correct and his half-brother turns out to be an abuser. Caz attracts abusers and users. He wants them to take care of him. Caz needs to take some risks, but the tasks he has before him, at this moment, are huge. How do I encourage him to try new behaviors, while still being safe? I've not had enough time with him to do the skill building necessary to prepare him for the upcoming events...

The hairs on the back of my neck are standing up and I have goose bumps. I wonder what my body is telling me. Gosh I wish I had more time to prepare him and to help move slowly and cautiously toward his new goals. The trial is looming and it could send him into a tailspin.

I summarize what I've heard. "Caz, you're exploring many important issues, and I wonder whether you feel prepared to sort them out. Your grandfather's death is an incredible stressor. He was very supportive of you and loved you. Then there's the issue of finding out your mother was raped, had a baby, and died of AIDS. Finally, you've just met your half-brother. You don't know him and you're right to be wary."

Caz isn't listening to me. He's looking to my right and appears frightened like he's seeing a ghost, yet intrigued at the same time. I speak softly so as not to startle him. "Caz?" No response. "Caz?" He blinks a bit, but continues to stare past me at the wall. "Caz, are you ok?" He continues to be quiet, but then he holds one finger in the air as if he's telling me to wait a minute. I sense something unusual is happening, but I don't have a clue. I continue to feel tingling, like a light current of electricity is running through me. I wonder if Caz is feeling something like this. What's going on!? Something is happening, and I am not in control. I DON'T LIKE IT! Wait a minute. Take a deep breath, I say to myself. What are you feeling? I don't feel scared. I'm just not in control of the situation, and I can't gently get Caz' attention. Ok, Lisa, slow down and wait.

Caz is quiet, not moving a muscle, and still looking past me. I shut up. My therapy mantra is "When in doubt, shut up". I give him the space he needs. Five minutes pass. Now I'm really getting uncomfortable. Is he having a psychotic episode? Is he sick? I don't think so. He looks calm, serene. He knows I'm here because he held up his finger telling me, 'Just a minute.' He actually looks peaceful and content. His face has a softness that causes him to look almost childlike. He is looking at his hands and turning them over. I wait. More minutes pass. Then he very slowly turns his body in my direction as if he were going to break a spell if he moves too fast. "He's here." he whispers.

"Oh my, gosh", I say to myself, he **is** having a psychotic break! Caz' mouth begins a slow curve upward that resembles a smile... or indigestion... or pain, I can't tell. He lifts his head millimeter by millimeter and makes eye contact. He's smiling, but also has a hint of questioning on his face. "I think my grandfather is here, or was." Caz speaks in a hushed tone, as though his voice is going to disturb the dead. Holy crap! What do I do with this? I was concerned that Caz may not be handling the additional recent stressors placed on him as a result of his grandfather's death. I may be correct in suspecting hallucination. . . or is it something else? I felt the hairs on my neck stand up and salute, too. I sensed some kind of holy ground being established. What if his grandfather was in the room? Ok, right now, it doesn't matter what I experienced, I need to focus on Caz.

"Caz, can you tell me what you experienced?" Good question! Brilliant! Nice dodge.

"I dunno exactly how to ... the hairs on the back of my neck and arms stood up, and then, I got goose bumps. Then I felt like there was a, a, presence in the room. Weird." Caz looks down at his hands, turning them over and then back again several times.

A lot of questions are running circles in my head, and I sense Caz' struggling to find words for his experiences, too. I remain quiet, though I'm aware of my heart pounding and I wonder if Caz can hear it too. After a few minutes, Caz takes a deep, long breath. "I've felt something like this before when I prayed. At those times, I felt loved, cared about, compassion, and I never wanted it to stop. Same thing happened here only I know it was not a prayer experience because you and I were talking. I **knew** my grandfather was standing behind you, then came closer to me, and stood beside me. I kept getting an impression that my hands are important. I don't know what that means. I didn't dare breathe for fear he'd leave. Didn't you feel it?" Caz' eyes are now wide with wonder and awe.

Oh, great, now what do I say? 'No" would be a lie. 'Yes' feels like I am entering into a collusion of a delusion. But, the fact is, I felt the same physical symptoms Caz did, and at the same time. "Caz, I could see you were deeply moved by the experience. Can you put words to it?" Whew, dodged another one, I think.

What's wrong with my profession that I can't reveal what I'm really experiencing?

Caz is still looking soft and awe struck. "I know my grandfather was here. I felt his love. I sensed he wanted me to heal, and grow, but I didn't hear a voice or anything like that. Just an impression that it's time for me to move forward. I kept thinking that I wish my mom was with him and then I felt a gentle breeze pass by. That's all. It was very short, a few seconds. Silence.

"Caz, are you aware of the time?"

Caz turns to see the clock and recognizes that 15 minutes has elapsed. He stares incredulously at the clock. "It felt like 30 seconds. I see that our session is over. I will see you next week." He got up abruptly and was gone. I had no chance to say anything in response.

What the hell just happened? Are we sharing tactile hallucinations? Was his grandfather here? I believe in God and attend church, but I get a little antsy when others feel spirits, hear God's voice, etc. Perhaps I'm skeptical and suspicious because that's never happened to me. I wanted it to, when my daughter died, but nothing occurred that gave me a sense of peace. I felt left alone with my grief and even wondered whether God loved me any more. If Caz' grandfather "showed up," why didn't my daughter come to comfort me? Perhaps she did and I wasn't sensitive enough to pick up the vibes. I did today, though. Why would I feel Caz' grandfather and not my own daughter? I admit that if Caz' grandfather did "visit" him, I am a little envious and grateful. Envious because he had an experience I didn't have with my daughter and grateful because I sense Caz may have received a gift.

I have several colleagues with whom I consult when I reach a dilemma like this. We share our vulnerabilities and concerns about our work over lunch, but I don't know whether I can share this one. They may think I'm walking off the high dive into the proverbial deep end. I don't care. I need someone's input. But, which of my friends can I trust not to jump to judgment and commit me to a mental ward? Larry! I pick up the phone while the atmosphere is still charged and call Larry, and of course, I have to leave a message. I jot down Caz' case notes. I don't want to forget what happened and the impact of how I felt in the session. I also prepare for the next client. I have to pull myself together to see four more clients. I utter a prayer that they're all going to be talking about their run-of-the-mill neuroses. My prayer was answered.

Heebie-Jeebies or Something Else?

How can I be tired when all I did was sit all day? Six messages are on my voice mail: my mother, two calls from a friend wanting to make a referral, two hang ups, and LARRY! I call him immediately. Larry is his happy-go-lucky upbeat self. After the usual pleasantries, I explain what happened in my session today. Larry listens quietly for the 10 minutes it takes me to tell the story. Then comes THE QUESTION. "Larry, am I going crazy?"

"Lisa, have you never felt something like this before?"

"God, no Larry!"

"I think you have. You're very intuitive and have gut reactions and feelings all the time."

"Well, that's true. But, Larry, this was so weird. I felt the hairs on my neck and arms stand up. I felt the electricity in the room. At first, Caz said nothing, but then he said the hairs on his neck and arms stood up and he felt an electric charge. We experienced the exact same physical feelings at the same time."

"Listen to me; you've just had a very important experience. Don't try to pathologize it. You need to embrace it as a spiritual moment. That moment may do more for your client than 20 sessions."

"Have you ever experienced something like this, Larry?"

He's quiet a little too long and I know I made the correct decision in calling him.

Larry sighs, "Ok, if I tell you, do you promise not to tell anyone else? I don't want to be seen as a nutcase."

"Nice clinical word, Larry." He laughs. "Okay, I promise."

"I had a client who lost her son to suicide. She collapsed at his funeral and ended up in our local mental hospital, where I was working. She was diagnosed with Brief Reactive Psychosis in those days. She was non-communicative and my job at the hospital was to be her therapist. I tried everything to get her to communicate with me, but she just sat everyday in a semi-catatonic state. She dressed, bathed, ate, and walked about, but she did nothing else. One day we were sitting in my office saying nothing for 45 minutes. It was a freezing cold day and the hospital was having difficulty keeping the heat going. We were all wearing coats and scarves, and gloves in the hospital to keep warm. As I sat there, she said, 'He's here.' I swear to God those were the first words she said since coming to the hospital. I began to get warm and figured the heat had been fixed. So I started taking off my gloves, scarf, hat, and coat. She also was taking off her outer garments. As the room warmed up, so did she. She began to talk, telling me that her son is ok. 'He's not in hell. He's in a good place and learning about mental illness.' She said he feels love and wants me to stop blaming myself.

"Lisa, you know I believe in a supreme being and an after life and all that, but I don't think about it very often. I'm not very religious, I'm Jewish, but it is more a cultural thing with me. I believe Jesus was the Messiah and we Jews missed the boat. I do yoga and meditate. I don't fit anywhere. I figure, life is what it is, and I can only interact on this plane.

"Ok, here's the strange part. After she stopped talking, I heard a man's voice say the word 'bugs' just as clear as day, but there was no one in the room with us.

My client looks up and says 'My son just said that I have to take care of bugs.' "I thought she was talking about getting an pest exterminator. So being the excellent therapist I am, I repeated the word with a question mark. 'Bugs?' She said, 'Yes, Bugs is our special nickname for my West Highland Terrier. We call her Bugs because she has big ears and looks like Bugs Bunny." We both laughed and then she said, 'Thank you for believing me.' And she got up to leave. I guess she knew the session was over. I felt like I was in a fog. I was not able to sort through what had happened. She picked up her coat, etc. and we walked out of my office into the same cold that had been there when we walked into my office. It was freezing in the entire building. She didn't seem to notice or care. She just walked away with her coat over her arm, saying she'd see me tomorrow. I turned around and walked back into my office and it was **freezing** in there, again."

Larry's clinical tale stunned me. How many times have these events happened to me and I've just blown off the event as "weird". An emerging sense of gratitude warms my core. I have been privileged to experience this wonderful event with Caz. I'm not crazy and neither is Caz. We were gifted with a presence that was trying to help him. Perhaps this therapeutic process doesn't always have to be solely my responsibility or my client's.

"Thanks, Larry. You are the best! I'm beginning to think I don't rely on the spiritual realm enough. I pray to God, but I often forget there are beings who hang around trying to help us. Perhaps I'm too egotistical to recognize their power and their ability to help me."

"Hey, maybe you need to go spend some time with Native Americans. Sleep well, Lisa." Larry hangs up and I am still holding my phone. I promise myself I'm going to read up on spiritual events or interventions. There is a book about everything, and I hope there's one about this. I pause. Maybe Larry is right. What I need to learn may not come in a book.

I'm dieting again. I want to look like Bally from the neck down, so I have rabbit food for dinner. As I munch on the tasteless salad hoping I'll lose some weight by tomorrow, I realize working with Caz may teach me as much as I'll teach him.

I call Mom. She's 80 years old and lives alone. My father died several years ago, and my sister and I tried to talk Mom into selling the house and moving in with one of us. She's as stubborn as I am. She refused, adamantly. We broached the subject of a retirement community. Nope, no way! She lives a plane ride away from both of us, and we worry that if anything happens, we will be the last to know. Her retort every time one of us brings up our mutual concern is that she has all our phone numbers on her fridge and someone will call. Sigh. Mom simply was checking in…her health, her bridge games, the latest funeral she attended, did I see *Heroes* this week etc. Then she says, "Did I ever tell you that I wake up in the middle of the night with someone playing with my toes?" "WWWhhhaattt?" was all I could get out. "Yea, I think it's your father, but it could be my brother. I'm not scared or anything. I just don't know what to make of it…. Hello?… honey are you still there?"

"Yes Mom, I'm still here. Umm, did you tell the doctor?"

"The doctor? Why would I do that?"

"Well, it may be something medical…like toe fungus."

"Mary Elizabeth, it's not toe fungus, Marty has that and she tells me the symptoms all the time at bridge. I can recite them by heart. I don't have toe fungus. Someone is playing with my toes, and it wakes me up. Have you ever heard of a dead person trying to get someone's attention that way."

"Uh, no Mom, I can't say that I've heard that one."

"I was just wondering because you hear lots of strange stories all day. Anyway, Marty's here to pick me up for Poker night. I gotta run, or at my age I better walk! Love you honey." She hung up as I was saying "Love you too, Mom."

The timing of the phone call with my mom gives me the heebie-jeebies. Someone or something is trying to get my attention.

Bally's Pictures
A Hint About Her Identity?

I have the pictures but I'm afraid to look at them. Carly said she got information just from looking at them. That sounded ominous. What did she see? I'm a little uneasy about doing this alone. Should I take them to Lisa or should I look? I can't stand waiting…The shop did a great job! The pictures are crystal clear. I sift through them, one by one, looking for telltale signs of what my family was like. The very small picture Lisa and I looked at last week, was now a five by seven. I can clearly see Little and Dad and Mom. Mom and Dad are not touching at all. Sad. Was Dad having an affair with Little? How can I find out? I can't ask Mom. Too invasive. She might have been so naïve that she was clueless. My question could really hurt her. My eyes catch Little's face. My stomach is in knots. Now I know why she looks familiar. **She looks like me!** Could this be a simple genetics thing? Or…or….is Little my mother? Oh my God! Is this what Carly was hinting about? Is that why Dad favored me? Carly and Atlee always said that I was his favorite. Is that why? I look intently at the picture to see if Mom is pregnant, but I don't think she is. If she was, she would have been about five months along herself. She doesn't even have a little bump. She's so tiny that if she were five months, she would show. Wait! What if the picture was taken two months before it was developed? That would explain the date on the back and why she wasn't showing. That must be it. I need to talk to someone, and I don't see Lisa for a couple of days. I call Carly. She answers. Thank God.

"Hi Carly, it's Bally. How are you?"

"I'm fine Bally, and you?"

"I'm good…no I'm not. I lied. I'm looking at these pictures and I'm confused and, I gotta tell you, a little scared."

"Can you see the resemblance?"

"Yea, and the only thing I can figure out is that maybe, just maybe, they took the picture two months before they developed it."

"Which picture are you looking at, Bally?"

"The one with Little, Dad, and Mom."

"Did you see the one with the whole clan?"

"Yes. Why?"

"Go back and look at it."

I pull that picture out and put it side by side with the other one. "Holy crap! Carly, what was going on in our family?"

"From what I can see. Little is your mother, Sassy is mine, and Mom is Atlee's. Now there may be some genetics and timetables at play here, like you suggested, but my guess is Dad had three wives or one wife and two consorts.

"I look more like Sassy than Mom. When we were kids, I didn't see it, but now that we are adults, I look like the way Sassy looked as a young adult. You're a dead ringer for Little except you're a little taller and have Dad's lighter eyes. Atlee has always looked more like Mom. And Dad treated Mom and Atlee horribly. He seemed to treat us more lovingly. I always thought it was because Dad liked girls more than boys. But, now I'm not so sure. Mom's always been dependent, meek, and weak. Was she a patsy for Dad while he was free to look elsewhere?"

I'm shaking as Carly explains her hypotheses. Something inside of me says she's right, but I have little data except the pictures.

I need to shift to my business woman façade to take care of the anxiety. Jump in with a solution. "How can we find out?"

Carly pauses to think. I'm pondering, too. Carly speaks first. "Bally, do you think we should contact Dad? I know we haven't seen him in years, and none of us are close to him, but he'd have all the information we're seeking."

"I don't know Carly. Thinking about seeing Dad again after so many years feels like ...um... I don't know what it feels like. Do **you** want to see him again?"

"Not really. When he left Mom, I was furious. She'd taken care of him after he went blind, and he just walked out to be with someone else."

"Yeah, I know. But, what really pissed me off was when Mom came into some money, and he tried to get back with her."

"Yeah, me too. But, Bally, this seems important, and I need answers and closure. I don't know if you and Atlee do... I always felt sorry for Dad, because of his sight loss, but at the same time I hated him because he played us against each other and treated Mom like his slave. If he also had us by three different sisters then he is one sick pup."

"I don't know if I want to know. But, if he did have the three of us by different women, then that explains a lot about the dynamics in the family. Maybe on some level we've known this all our lives."

"What do you mean, Bally?"

"I've always been so fricking angry and irritable, and I use people the way he does. Jees I've never admitted that before. Maybe this counseling stuff is working. I'm sorry if I was obnoxious with you. I do kinda love ya, ya know."

Carly is sent into peels of laughter. She acknowledges she felt anger at me, especially when we were teenagers. She believed I was Dad's favorite, spoiled, and got away with murder because of my looks. Makes sense. I, too, felt I was treated special by Dad. I thought it was because of the way I looked, but maybe it was something else.

"Well, you know what, Carly? Let me think about this. I'm kinda freaked out by the possibility. I'll get back to you. We've waited this long. We can think about it for a while longer. Why don't we try to find Atlee, too."

"You mean if he **wants t**o be found."

"True. I bet Mom keeps up with him."

"Probably. I'll call Mom and see if she has his most recent phone numbers. And Bally, thanks for being a partner in this family excavation. I have felt alone with my suspicions and feelings."

"Believe it or not, Carly, I thought I was the most f'ed up of the three of us. I thought you had the perfect life with your husband and kids."

"I do have a good life,... but, I'm not happy, and it has nothing to do with my family. It has to do with how I feel about myself... as a person."

"Wow, YOU? I'm surprised you feel like I do. I thought you were happy and settled and content. I never thought of you as having problems or drinking. I thought that was my bag."

"But, Bally, you're very accomplished in your field. I thought you couldn't make a marriage work because you didn't put up with other people's garbage and so you divorced them rather than work on the marriages."

"Actually, Carly, **they** all divorced **me**. I just told everyone I divorced them. I'm a raving bitch who is also a drunk. I can be the most charming and entertaining woman on the planet when I want a man to notice me or fall in love with me, but I don't know how to stay in a loving relationship. I guess I'm more like Dad than I'd like to admit."

"Did you tell your shrink all this?"

"Hell, no! I have to make her work for her money!"

Carly is silent. I just crossed a line and revealed my sarcastic bitch self. Do I care? Not really but at least I can pretend to care what she thinks of me. "I'm sorry. I didn't mean to be snotty. I get flip when I get scared." That's it use a 'poor me' feeling to obtain sympathy. "I like Lisa, but she's not in the same social class as me. She's kinda frumpy." Crap! I still sound snooty and judgmental. I can't get anything right. Change the subject, take her mind off it. "Maybe this excursion into the past will help all of us."

"Right. Let's hope." Carly sounds irritated, and she's dismissing me.

"I'll call you after I think about whether I want to contact Dad, and you call me if Mom has a way of contacting Atlee. Ok?"

"Ok. Bye."

"Bye."

Bally Charges Ahead
Lisa Reserves Judgment

"Hi Lisa, how are you?"

"I'm fine."

"Well, I've had a hell of a week."

"What's happening, Bally?"

"Well, I want to show you the photos I had digitally enhanced." I pull them out of the bag and lay them on the side table next to Lisa. "The two pictures I want to focus on are these." I pull two pictures out, the one of pregnant Little, Dad, and Mom and the one of the entire family. I sit back to observe her as she looks closely at the pictures. She's taking her time. Isn't she smart enough to get it? Can't wait for her response. She's taking too long. "Do you see the resemblance?"

"Between...?"

"Between me and Little?" Exasperation!

"Sure. What do you make of that?"

"I think she's my mother. Based on the date on the back of the original photo, my mother would have been five months pregnant with me at the time of the picture. My mother is clearly not five months pregnant and Little is. Also, I look just like her."

"I can see what you're talking about and how you arrived at your conclusions, but there are other explanations."

"I know, I know. The date stamp on the back may be off because they didn't get the pictures developed right away and mom's three months pregnant. Duh! But, there's more and this you'll have to take my word for."

"Ok."

"Well, see this other picture of the entire family?"

"Yep."

"The woman in the middle is my other aunt, Sassy. She's a dead ringer for my sister. I didn't look at her because I was trying to figure out my own lineage, I always look at myself first, kinda narcissistic, huh?" (I don't wait for an answer. I don't want to hear what she really thinks.) "But, my sister told me to look at Sassy." I point out Sassy. "Here's a picture of my sister Carly." I hand her the picture. "Now, you'll have to believe me about the next piece of information. My brother Atlee looks like my mother." I sit back and see if Lisa draws the same conclusion, but she'll just dump it back on me anyway.

"So what are you saying?"

SEE! I knew she'd dump it back on me. "It's not just what **I'm** saying, it's what my sister thinks, too. Dad was married to my mother and had affairs with her two sisters and therefore the three of us have the same biological father and different biological mothers, but the mothers are all sisters."

"That's an awful lot of information to take in."

"It is and I've had a couple of days to think about it, so I have a head start on you. If this is true then it explains a lot. It explains why my brother was treated badly by my father. In all the pictures, Dad is never standing next to my mother. He seems to be relating to my aunts, especially Little."

"That's true. Based on these two pictures, he seems to be standing close to your aunts."

"It also makes my flash of memory make sense where Dad is stroking Little's thigh."

"That's true too. What was the relationship like between your parents?"

"Non-existent."

"According to what you just told me they have a child, wasn't there some marital connection."

"I'm not sure. I never saw them kiss or hug. From the time I can remember (age 12), they slept in separate bedrooms. Mom always said it was because Dad snored, but I never heard him snore."

"How does Carly feel about this possible discovery?"

"She was eager to know if I saw what she saw. We talked about how to proceed from here. That's what I want to talk to you about."

"Ok."

"Well, first a few things we haven't discussed yet."

"Ok."

"My father clearly favored me. I'm not bragging or anything. In fact I thought it was pretty shitty to favor one child. I never felt good about it, but I sure enjoyed the attention. I didn't know why I deserved his favor over the other two children. I never **did** anything to deserve it, except for how I looked. I look like my aunt. And yet Dad kept telling me how special I was, but then he was always critical of me, too. Always picking on everything I did to make me conscious of appearing perfect to the outside world. You know how dads usually don't like to see their daughters dress seductively? Well, my father encouraged me to dress sexy. He liked it when others looked at me. Mom was never allowed to criticize me or correct my behavior. I felt special from Dad and neglected by her all at the same time."

"You felt like you were favored and not good enough all at the same time with your father. Did you feel your mother loved you?"

"She was sweet and kind, but she let me get away with stuff because of Dad. She hardly interacted with me because...well, I think she was afraid if she did she might say something to me that would infuriate Dad. This led me to believe I was Miss Perfect, and yet, I knew I wasn't. My entire persona was a phony façade.

"I always thought Mom was passive, a push-over, but if I wasn't her biological daughter then she may have been told by Dad that she didn't have the right to parent me. And I know she was afraid of Dad. I remember when I was a teenager. Mom never told me what I should wear, how I should act, when I should study...I thought I was lucky because my friends' parents were all over them. My brother was being parented by Mom, but I wasn't. I was relieved, but I also thought she didn't care about me. Now I wonder if Mom was told to lay off and she did what she was told.

"Carly wasn't parented by Mom either. But, Carly was the goody-two-shoes anyway. There was no need for my mother to worry about her. Come to think of it, when I snuck in at three in the morning, my mother was never waiting up for me. I remember she was upset with Atlee for coming home passed his curfew, but I blew my curfew to bits as soon as I was 14 and never heard a word."

"Not even from you father? I thought he would have had you on a shorter leash."

"Well, you see, Dad wasn't home much because he traveled a lot. I was more careful when he was home."

"What did your father do for a living and where did he travel to?"

"I think he was a salesman, and he was gone Monday through Friday most weeks out of the year. He also had weekend events to attend. I don't know where he traveled, but I got the impression it was most of the Eastern seaboard."

"Where did your aunts live?"

"A very interesting question! I always assumed they lived far away like the Philippines, but they were born and raised here. I must've thought they lived far away because I didn't see them. I only have that one flash of memory. I have no idea where they lived or where they are now.

"That's amazing."

"Why?"

"Because if your premise is accurate and Little's your mother, then it might have been very difficult for her to turn you over to your mother to raise. Can you obtain some of this information from your mother?"

"That's the hitch. It's what I want to talk to you about. Mom seems frail, and, I don't know how to say this, um, she seems like she isn't with-it. She loves for me to call, but then we really don't have a conversation, not a real mother-daughter conversation. She keeps everything superficial, and then she asks me to call again. She may not have enforced rules or punished me, but she did feed me, hug me, wash my clothes, etc. She acted like a mother even if she wasn't my mother. If I delve into all this with her, I'm afraid I'm going to hurt her and hurt her bad. She doesn't deserve that. Also, I don't know how much she knows."

"If she didn't give birth to you, I'm sure she would know that. Are you saying she may think your father adopted you and Carly?"

"I never thought about that! She…just…might! This is such a load of crap."

"What about your father? Is he still alive?"

"Yes, he left my mother years ago, turned his back and walked out. I think he arranged for her to be taken care of financially but only minimally. She lived in a small one bedroom apartment in a not-so-great part of town. She worked in a bakery and worked 50 hours a week for minimum wage just to make ends meet. Then her parents died, and she came into some money. She was able to buy a condo and furnish it. Now she lives on social security and the little money she put away. She's financially fine now."

"Bally, how do you feel about your mother, at least the woman who raised you? Do you love her? Do you feel sorry for her?"

"I don't know. I mean…I love her. She's really a sweet little lady, and she made sure I had everything I needed to begin life. If she failed at all, she failed to set appropriate boundaries with me and failed to restrict my activities that were very self-destructive. I hate to say it, but I don't know how smart she is. It's very possible my father manipulated and coerced her into doing what he wanted."

"I can see your dilemma. Back to your father. Where does he live and is he still working?"

"No, he went blind 20 plus years ago and lives on disability. He has some investments, at least that's what he said years ago when he left my mother. I don't know if it's true."

"You never told me about your father's blindness. He went blind when you were around 20 and then left your mother?"

"He went blind when I was about 16 or 17, then when I was around 21, he left my mother for another woman. I never knew who she was and never met her. Then when Mom inherited money, he tried to worm his way back into her life. He was still living with the other woman, I don't know whether he married her or not, but when he tried to cuddle up to Mom again. Atlee, Carly, and I supported Mom and tried to keep her from taking him back. That set up a really difficult time for Carly, Atlee, and me. Dad was furious that we told her she was crazy for even thinking about taking him back. One day, Mom said to Dad, 'No thank you.' Can you imagine that? He was pressuring her to move back in and she was not saying 'yes' or 'no'. Then the three of us rallied around her and tell her, in no uncertain terms, she should never take him back because she could never trust him again. I remember, Atlee saying, "Mom if you let him back for a few years and he decides to leave again, He will get ½ of what you have."

Mom never reacts to things, she just listens. We thought she was not hearing us, and we hounded her for a week while she was trying to decide whether Dad could come back. Then one day she demurely says 'No thank you." And Dad stormed out and none of us have ever seen him since that day. Mom still talks to him every now and then. But, Carly and I don't know where he is. One time, Mom told us that he moved far away and is living on social security in a small apartment. That's all I know."

"If you can find him, are you and Carly considering contacting him and confronting him?"

"Yes, and we only have a vague sense of where he might be living so we would have to involve Mom. And of course we need to find Atlee, too."

"You don't know where your brother is either?"

"Not really. Carly seems to think Mom knows. Carly's calling her to ask Mom to get his phone numbers."

"So you are starting with finding Atlee?"

"Yes. When Carly and I talked about whether to find Dad, we realized we should be a united front and so we want to involve Atlee, too, if he wants to be involved." Long pause. I'm exhausted with all this. "Lisa, am I doing the right thing? I mean, all this started because I wanted to know more about my family and to retrieve some memories. I feel like I'm sitting on a run-away horse. It's getting out of control. Part of me doesn't want to delve into this shit, and part of me knows I gotta find out."

"That's quite a dilemma. How will you decide?"

"Well, I'm hoping Carly will find out more about where Atlee is. If she does then we'll give him the information we have. If he agrees with us then I'm hoping we can all go to Dad with our information and see if he confirms what we suspect."

"And if he confirms what you suspect. Then what?"

"I think I'll be in therapy a long time!" I laugh. Lisa smiles. "I have a lot to think about, but I have to wait until Carly does her part and then I guess we'll take this one step at a time. Same time next week?"

"Sure. See you then."

Jumping to Conclusions?

Bally might be jumping to conclusions before she has all the information. That's her typical style, but she's also highly intuitive and is usually correct. If her aunt turns out to be her mother, then her entire sense of self is in jeopardy. Her very identity would be shifted from what she has known all her life to a total unknown, a reformation. Her rage will probably be turned on her father and possibly her aunt/mother. If she finds out her mother was part of the conspiracy, she would have no parental figure in her life she could trust. Carly and Atlee would be grieving and going through similar self-reflections…Who am I? Why did this happen? Who is to blame? So she may feel very alone in her grief.

Bally's openness to therapy is refreshing but I'm cautious. She **seemed** genuinely interested in talking with me, but Bally is a chameleon who changes her reactions as quickly as she changes her underwear.

Atlee and the Evidence

I don't think I have talked to my family more than five or six times in the last five years. This month I've talked to my mother and sister 10 times. Mom is playing coy and every time I broach the subject of the pictures and contacting Atlee, she politely tells me to call again soon and hangs up. Is she getting the idea we're on to the charade that our family's been perpetuating for years? Carly is now convinced that what she originally unearthed a few weeks ago is correct. She was able to get Atlee's phone number and called him in Seattle. Atlee and Carly have been playing telephone tag. Carly thinks we should jump on a plane and go see Atlee together. I'm usually the impulsive one, but Carly's running fast with the ball. I'm letting her. It feels good to have someone else (who is competent) take up the reigns. I've always felt a great sense of responsibility and

I'm tired of leading the charges while others stand back and watch, and then criticize. Also, my co-workers drop the ball all the time, knowing I'll tidy up their errors and make things happen. I've come to believe this is my role in life. I'm finding out quickly that being a follower is ok at times, so I've been letting Carly lead. She's like a wild Amazon woman on a stallion.

I keep staring at the picture of the family. If Carly and I are both wrong we'll feel foolish. At least we'll feel foolish together and because we haven't involved too many people, we'll only feel foolish with a handful of people. Lisa keeps encouraging me to go slow and not jump to conclusions, but I can't make sense of this any other way. The phone rings. Caller ID says its Carly.

"Hi Carly."

"Hi Bally. I know you have Caller ID, but I gotta tell you, it still feels funny when you answer the phone that way."

"Yeah, it still weirds me out too when someone does that to me."

Long pause.

"I just spoke to Atlee."

"And.."

"Are you sitting down?"

"Yes."

"He's always known he was mom's son and we weren't."

"What!?"

"He says, one time when Dad was drunk and angry at him, Dad spilled the beans. Atlee knew then this family was a sham, and it was psychologically dangerous to stay around. That's why Atlee fled the house as soon as he was old enough and never went back."

"Holy crap."

"That's **exactly** what I said when I got off the phone with him."

"Where does that leave us, Carly?"

"We need to go to Seattle to see Atlee."

"Why?"

"He has evidence."

"What kind?"

"I don't know. All he said was he had the goods on Dad, and he'd love to share it with us if we wanted. He invited us to Seattle. Evidently he just started a new job and he can't take time off."

"Carly, I can't take time off either. I'm on thin ice at work because of my past drinking, running out of sick leave, and then needing time off because of the accident. We need to do this over a weekend."

"Ok. When?"

"Let's go to Atlee's over the holiday weekend. That way we'll have more time."

"Do you want to wait that long?"

"No, but it's a long flight to Seattle. We need the time to travel and be there and figure all this out."

"Ok. I guess I can be patient. I don't know how you can, though."

"Hell, this is churning me up. I haven't slept well. I stay awake thinking of all the possibilities and now you're telling me what we suspected is true! I know I won't sleep now."

"This thing wakes me up in the middle of the night too, Bally. I just want to get some closure and soon."

"Yeah, me too. But, I'm stuck at work. I just can't get another day off. Perhaps, I need to learn patience anyway."

"You've never been a patient person, Bally, but now I'm the one who has no patience. I want to call the airlines and go now!"

"Ok, let's do it this way. You call Atlee and find out what weekends are good for him. I'll work on my boss and see if I can get off a little early on a Friday or ....even better, I just remembered! I think we have a client in Seattle I can see. Call me with the dates, and I will go to work on my boss."

"You got it. Bally. I'll call him now."

"Carly, not now, it is six a.m. in Seattle."

"Ok, I'll give Atlee two hours to sleep and then I'm calling."

Our laughter feels good. It breaks the tension. I may be getting my broken family back together but in the weirdest way possible. Finding out we're only half siblings is bringing us closer. Life's weird.

I call Lisa and leave a message that I found out my suspicions are true and I'm planning a trip to Seattle ASAP. I give her a heads up. I might need to cancel or change my Friday appointment. I wonder what she will say when she gets **that** message. She'll know **I** was right all along and **she** was cautious and wishy-washy.

Bally's Charging Ahead

Bally called this morning and left a message that her mother is not her mother. Evidently only Atlee is her mother's biological child. She and Carly will be heading to Seattle soon to retrieve the "evidence" from Atlee. My gut told me she was right in her conclusions, but I was hoping she'd have a bit more time to process the information. She sounds eager to learn what "evidence" Atlee has. I call her back and leave a message giving her some alternative times for a session this week and next if she has to change her Friday appointment.

Chapter Five
Archeological Excavation and Pay Dirt

In the second stage of recovery, the survivor tells the story of the trauma. She tells it completely, in depth and in detail. This work of reconstruction actually transforms the traumatic memory, so that it can be integrated into the survivor's life story.

(Herman, 1992, p. 173)

Caz' Efforts
Cognitive-Behavioral Techniques

My eyes open at 8:30 a.m. I woke up...on my own! But, I still feel the draw of sleep. If I close my eyes for a few minutes, I will be back asleep. Dad usually calls me to get up at 8:45. Should I sleep the extra 15 minutes or surprise Dad and get up now? My body wants to go back to sleep, but my mind says 'get up'! I close my eyes and drift back to sleep.

Dad's shaking my shoulder and yelling in my ear to get up, it's 9:15. Damn, I wish I hadn't gone back to sleep. I'm never going to be like other people. Crap and bummer!

I'm going to make up for the "back-to-sleep" decision this morning. I'll do something special for Dad and Rom today. I haul my ass out of bed, eat a bowl of Cheerios, and prepare to walk the dog. Cocoa becomes excited when she sees the leash. She spins around and around tripping over her lanky legs. While we're walking, I have time to think and pray and do the exercise Lisa suggested. Cocoa has time to pee and poop. Tackle Lisa's exercise first. Let's see, I am supposed to say "nice things" to myself. Ok, here goes, "I am a child of God's." That's a good start and a true statement, heard it at church since I was three. "OK, next, I'm tall." So what? Is that a good thing? Shit, I don't know what to say to myself. I can find boatloads of stuff I hate. Why can't I find something I like? Pause, Think, Pause, Think. I guess I can be funny sometimes. I'm compassionate to others. When I do a job, I like to do it well. I'm trying to recover by going to counseling. I'm sensitive but sometimes too sensitive. In fact my sensitivity gets me into trouble because I over-identify with others and sometimes make an emotional fool out of myself. STOP! Hell, it's easy to slip into the cesspool! This is harder than I thought. When Lisa suggested it, I thought this was a stupid, juvenile exercise. It's not! I'm so used to being critical of myself I can't stop. Ok, get back to the positive. I'm brave for agreeing to testify against Belle. That's true, lots of others are too afraid.

I'm out of ideas. Stupid exercise. I don't have enough good things to make this work. I'll just have to repeat the same crap over and over. I'm funny. I'm compassionate. I'm becoming mentally healthy. I'm sensitive. I'm funny. I'm brave. I'm compassionate, becoming mentally healthy, sensitive, brave, funny. The walk is 20 minutes long and I repeat my positive traits over and over until I'm bored. Cocoa hangs her head and looks out of the corner of her eye at me as if to say, "I think you've lost your dog biscuits." We arrive home, with her poop in a bag and our tongues hanging out. Cocoa heads for her water bowl and drinks, slurping the water and dropping it and her saliva on the floor. Yuk. Then she flops on the floor and sleeps. That reminds me, I would love to lie down and nap too. NO! I'm going to do something productive. I'm going to cook! My mother kept a recipe book, and I saw Dad look up a recipe several weeks ago. It's got to be here somewhere. I want to make her famous manicotti. I search and find the book, on the top shelf of the cabinet over the oven. It's really old and I carefully open the cover. (Another good trait, I'm careful with things that are not mine. Belle taught me that. I hate that Belle had a positive influence......STOP!!! This cognitive exercise is hard!)

The manicotti recipe is dog-eared. Easy to find. Her handwritten notes and reminders are in the margins. I touch her pen scribbles and my fingers linger there as the emotion builds. I feel a catch in my throat and a sound develops deep in my being and finally makes it to my mouth, "Mommy!" I sob as I collapse in the kitchen chair. Cocoa wakes up, saunters over, and puts her head in my lap. I grab her around her neck, slide to the floor, and sob in her brown fur. Stroking her head brings more emotion to the surface. "Grandpa!" I look down at her and another name escapes my mouth, "Gillian". The tears finally stop and I feel I vomited something that had been buried for a long time. I look down at Cocoa's face. My tears have plastered her left ear to the side of her head. She looks kinda lopsided and a small smile creeps on my face, "Well, Cocoa, I can add another positive trait to my list. I'm a good crier!"

Lisa's Informative Dream

A disturbing dream interrupts my sleep at 3:30. I'm trying to hold on to the dream by lying very still and not lifting my head off the pillow. I grab the pencil and paper I keep beside my bed so I can write down my dreams before I lose them. I learned this technique in a dream workshop I took several years ago. "Don't lift your head up, just write," my teacher said in a thick Italian accent, "or you'll lose the dream".

In the dream, I'm in my garden fertilizing, pruning, watering, and weeding. Every time I do a task, a mad fox with saliva dripping from its mouth destroys what I've done. I'm getting frustrated and angry so I begin to swing a hoe at the fox, but it deftly jumps out of the way of the hoe, snarls and laughs at me. I work harder as if I'm in fast forward mode, and the fox doubles its effort to thwart my progress. I'm determined, but I'm beginning to tire. Then the fox jumps up and rips my heart out and I awaken. My heart is pounding and my head is throbbing. It doesn't take Freud, Jung, or Perls to figure this one out! I'm feeling incompetent with Caz, Bally, and Noelle. Intellectually, I know my other clients are doing well, and also I'm doing what I'm supposed to do to assist them in achieving increased mental health, but it seems every time I help them take a step forward, a major setback occurs. My work feels futile. Sometimes I feel frustrated with each of them for not putting forth the effort that's needed. Sometimes, their progress is thwarted by events in their lives, which seem to conspire against them. Sometimes, I'm angry with myself for missing a clue. To be honest, I am angry at God, too. These three clients have been through hell most of their lives. They didn't cause their young lives to be damaged. They can't help they're not capable of doing the work as fast as I'd like. BUT, can't they catch a break? God can't you let them experience some success? Let they feel some encouragement? Ahh! That's the word! They are **discouraged** people and I'm taking on their discouragement. The word 'discourage' means to lose heart. That's exactly what happened in my dream, I lost my heart.

I can't give up on them. But, I can't stop them from giving up either. If my dream is reflective of my mental and emotional state, I'm losing ground. "Dear God, help me!" I whisper. I'm filled with conflicting emotion. I'm tired, discouraged, frustrated, but determined. I'm not going to give up. My family always refers to me as tenacious (actually they call me stubborn). But, there have been a lot of set backs that have been out of their control. They all definitely need a break. Perhaps if I'm incapable of creating the atmosphere of change with these clients, and they're incapable of changing without help, then God needs to get more involved.

I cannot do this by myself. I need help." My voice cracks, "Please help me help them." Amen! I don't know if the Amen on the end was just a knee-jerk response to my religious upbringing, but it sounded funny attached at the end of such a short prayer. I don't know what else to do or say. Perhaps I should have asked for God's help earlier. As I fall back asleep I muse that I'm focusing on my most difficult clients who are floundering rather than the other 20 who are making progress. So human to see the storms and not the rainbows.

ARRRGGHHH!! I feel hung-over after my disturbed sleep. I don't want to get out of bed, but I do. This is what Caz feels every day of his life. What an awful feeling! But, why do I get up even when I don't want to and he doesn't? Perhaps because I have a purpose? Perhaps because I have hope? Perhaps I don't feel as badly as he does in the morning? A cup of tea helps. What else? I look forward to something during the day. I'm seeing a friend for dinner. What else? I can plan my life so I can go to bed early, and that fools me into thinking the day's shorter. Anything else? I'm reading a great book and look forward to picking the book up sometime today. Hmm maybe Caz needs to explore how getting up in the morning could be a time to look forward to something during the day.

Well, I have one idea anyway. It seems very cognitively and behaviorally-oriented. Caz may not like it, but it's worth a try. I'll see how well he does with the other cognitive skill building exercise I gave him. He didn't seem thrilled with it. Most clients don't like the exercise. Most don't even do the exercise. Usually, when clients begin saying affirmations, they first report "It didn't work." Then I have to encourage them to continue. The ones who continue usually begin to feel better about themselves in a month. Did he do the exercise?

Since I'm exhausted and in a numb mood today, I am going to do one of the chores I don't want to do. Why mess up a **good** day with an unpleasant task? I call the board that licenses psychiatrists. I get a secretary who listens to half my question (I never did get a chance to name the psychiatrist) and then cops an attitude. She basically tells me the Board doesn't want to hear about ancient history. She says that Caz or his father should have filed a complaint years ago. The statute of limitations has expired. I ask her if she's sure I don't need to file a complaint and she responds curtly "Yes, I'm sure."

My first reaction is to feel irritated, but then...hey, perhaps I'm off the hook? I tried to find out what to do and was rudely dismissed. Do I have to make life miserable for myself and continue to carry the banner of justice and fairness? Obviously, I don't need to go further, but perhaps Caz does, or maybe Stewart? I still think someone needs to let the psychiatrist know that because he did not report the abuse, the consequences for his patient and many other boys were horrible. I pick up the phone and call the psychiatrist. It's 8 am and I know I'll have to leave a message. Good, I don't want to do this anyway. To my surprise, Dr. Paul answers the phone. I gulp and introduce myself as Caz' counselor and remind him of the Release of Confidential Information I sent to his office so that we could touch base about Caz. Dr. Paul is silent a moment, then he says. "I should have reported the abuse years ago. I feel terrible about what Caz had to endure because I failed to act. I have to live with this the rest of my life. And now the press is reporting the arrest and trial events. I can't get away from it."

"Neither can Caz." I say softly.

"You're right, I was only thinking of myself."

"I just want you to know I was going to report the incident to your licensing board. However, the woman I spoke to said they didn't want to hear about 'ancient history'. I guess there's a statute of limitations ...I think enough people have suffered because of Belle and I think you are one of those who is suffering."

"Thank you." He whispers. "I think it may come out anyway at the trial."

"Well, I hope you find peace."

"Me too. By the way, I haven't seen Caz in a long time. How is he doing?"

"As well as can be expected."

"Tell him...tell him, I'm sorry."

"Perhaps you should tell him yourself."

"You're right. I'll call him. Maybe it will help him to know how very sorry I am."

"It just might. Nobody has ever apologized to him for all the pain he has suffered. Good-bye."

Amazing. I was angry at Dr. Paul for his failure to report Belle, but I misjudged him. I had him defined in my mind as a haughty, uncaring narcissist, but he was deeply wounded by his error of inaction. I feel sorry for him. If I had made the error, I would have felt the same way, responsible and yet praying no one would find out. Sounds like he's learned from this experience and that's what counts. We cannot change the past, and I doubt he'll ever fail to report again. I learned too. I will be much less hesitant in the future about reporting abuse.

Caz
"This is too difficult."

I tried to be more upbeat this week and I can honestly report to Lisa I worked on saying positive things to myself. I hope she'll be glad to hear I tried. See, I'm being positive, even though it feels phony. While Dad's driving me to counseling, he drops a bomb. "Caz, when are you going to get your driver's license again?"

Hell, I'm not sure I want my driver's license again. I feel safer with Dad driving me, but clearly he's getting tired of being my chauffer. I shrug my shoulders like I did when I was a kid. I feel immature and stupid. Nothing 'good' to say about this conversation.

Lisa is dressed in a pink suit today. When I comment on her outfit, she says she's meeting a friend for dinner tonight. I feel jealous of the friend. I would like to go to dinner with her, which reminds me; I have no friends and the only social stuff I do is with my father and brother. I can't do this positive crap, I always end up seeing the worst in every situation..

I guess that's a good place to start the session today. "I tried to be more positive this week and I think your technique created a couple of changes. But, no matter how many positive things I said to myself, I ended up in the negative crap. For example, I had a blowout crying jag just after I repeated nice things to myself for 20 minutes."

"What was that about?" Lisa asks.

"I had taken the dog for a walk and kept repeating my positive traits. I think the dog thought I was crazy." I laugh. Lisa just smiles. "Then I felt energized a bit and decided to make dinner for Dad and Rom. I opened my mother's cookbook and turned to one of her favorite recipes, manicotti. I saw her handwritten notes in the margin and began to cry. The crying led to grieving her death, the death of my Grandpa, and the death of Gillian, my golden retriever."

"What happened then?"

"I cooked the manicotti and it was good. My father and Rom were pleased."

"So while you had a crying spell, you were still motivated enough to cook a good meal. What did that feel like for you?"

"Proud, I guess, and....glad I did it." I say, with my usual shrug.

"You **guess** you were proud?"

"Yeah I was proud."

"You know, Caz, you use the phrases 'I guess', 'I tried', 'I don't know' a lot. Can you sense the tentative, ambivalent nature of these words?"

"Yeah."

"Words are important. They change the way we feel and think about things. For example, if I saw you tomorrow and you asked me how tonight's dinner went and I said, 'I guess it went ok.' or 'I don't know.' or 'I tried to have fun.' What would you think?"

"I would think you had an ok time, not great."

"Exactly."

"What do you think saying these things would do to my memory of the event?"

"Probably create a memory of being ok but not great."

"Exactly. If the food was great and the company wonderful, but my car was towed and I swoop all of those experiences together and say, 'I guess it was ok' then you would assume what?"

"I would assume everything was mediocre." I offer weakly.

"So, words are important. That's why what you say to yourself is important. Words define us and change our perception and create perceptions."

"You know, the week my grandfather died, we were going to talk about God."

"I remember."

"Are words important to God, and part of all that stuff?"

"Part of all what? You just used a qualifier that diminished your question, Caz"

"What do you mean?"

"If I ask you the question, 'Are words important to God?' how impactful does that feel to you on a scale of one to ten with one being not at all and ten being WOW."

"I'd say an eight."

"Okay. Now listen to your statement. 'Are words important to God and part of all that stuff?' How strong is that statement?"

"I'd say a four."

"Why?"

"Because I trailed off at the end. In English classes they told us not to write like that."

"Yep. Why?"

"It weakens the premise."

"Now ask the question using potency."

"Are words important to God?" I say stronger and louder.

"Say more about that."

"Well, in the book of John, it says, "In the beginning was the Word, and the Word was with God, and the Word was God.' John is referring to Jesus."

"I never thought about that, Caz. But, you're right. John used the Word to define who Jesus was. What do you think about that definition of Jesus?"

Lisa always turns my words and thoughts around so I have to think about them. Well, since we're talking about the importance of words, she doesn't **always** do that but a lot.

"I'm really not sure, but I think if Jesus is the Word then words are very important." I confess.

"Then how can you use this information?" She asks.

See she did it again! Turned it back to me.

"I'll have to think about it. But, right off the top of my head, I would say, if I'm using words to describe myself, then I would be better off using positive words."

Lisa thinks for a moment and then says, "I agree. I wonder if this may even go deeper for you. If we agree that words are powerful and, theologically this makes sense to you, then what you say to and about yourself, your life, and others will define how you feel about you, your life, and others. Is that going too far for you?"

"Not sure. I can see how I use words to beat myself up and when I do, I feel worse. If Jesus is the Word then a word is holy, and I should think before I use them."

Lisa continues, "I see your point. However, to really bring it home, let's talk about what words have injured you."

"Well, when my brother called me a 'freak', the word really hurt. And when they told me I couldn't get into graduate school, it devastated me. They didn't care enough to talk to me as if I counted. They shouldn't have treated anybody like that."

"Who is 'they', Caz?"

"Dr. Crete and Dr. Reese."

"Name them."

"Dr. Crete and Dr. Reese didn't care enough to talk to me with respect."

"Excellent.

"Caz, when you said the words 'They shouldn't have treated anybody like that.' What just happened?"

"I, um, I generalized it and didn't use the more powerful statement. 'They shouldn't have treated ME like that.'"

"Great! I just had a thought you may like. Remember when Jesus was talking to his disciples and he said something about their not feeding him or clothing him? And then the disciples say something like, 'When did we not feed you or clothe you, Lord?' Jesus says…"

I interrupt. I know this! "'When you meet another person who needs food or clothing and you do not feed them or clothe them, then you are not feeding or clothing me.'"

"Good point, Caz!"

"I think he actually says something like 'What you do to the least of these, you do to me.' So if Jesus is the Word and he's telling us that others are 'Words' too, then how we talk to people and treat people, in some way, impacts our relationship with him?"

And remember, you're a person, too. You count. How you speak to and treat others is important, but how you speak to **yourself and about yourself** is equally important." This not just psychological mumbo-jumbo, this is about deeply caring enough about yourself and others to be kind, loving, and gentle each time you talk to other people and to yourself. This fits your Christian faith. Right?"

I am stunned. She's right. I deserve to treat myself and others better. We're all 'words', just like Jesus is. I need to make some changes, no matter how long they take. I lift myself out of the chair and become very business like. "Thank you for sharing your thoughts today. I'm going to put this information to work right now. How's that for being less tentative and yet more positive?" I laugh.

"That's great, Caz. I hope you have a good week."

"Have a great dinner with your friend."

Lisa
Caz' session

Whew! I was not sure where he was going with the reference to John when we were talking about the power of words. But, as he talked I started to realize how often the Bible emphasizes the use of words as important. After Caz left, several ideas flashed in my mind, like how Jesus spoke words while he was healing people, how in Genesis God speaks creation into existence. I have come to appreciate and love using words to help people express themselves. I have seen how using negative words creates and sustains negative behavior. However, Caz' question about the theological connection with words opened my eyes to other possibilities that support using positive statements to overcome the negativity. Cognitive-Behavioral theorists would be proud of Caz today. They believe talking to ourselves in positive ways creates positive change in us. In Caz' case talking positively about himself is important and could produce change, but he also needs to think positively about others and life in general. Maybe this session was an inauguration.

A Surprise Phone Call

After the session, I felt more hopeful. Perhaps there is something I can do to make me feel better about myself, and maybe my life. However, I don't know what to do with all the other stuff that defeats me. One thing I haven't shared with Lisa is what a lazy bum I am. It's easier to keep speaking to myself in the same negative way than to correct myself constantly. And it'll take constant correction to turn this 'negative crap' around. I'm fighting an uphill battle like the Greek mythical character Sisyphus who's condemned to push a huge round bolder up a hill everyday only to have the Greek gods push it back down at the end of the day making him start all over. I hope Lisa is right about how speaking positively to myself will get easier with each day, but it's a hell-of-a tiring rock to move right now.

As I work on gathering a grocery list together, the phone rings.

"Hello."

"Caz, this is Dr. Paul."

My heart almost stopped beating for a moment.

"Hi Dr. Paul."

"Caz, I want you to know how I'm very sorry I am that I didn't believe you about the abuse that was going on with you and Belle Surte, and the other children. I could justify myself and give you a lot of reasons why I didn't take it seriously, but they would be, just that, excuses. There are no excuses. I should have reported to the authorities what you were telling me. At very least I should have told your father. I was wrong and I want you to know you deserved the right to be believed. I can only hope you will be able to work this all out with your therapist. She seems very competent and ethical. She also was very gentle with me, when we talked briefly."

"You spoke to her?"

"Yes, she called me. You signed a release of confidential information and she called me."

"Wow, I don't know what to say. Um, thanks for apologizing. I've been blaming myself for not being more forthcoming with you about, you know, what Belle was doing to me and the other boys. I thought it was my fault, that I couldn't convince you about the abuse."

"No, Caz. It was never your fault. You left me many hints. I should have believed you and followed through. Once again, I am sorry."

"Thanks. It means a lot to me that you called."

"You're welcome. I hope you get better, Caz. I really do."

"I'm working on it. Bye."

"Good-bye."

Wow, what a surprise! I never thought a psychiatrist would apologize to me. I always think I'm the one who screws up. I accept his apology. Now, I need to let myself off the hook, like he did. He said I was clear and gave him the information he needed. I didn't think so. Why do I always think I'm the one who's wrong?

Lisa
Noelle's session

Noelle is late. First time that's happened. She's usually extremely punctual. It's her leaving that's the problem. I hope she's ok. I decide to use the time to make phone calls to the insurance companies who haven't paid me for sessions or who haven't gotten back to me about requests for additional sessions for clients. This part of my job is a nuisance, but it has to be done. I can spend hours on the phone each month just trying to get paid. That's time I could be seeing clients or keeping up with the newest information in the field. I've thought about dropping off of the insurance panels, but then I'd only have the wealthier clients who could afford to pay me out of pocket. It doesn't seem fair to those who need to use their insurance. Quite a quandary. I've been holding for 15 minutes and Noelle walks in. She looks disheveled and tired. There's an unusual look about her. She's always extremely neat and punctual. I hang up. Sigh. I'll call back later.

"I'm sorry, I'm late. I didn't sleep gud last night an' overslept this mornin'. I called in sick an' went back to bed an' almost missed our appointmen'."

"Are you ok? Are you coming down with something?"

"No, I jist kept havin' one bad dream afta 'nother."

"I see. Are you up to talking with me today? If not, we can reschedule."

"Yea. I gotta confession." She's out of breath a little.

"Ok."

"I didn't tell you 'bout 'nother counselor I saw many years ago."

I'm thinking back to her intake form. She checked the 'no' box where it said 'Previous Counseling?' She also checked that she wasn't on medication.

"I saw a shrink many years ago. He gave me meds an' fell asleep during our sessions. I stayed six months an' then one day when I was seeing him, he fell asleep. I usually jist waited and he'd wake up. This time, he snorted an' woke himself up."

I can't help it. I tried not to smile, but she's really funny when she tells stories not associated with death. I smile and put my hand over my mouth, trying not to laugh, but she sees me holding back. Noelle then does something I have never seen before. She laughs. It gives me permission to laugh, too, and I feel a stronger bond has been established. Will she be afraid this bond will kill me and run?

"Dr. Brown wuz a nice man, but he jist couldn't stay awake when I wuz talkin'."

Oh my! I didn't know she saw Dr. Brown. He died a few years back of a heart attack. Do I tell her? Does she know he died? He may have been ill when she saw him, and that's why he couldn't stay awake. Will she think she killed him? I'm going for it.

"Noelle, I knew Dr. Brown. He was a great psychiatrist, but he was very ill, probably around the time you saw him."

"Yea, I knowd he died"

"He died of a heart attack years ago. He was evidently very ill with a heart condition."

"I thought I wuz boring him and that's why he slept through our sessions. Sometimes, I would just tiptoe out and close the door. Leeza, you don't seem bored with me. Why not?"

"Noelle, You are definitely not boring. Dr. Brown was ill." I'm pausing to see if she blames herself for killing him.

She appears to be struggling to say something. Long pause and then, "I didn't kill him."

"Right."

"I didn't care 'bout him that much to kill him."

"I see."

"I'm worried 'bout you though."

"I appreciate that." Long pause. "Did he prescribe medication for you?"

"Yep, I'm still takin' Paxil an' Klonopin."

"What symptoms was Dr. Brown treating you for with those drugs?"

"I wuz depressed, at least that's what ma old boss said. I never smiled. Maybe that's why he thought I wuz depressed. I didn't feel depressed, but I did feel anxious, though. I wuz always lookin' around for who I'd kill next."

"After Dr. Brown died, who gave you the medications?"

"My reg'lar doctor."

"Your internist?"

"Yep."

"Would you give me written permission to speak with him?"

"I guess. I knew you'd be askin' me about dis if I told you. I wanna stop takin' dem meds. Yesterday I din't take my med'cine. Today, neither."

"And do you think that's why you didn't sleep well?" Noelle shrugs. I'm getting the form out of my file cabinet and handing it to her to complete and sign. I sit back down while she fills it out.

"Noelle, I'm not a medical doctor, but I don't think that suddenly stopping medications without talking to your doctor is good for you. Would you continue taking them until you see your doctor and I have a chance to talk with him, too?"

Noelle nods slowly as if considering what I'm asking but is not sure she wants to agree. "I hate takin' 'em." She says. She signs the form.

"I understand, but for now, please don't stop cold turkey. It could be dangerous."

Noelle's eyes are filling with tears. This time there is no dam breaking, she's feeling something. I wait.

"I can't function wiffout 'em. But, I don't wanna take 'em neither. Takin' 'em makes me feel like I'm crazy." She's whining like a five year old.

"I understand. Let's just not do anything until we consult with your doctor. Ok?"

Noelle sighs and nods. I don't know where to go from here. I would like to know why her hair is white. I would like to know more about her relationship with Dr. Brown. But, she seems a little too fragile today, maybe next time.

"I'm too tired to work."

"Ok."

"Can I go now?"

"Sure."

She stops in the middle of rising out of the chair. "My hair fell out when I was 18. Then it grew back white."

I nod. She sighs a deep sigh.

"I'll tell you 'bout it next week. Ok?"

"Ok. Please take your meds for now."

She nods and this time she leaves slowly, not running away like she did before when the heat of the sessions scalded her. She got up like she needed to go back to bed and quietly left.

I pick up the form and call her medical doctor knowing I'll have to leave a message. Damn, I get a telephone tree. "For Dr. so and so press one….etc." I press the three as indicated, and I get another tree. "For medication refills press one, for an appointment press two, for results of a test press three, if you are calling from a medical doctor's office press four, to repeat this menu press five." Why is it that no matter how detailed the trees are, I never seem to fit the categories? I press four, seemed the closest to why I'm calling. I get another tree! "To have Dr. Retter return your call, press one, for…." I press one. I hate this telephone tree nonsense. I finally get a recording where I can leave a message. "I am Sue, Dr. Retter's secretary, I am out of the office or on another call. Please leave a message at the sound of the tone." BEEP. "Dr. Retter, this is Lisa O'Hara calling. I'm a licensed clinical professional counselor, and I'm seeing one of your patients, Noelle Holly Kilpatrick." I stop for a second and consider her last name. "She has shared with me that she's being prescribed medication for depression and anxiety. I would like to speak with you. My number is 410-555-6263. She arrived today for her appointment and had not taken her medication yesterday or today. She was not feeling well. Please call me at the above number or my cell." I leave my cell phone number and hang up.

Damn, why didn't I see it before? Her last name has Kill in it. Does she unconsciously associate her name with the deaths?

I'm sitting and pondering and writing my case notes to document the medication issue when my cell phone vibrates. I answer it "Lisa O'Hara."

"Dr. O'Hara, this is Dr. Retter. My secretary just picked up your call and thought this was important."

"I'm not a doctor, Dr. Retter. I'm ABD. Please call me Lisa. I'm calling about Noelle."

"I'm Fritz. Yes, I'm glad she's seeing you. I've been concerned about her ever since Patrick Brown died. She'd been seeing him, and he dropped dead while seeing her. She seemed to think she'd killed him. She was very distraught, therefore, I continued the medication he had prescribed. I've been telling her for the past few years to get into counseling. I even threatened to discontinue her medication unless she saw someone, but she'd insist the medication was working. She's on a hefty dose of Paxil and Klonopin. I would like to reduce them both slowly once she's better. Also, I'd like to try her on some of the newer medications."

I'm sitting and listening, but my mind is on PATRICK Brown. Noelle KILPATRICK thinks she might have KILLED PATRICK? "I agree with you. She seems zombie-like. Could that be a side effect of the medications?"

"Sure the Klonopin is four times the regular dose. I don't have her chart in front of me, but she can't sleep without it. I've tried several other medications for sleep, but she claims she can't sleep on any of them. I suspect she has nightmares, but she denies having them. Would you please suggest to her that she make an appointment to see me?"

"I just did. She left my office a few minutes ago. Would you call me after you see her, and let me know if you decide to change the medication dosage or the medication itself?"

"I sure will. I'm glad she's finally gotten into counseling. Having your psychiatrist drop dead in the middle of a session must have been traumatic."

"I'm sorry. The way you just said that it sounds like she was in the room when he died."

"She was. His secretary was a good friend of my wife's. I knew he was ill for quite awhile. Noelle was in the room having a session when he died. My understanding is she called the paramedics and his secretary from inside his office, and then opened the door and left without a word."

"She hasn't told me **that** story, yet. She's told me a lot of others though. She's had to deal with a lot of deaths beginning at age four."

"I didn't know that."

"She plays her cards pretty close to her chest. Has she told you she doesn't get close to people because they die and she blames herself?"

"No, she hasn't, but then, I don't get to spend a lot of time with my patients."

"I understand. Please keep in touch."

"I will. You do the same." I said the perfunctory phrase, "Have a good day." And I hang up. WOW! Noelle, how in the world have you coped all these years?

Noelle's Medication

I gave Leeza permission to call my doctor 'bout my meds. I hope I can trust her. Will she tell Dr. Retter I stopped taking 'em? Will he fire me? I hate them meds, but I can't function wiffout 'em. I just wanna feel normal. I'm scared to share too much wiff Leeza. She picks up on things too fast. I'm sure someday she'll ask me 'bout dreams. If I tell her I can't 'member any, will she leave me alone 'bout dreams? I doubt it. I like her, but she scares me. I can't hide from her like I can from others.

Caz' Nightmares

For two days now, I have concentrated on only saying good things to myself and others. It's easier to say nice things to others, than to myself. But, I'm working on it.

However, as my positive self talk has increased, my dreams have become more scary. Actually, I am having horrible nightmares. Maybe they're getting worse because Belle's trial is coming up in a few weeks. Also, I saw another person who was one of 'Belle's boys' in the supermarket. He nodded and I nodded back, but we didn't speak. When I've seen him before, we do our perfunctory nodding, but this time, he looked like hell. He was thinner and his eyes were like zombies' eyes, dead. I can't get him out of my mind. I don't know what's going on. I'm trying to be good to myself, but then these nightmares...what the hell is happening? I need to see Lisa. I thought we were making progress with this cognitive stuff, but all of a sudden, I'm not sleeping well again.

Heads up from Pastor Craig

Pastor Craig calls today. He doesn't have time to talk, but he wants me to know some of the men in his congregation are talking about some additional abuse that took place in Belle's house and it's not being made known to the public. He doesn't know of what it consists, and he does not know whether Caz was a part of this abuse. He was told about it from either Frick or Frack; he couldn't remember who my Frick was and who was my Frack. He wanted to give me a heads up in case Caz has additional difficulty not explainable by the abuse he revealed months ago. Great! (said facetiously) I thought things were going a little better, and now there's a possibility a different form of abuse was going on at Belle's? Remember, God, you were going to make the therapeutic journey a little easier for Caz... Remember?! This could **not** have occurred at a worse time. A holiday weekend is right around the corner and that means fewer days to fit in clients. In addition, Caz and I agreed to begin talking about his testimony. He's meeting with the district attorney right after the holiday and the trial starts a few weeks later. Was Caz involved in more abusive activities than he originally reported? I pray he was not.

Bally'
Family Crisis

My last session with Lisa went as expected. I was talking a bazillion miles an hour explaining about how Carly and I are going to see Atlee in Seattle. Lisa was her uncommitted and cautious self. She explained she was worried about how all this information was going to affect me. Maybe I'm missing something, but I don't see how I could be much worse. I've been divorced five times, I have a f'd up family, I'm a drunk in recovery, and I have scars that may fade over time but still look pretty awful now. What's a little more intrigue going to do? I'm chalking her concern up to her being weak in the face of extreme adversity.

Carly calls with Atlee's weekend availability. I quickly contact the client in Seattle who's thrilled I can come out for a couple of days and do some training. My boss is a little taken back that the Seattle client asked for training, but he's ok with it and asks when I'm leaving. I give him the dates and pray the client doesn't call my boss and tell him it was my idea to go to Seattle. I'm walking on thin ice here. I can usually talk my way out of "mix ups" I create, but I hope I don't have to this time. I've been feeling a little less confident about my skills lately. I think the family revelation has stopped me in my tracks and I'm taking stock of my life. I find I'm valuing honesty where I always valued slickness before. Lisa seemed to imply I was "finding my conscience." That's exactly how I feel. I've lived with lies and deceit since I was in the womb. Therefore, I continue to do so at work, in my relationships, perhaps even with myself. I'm seeing how sick this is, and I don't want to be like my father anymore and maybe even my mother and aunts. In my attempt at being honest, I'm developing the little white angel who sits on my shoulder and whispers in my ear. I used to only have the tuxedo clad angel devilishly telling me how to connive and tweak the truth to get away with stuff. This small deceit about Seattle with my boss is bothering me and it wouldn't have bothered me three months ago. I would've been able to look him in the eye and lie and feel a thrill when he couldn't prove I was lying. It would be my word against the client's, and he would have to trust me. That never meant anything before. Now I want his trust. He went the distance with me after the accident and I want to go the extra mile for him. I'm going to try to sell the Seattle client on our newer services so the trip will not have been in vain. That might assuage my guilt a little. I could tell Lisa disapproved by the look on her face even though she didn't say anything, but I told her she cannot expect me to go from being a lying, conniving, in-it-for-me, witch to a perfect picture of purity in one day. One day and one step at a time. She still wasn't convinced. Crap. I hate that what she thinks **of** me matters **to** me.

The date is set. Carly and I fly to Seattle on Saturday and spend the weekend with Atlee. Then on Monday and Tuesday, I'll stay to work. Carly's taking a red eye back to Texas on Sunday night. This trip feels huge to me. And I'm excited and scared, real scared. So scared that I have the runs.

In fact, I'm scared enough to have bought a six pack of beer and decided to drink it to settle my nerves, but I haven't. I even poured one, smelled it, called my sponsor, and poured the beer down the drain. The other five are cooling in the fridge, just in case I need them. I'm afraid of having Carly and Atlee see my scarred face, of facing my past, of my boss finding out I pushed the trip on our Seattle client, just so I could get my flight paid for to fly out there. I think all this turmoil deserves a drink. But, I'm not going to do it, at least not today. I hate my addiction but love drinking, and the way it makes me feel. I busy myself with packing. That helps. Going to bed early helps too.

Caz' Reflection

I'm glad this week is over. I didn't sleep well at night so I slept most of my days away. Did just enough to keep my father and brother off my back. I'm on my way to a session with Lisa. These dreams really bother me. They're very disturbing. They seem real, but I can't tell if they're memories and I'm dreaming about them or whether they are just bad dreams.

Lisa's sipping a cup of something hot that smells like hot chocolate. The smell makes we wish I had gotten up in time to eat breakfast. On second thought perhaps it's best I didn't eat. The dreams turn my stomach. I'm clutching my dream journal and dreading this, but I hope talking about them will make them go away. But, what if it makes them worse?

"Good morning." Lisa smiles.

"Hi." I respond.

"You look like you don't want to be here."

"I want to be here. But, I need to talk about some recent dreams. They're pretty nasty. Truth is, they scare the shit out of me, and I can't go back to sleep. Before I start though, I want you to know I've been working hard on my positive messages. However, I'm aware I'm able to use positive words and messages with others better than with myself. Is that normal?"

"You've always reported having a better relationship with others than you did with yourself."

I respond simply, "True. Hmmm."

"Ok, here goes, I am dreading this. Oh, wait, first I want to thank you for calling Dr. Paul. He called me and apologized. Can you believe that? Someone actually apologized to me!"

"I'm glad he called you. He felt awful about not reporting the abuse. I felt sorry for him. Hopefully, apologizing to you gave him some relief from his guilt."

"Yes, me too. I've got to get through this next part, okay?"

"Go for it."

"I've had three dreams in the last few days that have been repetitive. I don't understand why I'm having them now. Could saying positive stuff make for bad dreams?"

Lisa takes her time responding. "That's not usually the case. But, if you are feeling stronger, then your unconscious may be telling you it's ok to deal with additional negative events. Do you think these dreams are related or are they separate?"

"I don't know, but they feel all part of the same story. Actually, I had similar dreams when I was in high school and again in college, but they stopped and never reoccurred until now. They started up again when I saw one of the godbrothers in the grocery store. He looked awful. Drawn, thin, haggard, like he wasn't sleeping either."

Lisa suggests that I tell all three dreams before we discuss them.

> Dream #1: I'm 12 and at a house that I don't recognize but I know it's not Belle's. It's bigger and has many rooms. In each room there's screaming, but each voice is different so I know there are several boys there. I don't want to go into the rooms, but the person I'm walking with keeps encouraging me. She says it's a game and the screaming's just part of the game. Doesn't sound like any game I want to play. We arrive at a door and she opens it for me. I don't want to go in, but I don't know why. I just have a really bad feeling. I

break out in a cold sweat, as she gently pushes me through the door, I scream and wake up.

Dream #2: This time I'm naked and strapped face down on a table. A woman's wearing a mask and she has some kind of surgical instruments in her hand. I don't know why I'm in this place or on the table, but I know it's going to hurt so I must have gone through this before. I feel a searing pain in my butt and I scream and wake up.

Dream #3: I'm in a small bed and there's a woman sitting on top of me. She's laughing, tickling me, and telling me to relax, but I can't. I don't know who she is. I've never seen her before. She lifts up her skirt and has no underwear on. She keeps telling me not to cry or she'll pee on my face. I can't stop crying, and I won't open my eyes. Then I taste the saltiness and I know she peed on me. I'm gagging and crying. She's laughs. My eyes are closed. I can't look, then I feel something gooey being painted on my face like war paint and, at first, I don't know what it is and then I smell it. She has painted my face with crap. I hear her laughing hysterically.

Lisa is silent. Her complexion is green, or maybe it's her green blouse reflecting on her face, I can't tell. She takes a deep breath and asks THE question. "Do you think these are dreams or memories?" I start shaking as if I'm cold, but I'm not. I feel tears gathering in my eyes, and I can't stop them. I know these events are memories, but they've made their debut in dreams. I tell Lisa I don't know the three women. One was tall with dark gray hair, one was short and had light brown hair, and one was average height, obese and had dyed blondish red hair with dark roots.

I feel I'm losing control, but I'm trying to hold back the sobs. I feel like I'm in a tunnel. Will this abuse story ever end? How will it end? Will I have to die to get it to end? I shake and cry. I'm melting on to the floor. The three memories are flashing over and over again in my head like strobe lights. Reliving the horror. Losing touch with where I am and who I'm with. My eyes close to stop the intrusion of the memories, but it doesn't work. I finally give up and let the memories come. Dear God, if there are any other horror stories please let them emerge now and let me be done with this. I feel like I do when my stomach aches and I know I'm going to throw up. I hate to vomit and I fight it and fight it until my body does what it needs to do. Once it's over, I feel better and I wonder why I ever postponed vomiting. That's how this feels. I fight the emerging of the flashbacks. I hate them and so I fight and I fight until I know I cannot win the battle and I yield allowing them to vomit their images in my brain. All of them, all of them, all…of…them.

They begin to subside, and I'm drained. I open my eyes and find myself sitting on the floor, my head on the seat of the sofa. How long have I been sitting there? Lisa's quiet and I see compassion on her face. I'm not sure if there are any more embedded memories in my unconscious, but I want everything out, NOW. I can deal with what I know, I can't deal with what I don't know. I'm tired of being ambushed by my own mind and body. Lisa softly asks me if I'm ok. I nod. She assures me I don't have to talk about the memories now, if I don't want to. I say I don't want to talk about them now or ever. "The memories flooded and overwhelmed me like the dream did, but this time I know they're memories. I hope this is the end of the abuse revelations.

Lisa gives me space to just sit quietly. When I finally get up off the floor and sit on the sofa, Lisa asks if we could have a family meeting…only when I'm ready. I don't care, whatever. She also says that these newly revealed memories need to be reported to the police who are working on Belle's case. I agree, but I can't do it. I ask if she would call the detectives. She agrees. I need to leave. I have to get out of here. I try to stand up, but my legs feel like rubber. There's no energy left in my body. I just want to sleep, but I'm afraid to go to sleep. Lisa gives me a glass of water, and the time I need to recover. After about 15-20 minutes I begin to gain some strength. I hear the door bell announce another client and I slowly get up and gingerly walk out of her office as if I have just had an operation on my entire body and mind. I feel sore.

The doorbell had announced not Lisa's next client but my father, who was concerned when I didn't come out to the car on time. Dad looks at me and takes three huge steps toward me to support me. I'm grateful for his help. I'm beyond being embarrassed. I see now how mentally ill I really am and accept his assistance. Dad's insisting I tell him what happened. I can't, I'm too weak. I look to Lisa to explain. I hear Lisa telling my dad I recovered some very disturbing memories that first emerged as dreams but are now being manifested as flashbacks. Dad looks puzzled. He says, "I thought he had complete memory of his time with Belle." Lisa says, "These memories happened during the time Belle was abusing Caz, but they don't involve Belle." Dad looks like he's going to cry. He's almost cradling me in his arms and that's quite a feat considering I'm six-six and dad's only six foot. Lisa asks my dad if he would be willing to have a family meeting with Rom and me, and Dad agrees immediately. Bless him. All this conversation sounds muffled a bit and removed from where we are. I almost feel like I had an accident, and the paramedics are talking around me and I hear their muffled voices. He and Lisa agree on a different time for the family meeting so I don't have to give up my individual meeting with Lisa. Dad helps me out of the office. I just want to go home. But, this time, I don't want to sleep. The dreams may return. Perhaps the dreams are what I was avoiding by staying awake at night until the wee hours?

Caz' additional abuse

I'm grateful Craig gave me a heads up about the possible additional abuse. I call Craig, the police, and Helen. They will all have to get back to me. Previously Caz' flashbacks had been mild. He faded a bit, recounted the memory, and became agitated. Today was totally different. He entered a trance-like state in which he had narrowing of awareness of his immediate surroundings. He lost track of where he was and relived the abuse. He whimpered, cried out, and begged for it to stop. Caz is disabled for now and I need to bring his family on board so they stop pressuring him to change. I need to stop putting pressure on him, too. Caz is an intelligent, funny, engaging, and caring person. He comes across as someone who should be able to drive, hold a job, and perform routine life skills. However, the nightmares, intrusive thoughts, and overwhelming flashbacks totally impair his ability to engage consistently in the most minimal life task. I don't want to make excuses for Caz or give him an excuse to stay in bed, but his family has to realize how impaired he is, for now. With the trial looming, he will need their support, not their criticism and pressure.

As I'm writing my case notes, Helen calls. I explain what happened to Caz in my office and she sighs. "I hoped, since he had memory of his time with Belle, he'd escaped the debilitating flashbacks that intrude spontaneously on clients who have amnesia." She asks if I think she might need to change his medication for now. I tell her I'll see him in two days with his family and I'll check in with him and see if he needs to increase his anxiolytic medication temporarily. She agrees it's a good plan and tells me I'm doing a great job with Caz. I thank her and hang up feeling supported. It's nice to hear, but I'm still second guessing myself. This case is an extremely difficult one. The abuse of a child usually creates a client who has multiple diagnoses and recalcitrant symptoms. With the trial looming he could be in danger. Damn. His rainbow was taking shape a bit, and now this new revelation shattered him and I felt him fade away, hopefully only for the moment.

After seeing three more clients, I have a break and call Craig again. He answers the phone and breathes a sigh of relief when he hears my voice. "I've been trying to reach you, but your voicemail kept kicking in. What's up?" he asks. I tell him Caz has recovered additional memories that are quite disturbing. I suggest he may want to do a pastoral visit with Caz, especially with the impending trial. Craig agrees and thanks me for being open to the importance of pastoral care. So much affirmation in one day! I thank him for the heads up on the possibility of additional forms of abuse. It helped me to be prepared for what happened today. As I hang up I hear my doorbell ring signaling the arrival of my next client. I walk out of my office to greet Noelle and to my surprise Frick and Frack are standing there. Detective Bentley (Frick) and Detective Lang

(Frack) want to talk. I think it's about time I honor them with using their real names instead of my sarcastic names. After all, words are important! And, we are all on the same side. I just didn't like being played like a fool the first time we met. This encounter is entirely different. They are more collegial and open. I explain I have a client in a few minutes, and I'm not available to talk until after my last client leaves at 8 p.m., then I have to go home and feed my poor, neglected dog. They ask if they could drop by my home at 8:30, and I agree. Why not? What's one more hour in a long day?

Lisa and the Detectives

When I arrive home at 8:10, the detectives are sitting in their car outside my house. Well, at least Baltimore's finest kept all the bad guys away from my house tonight. Either that or my neighbors are having a rumor heyday wondering what kind of trouble their shrink neighbor has gotten herself into. I welcome them in and offer coffee, tea? I stopped short of saying "me", I was too tired anyway. I explained to the Dynamic Detective Duo that I had a session with Caz in which additional abuse was remembered. I also told them the abuse involved three women Caz does not know, and the newly recovered memories involve a different type of abuse than Belle preferred but may, in some way, have involved her as the initial contact. They asked me to be specific; clearly they were looking for confirmation of another accusation. I took a deep breath. This is not the kind of conversation one likes to have with two men in your living room. I took the plunge, hoping the description didn't embarrass them, or me. When I was finished, they looked at each other, closed their notepads, thanked me, and left. I felt like I just had coitus interruptus. I thought this was a two-way street. I share, they share, we chat, share conjecture, run some possibilities up the flagpole, plan a stake out, nab the bad gals, etc. Instead, I got a hit-and-run. Well, at least I have the rest of my evening to relax. But, I'm charged up now. I want to be a junior cop and get these predators. I made a hot fudge and chocolate ice cream sundae for dinner instead. If I can't grab the bad gals, I'll grab the bad cals. Don't judge me, I had a good lunch, and I'm tired. I deserve this after the day I've had. Ok, I feel guilty, but not guilty enough to stop. With all this chocolate and sugar, I am really going to dream tonight.

Chapter Six
Things Seem to Get Worse Before They Get Better

When the platform of assumptions collapses under the deadly weight of a horrific event, everything else goes down with it, and suddenly there's no place to stand. It's as if the world has broken its promise revealing itself to be capable of devastating chaos and cruelty.

(Naparstek, 2004, p. 37-38)

Noelle
Sessions with Dr. Brown

Noelle is exactly on time again. I fantasize that she arrives early, sits in her car until 30 seconds before she is supposed to be here, and then walks from her car to the office and (ta da!) she arrives exactly on time. She looks blank, but I know there is much behind that veneer.

"Hi, Noelle."

"Hi." She says morosely, hanging her head.

"I talked with Dr. Retter this week. He wants you to schedule an appointment to talk about your medications. Have you continued to take them as prescribed this week?"

She nods slightly. Should I take this to mean she didn't her medication every day?

"Dr. Retter says you have been on those medications for quite awhile now, and there are some better ones on the market that might work for you."

Sigh

"You seem down today. What's going on?"

"I'm down ever' day."

True, but ...she seems more lethargic.

"You just seem more lethargic."

"What's that?" she asks with a sneer, as if I were stupid for using the word.

"It means you don't look as though you have much energy."

"I don't."

"Do you know why?"

Shrug

"We're back to where I'm asking all the questions, and you're just shrugging or nodding or giving me one-word answers. Has something happened?"

She looks me in the eye for the first time and it is intense. "Did you tell Dr. Retter what I'm talkin' 'bout in here?"

"NO! I told you I would just talk about your medication and your transfer from Dr. Brown to Dr. Retter when he died. Why do you ask?"

"Other people made promises to me an' didn't keep 'em."

Oh my, some paranoia emerging. "I keep my promises. I make mistakes sometimes because I'm human, but I kept my promise to you. Dr. Retter said he's glad you're seeing me, and he'd like you to come back so he can assess the medications."

"Humph." She looks like she doesn't believe me. Is this a way to push me away so she doesn't kill me? Or is she really a bit paranoid?

"I wonder...are you acting this way to keep me from getting close to you because you're afraid you'll kill me?"

Noelle looks wide-eyed. "How'd you figger that out? You're scary! It's like you read ma'mind."

I smile and chuckle at her innocence. "I can't read minds, but it seemed logical." I shrug. "I am confused about one thing though. You said you didn't feel responsible for Dr. Brown's death because you weren't close to him. Yet you saw him for how long?"

"'Bout three years."

"He seemed like a nice man, very fatherly. I liked him. You didn't?"

Long deep sigh. "I didn't see him but once a month at the beginnin' an' then once ev'ry three months afta that. I guess I didn't git to know him very well."

"I see. How did you feel when he died?"

Tears are gathering. She looks down and then away as if she doesn't want me to see them, but it's too late. They're falling on her silk blouse turning the pale yellow blouse gold on the spots where they land. She makes her mouth a line again. Who does she remind me of? Why can't I think of it?

"I...saw....him.....die."

I sit in silence. Of course I knew this, but I can't say Dr. Retter told me. She wouldn't understand that he thought she'd already told me the whole story.

"That must have been awful. Can you tell me the story?"

"I had an 'ppointment an' he died."

Short and to the point but that won't get her to grieve.

"You mean that you were in the room when he died? Or you were in the waiting room? Or...."

"He'd been fallin' 'sleep on me. I thought he was just rude, but he seemed nice. I didn't know he wuz sick. I wuz angry wiff' him an' when I went that day I decided to ask him to stay awake. I sat there tryin' to git my courage up an' then he looked at me... funny-like... an' his eyes rolled back. He grabbed his chest. An' he fell outta his chair."

"Oh, my! Noelle, I'm sad you had to see that."

"I thought...Now how could I have kilt him? I didn't feel close to him. Then I thought maybe my anger kilt him. Maybe my ability had... whut do ya call it? Mutated?"

Now I understand! She thought she had killed him, but this time with anger.

"What did you do?"

"I went to 'is desk an' called 911 an' his secretary an' then I lef'. I jist walked away."

"You must have been very confused."

"I wus until I realized he'd been sick a long time and I didn't' kill him. I wus jist the unlucky person he died in front of."

"But. wasn't it sort of traumatic to see someone you know die in front of you?"

"No more trymatic then other deaths."

"I see."

"Noelle, I think most people would feel very scared, hurt, confused if something like that happened to them. Why do you think you just walked away?"

"Cause I seen a lot worse than that. He was a sick old man who died. It happens. It's the others that's hard."

"Um, Noelle, you didn't mention your name and Dr. Retter's have something in common."

"What?"

Is she kidding me or making me explain? Does she not see it?

"Well, his first name was Patrick and your last name is KILL PATRICK."

Her eyes got real big. "I n'ver put that together. But I didn't kill him, I swear."

"I believe you, but do you believe you?"

"Yea, I think so."

She seems to be talking openly, and I'd like to see if she'll stay longer this session, so I ask her the question she posed to me at the end of a previous session. "Do you want to tell me how your hair turned white?"

"Not really."

"You teased me about not asking you about that."

"I don't tease."

"Oh."

She has retreated back into her very cold, grim mode again. Not that she's ever been warm, but she does melt around the edges a bit here and there. She picks up her purse and puts it on her lap as if she is going to run again… or just in case she wants to leave quickly. She's looking at the couch in my office (the one that Caz sits on) almost like she's trying to picture another client on the sofa. She sighs. She sighs again. Then she looks scared, and she begins talking in a low voice and I can barely hear her.

"I live in Chase, Maryland." (Pause.) "Do you remember the train wreck on Jan'ry 4th, 1987?"

"Yes."

"Well I live near the place where the train wreck occurred. The cross streets are Birdwood and Redbird an' I live near dere."

I decide to remain still for fear I will say something to spook her.

"The train wreck happened in early Jan'ry an' it wuz cold, really cold. I didn't wanna go out, but I didn't have any food af'er the holidays. I decided ta go ta the grocery store. It was a little before 1 o'clock in the afternoon. I put on my red coat an' a scarf an' gloves an' boots an' hat."

She stops talking and is looking at her hands, picking at her nails. I cannot interrupt her even though I have a dozen questions already.

"I git in my car an' begin drivin' an' I have ta go near the train tracks to git to the closest grocery store. As I git near ta the tracks I hear a train whistle (I hear them all the time), but this time it's intense an' long an' it doesn't stop an' I know something's wrong. I hear another train sound an' then I see the engineer leaning out his window. He looks terrified. I look down the track, the other way, an' I see 'nother train comin'. THEY ARE GOIN' TO COLLIDE! OH MY GOD! THEY ARE GOIN' TO SMASH INTO EACH OTHER. WHAT CAN I DO! WHAT CAN I DO?" Noelle is screaming at the top of her lungs, her eyes are wide an' her face is ice white. "NOOOOOO."

She is breathing heavy an' tears are falling, but there's no crying sound. "He jumped. The conductor jumped."

"Was he safe?" I asked as if I was seeing a movie and needed to hear the end.

She doesn't answer. She runs away.

She saw the Chase Train Wreck! I knew there were a couple people who witnessed the actual collision, but I had no idea Noelle was one of them. How traumatic for her! And on top of all the other deaths she experienced. This one is different though. She didn't know anyone on the train. Did she?

Noelle Decides
No More Counseling

I can't do this counselin' thing anymore. I almost lost it in dere. No matter how kind Leeza is, the relivin' part of ma'life sucks. Will it help? Can she help me? Will she die if I let her try? Can I bear 'nother death? I'm not goin' back. Period.

Lisa
Reflection on Noelle's Session

In think Noelle holds the record for the shortest sessions I ever had with clients. She just can't stand the pain of the memories. The train incident must have been horrible. I remember it well. I was taking PhD courses in graduate school and I was in a class that started in January. One of the students in my class was a paramedic on site that day. He said it was the worst accident he had ever experienced. But, on the positive side, he said the people who lived along the tracks were wonderful. They cooked food out of their freezers for the workers and invited them into their homes to get warm and have coffee. Some of them had been home when the trains collided and had been the first people to help the walking wounded. They had even taken sheets off their beds to make bandages. And now, here I am, hearing the story again but from an eye witness.

Noelle called and cancelled her next appointment. Claimed she wasn't feeling well. I'm sure she's somatizing her pain. Either that, or she's too afraid to relive more experiences. Perhaps she needs a rest from counseling. I hope she comes back. I can see her making some small efforts that could lead to improved mental health...if she'd just trust me and the process and stay the course.

A Written Guarantee

I tole Leeza I was sick, but the fact is I'm sick and tired of trying to get better. I can't help what's happened ta me, but I can help whether I wanna deal wiff this stuff. And I don't! I don't know if I even want to be in counseling anymore. I can't see myself sharing more stories unless dere is a guarantee I'll feel better. Dat's what them shrinks need – A written guarantee that talking 'bout your feelings and stuff works. If it doesn't, then you git your money back! And a warranty that, if in the future, dem nightmares and memories come back and git to you, then they should see you for free. That's it. I'm gonna tell Leeza the next time I see her. Crap.

The Rheems
Family Session

Caz, Rom, and Stewart arrive for the family meeting. Caz looks refreshed, but Caz' shorter version of himself, Rom, is squirming and looking uncomfortable. I'd bet he's never been in a counseling session before and knows he should be talking to someone about his panic attacks. Stewart looks like he's ready for a dressing down. What do people think goes on in counseling? I should have brought a whip and chain and hung them on the wall. That would really scare them. I begin by explaining why I wanted to talk to everyone. I spent some time explaining what Posttraumatic Stress Disorder (PTSD) is and what the symptoms are. They all recognized at once that Caz suffers almost all of the symptoms. But, as I laid out why and how the diagnostic symptoms manifest, both Stewart and Rom begin to wiggle in their seats. Stewart spoke first.

"Doesn't almost everyone have some of these symptoms? I mean, when my wife left, one could say I was traumatized and I avoided women out of fear I would choose poorly again. Wouldn't that qualify as avoidant behavior?"

Good point. I have an opportunity here and I don't want to blow it.

"Any time we experience a tragedy there's a certain amount of trauma and pain that goes along with the event. However, everyone reacts slightly differently. For example, when you arrived home and found your two small children alone, scared, and hurt, and then found your wife's note, there was trauma to you and the boys.

The trauma caused each of you to manage the memory of that day in your own way. One of you may relive that day, especially when you are under stress. One of you may avoid all mention of mothers, hate mother's day, swear you'll never marry, etc. One of you may experience numbing, not recall important aspects, or feel detached. If you don't deal with the symptoms when they first occurred, then they may reoccur leading you to develop coping strategies that can impede parts of your life, like avoiding women, suppressing emotions, trying to be perfect. You may also develop other symptoms like anxiety, panic attacks, depression, or obsessive compulsive symptoms. Would you survive? Sure, but your quality-of-life might not be optimal and you could feel vulnerable. However, when a person experiences repeated trauma as a small child, and there's no way out of the situation, and the trauma involves physical and/or sexual abuse, then the symptoms are usually much worse and compromise any attempt the person may try to "get on with life." There are usually co-morbid disorders such as depression **and** anxiety **and** substance abuse. The more intense and lengthy the abuse, the more pronounced the symptoms. Also the younger the child plus the presence of other trauma, like a vanishing parent, usually exacerbate the trauma symptoms.

Rom is next to speak. "So all of us were traumatized by Mom's leaving, but Caz got the worst of it because of his abuse by Belle? That's why he's more depressed, anxious, scared, and can't sleep?" Caz gets up and hugs Rom and simply says, "Thanks for understanding." Rom looks stunned but smiles.

Stewart wants to fix it. "What can we do?"

I turn to Caz and ask, "What can they do, Caz?"

Caz looks surprised I turned this over to him. He stammers around awhile and then says, "Try to understand. Some days are really crap for me and some are ok. I can have dreams that keep me from sleeping at night and then I'll have a very difficult time getting up in the morning. Dad, I want to learn to drive again, but I'm scared. I don't have any confidence in myself, so let's take it very slowly. Praise me when I do something well, don't jump on me when I fail. This month is going to be bad with the trial coming up. I may have a lot of flashbacks when I testify. I may feel like running away. Please help me." Caz stops and takes a breath and says. "I love you."

Rom and Stewart both nod and Stewart asks if Caz wants them to be in the courtroom for support. Caz answers, "I don't know. Let me think about it. I don't know whether I want you to hear all the details of the abuse."

Rom and Stewart agree. I'm not sure how much further to invite the men to consider more counseling as a family, or individually. I'm afraid they may see me as pushing the counseling agenda. I drop the suggestion for now.

I finish the session by asking them to tell each other how they feel when one member of the family does them a favor or lets them down. They get into this and discover more about themselves individually and as a family. At the end I offer to make a referral if anyone of them or the family wants to pursue additional counseling. They all nod. This family nods a lot!

Stewart's Insight

I had no idea how destroyed Caz was by his mother's abandonment. I think I was too wrapped up in my own pain. I couldn't attend to the boys the way I should have. Perhaps if I had taken the referrals offered to me 20 years ago, some of this mess could have been avoided. I didn't mention this in the session but I feel responsible for Belle's abuse of Caz. I was overwhelmed back then trying to work and raise two little guys who lost their mother. When Belle offered to take Caz to her home to play with other kids, I trusted her and was relieved to have a breather. Rom was an easy kid who had lots of friends and did what he was told, but Caz was more difficult because of his ADHD and learning disabilities. I had to ask him to do everything twice and still had to follow up with him. I was also extremely hurt (Lisa would say 'traumatized' by my wife's leaving. This whole thing feels like it's my fault.

I never had a good relationship with my mother. She was controlling and not available. She abandoned me in her own way. I remember the day I broke my leg. It was the 4th of July and my family was hosting a large backyard barbeque. I was riding my bike, fell, and broke my leg. A neighbor called my parents and an ambulance (there was no 911 dispatch in those days). My mother was furious. She accused me of destroying the party on purpose. She said I always did my best to ruin her life. I curled up in the hospital bed and cried. The nurse came in and thought I was crying because of the pain and gave me a needle for the pain. It worked. The pain, both physical and psychological, went away with the drug. So in some ways I understand Caz' viewpoint. He was always testing us beyond our patience, and we didn't know why. Now I understand what ADHD and learning disabilities mean. He can't help himself sometimes just like I couldn't help breaking my leg. I wonder, after all this time, if I should try a little counseling. It certainly was not what I thought it would be like. I thought Lisa was going to tell us what we should do to make life better for Caz, or she was going to blame us in some way. But, she focused on how we all could work together to make life better for all of us. I gained some insight into our problems, too.

Maybe I will take the referral. I might be able to understand better how my mother's blaming me for ruining the party turned me into a person who blames myself for every bad thing that happens, like when my wife left. I really will think about it.

Rom's Resistance

Uncomfortable is the word for counseling. I thought any moment the conversation was going to turn towards me, and I would be blamed for Caz feeling bad about himself. I treat him like garbage some days when he frustrates me. Sleeping all day while I bust my ass to help Dad make ends meet! I get pissed off. I was abandoned too, but I pulled myself up by my bootstraps and moved on! I could never understand what was wrong with him and why Caz couldn't do the same thing I did. I can see how Caz got the worst of our life together, and I'm going to try to be kinder. I know Lisa wanted me to think about getting help for my panic attacks though I don't know how she would know that I get extremely anxious at times, maybe Caz told her. I just can't see myself sitting with a stranger and unloading. I'll go to any future family meetings if I'm asked, but that's all I'm gonna to do. I'll also attend court if Caz wants me to. It's the least I can do for my brother. But, counseling for ME, no way!

The Walk-Through

My father and brother have been less critical in the last few days since the family session. I didn't get the impression that Rom was crazy about counseling, but he did participate and hasn't been as mean. If this attitude continues, then I'd like to have him in the courtroom. I definitely want my father and Lisa there, if she can clear her schedule. Pastor Craig is definitely coming, and I'm glad. Pastor has supported me these last few months by visiting me when I was down and bringing me communion, and praying with me. I think he's helping Dad too. Several times, Dad said he was going to church to talk to Pastor Craig. Maybe they're doing a little counseling, too. He doesn't admit it though.

In today's session, I ask Lisa to help me prepare for court. She agrees. However, she doesn't seem happy when I tell her I want to go to Belle's house to refresh my memory. She's concerned I will be flooded with flashbacks and not be able to keep it together on the witness stand. I disagree with her. I think visiting the house without Belle there will bring some closure to 8 years of abuse. I also have some very good memories of those years in that house. She recommends I think about it, and then, if I decide I still want to go through Belle's house, I can call the prosecutor to ask for permission. I tell her I know how to get into the house without anyone knowing because I know the house inside and out. Lisa becomes more directive than I've ever seen her. She tells me I'm embarking on some "self-defeating behavior", and she describes a consequence I hadn't thought about. Lisa says, "What if you 'sneak into the house' and a neighbor calls the police and you're arrested for illegal entry or trespassing?" I have to admit she has a point, but I tell her I don't care. Well, then she really stomps on me. "You know, Caz, one of your problems is you don't care about yourself. You have been abandoned, abused, criticized, and betrayed. So you think if others don't care about you, then you don't need to care about yourself. You need to start caring about what happens to you and think about the consequences of your actions." Those weren't her exact words, but that's what I think she said.

I just don't want to follow other people's rules. Other people, especially people in authority, haven't been reliable for me. I know, if I ask permission, I'll be denied, and I'll have to appeal and go through all kinds of hoops to get what I know I need in order to testify well. Because I find life to be difficult and exhausting, I frequently try to circumvent the system or I give up. For example, I used to have a driver's license, but when it was time to renew, I didn't have the money. I asked Dad to help me and, at the time, he was annoyed with me for leaving school, so he said I should work to get the money. I called the Motor Vehicle Administration and asked what I should do if I don't have the money, and they said I could fill out a form asking for assistance. They didn't send me the form in time, and I just let it lapse. Dad said I was lazy, but I just don't have the energy to deal with all the red tape of today's world. Lisa's looking at me for an answer. "Ok," I say reluctantly, "I'll call the prosecutor and ask for access to Belle's house, but I'm certain he'll say 'no'."

I feel discouraged after the session. I'm tempted to walk to Belle's house and see if there's an easy access that can't be seen from the street. I take Lisa's advice instead and call the prosecutor. He's intrigued by the idea. I wasn't expecting that! He says he has no reason to deny me my request, but an officer will have to be with me. I'm ok with that. Could it be that easy? He says he'll get back to me. I call Lisa and leave a message saying I had taken her advice and called the prosecutor.

Three days go by without a call from the prosecutor. Figures! I'm scheduled for a meeting with him in a week to go over my testimony. I don't know what to do, call him again or wait. I don't wait well. I call Lisa and ask her advice. She talks to me for 10 minutes and asks me a lot of questions about why I'm in such a hurry to see the house, and I honestly don't know. Crap! Ok, I'll wait.

The meeting with the prosecutor's a little unnerving. Dad takes me, but he waits outside. The prosecutor asks me lots of questions, and I answer. Then we go over what the defense attorney might ask me. When we are done, he invites Dad back in and he takes us to the courtroom to see the set up. I even sit in the witness chair and see where Belle will be sitting, which helps me picture it in my mind, and calms me. Sometimes not knowing stuff is worse than knowing what to expect. When we get back to his office, I ask him again if I can go to Belle's house. He says the judge has agreed to allow all the victims to walk through the house, because the abuse happened when we were young, and Belle is in jail. We've been instructed not to discuss any memories if we run into each other. The house will be open from 10-12 on Friday, and any of us who are interested may walk through. A police officer will be at the house to let us in. I ask if Lisa or Dad can walk through with me, and he hesitates, but then agrees one of them can go with me. I wonder if this is a special instance or if in other trials the victims are allowed to visit the scene of the crime.

At my next session with Lisa we primarily focus on the trip to Belle's house and the court date. Lisa appears pleased I went through channels. I guess I am too. I learned that not every situation creates a huge process of red tape. Lisa makes space in her calendar to go with me to Belle's. She uses one of her relaxation techniques she taught me months ago to help me get ready to see the house. We agree to meet at 10 a.m. on Friday at the house. Then we discuss the trial and the fact I was able to see the courtroom. She asks me if I had any feelings as I was sitting in the witness chair. I respond, "It felt surreal. I kept trying to picture Belle sitting at the table and wondering if she'll be frowning in disapproval or smiling to remind me of our relationship."

"Which would be worse for you?"

"I think seeing her frown would be worse because I've always tried to please her, and even though I don't need to please her anymore, I think the internal pressure will be bubbling up to be that little boy again." We do another guided imagery in which I see myself confidently walking into the courthouse, entering the courtroom, taking the witness stand, seeing Belle, telling my story calmly, and answering questions. No matter how aggressive the defense attorney gets with me, I see myself thinking before I answer the questions. Also Lisa gives me a number of escape hatches like asking the judge for a bathroom break if I feel overwhelmed, using the water that's provided to buy time if I'm asked a difficult question, and telling the judge I'm having flashbacks and need a break. I feel more confident after the exercise. Lisa suggests I do the visualization myself at least twice a day. Yuck! I hate homework. Probably will try it but I doubt I'll do it.

It's Friday, my insides turn to hominy grits as Dad and I approach Belle's house. I keep picturing it in my mind -- the house as I remember it. As dad turns the corner, the house, which played such an important role in my life, appears. I'm stunned. The house and grounds have deteriorated. Two-foot high weeds, overgrown bushes, and large fallen branches are everywhere. A couple of windows are broken. The house doesn't look welcoming like it did 20 years ago. It also looks smaller than I remember, and darker. While Belle's house is only three miles from mine, I always avoided driving down her road, and I asked Dad to avoid the house when he was driving. So I hadn't really seen the house in several years. I'd catch it out of the corner of my eye when we drove down a cross street, but I'd look away.

Sitting in Dad's car in front of her house, the memory of seeing Belle's house for the first time emerges. I was a very excited but hesitant six year old boy. I feel the dread of having to approach the ghosts that lie within the house. Maybe Lisa was right, this might be too difficult for me. Lisa parks her Green Toyota Prius next to us. Funny, I always pictured her driving a BMW or a Lexus. When she steps out of her car and stands next to my window, she looks intently at me through the glass. Her intense look inquires whether I still want to walk through the house. Maybe she's not sure about my ability either. I nod solemnly and get out of the car. Walking up the brick path to the front door, I feel myself shrinking into a six year old child and I feel the tug of wanting to run back to the car, and yet the pull of wanting the phantom chocolate chip cookies I can smell as I approach the door. The door seems much smaller than I remember. The shrinking and growing Alice in the *Alice in Wonderland* book comes to mind. Belle used to read it to us, acting out all the voices. "Off with her head" she would announce as she waved her hand like the queen.

The police officer opens the door for us. (He lets Dad in too, even though he wasn't on the list.) None of the other witnesses are there. Once inside, I feel like the abused child who both dreaded being there, yet needed to be there for companionship, laughter, pony rides, dogs, and games. I'm aware of Lisa's eyes watching me carefully. She doesn't speak but seems ready to jump in if I begin to have flashbacks like I did in her office. The great room also looks smaller and as I take in the scene I feel myself transported back in time. I hear the laughter and cheering of boys who are playing the early elementary computer games. I smell the apparition aroma of spaghetti, fried chicken and warm bread that are welcoming me back, and I feel the yearning of the little boy who needs a mother's home-cooked meal. But, the dust and rubbish bring me back to reality. I move to the patio and pool area.

The pool looks disgusting with green mold on the edges and debris floating in the water. There's even a dead squirrel floating on top. I close my eyes and hear the yells from boys doing cannonballs into the pool and see boys jumping off the diving board. I hear the sounds of kids playing Marco Polo until we were hoarse. All these sounds and images in my head intrude to remind me of the past. The stables are devoid of the horses I loved, but there's still the faint smell of manure and hay. I close my eyes and hear horses snorting and see them pawing the ground. I remember their ears standing up as we approached them with apples and carrots.

Lisa and Dad look around, but they say nothing as I continue walking through the gardens and back into house through the kitchen. I'm absorbed in my memories.

Going upstairs begins to release some of the darker memories. My old bedroom still had the same bed and dresser, that were mine temporarily. The bedspread is different, a faded Raiders of the Lost Ark. The memories are flash flooding my mind, but they are just memories, not flashbacks. I'm surprised and impressed with myself. I'm not having the intense physical sensations I've had before when thinking about the abuse. However, I've not entered the room where most of the abuse with Belle happened, the master bedroom. That's next. I pause at the door and feel the excitement and dread, which had always been a part of the weekends at Belle's.

I open the door and step in. Predictably, the room feels smaller. I was less than four feet tall when I began to visit this house. At well over six feet, the entire place, including the memories, seem to shrink to a four foot size.

I'm astonished! The room is exactly the same, the furniture, the pictures, the small knickknacks. I remember the picture centered over the bed; a scene of thick evergreen woods with a small path winding through the trees and yellow flowers on either side of the path. I would always see the picture when having sex with Belle and, even when I was with high school girls I saw it in my head. During sex, the woods caressed my mind, whispering 'You are special to be invited to this place of love", and, in the darkness of the forest green paint, I relived losing my virginity over and over again. I can see Belle, opening her robe to me, and I feel the gentle touches. I experience the genital stirrings that occurred each time with Belle, but no panicky flashbacks surface. I know where I am, and I'm in control. I could never have walked through this house six months ago. Wow, I say softly to myself. Lisa hears me and checks on me. I give her a hand signal saying I'm ok.

We all descend the stairs together. Lisa and Dad are in front of me. They think we're done with the walk-through, and they continue to the front door to leave the house. However, I step into the small den off the great room. I know it's there, but they miss it because the door is tucked around the corner. This room has the most negative energy for me. In here, the boys were instructed by Belle to "pleasure each other." I believe this is where my homosexual urges were born and my self-hatred was solidified. The sex scenes flood my mind, but the raw, angry, confusing excitement is missing. I simply feel disgust. This woman forced us to do unmentionable things, in order to be allowed to return for the other benefits. I remember as a kid feeling more sexual energy during this abuse than with Belle. I just realize why. With Belle the abuse involved loving caresses, tenderness, and kindness from a caring mother-figure. With the other boys, it was demanded, forced, exhibitionistic, and forbidden. There was also more shame, guilt, power, and embarrassment. From somewhere deep in my core, hatred stirs. It's not only hatred of myself but also, for the first time, of Belle.

I don't know why certain sexual images or acts are more tantalizing than others, but I now understand that feeling sexually aroused is not love. It also does not make or define a person as gay, bisexual, or straight. I have to define that for myself, when I discover who I am apart from the abuse.

Dad and Lisa quickly discover I'm not behind them and return to find me. I sense them standing outside the door, respectfully standing back and not talking. I tremble inside as if my organs are again being liquefied. The memories ooze out through my pores. The hatred, disgust, and guilt begin to overwhelm me, and I tremble like I've been left out in the cold. Hell! I **have** been left out in the cold. I have been left out of having a 'normal' life. Both come to my side and quickly walk me out of the house.

Earlier, Lisa and I had set up a session immediately after the walkthrough. I'm glad for the time. She lets me take the lead in the session. I need a few minutes to collect my thoughts. I sit forward with my head down and my forearms resting on my knees. I study the blue carpet trying to get my mind to focus on something other than that house. Slowly I regain my emotional footing,

"I'm just now realizing, that I needed mothering so much, I allowed the abuse to continue with Belle even though I knew it was wrong. I'm ashamed to admit it, but I looked forward to our private time together because she always held me tenderly and said she loved me. That's why it didn't feel like abuse because it fulfilled a need deep inside of me...for a mother's touch and love." A tear falls on my knee, and I ignore it. "The abuse with the guys is another matter. I felt directed to perform different sexual acts and if I didn't, I wouldn't be invited back for the fun part or the tender moments. It also has made me question whether I am gay, straight, bisexual, or perverted because I was aroused during all types of sex. It seems my body automatically responds to certain touches, images, and thoughts even if I don't want it to."

She smiles and looks tenderly at me as if I was a little boy who had just seen his first rainbow. "You were a normal kid in an abnormal situation, Caz."

She's right. I do a number on myself, too often.

"You seem to be doing well considering you just walked through Belle's house for the first time since the abuse". I nod, she's right. "Do you think you're ready to testify? Are you ready to say to Belle what you've just said to me and yourself?"

I pause and think about it. "Yes. But, I'm anxious."

"Of course you are. You wouldn't be a NORMAL human being if you weren't."

Lisa
The Walk-Through

I'm impressed with the way Caz walked through Belle's house. He was cool, calm, and pensive. I could see he was remembering some of the events, but he never lost control. The control was not forced either. It didn't seem like a determined, hang-on-for-dear-life control but a quiet, relaxed control. I'm not sure what I expected, but I was surprised how calm he was. The insights that came out of the walk-through were remarkable, too. I had the feeling the small needy child was growing up into a pensive man right in front of my eyes. Sometimes, therapists spend months with clients and the progress is slow but deliberate. There are no bells and whistles and "Aha!" moments, just inches of progress each week. And then there's a day when the client or the therapist realizes the work of therapy has really made a difference. There are other times when there are the horns, shouts, and rapid change right in front of your eyes, and that's amazing. But, most of the work happens slowly. Seeing the progress is what keeps me in the profession and reminds me how powerful the mind is when the tumblers fall into place. I'm not saying Caz is finished changing or even free from his self-defeating behaviors and thoughts, but something important shifted inside of him, and despite the backslides that are sure to come, Caz is different than he was a couple of hours before. It's always a privilege to observe a shift like that.

I only wish Caz could have testified right there and then. He was like a pump that had been primed. Unfortunately, our judicial system, for all its well-intentioned protections of the defendants, also grinds slowly and thus burdens those who are going to testify. The trial has been postponed, or 'continued' as they say in court.

Another couple of weeks will pass before it gets started. I sense Caz' disappointment. He felt ready, and now he'll wait. Sadly, the week of the trial I will not be able to attend. I have a vacation that's been planned and paid for over a year and involves two other people. If I were vacationing close by, I would take a day out of my vacation and attend, but I'm going to St. Croix. I sorely need this vacation. Why am I trying to convince myself it's ok to be gone for the trial. Am I too enmeshed in this case? Am I losing my perspective?

Caz and I meet each week and discuss a variety of issues, but the major one that's looming is the trial. He's scared because I will not be there. However, he has lots of support from Stewart, Rom, and Craig. He decided he doesn't want his grandmother to be there. She offered, but he's too embarrassed for her to hear the testimony.

Noelle
The Chase Train Story, Continued

I'm not a gambler, but I bet Noelle's having second thoughts about returning, knowing she's going to have to finish the Chase story. If that's the case, then I bet she doesn't show next week, after having cancelled this week. She seemed tentative about rescheduling the appointment when she left her message. However, I did tell her that the following week I'll be on vacation, so let's see if she decides to show up for one more session before she gets two week off.

Today is Noelle's appointment, and I'm waiting for her to arrive. She's one minute late, a rarity for her. Wait, here she comes. She's dressed totally in black and is dragging her shoulder bag behind her. Head down, shoulders forward, spine bent, like she's carrying all the planets on her shoulders.

She says nothing as she brushes past me to sit in "her" chair. Normally, I would see this behavior as rude, but I understand that Noelle doesn't want to be here. I wonder if her boss made her come today. I sit quietly and let her take the lead.

She's sitting with her head down, both feet on the floor, toes turned toward each other and heels out. She's not making eye contact and is even paler, if possible. She's in a dark hole of trauma.

I'll not intervene. She has to find her own way of talking about this.

"The engineer died." She whispers. I'm trying to get the context in which she was saying this and then realize the last thing she said two weeks ago was something like "He jumped." I then asked "Was he safe?" It was almost like the two weeks never happened and she's continuing the session in a time warp. She's answering my last question.

She begins gagging like she's going to vomit, I look around for the trash can in case that happens, but all that comes out is a very small frail answer. "He jumps an' lands on a guide wire an' is cut in two. I see his face as he jumps an' as he dies." She's building emotion and volume as she continues telling the story.

"Then his train goes past me up tha tracks an' the trains collide. I see it happen. I see it happen! I couldn't do nothin'. I jist stand by ma car in shock. One of the engines is completely disintegrated on impact. The sound is …is… unbelievable. Then I see people comin' outta their houses. Screamin', yellin', and tryin' to reach the people still in the train. Lots of passengers are walkin' around dazed an' bloody but alive. The whole thing takes maybe one to two minutes. Dat's all an' it's over 'cept the trains look like some huge toys piled on top of each other. I think for a minute maybe God was playin' trains and crashed dem into each other like a little boy would do. Stupid thought. Probably go to hell for that thought.

"Passengers who are alive are lookin' for their kin. I can still smell the diesel fuel. I can still hear the screams. I can still see his face when he dies. I hate the first week in Jan'ry." She takes a long breath and then starts again but this time in past tense. "At first I thought I died in the wreck cuz everythin' looked so, so not real. Like I wuz a ghost watchin' the chaos."

"What did you do?"

She follows my lead but shifts into present tense again. "I start walkin' towards the wreck. I hear the sirens screamin' an' a helicopter's comin'."

She looks up at the ceiling like she can see the helicopter. "People rushing by me, tryin' to help. But, I can't help. I can't take it in. A man grabs me an' clings to me. He is screamin' 'Where is my wife? Have you seen her? Where is she? Is she dead?' I mouth the words 'I don't know.' But, nothin' comes out. I feel my entire being' numbin' an' den I puke."

I feel a tear rolling down my cheek, and I didn't even notice until it hit my arm. Noelle has seen more pain in her short life than most see in 10 lifetimes. My countertransference is really percolating. My daughter died in a helicopter crash and while I wasn't there, I often think of the people on the ground who watched the helicopter go down. I wonder if they could see her face in the window, terrified and then gone. I think about 9/11 and those who heard their loved ones calling on their cell phones for help or saying goodbye.

I wonder, too, if I will be able to continue to see Noelle. Will I be too engaged with her now that I know she saw something horrible, something I envision in my daughter's death? Or will I be too aloof, not wanting to hear any more from Noelle about stories of death? One tear falls. Noelle notices my tear before I can wipe the track away without her seeing it. What's going to happen now? Will this scare her? Repulse her?

She smiles! Oh, my holy God! She smiles and turns her head at an angle and nods slightly as if to say 'Thank you and it's ok'. I don't wipe the tear. She's not wiping hers either. Her crying is not the same type of tears that burst out of her in our first few sessions but are tears that seem appropriate to honor those who died and those who went through the tragedy with her.

"You ok?" Noelle asks.

"I'm ok. You?"

"I'm ok. Tired. Like drained. But ok."

"What do you do next?" I stay in the present, but Noelle shifts to past tense.

"I walked back to my car an' went to the grocery story on the other side of town. I had to drive 20 minutes to get to dis one, but at least it was away from the train."

I'm incredulous. "You went to the grocery store?"

"Yea, but, I got lost in tha store. I couldn't find ma' way back to the front after I had wandered around pickin' up stuff. I forgot where my list was an' couldn't remember anythin' on it." She pauses for a long while remembering then shifts to present tense again.

"I keep smellin' diesel fuel an' then realize **I stink of diesel fuel**. None wuz on me, but it must have perm'ated my clothin' like cig'rette smoke duz when you're 'round it. It makes me sick to my stomach. I start to panic an' I run out of the store an' get in my car, but I don't know where to go. If I go back home I'll see the wreck, I'll smell the fuel. I may not be able to git back to my house cuz of the 'mergency 'quipment. So I call ma friend, Robin. I met her in one of my college classes."

She shifts to past tense again. "I was goin' to Harford Community College at the time an' knew a few people. I was dere for a semester when dis happened. She heard me sobbin' on the phone an' tole me to come to her house an' I did. She lived with her parents an' they had the TV on watchin' the news, breakin' story. I tole them what had happened an' they didn't believe me at first."

I'm very aware she's shifting in and out of past and present. She's living part of it and relating the other part. "How did you know they didn't believe you?"

"I can tell. They kep' pumpin' me for information. When I tole them what I saw dey kep' sayin' the news didn't say that or this. It was true, the news reporters weren't dere when it happened an' then it wuz chaos. Dey kep' lookin' at me as if I wuz makin' up my story to git sympathy or somethin'. After a week or 10 days, the news stories got most of the information right an' dey knew I wuz tellin' the truth, so I lef'."

"Why did you leave?"

"Didn't trus' dem anymore cuz dey didn't trus' me."

"Where did you go?"

"I went back to my place, but everthin' had changed. The trains wuz gone, but it still smelled like fuel for a long time. I went back to school, but I couldn't concentrate After the semester, I dropped. I went to secretarial school an' got my AA degree there."

"And your hair?"

"Oh, yea. Afta' the wreck, all ma hair fell out. Took 'bout three weeks, but I wuz pretty bald so I got a wig at Kmart."

"Were you concerned? Did you see a doctor?"

"Yea, I saw one of dem dermatology guys. He said it wuz the stress of seein' the wreck. He gave me some kinda ointment an' I had to put it on two times a day. Then about three months later, my hair started growing in, but it was white. I was only 18 so I put a rinse on it to be blond. The rinse doesn't last long an' I didn't have no money to go to a hair dresser every month, so I finally stopped."

We sit in silence for a long time.

Then abruptly she stands, wipes her face and announces, "Leeza, thanks for listenin', but I gotta go back to work."

"Are you ok to go back to work?"

"Sure, See ya'."

"See ya' in two weeks, Noelle."

Noelle
Thoughts about the Train Accident

I never thought I could tell dat story to Leeza. I didn't think I could get through it, but when I looked up an' saw her tear, I knew she was the one who could hear me tell the story an' maybe help. She b'lieved me, an' she could feel what I was feelin'. I don't know why I told her the story in the first place. I could have wifffheld it. I had enough death and pain to account for ma'problems in life. But, I impulsively sprung it on her and challenged her to ask me 'bout ma'hair. She seemed really moved by ma pain. I liked that. Sometimes shrinks sit an' look like puppets, no expression, an' then they ast stupid questions like, 'How did dat make you feel?' or they say stupid things wiff a stone cold face like. "Dat's interesting." I hate when dey do that! Dey don't give you no feedback.

I'm scared though. I'm feelin' closer to Leeza an' that's dangerous for her. She don't seem scared of me. I wonder why? She should be,... but she seems more inter'sted in helpin' me than protectin' herself. Dat's real stupid if ya ask me.

I went to see Doctor Retter an' he said he's glad I'm seein' Leeza. I shrugged like I don't care, cuz I don't want 'im to know I like her. He also changed my medications. Less Klonopin, more antidepressant, an' some sleep med'cine I seen on television. Makes ma'sleep feel like la la land.

Lisa's Assessment of Noelle

I can go months without an extremely challenging, heart wrenching case and then I will get several in a row. This year I'm being challenged by Noelle, Bally, and Caz. Noelle is a client with a death-ridden past. Death has haunted her and doesn't seem to let up. I like her a lot, and she'd find that troublesome, I'm sure. She's showing her sense of humor more, and is opening up and freely sharing more. I get bits and pieces of her story, and I have to fill in the gaps. Whereas Caz tells me everything and in pretty logical order and detail. They are different in so many ways, but they share a common theme...they're both extremely injured people. People adapt in different ways to traumatic situations. I'm thinking about calling a friend for a consult or lunch or both, but, looking at my schedule, I don't see a lunch time available.

Noelle's been difficult to bond with and difficult to diagnose. Because of her experiencing many deaths and the subsequent fear that she causes the deaths, she has developed strong avoidant behaviors though it's an unusual presentation. Overall, she has social inhibition and feelings of inadequacy. However, this social inhibition and inadequacy are based on her belief that she kills people she cares about. She doesn't care about people enough to worry about criticism or disapproval. Also, Noelle avoids and is unwilling to get involved with others but not because she is uncertain of being liked. She is simply afraid **for** others. She shows restraint, is inhibited in new interpersonal situations, and views herself as socially inept. Her beliefs that create her symptoms could be a defense against harming another, or they may be a cover up for the fear that she may be abandoned again.

In her infantile belief system, she may have felt that her family members who died didn't believe she was worth living for. Is it safer for her to believe she had a hand in their deaths, than to believe that those she loved died as a way of rejecting or abandoning her? I've often looked at the way children interpret their world and marvel at how they will create intricate belief systems to overcome the feeling that they are somehow 'less than' other children. I remember one such woman I was working with whose grandmother ridiculed her from the time she was about two until 22 when she graduated from college and entered counseling with me for panic attacks and depression. The woman believed her grandmother was one of the most wonderful grandmothers in the world. When I asked her how she reconciled the disparity between the grandmother who belittled her, embarrassed her in front of her friends, and denigrated everything she did, with her belief that her grandmother was wonderful, the woman shrugged and said, "Grandmother knew what she was doing. She was mean to me to make me stronger. So that when the world treats me that way, I'll be tough and prepared." On a conscious level and maybe preconscious level, my client believed what she had indoctrinated herself to believe for 20 years. Yet her body was speaking to her in an entirely different way. Her body was saying, "You are no good like your grandmother said." Thus her depression, panic attacks, and suicidal thoughts were talking to my client about the reality of Grandmother's verbal harassment. The reality was her grandmother didn't treat her well and this treatment was not meant to toughen her up but to harm her. In some ways, I wonder if Noelle's experiencing a discrepancy, too. Only time and careful listening will tell. My first obligation to Noelle is to help her emotionally survive telling her stories and then I must survive to show her that her belief that she has the power to kill people is built on a misperception.

I'm heading to the store for food because my pantry is bare and I need a few things before I leave on my trip. My favorite store is four miles from my office and two miles from my home. I love the store, but I often run into clients there. Because I have been working as a counselor in the same location for many years, I've seen a number of my town's citizens as clients. A lot of people know what I do for a living, even if they have not been clients. And so I have a rule I share with clients when we begin working together. The rule is ...if we run into each other in a public place, I will not acknowledge my client unless she or he acknowledges me first. That way, if my client is with someone and doesn't want that person to know who I am, then she is free to act as if I am a total stranger. It has worked most of the time. There's always the client who will blurt to the whole world that she is in counseling with me, but clients are not bound to confidentiality like I am.

I select very healthy meals for the next few days (I'll be on a beach in a bathing suit!) and then head for the ice cream (Just a little bit). I hear a grating voice I instantly recognize and say to myself, "Why does it have to be HER... and she caught me not looking over the vegetables... but the **ice cream**". Jenna is a beautiful 50 year old woman who looks 35. She goes to the gym four times a week, jogs every morning, and only eats organic food. She always has the latest information on how to stay thin, young, and fit. She offers this information to whoever will listen and to many who tune her out. I saw her several years ago when she was going through a divorce. Her husband of 15 years said he couldn't stand her obsession with her body. She sought counseling to affirm she was right and he was a jerk. Actually, I met him when he came to a session with the two of us, and I liked him. His Asian ancestry had grounded him in reasonableness. He said to me, "I believe everything should be taken in moderation, including moderation. If I go the movies and eat a tub of popcorn once a year, it's not going to kill me, and I may be mentally healthy for indulging myself every now and then." Jenna rolled her eyes and shook her head. "I haven't had movie popcorn in 15 years. I won't put that stuff in my body!" I wanted to ask, "Why? What's wrong with movie popcorn every now and then (except it gets stuck in my teeth)?", but I resisted. I knew she would use that question as an opportunity to stand even higher on her soap box.

Now here she is standing next to me, exclaiming how **long** it had been (I was wishing it were longer!) and how **was** I, was I **still** counseling nut cases like her (Nope, she was one of a kind), remarking I **had** lost weight (I couldn't remember if I had since the last time she had seen me.) and tsk, tsk about the **pint** of Cookie Dough ice cream I had in my hand. (Jenna has a penchant for emphasizing one word in each sentence as she speaks.) I decided to follow her penchant. I lied. I said it was for my **mother** who is now 75 and **loves** her ice cream. (I can't believe I lied and I can't believe I am talking like this, ...but it's fun.) I'd like to have said, "Yes, I like to indulge my sweet tooth every now and then. You should try it sometime." But, I didn't. Instead, I blamed my poor defenseless mother. I keep trying to back up and excuse myself, but she keeps talking about **preservatives,** seaweed, and the latest **fabulous** vitamins. I place the ice cream next to the fresh, organic spinach I'm buying for a salad, but she doesn't notice the spinach or the tomatoes or the yogurt, only the ice cream. I try backing away and she moves closer. Finally, I've had enough. I open the ice cream freezer nonchalantly, the door hits her arm and she jumps away as if even touching the freezer may put pounds on her. I grab three more pints, smile, and make my get away. She didn't miss a beat. She turns to the lady who's standing next to my cart and begins a conversation with her about **organic** ice cream being a misnomer. The woman gives me a "Please help me!" look, but I can't rescue anyone right now, except myself. I give the poor defenseless woman a look that says, "You're on your own."

I drive home with more ice cream than I wanted to purchase (but pleased none the less). Forget about Jenna. I can't get Noelle out of my head. I realize Noelle presented a new death story that has possibly created extreme trauma symptoms for her. That may account for some of her recent increased anxiety and depression. I wonder if she knows she has Posttraumatic Stress Disorder symptoms and what it means for her. I wonder if she thinks she killed those people on the train or if it has dawned on her that she didn't even know them, let alone loved them.

A tiredness that's more than just physical overwhelms me. I need a break from the pain of the world. My usual diversion is either reading or good television. Tonight the program *24* is on and I'm an avid watcher. One would think after hearing painful stories all day, the last thing I would want to do is watch an intense program like *24*. But, I find it takes me away from my real world and transports me for 60 minutes into another world. This week's show involves Jack in the midst of another one of his impossible situations. He always has one or two people who will come through for him and upload information to his phone or other portable device. As the camera pans to reveal the Counter Terrorism Unit staff, I gasp. There she is...Noelle's look-a-like, Chloe. They have the same scowl, the same set of the mouth, similar body style, and same hair. The only differences are Noelle's hair is white and short and Chloe's is brownish and longer, Noelle's eyes are bigger and lighter, but both are set in a perpetual frown, all you can see are their eyebrows and a straight line for a mouth. I've been trying to figure out who Noelle reminds me of, and here she is, her look-a-like staring fiercely and defiantly at the latest person who tells her to not do something or other. And of course she disobeys them, for Jack! I wondered out loud if Noelle has ever seen the program. Well, at least that mystery is solved. It had been bugging me for weeks. Ahhh, I can sleep, now. The show *24* (and the cookie dough ice cream) did their jobs.

Lisa's Consultation Vacation

My two friends, Maggie and Milly have been packing and unpacking for weeks. I don't have time. I just throw everything I think I need into two bags the night before. I'm sure they'll have whatever I forgot, and if not, then I'll buy what I need while I'm there. Maggie and Milly are therapists, too. We consult with each other and support each other when we feel we're too close to a case and lose objectivity. Perhaps I need to share my feelings about Caz and missing the trial. I could also use their input on Noelle and Bally. They seldom mince words and will surely set me straight if I need it. I hate to ask them to use their skills while on vacation, but I would do the same for them.

The first day on the beach is too intense for my untanned body so I rent a cabana for the day. Maggie is swimming and Milly joins in a beach volleyball game and with each smack of the ball she is looking more sand burned. I'm reading a Janet Evanovich novel and find myself laughing out loud, forgetting others can hear me. I put my book down to stretch, just in time to see Maggie fly by in a parasail. Maggie is squealing with delight.

We call it a day and return to our timeshare. When I step in the shower I realize, despite the cabana and # 45 sunscreen, I still got sunburned a little. I promise myself to be more careful. My dad had several skin cancer operations before he died because he worshipped the sun. He died of a heart attack though, not the cancer. Maggie and Milly are very red, but both soothe their pain with an aloe-based product and declare the sunburn was worth it. They had a blast. We made reservations for a dinner on the beach.

The timeshare has a wonderful gourmet casual restaurant right on the beach, and the tables are spread out for privacy. I want or need to talk about Caz, but I don't want to bring up business on vacation so I sit listening to the steel band and remind myself I'm several hundred miles away from home and I can relax. Maggie nudges me. "Hey, gal, what's up? You've been quiet all day, with your nose in a book. Are you ok?"

It's wonderful being with friends who are so healthy that they don't assume you're angry because you are uncharacteristically quiet. I'm grateful for her question. "I have a couple of very difficult client situations right now and they're going through a lot while I'm gone. I can't seem to get them out of my mind."

It's Milly's turn. "You always have several clients who are in crisis. How are these different?"

"That's just it. I don't know why they are hanging in my mind. Maybe it's because they've had such rough lives, so many horrible things have happened to them. I don't know how they survived. Just before I left, one had a major breakthrough and I saw him change right in front of my eyes. He is almost 30, but he looks like a little boy in a man's body. During the breakthrough his countenance changed, and he now looks more like a man. He has a long way to go in therapy, but he definitely shifted psychologically."

Maggie looks pensive. "So what? You've had clients change quickly before. The moment is magical, but what's different about this guy?" Milly has leaned in to hear my answer. "I don't know what to say." I take a long pause, a very long pause. Both women hang in there with the silence. They're such good therapists, they're giving me the space I need and somehow that's making it easy and yet difficult because I want to say something brilliant. Nothing emerges. I sigh and lean back against my chair. I feel tears in my eyes, but I don't know why. They're still quiet. They probably can see I'm working on something. I keep asking myself, what are the tears about?

Finally, Milly asks what I was asking myself, "What are the tears telling you?"

"I know there's something very deep I'm feeling about the client and his trials, but I can't put my finger on it."

Milly gentle prods a little further. "What's the one word that comes to mind when you think of this client."

"That's easy. There are two....loss and abandonment."

Both Maggie and Milly look at each other knowingly.

"What !?! What !?!" I say a little too loudly and the couple at the next table turns to look.

Maggie tries this time. "Lisa, what are the words you think of when you think of Grace's death?"

Wham. Right upside the head and I needed it. Maggie and Milly look surprised when I smile. "Of course that's it. Grace's death was the worse time in my life. I wasn't sure I was going to make it through the days and nights that first year. I felt the loss deeply and will never stop grieving, but it was the feeling that she abandoned me that hurt the most. We were 'the girls' in the family, and then all of a sudden we were not 'the girls' I was the only 'girl'. I felt sadness and anger and still do. My client's mother walked away one day and didn't return. He just found out she died. He has often said the words 'abandoned' and 'loss'. Those words have really resonated with me, and now I know why. I believe he can feel my deep empathy because of what I've been through. However, he has much more going on, abuse, rejection, several diagnoses. And while I'm gone, he's facing one of the most important moments of his adult life. I feel I have 'abandoned' him. Is he feeling a sense of loss because I'm gone? Does he blame me for having abandoned him in his hour of trial?"

I feel better. I know what the issue is for me. I feel like a mother to him, and I've abandoned him. Of course it's not true, but the feelings are the same, and they were haunting me. I order a glass of wine. I'm on vacation.

Maggie feels the need to check in with me. "Lisa, you know you could have wasted your entire vacation feeling crappy about having left this man to fend for himself. We all have these clients that pick at our scabs." Milly whines, "Yuk! Couldn't you come up with a different metaphor!" The laughter at our table attracted some more stares and smiles.

Maggie gets serious again, "You have been through a lot in last few years, and you've managed fairly well, but you still seem to be, let me see...how should I say this, vulnerable and maybe hurt by God?

"Yeah, I'm still a little angry at the big guy. Oh my gosh! I feel abandoned by God!"

Maggie smiles, "You are just filled with insight tonight. I didn't see that one coming at all. Before your daughter died, you seemed spiritually centered, but since then, you seem to go through the motions of being a religious person, but your joy of spirit has been diminished. Am I at all on track?"

The tears start again. "Yes, I feel anger and resentment that I'm all alone, abandoned by the One I trusted in the most. My problem is I don't feel open enough to connect with God. And maybe, I'm too irritated at him. If God wants to connect with me then he or she is going to have to work a little harder. I pray and nothing seems to come through from the spirit side."

I look out over the crystal clear aqua water and the sunset that has turned the sky pink and yellow and I know this is going to be a vacation I will forever remember. For the rest of the trip, I forget about everything back home. Noelle is struggling with her death issues, Bally is struggling with her alcoholism and family of origin problems, and Caz is testifying before the world about his abuse. They will all need me when I return to work. Therefore, I need to nurture myself so I'm a relaxed and healthy person next week. I also left each of them the name of someone I trust in case they need to see someone before I return.

The food continues to be delicious and delights us each night, and the company of two dear friends allows me to regress to being a teenager. We laugh until we cry, play games, walk on the beach, and fantasize about who would find the man of their dreams first. It's silly and fun, and I don't want to return home, yet. Neither do they. On the last day, we make a pact that next year we are going away for two weeks. I feel relaxed. I never want to lose this vacation feeling.

Chapter Seven
Transference

Herman (1992) suggests that if early trauma is repeated in adult life, it erodes the structure of an already formed personality. If, however, repeated trauma occurs in childhood, the trauma forms and deforms the personality.

Caz
The Walk-Through

The walk-through of Belle's house was really strange for me. I was surprised at how calm I felt. I expected I'd have a lot of anxiety. I had been practicing the relaxation exercises Lisa taught me, but I really didn't think they would work well when I went to Belle's house or when I was testifying. I believed the experiences would overpower my ability to relax. I guess this counseling stuff really does work. I felt different, like I was seeing the rooms from an unusual perspective. I could see the faces of the other boys who are now men, but are still boys in my mind. I could smell Belle's cooking. I could hear the laughter, but it seemed like I was watching a movie not reliving it. I think the best thing that has come out of the walk-through is my confidence has increased. The worse thing is I felt the love and caring Belle showered on me, and I miss it. No one in my life has treated me like she did. I long to see her smiling face and have her ruffle my hair as she hands me a cookie. I'm embarrassed to say I even have fantasies sometimes about Lisa being my mom and baking me cookies and kissing my cheek.

I could tell my Dad was relieved that there were no flashbacks. He didn't tell me he was proud of me, but I could sense from his expression that he was. I wonder how he will feel when I'm testifying, and he hears all the sordid details.

Scheduling a session with Lisa immediately after the walk-through was a good choice. It grounded me after re-experiencing the memories of the house. I wonder what magic happens in counseling that helps me get stronger and more confident just by talking. Lisa said I've been growing up. I'm no longer the 10 year old boy who was injured. I had a birthday this week. I'm now a 29 year old man who is still injured but stronger. I'm now "going-on-30". Time to act like a man even though I don't feel like one. I'm still scared, uncomfortable in my skin, and too sensitive. I just want this testifying crap over.

This week Lisa's been on vacation and so I didn't have a session. When she returns, I'll be able to tell her about another postponement of the trial. This means she'll be able to be at the trial with me after all. I've come to rely on her for support, and I couldn't imagine what testifying would be like without seeing her in the courtroom. Am I too dependent on her? I feel anxious just thinking about not having her in my life.

Post Vacation Reconnection

Driving up my street and seeing my house coming into view after vacation is always strange for me. I get a weird sensation that the house disappeared while I was gone and then reappeared just before I turned the corner. I remember taking a philosophy class in college and the question the teacher posed was "If a tree falls in the forest and no one is around to hear it fall, does it make a sound?" We debated that for an hour, and of course there's no answer, but sometimes, I wonder when I'm away, if everything stays the same as when I'm home or do things pop in and out of existence?

I also wonder why I think about this stuff and whether anyone else ponders questions they were asked in college many years before. I guess I've always been a philosopher at heart. Either that or I'm warped.

I pick up my messages, and find out the trial had been "continued" again. Caz, of course, is delighted, this time. I'm glad Mother Justice has paired up with Mother Time, and the postponement is going to work out for Caz. I have an appointment to see him tomorrow. We were going to debrief his court experience. But now we can go over his testimony. While I was gone, he saw the D.A. again to review the questions that would be asked. I hope the D.A. also primed Caz again for the cross examination. I'm more concerned about how he will do under the defense attorney's cross. That's the toughest time in court for a witness.

Caz looks a bit worried as he enters the room. He's not smiling, and he's chewing his lower lip. I ask how he's doing, and he manages a little smile and replies, "I'm ok. I'm scared, but I'm ok." He takes many minutes telling me all the things he did while I was gone. He ends with, "I have been praying a lot."

"What have you been praying for?" I ask.

"At first, I was praying Belle would take a plea bargain and none of us would have to testify. When that didn't happen, I started praying for your safe return" "Thanks. Let's talk about the trial. How do you want to appear on the stand?"

"I want to be confident, clear, and in control of my emotions. I guess that's a lot to ask."

"I don't think so. How confident do you feel right now?"

Caz' lower lip is trembling a bit. He tries to stop it by biting down on it and it starts to bleed. He grabs a tissue and holds it to the cut. He smiles slowly and sheepishly.

"I guess I don't want to do that next week."

I smile and nod. Caz continues, "I feel confident sometimes and not confident at others."

"What about your testimony makes you feel confident?"

"I feel confident I can answer the questions of the D.A. He and I met while you were on vacation, and his questions are pretty straight forward."

"What makes you feel not confident?" I'm guessing it's the cross examination, but I can be wrong.

"I am scared of the defense attorney, Mr. Young. He's suppose to be a shark and goes for the throat. I have no way to prepare for Mr. Young's questions. I really need to be calm. I'm also afraid I could experience flashbacks."

"If you had a flashback, would that be awful?"

"I don't know. I would be embarrassed, I guess. And, I may not do the job the D.A. wants. I would feel I had let him down."

"If you have a flashback on the stand, would it detract from your testimony or give credence to your testimony that there was abuse?"

Caz looks intrigued. "I'm not sure. I guess it would be normal, and it might even help the prosecution's case. I never saw it that way. The prosecutor just keeps saying I need to tell the truth in my own way, to be real and genuine. If I have a flashback, that would be real. I might be embarrassed, but it would be a result of the abuse." He shrugs like 'so what?'

"You really processed that information well Caz. Can I ask you another question or do you need some more time on the fear of flashbacks?"

"No, I'm okay, go ahead."

"I can understand you are concerned about being a good witness for the prosecution, but you're not the only one to testify, right?"

"That's true."

"There are about 20 other men and boys who are going to tell their stories, right?"

"That's true. There are 19 in addition to me."

"And you are one part of this orchestrated testimony by the prosecution."

"Yes."

"Caz, are you taking too much responsibility on your shoulders?"

"Probably. I'm always trying to do what's right, but I fail more than I succeed, so I'm worried I'll let him down. I guess I can do my best, and let the chips fall." Caz pauses and seems to be done with that, too. This is going way too quickly. Is he really processing this information quickly or is he trying to please me? Or am I that good, now that I'm relaxed? I wish! No, I think Caz is really working hard and perhaps has been working for the week I was gone. Good for him.

"What else bothers you?" I ask.

"I'm going to be giving gruesome details, and my dad and brother will hear this for the first time. I'm scared I'll gross them out."

"You're caring about how they will experience your testimony and how it will affect their view of you?"

"Yes! That's it. I wonder if they will look at me differently after I testify. They know generally what happened, but they haven't heard the details. Once they hear the horror I lived through, I wonder whether they will be affected by the information. They may feel sorry for me and treat me differently after I testify."

"I wonder what you could do to assuage their reaction."

"What do you mean?"

"Well, would there be a way to prepare them for your testimony?"

"You mean by telling them what they're going to hear before the trial?"

"That's one possibility. Do you think it would help?"

"I don't know." Long pause while Caz considers this. "I would have to go through the story twice then, once with them and again at the trial."

"That's true. But, it would also be a practice run for you. What would be better for you? To only have to tell the story once or to tell it twice and have your dad and brother know in advance what your testimony will be?"

"I'm not sure. Have to think about that one, 'cause Rom and Dad would have to hear the story twice too."

"What do you think you should do about this dilemma?"

"Dunno."

"Would it help to talk with them about this?"

"Probably. Maybe they don't want to be prepared."

We are both quiet for a minute. Caz looks pensive as he picks at one of his nails. I wonder what I would do in his place. Caz looks up and starts to say something and then puts his head down again. I remain quiet, giving him space to process.

"I want to thank you for hanging in there with me."

"You're welcome." I reply.

"I know this is your job, but I think you have gone the distance with me."

"Thanks, Caz. I'm glad you're feeling supported."

"Well, I think I better get going. I will talk with Dad and Rom and let them know what we talked about and let them decide whether they want to hear the testimony before we get to trial."

"Be good to yourself over the next few of days. I'll see you at the courthouse."

"Ok."

Caz Prepares to Testify

Should I tell Dad and Rom the details of the abuse they're going to hear in court? I wasn't going to, but after talking to Lisa, I understand I'm not the only one who's going to be affected by the testimony. I already know the details. I just have to say them in court out loud. But, Dad and Rom could be caught off guard by the content of my testimony.

On the way home in the car, I talk with Dad about my conversation with Lisa. Dad listens, and then he gulps really did a gulp thing and his eyes even bulged a bit. He said he couldn't speak for Rom, but he would rather know what to expect. I'm surprised. Dad doesn't usually want to talk about things that cause pain. He didn't want to talk to Rom and me after Mom left. He even shut us down a couple of times when we were crying about Mom's leaving. But, now he's saying he **wants** to hear my testimony, **twice**? We talk generally about the trial as we drive, but we don't get into specifics about my testimony. I wonder what Rom will choose? It's possible Dad will want to know and Rom won't. I am starting to dread this conversation. As we near home, I see Rom's car. He's home early. Shit, no time to prepare. I notice Dad's hands are shaking as he parks the car. Never dawned on me I'm not the only one who's scared.

After dinner, I broach the subject with Rom. He throws down his napkin and storms out without saying anything. Dad and I look at each other. I don't know what to say. Dad breaks the silence. "How bad is it, Caz?"

"It is pretty awful, Dad."

"I need to hear a bit of it and then I'll decide if I want to hear more."

"Fair enough. That's a good idea."

I tell Dad the first part of the story where Belle first fondled me when I was putting on my bathing suit. Dad remains quiet. Out of respect, I ask him if he wants me to continue. I would never have thought about asking permission before, but I learned this skill from watching Lisa do this with me. Dad says for me to continue. I tell him about when Belle had me insert my fingers in her, and I wiggled them. Dad has a catch in his voice, but he tells me to continue. I tell him about the first time Belle had sex with me when I was 12. Dad has tears rolling down his face and says, "You were only 12?" I nod. He shakes his head. I tell him about how Belle forced us boys to have sex with each other. Dad's getting angry. His face is the color of a tomato. He pounds the table with his fist and grabs me and holds me while he cries. I'm sobbing, too. Dad keeps petting my head as if I were a dog. When we part, we both blow our noses, and then we hear Rom just outside the door to the kitchen. Rom is screaming and pounding his fist on the wall. He kicks the wall and keeps saying, "That bitch, that bitch!" Dad and I get up and go to Rom and we all hold each other and cry. I feel sorry for us all. I was abused, but my family's suffering, too.

The Trial

Today Caz will testify in court against Belle. I cleared my calendar which means I will have to work longer hours on the other four days this week. My stomach is a little queasy. I wonder how Caz is doing. On my way to the courthouse, I pass an elementary school and when I stop at a school crossing and watch the children entering their school building. Some of the children appear to be about six years old, and I imagine how their lives would be different if their mothers were to abandon them right now. There are some children who look to be about nine and a few who look older, possibly 11 or 12. I keep looking at the boys trying to picture them being asked to perform sexual acts on a 45 year old woman. I just can't imagine what it was like for Caz and the rest of Belle's victims. Then, it hits me. Some of these children **are** being abused. The statistics are staggering. By the time a girl turns 18 there is a one in three chance she will have been molested in some way, probably by someone she knows. By the time a boy turns 18, there is a one in seven chance he will have been molested (Bass & Davis, 1988; Russell, 1986).

There are 50 kids milling around so the statistics say between five and twelve of these children are currently being abused. Right now! No one stands out. There's no sign on them identifying who they are. Some of them will never get the help they need. One of them may be the Caz in my future caseload. Which one? I shudder and drive on.

The courthouse is new. I've been in the old one for custody cases, but this is my first time in the new courthouse. Caz will forever be engraved in my conscious as the client who introduced me to the large white building with the fountain outside. Parking's a nightmare. New building, old parking garage. Now I need to find the courtroom. After going through security I have no trouble finding the courtroom. The hall is packed with frightened looking men and boys and their families. The press is being cordoned off from the witnesses, thank God. They are calling out to the men and boys asking for comments. Everyone is ignoring them. Again, thank God.

The press becomes loud and noisy when Belle and her attorney arrive. They try to avoid the press and make their way across the highly polished marble floor. Belle is smaller than I thought she would be. Seeing her through Caz' eyes, I felt her immense negative power. I expected her to be larger than life. She's short and she weighs no more than 120 pounds. She used to be a redhead, but the gray is overtaking the red. She's dressed in a suit and is wearing a bit too much makeup. She looks incensed and combative, like she's trying to convince everyone she's innocent and she's going to prove it. She passes close to me, I sense the incensed/combative façade is just that, a façade. She's terrified. She could spend the rest of her life in jail. I feel sad for her and at the same time irate enough to think. "Good, let her go to jail and possibly be molested herself." What an awful thought! I feel embarrassed. I'm human.

Caz' six foot six frame stands out in the crowd, and when he spots me, he waves his arms above his head and I acknowledge him and make my way over to where he and his family are standing. Caz lets me know he'll be held in a waiting room until it's his turn to testify. He gives me a tag, which allows me to go into the courtroom. Caz says he'd like to have one person with him at all times for support. Wow, he's telling us what he needs. That's quite a shift. Stewart, Rom, and I will be rotating the Caz-sitting duty. I wonder if Caz shared the abuse details with Stewart and Rom. As if reading my mind, Caz leans over and whispers, "I've told them about my testimony." I sense some family camaraderie. Rom and Stewart are going to be in the courtroom first. I will sit with Caz. At the first break, we will rotate. Caz brought a book to read and a deck of cards. He's thought through this day and has planned the details. Pastor Craig joins us, and Caz gives him his tag. Pastor Craig looks somber as he hugs each of them and shakes hands with me. An announcement says the trial will begin in five minutes. Pastor Craig takes charge and says, "Let us pray." Pastor Craig begins to pray for justice, wisdom, and truth. The entire hallway has become quiet and I steal a peek out of the corner of my eye to see what's going on. The other victims and family members, most of them are from Craig's church, are praying too. Everyone is listening to Craig's petition. Until that moment, I had not realized how much Belle's behavior had impacted the church's congregation.

Craig stays with Caz and me for awhile before he has to 'visit' other members of his congregation who are also waiting to testify. Caz and I do the small talk thing because there's no privacy. He asks more about my vacation and tells me a funny story about his dog. We only have to wait two hours before Caz is called. I enter the courtroom and Craig catches up with me. Rom and Stewart are already in their seats. Caz grabs my hand and squeezes it just before he walks down the aisle. This is the moment Caz has been dreading and preparing for.

Caz is sworn in, and the prosecutor begins asking the traditional identifying information. Caz looks calm. Then comes the questions about how he met Belle, when he was invited into her home, what he experienced at first. The prosecutor asks Caz to tell his story of the abuse. An open-ended question I thought would scare Caz, doesn't. He calmly launches into the story he told me months ago. The prosecutor interrupts him several times to clarify a point, but mostly this was Caz' story to tell, and the court allows him to continue. The defense attorney objects once or twice when the prosecutor asks a question that seemed reasonable to me but was somehow offensive to the defense. After an hour, Caz stops talking. He's a cucumber! So cool and matter-of-fact. Now the tough part starts. The defense attorney, dressed in an expensive navy blue pinstriped suit with a red striped tie, asks Caz whether he was a willing participant – Yes or No. Caz answered 'yes' and tried to say a 'but'. However, the defense attorney whines "Your Honor please instruct the witness to answer "Yes or No". Caz says, "Yes". The next question is whether Caz was responsible for abusing teenage girls. Caz says, "No!"

The prosecutor objects, but the doubt is placed in the jurors' minds. Caz is shaking slightly and he remembers to use his water as a diversion. The questions come fast now.

Do you love Belle? Caz, "No".

Did you love Belle? Caz, "Yes".

Did you enjoy going to Belle's house? Caz, "Yes".

Don't you suffer from mental disorders and are on psychotropic medication that keeps you from being psychotic? Caz, "Partially correct." (Good for you Caz!)

The defense attorney whines again, "Your Honor, please direct the witness to answer 'yes' or 'no'." The judge leans over to Caz and says, "If he asks you a question that requires a yes or no then please answer yes or no."

The defense attorney asks again, "Do you have a diagnosed mental disorder?" z, "Yes."

"Do you take medication for this disorder?"

"Yes".

"Have you ever been psychotic?"

"No."

"You haven't? Are you sure?"

"Yes."

"Do you know the penalty for perjury?"

"No." The courtroom laughs and the judge bangs his gavel.

"Don't you feel the experience you had at Belle's house was a wonderful introduction to sex?"

Caz, "Yes, at first." (He snuck in the 'at first'. Good for him.)

"Aren't you making up the abuse in hopes of bringing a civil suit?"

An objection from the prosecutor. The question was withdrawn.

The prosecutor redirects, and Caz is able to explain he loved Belle because she was a mother-figure to him, he loved going to her house to play with the other children, and at first he thought all children were introduced to sex the way Belle did. He didn't have a mother, so he didn't know what she was doing was wrong. He realized later she was abusing him. He also explained that as a result of the abuse, he suffers depression, anxiety, and posttraumatic stress disorder. Because of the disorders, he takes medication. The flashbacks and dreams are awful and he has been on several potent medications to help him sleep and to be less anxious. However, he has never been psychotic.

Caz is on the witness stand for over two hours. He looks a little shaky at times but for the most part, he's a great witness. When he's excused he takes a deep breath and looks right at Belle. At first he looks angry, but then he softens to sadness when he gets up to leave. As he leaves the stand, his eyes look at Belle again and then they freeze on a woman behind her. He keeps walking, but he can't take his eyes off the women directly behind Belle. Rom, Stewart, Craig, and I walk out with him. We are congratulating him, but he doesn't seem to take notice of our celebration. He then asks to see me alone. I walk away a few feet and Caz says, "I believe the woman sitting behind Belle is one of the other women who abused me."

"Are you sure?" I ask.

"I can't be sure. It was over 15 years ago and she's aged, but I'm pretty sure. What should I do?"

"I don't know." I reply. "Perhaps talk to the detectives who are investigating?"

"Yea, I can do that, but I don't want to falsely accuse someone."

"Tell the detectives that too."

"Ok." Caz replies.

I'm concerned about him. He looks tired and ready to cry. "Are you ok, Caz?"

"I'm ok. I'm glad it is over. I just wish I hadn't seen that woman."

Pastor Craig says 'goodbye' to Caz with a hug and goes back in the courtroom to show support for the other victims from his church who are testifying. Stewart and Rom take Caz by each arm and lead him out of the courthouse through a back entrance to avoid the press. I decide to go back into the courtroom with Craig.

The next three witnesses basically confirm what Caz has already told the court.

They were a little younger than Caz but have similar stories. Both of them talk about having PTSD and depression. Two never sought counseling because of embarrassment, but both have alcohol and drug problems and are in NA and AA.

The other man had been in counseling and found it helpful.

Court is recessed for the day, and I get up to leave. The dynamic duo detectives spot me and catch me before I could exit the building. They tell me Caz and one other man were the prosecution's best witnesses because they both experienced all the abuse Belle dished out. I want to reply sarcastically "Lucky him." The detectives further comment that Caz held up well on the stand, and they were pleased with his testimony. I tell the detectives I am glad to hear they are pleased. They ask if I would pass the compliment on to Caz. I reply I think he would like to hear it directly from them. They nod. I hesitate and then decide to take a risk. "Detectives, you may want to speak to Caz directly for another reason." They look puzzled, but then the detectives look at each other and nod in unison. There's a lot of nodding going on in this case. I wonder if it's catching. They each hand me their cards even though I already have them and say, "If you see him first, have him call us."

"Thanks." is all I can get out.

The drive home is foggy. I keep replaying the various testimony I heard. I wonder how Caz feels. I'll know in a few days when I see him again. I'd love to process what I saw, felt, experienced today with a colleague, but I can't. Everyone's working with clients. I'm too tired anyway, and I have a long day tomorrow. A hot bath and cup of Chamomile tea, a good book, and bed.

Bally Meets Little

The plane trip is long but easy, and I arrive earlier than Carly. I'm supposed to wait for her and then we'll rent a car to drive to Atlee's. I study the map and pace as I wait for her plane to arrive. Finally, I see her entering the baggage area and wave, she smiles, waves back, and approaches me for a hug. Gosh, I haven't seen her in several years. She is thinner and older. I'm the same weight, but I have the scars. Carly has tears in her eyes as she hugs me. She stands back and holds my arms looking at my face. Then she touches my scars. I recoil. Carly says, "Bally, the scars aren't as bad as you think. In a year they'll be faded and a little makeup will cover them. The way you described them, I thought you would look like Frankenstein's monster! You are still very beautiful."

How does she always know exactly the right thing to say? It's a gift she has. I usually say the worse things. I need to take a page out of Carly's book. Her luggage arrives, we claim our rental car, and take off for Atlee's. I drive. Carly navigates. We take a few wrong turns but find our way to Atlee's small cottage deep in the woods with a stream running down the right side of the house and around back. A perfect place to hide from the world, among huge pine trees.

Atlee must have heard our car approaching the house on the crusher run driveway. He opens the front door and jaunts to the car. "Hi, ladies, welcome to the rustic west." Smiles and hugs belie the trepidation I feel, and I suppose Carly and Atlee feel, too. Atlee helps us with our luggage and shows us to our bedroom on the second floor. I haven't slept in the same room with my sister since I was 16. This feels surreal and, as Lisa says, regressive. After unpacking, we head downstairs where Atlee's offering us iced tea and is talking about dinner plans. I wonder if the iced tea is a sign he knows both Carly and I have a 'wee' bit of a problem with alcohol. How's that for denial. **Carly** has a wee bit of a problem. I'm a ragin' alcoholic.

His house is a log cabin cape cod. There are three bedrooms, two up and the master is on the first floor. That one is Atlee's. The other bedroom upstairs belongs to his son, and I still cannot remember his name. I'm hoping someone mentions the child so I won't embarrass myself. He's not home and I can't even say, "Hey, where's _____?" So I remain silent and comment on his back woods taste in decorating, which I never thought I'd like. But, sitting on a couch in front of a fire, I feel warm and comfortable and at home. Perhaps I will convert from stylish, uptown, white leather and oriental carpets to bearskin rugs and wrought iron end tables with glass tops. The quiet is deafening, I have to break the ice. "Atlee, how did you decide to move to Seattle and live in the woods?"

"I've always wanted to hide from the world, and this seemed like a good idea. I moved several years ago. He shrugs. I work out of my house, Danny is secure and happy, and the cost of living is low. The only draw back, as you probably have noticed, is I have to drive 10 miles to the closest town, grocery store, post office, etc. I have to plan ahead, especially in the winter when a snowstorm can isolate us here in a flash. But, I have plenty of wood, a mountain stream, and as long as I stock up on groceries, we can survive a week without getting scurvy."

"Does Danny like it?" asks Carly. Thank God she mentioned Danny's name!

"He's 12 now, and he doesn't remember the Chicago area very much. He likes that I'm home more, and he has great friends. In fact he and two friends are out somewhere in the woods right now."

"Doesn't that frighten you?"

"At first it did. When he turned nine, he wanted to join the other kids in what they call "a forage." They track animals and shoot pictures, they build small dams, climb trees. You know, boy stuff. The only thing I worry about are the cats and bears." He says nonchalantly.

"Holy crap, Atlee! That sounds like a lot to worry about."

"Tell you the truth, I worried for awhile, and then a friend of mine from Chicago wrote one of those Christmas letters. And in it she wrote about how her daughter was approached by a man in the parking lot of a mall, asking her to help find his cat. She didn't fall for his act, but another kid did and that kid was raped and left by the road. She also mentioned 'a nuisance break-in' to their condo, and I felt more and more secure here as I read the letter."

"But, how do you know your son is okay in the woods?" Carly looked as shocked as I felt.

"He has a cell phone and a rifle. He's a good shot, and I learned to trust him."

Carly shakes her head. "It's a whole 'nother world you're living in brother!"

"Took some getting used to, but I feel very safe and secure. One ring of that school bell on the post beside the front door and my neighbors would be here in minutes and with guns."

"Have you ever had a scare?"

"Nope. I see bears and other animals all the time. They leave us alone, and we leave them alone. The only thing we had to learn is how to manage our garbage."

"Why?"

"If the bears associate us with left over food, then they would be hanging around all the time, getting into our garbage cans. So we bury our garbage deep or we haul it out, depending on the season. By doing this, the bears don't associate this place with food."

Everyone is silent for a few minutes. I break the silence. "I admire you, Atlee."

"You do? Why? I've always been the outcast in our family. I was the only boy, the only child of our mother, the only child hated by our father. I was one screwed up kid and young adult. I just wanted to get on the next space shuttle and leave this planet. This place is my way of 'getting lost'."

"You've made a niche for yourself here. You're raising a son by yourself, and you've learned to survive, without the world."

"I wouldn't say without the world exactly. I'm a computer geek and I need the world to stay connected with computers so I can make a living. But, I have found a way to straighten out my insides. It took a long time to forget Dad and learn to love and trust myself. I did a lot of therapy when I lived in Elgin, Illinois."

That really took me back. The whole world seems to be seeing shrinks. "I can really relate. Except, I haven't learned to love and trust myself...yet!"

Carly looks at me and then Atlee as if trying to decide how much to share. "I love and trust myself, but I'm not happy. I have a great family and financial security. I like my job, but nothing seems to make me happy. I just exist."

Atlee and I both know what she's talking about. We nod in agreement.

Atlee breaks the silence. "We're all products of Dad's loin, but we had three different mothers. What a mess."

"Are you positive, Atlee? Carly and I are basing our belief on some pictures, but you said you had proof."

"I do have proof."

Carly is wiggling in her chair. "What kind of proof?"

"The best kind. Little lives in Seattle, and I've met with her several times. Sassy lives in Portland. I've seen her a couple of times when she's visiting Little."

I wish I had a picture of Carly's and my faces. We are both sitting forward in our seats with our mouths hanging open. "No shit!!!" was all I could say. Then Carly and I turn to look at each other. We never expected this, but now, we know why Atlee wanted us to come to Seattle and not to Carly's or my place. This really changes my plans for the weekend. I am going to see Little, if she'll agree. I can see Carly has the same resolve about Sassy.

My insides are shaking. "Do you think they'll see us?"

"They're both coming for lunch tomorrow. I took the liberty now that you both figured out our "little" family secret. I figured getting all this out in the open helped me, it might help you two. If you don't agree, then they're prepared to stay home."

"NO!" Both Carly and I shout. I continue, "I want, need, to see Little. I need answers." Carly is nodding.

"I thought you might. That's why I invited you here and I have to admit, I lied to get you here."

"You lied?" Carly is incredulous.

"Yeah, I didn't just start a new job. I'm self-employed. If I wanted to take off for a couple of days and fly east or south to your homes, no problem, but I knew as soon as you heard that Sassy and Little live here, you would have said, 'Why didn't we meet in Seattle, then?' "

"You're right. But, why didn't you tell us this on the phone? Couldn't you trust us?"

"The phone didn't seem to be the right place to break this to you."

We're all silent. Taking in this news is like seeing the planes flying into the World Trade Center. I can see it happening, but it doesn't make sense yet. "I feel like I'm living in a *60 Minutes* or *48 Hours* TV special." Both of them laugh. Carly takes a sip of tea.

Atlee goes outside and rings the school bell three times. He returns casually and heads for the kitchen. "Danny will be here in few minutes, I'm going to start dinner."

I pipe up "Let me take us out to dinner."

Atlee smiles. "Closest restaurant, that's any good, is over 15 miles away and there's no highway. Takes 30 minutes. We cook for ourselves here. I won't poison you, I promise."

Ten minutes later, Danny bursts through the back door. "Dad, I'm starved. We found the beaver dam again. They built 'nother half mile upstream. I think she's pregnant. Waddling a bit more than usual. What's for dinner? Did my aunts get here yet?" All this was said while taking off his boots, coat, gloves, hat, and putting down his rifle. Atlee nods his head toward the living room, and Danny turns to face us. A smile bursts across his face and he runs to hug both of us. What a wonderful young man! He chats with us while Atlee performs magic in the kitchen. Danny, Carly, and I tell each other all about our lives. Danny asks questions as if we live in Europe instead of the other side of the same country. He wants to know what the kids listen to, what new electronic devices we have that he doesn't. He doesn't seem defensive or jealous of our lives, just interested. We find out the last movie he saw on the big screen was the most recent Harry Potter flick. He had read all the books and many, many others of the same genre. He keeps asking his father if there's anything he can do to help him. Atlee always says "No." So Carly and I don't bother to ask.

Dinner is fantastic. Fresh trout with a sauce I could have drunk with a straw, stir-fried potatoes with fresh dill, and fresh asparagus. "Where did you learn to cook?" I ask. Atlee replies it was out of necessity, because they live far from civilization...and restaurants. Dessert was homemade chocolate éclairs, only he made them round instead of long. No wine on the table. Just water.

After dinner my eyes feel heavy. While it's only 9 p.m., my body clock says it's midnight. I excuse myself and go to bed. I can't take in one more piece of information. I'm exhausted, physically, emotionally, and cognitively.

I awake to the sounds of the forest, birds, and wind in the trees. Carly is still asleep. I don't know when she came to bed and what conversation I missed last night. I look out the window and see Atlee in a plaid shirt and jeans, collecting wood for the fireplace. How trite and yet so cool. What a beautiful place. I could stay sober here.

Before anyone gets up and uses up all the hot water, I jump in the shower. As the water falls on my face, I think "Today I will meet my biological mother. Today I will find the truth. It might be difficult to hear but at least I will know what really happened over 40 years ago." My insides feel jumbled like a tossed salad. What happened to the confident, maybe overconfident Bally who swooshes into business meetings with an air of determination? I have dealt with men and women who are wealthy, powerful, and influential and never had so much as a drop of inconvenient gastric juice. Now I'm facing my biological mother and a story I cannot even begin to imagine and I feel myself liquefying. I just want this over. Then I can spend the next 50 years in therapy sorting it all out. When I get back to our room, Carly's up. She looks like I feel. "Bally, maybe we're making a mistake by being here. Our mother is the one who raised us, right? Sassy and Little aren't our mothers, they're our aunts. Even if they bore us into the world, they never took care of us, fed us, bathed us, stayed up all night with us when we were sick. Our **mother** did that."

"I agree. But, there's more to this story. It's about our identity. We have a mother **and** a biological mother and a father who figures into this somehow. Look, Carly, I don't want to be in this position either, but I am, and I have to find out what happened."

"You're right, I'm just scared, that's all." She whines like a little girl.

"Me, too."

"You, Bally? You're scared?"

"Yeah, I'm apprehensive. I don't think I'm going to like the story they have to tell. Don't you wonder why they want to meet us, now, after all these years."

"Good point. I'll meet you downstairs. I'm going to take a shower."

"Ok."

No one's in the living room, dining area, or kitchen. Atlee is not in his room, the door is open, bed made. His truck is missing too. I guess he ran some errands. Sounds like errand running can take all morning based on what Atlee said last night about how far away everything is. I'm not sure I'd like having to drive 30 miles for a stick of butter. Yet, here…I feel quieter inside, relaxed. Is it because I'm away from work and in a place that looks like God enjoyed making? I look around the kitchen for something to eat and found a note. "Carly and Bally, I had a couple of chores to do, please eat whatever you want. There's raspberry Danish in the fridge as well as fruit, eggs, bacon, English muffins, and oatmeal. Help yourself. I'll be home by 11:30. S and L due to arrive at 12:30. Love, A."

I begin to make breakfast and Carly joins me, reads the note, and pops an English muffin into the toaster. "What are we going to do for the next two hours until Atlee gets home?"

"Dunno. You want to go for a drive or a walk?"

"You mean walk around looking for bears?"

"Good point."

"Hi." Danny appears in the doorway. "What's for breakfast?"

"Looks like anything you want."

Danny grabs an apple and begins boiling water for oatmeal. This kid makes good decisions. I would've opted for the Danish at his age. "You want to do some site seeing?"

Carly and I look at each other and shrug. "Sure." In unison.

"Want to see a beaver dam?"

Carly and I look at each other, again. "Sure." In unison again.

"Great! They are so cool."

After breakfast we dress in our most rugged clothes and head out through the woods. Danny points out lady slippers, an Indian pipe plant, and deer hoof prints. The light beams streak through the trees and the forest looks like a movie set. The trees are huge in diameter and in height. They block most of the sun except for the persistent sun beam that makes its way to a point on the forest floor. Danny's a superb guide. He suddenly stops and holds up his hand and motions for us to get down and be quiet. We obey.

I've never seen a beaver outside of a zoo. They're amazing in the wild. I can't take my eyes off of them. They keep busy all the time and never notice they're being watched. Swim, dive, push sticks around, grab some wood, swim, dive. The female emerges from the den and she does indeed look pregnant. I want to ask a question about how long a beaver is pregnant, but I know to ask the question may make the beaver aware of our presence. So I stifle my question and remind myself to stay in the here and now. Stop intellectualizing and just BE. Carly has tears in her eyes. I have no idea how long we lay on the forest floor watching them. I lose track of time, something I never do. This child, my nephew, is teaching me something I never learned – how to be in the world without analyzing it. Then something inside of me feels a longing like I lost something I'll never recover. I lost my childhood. I was forced by my father to act like an adult from the time I can remember. I kept telling Lisa I have very few memories, but right here, with my nephew on my left and my half sister on my right, watching beaver do what beaver do, I remember. My father criticized the way I dressed, ate, crossed my legs, wore my hair, kept my room, etc., etc. I was never allowed to be a kid, to roam the woods, color outside the lines, or watch animals for an hour. I had to account for my time. Not that he made me keep busy with chores (others did those), but I had to be productive, everything he deemed nonsense was a waste of time. I was trained by the age of 12 to be a business woman. I was never a kid. I was a little adult, and I was enraged, but I stuffed the feeling. I put others down, criticized their dress, work, behavior, and yet, I wasn't in control of myself. I was an organ grinder's monkey, but a very well-trained monkey. No wonder I'm a bitch. A successful, well-dressed, perfectionistic bitch who does not waste time. I am a work-a-holic. No wonder I drink. It's the only thing I do that doesn't make sense, is self-defeating, and is the one thing my father would disapprove of. I feel like I have chains wrapped around me. Will the upcoming meeting unchain me or make the chains tighter? Larger? Heavier?

Danny's motioning to me to quietly back away from the stream. I obey as if he were a much older person. He has a quiet assuredness about him that commands respect, but he does not demand it: we simply follow him because he's confident, knowledgeable, and happy. Atlee has created an atmosphere that stimulates his son's growth, not stifles it. Danny's flourishing. I, on the other hand, make lots of money and am withering. Carly is quiet. I wonder what she's thinking. The forest floor is clean of debris, no bottles or wrappers. And the trees! They are magnificent. They look like they will protect us. That's what a parent should do for their children, clear the debris and protect them so they can grow into who they're meant to be, not force them into a perfectly constructed topiary.

As we walk back, everyone is quiet, and yet, not uncomfortable. The silence seems right in this place. Danny smiles at me as we walk and then beckons us to leave the well-worn trail and walk through the forest. We walk for several minutes and then the trees stop, and there is a field of flowers, and then, Mt. Rainier in all her glory. The sky is robin's egg blue, the clouds are white, and the mountain looks pristine, like a coffee table book's picture. It takes my breath away. Carly speaks first, "Wow, I feel like I could walk across that field and right up the mountain side."

Danny nods. "Even though Mt. Rainier is many miles away, I feel I can touch it. Brings perspective, doesn't it?"

It's now my turn to feel tears in my eyes. For the last hour, I forgot all about the upcoming meeting, the fear, the questions. Everything in the world feels right, just as it should be.

We arrive back at the house at 11 which gives us time to freshen up, but I decide not to change into my more classy clothes. Last night I planned to "dress" to meet my biological mother, but I've changed my mind, and I stay in my jeans and sweater. Atlee arrives home with Sassy. She looks at me and catches her breath. "Oh, my! You look like Little did 30 years ago. You must be Bally."

"I am."

"And you're Carly?" She says turning to Carly. Carly nods. "I am your biological mother. I'm sure you have a lot of questions." Carly nods again. Sassy continues, "Little should be here soon. We'll explain everything then."

Danny interrupts the uncomfortable situation by asking if he could get everyone something to drink. We all place our orders with our 12 year old waiter, and he disappears into kitchen. Sassy goes to Carly and takes her hand like one would do to a small child. She guides her to the couch and indicates Carly should sit. Carly obeys. Then Sassy sits beside her and hugs her. Carly lets Sassy do this. Tears choke my throat. I turn away from the scene before I lose control and wait at the window for my mother. I don't have to wait long, a black car turns down the driveway, and a very attractive Filipino woman slides out of the car and walks to the door. Little is not little. She is tall, lanky, and self-assured. She reminds me of myself; the way she walks and holds herself is very like me. She does not seem nervous at all. Quite the opposite. She looks like she is headed for a purely business meeting. I open the door just as she knocks, and her startled reaction is the first sign that Little may have been on edge. That or...she is shocked to see how much I look like her. I don't know what to say, and she doesn't either, so I say "Hi, I'm Bally, you must be Little." That's it, girl, take the initiative.

"Yes, hi Bally. I haven't seen you since you were a baby."

Well, that exchange could have happened to anyone who hadn't seen each other in over 40 years. It was not an exchange one would expect to see between a biological mother and her daughter. How different the first exchange was between Sassy and Carly! I guess I'm a lot like my biomom. I go right for the intellectual, the impersonal, the polite exchange when I'm emotionally unsure of the situation. I have a split-second of insight… this defensive attitude keeps me isolated. Carly and Sassy are sitting together and Sassy is looking at Carly with affection. Little is now chatting with Atlee and giving her drink order to Danny. This could be a polite cocktail party.

Oh, no! Who's going to begin this uncomfortable reunion! Am I supposed to say something? What would I say? I guess I should start with explaining how Carly and I saw the pictures and recognized the resemblance. I begin rehearsing in my head what I will and will not say. Stay away from Carly's drinking and driving, mention my accident briefly so they understand how I got the scars, stay away from the word 'therapy'. As I'm standing alone in a corner rehearsing my speech (Little never reconnected with me after the initial exchange), Atlee stands and begins. Thank heavens! The pressure's off me.

"This has been quite a journey for all of us. When I moved to Elgin, Illinois, I was running away from my childhood memories, then I found out I had family in Seattle, Sassy and Little and a bunch of little sassys and littles." Chuckling from everyone. "I called them when I was settled and invited them to my new home. As you can imagine, they were very surprised when I called them. He turns to Carly and me to explain. Both Little and Sassy thought we would never want to see or speak to them. They thought we knew the family secret and chose never to be in contact. When I first saw Sassy and Little, I knew the truth. Just look at you four. No one would ever doubt you were closely related. I explained to Sassy and Little that we three had been sheltered from the truth of our parentage. We were never told nor did we see any pictures. The recent turn of events occurred when Carly asked my mother for some pictures of her when she was a small child. My mother innocently sent her pictures, pictures of Sassy and Little when they were in their late teens. Looking at those pictures, Carly came to the same conclusion I had when I first met Sassy and Little. Then, Bally was in an automobile accident, and as a result she entered counseling to deal with her trauma. As a part of the counseling, her early childhood came up and Bally decided to find some pictures, and she called my mom and Carly. When she saw the pictures, she also believed there was an untold story that went back over 40 years. Carly and Bally found me, and of course, I already knew what they were just discovering. They decided to get together with me to discuss their suspicions, and I have surprised them by inviting Sassy and Little here today. I think we're all in agreement. We want to know the truth about our parentage . We need know who we are, and why our lives have been forever changed by the events many years ago. Who wants to go first?"

To my surprise, Little raised her hand. "I do. The events that unfolded over 40 years ago have impacted everyone in this room. We are all victims of a mad man, a culture that allowed us to believe that men are superior to women, and a code of silence that's just now being broken. Sassy and I agreed I would tell the story and then we will stay as long as it takes to answer questions and hopefully create an open and honest atmosphere in which healing can occur. The story begins in the Philippines where Gladys was born. After her birth, our parents immigrated to the U.S. and the two of us were born shortly after. I am two years younger than Gladys and Sassy is 14 months younger than me.

Gladys was the first to marry. When Cameron asked my father for Gladys' hand my father said 'yes and I want a male grandchild right away, I am getting old'. Cameron said he would produce an heir immediately. Cameron was a man who always believed he should get his way. He boasted openly he always got what he wanted. My father also was cut from the same cloth. However, Cameron was soon to be disappointed. Gladys and Cameron tried and tried, and they couldn't get pregnant. My father grew impatient and blamed Cameron for not having 'what it takes'. Cameron was incensed and humiliated. He blamed Gladys. There were horrible displays of temper. My father then offered me to Cameron, as a surrogate. I was terrified and dead set against this and said so, vehemently. My father didn't listen, and my mother didn't help me. They set up several secret times when Cameron and I could be alone, but I began avoiding Cameron. But, Cameron wouldn't give up. Then one day Cameron caught me and raped me. I fought him, but he was too strong for me. Later I found out my father knew

I was avoiding Cameron and arranged for me to be home alone. Anyway, I conceived right away and had twin sons. My pregnancy confirmed, in Cameron's mind, that Gladys was the one who could not get pregnant so he emotionally divorced her. Everyone was happy, except me and Gladys. Cameron was ignoring her and I was not married and had twin boys. However, once they were weaned at six months, my father took the boys from me and started raising them as his own. I was devastated and relieved all at the same time. I was young, unmarried, and was living in my father's home. There was no future for me. I tried to find a job, but I had no skills. However, Cameron was furious. He wanted to raise **his** sons, but he had no claim to them and there was no DNA testing in those days to prove he was the father. My father and Cameron saw me as a bitch and arranged for me to be home alone again. Cameron raped me again. This time I did not fight, and thank God I didn't get pregnant. A few weeks later, Cameron forced himself on me a third and final time and I had you, Bally. My father wasn't interested in you because you were a girl and so Cameron took you and raised you. Gladys finally had a child, and she was very happy. I don't know if Gladys knew Cameron had three children with me. She thought my father was a gracious man to take my two sons and raise them as if they were his sons instead of his grandsons. She also thought Cameron was helping out by "adopting" you. Shortly thereafter, I left town and disappeared from the family. That's when I moved to Seattle. After I left, Cameron had no one to have sex with because he had rejected Toto. I was gone, so he turned to Sassy. Sassy was also raped by him and then, and only then, did she understand what had happened to me. She told me later she thought I was a 'loose woman'. Well, she also became pregnant and Carly was born, but once again, my father wanted sons, so Carly was given to Gladys, too. At my prompting, Carly also decided to leave home, and she came here to live because I was here. She moved here shortly after your birth, Carly.

"Cameron must have been outraged when he discovered he had no easy sexual partners left, so he turned back to Gladys and she conceived Atlee. I wouldn't be surprised if he didn't rape her too. All through the pregnancy, Cameron called him "At Last" and

Toto hated Cameron for mocking her that way. When the chance came to fill out the birth certificate, Gladys wrote ATLAS which quickly became Atlee, a nickname. I never saw my sons again, and they don't know I'm their mother. I also married a very nice man here in Seattle and had one daughter. He died a few years ago.

"Carly and Bally, I, too, have been through therapy, and I found it helpful, but I still have difficulty trusting people, especially men. I keep to myself which means I'm alone a lot and isolated from the world. The scheme my father and your father hatched destroyed my ability to connect with people. I have had to work hard to trust others.

"Sassy also married and has two children who live in Canada. All of them have been informed of this meeting and why it's occurring. They would love to meet you when you return for another visit.

"I just want you both to know, I'm sorry you have been injured. I was hoping that by my leaving town, you would be raised by Toto, who is a sweet and innocent woman. When everyone else was avoiding me and looking at me as if I was a tramp, she never judged or blamed me, or Sassy for that matter. She just took the two of you into her life and raised you as her own. When she became pregnant and had Atlee, she was overjoyed, but Cameron was not. He had grown angry at her for the failure to conceive early in their marriage. He was horrified that his only son came from her. Consequently, he treated Atlee horribly. Now you may be wondering how I know all this since I left town and never returned. Well, Sass and I had two confederates. First, I told Toto what had happened and how she got the two of you as her daughters, but she never talked about it a lot. However, she would call me and Sass, when Cameron was traveling, to keep us informed as to your progress. Secretly, she sent us pictures and stories about your accomplishments. My mother was another confederate, who also kept in touch, without my father knowing it. She took her secret contact with both Sass and me to her grave. Sassy and I want you to know we're very sorry for the part we have played in causing you pain. We both thought we were doing the right thing in leaving and establishing ourselves in the northwest. In hindsight, we wish we would have had the nerve to take you with us. But, in those days a woman who was an unwed mother was seen as tramp. We believed you would be better off in Gladys' care and we knew she would be a loving mother. She is sweet and kind, but she is like our mother, passive and accommodating to her husband. She never complained though I suspect she was hurt and angry. Some of her personality traits are cultural, but some of this is her dependency. Please believe us when we tell you it never occurred to either of us that Cameron would be a terrible father. I guess we thought that because he wanted children so badly, he would treat you well."

Sassy speaks up. "Bally and Carly, Little and I have never stopped loving you or praying for you. We have known of your successes and failures, your careers, and of your children, Carly. We never wanted to be separated from you, but we both realized independently we could not fight both our father and yours and, if we tried, we all would have been severely hurt. We just now found out how injured you have been, but even though we believed that leaving you with Toto was right decision, we regret it. Please let us try to make up for some of the time we have missed. We do not want to take any of your love away from our sister. We love her and we honor her for having raised you, but if you can find it in your hearts to forgive us, we would love to play a role in your lives, even a small one."

Sassy burst into tears and hugged her mother. Little and I are standing in opposite corners as if we were ready to enter a boxing ring. I don't know what to think and I certainly don't know what to say. I have many feelings and thoughts coursing through my mind and body. I can't sort through them, so all I do is nod. Then it dawns on me; I have two older brothers. "Excuse me, but who are my older brothers? Do you know them? Have you seen them?"

Finally, there is a fine crack in Little's armor, she wells up with tears and turns her body 90 degrees so I can't see her emotion. Sassy sees it and jumps in. "Your uncles, er, brothers have never been told you are their sisters. According to our mother, they were kept isolated from Toto and Cameron and you three. They also have been told that both Little and I have died. Reconnecting with them will be very difficult because our parents are dead and cannot verify what really happened. Also, we don't know if they are like our father or not. We assume they are more western and modern in their cultural beliefs, but we don't know if they would hate us for the deception and abandonment."

I'm going to take a leap. "Little, do you know their names, where they live, and most importantly, if I find them, do you want to know? Do you want them to know about you?"

Little thinks for a minute and then, just like I would do, she makes a sound decision. "I think we need to take this one step at a time. We have to get to know each other and then discuss if we should search for my sons. I suspect Toto knows them. She still lives in the same town, and she was close to both of our parents when they died. If they are still living there, she would know, but we haven't spoken of them in years." Little begins to cry softly. I don't know what to do. I'm scared to reach out, but I want to. I look at Atlee. He nods in Little's direction so I walk across the room and touch her shoulder, and she and I hug and cry for what seems like an eternity but was only a minute. Then as if on cue, my anger takes over. I break our embrace and say loudly, "Son of a Bitch! My father's a monster, a rapist, a fraud. I hate him."

Did that come out of my mouth? Who cares! I keep going. "Who died and made him God? How did he think that his taking what he wanted was the right thing to do? He treated Mom, Gladys, like a slave AND SHE LET HIM! This is such a mess. What am I going to say to Mom?" I look to Carly and she shrugs her shoulders. Big help. "Do you think Mom knows we have discovered the truth?" Carly weakly offers, "I don't think so."

Little says, "I'm not sure. She sometimes acknowledges what happened and sometimes she pretends not to know. When Atlee decided to move here, she was the one who told Atlee where we were living. That's how he found us. But, then I will call her, and she will ignore me when I refer to my pregnancy and the six months I had you."

"We'll have to think this through. Atlee, do you keep in touch with Mom?"

"A little. When I call her, she only stays on the line about two minutes and gets off quickly. I never told her what I had discovered. Did either of you talk to her about this meeting?"

Sassy and Little indicate they hadn't.

We sit in silence. What to do? How much to do?

Atlee offers lunch with continued conversation and everyone, though emotionally exhausted, agrees that food might help. The discussion grew more lively the more we ate. We brainstormed everything from dipping my father's dick in molten lead to doing nothing except to continue to be in touch with each other. Finally, I said something that doesn't sound like me. "There's been enough pain. For now, I'd like to spend sometime with you all and reconnect. We can decide later, slowly, if we bring our uncle-brothers on board. However, I, for one, do not want to hurt Mom. She has done nothing wrong, except not fight against her husband's decisions and demands. She raised us, and she deserves our respect. However, that said, I would like to confront my father, with or without you all. I think he needs to know what a mess he has created, and that we are going to straighten it all out...and heal."

Everyone is silent. Carly and Atlee are thinking. Carly quietly says, "I'm in." Atlee nods. Then the surprise: Both Little and Sassy agree they want to be there when we confront Dad. The question that lingered in my mind is whether Dad, and I use the term loosely, will contact Mom and tell her what we have done. That would hurt her and she may not want to see us again. What an incredible pile of crap!

Carly asks me the question I need to take back to Lisa. "Bally, I always thought you were the most like Dad. I don't mean to be disrespectful or to hurt you, but you seemed to buy into his demands and expectations. (Atlee is nodding.) How has this changed you?"

All I could say is, "I don't know. What I do know is **I have to change** before a group of angry people descends on me and calls me to task for all I have done to them." I didn't mean it to be funny, but everyone laughed.

It's only 3 p.m., and I'm wiped out. I think everyone else is tired, too, because the conversation changes to lighter topics like do we have pets, what are Carly's kids like, who went to college and where, etc. I'm surprised to see that Danny is still listening. He's quite an impressive young man. Apparently Atlee keeps nothing from him.

We make plans to contact each other, and I agree to set up a way we can all communicate. Atlee suggests we bring Mom on board before we confront Dad. He offers to visit Mom with Danny and gently let her know what has transpired. He says he will give her one piece of information at a time so as not to overwhelm or scare her. We all see her as fragile, and we are worried about how she will handle this revelation. Little says she wants Mom to know we all love her and do not blame her for what happened over 40 years ago. I have no doubt Atlee will handle this task perfectly. I have grown to trust him over the last 24 hours. His communication skills are excellent, and his parenting skills are superb. I'm envious of his life.

Sassy and Little are preparing to leave, and I don't know how to approach Little. Carly and Sassy are embracing, and I want some of that too. I go to Little and hold out my arms. She hesitates and then enfolds me in her arms. The embrace is sincere but is a much briefer one than Carly got from Sassy. I'm trying not to internalize Little's attitude toward me as rejection, but I can't help it. I'm keeping my focus on the fact she has been raped three times by MY father, and she doesn't trust anyone, especially someone who is carrying my father's genes. I keep saying to myself, "Go slow." But I want what Carly has with Sassy. Why can't I find love? More issues for Lisa-time.

I feel like I've been wrestling an alligator all day. The alligator is myself. I want to blow up and yell and scream and drink, because I've been holding almost everything in all day. I'm emotionally, intellectually, and physically depleted. I feel like I've been to the bottom of my being and am scouring the crap out of me. I try to nap, but I can't turn off. I replay the events and conversation of the day over and over. I wanted to ask Little about my memory flash of Dad stroking her thigh. She kept saying he raped her, but my three year old memory saw something different. Did I misunderstand it? I was only three. I thought she was enjoying it, but perhaps that was my childish view of the event. If I understood Little correctly, she left our home town before I was one, so why do I remember that incident? Did I make it up? Anyway, today didn't seem the right time. Maybe another time. I'm ready to go home, why did I ever think I needed more time here? I feel like I've run a marathon and now need to replenish my body and mind. But, nothing turns off. I keep trying to rest, but I can't, the day's events keep replaying like a bad song I can't get out of my head. I start for the stairs to find a book to read, but as I approach the top, I hear Atlee and Carly talking. I sit down on the top step to listen.

Atlee is speaking. "...didn't know Bally has had difficulty staying in a relationship. She is so beautiful. I can understand why men are drawn to her. Seeing her with Little, I see her cool, defensive manner was passed on. Little seemed a bit shut down with Bally. Was Little protecting herself? Was Bally a reminder of her pain?"

Carly asks, "How did Little respond to you when you first met her?"

"She's always been less warm than Sassy, but, to be fair, she was the most harmed by our father. She bore three children she didn't want and had no support from her mother or father. She was used and abused. I guess it accounts for her restraint. But, I think she was more restrained with Bally than she was with me the first time we met."

"Do you think Bally was too much of a reminder, or that Bally looks so much like her that she was overwhelmed?"

"Carly, I honestly don't know. I just see her as very damaged. Bally has the same feel to her. Both keep their defenses up. However, Bally is warmer and more compassionate than I expected her to be. I like her."

"She's usually all 'business', but recently, I've seen a change in her. She's been more concerned about me and Mom. Maybe the recent events have begun to change her view of the world. I know I'll never be the same. These last 24 hours have awakened in me the person I always wanted to be and never could because I didn't know who I was. I plan to use this experience to find the happy Carly."

"Good for you, Sis. That's why I came to Seattle. I had no idea what I would find here, but I knew I wanted to be different and to raise my son differently too."

"He's great, Atlee!"

"Thanks, Carly. I think he's special too."

"What do we do from here, Atlee? I'm assuming you're planning a visit to Mom's."

"Yes, that's first on my things-to-do list. What'll you do?"

"I'm going home tomorrow to Texas and spend time in therapy uncovering the real me and find out who I am, separate from my parents. And I'll help Bally and you confront Dad."

"Sounds like we have a lot of work ahead of us, Carly." A long pensive pause ensues.

I cannot be left out of this conversation. "I agree. I feel scared of the journey ahead. I don't know how begin. I hope my therapist has a clue about how to help me."

Atlee and Carly look up at me, and realize I've been listening. I can see them running the tape back in their minds to assure themselves they didn't say anything bad about me. Lisa would say I'm jumping to conclusions. Together we make a plan to confront Dad in a few weeks. I feel my stomach turn to mush, but I also feel the vindictive part of me dancing with glee at the opportunity to confront him.

After dinner and some chit-chat, I go to bed, and Atlee prepares to take Carly to the airport. We all hug and hug again and make plans to talk soon. I'm crashing and am glad they didn't want me to make the trip to the airport. I've not prepped my presentation tomorrow. I thought I would do my typical lectures. I've done them several times. Should be a piece of cake. Ahhh. Sleep.

Arrrghh! My alarm! I know I only slept two minutes. The clock proves otherwise. A shower sorta wakes me up, but I feel hung-over, even though I had nothing to drink. Atlee offers me coffee, breakfast, and directions to downtown Seattle, one hour away. I take off and have no problem finding my way, thanks to his directions. I don't feel well enough to work, but I have to play this lie out, now that I'm here. The building is impressive: seven stories of glass, lobby with fresh flowers, and security guards. I ask for Mr. Windress and the receptionist asks me politely to "have a seat". Wow! I notice the large picture window that frames Mt. Rainier. At first I thought it was a huge photograph. I feel drawn to that mountain as if it's calling me. Standing in front of the window I feel bathed in the call of the mountain. I could get lost up there! Since Mr. Windress is keeping me waiting, I try to read my notes, get in the groove for the presentation. I can't, so I go back to the window and begin a mantra, "I have to pull this off... I have to pull this off." All this does is increase the pressure. I've never gotten the meditation thing down.

Mr. Windress is friendly and chatty. We met a few years ago and I noticed he had aged quite a bit. He keeps looking at me. I'm used to men doing that. SHHHHIIIITTTT!!! I forgot to use the professional make-up on my scars. He's not admiring me, he's trying to figure out how I got my scars. My heart pounds. I feel totally naked, like it's one of those dreams where you are butt naked and can't cover yourself up. I can see him trying to decide if I had the scars when he met me before or whether they are new. He keeps looking at my face, but he wisely says nothing. This isn't going well. Now, I'm exhausted and naked! Can I do this?

My head begins to pound as I set up my PowerPoint presentation. What the hell. I'm ready to go. Mr. Windress greets the employees as they walk in the room. I feel myself go into automatic drive and begin to feel better. After about an hour of presenting information I asked everyone get into small groups of four or five for a practice session. Mr. Windress approaches me as the employees dutifully obey. I smile at him expecting him to compliment me on my presentation. I usually get accolades,... but he doesn't.

"Bally, you presented this material four years ago. A few of our employees haven't seen it because they are new, but most have seen this before. Are you going to give us a chance to see the newer computer program products your company is sending us?"

My heart is racing. I didn't have any memory of doing this presentation with this client four years ago! I know I lost a year or two of my life while drinking, but I was sure I knew this client's level of training. Shit, did I bring the brand new stuff? I search my bag and come up with a few slides and ask they be copied for me. Mr. Windress looks annoyed, but he calls a secretary and asks him to come to the conference room to make some copies. While the copies are being made, I feel ready to continue the practice session, but I upped the exercise to include the next level of learning. Most of them nodded and proceeded with the exercise.

After the morning session, I called for a lunch break. Mr. Windress told me where I could get some lunch. Not a good sign! Usually, the company executive TAKES me to lunch. Ok, Bally, make good use of the situation. I call my secretary, and tell her I need her to email the newest product information. I can't get to my copies of the slides because they are on my home computer. But, I did get enough of the material to put together some slides with bullet points. I usually have slides that are dense with material, but I have no time to type content-filled slides. I'm familiar with the new products but not real comfortable with these products without my slides. I gotta pull this off! I'm emotionally depleted, physically exhausted, and intellectually I'm not feeling sharp.

I return from lunch and observe Mr. Windress talking animatedly with three employees. They stop talking when I approach. I go into overdrive, and present with animation, jokes, and graphs that seem to satisfy them. The afternoon goes ok. I feel my adrenaline kick in and I work hard, but I still feel incompetent. However, the copied materials are excellent and the slides are ok, not great, but good enough. At the end of the day, the group begins to come alive with the new materials and ask intriguing questions. This is where I shine and I feel redemption is at work. The group responds well and is genuinely excited about the products... and I hope the training, too. I don't hand out the feedback sheets. I don't want to hear the critique.

The day's training is over. Mr. Windress tells me he is pleased with the new information. He then drops the bomb. "Do you have any additional information to present?" I finesse the answer, I explain I was surprised by the excellent background and skill sets his employees have. I told him I have more information on programs that are being introduced later this year, and I could come back another time and bring these exciting new programs, but for now, I can only give an overview tomorrow. He seems satisfied and displeased at the same. He kindly lets me know he will not need me tomorrow.

Besides being personally exhausted, I am beating myself up for not researching this company's level of training. I heard Mr. Windress' excitement over my willingness to do some training as an invitation to introduce our products and services, but his employees were well trained already. He wanted **new** products and services. How did I miss this? I've never been out here before. Mr. Windress had been to Baltimore before, but not in the last two years. Did **he** do the excellent training of his employees? Had someone else from my company been here? Maybe while I was in rehab? Crap. I think I pulled this off, but the next time I will know to bring the most up-to-date sophisticated programs, even if I don't think I'll need them. There's no offer for dinner, another hint he's not thrilled. I can package this with my boss as a lack of communication with Mr. Windress. I can sorta explain that he gave me the impression he needed one level of training when he actually needed another. That's it! I think that explanation will fly. However, I'm leaving a day early to return to Baltimore and that means I failed.

The drive back to Atlee's house allows me the time to process more. I'm not at the top of my game anymore. I gotta get this family stuff behind me so I can concentrate. I also need to go back to my basics with my training protocol. Ok, give myself a pep talk. This is salvageable. I think.

Atlee sees the look on my face and can tell I'm not pleased with the day. He's willing to listen and process, but I'm not in the mood. I dodge his desire to help and tell him I need to leave for home. He asks no more questions. I change my flight to take the red-eye back to Baltimore.

I drive to the airport, return the car, and fly through the night. I need sleep but can't. I have too much on my mind. I may feel better if I get back to Baltimore and talk to my supervisor before Mr. Windress does. This kind of stuff used to energize me, but I have nothing left in me and all I feel is despondent. God, I need a drink! Here comes the flight attendant. I want a drink, but I order a Sprite.

My flight goes well, arriving on-time at 5:00 a.m., 2:00 a.m. Mr. Windress' time. I shower, dress, eat, and leave for the office. Even though it is 8:00 a.m., the office is busy. However, Ron is not in the office. I wait, tapping fingers and feet, a sign of my anxiety. I can't stand this waiting…I answer all my emails and voicemails. I also plan exactly what I am going to say about being home a day early.

At nine, Ron walks in and looks surprised to see me. "Hi Bally, I thought you were in Seattle."

"Just flew in. I was so damn good I crammed two days of training into one."

"Sounds like you had some good students, too!"

"There was a minor miscommunication about the level of sophistication of his employees. They were more skilled and informed than Mr. Windress indicated, so when I prepared to make the trip I planned to cover material they already had. When I recognized the communication problem, I quickly switched the presentation and arranged for the newest more sophisticated program information to be sent to me yesterday. I think I left them wanting more, and after my presentation, they can handle the most up-to-date, high-level products."

"Good."

Ron walks away.

I go to my office and breathe, breathe, breathe.

I'm preparing my report when my phone rings. "Bally, could you come into my office, please." Shit, it's Ron. "Sure."

My mouth is dry and my heart is pounding. I'm nauseous.

"Close the door, Bally."

"What's up?"

"I just spoke to Jack Windress. He says you were unprepared, had him make copies, and seemed preoccupied."

"Well, I was prepared for a Level Three presentation, but after an hour of presenting at that level, I realized most of the employees were at a higher level of expertise, so I shifted immediately to a level five presentation. However, I didn't have the level five handouts so I had his secretary copy them for the rest of the day. I then waved off lunch and spent the hour reviewing the additional slides (didn't tell Ron I needed to MAKE the slides). The participants seemed to be totally engaged and actively asked questions. I think I salvaged the afternoon, and more than that, I set him up for the major programs we are introducing next month."

"Jack expected the new programs to be introduced at the workshop yesterday. He seems to think the two of you agreed on that over the phone."

"Gee, Ron, I don't think so. I would never have promised that because the new program changes aren't going to be ready for two more months and then we have to be trained on them first. Where would he get that idea?"

"I don't know Bally, but he did. Did you have another reason to be in Seattle?"

"What do you mean?" (Always make them explain.)

"Have you met someone and you wanted to go to Seattle badly, badly enough that you may have misrepresented what you could do for Jack's company?"

"Ron! I am hurt. Do you think I would be that unprofessional? No, I have not met someone, and I didn't go to Seattle for a rendezvous with a love interest! Good grief. It was a simple mistake. Jack failed to communicate the level of expertise he needed, and I failed to clarify."

"Ok. I'll send someone out there next month to give them the new training for free. That should make up for yesterday."

"I could do it. Would give me a chance to make things better."

"No, Jack specifically asked I not send you. He thought you were distracted, unorganized, and not prepared."

"Really? And I busted my butt to shift my entire presentation in order that he would get a higher level of training for his employees. In addition, he had both extremely well trained employees and novices at the training. I had difficulty meeting everyone's needs in the same presentation."

"Ok, Bally. Let's drop it. But, do not call Jack, and do not try to go back there to make things right. I'll send someone else next month. Got it?"

"Got it. But, I feel Jack is sullying my reputation when he was partially at fault."

"Bally, let it go."

I turn on my heels and leave.

Post Testimony Stress Disorder

I passed my driver's license examination two days ago, and I'm driving to Lisa's!

Dad lent me the car. I dropped him off at work and I feel free! I don't feel like a little kid anymore.

Lisa's running late with another client and I'm getting irritated. This is **my** time, and she's allowing another person to infringe on my session. I'm reading an article in Newsweek to keep from knocking on the door. When her door finally opens, an attractive woman emerges. She is darker skinned, Asian woman and she's beautiful! I can't take my eyes off her, though I'm trying not to stare. She's been crying, and her eyes are puffy, but she's still gorgeous. She looks at me, and I look at her. We are probably both thinking the same thing. "What is **your** problem, that **you** have to be here?" I'm annoyed with Lisa. She never runs late. Will I get my entire 50 minutes? Lisa waves me in.

Lisa apologizes for running 10 minutes late. She says she had an emergency, but I'm not to worry, we will have our entire session. Why didn't I trust her? I feel stupid. Of course she's going to take care of me. I tell her that I got my driver's license and her face lights up. "Good for you!" she says. We debrief the testimony. I ask her how she thinks I did, and she says I was articulate, clear, funny, and focused. I felt the same way, but I felt sick when I saw that woman behind Belle. Lisa explains that the two detectives would like to talk to me. I'm stunned. How did the two detectives know about the woman behind Belle? Lisa's trying to explain how she ran into the detectives and she told them they should call me. She gave me their cards. I'm irritated at her for going behind my back, and I say this. She looks a little hurt or guilty I can't tell. She explains she did not tell the detectives anything except I wanted to talk to them. She's confused as to why I am irritated. I apologize and tell her I'm really pissy today. She still looks a little confused, so I tell her it's ok she told the detectives to call me. I'm turning on the one person who has my best interest at heart. She has never done anything that deserved my irritating comment. Why am I acting this way? Should I talk it out?

"I don't know why I am crabby. I have been in a weird mood ever since I finished my testimony. Maybe I have PTSD, Post Testimony Stress Disorder." Lisa laughs. It feels good to know I can still make her laugh. "I have been gearing up for this trial for months. I dreamed about it, worried about it, recovered memories, taken medication, worked on 'my issues', and now what am I going to do?"

Lisa responds, "Live?"

"What do you mean? Aren't I living now?"

"Depends on how you define living. You've been working hard on yourself. For what?"

"I honestly don't know. What I do know is I can't identify the woman behind Belle and go right back to court again. I'm too tired. I'm done with this, and I want to move on. I just don't know how."

"During the last six months, have you dreamed about what you would do when the trial was over and when you were healthy enough to move on?"

"I've thought about it, but to tell you the truth, I don't think I can hold down a full time job. I just don't have the energy or the ability to concentrate all day. I want to do something, but I don't know what. I doubt I will ever be able to work full time."

"Perhaps you need to take one step at a time. Let's talk about what you think you could do."

"I like to work with my hands. I've enjoyed the gardening and the cooking I've been doing at home. I've turned into a frickin' housewife! But, I can't cook for a living. The pressure is too great. I'd get fired if I had a flashback. I don't think Dad's going to support me for the rest of my life."

"If there's a job with little pressure, where you could work with your hands in the yard and earn a living, do you think you could find the energy to try?"

"Sure. But, I can't imagine who would hire me under those conditions. God would have to work a miracle."

"For now, why don't you just stay open to the possibility of finding an experience like that."

"Are we talking about using words again? Like talking about it will make it so?"

"I'm saying if you don't open up to the possibilities and use words to define what you want, you may not recognize the opportunities when they arise, then you will not move forward. Saying what you desire to yourself will create awareness in you so you will see the prospect when it occurs."

"Sounds like a lot more work to do."

"When I first mentioned the exercise of saying positive things to yourself, you thought I was crazy, right?"

"Sorta."

"What happened when you repeated positive things to yourself?"

"I began to feel stupid at first, then I started to feel better. I hate to admit it, but I think complimenting myself gave me the boost to testify."

"Okay, then why wouldn't you want to think positively about finding a place where you fit in the work world?"

"I'm too tired." I whine.

"Is that true or are you telling yourself you're too tired?"

"I dunno."

"You've worked hard and met many challenges. You've testified against your abuser and you were GOOD. Why is this step of looking at your future career getting you down?"

"I've had too many failures in that area."

"I don't mean to sound like a Pollyanna, but what if you looked at the jobs where you were fired and figure out what you did and didn't like about those jobs. Perhaps they have something to teach you."

"I'm not up for this right now. I have to find out what happens to Belle, whether I will be called back to the stand, whether the woman behind her was one of the other women who abused me."

"Ok, but, I'm concerned about you. You seem depressed or discouraged. You got your driver's license and it hasn't helped you to feel better."

"I feel good about my driver's license, and I felt good on the stand. I felt I did a good job. I even looked Belle in the eye and didn't melt. Then I saw that woman sitting behind Belle and all the good, competent, strong feelings left. This is stupid. I don't even know whether that woman is the person who tormented me."

"How could you find out?"

"What? I don't know. I guess I could talk to the detectives."

"That would be one way to start. What if you found out the woman sitting behind Belle has nothing to do with the abuse? What if she was a newspaper woman?"

"Then I'd know I was wrong."

"How would that affect you?"

"I'd feel better. Hmmm. I get your point. I have unfinished business with my testimony. I'll call the detectives."

"Ok, see you next week? Same time?"

"Sure, but, now I can come anytime because I got wheels!"

Chapter Eight
Here We Go Again

The victim of human-induced trauma comes fact-to-face with the existence of evil, with the understanding "...at a deep experiential level, that one's terror and pain were intentionally caused by another human being"
(Janoff-Bulman, 1992, p. 78).

Lisa's Pathetic Day

Caz confused me today. I expected he'd be riding a wave of feeling competent. Instead he was down, dejected, and had low energy. I tried to motivate him, and I think I did get him to consider some alternatives, but he sure didn't jump for joy. Between Caz, Noelle, and Bally, I'm really feeling drained, almost like I am taking on some of their discouragement. Today was not a good day. The **best** thing that happened today was I ate spaghetti for lunch and **didn't** dribble any sauce on my blouse. How pathetic is that? Gee, I'm sounding like them. Sigh.

Caz
Testify Again?

What is wrong with me? I know I frustrated Lisa. She's always been straight with me, so why was I angry at her? Hell, I'm angry at everything. I will contact the detectives. Hell, call now, bozo.

The detectives agreed to come over in an hour. I'll tell them my story and see what they say. I'm probably making too much of all this crap with the woman in the courtroom anyway. I'm headed for the shower and a snack. Perhaps it will perk me up before the detectives arrive. I finished my shower, but the detectives are early, so it looks like the Double Stuff Oreos and milk have to wait until later. They enter wearing matching trench coats. I have to look outside to see if it is raining. It isn't. Trench coats? How trite? I lead them into our living room, where we first met to talk about Belle, but this time they choose to stand, hands folded over their genitals. Why do men stand like that? Protecting their manhood? From what? They look at me expectantly. I stammer, "You probably can't answer this...it's been several days... and people change seats a lot,... but do you know the woman who sat behind Belle, the day I testified?"

Detective Bentley leans forward and asks, "Why are you asking?" Detective Lang doesn't move a muscle.

"I think I know her."

Detective Lang now also leans forward. I can see why Lisa called them Frick and Frack. They don't look alike, but they act in tandem. Detective Lang says, "Where would you have come in contact with her?"

Ok here goes. "I may be wrong, but remember the memories I recovered from my dreams in which three different women abused me?" Both nod together and shift their feet. "Well, she resembles one of the women. It's been about 15 years, but she sure looks like the woman who smeared crap on my face."

Frick looked at Frack. Frick speaks, "If I told you she's Belle's friend and has not missed a moment of the trial, she's been sitting behind Belle the entire time, would it help you?"

"I don't know. I only know she resembles the woman who abused me."

"Caz, if we find out she is the woman who abused you, would you testify?"

There's that work again...TESTIFY! I'm feeling nauseous (glad I didn't eat the Oreos) and scared. I hedge, "I might, if I was sure she was the woman who abused me." I don't believe I'm volunteering, again!

"If we found pictures of her 15 years ago, would you be able to identify her?"

"I probably could identify her if I saw her picture from 15 years ago.

The detectives nod and smile. They pull out a picture and show it to me. I feel light-headed, almost faint. The room feels like it's becoming a tunnel. I nod. "That's her." I say as I reach for a chair before I fall.

The detectives tell me Belle's trail is ending tomorrow and the jury will get instructions. They also asked if I wanted to be there when the verdict came in. I said I did. They left promising to get back to me 'real soon.' I'm beginning to appreciate these guys.

I call Lisa and leave a message explaining that the mystery woman is who I thought she was, and that Belle's trial is going to the jury tomorrow.

I didn't sleep. I kept dreaming of the woman and her hideous abusive act. At 9:30 my dad shakes me to tell me the jury's just received their instructions from the judge. I take a deep breath trying to get more oxygen to wake me up. Today could be the culmination of a long journey. I keep busy all day to block Belle out of my mind. At 4:30, the detectives call to say the jury is back, and they're picking me up. I dress and wait.

The courthouse looks different to me. I'm there to hear the verdict, not testify. The jury, seven men and five women, files in silently, and the judge asks if they've reached a verdict. The forewoman says they have, and she begins to recite the charges and verdict for each, count one – guilty, count two – guilty, count three – guilty. I fade back to Belle's happy house with kids laughing and clowning. And then the abuse clouds in around the edges of my memories. I return to the courtroom when I hear the judge thank the jury and reiterate that Belle was found guilty on all 20 counts of child abuse. Belle was trembling and crying. She will be sentenced in two weeks, but she's going to jail, it's just a matter of how long. But, it may be for the rest of her life. I keep trying to get a glimpse of the woman sitting behind Belle, but I can't see her face. She hangs her head and quickly leaves the packed courtroom. As the detectives are walking with me out of the courthouse, they excuse themselves for a minute and walk over to the woman, whose name I now know is Ann, and arrest her right there in front of me and escort her to a waiting police vehicle. The police car speeds off to booking. The detectives return to me and Detective Lang says with a smile, "We have confirmation that she abused two other men, too. You cinched our case against her. We thought you deserved to see her arrested! You didn't see Belle arrested except on the news."

My emotions are on a roller coaster ride. I'm relieved Belle's trial is over, but oddly, I'm sad for her. I'm also angry at her. I'm confused by the quick arrest right in front of me. My feelings are clear about Ann. I feel hatred toward her. I don't have the fond memories of her I once had for Belle. And I'm worried I'll have to testify again. Why does the very word testify bother me? It sounds too much like testicles which reminds me of the abuse.

I will *testify* if I have to, but I feel the need to get on with my life. Having another trial to go through will hold me back. Will I have the fortitude to *testify again?* Will I have to go through this with the other two women if they are named? The detectives seem clueless as to how this whole thing is affecting me. One of them says, I think it is, Detective Lang (I get them mixed up.) "Look a little happier, you helped us get justice done!" I offer a weak half-hearted smile.

Then, out of the blue the press notices me and swarms me like flies on shit. They're all talking at once. I don't know where I get the strength, but I raise my hand and they all fall silent, standing with their arms stretched out toward me, each with a microphone in his or her hand. The looks on their faces are of anticipation, like I'm going to say something profound. I don't have a clue what I'm going to say, I just wanted to stop them from swarming me.

Maybe shit should take notice – it worked to stop the press, maybe it would work to stop the flies. "Belle's been found guilty. I knew she was guilty because I was a victim of her deceitful life. All of us who have been abused have been harmed beyond comprehension. Our lives have been damaged and many are beyond repair. I'm sad today. Belle was a warm, loving person who took advantage of her position of power to get her own needs met using innocent children who trusted her. I pray she'll come to grips with what she's done and seek God's forgiveness. As for me, I just want to try to recover from this tragedy and move on with my life."

With that, I look at the detectives who flank me left and right and usher me past the swarm of microphones and cameras attached to bodies and loud voices shouting questions. Getting into the car and shutting the door is a blessing, the voices and faces are still persistent but much reduced. I fall back across the seat, close my eyes, and try to shut out the world.

I withdraw into silence as the detectives drive me home. I need an extra session with Lisa, NOW! I call to see if she can fit me in, and she can't, but she offers me a session in two days. I know she's busy, but, gosh, can't I get at least a few minutes? I take the one in two days.

Noelle's Dislike for People

Ma boss is drivin' me crazy. He keeps sayin' he can see changes in me, but, for the life of me, I don't know what he means. I don't **feel** different. He probably is lookin' for stuff, now that I'm goin' to counseling every week. Now he's pressurin' me to go out with him agin. Jeeze. Can't everyone leave me alone! It'll never work between us, anyway.

I haven't tole the story of the train wreck in years. When it first happened, telling the story was 'ddictive for others an' in some way for me too. I felt a little less stressed each time I tole my story. Then there was a point when I couldn't stan' to talk about it, cuz it brought up too many mem'ries. Besides I hate when people get high on the gory details. No one really cared about **me**, how it affected **me**, how **I** might be changed forever. One time when I wus talkin' 'bout the wreck an' how my hair turned white a woman said to me, "Gosh honey, now you won't have to highlight your hair anymore." I wanted to scream, "I never did highlight my hair ya insensitive jerk." But, I just gave her a weak smile an' lef'. As I lef', I heard her say that since the wreck, I haven't been right in the head an' I caught a glimpse of her in my rear-view mirror as she touched her head.

I think I hate people. Leeza might be diff'rent. Leeza's concerned more 'bout me than the gory facts. Well, Gerard might be ok, too. And Dad's a good man. But, that's it. Only three people in the whole world.

Now I think 'bout it, people always make weird remarks when someone dies. When I was four an' my Gran died. One 12 year old kid said to me, "Old people die, an' it's just as well, makes room for the rest of us." When my nanny died, I went to the funeral an' as I was wanderin' 'round I heard things like "I heard she was stripping on the side to make money. Everyone knows you can't make money as a nanny." "Her parents must be just sick with grief. But, maybe they can have some consolation now that she's not out at night." When my teacher choked on the bone an' died, people were really nice. But, I heard one person say it was ironic how she died. She had died because she was a glutten, choked on food. She was a little plump, but she was beautiful. How dare they! People're cruel. I'm sure I've been the butt of jokes too. I don't care....yeah I do.

Lisa
Session with Noelle

Noelle is dressed in more colorful clothes today. She also looks like she may have tinted her hair a little. Her hair looks more blonde than white. And I think she is wearing mascara. Should I mention it, or should I not embarrass her by pointing out my observation? Knowing Noelle, I will keep my observations to myself.

"What would you like to talk about today?"

"Ma boss."

"Ok. Go."

"He's pressurin' me agin to go out wiff him. He sez I'm lookin' better an' actin' better."

"What does he mean by that?"

"I don't know."

"Have you been dressing nicer, wearing more make-up, or doing something that might attract his attention?"

A shrug. I will take that as a 'yes'.

"What are you doing? And more importantly, why?"

A long pause, a boring long pause. She's pulling at her short hair as if she wishes it were longer and that pulling on it may quicken the growth process.

"I tried some stuff."

"Stuff?"

"Yea, I had a make-over at the Towson Mall."

"You mean like make-up an' stuff?"

"Yea, this lady, she did my make-up an' then another department did my hair an' then I had a clothing consultant help me pick out some clothes."

"Do you like what you see when you look in the mirror?"

"Yea."

"And your boss noticed."

"I guess."

"Do you like that he noticed your changes?"

"Yea, in some ways I like it, but he's goin' too fast. I can't do anythin' different wifffout him sayin' somethin' like... 'That counseling is sure working for you. You look hot. Let's have dinner.' Stuff like that."

"And it makes you uncomfortable?" I am trying not to smile!

"Yea."

"Why?"

"Pressure. He's getting' too close. I could kill him, you know."

"Yes, I know." I decide to agree with her this time.

"Why take the chance?" She shrugs.

"I don't know." I'm saying things to throw her off a bit and make her think.

"Really?"

She seems surprised at my answer. Good.

"Yea. Why take the chance you might kill him?"

"I thought you didn't b'lieve that stuff about my killin' people." She is off center a bit and confused.

"I don't. But, you do."

"True." Long pause as she considers my new stance. "But, what's he seein' I don't see? Why does he think I've changed?"

"What if you're feeling a little less depressed, a little less anxious, and less burdened by all you've been through?"

"But, all we did is talk."

"We've done more than talk, Noelle."

"We have?"

"Sure, you've told many stories about how death has affected you. You've grieved and relived some of it. You've laid down some of your burden. Do you feel it?"

A shrug. I'm going to ignore the shrug and wait her out. Long pause. She's looking uncomfortable, and she wants to say something, but she's fighting herself.

"Ok."

"Ok what?"

"I've felt less bottled up inside."

"Is that what it was feeling like to you? Like you were burdened by all the grief and memories and couldn't hold them any more?

"Yes." Hmmm, she usually says "Yea."

"How do you feel now?"

"A little lighter." She looks like it too.

"And I didn't die." I remind her.

"Not yet."

Yipes! She sure knows how to throw ice water on me.

"Your boss hasn't died, and I haven't died."

Begrudgingly... "No."

"So how much more crap do you want to drop in here?"

"All of it. But, I'm scared."

"Scared?" I reflect back, picking up on the most important word in her last sentence.

"Yea."

"What are you afraid of?"

"That I won't know who I am if I don't carry this pain."

"Wow, Noelle, that was profound!"

"It wuz?"

She has no idea what she just said, so I reinforce. "It was extremely profound!"

"How?"

"You just realized that carrying your grief has defined you all these years. You don't know who you are separate from the grief and pain. But, you can find out and it could be fun."

"Right!!!" Sarcasm "Sure." More sarcasm.

"Yep." Using her word. "Did you enjoy your day at the department store?"

"Kinda. I liked feelin' special an' pampered, but I wuz uncomfortable by the attention. I kept thinkin', 'They don't like ME, they're just doin' this 'cause they're bein' paid to do this.'"

"Did you ever see anything in their behaviors that confirmed your belief? Like did you see them roll their eyes or sigh?"

"No."

"So you have no reason to believe your current suspicions are accurate.

"No."

"In fact, you don't have reason to believe that your past suspicions or fears are accurate. The fears have always been with you...fears about how others don't really enjoy being with you, or they may reject you, or they may die and abandon you."

Silence, fumbling with the fabric on the arm of the chair.

Eventually, she nodded.

"Is it possible your fears of being abandoned, or not liked by others, are those of a four year old child, not the wisdom of a 40 year old woman."

"But, those memories are real."

"Of course they are. But, the interpretation of those memories belong to a four year old and may not be as accurate as the memory."

Tears are glistening on her mascara-laden lashes. "It's difficult to let go of those memories or beliefs."

"I know it is."

"You do?"

"Sure. We all have information from our early childhood that's not quite accurate and we build our world-view based on memories, and our interpretation of them. Most of these memories are impossible to understand at such a young age. But, they impact us and we act as if our interpretation is true. A lot of the time, our assumption is not accurate. Therefore, we have to look at these memories and decide as adults that the events are not going to define who we are any longer."

"I'm leaving now. I believe you, but I can only take in so much at one time. You understand?"

"Yep. See you next week."

I'm getting comfortable with Noelle not staying for the entire session. At first, I felt I wasn't earning my hourly fee. But, now I use the time to write my case notes and make phone calls. Oh-oh, I was going to call my friends and have lunch and mull over stuff. Calls go out to Maggie and Milly, but I have to leave messages on their cell phones. As I look over my notes from Noelle's earlier sessions, I can see her progress. She had no insight, no desire to be in counseling, no inclination to share. Now she has some insight, wants to be in counseling, and shares a great deal. I wish I had a magic wand and could wave it and all her fears and odd beliefs would vanish. I could make a fortunate with such a wand! Unfortunately, we are built to have to process and process until we "get it".

Life Was Easier Before Counseling

Life wuz easier b'fore counselin'. I got up, fed my cat, took a shower, got dressed, drove to work, worked for eight hours an' then drove home, fed my cat, watched TV, an' went to bed. I blocked all the past an' present crap from my mind. I blocked relationships. I blocked plans for my future. I wuz content to do this routine for the rest of my life, if everyone would jist leave me alone. Don't get me wrong, I wanted relationships, but they jist are too difficult for me.

Now, I gotta deal wiff stuff. Tellin' my stories or mem'ries makes me think about my life an' feel the pain I worked hard to shove. Now when I get up I gotta think about what I'm going to say to ma boss, to Leeza, to myself. Some days I wish hadn't started this counseling stuff. It's hard to work on this garbage. I have dreams, flashbacks, dread, anxiety, an' I feel depressed when I git overwhelmed. Leeza sez I'm makin' progress. But, progress toward what? Do I trust her judgmen'? She seems to know what she's doin'. I hope she does. Cuz this crap hurts alot.

One gud thing though, I wanna pretty myself up. I'm startin' to believe that maybe I don't kill people I like. Nothin' has happened to ma boss or Leeza or ma'cat...or ma'father. Is that progress?

Caz Talks to His Emotions

These last two days have been the longest ones of my life. I tried to sort through my feelings, but every time I think I got one nailed, one more pops up to confuse me sorta like one of those long balloons if you grab one end, the other end gets bigger. I hope Lisa can help me figure out why I'm confused. I have no appetite, I can't sleep, and I'm not even soothed by mindless television programs. My dad and Rom have been quiet, letting me be. The press has been running my now famous statement over and over. I fear watching television because I hate seeing my talking face on the screen. Leaving the house is awful. The press is still lingering outside my house, but there are fewer of them. They ask me a question or two as I walk to the car, and I repeat the same information I said outside the courtroom. I'm hoping they'll become bored if I just say the same stuff, and it seems to be working. I've seen Pastor Craig and the Bishop on television making remarks about how the church acted swiftly when the charges were made against Belle. Even Grandma called to say her T.V. stations picked up the story, and she saw my interview. She told me she was very proud of me. But, she has to say that, she's my grandmother. Still I'm grateful for her support. She offers me the opportunity to visit her for awhile until things calm down here. I thank her and tell her I'll think about it. Is that running away? I don't know what to do.

Lisa's dressed casually today. Maybe she likes the casual Friday trend. She looks cute in her jeans and top and I tell her so. She ignores my comment about looking cute. Instead, Lisa says Fridays are her day to see emergency clients and others she can't fit in on Mondays through Thursdays

"What's up?" she asks.

What's up? What does she think is up? I just went through a trial of grossest proportions and watched another woman, Ann, get arrested right in front of me. Ann looked right at me and had no idea who I was, even though she helped to destroy my childhood. The press has been relentless. I'm a mess! "Lisa, I'm confused. I can't sort out the feelings about the events of the past few days."

"Well, how about laying all the feelings out, and let's sort through them?" Lisa doesn't seem as sharp today. "Of course we're going to get all the feelings out and sort through them, does she think I'm totally new to this process?"

I can't say that to her, she's trying to help. What's wrong with me?

"Lisa, I feel relieved that the trial's over, sad for Belle, anger and hatred at Ann, confused by the quick arrest, proud of my statement to the press, worried that I'll have to testify again...." Lisa looks confused. Now I understand why she's not in tuned with me. She doesn't know anything about what's happened! "Haven't you been watching the news?" Lisa says she's been too busy. She hasn't turned on her television in a week.

"I'm sorry. I just realized you're unaware of the recent events. Let me catch you up. After I left you, I called the two detectives and they came over to my house and showed me a picture of the woman who was sitting behind Belle at the trial. The picture was one that was taken about 15 years ago. I was able to recognize her right away as the woman who smeared shit in my face." Lisa nods, "I knew that part."

"Well," I continue, "then the detectives called me to let me know the jury was in and they would pick me up. They took me to the courthouse to hear the verdict. The jury found Belle guilty on all 20 counts. Then Frick and Frack arrested the woman, Ann, right in front of me. I think the detectives were pleased with themselves and wanted to surprise me with the arrest, but I went numb. Then the press recognized me and swarmed me like bees (I didn't want to say 'shit' twice in a row) and I made a statement, a really good one too. They're still camping out on my street, but it's gotten less in the last two days."

Lisa's back to her normal self. I can see the empathy in her eyes. "I can understand why you're confused."

"You can?" I blurted out too loudly.

"Sure, you've had multiple mini-traumas surrounding the Belle case. You did a great job of testifying, but it came with a price tag of having to repeat to the world what happened to you and the defense attorney tried to impugn your reputation. That had to hurt. Then you see Ann and a whole new set of feelings pop up. While everyone else is celebrating your achievement, you're reeling from the experience. Then, hearing the verdict must have been a relief, an acknowledgement of your pain, but also a sadness that the woman you loved will go to jail, probably for a long time, maybe the rest of her life. On top of that, you're subjected to an arrest procedure of a woman you hate, and now you're concerned you'll have to testify at yet another trail."

"I am stunned. How do you do that? You got it after a few minutes and I have been processing for over two days."

Lisa shrugs, "This all makes perfect **emotional** sense to me. I'd be surprised if you didn't have these feelings." Then she leans forward and hugs me with her words and the world seems sane again. "Caz, you have been through hell. Hell is confusing with conflicting emotions tearing you apart. You've done a great job, but it's not over yet. Someday you'll be able to put some of this in a personal museum that you might visit every now and then, but for now, you've been rubbed raw from these experiences. Be gentle with yourself. I think you're the only one who expects you to be instantaneously well."

"You're right. I do expect myself to be instantly better. I keep thinking…after this, I'll be better, after that, I'll be able to put this all behind me. But, nothing ever feels over…this just keeps going like that damn irritating Energizer bunny. I also think my father and brother want this over and expect something to instantly happen that will make me all better. They've tried to be patient, but I still sense their annoyance. They think it's time for me to put all this all behind me."

Lisa looks amused. "You have a lot of good qualities and skills, but one thing you cannot do is read minds."

She is teasing me, but she is right. "I can't read minds, but I've lived with these two men all my life, and I can read them well."

"And you may be correct, but you may also be reading something into their behavior that's not there. What could you do to check out whether they are really expecting you to 'poof' be better or whether something else is going on?'

"I could ask."

"Yep."

"Ok, but, what do I do with all these conflicting emotions? Do I talk to them too?"

"Funny you should mention that. You can talk to your emotions!"

I roll my eyes, "Is this more therapist voodoo?"

"No, your emotions are part of you and each part can be addressed. For example, what if you have a sore on your foot? If you ignore it or complain about it, will it go away? No. You have to attend to the part of you that's hurting. You find out why your foot hurts, and then you try to alleviate the pain by wearing different shoes, going to the doctor, putting a Band-Aid on it, etc. Now let's do the same thing with your emotions. Let's start with one of them. Which one?"

"Dread. Dread about having to go back and testify. This time against Ann."

"Great, let's pay attention to that feeling. Where in your body do you feel it?"

"In my stomach."

"Ok, now feel the dread in your stomach. What are you feeling?"

"I feel tired. I want to sleep until I can't sleep any more. I want it to go away. I want to be soothed. I want to run away....like my mom did." I can feel the tears burning my eyelids. I feel the empathy for mom's predicament even though the situation's different. I can't speak.

Lisa's looking expectantly at me. She's waiting to see if I'll break the silence, but I can't. If I do, I will dissolve into a puddle. Finally she speaks, "Caz do you remember when you told me several weeks ago you wanted to make a change. You said your mom made a huge mistake. She didn't trust the people who loved her, so she ran away. You said you wanted to learn to trust the people who love you and not run away. This 'dread' feeling is making you feel like running away and running away is connected to your mom. Do you see why you feel confused and overwhelmed about this particular feeling?"

"Yes. Now I do. So I have to do what?"

"Nothing. Except say to yourself, 'This is a normal feeling, and it will crest like a wave and subside back into my ocean of emotion. You don't need to do anything. Just stay with the feeling for awhile."

We sit and sit. It's uncomfortable, but we sit and sit.

"How are you feeling now?"

"I'm feeling a little less anxious about it."

"Now put your 'Dread-I want to run away' feeling in that chair over there and talk to it."

"I feel silly."

"I know, but try it just this once."

I don't want to do this, but I'll try... for Lisa. I address the empty green plaid chair. "I hate you. I want to be rid of you. I feel the only way I can be rid of you is to run away, but I know you'll just follow me wherever I go. I'll never be rid of you."

Lisa says, "Good, now talk back to yourself as if you are Dread."

Now I'm really uncomfortable, but hey I've already embarrassed myself so here goes. "You could be rid of me if you talk to your Dad and Rom when you feel like running away. Putting words to the feeling will lessen me. You can also make a decision not to testify against Ann. They have two other men who will testify. Why should you bear the entire burden?"

I stop and look at Lisa. I suddenly realize the reason I'm feeling dread is because I'm being brave. If I didn't agree to testify, I would not be feeling dread. I have the option to run away from the next trial, not from my family, like mom did, but from the situation. I do have that option, but I'm choosing not to run. I'll testify if necessary. Until now, it never occurred to me I had an option. I explain to her the insight I just had.

"So what do you want to do?"

"I want to and need to be brave. There's been enough running away from pain in this family."

Now it's Lisa's turn to be confused. "What do you mean?"

"My mother was in a bind, and she ran away physically. My father was uncomfortable about being abandoned, and he ran away emotionally. My brother runs away from being uncomfortable, and he suffers panic attacks, which are worse than if he faced his feelings about Mom's abandonment. I want us to stop running away and start dealing with the manure others have shoveled onto us." I'm angry now, not scared.

"Wow, Caz!"

"I'll testify even though it will be uncomfortable. And I can talk to the part of me that's uncomfortable, right?"

"Yep."

"Thanks Lisa. Have a relaxing weekend."

"But, Caz, we have a few more minutes in your session."

"That's ok, I want to put some of this into practice with my family before I lose the momentum. I'll see you at our usual time next week."

Wee Forest Folk

That was quite a remarkable session. Caz was in crisis when he walked in, and he walked out determined. I wonder if he just experienced an internal modification, a turning point, in his search for health. Something definitely clicked for him. I've seldom seen him motivated to take on a homework project. This is the second time I saw rapid movement in Caz. I know Caz has made a lot of progress, but I'm very concerned about him. He's being bombarded with too much too quickly. I appreciate he has some energy to work on the issues facing him, but I'm worried things are moving too fast. He could become overwhelmed and not be able to handle his new decision. I guess I sound like a worried mother with an adult child who's going through a series of events, which could prove damaging if not handled the healthiest way. Caz is beginning to understand himself, and he's trying to take on his life events with a brave, determined attitude, but he's vulnerable to a set back. "Dear

God protect him and encourage him. I'll do my job if you'll do yours." How arrogant does that sound? Sorry, God.

I'm exhausted. I don't need any more emotional turmoil in my life for awhile. I need to laugh and dig in my garden, and read nonsense books, and shop. I left out eat, I definitely need to eat.

It's 11 a.m. on Saturday! I can't believe I slept that long. I must've needed it, but now I lost ¼ of my weekend. Good grief, I need to stop thinking negatively. Stop beating yourself up and enjoy the weekend. Ok, how's this? "Yea! I got to sleep until 11, Lucy didn't wake me up and the phone didn't ring. I have to practice what I preach and guess what? It worked. I decide to go shopping and buy something I love, a new mouse.

My ex-husband bought me a Wee Forest Folk figurine over 20 years ago, and they're the only collectibles I've ever enjoyed. Every birthday or holiday, my family gives me one, and I try to buy a special one for myself every now and then. The ones my daughter gave me have special meaning. After she died, I couldn't look at those particular mice for several months. Now, they're the ones I love the most. Today, I'll buy one of the 12 new mice that were introduced this year, but which one? My favorite "mouse" shop is Of Mice and Minis, a small collectible boutique just up the street. This is a dangerous trip. I'll be indecisive. I'll love them all. I'll have to eliminate 11 out of the 12, and each one is cuter than the other.

The glass case holds a myriad of old and new mice. The "mousers" are out in force inspecting the latest creations. I seem to be taking forever, but the shop owner doesn't mind. She loves the mice too. I've been buying mice there for years. My son says it's a sad commentary on how much I love the mice when the shop owner knows your name and calls you when new mice arrive. I make a mental note to comprise a list for my son for my upcoming birthday.

This year's mice are beautiful, but I spy one of the older mice I don't have. She's called Puzzled, and the figurine is a mouse putting a jigsaw puzzle together. She brings back memories of spending two weeks every summer at Kentucky Lakes, no phone, television, cell phones, or computers. Just a lake, a tennis court, a ski boat, and a beach. At night my kids and I put jigsaw puzzles together – happy memories. Puzzled will come home with me, but I grieve leaving the others in the shop.

That was just the diversion I needed. 'Mousing' reminds me of my daughter who loved taking me to this shop to pick out my newest friend.

Years ago when I first started collecting, I believed there was something wrong with me because I enjoyed these little guys so much. Could I be diagnosed as obsessive or compulsive? Then one day I discovered a couple of websites devoted to Wee Forest Folk and I realized there are thousands of collectors who enjoy chatting about WFF. I discovered, I'm not crazy. I'm a smart investor. These mice are increasing in value quicker than my stock portfolio. I'm brilliant! AND I can be gaga over the little guys.

I feel more relaxed and centered. Perhaps it's because I did something only for me, and I've forgotten about all my clients' woes for awhile. Sigh of relief. My weekend is starting out well. Now for the grocery shopping, gardening, and laundry!

Caz and Ativan

I know what I **want** to do. I just can't seem to do it! Everywhere I look I'm reminded of Belle and the abuse and I get cramps and lightheaded. Before I started counseling these symptoms frightened me, so I avoided places, songs, things that brought up the abuse. For example, Belle cooked us bacon for breakfast when we stayed over. When I smell bacon, I think of Belle and the abuse, and I can't eat bacon.

I felt all G.I. Joe gung-ho when I left Lisa's office. I felt brave when I was sitting with Lisa, but out in the world, there are too many triggers. I'm nothing more than a terrified little kid. Oh, crap! I just fell into the self-defeating talk again. Shit, it's too easy to defeat myself. I just want someone to rescue me. I want a person who will take care of me, wake me up, cook my breakfast, send me out to play, tell me what to do, protect me from others and myself, do all the difficult things that I don't want to do. I NEED A MOM! My stomach hurts so I pull over the car, double up, and bawl my eyes out. Do people who hurt kids know the long term effects? Do they care that someone will be harmed and that pain will follow them the rest of their lives?

The anxiety's building in my chest. My heart's pounding and skipping beats. I'm clammy, my hands are shaking, and I'm dizzy. It feels like I am going to jump out of my skin. I'm having a panic attack, I know it in my head, yet I'm still frightened. I know intellectually it'll subside, yet I feel like I'm going to die. Ten minutes later, it's subsiding a bit. I need some of Rom's Ativan! I run upstairs, and take some from the medicine cabinet before anyone gets home. I immediately take one while looking at the face in the mirror. The mirror betrays my feelings. The face does not look like I'm feeling anxious. It just looks tired. The Ativan's beginning to work, the anxiety's a little less. Or maybe it's all in my head. The feeling usually goes away after 10-15 minutes. What if I had waited a bit more? Would it have subsided anyway? Perhaps, but I don't want to experience **any** anxiety, even mild. I open the bottle and take out five more pills and put them in my shirt pocket and hope Rom doesn't notice that six of his thirty tablets are missing. I guess it depends if he takes one every day. If he doesn't, I'm home free. If he does, I'm screwed. He'll accuse me and I'll deny it. There'll be a terrible fight and Rom will always know I took them, but he won't be able to prove it. I've taken some of Rom's medication before but just one pill every now and then. He hasn't noticed, or if he has he hasn't said anything.

I need these, and I've asked Dr. Jamison for them, but she's refused. I guess she's afraid I'll abuse them. She's right I'll abuse them because **I need them**. I cannot function without some sort of anxiety medication, but she keeps saying the medication I'm taking should help the anxiety, but it isn't an instant fix. Five minutes has passed and I'm not as anxious, but now I feel guilty. I start dinner to ease the guilt. I should return the pills, but what if I need them? What if I'm driving tomorrow and I get another panic attack? I could return four and keep just one. But, what if Rom moves his medication and I can't get to one if I need it? If he confronts me, I'll lie. God, I'm a bastard! I hate myself, but I can't stop doing these horrible things. Everyone told me I was cool as a cucumber on the witness stand and I was a hero of sorts, but what they didn't know is that the real hero was Rom's medication calming me down. What would Lisa think? She would be disappointed in me like I'm disappointed in myself. Would she call Dr. Jamison? Probably. Would Dr. Jamison then believe me about needing my own Ativan? Maybe. If Rom confronts me I'll deny it, and then admit it and become very contrite. Then I'll tell Lisa why I did it and she will be sweet and understanding and then she'll call Dr. J. and I'll get the meds I need. This could work. I might lose some respect from everyone, but I'll get what I want, oops, need. I can chalk this up to the stress of the trial. Yeah, that's it, the trial!

Dinner's in the oven and I lay down for a nap. I know I'm not supposed to do this, but I'm feeling tired, perhaps the panic attack and the Ativan made me feel sleepy. I take the five pills out of my pocket and slip them between the mattress and box spring. No one will find them there. It feels good to be slipping off to sleep. I'll have to get up just before Dad and Rom get home so they won't know I slept during the day. I set the alarm for an hour.

I'm awakened by Rom screaming in my face to give me his pills. Dad's standing in the doorway and doesn't know what to say or believe. He's looking from me to Rom and back again. I state calmly, "I don't know what you're talking about." At the moment, I really don't know what he's talking about. I'm groggy from the nap and my alarm didn't go off. Then I remember the Ativan. Shit. Rom has his hand out and demands I return the six pills I took. "Caz, I've been missing a pill here and there, but I thought I may have messed up the count. Then I thought you had taken them, but I could never prove it. So I started counting them each day. But now, there are **six** missing and I know you didn't ingest six all at once or you'd be zonked. And I counted them last night, now, give them back!"

I still feign innocence, but he's relentless. Rom is standing over me with his hand out and screaming over and over, "Give me my pills." I can't take his screeching so I reach between the mattress and box spring and give him two back. He erupts, "You took four today!? Are you crazy?" Now Dad is getting angry too. They storm out believing I had taken four Ativan today. But, I still have three hidden they don't know about. I hear Dad downstairs trying to calm Rom down and talk on the phone at the same time. Then I realize he's calling Lisa. Oh, no! I wanted to tell her myself. I can tell her the story so that she feels compassion. Dad's going to get her angry at me. I fly downstairs just in time to realize he'd left a message for her. I'm screwed. She's not going to trust me ever again. I begin to cry, "Dad, I would've told her, you didn't need to rat me out." Dad looks me straight in the eye and says, "Caz, we've been very understanding of your PBST, or whatever it is, but this is a criminal act and I'm not going to let you continue taking medication that belongs to someone else, sleeping all day, doing just enough to keep me from complaining, but not enough to get better. I know you're a very sick person and most of it's not your fault, but TAKING ROM'S MEDICATION IS YOUR FAULT. You cannot blame your mom or Belle or the other abusers. You did this all by yourself. You disgust me. GET OUT."

I can't believe what I'm hearing. Dad can't throw me out. He loves me and he knows I'm trying. "Dad, I made a mistake. I had a panic attack and I needed something. I felt like I was going crazy." Dad isn't buying it. "That accounts for one pill only. Also, why didn't you call Lisa or Dr. Jamison? Why didn't you call me or Rom and tell us what was happening?" Dad's furious and his face's the color of my radishes.

I need to get him to calm down. I'll go into my little boy act, "I don't know. I was scared and I just wanted to get the anxiety to go away. I over did it, but I didn't mean to." Where's Rom? He left the room briefly and has now returned. He's frigid, angry, and leaning against the door frame with an expression that fries the ends of my hair. Dad stops and looks at Rom who casually and slowly opens his hand to reveal my other three pills. I am **so** screwed! I feel a rush of anxiety, my heart starts beating fast, my head is spinning and....

Caz
Concussion Trauma

I've never been that angry and scared all at the same time. I see Caz' eyes roll back in his head and his whole six foot six body waver for a minute like a tree that's cut and ready to fall but doesn't for a few seconds. Then he falls and hits his head on the edge of the oven. Blood is spurting everywhere and Caz is totally unconscious, his face is pressed against the floor where his blood is pooling. Rom calls 911, while I try to stop the bleeding. The ambulance takes 10 minutes to get here, but thank God the police arrive first. They apply pressure and the pool of blood is not growing as fast. I tried to apply pressure, but I guess I wasn't applying enough. The paramedics arrive and are assessing Caz' injury. They ask me what happened, and I only say Caz passed out. Rom glares at me but says nothing. The paramedics inform me they're taking Caz to Greater Baltimore Medical Center and we should follow in our car. I nod and begin to leave when I see I'm covered in blood. I wash my hands, arms, and face. Rom gets me another shirt. The neighbors are gathering and look concerned but no questions.. Rom drives while I use my cell phone to call Lisa, Dr. Jamison, and Pastor Craig. I leave messages for all of them.

Pastor Craig is the first to return my call. He agrees to meet us at the hospital. By the time we arrived, they'd already taken Caz in to the back room. I tell the hospital registrar that my son has no insurance, which doesn't seem to matter to them. Another thank you to God. Pastor Craig arrives minutes later and asks what happened. I tell him everything. I cry. Rom cries and curses and then apologizes to our pastor who just shrugs and continues asking questions like did I called Lisa and Dr. Jamison. I told him I had.

It's been an hour and I can't stop my angry tears. I think I may become dehydrated. Craig nudges me to look up. When I do, I see Dr. Jamison walking toward me. She explains she was in the hospital for another reason and picked up my message that we were on the way to the emergency room. I had to repeat the entire story to her and she listened, nodded, and then went to see Caz. Another hour passes and Lisa calls. I take a deep breath. I'm dreading telling the story all over again. Craig rescues me. He tells Lisa the story and then hands me the phone. She asks how I'm doing. I don't know what to say. I feel I caused this by telling Caz to get out. Lisa's understanding. She says I had every right to be angry. I guess that's true. Caz broke the law, lied to Rom and me about how many pills he had taken, and then tried to deceive us further by withholding some of the pills. Why do **I** feel guilty, then? She asks how Rom is doing. I start to say Rom is really angry, but Rom, who has been pacing, leans over me and spits words into the cell phone near my ear. "He's a bold-faced liar and con artist and I want him out of my life. And maybe he needs another g. d. therapist, too." Lisa is quiet on the other end. I'm embarrassed by Rom's outburst, but I can't blame him. I'm fried with angry and disappointment myself, but I'm still worried about him. Lisa asks that I keep her informed. I promise I will.

A ½ hour later a nurse beckons to me. Rom refuses to see Caz, so I go in alone. Dr. Jamison is standing in the hall talking with another doctor as I approach and she nods to a quiet corner and I dutifully follow. She tells me Caz has a concussion and is still unconscious. The doctors have ordered a series of tests to see how much trauma (there's that word again) his brain sustained in the fall. Caz will be spending the night and possibly will be in the hospital a few days depending on what they find out from the tests. She says she'll revisit the need for a faster acting anti-anxiety medication when he's released from the hospital, but she's concerned he'll abuse it. Obviously she had been right in not prescribing the meds the first time. She has a good point. She says she is going to read him the riot act and monitor every pill for awhile until he builds back trust.

I don't know what to think any more. I need to leave this in her hands. Dr. Jamison excuses herself and tells me to have Caz make an appointment when he's out of the hospital and she leaves us.

I ask if I can see Caz, and the doctor nods, "Sure, but he's still unconscious."

"I understand." I reply.

Caz looks small in the bed with the machines beeping, IV tubes, and oxygen mask on. He's unresponsive when I touch his hand and stroke his forehead. I say I'm sorry, but I don't know what I'm sorry for, I just know I am. I've made many mistakes starting with not allowing Rom and Caz to grieve after their mother left. My tears are falling on his face as I whisper "I want you to get better. I love you." I haven't said those words to him in a long time. In fact I can't remember when I said them last. Perhaps that's what he needs to hear right now, if he can hear me at all.

Pastor Craig was allowed to see Caz, too. He says a prayer and lends support until Caz is formally admitted to the hospital. The ER doctor tells us to go home and rest.

I push through the huge white doors that separate the emergency room from the waiting room. Rom is crying and Pastor Craig comforts him. Thank heavens Rom finally feels something other than anger. We ride home in silence. Opening the front door yielded dark, acid tasting smoke. The smoke detectors are screaming a warning to the only occupant of the house, the dog, that there's danger. Cocoa's running around the house like a rabid animal, whining, wiping at her burning eyes on the rug. I realize the oven is the source of the smoke. The casserole Caz put in the oven had burned to a crisp and ruined the pan and possibly the inside of the oven. I throw the casserole and dish out the back door into the dirt, turn off the oven, open the windows, let the dog outside, collapse on the couch, and cry again. I don't think I've ever cried so much in one day in my life, even when my wife left I didn't' cry this much. Maybe I'm making up **for** holding it all in for all these years. Rom's sitting in the recliner stunned and in shock. He lets Cocoa back in and we fall asleep in the living room, me on the sofa, Rom in the recliner, Cocoa on the rug. The phone rings like an alarm clock at 8 a.m. In my groggy state, I thought the smoke detector was going off again, but it was the hospital calling to say Caz is waking up.

Rom and I shower, call in sick, and leave for the hospital. Caz' room is dark and he's asleep. Some things never change! We wait three hours before anyone talks to us. The staff neurologist tells us Caz sustained a frontal lobe hematoma, whatever that is. He may require surgery if the swelling doesn't subside soon. The fact he was conscious for a little while is a good sign. I tell Rom to go to work while I stay at the hospital with Caz. At first, Rom fights me saying things like he doesn't want to leave me alone, what if Caz takes a turn for the worse, etc., but I know Rom doesn't want to be here. He's just putting up a fight for my sake. I convince him I'll be fine and promise to call if anything changes. He leaves. I think he's glad to be leaving. To tell you the truth, I'm grateful he left. I need to be alone to sort out some stuff. I call Lisa and ask if I could see her.

She calls back an hour later and tells me to come at noon. I suspect I'm taking her lunch hour, but she never lets on.

I spend three hours sitting beside my son. My son, who's been damaged by his mother's abandoning him, damaged further by a mother figure who abused him, hurt further by three women connected to Belle, harmed by my unavailability, and injured by several others who judged him harshly or who betrayed his trust. His problems have been further exacerbated by the recent trial and media attention. I'm in the middle of sorting all this out when I realize I need to leave to see Lisa.

She sits quietly and allows me to talk. I explain that Caz has been awake twice for about 30 minutes but then falls back asleep. The doctors are debating whether they need to relieve the pressure in his brain. Lisa nods, "How are **you** doing, Stewart?"

Burning tears are falling. "I'm trying to sort through this mess, not just what happened last night, but what's been happening for the last 20 years."

"And what have you come up with?" Lisa asks.

"Caz has not only been abused but neglected."

"Say more about that."

"I'm trying to put this into words, but I'm having difficulty. Their mother's abandonment was traumatic, but then I emotionally neglected both Rom and Caz not only because I was hurting, but also because I was the bread winner and mother, nurse, tutor, and housekeeper. I didn't have enough time, so I let Belle take Caz, thinking it was ok. Belle abused him, but in some ways, she was neglecting his real needs. Something like that."

"You mean she neglected his need for honest intimacy, caring, and mothering? She pretended to give him what he desperately needed, but it was all dishonest."

"Yeah, she was neglecting him, too, in favor of her own needs. Then his psychiatrist gave him medication but ignored what Caz was saying about Belle. And he didn't report the abuse. That's more neglect. His counselor did the same thing. His adviser at school was focused on putting Caz down, and she ignored Caz' needs and neglected to report the abuse."

Lisa listened to me go on and on for 45 minutes. It was like a cleansing and a confession. She never judged. I can see why Caz has grown fond of her.

Lisa finally gets a chance to say something, "Stewart, you're doing a lot of powerful processing of your life with Caz and Rom. Talking with someone about your experience may help."

Tears are welling up again. "You're right, Lisa, can I get a referral?" I was as surprised as Lisa at my request, but she wasted no time in pulling out her card and writing two colleagues names and numbers on the back and handing it to me. I believe this is the right next step. I only wish I had taken this step into self-exploration 20 years ago. Her final gift was a question. "Have you told Caz this?" I shake my head, thank her for listening, and leave.

I return to Caz' room and begin to pour out my heart the way I did at Lisa's office. I say everything. Everything that's been bothering me all these years. After fifteen minutes, I pause to catch my breath and from the bed came Caz' voice, "My whole life has been a stench of neglect." Caz has been listening, for how long I don't know. I try to hug him through the tubes and wires that are hooked up to his body.

We laugh at my fumbling, "Caz, that's the perfect title for your book." Caz laughs and whispers hoarsely. "Who'd read it? Who'd want to read a sad, desperate, abusive story like mine?"

"I think a lot of people would be interested in what you have been through. Pastor Craig has called your story 'compelling' and he's right. Many people could've made a difference in your life and failed to help you. Perhaps another person, reading your story, may recognize what he or she could or should do for another child who's experienced what you have and intervene quickly."

Caz smiled, "Then you write it or better, tell Lisa to write it. I'm a lousy writer. Besides, I don't want any more reminders of my sad, sad life."

This time Caz stays awake for 90 minutes before he falls back asleep. When the doctor drops by at six p.m. He tells me the swelling is subsiding, There will be no surgery unless Caz does not continue to improve, which he does. Four days later, I take him home. His first statement as he walked in the front door is, "It smells like smoke in here. Have you guys taken up smoking?" Even Rom had to laugh.

Caz' Regret

What a jerk I was -- a complete asshole to take those pills from Rom. What was I thinking? Gee, I sound like Dr. Phil. I'd like to believe I wasn't thinking... but if I'm honest, I've been carefully manipulating a way to get Rom's medication without his knowing it. I manipulated everyone, including myself. I can't believe my family, Lisa, Dr. Jamison, and Pastor Craig are hanging in there with me. Dr. Jamison added Klonopin back in to my medication cocktail. I don't get the intense rush of relief I get with Ativan, but I'm less anxious. She read me the riot act about how dangerous it is to take someone else's medication. She nailed me when she asked, "What if the Ativan had reacted negatively with one of the other medications you were on?" I hadn't thought about that. She also told me if I ever did anything like that again, she would not continue as my psychiatrist. At first I didn't believe her, but then she pulled out a piece of paper and wrote a contract stating I would never take any medication except what has been prescribed to me by her or my physician. If I do, then our relationship would be over. She signed it, and I signed it. She's a serious dudette!

Lisa was more gentle, but she was still insistent I never take any medication except my own. She also pointed out how manipulating people often bites a person in his ass. She didn't say it exactly like that, but that's the gist of it. She made it clear If I needed something, I was to ask straight out. I was to state what I need. I may or may not get it – that's life. I agreed, but this is new to me. I've never operated honestly before. My life trained me to manipulate others to get what I want, because I couldn't count on other people to listen and to have my best interest in mind. Another new task to learn!

I'm really getting tired of all this pain and having to learn stuff most people get in childhood. And the concussion left me with headaches that blow the top of my head off. I'm tired, really physically tired. The doctor says it's because of the head injury.

Also, I'm listing to the right when I walk. I can't read. I mean, I can read the words, but I cannot understand what I've read. I need to read over and over again and still it's like reading Greek. I also have some compulsive acts like lining up things. Yesterday, I was setting the table and I lined up the forks, knives and spoons on the placemat and then realigned them, then measured with my fingers to be sure each one was perfectly placed. When I'm talking I lose track of what I was saying and I search for words, simple words, I've known all my life. The scariest outcome of the concussion is I'm not retaining information. Yesterday, Dad asked me to go the drug store and get shaving cream. I walked to the wrong store and forgot why I was there. I've been told all these symptoms are the result of the brain injury. Lisa called these symptoms Post-concussional Disorder. If they don't improve in the next month, I will need to do some sort of brain therapy. Great! More work for my brain. At least this is cognitive brain retraining and not the emotional retraining crap. I'm getting tired of trying to change myself.

I still see Lisa but not as often. Just the work of getting dressed is exhausting. Oh, yeah, and I can't drive for a few weeks. The emotional work wipes me out for the rest of the day, so Lisa and I are only seeing each other when I call which is about every 14 days. I miss seeing her, but I've only myself to blame. If I had not taken Rom's meds none of this would've happened. I'm trying not to blame others for my life. I still try to manipulate Dad using my emotions and the "poor me" attitude, and then I catch myself and back off. Other times, I go ahead and manipulate him. He feels guilty for telling me to 'get out' and that makes it easy to get him to do what I want. Three days ago, I wanted some of my favorite ice cream, mint chocolate chip. I'm not allowed to drive yet, so I had to ask Dad to drive to the store which is five miles away. Dad told me he would get some tomorrow on his way home from work. I did my best to look sad and disappointed. I even told him I could get a cab (how I was going to pay for it, I didn't consider.). He sighed a huge sigh and drove me to the ice cream store. I got what I wanted. I didn't feel great about it, though. I realize I was using Dad just like I was used by Belle. Well, maybe not "just like I was used", but I did get him to do what I wanted. I felt powerful and guilty at the same time. I wonder if Belle or her "ladies" ever felt that way?

A Therapeutic Holiday

Sometimes, when I'm doing intensive psychotherapy with a client like Caz, a therapeutic holiday is called for. Counseling becomes too intense for too long and the good work that's been done seems to unravel as the intensity continues. I was beginning to feel that Caz was moving along too fast, that his previous work had not been metabolized thoroughly. He was pressuring himself to complete issues in a few sessions that had taken 25 years to develop. His fall stopped the intensity of our work together. However, Caz may need to take some time off from therapy and work on some of his more concrete life issues, like learning a new skill or developing or repairing relationships. In addition, Caz must focus on his physical healing which will be slow.

I might have also pushed for progress too quickly, because Caz was pushing himself. Much has happened in the months we have been seeing each other. He has made some progress on his PTSD and depression, but his personality traits undermine his progress and this will take much longer to address. His dependent traits are ingrained. He is still seeking the mothering he lost at six. He's been trying to get some expression of love out of Stewart and possibly Rom. He's also very dependent on me. How can I disallow Caz' dependency on me before he has others who are available to meet his emotional needs? At least now he's aware he manipulates others to get his needs met. He even knows when he is doing it and why. However, he has difficulty stopping his impulse to proceed with the manipulation. Sometimes when he isn't manipulating to get his needs met, he too quickly defers to others because he wants to be liked or loved. When he isn't manipulating and deferring, he is demanding, just like a small child. Caz focuses on getting his needs and wants met and ignores others' needs.

When I think of Caz, I think of someone who is dejected, defeated, gloomy, pessimistic, and unhappy. He expresses very little joy in life. He believes he is inadequate, worthless, and has little self-esteem which is evident in his critical, self-blaming, and derogatory remarks. He broods and makes critical, judgmental remarks about himself. He is very prone to feeling guilty and remorseful.

The most irritating traits to his family are his passivity around fulfilling his routine chores and self-care. He constantly complains he's misunderstood and unappreciated. He plays the "poor me" and "why me?" cards frequently. He also vacillates between defiance and contrition.

No wonder I have been struggling with Caz' treatment. His personality traits transcend across several diagnoses and his symptoms are intertwined in his behavior, feelings, and thoughts. His multiple traumas, which resulted in PTSD, coupled with his learning disabilities and ADHD, set him up for a complicated and difficult life. But first, Caz also has to heal from his brain trauma. Then he's facing testifying at Ann's trial. Then perhaps he'll be able to address more thoroughly his on-going issues.

He's been hurting deeply all his life so learning new life skills are not going to happen overnight. I don't know why I was allowing him to push himself forward so quickly. He felt like a man on fire and now the flame is greatly diminished. Slowing down could be the best solution for him at this point.

It's 10 p.m. and sleep is calling to me. A loud knock on my door startles me. I hate opening the door this late. "Who is it?" The detectives are at my door! Don't they ever sleep? I open the door to Detective Lang and Detective Bentley. "What's so important that you two are out in the middle of the night?" I ask, pulling my robe closer around me.

Detective Lang says, "We thought you'd like to be the first to know Ann has taken a plea bargain and there will be no more trials. She gave us the names of five other women who were involved in the "Belle-ring" and they all accepted plea bargains. Caz will not have to testify again.

"This happened just now? At 10 o'clock at night?"

"Well not really. It happened a few hours ago, but the ink on the signatures is now dry and we wanted to share the good news with you. We thought we owed you one." said Detective Bentley.

Detective Lang continues, "We thought you'd like to be the one to share this with Caz. We heard he took quite a fall and has a concussion. We didn't want to wake him, but we wanted to share the good news with someone. So we chose you."

"Thanks, this is good news, indeed. I'll call him tomorrow. But detectives, you scared me knocking on my door at this hour. A phone call would have sufficed."

Detective Bentley nods and apologizes. "I guess we were too enthusiastic to sleep." Both detectives exit my front door, then detective Lang turns to say, "This was quite an ordeal for everyone. We all 'dun' gud.'"

I wave and smile and they do the same.

What a wonderful gift. I guess God heard my plea on behalf of Caz and, she came through!

The next morning I awoke feeling like I had dreamed the detectives' late night visit. I knew I hadn't, but I fell asleep so quickly I didn't have time to think about the implications. The drama's over for Caz. Now he can really begin to heal and move on without having to relive the abuse again in another public trial. I decide this news is too good to sit on. I have a break at 10, and I will drive to Caz' house and tell him the good news personally.

After seeing two clients, I begin driving to Caz' house. As I round the corner, I see Caz open the front door to retrieve the paper. He's still in his pajamas and robe. I'm dismayed. I thought he was trying to get up at nine when his father and brother left for work. What am I doing? I'm going to a client's house without invitation and for what? To be the first one to tell him some good news? Lisa...THINK! "Shit", I say out loud and turn the car around. However, I'm too late, Caz sees my car and waves. I keep going. I'm way too invested in this case. I need help to sort this out... again.

Returning to my office, I immediately make a soothing cup of tea and sit down to think and feel through why I'm over involved with Caz' situation. I know about the abandonment stuff. I figured that out with Maggie and Milly. But, what else is going on? I see my message light is blinking. I have a feeling it's Caz. It is. "Hi Lisa, I saw you driving down my street (good, he didn't see me turn around.). Did you need to see me? (Ouch, did **I** need to see **him**?) Call me if you need something. If I don't hear from you, I will see you in two days for our appointment.

I call a friend of mine who supervised me years ago. She knows me well and worked with me when my daughter died. I offer to take her to lunch on Friday. Sally accepts. I tell her I have some CT stuff, that's what we call it when we don't want to say countertransference. Somehow CT sounds less intimidating. Countertransference occurs when a counselor ascribes to a client her own thoughts, feelings, behaviors, values, etc. that belong to someone else. Countertransference can interfere with our work. It's usually our "stuff" to sort out and as a therapist, when CT emerges, I must attend to it. We all have feelings about almost everything. It's the sticky ones that cause us to drive to a client's home without thinking about it first.

I call Caz and he answers immediately and starts explaining "I have a bad cold so I haven't gotten dressed yet," he says through a very stuffed up nose. He probably thought I had seen him still in his pajamas at 10 a.m. and wanted to clear up why.

I remain neutral and professional. "I have some good news."

"What is it?"

I explain that the detective duo dropped by my house last night at 10 o'clock to tell me Ann, and five other women she named, all pled guilty and accepted plea bargains. There would be no more trials. Caz shouted, "Yes!!! God does answer petitions. I was prepared to testify, but I don't know what it would have taken out of me. I'm very relieved." I smile at his reaction and tell him to take care of his cold and I will see him in two days.

I hang up and still can't believe I even thought about driving to a client's home unannounced! If I hadn't turned around, I would have been standing in his doorway with him in his pajamas. He may have even hugged me for bringing the good news. What was I thinking? I know exactly what I was thinking. I was letting my ego get the better part of me. I wanted to be the one to tell Caz about the plea bargains. I wanted to share the good news. In therapy, I have been confronting his self-defeating behavior, now I was going to make him feel good. I need to reign in my countertransference.

I'm losing perspective. Sally is a good choice for a consult.

No More Testifying
Now What?

I'm unsure how I feel about the conclusion of my abuse saga. The good guys won and the abusers went to jail. I bet they don't regret what they did but do regret getting caught. I feel sad for Belle, but she got what she deserved.

The most remarkable parts of this journey are the discoveries I've made about myself. I'm not as good a person as I thought. I always saw myself as a poor little victim who hardly ever did anything wrong. I've always thought others were the evil ones who abused, abandoned, neglected, gossiped, lied, deceived, and used others. I knew I sinned, but I saw my sins as insignificant. I took the Lord's name in vain, I didn't study for a test, I had sex, or I told a lie. I never saw how the abuse taught me to look at life through self-centered and pessimistic lenses. I only thought about how I could get others to meet my needs by playing the victim, how I used any tool necessary to get people to do my bidding or walk on eggshells so they don't upset me. I demanded people be perfect when I was not perfect. I demanded that people meet my needs, but I never made any effort to meet theirs. I wanted to do what I wanted when I wanted and make others feel guilty if they didn't help me. I'm a louse

Lisa has me talking positively to myself. At first, the idea was repugnant now I like talking positively. But then, I realized the positive things I was saying were small potatoes compared to the really horrible side of me. I was deceptive, I abandoned my self-respect. I neglected my family by sleeping all day. I lied. I stole. I deceived others, and I used others. How am I that much different from Belle and her cohort? I'm not. I just didn't abuse children. I'm having a difficult time living with myself right now. Healing from the fall has given me a lot of time to think. I can't concentrate on reading. I can't sleep well because of the headaches. I can't walk a lot or do anything a lot. I can only watch television for so long and then my head hurts. Therefore, I have many quiet hours, time to reflect on myself. Funny, the one who previously only thought of himself, now only has time to think of himself. And, I don't like what I'm feeling or seeing inside. I've been praying God would help me. Is it possible God has really answered my prayers by letting me sink this low? As a result of this self-reflection time, I have more compassion for others and I'm embarrassed by my actions, especially over the last several months. I feel bad about how I treated my father and brother. Then I blamed **them** when they got angry at me. What an asshole I am!

I haven't had a session with Lisa in awhile. Haven't felt well enough, but I have an appointment tomorrow. I will 'confess'... the phone rings and awakens me out of my thoughts. I'm told by the prosecutor's secretary that Belle will be sentenced today...in case I wanted to be there. I do, but how will I get someone to take me with such a late notice? I still can't drive. I call the detectives and ask politely if they could pick me up. They say it is their pleasure.

This is the fourth time I have been to the courthouse in six weeks. The prosecutors' prep, Belle's trial, Belle's verdict, and now the sentencing. Sitting with the detectives feels safe, but safe from what? Belle's sentence is three years for each count. That's 60 years in jail. She will be eligible for parole in 30 years when she's 90. My brain fell to my stomach, not because I'm angry or sad for her but because of the waste of life. Many have been harmed, not just the boys she molested but their parents who trusted her, the church members who believed in her, the spouses of the victims, their children, etc. My God! One person can affect so many people in such negative ways. If one person can affect that many in a negative way, then can one person affect many in a positive way? Sure! But, why is it the impact of negative works seems stronger than the impact of good works? Since my concussion, I'm becoming more philosophical even though I can't remember to brush my teeth or empty the dishwasher! It's not that I don't want to do these things anymore, it's that I don't remember anymore. God, I hope this isn't permanent.

Belle will be in prison for the rest of her life and, as a pedophile, she may suffer at the hands of the inmates. My understanding is inmates hate child abusers, especially sexual abusers. The judge speaks harshly to her, but because she has no "priors", he's sending her to a minimum security prison.

Lisa
Consultation with Sally

Waiting for Sally at a seafood restaurant in Timonium I look over the appetizer menu, but nothing is awakening my appetite. This place has the best jumbo lump crab cakes in the Baltimore area, and yet I don't feel like indulging myself. She is a few minutes late, but that's Sally! I keep wondering how I will approach talking about my issues with Caz. Sally is usually very insightful and very direct. Sometimes I don't appreciate her laser brain, but today I need her to focus on my sore spots and zap me. I feel safe in her presence and know that no matter what she comes up with, she has my best interest at heart. Sally appears at the restaurant door, flashing her famous wide grin. Her dark brown eyes look black and give her an exotic look, especially when she colors her hair auburn like it is now. Sally and I hug and kiss each other on the cheek, our normal greeting. She apologizes for her tardiness. I accept, telling her that it's given me time to think. "Sounds ominous," she reflects.

I explain what happened when I started to drive to Caz' house ending with "I know I took a risk, the thing is I didn't even know I was stepping over a boundary. I'm usually careful. What happened?"

Sally says, "What do you think happened?" Before I can answer, the waitress arrives for our drink orders which gives me time to think. Sally and I both order iced teas and then she looks expectantly at me. "I think I got caught up in a supportive relationship and forgot my therapist-client relationship. I know I needed to play both parts, the supporter of 'C' as a witness in an abuse trial **and** his therapist too. The trial took me out of the therapy room and placed me at the courthouse and at Belle's house. I was right to enter into the in vivo work, but somewhere the boundaries were lost or crossed. I didn't even think to pick up the phone and call 'C'. I just started out for his house. The funny thing is I had never been to his house and I still didn't think two hoots about arriving on his doorstep with the good news. Perhaps I was set up by the 10 p.m. detectives' visit."

Sally looks doubtful. "I think you're looking too superficially by considering the behavioral aspects. I think you may need to look at the emotional part of how you're somehow connected to 'C'." LASER BEAM!

She's right. I'm dodging the question. Maybe, some free association will help. "Let's see. 'C' is an extremely challenging client. He challenges me on every level: emotional, intellectual, spiritual, physical." Sally raises her eyebrows at the word 'physical'. I continue, "C exhausts me and sometimes when I'm around him I feel tired just thinking of all the elements of his story I have to address. I become overwhelmed thinking about what he's had to deal with. I even dream about him. I'm always looking for the one thing I can say that would allow him to see how he mistreats himself and others, but nothing has worked." Sally smiles as she attacks her salad. "Nothing has worked?"

That was a stupid turn of a phrase. "Of course I've been effective and he's quite insightful. He has great ideas and makes progress and then stops, retreats, and blames others for his lack of progress. He's frustrating his father and brother and at one point they were ready to kick him out of the house. It's not that 'nothing has worked', it's that nothing changes permanently. It's like he's doing things I suggest just because I suggest them, but then he stops doing them and falls back into old habits. He doesn't see **he** is now his problem, not his mother, father, brother, abusers, etc. He doesn't get it." Sally mumbles as she eats some bread, but I hear her question. "Why don't you tell him that **he** is the problem?"

"He may flee if I confront him like that, and he needs a lot more time in therapy. If I blow it and confront too soon, he might leave counseling and I'll be just one more person in a whole line of people who have not supported him when he feels he needs it most."

Sally asks the obvious question, but sometimes I need to hear the obvious. "Do you think he's that fragile?" I honestly don't know how to answer that. I use my food to think about the question. "I don't know. I hate when clients say that to me and here I am saying it to you, but I honestly don't know. He appears fragile, but not as fragile as he was when he first came to see me. He has more insight and is beginning to be more honest with himself, but he still seems fragile. I'm afraid if I confront him, he'll leave before he's ready. OH MY GOSH!! I just realized why I'm connected to 'C'. I didn't confront my husband about his lack of attending to our relationship after our daughter died. I wanted to ask him to seek counseling, but I was afraid he would run away. I wasn't available to him because I was grieving myself, but I was at least there if he wanted to unburden himself. He tried to act as if nothing bothered him and yet I could sense he was one step away from collapsing into tears. When I did confront him about his lack of grieving and not participating anymore in our relationship, he left."

Sally lifts her fork in a gesture that said, "So there you go. For you, confrontation after a trauma has yielded abandonment in the past."

Amazing how this counseling stuff works! The parallel process is incredible. What my client experiences, I experience or have experienced. Same melody, different verse.

I leave feeling better but still don't know what to do. I understand why I let my boundary down with Caz. I was combining my feelings about my ex-husband's leaving with the possibility Caz' would flee. However, Caz needs to be confronted about his behavior, but, if I do, he may run just like my ex-husband did. The relationship with Caz started feeling familiar, and so I did with Caz what I did with my spouse. With Jay, I would have wanted to see his expression if I had something exciting to share. I wanted to see Caz' expression when I told him there would be no trial. I need to reset my boundary.

Rape, Lies, and Manipulation

Crap, Shit, and any other defecation procedure I can think of. I'm in a funk. Too much to deal with. The job is a pain, and I used to love it. The political stuff used to energize me, and now it drains me. I wonder if I have sprained my emotions, and I'm spiraling out of control. I've reached my coping limit. I'm due to see Lisa today, but I don't feel like going over what happened in Seattle again. Lisa doesn't usually make me feel better. She usually makes me think... and feel, oh God, she'll ask me how I feel! I can't do it today!

I'm sitting in my car in Lisa's parking lot, but I don't want to go in. But, I can't stand her up, and it's too late to cancel. Shit. I get out and slam the door.

Lisa's waiting, but she doesn't complain when I'm late. She just looks at me expectantly like I'm supposed to tell her what happened.

"I don't want to talk about it. I'm too frigging tired. The trip was more than I expected and I haven't slept since yesterday, I blew the job out there, and I'm emotionally overwhelmed."

"Sounds like an awful experience for you. What are you doing to take care of yourself?"

"Nothing except think and cry."

"What are you thinking about?"

"How my life is f'd up. Little is definitely my mother. She was raped by my father three times and has two sons older than me. All three of us are the products of rape. It's a long, long story, and I can't go into it right now. Suffice it to say I got the whole story and it's tragic. My father is a rapist, my grandfather was a sexist and a manipulator, my mother and grandmother played patsies to their husbands, and I'm too much like Little. She's cold, aloof, and controlling…but still, I liked her. She's a tragic figure and is probably suffering as much or more than I am. I saw my brother… now, my half brother, Atlee. He's been working on getting his life together, and he's been very successful…."

"Wait a minute. You saw Little?"

"Yes and Sassy. Oh, that's right you don't know. I always think you can read minds. (Lisa smiles a little.) When Carly and I arrived, Atlee announced he had been in contact with both Sassy and Little who live in the Seattle/Portland area. He had invited them to meet us. Both Carly and I were blown away that they both live in the area. That's why he moved there. He wanted to leave the Chicago area, some little dumb town like a watch name, Timex or Elgin or something, and he found out from Mom that Sassy and Little were in the Northwest and he moved there.

"I'm really tired. Let me explain, no let me sum up. My father married my mother and she couldn't have children, so my grandfather arranged for my father to have sex with Little and she got pregnant twice, twin boys and me. My grandfather, who only had daughters, took both of Little's boys away from her to raise them as his own. Little was young, maybe 20, and she believed she had to do what her father said. My father was furious when his sons were taken to live with my grandfather, so he raped Little again, and Little had me, my grandfather wasn't interested in a girl so my father took me and gave me to Mom. Little was humiliated, being an unwed mother, and was also fearful if she stayed, she'd be raped again. So she left town and hid in the Seattle area. Dad then turned to Sassy and raped her and she had Carly. Sassy left town at Little's urging and my father took Carly and also gave her to Mom to raise. Then apparently he needed an outlet for his sexual "attentions" and turned to Mom for the first time in years and she got pregnant with Atlee. Dad wanted a son and was furious Mom was the one who gave him a son, so he resented Mom and Atlee. Treated them like used lumber. That's why Atlee left home when he was 18 and never went back. He cut all ties to the family except for Mom."

"You've had quite a weekend. Take a breath. Another. Another. Did anything positive happen?"

I hate when she does that. I'm churned up and want to stay hyper. But, the breathing did settle me down. "Seattle is gorgeous. Carly and I took a walk through the woods and watched a family of beavers with Atlee's son, Danny. He's a cool kid. Also, we all got to meet each other and hash out what we wanted to do. We've decided to confront Dad, all five of us together."

"What's it like for you? To find out who you are and why you are who you are?"

"I don't want to be rude, Lisa, but I don't have an friggin' clue right now. I'm too tired and overwhelmed to sort it out."

I hesitate trying to decide whether to tell Lisa about the chaotic presentation. What the hell! "I also stayed for an extra day, and did a seminar so my company would pay for my trip out there. I was prepared to stay two days, but it all went poorly. I was too stressed out, I wasn't prepared, and I didn't do a good job. I've had to cover my butt with my boss and I know if he figures out I used his company to get myself to Seattle, he will fire me. So I'm living hour by hour hoping he doesn't find out." There, it's all out. Now watch Lisa lecture me about my deception!

"That's a lot of pressure on you. Are you ok?" She's a tricky one. I can't figure her out!

"No, but I'm making do." Tears fall on my designer suit. "I need to go to Aruba or something and get de-stressed."

"Are you sure you're ok? You have experienced a life-altering event that redefines who you are. Finding your mother, finding out your father is a rapist, reconnecting with your siblings, deciding to confront your father and fearing being caught by your boss. How are you taking care of yourself?"

"Duh!! I'm not! You forgot I'm still in recovery and I had an accident. I'm a mess. I'm looking forward to confronting my father with my biomom and my sibs, though. The son of a bitch screwed up eight lives and should pay for what he's done."

"A **little** anger can be energizing, but Bally you're way over the top with stress and change. Again, how are you planning to take care of yourself?"

"I'm not. I can't turn my mind off. I tried sleeping on the plane, but I couldn't sleep. The weekend events keep doing Twilight Zone reruns in my head. I wish I could make them stop. When I'm not thinking about the weekend, I'm thinking about confronting Dad or worrying about losing my job. I wish I could just lie down and go to sleep and not wake up to this nightmare of a life!"

"Bally, I need assurance you're not going to hurt yourself."

"What? And miss the major scene in this tragic movie where we confront my Dad? Not on your life! I gotta see this! Little and Sassy and their rapist together with their bastard children! I wouldn't miss this for the world!" I laugh wickedly, and a little too loudly.

"I'm serious. I need assurance you're not going to hurt yourself, including not drinking."

"Ok, ok, I am fine. I'm over-the-top stressed, but I am not suicidal."

Pause. Lisa's not budging.

"I'm not going to hurt myself, ok."

"Ok. No plan?"

"No plan."

"No means to hurt yourself like a bottle of pills or a gun?"

"No means."

"And no desire?"

"No! I'm on a mission to see my father pay. Ok?"

"Bally, this is a very tough time in your life. All you thought you knew about your family and yourself has changed. People are usually very fragile and vulnerable during times like these. Promise me you will call me if you feel like hurting yourself or someone else. If you can't reach me, go the nearest emergency room."

"Lisa, I'm ok. Stop worrying."

"Ok." She relinquishes.

"Look I don't want to be rude, but I can't keep my eyes open. Can we cut this short? You helped me decompress a bit, and I think I can sleep now."

"Ok. But, I wonder if you see the similarity between your chaotic emotional experience with your family and the chaos in your professional presentation."

That got me interested. "What do you mean?"

"Well, you and Carly went to Seattle expecting to simply meet with your brother and discuss the possibilities of finding your mothers. Then Atlee throws you for a loop by springing a meeting with Little and Sassy on you. You weren't prepared for this switch. Similarly, you went to Seattle, expecting to simply present a workshop, but when you arrived, you find out there's a switch, a need to present different material and you weren't prepared for this switch either."

"Life imitates life?"

"Exactly."

"Are you saying I need to learn to be prepared for the bait-and-switch experiences that happen in life?"

"I don't know that's what I'm saying. I don't know we can always be prepared for life's twists and turns. I'm saying our lives often are filled with patterns from which we can learn."

"Lisa, did you just mean to make a rhyme?"

Lisa smiles, "No, but I did, didn't I? Sorry."

"Ok, back to me. What do you think I have to learn, except crisis management?"

"I wonder if you could look at this experience as one that could teach you how you usually anticipate and respond to unexpected situations, then learn a different way of responding."

"Do you think I could have been more prepared for Little's appearance?" I am annoyed and show it.

"No, but when you realized you had been thrown for a loop, emotionally, and you were overwhelmed, you could have said to yourself, 'I am not in a good place, I'm tired and feel sick.' And you could have called in sick to take care of yourself. But, you plowed ahead and repeated the same defeating chaotic pattern in your business life that you were already dealing with in your personal life. This is not uncommon...we do this to ourselves."

"It never occurred to me to stop and re-group." I   yawn boldly!

"Exactly. When do you want to return?"

"In a week?"

"Are you sure you don't need something sooner?"

"Ok. Sure. Can I see you on Thursday after work?"

"Sure. How about 5:00."

"Fine."

"Sleep well."

"Thanks."

Lisa
Bally's Discoveries

Bally is one tough woman, but these latest discoveries about her family could be the most difficult for her to assimilate. She has support from her sister and her brother, but the revelations about their father and the tasks upon which the three of them are embarking are psychologically dangerous to them, especially to Bally. The temptation to drink could overwhelm her ability to resist. I should've mentioned to her to call her AA sponsor.

I call Bally, but she doesn't answer her cell phone so I leave a message. I hope she doesn't try to handle her recent experience all by herself. On Thursday, I want to follow up and find out more about how she got along with Little. How are they alike and how are they different? I also want to explore the walk through the woods and maybe do some guided imagery to help her relax.

Bally's Dilemma

At first I was irritated with Lisa for bringing up how I charge ahead without taking care of myself. This is a pattern I was taught early in life by my father. I thought she was blaming me, but when I thought about it, as I was driving home, I realized she was offering me a way of looking at my life I had never considered. I've been taught to push through everything with sheer determination. When I'm stressed or sick, I always get myself into trouble because I pretend I have things all together, but I end up making more errors so I have to blame or manipulate others in order to avoid taking responsibility for myself. It never occurred to me I could stop and take care of myself and reflect on what's happening. I'm not sure how to do this, but I'm sure Lisa has some ideas. She always does. God, she's annoying.

As I fall asleep I think about how it never occurred to me to see the meeting with Little as overwhelming me. I simply charged into a business presentation feeling awful. My father taught me well. His mantra was be strong, don't admit weakness, taking care of self is stupid, just get the job done. And if you have to lie, cheat, or blame others, do so and don't let them see you sweat! How will I ever get his crap out of my head?

I slept! I feel much better but a little hung over because I took a sleeping pill. I know I shouldn't have done it. Lisa would not approve, but I'm fine. I won't tell her. Wait! I don't know what Lisa thinks. Maybe she wouldn't disapprove and even if she does, so what? I was taking care of myself. She encourages me to do that! I slept well. I needed the drug. I don't remember any dreams, and I never got up to pee.

I think I can work today, after I get some coffee. I hate the fact that bitch is in my head. In some ways she's like my father. I hear her voice instructing me like I hear his. Some days she's like a song in my head I can't stop. Do shrinks know how much power they have?

The phone is ringing and interrupts my thoughts. "Hello?"

"Hi Bally."

"Hi Atlee. Hey, I'm grateful for your hospitality last weekend. I felt so bad as I was leaving that forgot to thank you properly. I'm impressed with your lifestyle in Seattle. I envy you. You're an excellent father. Loved Danny. Please thank him for the experience with Mr. and Ms. Beaver."

"You're welcome. I'm glad we got everyone together. I think we got some perspective and truth about our heritage, instead of lies and secrets. Listen, the reason I'm calling is to tell you I'm planning to see Mom in a couple of weeks and already made plane reservations. She's excited to see me and Danny. I hope she still feels that way when she finds out why we're visiting."

"Yipes that was fast. Hey, I know you can pull this off with Mom. You're the most thoughtful and kind person I know, and if anyone can break through her denial, you can. Let her know that we all love her and do not want her to feel any guilt. She was a great mother. I wish I had been a better daughter."

"That's why I am calling. Do you want to be there with me?"

CLOBBER! "Er....I don't think I'm the best one to talk to her about this. I think you are."

"What if I told you Little's coming with me? Would that change your mind?"

"It might. Let me think about it. Things aren't going well at work. I've been very distracted by all the personal stuff. I'll call in a couple of days and let you know. Ok? Thanks for asking me."

"You're welcome. Let me know, ok?"

"Ok, bye."

Crap, I don't want Little confronting Mom using her frigid, silent stance. Should I go? I'll put my job in danger if I take off any more time. He did say, "Weekend." Maybe I can squeeze out of work a little early. These cross country flights with two hour pre-flight arrivals at the airports are energy killers.

The internet reveals I could catch an 8:00 p.m. flight on a Friday and arrive at 9:00 p.m. That means I gotta be at the airport at six which means I must leave the office at five because of traffic. Geez it's going to be tight. Can I really do this?

I'm already tired. Damn, damn, damn. I can't let Little treat Mom the way she treated me in Seattle. Can Atlee handle this all by himself? Am I rescuing? You bet your ass I am! I click the send button buying the ticket.

Chapter Nine
Perspective

...a situation in which a patient is seeking help from a...therapist represents precisely the sort of trigger that activates the attachment system.
(Brisch, 2002)

Bally's Dilemma Continues

"Lisa, I don't know if I'm doing the right thing or not."

"Could you be a little more explicit for me?"

"Oh, sorry, I still think you can read my mind. Atlee called and he's jumping on this thing about visiting Mom. He's going to see her in a couple of weeks and explain everything to her. He's also planning to ask her where Dad is. Little's going with him. I feel like I gotta be there. If Little treats Mom the way she treated me, Mom could really get hurt. Not worried about Atlee. He's cool and so is Danny, but Little, she's got an icicle hanging from her nose and each nipple."

"So you're wondering if you should go because....?"

"Am I rescuing Mom? Or more to the point, am I protecting her from Little? I wish Sassy were going instead. She's so sweet.

Interesting. Their names don't match their personalities. Little is much more sassy and Sassy is a sweet **little** lady."

"And you're going in order to protect your mother?"

"That's it in a cashew shell."

"If you don't go, and Little gets out of hand, then what will you feel?"

"Crappy. Like I let Mom down."

"And if you do go and Little gets out of hand, then what would you feel or do?"

"I would feel like I could ease the tension and protect Mom, explain to her how Little's been very hurt and damaged by Dad, and she doesn't always care if she hurts someone else."

"Are you talking about Little or yourself?

"Crap, Lisa, I'm talking about Little!"….Long pause…"But, I could be talking about me, too."

"How so?"

"I'm hurt and damaged too, and I feel rage almost every day, and go off on the nearest person."

"That's quite a revelation, Bally."

"I've known it a long time, just never acknowledged it. I'm trying that 'name it, claim it, tame it,' thing that what's-his-name said, Young?"

"You mean Carl Jung?"

"Yea. Him. We do the Myers-Briggs Inventory at work. Cool stuff."

"What did you just do?"

"I named it and I'm taming it, I hope."

"How could you be sure?"

"Don't know."

Long pause and I know Lisa's not going to rescue me. I used to feel funny when we would sit in silence while I thought, but this is the booby-hatch room where I need to process my shit. The pause continues.

"I could start with you and apologize for how I treated you a couple years back. I was a drunken, angry bitch back then. I'm sadder now, but not as angry, except at my father, and he deserves my anger." Lisa nods.

"Bally, you've been very hurt by your father. Hurt in ways that few people can understand. He hurt you to your core, your very identity. That hurt spewed out everywhere and at everyone. Now, you're reigning in the anger at others and focusing it where it belongs."

"Yea."

"You've apologized to me. I accept your apology and am grateful that in the last month you've begun to address the core issues and not the superficial ones like 'Did **I** want to see you or did **you** want to see me on a particular day?' You see, that was keeping you from feeling the intensity of the rage at your father.

"Yea, I know that now, but it felt good when I was the towering inferno. I could blame everyone, my ex-husband and you topped my list." Another long pause." I think he would be a good one to try out being honest on...if he would see me."

"Would that give you some perspective or closure?"

"I'd like to see what he has to say if I apologize and explain all this. My hunch is he will forgive and smile that know-it-all crappy smile of his and say something like... 'It's nice to see you taking responsibility for yourself, Bal.'"

"And what would that do to you?"

"It would irritate the hell out of me because I don't like it when anyone else has the answers that I'm seeking. I feel dumb and stupid and...and..."

"Vulnerable?"

"You sure go for the throat! But, yes."

"What do you want to do?"

"Well, I already made my flight reservations. So I'm going. But, I think before I see Little again, I'd like to try out my insights and new tactics on my ex and see if I can keep from losing my temper."

"Are you ready for this?"

"I think so. I was surprised at how easy it was with Ron, my boss, after he fired me when I had the accident."

"An ex-husband carries a lot more emotional energy."

"True, well, but, you know, we used to be good together. I was better with him than with any of my other husbands."

"Why was that?"

"Because he's one of the good guys. It irritated me that he could easily nail me when I was acting out. He understood me and maybe even had some insight into why I was the way I was. He still loved me. I'm the one who did the pushing away. I couldn't stand it that he saw through me." Long pause. "I think that's why I didn't like you. You could see through me. I'm used to people not being able to see through me because I'm good at bullshitting, lying, and manipulating. Like right now I want to run away from you *real bad*, but I'm forcing myself to sit here and deal with this crap."

"Good... for... you."

"You don't have to placate me like a little girl."

"I'm not. I am saying what you are doing is Good...For...You."

"Do you just make this stuff up as you go along or are you really that quick on the draw?"

"I don't know what you mean. I don't play games, Bally. I think you're doing what is good...for...you. When I see someone making different decisions that they are proud of, I believe in supporting them."

"I don't know what to say to that. I'm so used to dueling, I don't know how to have an open and honest relationship."

"I think you've already started."

"Hmmm. Well, I'm going to call my ex and have a conversation that does not end in screaming, blaming, and name-calling. If I can pull that off then Little should be a cinch if she acts up. Hey, I need to run. I've taken advantage of my employer a bit too much recently so I'm making sure I get to work on time, come back from lunch on time, leave after other people do, etc. One additional thing before I go...remember the memory flash I had where my father was stroking Little's leg?"

"Yes."

"Well, it couldn't have happened."

"Why not?"

"Because Little left home when I was less than a year old."

"Hmm."

"I haven't asked Little about that memory but I would like to. Do you think it is a good idea?"

"If you couch it in a puzzling way. You know, like, 'I have a really weird memory flash that couldn't have happened, but I remember it. Can you shed any light on this for me, Little?'"

"Aha, I gotcha. Sort of like **musing** about it and not **accusing**."

"Right. Excellent."

We make another appointment and talk about our goals for next session because I'll be heading off to see Atlee, Little, and Mom after that session. We also make another appointment for the Monday when I get back. Crap, I hope I can do this. I feel if I had another six months in therapy, I might be stronger to confront all this, but it's coming fast and furious. The uncovering and self-reflections are overwhelming. I wish I could be like Hiro on the TV program, *Heroes,* and scrunch my face up and stop time for a minute while I think things through.

Bernie and Bally
The Glass Menagerie

Bernie was surprised I called. He agreed to see me but in a public place. I guess he wanted to be sure if I was going to kill him, he'd have witnesses. Not that being in a public place has ever held me back from flipping out and saying anything I want.

We agreed to meet at the Glass Menagerie, an upscale restaurant that was our favorite during the years we were married. It's a quiet and serene place, maybe that's why he selected it.

As usual, Bernie is waiting for me, even though I'm not late. I often wondered if he has a tracking beam on people. He always knows exactly when to arrive somewhere, so to be in the perfect spot, **right before** the other person arrives. This annoying behavior of his makes me feel like I'm late and I'M NOT. I hate that about him. Whoa!!!! Let's not go there Bally. I wave and smile. Much better. Let's (what does Lisa call it?) reframe the situation. Bernie values me enough to show up on time and not keep me waiting. How's that?

"Hi Bal. How are you?"

"I'm fine. Thanks for seeing me. I have a favor to ask."

The maitre d is seating us at a corner table. I wonder if Bernie asked for it.

"I don't know whether you can see the scars, I have a lot of makeup on them."

Bernie looks closer and nods. "How did you get those?"

At least he didn't ask "What did you do?"

"Right after I saw you in the coffee shop, I had an accident in the car. Wait, that's not exactly true. I was enraged at you and I went to my car, got in, slammed the door, and flew out of the parking space and hit another car. I ended up in shock trauma the rest of the day and night and almost lost my job because my boss thought I'd been drinking. When he found out I hadn't been drinking, he let me keep my job. But, I have these battle wounds to remind me of how potent my temper is. My insurance company is paying everything but will be "dropping me from their insured list". I just got the notice."

"I see. The scars aren't bad. You're still the most beautiful woman I ever saw."

"That's what I want to talk to you about. You say I'm the most beautiful woman you ever **saw,** but I've been working on being a beautiful person inside and I gotta tell you it's excruciatingly hard. I want to quit therapy every other day. Some days I like seeing Lisa and some days I dread seeing her because I have to look at ME and not in a glass mirror, but in my self mirror, the one she holds up to me." This is getting uncomfortable. I look around casually, as if I'm describing the wall hangings, not my innards. HOLY CRAP! There are mirrors on all the walls. I never noticed this before. Are they new? Everywhere you turn, there's glass, crystals, mirrors. GLASS MENAGERIE, of course. Did Lisa call him and recommend he take me here so that I'm surrounded by what I need to face? Face? Oh my God! This is too weird. I can't get away from ME.

"Bally? Where did you go just now? You ok?"

"I'm ok. I was just thrown by the fact that we were talking about being **seen** and I hate looking at myself in the mirror and here we are in the GLASS Menagerie. Creepy, Huh?"

"I see your point. You're really looking at life differently aren't you?"

"What do you mean?"

"You seem different. Less sure of yourself. More aware of your surroundings." The unobtrusive waiter arrives and pours water.

"Well, let me tell you what's happened since I saw you in the coffee shop and what I'm facing in the next several weeks." Facing. There's that word again!

"I'm glad to hear you out, but why me?"

"I need someone who knows me well and can help me look at myself and challenge me before I leave to see my mother in 10 days. I need to practice dealing honestly and directly without manipulating or losing my temper. So I chose you. I have always admired how well, well, um, grounded you are. You're even-tempered and you challenge me. I know, I know, I used to hate that about you and would go off on you. Tonight, I need you to challenge me and I need to remain calm and not jump to conclusions. Lisa and I've been working on this, but I'm facing some real crap, Bernie, and I gotta be good, real good."

Our waiter takes our drink orders. I almost wish we weren't in a restaurant. As soon as I get my ideas together we get interrupted. At least the waiter is a professional. He's barely noticeable. Still, it's constant interruption and I'm losing my courage.

Bernie notices how uncomfortable I am and turns to the waiter. "Frank, I have a request. Can we give you our entire order now and you just bring each item as we finish one course and need to start another? We need to do some talking and the constant ordering may interrupt our flow of conversation. Would you do that for us, please?"

God, Bernie is classy and smooth. Why did I ever let him go?

"Of course sir."

We order everything from appetizers to dessert and Frank disappears. Over the next hour as I explain everything to Bernie, I hardly notice Frank's presence. He's getting a great tip!

When I'm finished laying out the last two months, I sit back. Bernie, the smooth, unflappable Bernie, has his mouth open. "Good grief!"

I always hated that Bernie didn't cuss. He was always the gentleman. If there was anytime he could've said Shit, Damn, Crap, this would have been it, but all he says is 'Good grief' like he's Charlie Brown or something. He sits back and puts his fork down and looks at me.

"Bally, I've always suspected you were hurt in childhood, but I had no idea what it was, because you never shared anything of yourself. You just kept saying your childhood was "fine". I thought you were spoiled and I'm sorry I responded to you as if you were spoiled. I wish I had looked deeper, perhaps I could've helped somehow. Wow! What a story. But now, what're you going to do?"

"I'm just putting one foot in front of the other. My next task is to make sure Mom doesn't get hurt during our inquisition into this mess. She must have known what was going on and yet, she's naïve and maybe she just took Dad and Grandpa at their word. I'm also concerned about Mom now that I know Little is going to be there. She can be brutal."

"Who does she remind you of?"

"Me of course! At least the me I hated. Now I don't hate me as much, but I sure don't trust me, not like I want to."

"I understand, but you're doing great. Keep up the good work. I can see the Bally I loved, emerging right in front of my eyes. I hope you can see her too."

"Sometimes, for a few minutes, and then she fades. I'm working on it." I KEPT MY COOL! YES!

Dessert arrives.

"So Bernie, what are you up to?"

"Nothing quite as exciting as you. I've met someone and it's getting serious, but I'm not going to jinx it by sharing."

My stomach just sank through the floor and the dessert I was enjoying now tastes like cardboard. Months ago I would have blamed the restaurant and demanded that the waiter take it off the bill. Today, I know it's not the dessert or the mirrors, or Bernie but me. It's me, all me. I've been the victim of my childhood and now I continue to victimize myself and others. I feel like crying or yelling or throwing something, but this time I just sit and smile and in my most sincere voice I tell Bernie how happy I am for him. I wonder...does he see I'm crying inside? If he does, he doesn't say anything. If he doesn't see my pain then I'm getting better at being with people without bleeding all over them. I guess this is an improvement. I feel phony, but I also feel good that my distress doesn't show.

Our dinner ends, no crying, cussing, anger. Just a pleasant goodbye and a kiss on the cheek. Friends.

Lisa
Yearning To Be Me

I've lived alone for several years now, and I don't know how I would cope if I had to share every evening and weekend with someone. I need the space and the quiet after dealing with clients all day. My dog doesn't demand a lot of attention, just a head pat, a belly rub, a walk, and food. Then she's back to sleep. Some days I envy her life.

Lucy's a mutt I adopted from the SPCA. The lady said she was abandoned. The vet thought she's part "duck toller". I had no idea what that was but have come to find out it's a breed well-known in Canada. She looks like a miniature Golden Retriever except she has a mottled colored coat. She's been a gem since the day I adopted her, very good-natured and patient. She has to be, with my lifestyle! She has her leash in her mouth and is sitting by the door. Guess she wants or needs to go out. We walk a mile or so and she sniffs and squirts her way around the neighborhood, leaving pee mails for the dogs that follow us. This is my time to stop thinking for a ½ hour. The sun's setting and the sky is brilliant blue and pink. I wonder if that's where the expression "Sky blue pink" comes from. I never knew what it meant. I take a deep breath and close my eyes and let the wind play with my hair. Lucy's found something that entreats her to sniff it, and then she pees on it. Why can't life be this simple and peaceful all the time?

I want, no...need, to plan another vacation, but this time, I want to go to the western part of the country. I have never seen the Grand Canyon or Glacier National Park. I wonder if Milly and Maggie are up for a vacation like that instead of a cruise or an island in the Caribbean. I love playing with them, but I need something more meaningful or spiritual this time. I don't know why, but recently I've started thinking less about religion and church-going and more about just being with my Creator and listening to nature. In fact, it's more than just an interest, I am feeling "called" to explore the world, shut-up, and listen.

Tonight my back is squealing at me for some Motrin and I accommodate it. The phone rings, and I don't want to talk to anyone right now, especially a salesperson. The answering machine picks up the call and I recognize Maggie's voice. I catch her before she finishes talking and hangs up. "Hey, Mil, what's up?"

"Hey girlfriend, Milly and I want to know whether you are up for a meal and movie this weekend. Sounds like you have some CT stuff with a client. I caught one too, and Molly's overwhelmed. She says the stars are in retrograde or something. I have no idea what she's talking about."

"Sure, let's do it. I'm free most of the weekend." Calendar comes out of my briefcase.

"Let's do lunch and a matinee this Sunday. Can we meet at Millstone Grill say around noon?"

"You're on. I'm writing it on my calendar as we're talking. Do you want to call Milly or shall I?"

"I will. I need to refer a client to her anyway. Ta ta for now."

Hooray, what a great treat! Milly and Maggie are my touchstones for reality checking and vice versa. Maggie's dating someone now making it more difficult for the three of us to get together as much as we used to.

The weekend's off to a good start. I slept until Lucy brought me her leash which was at 8:45. Bless her for letting me sleep. I don't remember any dreams and I feel rested. I try to put all my clients' needs out of my head and focus on my own. So far, so good. I call my voicemail and "no messages". Yeah!

Saturday is filled with the normal catch up chores: groceries, bank, post office. Sunday morning is church and then Millstone Grill.

Milly's sitting at a quiet table in the back. Maggie hasn't arrived. Milly waves at me. I haven't seen her in awhile and I think she's lost a little weight. She says she hasn't and it must be the clothes, but she thinks it was a nice gesture on my part.

"What's up with you?" Milly asks as she munches on a breadstick.

"Got another very interesting client and I think I'm ok working with her but she has something in her background that's similar to mine and I want to check it out with you and Maggie."

The waitress arrives and takes my iced tea order. Milly says "Ok. Give it up!"

"I have a client who saw the Chase train wreck that happened over 20 years ago, but of course, she remembers it like it were yesterday. She has a history of deaths in her family and she blames herself for those deaths. I think I have a handle on that part, but when she told me the crash detail by detail, I lost my attention for a few minutes and my mind flashed to what my daughter would have gone through in the last minutes of her life. I wondered about the people who saw my daughter's helicopter go down."

Maggie arrives and apologizes for her lateness. Milly waves at the waitress and she arrives and takes Maggie's drink order. Milly kindly fills Maggie in on my dilemma. Both of them turn to me and listen to the story of Noelle. When I'm through Milly sits back and says, "Whew!" Maggie is shaking her head. "I remember that train wreck and I had a few clients who were working on their own trauma and had to discuss the wreck because it kicked up their own stuff. I haven't met anyone who actually saw it happen, though. Are you sure she's telling you the truth? Could she be trying to get your attention, knowing that this story would certainly engage you?"

"I don't think so, but I never thought of that. She's been a very reticent client. She's being forced to come to counseling, and she's told me several stories of deaths she's experienced over her life time. She believes she's jinxed and causes people to die when she gets too close to them. She's had difficulty connecting with me because she's afraid if she likes me, I will die. I believe her, about seeing the Chase Train tragedy. But perhaps, I need to look at whether she's telling me stories to keep me engaged. Wow!"

"I could be wrong, Lisa. I didn't know all that background before I blurted out my first impression." Maggie stops to take a sip of her Diet Coke and then continues." I just haven't heard that there were witnesses to the actual crash. And the story about the man being cut in half, that didn't make the papers or the news. I have to wonder why."

"Maybe they were protecting the family from the media?" Milly says. "I could do some sleuthing and see if I can find out if there was a witness and maybe I could find out about the engineer."

"Thanks. Even, if I find out she's telling the truth then I'm still left with my CT stuff. Does it sound like it is getting in the way of working with her?"

Maggie considers this briefly. Milly's quiet. "Lisa, I heard several stories associated with the Chase incident. I had nightmares for weeks. It sounds to me that your brief thought of your daughter is not interfering with your ability to work with this client. In fact it may help you work with her. You understand what she experienced far better than Milly or I do."

Milly leans forward and nods her head in agreement. "You know, I'm not as worried about your feelings about your daughter's death as I'm about this client's insisting if you get close to her, then you will DIE! Doesn't that give you the willys?"

Only Milly can be that blunt. "I've been dealing with this client now for months and at first I felt a bit uneasy, but it seems routine now. She believes she kills those she cares about. Her past plays this belief out perfectly and it's been reinforced over the years, so she stays clear of people. But, she has a father who's still alive, a boss who wants a more intimate relationship with her, and both of them are still kicking, so I guess I just didn't give it much credence."

Maggie laughs, "You are a better person than I am! I would've referred her to a friend I didn't like."

Milly shakes her head. "Maggie, you are a trip. Lisa, I'm concerned for you because I'm looking at this from a quantum field perspective. In quantum physics, scientists are beginning to prove that we can think our way into and out of situations. If you think a thought like 'I am a happy person', we know that Cognitive Theory says you will eventually feel happy. But, quantum theory shows it's not just changing the internal messages or the brain waves that makes us see things differently, but it actually creates a vibration, which affects your body, your mind, your spirit, and the world around you. I can give you some books if you are interested. There's a lot of scientific research and data supporting this theory."

I'm intrigued. I've always believed we can affect ourselves with our thoughts and beliefs but to affect others too? That could revolutionize my counseling practice. "Give me an example." Maggie's intrigued too.

"Let's see, there are many. Ok, here's one experiment I can quickly access in my aging brain. There was an experiment where the researchers paired up several people on paper, and then when they arrived at the lab, they put them in separate, sound-proofed rooms. They never introduced the people. They only told them they were being paired with another person who's in another room. Then the researchers hooked up the subjects to EEG machines. They monitored their brain waves. Soon the pair's brain waves were in synch. And the person with the stronger, more calm brain waves, always brought the weaker person to their level."

Maggie and I look at each other and both of us say at the same time. "I want that book!" Milly says she will email us a list of books to read. Milly continues, "Lisa, make sure, when you're working with this client or others, that you're centered and calm. You should project yourself into the future and see yourself as a healthy person. This client is projecting you to die. Who's stronger?"

I sit back. She's right of course. I've assumed that Noelle's so injured she doesn't have much personal power, but she's convinced she has the power to cause people to die, so her belief may be more powerful than my belief that she doesn't have this power. It won't hurt to project myself into the room with her as one who's **not** going to be one of her victims. Even though she would not wish me harm, her very belief may be giving her power she doesn't even want.

The rest of the meal belongs to Maggie and her client who has a tendency to manipulate her and everyone else. Our movie choice was mediocre, but I didn't go to the movies to be wowed, I went to be with friends and forget about my job for the time being. It works. I feel a buzz of contentment as I drive home. Lucy however, does not look happy with my absence on a weekend. She keeps nudging me to play ball. Why does it take a dog to remind me what life is all about?

When I adopted her, a lot of people kept warning me that she would tie me down. I hesitated, but then realized I needed to have a reason to come home, I needed to stop working and play more, I needed to slow down. Lucy has helped me do all of the above. I hug her and nuzzle my face in her hair and then sneeze. She looks like she's smiling. Laughter is good for the soul.

Noelle's Fear

Ma boss is pressurin' me more an' more to go out wiff him. I'm scared to say 'yes'. I haven't been on a date for over 15 years. Last one wuz a disaster. It wuz so bad that I went to the rest room an' never returned to the table. Ma boss is nice enough, but I can't even think about him as a possible date. Besides if we don't like each other after the date, then will I lose ma'job?

Quantum Physics and Lisa's Sessions

I'm doing what Milly suggested, meditating before Noelle arrives for her session. I need to be strong and project positive 'vibrations' to Noelle to counter her negativity. I feel a little silly because I don't know what I'm doing, but I have a sense I need to quiet myself before each client and project intentions for a good session. That's about all I got out of my conversation with Milly and Maggie. I need to read more to find out if there's a magic formula for this focusing, intentional stuff. I'm picturing Noelle and seeing her changing her mind about killing people. I see her opening up like a rose and understanding that her belief that she can kill people isn't justified. When I do this I see the grim set of her face softening and then smiling the way she did a couple of sessions ago. When she smiled she looked like a different person.

Noelle is dressed all in brown today and she looks like a tired Hershey bar. No eye contact. She just walked by me, entered the office, and sat down.

"Hi Noelle, how are you?"

"Ma boss keeps askin' me out. I'm not interested, but I'm afraid I'll lose ma'job if I keep turnin' him down."

"Noelle, would you share with me your boss' first name so I'll know how to refer to him?"

"Gerard."

"Ok, you say Gerard keeps asking you out, but you're afraid to accept. Could you say why you're afraid to accept his invitation?" I mean do you like him or do you just want to work for him?"

"I like him, an' if he weren't ma boss I would consider dating 'imp, but Gerard is, is, ma boss an' I'm afraid I'll lose ma job if he doesn't like me after we have dinner."

"He's asking you to dinner? Is he considering it a date?"

"I don't know."

"I see. Could you clarify this with him before you make your decision?"

"You mean just because he's asking me to dinner, he may not see it as a date?"

"Could be. I don't know. Do you?"

"I assumed he wuz askin' me out on a date."

"What gave you that idea?'

"I don't know."

"Did he say, 'Noelle, I'd like to take you to dinner?"

"Yea, like that."

"Did he say anything that led you to believe that this was more than a boss who wanted to take his employee out for dinner?"

"No. but, he smiles all the time like he's int'rested in me."

"Are you worried if you go out to dinner and you like him and he likes you then he'll be in danger?"

"Not really, I mean, not as much any more. I'm more afraid he won't like me or will push himself on me."

"What do you want to do?"

"Maybe I'll tell him, 'I'll go out to dinner wiff you, but it's got ta be strictly business.'"

"If he agrees, then will you be ok with that?"

"Yea, I guess. At least that way I'll feel like I'm settin' the rules.

"Ok."

Pause

"Noelle, how do you now perceive your ability to kill people versus when you first came here for counseling?"

"I can see your point 'bout the deaths not bein' my fault an' all, but I keep thinkin' it's my fault an' then I gotta disagree wiff ma'self. I feel like I'm arguin' wiff meself all the time."

"What does that sound like? Your conversation with yourself?"

"I say, 'Noelle, nobody b'lieves you when you say you kill people so maybe everyone else is right an' you're wrong.' I answer myself... 'but that's what's happened all my life. I love, they die."

"Then what happens?"

"I then say somethin' like... Maybe I'm jist not lucky. Maybe the people died becuz ...they jist died. Maybe I don't have nothin' to do wiff it. I jist love people an' they died, not that you love people an' **cause** them to die."

"Do you believe what you are saying?"

"I'm startin' to. You pointed out that ma father's still alive...."

"Instead of talking to yourself in a back and forth mode, let's come up with a statement that you can say to yourself frequently. Would that be easier than arguing with yourself?"

"I guess."

"Ok, what statement would capture what you want to believe."

"Umm, maybe somethin' like. I don't cause people to die. I don't have that power. If someone dies it jist means that they died. I didn't cause it."

"Sounds good to me. How does it sound to you?"

"I'd like to believe it."

"Let's try it for a week and see what happens."

"Ok."

"Did you say anything special to yourself when you were in the vicinity of the Chase train collision?"

"That inciden' really made me think. I was there, but I didn't know any of them people so how could I've cared 'nough about them to cause 15 deaths? Besides, I can't bear to think I had anythin' to do with that."

"You couldn't bear to think that you caused the deaths of the people on the train, but you could bear to think that you caused your mother's, grandmother's, brother's deaths? I wonder why?"

Noelle is sitting quietly thinking. She looks up. "I dunno. What do you think?"

"I'm not sure either but I wonder... and it's just a guess... if you felt abandoned by others who died and it's easier or safer for you to think you are a murderer than to believe they abandoned you."

Noelle looks stunned. I can't see by her face if she is intrigued, enlightened, or enraged. "I dunno. I guess. I'm feeling anxious. I have to go."

"How about just staying with the feeling and not running away this time."

Noelle is shaking slightly, then she closes her eyes and begins breathing deeply. Then she opens her eyes and simply says, "Ok." She just kept herself from fleeing! Pretty good control. She pauses, picking at the chair arm. Looking at her purse. For some reason I don't think she wants to leave. I think she's processing information.

"Leeza, do you think I'm stupid?"

That question came out of the blue! "Why would you ask that?"

"How did you learn to talk gud?"

"Do you mean using correct grammar, or putting words together, or what?

"You say 'xactly what I'm feelin' an' when you say it, it sounds better than I would if I try to say it."

"I see. I learned some of it in college, and I practiced in graduate school.

Why? What's going on?"

"I wanna go back to school an' git ma degree."

I never thought she had any aspirations like school. She seemed stuck where she was, and yet safe in her stuckness. I think we just turned another corner. First she demonstrated control over her feelings of wanting to run and now she's thinking about returning to school! "You finished one year and then dropped out. Right?"

"Yea, I din't do too gud. All I got were 'Cs' an' a couple of 'Bs'. The first semester wuz hard cause I din't know how to study real gud, then the second semester I had the train wreck thing goin' on. I don't even know if I'd hav'ta start all over agin."

"How could you find out?"

Shrug again. She's retreating after putting something important on the table. She's backing away from it. Should I say that?

"Noelle, I noticed you took a big step just then, bringing up one of your dreams, to go back to school. Then you started to back away from it. What happened?"

"Scared I guess."

"Taking a risk is scary. First, you had to look at your history with death, then you had to look at how you used your belief that you kill people as a reason to push people away. That took courage. Then you talked about the train crash and had to face that horrible experience. That took courage, too. Now you're thinking about finishing your degree. All these have evoked fear in you and all require courage. Change is hard and scary and sometimes difficult. The key is taking the first step. And you have."

"I'm tired of working hard."

"Work is hard, whether it is physical, emotional, or intellectual."

Sigh.

"Would you do me a favor?"

"Sure, Noelle, what can I do to help you?"

"Would you call Harford Community College for me an' find out what I hafta do to git back in?"

"What stops you from doing it?"

"I'm tired."

"Then maybe the time isn't right for you to be doing it."

"You're probably right. See you next week."

"Ok."

Darn, should I have agreed to make the call? She expressed interest in going back to school but she's not in an emotional place to make the phone call. She should do this for herself and not look to someone else to rescue her from her discomfort. If I call HCC, I'll be creating too much dependence on me. Tough call, but I made

Noelle's Homework

the correct decision. If she's too tired to make a phone call, then she'll be too tired to go to school. When she has the energy, she'll call on her own.

Noelle's Homework

Gotta lot of counseling homework this week. I hav'ta tell ma boss I'll go out to dinner wiff him. I hav'ta practice my statement that I don't cause deaths, an' Leeza wouldn't make the call to HCC for me so I gotta make that call, too. I'm startin' wiff Gerard. He's sittin' at his desk when I git back to the office. He waves an' I raise ma hand a little. Ok, here goes. I stand' there waitin' for him to acknowledge me, but he's lookin' at me like he's waitin' for me to say somethin'. I wish he'd ask me out agin. But, he jist looks at me expectin' like. How would Leeza do this. "I would like to go to dinner wiff you, Gerard, but jist business. Is that ok wiff you?"

Gerard smiles an' chuckles. What's he laughin' at? Is he laughin' at me? I quickly turn to go to my desk. My face feels hot, red. I'm 'mbarrassed. I must've done it wrong. Damn. Gerard speaks up. "How about tonight, Noelle?"

I don't look at him. "That would be just fine, Gerard. Thank you." "Oh, I forgot, I have ta feed my cat first. Could I meet you at the restaurant, please?" I enunciated each word the way Leeza does. Gerard is still grinnin'. I wish he'd stop that! It makes me feel like he's laughin' at me. Try again.

"Gerard, would you please stop laughing at me. I am doing my best to be polite, but if you keep laughing, I might kick your shins." I guess I shouldn't have said that last part.

Gerard stops laughing an' looks serious. "Noelle, I've been asking you out for a year and you kept pushing me away. Now you come in here and say 'yes' to dinner and you don't want me to smile?"

"I thought you wuz, were laughin', laughing, at me."

"I wasn't. I was happy. Don't assume you always know what others are feeling or thinking. You may be wrong and this time you're wrong. I'm happy and I'm smiling. I'm not laughing at you.

I feel stupid. I didn't know he wuz just laughin' out of happiness. I didn't know people did that. I thought the only reason people laugh is because someone said something funny or the person is laughin' AT another person. I guess I make too many 'ssumptions. More to ask Lisa 'bout.

What will I wear tonight? I kinda lied. I don't have to go home an' feed ma cat, I hafta go home an' change my clothes an' put some make up on. I hope I can do this dinner thing tonight. I have a jittery feeling in my stomach.

Gerard speaks up from his paper work. "Noelle, why don't you take the rest of the day off? You worked late last night. I'll answer the phones"

"You don't need to"....Gerard puts up his hand telling me to be quiet. "Go home and take it easy. I'll pick you up at 6:30. We'll go to Morton's Steak House. You like steak?" I put my head down, nod a couple times, pick up my things, and leave.

Quantum Science

I'm voraciously reading *The Secret Life of Plants* that Milly lent me. I also read *The Field.* If even 10% of this research is valid, then I need to rethink how I try to create movement or change in my clients. I also watched the movie Milly recommended, *What the Bleep Do We Know?* From what I'm reading and seeing, I need to do more than act like a trained professional who's empathic, I need to create intention in the room for a client to feel better and begin to improve. I've been praying and wishing, which are analogous to intention, that my clients would heal, change, grow, but I haven't imbued my thoughts, feelings, and intentions with constructive transformation. Instead I usually ask/beg God to help me and my client. That's good and reasonable, but there's scientific evidence that there are many possible outcomes for the client and she/he needs to declare what outcome is desired. Then both of us need to use our prayer intentionally to develop the avenue to achieve that outcome. Fascinating stuff! Why is this not taught in schools?

I'm resolute about creating a new ambiance with Noelle. She has a clearer agenda than Caz and Bally. Noelle wants to stop seeing the deaths that have plagued her as her fault. Even though Gerard and I have not died, she's still fighting the belief that we may not be safe.

While I wait for Noelle, I'm putting myself in a state of prayerful meditation and selecting a new image for Noelle; one that includes her feeling safe, happy, and certain she's not responsible for killing others. I've been doing this each day since I've read the books. I also spontaneously started tuning in to the weather. Our area is experiencing a drought, so I've been imaging rain falling and picturing myself fully enjoying its benefits. If I understand the research correctly, the more people who participate in creating an intention, the more potent it is.

The doorbell announces Noelle's arrival. I stop my reverie and greet her. She's dressed differently than in other sessions. First, she's wearing a dress, not a suit, and the dress is layers of colorful, light, and flowing fabric that moves when she walks. She's wearing makeup and her hair is curled. Her transformation is almost complete, except for her scowl. She needs to do something about that scowl. I think she's been doing it for a long time to keep people away, and she's unaware of it.

"Hi, Noelle, come in. Your dress is beautiful."

"Thanks."

"I don't think I have ever seen you in a dress before. You usually wear pant suits."

"Yea, tryin' somethin' new."

"How do you feel? Do you feel like your dress, light and flowing, or like your face, sad and pained?" I wanted to say, 'a grumpy scowl', but I didn't want to offend her.

"I feel like my dress. Does my face look sad, painful?"

I nod. "Are you aware of it?"

"No. I need a mirror."

I take her at her word that she's not aware of her face, and hand her a mirror from my purse. She looks in the mirror for a long while, turning it to several different angles. Then she snaps it closed and hands it to me.

"I didn't know I looked like that. I feel happy an' content for th'first time in years. Why duz my face look grumpy? Do ya' think ma'face is jist built that way?"

"I've seen you smile. I don't think it is structural."

"How do I change it?"

"Try relaxing your muscles in your face."

She closes her eyes and rubs different parts of her face. As soon as her face relaxes, she opens her eyes and she asks for the mirror again. The relaxation helped a little, but the muscles must be like concrete, set and hard. She looks at her reflection and continues to try to smooth out the frown. She looks up after awhile. "I guess I've been frownin' so long my muscles don't know what else to do." She laughs and I chuckle. She really has come a long way. When I remember the woman who gave me one word answers in the first session, and then ran out of the office halfway through the session, I'm amazed at her transformation. She seems like a different person, one who is transitioning from being laminated to being flexible.

"Could I make a suggestion that might help?"

"Sure."

"I wonder if you would be open to a deep tissue massage around your face, head, and neck?"

"I dunno. Does it hurt?"

"It can be uncomfortable until the muscles relax. However, after that there's a feeling of relief. Would you like some names of massage therapists?"

"Sure. I'll try it. I don't wanna look angry the rest of my life. I'm trying right now to not frown, but I don't know what buttons to push on my face to get it to relax."

"Ok, I'll give you some names of massage therapists and you can call them when you're ready."

"Ok, thanks." She pauses and thinks for a minute. "I had a 'date' wiff ma boss last week." She makes quotation mark gestures with her fingers when she said the word 'date'.

"You told him you'd go out with him?"

"Yes. I lef' here an' went back ta'work. He wuz in the office an' I took that as a sign I should let 'im know I would go out wiff 'im, but it had to be jist a bizness dinner."

"He agreed?"

"Yea, first he laughed an' I thought he wuz laughin' at me an' I got snippy, but he tole me he wuz laughin' 'cause he wuz happy. He took me to Morton's. Gawd the prices!" And she laughed again.

She looks like a totally different person when she laughs, not at all like Chloe on *24.*

"And?"

"We had a gud time. Took me a long time to r'lax though. I wuz tense, an' kept lookin' 'round to see if someone had seen us."

"Why?"

"I didn't want nobody to think we were a couple."

"Why not?"

She leans forward with a devilish smile on her face and loudly whispers, "I could kill him 'member?"

She's really a character! I never saw her as funny or engaging and yet here she is actually talking to me and kidding me about her presenting problem.

"Oh, yea I forgot!" I retort playfully. "But really, Noelle, what keeps you from taking his interest in you seriously?"

"I dunno."

"Is it because you still feel he's in danger? Or is it because you're afraid of being in a relationship and possibly getting rejected or hurt?"

"I'm 'fraid of a relationship. I don't know what to do, how to act. And I'm 'fraid of bein' rejected and tossed aside."

"Tell me about your previous relationships with men."

"Nothin' to tell. Never had one. No one wuz interested an' I wuz too 'fraid to be involved wiff anyone anyway."

"This is a new experience for you."

"Yep. That's why I'm skeptical." She stumbles over the word as if it's new for her. "I don't get it. Why's he interested? Does he have an ulter'or motive?"

She used a bigger word than she usually does. She's trying!

"You sat with him at dinner. What did you think about his behavior? Was he a gentleman?"

"Yea, he wuz very polite an' nice. We talked about work, mostly. I guess 'cause I said our dinner had to be all bizness. But, he tole me he wuz married once many years ago for two years an' then divorced. He wuz hurt and he never dated 'gain. He threw hisself into his work, an' he's proud of the company he's built. He hinted he wants to share it wiff someone, and he's lonely an' tired of jist workin'. Then he ast 'bout me. I didn't know what to tell him. I jist said ma mother died when I wuz young."

She squirms in her chair like she wants to say something, but is embarrassed. She whispers, "He kissed me when he lef'."

"What kind of kiss?"

"There are different kinds?"

"Well there's the kind of kiss a friend gives you when she greets you, like a cheek-kiss. Then there is a quick lip kiss. (I can't believe I am describing kisses to her. She is so naive. I guess she's still a virgin at 40). Then there's a passionate kiss, like in the movies."

"Oh, yea. I guess I didn't know you were talking about those kisses. Well, he sorta pecked me on the cheek. He wuz playin' it safe wiff me 'cause he wuz afraid I might run away."

"Think so?"

"I think he knows I'm scared an' he wuz respectin' my fear."

"He sounds like a nice person."

"Yea. I mean Yes."

"Would you go out with him again, if he asks you?"

"Yea, Yes. But, he hasn't. Maybe I blew it."

"Maybe he's scared, too?"

"Really? Why?"

"Well, you turned him down a lot before you said 'yes' and he may wonder if you had a good time at dinner. Did you tell him you had a good time?"

"No, I didn't think of it."

"Do you think that's a good thing to do? Let him know you had a good time, and you're open to doing it again?"

"That's kinda scary."

"I know. But, he can't read your mind and sometimes your body language and facial expressions are difficult to read, like we talked about earlier. You were feeling happy, but you had a scowl on your face."

"I guess."

"What's the worst that could happen if you let him know you enjoyed yourself?"

"He might say, 'Well, I didn't. We're not compatible." She trips over the last word.

"Is that the worst? I thought you were going to say he could drop dead."

Noelle starts laughing and doesn't stop. She's laughing so hard, tears are running down her face. I didn't think my comment was that funny!

She's wiping her tears away and still smiling.

"Leeza you're a hoot! But, ya know what's funny? I didn't think about his dying. I just wanted to go out agin. That's progress, right?"

"It sure is Noelle. What are you going to do?"

"I'm gonna find a way to tell him I liked the dinner."

"What will you say?"

"I dunno, I usually jist say whatever comes to ma mind."

"Does that work for you?"

She smiles broadly. "It never has!"

Now I'm the one who's laughing. "Ok, let's try something different. Let's prepare a small script. What exactly do you want to say?"

She gets serious now. "I wanna say. 'I had a good time last week.'" She looks at me for approval.

"That's a great start.?"

"How about, 'I hope I wuzn't too boring.' Would that be ok?"

I don't want to tell her what to say, but I don't think that statement's the best one. I play it safe. "Anything else?"

She sighs and thinks. "Maybe I could say that I think he's a very nice man."

"Ok, anything else?"

"Nope, not now."

"Ok, I like the first one and the last one. The middle one sounds like the old Noelle, always down and expecting the worst."

"That's kinda still the current Noelle."

"I know, but you're laughing and kidding and looking foxy. How about breaking out of the old Noelle, and trying on a new persona."

"A what?"

"A persona, a new personality, a happier one."

"You mean fake it till you make it?"

"Where did you hear that?"

"On TV."

"Ok, something like that." I'm still chuckling under my breath at her emerging sense of humor.

"Ok, this is a big step for me. I'll try it an' see what he sez. But, if he sez 'I'm not interested.' Then can I call you when I panic?"

"Sure. But, I'm betting he's waiting to hear from you."

"Really?"

"Just my gut instinct. I could be wrong."

"I hope your gut's right."

"Me too."

Our session continues with other topics she selected, but,…SHE MADE IT THROUGH AN ENTIRE SESSION!!!

"Well, our time is up for now." I say reaching for my calendar. "I'll see you next week at the same time?"

"Sure."

"And, Noelle, if this doesn't go well and you need to talk, call me, ok?"

"Thanks, I 'ppreciate it." She stops and turns around and corrects herself. "Thank you. I appreciate it." And she leaves, but this time she isn't running away.

Noelle's Script

I gotta git back to work. I usually don't stay for a whole session 'cause I git anxious and leave, but that session wuz gud, but now I feel guilty for bein' late gittin' back to work. Wait! Stop! I am **not** late. Gerard knows I have a session an' he knows it takes me 15 minutes to drive to Leeza's an' 15 minutes back. Why'm I tied in knots? 'Cause I usually don't stay the entire time? No, he'll be glad I stayed the entire hour. What is it? I think I'm really scared to say my 'script' to him that I practiced with Leeza and that's makin' me jumpy.

Gerard isn't even at the office! Why wuz I so tense? I seem to be my own worst friend. Gerard lef' a note on my desk! "Hey, you must have stayed for your whole session. I hope it went well. Call me on my cell if you need me. I'm seeing clients all afternoon."

Great! Maybe this'll be easier if I don't see his face. I call his phone an' his voicemail picks up. I try to sound upbeat "I'm back, jist wanted to let you know." Pause. "Umm, Umm, I really had a gud time at dinner last week. I think you're a really, really gud man. Umm, Umm, Bye."

Why did I say all those 'reallys'? I sounded dumb. Now I haf'ta wait for his response. Back to work. It'll take ma'mind off the call.

Three hours of hard work an' I only think about Gerard an' the message I lef' every now an' then. When I do think 'bout it, I get a little queasy feelin' in ma'stomach. At 4 o'clock, I start ta clean up for the day an' the phone rings. I absently say "Finance Associates" and hear Gerard's voice.

"Hey, again. Did you get my note?"

"Yea, I mean Yes, did you git, get, my voice message?"

"Yea, thanks. Would, umm, you like, umm, to do it again sometime but this time not just business?"

"I would. Thanks."

"I'll talk to you tomorrow and we'll plan something. Ok?"

"'Kay. I mean Okay. See ya."

"See ya."

I jump for joy an' dance an' twirl 'round the office.

Noelle's Voicemail Message

When I heard Noelle on my voicemail, I thought she had bad news about Gerard's response to her "script". Instead, she sounded as if she were floating three feet off the floor. I'm genuinely glad for her. It's been a few months since she started counseling, and it was a rocky beginning. I didn't think she was going to stick it out. I never thought I was going to see her smile, let alone laugh. But, she's doing better. These are the moments that make my effort feel worthwhile.

The Second Date

I'm feelin' stuff I never thought I'd feel. I'm happy for the first time in over 30 years. I keep tellin' ma'self I'm dreamin'. But, I'm not wakin' up. It must be real. I bought a new dress. That's two new dresses in two weeks. I usually don't buy two new dresses or anythin' new in a year. This one's aqua an' the minute I pulled it over ma'head an' saw ma'face come through the neck, I knew it wuz the one I wanted. It cost a pretty nickel, a lot more than I ever spent on a dress. It's beautiful an' I feel like a movie star in it.

Our date is Saturday, so I had to wait a few days to decorate myself. I got ma'nails done, an' while I wuz at the beauty shop, I had ma'hair done too. They colored it a little darker an' styled it. When I looked in the mirror I couldn't believe I wuz seein' me. I wanted to get the massage Lisa suggested, but no one could take me this week so the lady at the salon gave me a general massage and focused on my head and neck. It felt kinda weird to have someone touch me like that, but I think Lisa's right. When my face is relaxed, I look less grumpy. I hope it don't grump up again on our date.

Gerard's late! He's changed his mind. He's not comin'. He's forgotten me. He's dead! The doorbell rings an' Gerard is standin' there wiff a huge bouquet of flowers.

"I'm sorry I'm late. There's a big accident on 695, and I inched forward for half hour until I could get off and go the back way."

"It's ok. I wuz worried 'bout you, though."

"You were?"

"Yeah. I thought you wuz, umm were, in an accident or somethin' an' I got scared."

Gerard smiles an' then hugs me. "Let's go. We got a reservation. I called to let them know about the accident, and they're holding the table for us."

He holds the door to the car for me an' then notices my dress. "Gosh, you're beautiful!"

What! I can't believe it! No one has ever called me beautiful. No one. Not even ma'dad. He sez I'm cute but never beautiful. My heart's racin' an' I'm scared I'm gonna blow it wiff Gerard, so I pretend that I'm Leeza an' I try to say things like she does. "That's nice of you to say that, Gerard." An' I smile. I think I sounded phony.

He looks a little taken back like he is seein' me for the first time. Maybe I'm seein' myself for the first time, too, through his eyes.

Gerard takes me to this very classy restaurant in downtown Balmer. It over looks the harbor an' the waiters are wearin' tux. I've never been to a place like this an' I'm gettin' anxious about what fork to use. What do I do? I wanna run away. But, I'm not gonna. I'll jist watch Gerard an' do everythin' he does. Gerard excuses himself an' goes to the men's room. Well, I guess I can't do EVERYTHIN' he does.

Dinner starts wiff the tiniest little tidbits of food I ever seen. They taste like they are made by God. Then there's soup. Oh, no! I usually slurp an' spill soup. I'm shakin' inside an' I'm 'fraid I might not be able to control my hand. I refuse the soup, but it looks an' smells great. I don't wanna ruin my dress. Ruin the dress, ruin my evenin'. Gerard looks at me funny. "Don't you like pumpkin soup?" he asks.

"I think I'll wait for the rest of the meal. I might not be able to eat it all if they keep bringin' such gud stuff." Gud stuff? What a stupid thing to say.

"It's really good!" Gerard sez in a singsong voice, temptin' me. "Sure you don't want a taste?"

"No thanks."

I feel like I'm walkin' through a dream an' if I don't make all the right decisions, I'll wake up and Gerard will be gone. The waiter arrives to take our order an' I make it easy, a fillet, asparagus, baked potato. He asks about a salad an' I say "Yes." He then opens the menu an' points to seven choices. Good grief! I just point to one an' hope I made a good choice. This is hard!

The food wuz like nothin' I ever had. Gerard is shiftin' in his chair an' I wonder if I did somethin' wrong. I don't **think** I have. Do I have salad in my teeth? How do I find out? My Gran used to look at her teeth in the reflection of a knife. I'm not sure that I should do that, so I don't.

Gerard sounds serious. "Noelle, we've been working together for over four years, and I don't know very much about you. I know your mother died when you were young. Is your father still alive?"

"Yes, my father's still alive. He lives in Hagerstown. I don't git to see 'im much. He's a real estate agent an' he's busy most weekends an' that's when I'm free."

"Do you have any siblings?"

"I had a brother, but he died when I wuz a kid. It wuz an accident."

"Oh, I'm sorry."

Why do people apologize when they hear someone died? I never understood that.

"Any other family?"

"Just a few cousins an' aunts but they live in Virginia. I don't see 'em very much either."

"Do you live alone?"

"No." Gerard looks surprised so I quickly clarify, "I have a cat. He's a good cat. I've had 'im 12 years. He's gettin' up there... in years I mean."

Gerard nods and still looks like he's going to say somethin' serious. It's really quiet, and I'm uncomfortable. I try not to squirm or pick at something like I usually do. Instead, I look around, kinda like I'm admiring the decorating.

"Noelle, are you mad at me for sending you for counseling?"

Gosh, that's a strange question. I understand why he wuz taking his time before he ast the question. I don't know what to tell him so I'll use another Leeza phrase. "I hafta think about that. It's a difficult question." Gerard nods like he agrees with me. I take my time before I continue. I try to pick my words careful-like. "I guess at first I wuz hurt an' angry...an' scared, but I like Leeza and she helps me to see some things differently. Can I ask you a question?"

"Sure."

"Why did you send me? You jist, said I wuz **weird** an' I needed to go to counselin'. Why wuz I weird?"

"Well, you hardly talked. You came to work, did your work and went home. I tried to get you to talk to me, you know, small talk, but you just frowned, lowered your head, and answered 'yes' or 'no'. I tried to get you involved more in the business by asking you to go out to dinner with some of my business associates, but you just lowered your head and said 'No.' I don't remember saying you were weird though."

"You said, 'You get real weird sometimes.' At least I think that's what you said."

"Yea, I did say that. I'm sorry. I was frustrated. I wanted you to go out with me, but every time I broached the subject, you put a wall up and wouldn't talk."

"I thought you just wanted sex."

"You what?! Oh my God. I was trying to get to know you, and all you thought I wanted was sex?"

"Yeah. I'm sorry. I never wuz taught how to read people."

"Because your mom died when you were young?"

"It's a long story. Sometime when we have more time, an' we're not in a really nice place, I'll share it wiff you as long as **you** don't run away."

"Why would I do that?"

"Cause it's a really **weird** story."

He laughs. "Ok. But, how have you made such a change in just a few months? Is Lisa really that good. Or have you been working hard?"

"I don't know. I wasn't real cooperative at the beginning. I didn't wanna go an' I didn't wanna stay. I knew if I didn't go you'd fire me, so..."

"Fire you? Where did you get that idea?"

"You said it."

"No I didn't. I said if you didn't get some help I would be forced to do something else. I didn't mean fire you. I meant like ...I don't know what I meant. I was just frustrated. I've been trying to get you to like me for four years, but you acted like I was a fixture on the wall."

"Ok. I'm gonna, going to, tell you one piece of this story of mine so you will understand why I am the way I am. And why I'm tryin' to change. Ok?"

"Sure."

"I thought I had the power to kill people if I loved them."

Gerard had been sitting forward as he talked to me, but that statement made him sit back in his chair, kinda like distancing himself from what I said. Crap! And things were goin' well. I blew it. I hang my head and Gerard shakes his. "Noelle, I don't even know what kind of question to ask after that revelation."

I'm gonna run. I can feel it comin'. STAY I shout to my innards. Then more calmly, "Gerard, everyone I got close to as a kid, died. I thought I should never get close to anyone because if I did they'd die. I pushed you away, so you would be safe."

"Holy crap! I would really like to hear this story....when you are ready, of course."

"Even if it kills you?" I smile shyly.

"I'm not going anywhere...right now at least." He smiles. I like his smile. He also thinks before he asks questions. He seems to ask gud, good, questions. Maybe I should try thinkin' before speakin' more than I do.

"How did Lisa convince you that you were wrong?"

"I don't know, exactly. She wuzn't afraid of me for one thing. An' she listened an' didn't judge me for another. Then she started pointin' out I had made a bunch of 'ssumptions, no, she says I have 'basic misperceptions' an' she sez we all do. Mine is jist based on a lot of deaths. Others have dif'rent ways they misperceive things, I guess. Anyway, she made me feel more normal an' she's encouraged me to get closer to you. She's the one who encouraged me to tell you that I had a nice time wiff, with, you when you took me to Morton's."

"Good thing she encouraged you, because I didn't think you wanted to go out again. You never said 'thank you' or 'that was nice' or anything. I wasn't sure if you wanted to see me again, socially."

"That's what Leeza said. That's why I tole you I had a gud time."

"You know what Noelle, you're a very deep person. I knew there was more to you than just work. You always look angry and frustrated, but I could see the little hurt girl sometimes and **that's** why I sent you to counseling. What are you working on now? May I ask?"

"Sure. We just started workin' on my goin' back to school. I only finished one year at Harford Community College an' then somethin' happened an' I dropped out an' went to secretarial school. I wanna finish college."

"Good for you. How can I help?"

"Nothin'. I gotta do this myself."

"Can I give you flexible work hours so you can go to school?"

"You'd do that?"

"Sure. Why not? You're the most efficient, smartest assistant I've ever had. You do your work and I never have to remind you or correct your work. I want to support you if you want to go back to school and maybe you can then take on more responsibility and I could get **you** an assistant."

"Do you have the money to do that?"

"Noelle, I have a lot of money. I could retire right now if I wanted to, but I love my work. I hate the office work and the contracts and stuff. But, you're great at that. We're a good team. I want to help you, so let's do it. On Monday call HCC and find out what you have to do to get re-enrolled."

"Gerard, you're not doin' this 'cause you want to... expect me to... umm, umm."

"I'm insulted. You think I'm doing this because I want to sleep with you?"

I don't know what to say so I sit quietly an' say nothin', but I pick at the napkin in my lap.

"Noelle, do you think so little of me, and yourself, that you think that's the only reason, I sent you to counseling, have taken you to nice restaurants, and offered you flex time to go to school? I'm hurt."

I start to cry. I feel like such a louse. I run to the ladies room before I have a bugger hangin' from ma'nose. Gerard follows me but stops short of enterin' the ladies room. But, he doesn't return to his seat neither. He's waitin' for me. I catch a glimpse of him every time someone opens the door. While I'm in here I might as well pee. I get myself together an' try to walk out cool-like. As soon as he sees me, he walks over to me.

"I'm sorry." We both say at the same time. Then we look at each other an' burst out laughin'. He grabs me an' hugs me an' doesn't let go. "Noelle, I also want to pay for your schooling. No arguments. And you don't have to sleep with me either." Now we are both laughin' hard. I feel good and I want to flirt a little, but all that comes out is "Let's have dessert. I passed up soup so I'd have room for dessert."

Parallel Process

Noelle called me during the week, in between her sessions. I see it as a sign that her defensive shield, which kept her from getting close to me, is dissolving. That may mean she's begun to rethink her misperception that she's somehow responsible for other people's deaths. She also may be challenging some of her beliefs about herself that kept her from taking risks and being happy, evidenced by her returning to school, and dating. Perhaps I need to take my own counsel. I need to risk going on vacation, possibly alone to a place that will feed me, not just relax me. I need to go back to school and finish my dissertation. I dropped out after my daughter died because I had difficulty managing my practice, school, my failing marriage, my son's grief, and my own grief. Maybe I need to bring some closure to my education and bring some joy into my life. I don't know where I would find the time to work on a dissertation and also I don't know if I have time in my life for a man. I'm amazed at how my clients' issues can parallel my own.

Chapter Ten
Facing the Self

The core experiences of psychological trauma are disempowerment and disconnection from others. Recovery, therefore, is based upon the empowerment of the survivor and the creation of new connections. Recovery can take place only within the context of the relationships; it cannot occur in isolation.

(Herman, 1992, p.133)

Caz
The Abuser

I'm dreading my session, and yet, I need to see her. I've a sense of foreboding. I recently had some insight, but I know Lisa has a way of seeing stuff I've missed, and I'm afraid of what I may have missed. I need her to be honest, but I don't want to hear it, yet I need to hear it. CRAP! I felt better when I could blame others for my problems.

I can drive now – the first time since my accident. The headaches are less intense, and I'm not getting lost or confused anymore. Lisa's waiting for me even though I'm early. She welcomes me and

355

encourages me to catch her up on what's happened since our last session. I begin by telling her what I've been thinking about, that I'm not as good a person as I thought.

"I always viewed myself as a victim. I thought other people were the evil ones who abused, abandoned, neglected, and deceived. I didn't think of myself as a sinful person, because I saw my sins as small in comparison to others. I take the Lord's name in vain, I don't get up in the morning, or I tell a little lie. My abusive childhood has programmed me to look at life through my own broken kaleidoscope. So, as a victim, I only thought about how I could get others to meet my needs by acting the poor, poor, pitiful dupe. I felt that others owed me, and I demanded people be perfect when I'm not perfect. I demanded people meet my needs, but I never made any effort to meet theirs. I made others feel guilty if they didn't help me. Yet I didn't help myself.

"And don't forget, the positive self-talk was repugnant to me because I didn't believe it. But, then, I started liking the positive self-talk because it focused on ME! I rode that horse for awhile, and then I realized the positive things I was saying were miniature compared to the really horrible side of me, how I neglected my family by sleeping all day, how I lied, stole, and deceived others. How I used others. I'll finish this truthful tirade with the question, "How am I that much different from Belle and her cohort? Let me answer that. I'm not! I just didn't abuse children.

"I know I said I was finished, but I can't stop now. I've been praying that God would help me. I really think God answered my prayers by letting me sink this low. The experiences of the last several weeks helped me to have more compassion for others and to feel embarrassed about how I treated my father and brother. I need to hear how you see me. Do you see me as a victim or a victimizer?"

Lisa pauses and thinks. I'm waiting to hear what she has to say and I'm feeling anxious. Then she talks and she does that thing with her eyes where she is telling me the truth but hugging me at the same time. "I see you as a victim...and a victimizer. I'm not going to hedge, you are both. There is no doubt you were the victim of your mother, Belle and her cronies, your psychiatrist, college advisor, and even your father when he neglected you. However, from this experience you learned some negative coping mechanisms. Can you list them?"

She put me on the spot. "I learned how to escape reality by sleeping, playing sick and depressed. I learned how to manipulate people and get away with it by playing 'poor little me,' and I learned how to avoid responsibility. Do you know anything else?"

"Well, you learned how to lie. You lie by using generalities and not specifics when asked a question and you learned how to seduce others and not make it look like abuse."

"What?" I stammered. "When did I do that?"

"In high school. You proudly boasted that you used the talents Belle gave you to seduce girls. You convinced yourself that they wanted you to seduce them. I think Belle convinced herself that you boys wanted sex. And she convinced you that you wanted to have sex with her. But, in actuality, she was manipulating you and abusing you. I think you did the same with the girls so you always had a date and felt significant. Can you see how Belle seduced you and trained to sexually perform, and then how you used the training to seduce others? You were the victim and then the victimizer."

"Christ, almighty! I'm a monster just like her!"

"No! You imitated her. That's how kids learn. This was not your idea. But, you are now responsible to acknowledge your imitation of her with the girls and face yourself as the victim who was turned into a victimizer because you were brainwashed to think of yourself that way. But, the abuse has to stop with you, Caz. You have an opportunity to look at this situation and acknowledge it, and change it. We call this 'name it, claim it, and tame it.'"

"Lisa, I feel panicky. I know you're right, but to think of myself as a "Belle" is too much. I need to leave!" I get out of the chair to exit, but instead I take a deep breath. "Wait a minute. Didn't I already "name it" myself earlier in the session?"

Lisa smiles and nods. "You sure did. But, it might sound different, or more hurtful, coming from someone else."

"This is going to take some time to sink in." I sink back into the sofa.

"Of course it will. That's the claim it part. You just named it today and it will take time to fully claim it."

I can't fully grasp this conversation. I say I'm rotten and Lisa then agrees with me? She never does that. She always helps me see things in a positive way. She turns things around to help me feel better. But, she's not this time. Why? When I finally hold up a realistic mirror to look at myself honestly, she holds up the same god damn mirror!. That's not what I expected. I expected she would say...I was being too hard on myself. But, no, she's agreeing with me! What happened to my kind, caring therapist? I start to cry, but she still doesn't rescue me. The ugly **me** is still sitting in the room, not the victim me. She's not helping me. Why not? She's just letting me cry. Damn her! I hate her! I hate me! Why was I honest? I could have kept playing the victim. She was kind to the victim. Is this the way she has seen me all along and has been lying to me or manipulating me? "Lisa, do you really see me as the horrible person I laid out?"

"Do you?"

I HATE WHEN SHE DOES THAT!

"Yes and no."

"Say more."

I HATE WHEN SHE DOES THAT!

"I feel like I've caused all this crap that's happened to me."

"Caz, you're going too far in accepting all the blame. Try being more realistic."

"What do you mean?" That usually gets her to be more specific and it gives me time to think. Silence. She's not going to answer me. Why the hell not? My heart is pounding and my mind is racing.

"Lisa, why aren't you rescuing me?"

"You need to rescue yourself, Caz. You can't keep relying on others to do the work you should be doing."

"I can't take this reality stuff any more. I need to change the subject or I'm gonna run."

"It's your session, Caz."

"Ok, I want to continue with this conversation later, but I have something pressing to talk about. Please don't think I'm changing the subject to avoid what we were talking about, but this is important. My grandmother wants me to live with her for awhile. She needs help cleaning out my grandfather's things and getting the house ready to sell. I'm thinking about going up there for several months. I would have to leave soon. I can see positives and negatives to this."

Lisa asks me to list the positives and negatives, but it's easy because I have already listed them in my head. "The positives are 1. I can get away from this area where I have daily anxiety about the abuse. Not always flashbacks but a queasy feeling. 2. I love my grandmother and I think she will be the mother figure I need right now. 3. I would probably get up in the morning for her and it may get to be a habit I need to establish. 4. I would like to help Grandma. 5. I will be closer to my half-brother and have the opportunity to get to know him better. 6. I think Dad and Rom and I need a break from each other. There is only one negative. I wouldn't be able to see you on a regular basis." (At this point maybe I need to get away from Lisa, too.) I don't say this last part. "Because I'm seeing Dr. Jamison only once a month, I could come back to see both of you on the same day." (Once a month is probably all I can take of her right now.) I don't say this part either.

Lisa asks, "What about losing your support system, like Pastor Craig?"

"To tell you the truth, I would be relieved. I would miss the church and Pastor Craig, but I feel like a pariah there. People look at me funny."

"But, aren't most of the men and boys who testified members of your congregation?"

"True, but a lot of them have moved out of the church. Bryce and I were the ones primarily responsible for blowing the whistle on Belle. I think the parishioners are cool with what we did, but we are a constant reminder of the horror that occurred in their church. They need time to heal too and my absence may help them."

"I see." Long pause. "So what do you want to do?"

Part of me wants to **abandon** her, right now, and have her feel bad about what happened earlier in the session...and part of me feels bad that I'm leaving Lisa. She's been a great support to me and I've learned a lot, but I need a break and I need to clear my head of the last several months. "I want to live with Grandma for a few months and see if a change helps me to grow up and become more responsible. I know I'll want to stay in bed there too, but I'm hoping I won't be as resistant to Grandma's prodding me to get up as I am to Dad's. I won't know unless I try. Also, I really want to help Grandma out. I'm sure she misses Grandpa, and she's moving out of the house she's lived in for 45 years. That has to be difficult. Could I see you once a month when I drive down to see Dr. Jamison?."

"Of course you can. When would you be leaving?"

"Grandma wants to put her house on the market in three months, so I will leave here in six weeks and help her go through Grandpa's things, pack, and get the house and yard in good shape to sell."

"We have six weeks left before you leave. What would you like to accomplish in that time?"

"I have to give up smoking. Grandma will not let me smoke in the house. I need to learn how to forgive myself for the sexual activities I engaged in while in high school. I also need to forgive myself for how I lied, manipulated, and used my father and brother. I need to respect myself and others. I always thought I was better than others because other people hurt me so bad, but now I realize I'm no better." Shit, now I'm agreeing with Lisa!

"That's a lot of work for six weeks. Are you ready to make a plan as to how to accomplish these?"

"I haven't had a cigarette all day. I'd like to make an act of contrition for the sexual activities I pushed on the high school girls. I have a friend who's Catholic and he says, in his church, they do acts of contrition to make amends."

"Do you have something in mind?"

"No. But, I'm thinking about it. I don't have any money so I can't donate to a charity that helps young girls who were raped or something. I was thinking of volunteering."

"Volunteer work can be a great way to help others, and learn skills. With only six weeks left in this area, is there a short term volunteer job that needs doing?"

"I didn't think of that. I guess I can't start volunteering somewhere just to alleviate my guilt and then leave"

"You're right, that may not be the best idea, but perhaps you'll think of another idea."

"I'll think about it." I make another appointment for next week and promise to think about what I can do to reduce the feeling I'm a predator like Belle. Lisa hates that I called myself a predator. I really wasn't a predator. The girls and I were experimenting, but I used girls to get my needs met, and I didn't stop the sexual behavior when I knew it was wrong. I wanted to be a big shot, known for my prowess. And I liked the attention. Why can I be honest with myself, and yet I resent Lisa for being honest, too?

As I leave the session, I give her the finger. She doesn't see it.

Lisa
Caz' Decision

I don't know whether it's in Caz' best interest to leave Baltimore and live with his grandmother in Pennsylvania. On the one hand, I can see the move as being beneficial for Caz and, on the other hand, I can see it being a disaster. The outcome is up to Caz. If he continues to live with his grandmother in the same manner he lives with his father and brother, then the move will simply transfer his problems to another location and Caz will feel like a failure again. If he can overcome some of his self-defeating behaviors and thinking patterns, then the move could be a new beginning. My goals are to help Caz become more motivated to change as he is preparing for the move and to help him to see that his mother, Belle, the psychiatrist, and the college adviser each hurt him, but now he has to make a decision each day whether he is going to hurt himself. In addition, I need to help him rescue the little boy of the past as well as the Caz of the future. Over the months we've been working together, I've been talking gently to Caz about these things, and he has only heard my support and gentleness. He needed to hear that after the two most important women in his young live abandoned him and abused him. However, the time has come to be more assertive, without hurting him. Today, I let him beat himself up. I didn't rescue him and I could tell he was pissed. He wanted me to mother him. I felt he was trying to manipulate me into disagreeing with his beliefs. He played 'poor, poor, pitiful me' and I was supposed to say, "No, you're not that person." I didn't. I hope I haven't damaged our relationship. I saw an opportunity to keep him honest with himself and hold his feet to the fire and decide what type of survivor he's going to become. Will he continue to flounder, defeat himself, and hurt? Or will he decide to move into a different posture and thrive? A lot of the fundamental abuse work is ending, but the future-oriented work is just beginning. Perhaps I need to offer him a referral so he can continue his therapeutic work in Pennsylvania. Maybe he won't even come back to see me to get the referral. It was tough session for him. I hope I didn't do too much damage by refusing to collude with him.

Caz' Rage and Confusion

I think that session was the worst. The first half I tried to be honest and she let me stew. I hate her. That's not what therapists are supposed to do. She really was not on her game today. She was almost abusive. Maybe she's sick. Maybe something horrible happened that made her irritable. I thought Lisa was going to be really upset about my leaving town. However, she was cool. I wonder if she's glad to be rid of me. I felt things about her today I never thought I'd feel. I don't care if I ever see her again.

I **have** to stop thinking and talking like that. She's been my rock and she has helped me a lot. Maybe she's reached the end of her ability to help me. I just don't get it!

She seems genuinely supportive of my decision to leave, if I'm convinced it's the right move. That's what I like about counseling and what I dislike about counseling. I like the fact I'm supported in what I want to do, as long as it's healthy. I dislike the fact the counselor doesn't tell me what to do. I would like to be told "Do this or that and you'll get better." But, counselors don't usually tell you what to do. Then again, I wonder if Lisa said "Stop smoking!" would I listen to her and do it? I doubt it. I probably would just say, "What right does she have to demand I do something?" My father and my brother tell me what I need to do all the time and I don't give their suggestions the time of day. I say to myself, "They should walk a mile in my shoes, **then** they can tell me what to do." Lisa's tried to walk in my shoes more than anyone else and she seldom tells me what to do. She offers ideas and insights but doesn't insist I do things her way. I sometimes wish she would, yet I know I'd discount her advice. I'm the only one who knows what I need to do, and I don't even take my own advice. I am so confused. I don't know what I'm saying or doing. How could I hate her? But how can I see her again after she called me an abuser?

My father and Rom are encouraging me to go to Grandma's and help her. Do they want to be rid of me, too? Probably. I've really tested their patience. If I were them, I'd want to be rid of me too. Funny, it just dawned on me I'm the only person in the world I can't be rid of.

I'm enraged with her I could spit in her face. and I'm going to tell her next week, and that will be the last week I'll see her.

Lisa Confronts Caz Again
Self-disclosure

I have a queasy feeling as I approach my session with Caz. I'm going to take another risk today and tell him what he needs to do to be successful. If I don't handle this well, it could backfire and Caz could leave here and never return. What would be worse is Caz could be totally turned off by all counseling and never get the help he needs. This is risky, but I don't have the time to tiptoe around the topic

Caz enters the office with a non-committal look. He's still irritated about last week's session. I ask him what he would like to talk about today and he begins, "I want to celebrate that I haven't smoked in a week." I congratulate him on a job well done. He says he only had the cravings for about three days and then he only felt them once or twice a day and was able to ignore them.

"What else?" I prompt.

"I've noticed how much negative talk I'm still doing. I correct it every time, but it's like I'm on autopilot. I'm getting frustrated."

"You know, Caz, all growth and development is hard work. Each of us has to make a decision every day to go in one direction or another. We can browbeat ourselves into a puddle or we can encourage ourselves. The choice is ours everyday."

Caz looks down at his nails. He says nothing. I let him sit. After a few minutes, he says, "I don't think I have many choices. Some days I wake up and I feel ok. But, other days, I can't get out of bed. Some days I'm anxious. Some days I'm depressed. People don't understand. They just keep pushing me to change. I was injured by a lot of people and there's no one who knows what it's like to walk inside my skin. Not even you."

"You're right, Caz, I don't know what it's like to walk inside your skin, but I do know what it's like to walk inside my skin. Life is difficult for everyone. Bad things happen that make us not want to get up in the morning, not want go to work, or eat. But, we can't change the past, we can only change what we're doing this very minute. So if I'm depressed and I don't want to get out of bed, I have two choices – don't get up or get up. If I yield to my pain and stay in bed, I'm victimizing myself all over again. If I triumph over the pain and get up I'm making a positive decision for life and a future."

Caz yells at me. "YOU THINK YOU'VE EXPERIENCED PAIN! YOU HAVEN'T. YOU SIT IN YOUR CHAIR ALL DAY AND SMILE AND HELP PEOPLE, BUT YOU HAVEN'T BEEN THROUGH WHAT I'VE BEEN THROUGH. HOW DARE YOU TELL ME I HAVE TO DECIDE ABOUT MY FUTURE LIFE. I DON'T HAVE TO DO A GOD DAMN THING. YOU DON'T KNOW WHAT IT'S LIKE!"

And there it is right out in the room... finally. "Caz I don't know what it's like to be you. But, don't presume to know what it's like to be me. I've had my share of sufferings and one of them almost killed me. I wanted to lie in bed until I died."

Caz is beginning to cry. "I'm sorry. I didn't mean to yell at you."

"Yes you did."

"Yeah I guess I did. I hurt after last week's session. I was really hurt and I couldn't stand it some days. I didn't mean to hurt you. You have been great to me. But, Lisa, you can't sit there and tell me you've been hurt like I've been hurt."

"We're not going to play one-up-man-ship, Caz. My pain was unbearable and your pain is unbearable. We both hurt. The point is, the decisions we make on a minute to minute basis will either keep us ensconced in our past pain or rescue our future."

"May I ask what your hurt involved?" Caz is looking for a comparison. Now I have a real dilemma. Do I tell him? Do I risk self-disclosure hoping the knowledge will help him understand it's possible to survive? Do I sidestep the issue and let him think I'm being slippery or worse, deceptive? I only have five sessions after this one. I'm risking self-disclosure.

"My daughter died in a helicopter crash several years ago. She was an intern news reporter for the local television station and the plane went down killing all on board." Sharing this information grabbed at my heart, but not as badly as it did years ago. I have grown into my pain and now I can use it therapeutically. I hope it helps Caz.

He's silent and his mouth's hanging open. He begins to cry, hard and deep. Through tears, the snot, the slobber, he is trying to apologize.

"I'm so sorry. I'm an ass. I just thought your life was probably normal and you couldn't have suffered anything like I have. I'm sorry." Caz is pounding the chair and is slightly rocking back and forth.

"Caz, it's ok. I shared this with you, not to make you feel like an ass for asking but to show you that pain doesn't have to stop us from living a good life. You seem to think you're the only one who's been injured by life. Your father has. Rom has. Your grandmother has. I have. You're not alone. The difference between us is not whether we are injured in life but how we cope. You've given up. You want to be five again, to be a little boy like before your mother left, and you keep asking people to treat you like you're five. But no one will and you see this as a sign that we don't understand or care. We do understand. We do care. We just want YOU to care enough to fight for your future the way we have. Last week I let you decide whether you wanted to stay five years old and stay the victim or to be the adult and own the fact you've been a horse's ass sometimes. What did you decide?"

"You're a great counselor, Lisa."

"Thanks, Caz. I appreciate that, but you're side-stepping the topic."

"I don't know what to say."

"That's ok, just stay with yourself. Own the pain that was inflicted on you and your own errors like you did last week. But, now go further and don't expect when you own it, others will rescue you."

"How can you sit there and help others when you've been so hurt?"

"You know what? The best counselors I know have all had to deal with personal tragedy. Going through a horrible experience can make us strong and empathic. Learning how to overcome a tragedy is what makes us wise."

"Are you saying you and other counselors are glad for your heartbreak?"

"No, no one wants pain, but once it's sitting in front of you, and you can't ignore it or its ramifications, the healing can begin and the stronger you get. And then something happens and you can see how it's made you a better person. If you don't take that path, then you get stuck and can't move forward into the future that you believe God has designed for you. A very wise man wrote a little but powerful book on the subject called *The Wounded Healer*. His name was Henri Nouwen. His premise is you cannot heal if you have not been broken. You cannot help others if you have not felt your own pain."

"I **want** to heal, but I can't seem to make myself **do** the healing."

"I know the feeling. There's no easy way to tell you this, Caz, but wanting to heal is not going to heal you. Healing is in the doing. If you want to claim your rightful future, you must act each day. Action takes courage, and some days it takes a lot of courage."

"Are we back to getting up in the morning?" He rolls his eyes.

"We're talking about whatever you need to do to become the man you want to be. Getting out of bed when you don't want to is courageous. Stopping smoking when you want a cigarette is courageous. Doing menial chores is courageous. Taking your medication as directed..."

"...is courageous."

"Exactly."

Caz is quiet for a long while, and I sit quietly until he's ready to talk. Minutes pass and Caz sits with his hands in his lap, examining them as if he is seeing them for the first time. Quietly in almost a whisper, "I have been praying to God to lift this pain from my shoulders and make me better. He hasn't answered my prayers. Why?"

"That is the question of the ages, Caz. All the great thinkers and writers, have struggled with that question. So I don't have the answer, but I'll tell you what someone told me once when I was asking the big WHY? question. He said God's not an errand boy. God wants us to learn to handle life ourselves. He supports us and gives us strength, but he doesn't take away our challenges in life because in learning to handle our tragedy or pain, we have the opportunity to blossom. By praying to God to change our lives when **we are not working** to change our lives means we are simply acting as dependent children, not as competent adults."

"Do does God love us whether we work hard or not?" Caz scratches his head as if doing this will trigger some answers for him.

"What do **you** think, Caz? Stop relying on me for the answers to **your** questions."

"I don't know. Perhaps God loves us no matter what but is more proud of us when we work hard at life?"

"That's an excellent answer and it came from within **you**. When you look inside yourself, your innate skills begin to flourish. I can never answer the questions that are uniquely yours. I only have my questions and my answers. I do know this. I feel better when I'm using my God-given and acquired gifts. Life becomes exciting and challenging and fun. In life, there are always trials, but they can make us wise."

Caz is sniffling through our conversation. He recognizes our time's come to an end and he is getting up. "Thanks for sharing, Lisa. I didn't know about your daughter's death. I'm glad you told me. I'm in awe of what you have accomplished. I hope I can do even half as much."

"It all happens by taking a single step, one at a time, and it can start today. I'll see you next week."

Caz pauses at the door. "Remember the act of contrition I was going to try? I decided I needed to do an act of forgiveness instead, so I planted seven trees in our yard, one for each person who hurt me deeply. They are just twigs right now, but I'll nurture them." He turns and leaves before I can say anything.

I'm worn out. I hope I did the right thing by sharing my story with Caz. He seemed to be quite taken back by the fact that someone else has had a difficult time and was able to thrive in the end.

Caz' Resolve

I'm blown out of the brackish water! Lisa seems so together and yet she has suffered the greatest tragedy of all, the death of a child. How could she calmly sit there hour after hour hearing everyone's pain and complaints and still feel good? I guess it can be done. She must have been comatose after her daughter's death. Somehow she made it, though. Because of my trauma, I don't feel like doing the mundane things I need to do each day, either. But I'm going to make a list and do them. I **will** get out of bed by 9 a.m. I **will** take a shower. I **will not** smoke. I **will** do the chores around the house. I **will** take the dog for a walk. And I **will** stop thinking and wallowing in my abuse story. "God help me." I whisper.

Prior to today, I've taken Lisa's suggestions as just her academic knowledge about what I need to do, but now that I know she's suffered too, I see her as someone who might know something about life and how to turn suffering into meaning.

The world somehow seems different when I arrive home and start dinner. At dinner, I share with Dad and Rom what Lisa told me. Maybe I shouldn't share Lisa's personal information, but I want them to know. Dad remembers the news helicopter crash, but he didn't put together that it was Lisa's daughter. We are all quiet for a long while. I utter a prayer for her.

Lisa
Thoughts about Self-disclosure

I felt like I was lecturing Caz the entire session. I hope I didn't make a mistake. I have seldom shared as much personal information with a client as I did with Caz today but, I've no regrets. The sharing I did will either impact Caz and he'll work a little harder at overcoming some of his personality traits that keep him infantile, depressed, angry, and resistant to change...or not. I'm leaving it in Caz' and God's hands. I think I suffer the disease most therapists suffer. I think the client's growth rests mostly on my being able to develop a healthy, helpful relationship, to be insightful and informative, and to utilize my therapeutic techniques effectively. While all these are important, the most important element in change is the client's motivation to change. I can't MAKE a person change if they don't want to. I need to let my clients own their change. It's a little self-serving to think I'm the major contributor to a client's improvement. It's also self-defeating to blame myself when a client refuses to take the very steps he needs to take to improve his life.

Interestingly, if a client doesn't change, I'm usually the one doing all the work to find the one thing I can say to encourage him. If a client does change, I give away the glory to the client. This relationship is a two way tunnel. Even if I'm at the top of my game, I'm still not 100% responsible for the client's growth. On the other hand, there are days when I'm not working to the best of my ability and still the client improves. The counseling relationship is a complicated, interactive, intricate dance, but at the end of the session, the client is totally responsible for how he uses the information he gathered in counseling.

I don't know what Caz will do this week. I would like to say I'm optimistic about his effort to overcome some of his self-defeating behaviors, but I wouldn't go to the Pimilco Race Track and place a bet on him either way. His depression, anxiety, PTSD, and personality traits can undermine his progress and have many times. On the other hand, when he's determined and centered, Caz can make remarkable strides. It's up to him.

Caz
Emergency Session

"Hello."

"Lisa, this is Stewart. Caz crashed this week. The flashbacks are intense and he can hardly function. Can I get an emergency appointment for him?"

"Of course, Stewart. Have him come to my office tonight at 7:00."

"Thanks, Lisa."

Well, I guess that answers my earlier question. Caz didn't respond well to our session. He's regressed to being a little boy whose father had to call to ask for an appointment, just like he did the first session.

Caz looks like he has the flu. His eyes and nose are red, his hair is unkempt, he's wearing the baggy shorts and large shirt he wore at our first session. (Was that on purpose?) Caz sits, looking at the floor. I look expectantly at him.

Caz fiddles with the hem of his shirt. "I was encouraged by our last session. I know it was difficult for both of us, but I was hoping to draw on your wisdom to start making progress. Then, I stupidly watched the news two days ago and saw a report of a man who molested over 100 children. He kept a journal of what he did to each child. It bothered me, and I had flashbacks."

I'm sympathetic to what Caz's saying, but I'm not quite sure I'm buying this story. I don't know why. Just a gut instinct. I understand this news story was a trigger or cue for Caz' flashbacks, but the man who is sitting in front of me is not having flashbacks, he's deteriorated to where he was several months ago when he couldn't take care of his basic needs. I don't know whether to challenge the fact he called himself stupid for watching the news or to ask about the word 'bother'. It's a general word that could be taken several ways. I decide to go with the word 'bother'. "What bothered you about the story?"

Caz looks at me blankly and shrugs. "I don't know. It just bothered me." He sounds irritated.

"Well, did it bother you because you had flashbacks?"

"No, it just bothered me."

"Saying it bothered you doesn't give me a chance to understand what was going on inside of you. Were you depressed?"

"I felt sad for the kids."

"So you felt empathy for the children?"

"Yeah, I guess."

I'm really confused. For someone who needed an emergency appointment, Caz seems to be avoiding telling me what's going on with him. Is he toying with me to get my attention? I could go on questioning him and having him give me vague answers for 50 minutes. I'm unwilling to do that. I sit quietly. We sit for five minutes without talking.

This may sound like a trivial amount of time, but try sitting in a room with someone and saying nothing for five minutes. It can be difficult not to mention, boring. However, I use the time to watch Caz carefully. He looks at his nails, his signature avoidant behavior. He plays with his athletic shoelaces. He looks up but not at me. He looks past me to a picture on the wall. He looks at his watch and shifts his weight. I continue to look at him expectantly and remain quiet.

Finally Caz whispers, "I became excited."

I heard what he said, but I pretend to have missed it. "Excuse me?"

"I said I became excited." He says a little louder.

"What do you mean by excited?"

"What the 'f' do you think I mean? I had an erection."

"What does this mean to you?"

"I'm a pervert."

"Why do you think you're a pervert?"

"You said people who abused children are perverts."

I don't remember saying that, but I could have implied it, so I ignore the quote. I play dumb. "You're saying you're a pervert because you abused a child?"

"NO! I didn't hurt anyone like that. I just got excited, but that means I **could** hurt a kid, right?"

"No." I'm not buying into this. Now I'm sure he's playing me. He had an erection upon hearing of a man who abused a lot of kids,

100 of them. Belle abused about a 100 children. He is associating the two and I think he knows it. He wants something from me and he's playing coy. This side of him is really annoying.

"You mean I'm not capable of hurting a kid?"

He knows what I mean, but now he's playing dumb. I'll play this time. "Having an erection does not mean you are capable of hurting a kid. For example, when you had an erection, had there been a kid in the room, would you have felt the urge to take advantage of the child?"

"No!"

"So you don't think you could hurt a child, and yet you're upset because you had an erection and you wonder what it says about you?"

"Yeah."

I don't know why I'm not buying into this supposed set back. I should be inquisitive and helpful in sorting out his feelings. I think he didn't do what he promised to do this week and so he's playing the "Aren't I awful?" card to get my attention. He's acting too coy and doesn't appear all that upset. I could ask questions, which would give him attention. I could sit here, that would annoy him. I could affirm him, which would reinforce his infantile behavior. Hmm, what to do?

"What's really going on Caz?" Atta girl just call him out. Of course he's going to say, "What do you mean?"

Caz says, "What do you mean?" He has an almost too, too innocent look on his face. Aha, I was right he's playing games. He wants the supportive Lisa back not the one who is asking him to change.

"What's really bothering you?"

"I told you I heard of the abuse and I had an erection."

"I know, but we've talked about how your body simply reacts to certain images, memories, etc. So your body reacted the way it was trained to react. Why is that bothering you so much that your dad was concerned enough to call me?"

"What do you mean 'bothering me so much'?"

Yipes! I'm ready to explode. Instead, I quietly say, "I'm just repeating the word **you** used. Can you explain it now?" So there.

"I don't like feeling these urges."

"I'm sure you don't."

"I want them to stop."

"These urges are part of who we are. Accepting them as part of our human nature may help." Cripes, I'm lecturing him. "You can diminish them by turning your attention to something else. We talked about how to do that several sessions ago. Did you try it?"

"Yes, but it didn't work."

I know he didn't do the exercises we talked about earlier, but I'll play along again. "What did you try that didn't work?"

"I just kept watching television hoping the next story would take my attention away from the erection."

Aha! So he was passively waiting for the television to change the topic rather than actively doing something himself. I'm going to call him on this and he's not going to be happy. "So you didn't do anything to turn your attention away from your genital stirrings. Instead, you passively waited for the television to change the topic." Ouch, he's not happy. His look says it all. Then he changes his look to be more child-like.

"I tried." He says demurely.

"What did you try? We've talked about a lot of different coping mechanisms. We talked about taking a walk, reading a book, relaxation exercises, making a meal, etc."

"I didn't do any of those. I just wanted it to go away, so I concentrated on the erection going away."

"And what happened?"

"It didn't go away."

"And what happened?"

"I ejaculated."

"Did that help?"

"Yes."

"So tell me again why you're upset. Are you upset because you had an erection, an ejaculation, or didn't do the coping mechanisms that could have calmed you down?"

"All of it. I'm so damn disappointed in myself. Once that happened I haven't been able to get out of bed, do the shopping, clean the house, or anything."

"Caz, you had a normal reaction for someone who has been abused. Why did you let it destroy all the plans you had?"

He's beginning to cry. I'm trying hard not to feel too sorry for him, and yet he really was damaged by Belle and company and he probably isn't capable of sorting through what he should and shouldn't do. Am I cutting him too much of a break? Probably. I feel compassion for him, but, at the same time, he has a lot of information and skills we've discussed over the months and he could've used any of them to help him manage his feelings. And he didn't do anything. That's the dependent, passive side of him that gets him into trouble with others.

Caz says through the tears, "I just want someone to take all this away from me so I can be normal. I'll never be normal. I'll always react to child abuse in an inappropriate way because of the triggers that are etched into my brain. I'm damaged goods."

Oh, cripes! Now I feel terrible. Wait a minute! He just ran me off the road into the 'poor me' mine field. He's good! I know he feels like he wants someone to rescue him but he also knows **he** has to do the rescuing now. I have an idea.

"Caz, would you close your eyes for a moment and take three deep breaths?"

Caz complies...of course. "Now I want you to picture in your mind, one of the abuse experiences from which you wanted to be rescued. Can you see that?"

Caz nods. I'm always amazed at how quickly and deeply an abused person can enter a light trance-like state. I proceed. "I want you to feel the terror. Do you?" Caz nods and his heart rate and breathing frequency are increasing. "Now you hear someone coming to rescue you. You can hear the footsteps, but you can't see the person. You know a man's coming. Do you hear the footsteps?" Caz nods again. "You're feeling optimistic. This person can really help you. He's coming closer. You can hear him opening the door. You still can't see his face, but you can see him out of the corner of your eye and he's a big man. The person who's abusing you stops and backs away from you, out of fear of this man. Then, the man reaches down to help you... and you look up at his face.... And ... the man...(pause) is...(pause) **you**."

Caz jolts in his chair. He opens his eyes and looks at me. He's stunned. I think it worked. The problem has always been that Caz has been looking all his life for someone to rescue him. I've been suggesting all along that he needs to rescue himself, but he didn't buy it. He never embraced the fact that he could be his own rescuer. By doing a brief guided imagery, he has a new image of himself as the rescuer. Caz is quiet, not just 'not talking' but really quieter. He either has had an epiphany or he's at a loss. "That was awesome. You really had me going. I kept expecting my dad would show up or Rom or Pastor Craig. I even thought Jesus was coming, but I never thought it was going to be me, as an adult! Wow."

"How are you feeling right now?"

"I feel a little more centered and awe-struck. I want this to be true, but it was only an image, right?"

"Well, that's true. The guided imagery we just did gave you an alternative image. You are the rescuer and the victim. But, your brain doesn't know the difference between reality and an image."

"Huh?"

"I'll show you. Let's do one more exercise. This will only take two minutes. Close your eyes and picture your kitchen. Can you see it?" Caz nods. "Now picture yourself opening your refrigerator. Feel the handle in your hand. Feel the cool air hit your face as you open it. Do you feel the air?" Caz nods again. "On the shelf you see a big, yellow lemon. Do you see it?" Caz nods that he does. "Pick it up and take it to the counter. Find a sharp knife and cut it in half. See the juice flow onto the counter. Do you see that?" Caz smiles and nods again. "Now pick up one half of the lemon in your hand and feel the juice on your fingers as you do. Now bite into it." Caz made a face and I knew he could taste the lemon. He laughs, "That's amazing!"

I continue, "Your brain did that. You see Caz, your brain doesn't know the difference between a real lemon and an image in your mind of a lemon. It sent the same messages to your salivary glands as if you had really bitten into the lemon. So your brain can also think you are your own rescuer and it will respond to the image of you rescuing yourself, just like it did when you imaged biting the lemon. You have a lot more power than you think you do."

Caz is pondering this new information. I can tell by the tilt of his head and the squint of his left eye. "You've given me a lot to think about. I'll see you on Monday?"

"Sure." And he left.

People who have been abused as children are suggestible. They use a form of autohypnosis to manage their abuse memories by dissociating. It's a God-given gift of flight. This suggestibility is also one of their curses because it can lead them to be susceptible to people taking advantage of them. They are so eager to be loved and to please that anyone can plant an image in their brains and manipulate them. That's exactly how Belle controlled the boys. She gave them a set of experiences that were wonderful and implanted that the abuse was just part of the beauty of being with her. Abusers count on this susceptibility to keep their victims dependent. Belle used gifts and love, but some abusers use threats of violence to the victim, or someone their victim loves, if the victim dares reveal the abuse. The victims of abuse believe the perpetrator's threats because they are so susceptible to implanted suggestions.

What Caz will do with the experiences and information he gained tonight? I tirelessly wonder when some of what we have talked about will finally begin to gel with him so he can act. He seems to grab at pieces of our work and use them temporarily but never pulls it all together so that the whole counseling experience becomes more than the sum of the parts gained in individual sessions. I noticed I let out a huge sigh as I wrote my notes of the session. I don't expect a complete turn around or a miracle, just some forward progress, without a retreat. One can only hope.

Caz
Can I do this?

Lisa never fails to amaze me. Where does she get this stuff? I could really see my own face appearing in the image of the man who rescued me. I could really taste the lemon juice. Could she be right? Could I really help myself? That would mean there would come a time when I could do this myself and not need her or any other counselor. I'm sure there would be a lot of work to do, there always is. I wish the work wasn't so difficult. Consistency has never been my strong suit. I get sidetracked into thinking and behaving in ways that are not healthy. It's a habit. Will it take another 30 years to undo all the unhealthy habits I've developed? I'm exhausted just thinking about it. I'll have to ask her, but I bet she'll say mental health is hard work just like physical health is hard work. She'll say if you want to be mentally healthy then you have to work on it all your life. Why does everything have to be so hard? I wish I could live for a year with Lisa. She would be able to monitor me constantly and I'd improve faster. Maybe I'm fooling myself, but that's why I want to live with Grandma for awhile. I'm hoping she can help me while I help her.

Stewart's Desire

Maybe I'm experiencing wishful thinking, but I think Caz seems better this week. He seems more mature and focused. I'm trying not to get my hopes up, but there seems to be a subtle shift occurring. I'm probably just imagining it. Caz usually is better after a session with Lisa, then he falls back to his old routine.

I've been in counseling with Burt for the last few weeks. I didn't want to go at first, but I discovered that I like having someone I can talk to about my screwed up life. When I talk to others they're polite, but they don't know what to say... either that or they begin telling me what to do as if they are the experts on my life. Having a counselor allows me to say anything I want. The therapist can sort through the garbage and find the rose. I wish I'd done this years ago. I feel calmer and more in touch with myself. Hmm, maybe Caz isn't better, may I am?

One thing I noticed about myself over the years is I've avoided relationships with women. I was scared of abandonment. I blamed myself for my wife's leaving more than I thought. In the past, when I thought about dating, I would say, "What's the purpose? She'll only leave too." After talking about it with Burt, I feel more optimistic about meeting someone. In fact, I've met someone at work I'd like to ask out, but I'm scared she'll say 'no' and I'll be rejected again. Burt's encouraging me, but not pressuring me. I wonder what Rom and Caz would say if I were to go on a date. Perhaps I should ask them, but I'm afraid I might cause Caz to have a set back again.

Come to think of it, neither Caz nor Rom have dated much. Are they afraid of rejection or intimacy too? Or, and I hadn't thought of this until this minute, are they gay?

How would I handle it if both of them were gay? I guess with all we've been through together in our lives, being gay wouldn't be such a big deal. Our church's been through a lot in the last few years with the ordination of openly gay men and women and with the election of an openly gay Bishop. It's been a real struggle for our church and personally, I think it's much ado about nothing. The church went through the same outrage when we ordained women. The church will survive and so will I, if Rom and Caz are gay. They are my sons and I love them no matter what.

At dinner tonight I am bringing up the dating thing. I cannot walk on eggshells around Caz forever. We all have to get on with our lives. It's my turn to make dinner and I've chosen stir fry. It's quick and easy to prepare. That'll give us all a chance to talk when they get back from the movies. Come to think of it, tonight is the first time, in a long time, they've done something together. They seldom talk, so I guess a movie is good, they can be together and not have to share much.

Cutting up the vegetables gives me time to think about what I'm going to say. I have no idea how to approach the topic, but I want to be sharp. Ouch, like the knife. Perhaps I'll just slice through the crap, and say what's on my mind. The door opens, and the guys are home. I ask them how the movie was, and it sounds like Caz liked it more than Rom. Dinner's ready, and they sit down poking each other the way they did when they were little. It used to annoy the hell out of me then, but today, it feels good to see them joking and poking.

Dinner was quick, which gave me no time to think about what I'm going to say. I'm going to wing it. "There's something I want to talk about with the two of you." They both look at me with dread. "It's nothing bad, just something I'm considering." They both look relieved. "I'm thinking about dating again." Rom and Caz both give me huge smiles. I guess that means they approve.

After your mom left, I felt too damaged to date. I thought if she didn't want me, then no one would. I also was sensitive to the fact that I had two young boys to take care of, and I didn't want you to suffer if I chose a woman you didn't like. It sounds silly now, but that's how I felt. Anyway, there's a woman at work I'd like to ask out, but I'm scared. I'd like your input."

Rom is the first to answer. "Dad, it's about time! Go for it." Caz is nodding his head off. Wow, that was easy. Now for the hard part. "You two don't seem to date much are you feeling like I was, scared of women abandoning you? Or....are you interested more in...in... men?" I'm holding my breath. Rom again is the first to answer. "I'm not gay, if that's what you mean, but I'm afraid of women and rightly so. I'll know when the time is right for me to try a relationship." Caz is quiet and is shifting a bit in his chair. I fear I know what he's going to say. But I don't. He surprises me. "I don't know what I am, Dad. I have a long abusive past with women and mom's abandonment scared me. I guess all I can say is I don't know myself well enough to know if I'm gay or straight."

I'm grateful for Caz' honesty. I can see Rom nodding as if he understands. A reply is called for here. "Caz, I want you to know that no matter what you discover about yourself, I love you and will support you." Hmm, I sound like my therapist. But, that's not a bad thing.

Caz is tearing up and he's trying to stifle the crying by looking around the room. I feel closer to my sons because we had this conversation, but I don't know what else to say. It's a bit uncomfortable, so I ask if they'd like to play poker. Both of them break into grins and jump up to clear the table. "Leave the dishes for tomorrow morning." Our lives are becoming normal!

Caz
The Move and Sexual Orientation

Our meal, conversation, and poker game turned into one of the best nights we've spent together. Something's changing. I don't feel like I have sand in my gizzard any more. Dad seems happier. Rom isn't as grumpy. I feel closer to them and accepted. When I first decided to live with Grandma for a few months, I was thinking it would be good for me to be away from Dad and Rom. Now, I'm really going to miss them. There's a part of me that wishes I hadn't made the commitment to Grandma. But, she needs my help and it's the least I can do. Rom and Dad aren't free to help her like I am. I dig around in my closet to find Grandpa's engineer's hat. I need to wear this more often. It makes me feel like Grandpa, kind, funny, easygoing, helpful. This was a good week. No trauma, no arguments, just peace and quiet. I wish every week could be like this.

I see Lisa tomorrow and I wonder what I'm going to talk about. The trial's over, things are going well at home, I'm both scared and excited about helping Grandma. And Dad seems happier. Wow, he might date! That'll be interesting, but unfortunately I won't be around to see this historic event. Rom will have to fill me in. That's another thing that's going better. Rom and I are developing a relationship again. I guess I have a lot of good things to tell her but will that take up 50 minutes? For the first time since I started seeing her, I don't think I NEED to see her. What will we talk about?

I slept like a baby last night. I've had some good nights before, but they were few and far between. Last night was wonderful. No bad dreams and I feel energized. Plus, I don't have a lethargic hangover from the Lunesta. Maybe it's because I took it at 8:30. I actually made a mistake. I looked at the clock and thought it said 9:30 and took it, thinking I was taking it a half hour early, but as it turned out I was taking it one and a half hours early. Dr. Jamison and Lisa kept trying to tell me I was taking the Lunesta too late in the night, but I didn't listen to them. I would tell them I was taking it at 10, but I was really taking it closer to midnight and I wouldn't fall asleep until one. I didn't want to take the meds the way they insisted because I don't like going to sleep. However, I don't like feeling awful the next day either. Maybe I found out by accident they were right. I'll take it at 9:00 this week and see if taking it earlier really works better.

As I climb the stairs to Lisa's office, I'm wishing I had taken the elevator, the easy way, rather than exerting myself. Is this a metaphor for my life? I usually want what is easy? Climbing the two flights of steps is a test of my resolve to change. Interestingly, it didn't exhaust me, it invigorated me. Not smoking has improved my energy. Lisa sees me coming out of the stairwell and notices I chose to climb the steps. Does she notice everything? "Having a fitness day?" She smiles teasingly. I shrug and say, "I just felt like it."

I inform Lisa this was a good week and recount the information about Dad, Rom, and our dinner together. I end with reminding her we only have a couple of weeks before I leave for Grandma's. She nods. "How would you like to spend these last couple of sessions?" She asks. I tell her I want to stabilize. Where did that come from? I hadn't intended to say anything like that. It was like God put words in my mouth.

We talk about what stabilize means, what kinds of things I need to do, what kinds of thoughts I need to think, what types of skills I will use when things go awry, etc. This is a normal session. No hysterics, no flashbacks, no crises, no beating myself up. Did Lisa feel like she earned her fee today? I venture to ask her. She laughs out loud and then retorts. "Today's session is the first time I shouldn't have been paid **twice** for a session." She's quick on the draw. It feels good to laugh with her. When I look at her, I'm reminded of the pain of the last year and my whole life and I tell her this. She thinks for a minute and says, "You know, Caz, a lot of my clients say that. I become the person who helps them feel better, but then after they feel better, I become a reminder of the pain they endured. About that time we agree to fewer sessions. Usually what I hear clients say is 'I was on my way here and I wasn't sure what I was going to talk about. I didn't want to rehash more of my past trauma or hurt and nothing much is going on,'"

"I felt that way today."

"Then, perhaps being with your grandmother and seeing me less is exactly what you need. I know you feel 'unfinished' with counseling, but a break can be just as therapeutic. You can try out some of your new skills in a different environment."

"I'm feeling a little anxious. You have been my lifeline this year. You've rescued me from the edge of insanity. I don't want to stop seeing you, but I do need a break. I wish I wasn't going to be living so far away, then I could see you more frequently as I try out being ME, whoever that is."

"Change is scary. Even when we need it and want it. But, Caz, we are not ending our relationship. We are redefining our relationship. We worked hard and long on a very difficult set of problems. Not all of them have been ameliorated, but their intensity has been reduced. Now your task is to monitor your growth and enhance it when it needs some work."

Lisa pauses as if she wants to tell me something I may not like. "I wonder if you would like to try working with someone else, a counselor in your grandmother's town?"

"NO! No Way! I'm sorry, but the thought of starting all over again with someone else and having to tell that horrible, boring story again, does not appeal to me."

"Are you aware you just called your story 'boring'?"

"Yeah. Why?"

"Because I always got the impression that one of things that held you close to the abuse was the excitement of being at Belle's house."

"I guess you're right. But, now it seems dreadfully boring to have to share it again."

"That's quite a shift in you." (Caz nods.) "I'll tell you what, if you decide you need to see someone in Chambers, I'll make the referral and explain the situation to the counselor. That way you don't have to start all over again. Then you will be free to work on current problems in light of the past ones."

"Do you know someone in Chambers?"

"I do, actually. So call me if you need a referral."

"Okay...... Lisa, can I ask you a personal question?"

"You can, but I'm not sure you'll get an answer." We both laugh.

"You believe in God, right?"

She nods. I continue, "Do you understand why God allows awful things to happen?"

"Nope."

"Do you think God is only the God of Christians and everyone else is wrong?"

"What do you think?" She turns it back to me. Darn.

"No, I don't. I think God is much bigger than any one religion. We can't conceive of how big God is." But I have to stretch my concept of God to be able to incorporate me, a gay, mentally ill, injured person who has been a horse's ass because of my pain and suffering. I wonder why I had to go through all this."

"I don't know, Caz."

"So if someone says they're gay and others say that he's therefore an abomination of God's creation, you would say what?"

"I'd say that I wish you would speak in the first person and not the third."

"Lisa, you are tough! Ok. So…if I say I'm gay and others, therefore call me an abomination of God's creation, what would **I say**?"

"Yep."

"This is tough. The voices of other people who call me an abomination are really loud! But, I think, (Long pause) it's not their place to judge another human being for what they have done or who they are."

"So, Caz, you think that your mandate from God is what?

"To simply love everyone, and let God be God."

"So you don't think you are an abomination if you are gay?"

"No. I can only believe what I've read in the Bible. Jesus tells us not to judge others, that's God's job. He ate with sinners and He died for all of us, not just the righteous." We are both quiet. I feel proud of what I just said.

"That was beautifully said, Caz."

I think about asking another question, but I raise my eyes off my fingernails and tear falls down my cheek, and softly I say, "Thanks, Lisa. I really needed to hear that."

"You're welcome." Long pause while we sit in silence.

Lisa breaks the silence first. "Now tell me about your dad wanting to date. How do you feel about that?"

The session continues with current events and Lisa had some interesting points. She brought up the issue of looking for the positives as well as working on the negatives in my life. The last time she did this I was annoyed. This time, I could hear what she's saying. I need to count my blessings as well as see my life challenges. I will miss our sessions.

Lisa
Termination

If this were a Hollywood movie script, there would be a major, one last time, dramatic scene in which Caz was forever changed. Life in therapy is seldom, if ever, like the movies.

I remember watching Ordinary People and Good Will Hunting, two movies that deal with therapeutic issues. While they were better than most of the therapy movies I've seen, the dramatic moments in both movies where the clients are forever changed by a few words spoken by the therapists is a stretch. I wish that were the case. Therapy would be easy if I could find those magic word-bullets to fire at the client at just the right time and bingo they hit the mark and the client has insight and the client changes. Caz has had several of those moments, but he didn't immediately change and the changes didn't last forever. (Perhaps I'm not as good at therapy as the actors or writers?). He did however slowly change, slide back, change, slide back even more, lurched forward a lot only to slide back again. There were small shifts going on the entire year. The final major shift occurred with the rescue scene in the guided image, but it was not as dramatic as in the movies and he did regress after that remarkably happy week. He became very anxious about leaving me and his family and moving to Chambers to be with his grandmother. In fact, Caz reported to me he had a panic attack about 20 miles from his grandmother's house. He had to pull off the road and wait it out. At least he knew what to do, and he didn't panic about having a panic attack. He breathed and talked his way out of it. If he had been at home, I am sure I would have received a phone call.

Being away was the mother of invention for Caz. He had to use the skills we had talked about. He couldn't rely on his father, brother or me. His dependency traits were being challenged and he rose to the challenge. Now he knows he can manage by himself. Helen and I kept telling him he needed to rely on himself and use his new skills, but he wouldn't make the effort as long as we were there to rescue him. I, like Caz, wish we had had a few more months of working together before he left for his grandmother's, but the timing was not ours to construct.

Noelle's Tryin', oops, Trying

The date with Gerry (I didn't know he wanted to be called Gerry!) was the best social affair I've ever had. Of course I haven't had too many of 'em. Gerry's a real nice person. I don't know how ta fall in love, but I git a sense that to fall in love I have ta let go. I don't know how to do that. Guess I can ask Lisa.

I practiced speaking more clearly, the way Gerry and Lisa do. If I'm gonna to return to school, I want to talk like a college student. Over the years I've gotten, oops, become lazy with my speech. "Why bother?" was my motto. Now I see it's empowering to use proper English. I think one of the first courses I want to sign up for is English Speaking 101.

This speaking stuff's hard. I get a headache just trying to think in proper English. Maybe I can practice at work. Talkin' on the phone can help me practice. Hopefully it won't take too long before I'm put**ting** the 'g' on my ing words and pronoun**cing** all the syllables. I used to be better at speaking clearly, but I got lazy. Remember my motto was "why bother?" Now there's a reason or two, Gerry and college.

I can't wait to see Leeza. That feeling is sure a turn around for me. I used to hate Tuesdays when I first started seeing her. I used to make up excuses about why I had to leave the session early. Now the 50 minutes isn't 'nough, oops, enough.

Lisa
A Vacation She Didn't Want

I called some friends to arrange a trip somewhere and only four were available this summer, Milly and Maggie and two other friends I haven't seen in awhile. We met and we talked about various locations. After the meeting, my canyon and Yellowstone ideas were left on the cutting room floor and everyone agreed on San Diego. Weeks ago before I started reading the quantum science books, I would have fretted about finding someone to go with me and also getting to go somewhere I wanted to go. But, now I can see that things will work out the way their supposed to and I have to let go of trying to make everything happen the way I want it to work. Whoever is supposed to go with me will.

I start by making phone calls to places in San Diego and getting on the internet to see what accommodations are available. I found that we can stay at the famous Hotel del Coronado on Coronado Island if we share a suite. The prices are unbelievable, but a three or four way split makes it doable. I get the dates and call all those who said they were interested. Only Milly and Maggie agree to go with me, so I booked the resort for a week, put down the deposit, and made airline reservations for myself. I'm looking forward to the trip, but there seems to be something wrong. I wanted to do the canyons or Yellowstone or something. How did I get talked into another resort-type vacation? How did we end up with just one week when last year we said we'd do two weeks. I'm letting others determine **my** vacation. Perhaps, in the future, I need to take a risk and do something by myself, even though I'd feel anxious to be alone for a week. But, if I want to go, I just might have to suffer a little anxiety. For now, San Diego is the target of this year's vacation. I don't feel as excited as I did last year. Am I tired? Am I disappointed?

Noelle
Diction, School, and Gerry

"Hi Lisa. I have a lot to talk about today."

Lisa's smile welcomes me warmly. She asks me what I want to talk about and I tell her about my date with Gerry. I explain the entire evening including my running to the ladies room to escape havin' to deal with Gerry's bein' hurt about my assumption that he wanted to have sex with me. Lisa listens carefully and then in her classic style asks a good question.

"So, do you think Gerry is a person of interest for you?"

I had to laugh. "Of course he is. Most importantly he knows how weird I am and still likes me." We both laugh again.

I tell her about the massage and she nods. "I think it made a difference, but my face's so used to bein' in a frown that it'll take a few sessions an' a lot of practice smiling to change my 'countenance'.

I looked up the word in the dictionary and am trying to use it often to make it my own." Lisa raises her eyebrows and smiles an approval.

I also told her Gerry's gunna give me flex time an' money to go to school. She seemed very surprised at his generosity and affirms me when she says he must value me as a person and employee. I called Harford Community College and the admissions person said I needed to reapply and all my credits would transfer back in if I'm accepted. I'll only have 30 credits to take to get my AA degree. That means it might take me two years if I work full time.

Lisa nods. "That's really positive news, Noelle. How do you feel about Gerry helping you?"

"I'm grateful, and I'm scared to go back to school after so many years. But, I think I can do it, especially if Gerry is giving me time off and is going to pay for it."

"Do you feel obligated to him if he helps you?"

"You mean like continuing' to work for him or are you askin' me what I asked him…if there is a hidden meaning to his generosity?"

"Both."

"I'm a little concerned he may see this as a way to bond with me more than just as an employee."

"How do you feel about that?"

"I dunno. I mean, I don't know. I'm scared of relationships, but Gerry's about as nice a man as I've ever met. However, he made it clear he's interested in a personal **and** professional relationship with me. I'm a little concerned how we'll work it out if one of us decides we no longer want a personal relationship. One of us cud get hurt an' it'll probably be me."

"Why do you say that? **You** could be the one to decide that he's not right for you."

"Lisa, I've had three dates an' two have been wiff Gerry. I don't think guys are going to beat down my door at this stage to begin datin' me."

"But, it's also possible you could decide Gerry's not for you or that you prefer not to have a boyfriend at all. Can you conceive of that?"

"You mean can I imagine that?"

"Yes."

"No, I can't imagine saying 'no' to someone who wants to be wiff me."

Lisa nods, but I can see she's not fully convinced. "Perhaps if I grow more and get my degree, I'll have more confidence an' will find someone else, but why would I want to? Gerry's a good man and he clearly has gone the distance with me in the last four years. He's been very patient. My problem is I dunno...don't know...what love is or what it feels like. Out of the blue I ask..."Lisa do you think I can go every other week when I git back to school? I feel better. My life's goin' better. I feel more in control. I'm startin' to believe I haven't really killed people because I love them...."

"Noelle, you don't have to justify seeing me every other week. You've made progress and if you want to put some of your energy into school then you should do that. Let's see each other every week until you start school and then let's schedule every other week. Would that work for you?"

"That's great."

Our session ends with a talk about relationships and how not to jump to conclusions or make 'ssumptions. We also talked 'bout what love feels like and how to tell Gerry 'bout my past without overwhelming him. Gerry and I have a couple of outings planned for this week and I'll begin telling him 'bout my life and he'll do the same. Lisa's suggestion was "Go slow." It's a good one for me, but I think Gerry's more ready to jump into a romantic relationship than I am.

Bally's Trip
Toto's Reaction

Yesterday, I used the session to go over the upcoming trip and the various possibilities that could happen. I should feel much better after the preparation, but I don't. My family can always throw in a ring-a-dinger. That's my concern. Will I know what to do if something happens that I've not been able to plan for?

Driving to the airport and anticipating the endless check-in lines and the three hour trip makes me tired before I even park the car. I have to be psychologically ready, but is it possible to ever be ready for what's to come? A couple of weeks ago, Lisa believed I was ready to meet Atlee in Seattle, and when several 'surprises' occurred, I didn't do well. Why should this be any different? I think she's too optimistic. She doesn't know my total history of how I screw up every relationship. Well, she knows, but she hasn't lived it, I have. I've done better recently, but I'm still not in the best place to deal with 'anything' that may come up. I think Lisa's a Pollyanna. I'm more realistic. I'm still going over and over the same stuff when I find my seat and settle in. The sun will be setting in a little while, and I'll try sleeping on the plane.

Sleep doesn't happen, but I'm able to get to that twilight state. At least my body is more relaxed. Four hours later I'm waiting out on the curb for Atlee. The story of my life, always waiting on the curb of life watching others drive around living lives that seem happy. Oh, come on, Bally, stop it!

Atlee's waving at me. I must have been thinking intensely and missed seeing him. He's smiling, always the upbeat guy! Wish I could be like that.

"Hey, when did you get here?"

"Danny and I got in around noon. We had lunch with Mom and took a tour of the city. We met her neighbors. Little gets in tomorrow morning."

"Another trip to the airport for you. Poor baby!"

"Actually Little's renting a car. She wants the freedom to take off at times and try to look up some of her friends, if she has time. She seems pretty happy. Well, as happy as Little can be."

"What's your assessment of Mom? Do you think she knows anything? Suspects anything?"

"If she does, she's the greatest actress in the world. When we arrived, she acted happy to see me and Danny and she knows Little's coming to see her tomorrow. She appears genuinely excited. My guess is she doesn't know that Little is your biological mother. I could be wrong, though"

"How could she not? One look at a picture and you, Carly, and I all guessed the truth."

"I don't know, but my hunch is she trusted Dad and may love living in the world of denial."

"Then, our job this weekend is to tell her the truth and get her to believe us and also to make sure she's ok, not depressed, anxious, or overwhelmed."

"Yep. She hasn't even asked me why you, Danny, and I are here the same weekend that Little's returning after all these years. She hasn't put it together or if she has, she's pretending it's not happening."

"Wow. I feel awful about bursting her bubble of denial. How are you planning on presenting the truth to her?"

"Little and I talked and she's going to do it."

"NO!! She's cold and aloof. She'll never be able to tell Mom in a loving way!"

"Wait, wait, Bally, before you get upset, you haven't heard her plan. She's going to try to get your Mom to say how much you two look alike and lead the conversation that way."

"What if Mom doesn't see it. If she's in la-la land, she may continue to deny the truth, chalk it up to a weird gene constellation, like I did at first."

"If that happens, she's going to tell her gently with me there. Do you want to be there too?"

"Yes. But, I would feel a lot better if you told her. You have a really nice way of telling people hurtful stuff and still make them believe that "the sun will come out tomorrow." You ever think of becoming a counselor?"

"What? Why did you ask that?"

"Because my counselor can tell me to go to hell and back and it doesn't feel like it's such a bad thing!"

Atlee laughs. "No I never considered the social service profession."

"Atlee, I'm scared. Really scared."

"Want to know something, Bally? Me, too."

"Really?"

"Yep. I believe still waters run deep and I fear Mom's in denial. How deep does it go and how fragile is she? Has she always "known" on some level and just covers it up? Or will this be the biggest shock in the world to her? Could it send her over the edge? I have no idea."

"That's my fear too." And I can't hold back the tears any longer. I cry openly and loudly and Atlee rubs my shoulder and says nothing. We arrive at Mom's and I feel sick.

"Atlee, I don't know if I can do this."

"YOU don't have to do this. WE are going to do this."

"I wish Carly and Sassy were here, too."

"Me too, but having everyone around may have too much of an impact on Mom all at once."

Sitting in the car and looking at her condo, I say, under my breath, "This is it". I have to put on a face that will last until tomorrow morning. I've never been good about holding things in. I usually just blurt out stuff, and let others deal with whatever is inside of me. This will be one of the hardest things I will do, telling my mother that I know she's not my biological mother and watch her hurt. Christ Almighty!

Atlee has my bag and is starting for the door. My mind wants to run in the opposite direction, but my legs follow Atlee. I want to vomit, but my mouth smiles as Mom opens the door and hugs me. Then, I have my out...Mom says I look tired. "I am exhausted, Mom. I hope you won't mind if I have a bite of that wonderful pie you were cutting when I arrived, and then head for bed."

"No, not at all. You sleep. You need it."

Whew!

Bally
Confrontation

My eyes are heavy, like they're sealed shut. I pry one lid open and see that I slept for 10 hours, and still, I feel tired from the dread of what's to come this morning. It's 8:00 a.m. and Atlee said Little will arrive at 9:30. Shower, dress, make-up that's water proof, just in case of tears, and then...Mom makes me breakfast, first time in over 20 years. I watch her move around the kitchen. She's so cute.

Mom is only five feet tall and weighs no more than 100 pounds. She's 63 or 4. She doesn't look it (Asian skin is amazing!), but she acts 80. She shuffles when she walks and says, "That's nice" a lot. She doesn't want to talk about anything deep, but knows everything that's happening on 'her' Soap Operas. I don't remember a lot about her when she was young. She's always seemed old to me, but I thought it was because all parents seem old to kids. Now I wonder if she's been old all her life. Her movements, her talk, her dress seem very familiar, like she's been this way forever. Sassy and Little are much more…hip! Their ways of dressing are current, they walk without shuffling, and talk about current events. They are just a couple years younger but seem a decade younger. The trauma that occurred over 40 years ago affected each sister differently. Perhaps Little became angry, Sassy became empathic, and Mom grew old.

Mom's looking at me in wonderment like I was a new baby. "I love you Mom." I want to see if she responds. She does, she blushes "I love you too. Eat more, you too skinny."

"No I'm not, Mom."

"You skinny like Little was."

"I do resemble her a lot, don't I?"

"Yes, you always did."

"So what do you make of that?"

"Genes."

"What do you mean 'Genes'?"

"You have her genes."

I'm just about ready to ask her what she meant when Little walks in. Mom jumps up and runs to hug Little and Little returns the hug. "I so happy to see you! Been many years. You look the same…just like Bally…so pretty!"

"Toto, (Little uses Mom's Filipino nickname.) you always were good for my ego."

"We don't look like sisters at all. We look so different. I short, you tall, I look like my mom, you look more like Dad."

"Sassy looks like neither of us." Little points out.

"Yes, we all look like the different cultures we come from, so do my children. They all three look very different."

Little comes over and stands next to me and puts her hand on my shoulder and looks at my Mom. Little says, "Toto, do you see the resemblance?" Wow, Little wastes no time. I had opened the door slowly, but something tells me that no-nonsense Little is going to the heart of the issue. Is she pushing too fast?

"Yes. You could be sisters."

"There's a reason Bally looks like me. Do you remember why?"

Mom's face clouds over and she shakes her head. Little gently goes to her and holds her. "Toto?" Mom doesn't respond. "Gladys, it's time we all talk about the truth."

"I don't want to. I like the way things are."

"I know, Toto. But Bally, Carly, and Atlee all figured out the truth."

So mom did know!

Mom looks up at Little like a small child looking at her mother. She has a quizzical look on her face that slowly turns to pain and then to denial. Mom shakes her head as if to shake out the reality.

"You do remember. Don't you, Toto?"

Mom busies herself with dishes and keeps shaking her head.

Little pursues. She takes the dishtowel from Mom and turns her around to make Mom face her. "Gladys, it's over. Everyone knows and everyone still loves you and cares about you. We need to start talking about this again."

"I don't know what you mean."

"We talked about all this as I left town. The conversation was only a few minutes long, when I told you what your husband did. Do you remember?"

Mom hangs her head and starts to cry but says nothing.

"Toto, you remember? I told you your husband raped me three times. Shooter and Crabby were adopted by Dad as his own, but Cameron took Bally because she was a girl and Dad didn't want a girl, he had three already. Remember? I told you I was leaving town because my reputation was sullied. Our father and Cameron kept telling everyone I had loose morals and had three bastard children out of wedlock. That kept me isolated from others. No girl would be my friend and every man in town thought he could have his way with me. I had to leave to salvage my life. Remember?"

"Yes, I remember."

"Toto, Bally and I met after all these years. She's loyal to you as her mother and that's how it should be. She loves you **and** she wants to get to know me better. We are biologically mother and daughter, and I want to be able to talk openly to both of you about our relationship."

Mom's silent tears turn into wailing. She reaches for Atlee, not me. That hurts. I want to hold her, but he holds her and she cries. Danny enters the kitchen and begins to stroke her hair. What a kid! She cries as if there are 40 years of tears stuffed inside her. I'm not sure she's ever going to stop. I'm afraid she's going to cry until she turns to dust.

Then the anger erupts. She tears at her clothes and bangs her fist on the table. Atlee stops her from breaking her hand. Then she screams, a scream that is so heart-stabbing I can feel the pain down to my toes. Atlee continues to cradle her and now he is rocking her and speaking quietly to her. Little and I back off and hold hands. I don't remember when that happened. Tears are rolling down my cheeks, but Little is standing tall and tough. Yet, her moist eyes betray her toughness. She's being affected by Mom's reaction, too.

Seems like hours have gone by, but it's only been 30 minutes. Still every sob, tear, and scream reaches into my body and undoes something that's been riddling me with anxiety, fear, and anger for years. In its place the sadness and loss settle in. The years of torment! What a waste!

Everyone has been affected by my father's and grandfather's narcissism. They believed they were entitled to do whatever they desired to others, just to get what they wanted. They didn't care that other people were harmed.

Rivulets of guilt trickle through me. I've treated others as if I have the right to do whatever I want, too. I don't rape or lie (much) or hold others hostage, the way my father held Mom hostage to his demands, but I manipulate for my own gain and use anger to control others. I feel sick. I'm just like my father in many ways. Is it genetic or did I learn it from him? He doesn't deserve to live and maybe I don't either. I hurt a lot of people with my rage, but the one I end up hurting the most with my rampages is me. Dad destroyed others. Is there a difference?

Mom's calming down. Her face is in the crook of her right arm. Her body language is saying "I don't want to look at anyone, and I don't want anyone seeing me." I feel like I'm watching a dog I had several years ago. He used to hide his 100 pound body behind a 12 inch diameter tree by putting his head behind the tree. If he couldn't see me then I guess he thought I couldn't see him. I used to laugh at him every time he did that. Now watching Mom, I want to smile at her hiding her face from us while we can still see her entire body racked in emotional pain. But there is nothing funny about this. When she calms down, I go and kneel down beside her. I put my head in her lap and tell her I love her. She strokes my head, but I'm not sure she knows it's me. Without looking at anyone she goes to her room and gently lowers herself on the bed and curls into the fetal position. We let her be.

Little finally breathes a sigh of relief and turns away from us. Most of the secret is out in the open. We don't have to deny the truth any longer. Atlee looks pale and, with shaking hands, holds Danny. I need to take a walk. I leave, without excusing myself or asking permission. Walking down the quaint, cobblestone street, I try to make some sense of the 40 years of pain, denial, and suffering.

I also feel badly for Little. I never considered how the tight-knit community judged her back then. The judgmentalness and rejection made her leave her family and relocate 1500 miles away, and she never returned until today. Originally, I thought she left because she didn't want to be raped by my father anymore. While that was true, she was also ostracized. I guess she's entitled to her haughty attitude. It keeps the pain away and keeps others from getting close and hurting her. I can understand that. I use the same coping style, coupled with anger.

I don't know how long I walk and think, but it's dusk when I return home. I'm shocked to see Mom making dinner and acting as if nothing happened. The only tell tale sign is her swollen eyes. Little hovers close to her, but Mom's treating Little as if she is a visitor, not the woman who just unlocked a 40 year secret in front of her children. Denial is a wonderful thing!

I can barely swallow dinner. Little turns to Mom and says, "Toto, I'm sorry I caused you pain today, but we needed to get all this out in the open. Secrets kill relationships. But, I want to tell you one more thing then I want you to help Atlee, Bally, and me out. Ok?"

"Ok."

"Cameron also raped Sassy and Carly is her child. That's why Sassy left town too. She didn't wait to be raped again. She and Carly wanted to be here too, but we all felt it would be too overwhelming for you if all of us were here. They both would like to be able to call and visit and reestablish their connections with you."

Mom nods. Little lets a long silent pause occur. Then,

"Gladys, do you know where Cameron is?"

Mom nods. "Why do you want to know?"

"We want, no, need to confront him with the truth. We want him to see that we all know the truth and he isn't free to think he got away with his manipulation. I guess we're thinking in terms of sort of an intervention. We want nothing from him, just the satisfaction of seeing him and telling him he didn't get away with keeping the secrets.

"Will you tell us where he is?"

"No."

"Damn it Toto. You're still protecting him after all these years!?!"

"No. I not protecting him....I want to confront him first! Then I will tell you where he is."

We all look at each other. We're speechless. We didn't anticipate this from Mom. We ask her to tell us when she will go see him, and we offer to go with her. She rebuffs us all. She will decide and she wants to go alone. We cave. What can we do? Atlee googled him and nothing came up about his whereabouts. There was reference to some paintings, probably an artist with the same name. Dad's been blind for years. Clearly, Mom is the only one who's in touch with him.

The next morning, we all look like hell. Clearly none of us slept well. Atlee takes the reigns again. He tries to convince Mom he should go with her to confront Dad, but she clams up, makes her mouth a pucker, and shakes her head.

So, typical of our family, we ignore the yellow dinosaur in the room. The rest of the day, we drive around town with Danny and point out our schools, stadiums, etc. just as if we are a normal family. We end up at Mom's favorite restaurant. Everyone at the restaurant knows her. She flits from table to table and from waitress to waitress hugging and smiling. This is a side of Mom I've never seen, a happy, social, woman.

After dinner, Little drives me to the airport. Atlee and Danny stay one more night with Mom, but I'm glad I'm leaving.

Little and I are alone for the first time and this is the perfect opportunity to ask her about my memory flash of Dad stroking her leg, but I'm getting cold feet. I swallow and broach the subject just like Lisa and I discussed, not accusing her, but puzzled how I could have that memory when she left town before I was one. Little's mouth drops open and she slowly turns to me. She silently mouths the words, "Oh my God!"

"What?"

"When Toto was pregnant with Atlee, she had to be in bed for the last two months. But, she couldn't take care of you and Carly and stay in bed so Cameron asked your grandfather to fly my first cousin out from the Philippines for a couple of months to help with the two of you. Looking at Annie is like looking into the mirror for me. We are like twins. I have pictures of us together when she was out here one summer. Everyone thought we were twins. Your memory of when you were three is about Annie and Cameron, not about me and your father."

I'm trying to take this in. All I say is "I see, thanks for clearing that up for me." Little doesn't say anything but I can see my memory hurts or angers her, because her hands are shaking and she is holding back tears. I want to say something supportive or apologize for upsetting her, but I don't have an appropriate response. We hug awkwardly, say goodbye, and head for two different terminals.

Then, the ironic truth hits me. My mind is in like a tornado. Questions, hunches, reflections, blaming. The implications of this new piece of information is staggering.

I'm glad to be going back home. When someone calls to say we're scheduling the trip to visit Dad, I'll be ready to go, but right now, I just want to go home, sleep, do my job, and let everything I experienced go through my emotional filter so I can make sense of it all.

Chapter Eleven
Change

The influence of external reality on the formation of internal reality must not be neglected.
(Bowlby, 1988)

Contextualizing Grief

Bally enters my office looking extremely tired. Her walk is slow, her eyes are bloodshot, her face is devoid of emotion. For the first time, Bally looks her age. She drops her body onto my couch with a long sigh.

"I'm exhausted. I can't do this any longer. I need to get some closure on this family stuff. Help me process this past weekend and rid myself of it."

"How about bringing me up to speed?"

Bally tells me the story of her trip in excruciating detail, clothing, food, emotions, etc. After 45 minutes of non-stop description, Bally cries. Her agony fills the room. For the first time, she does not take the tissues and twist the corners into little points to dab her eyes. She cries with grief from the depths of her soul. She blows her nose loudly and wipes her eyes smearing her eye makeup and doesn't seem to care. Bally's defenses have been dropping over the weeks, but today she's making herself extremely vulnerable. She hurts and she's openly dealing with the pain she feels. There's no projection, misdirected anger, or flippant behavior.

Bally looks at her shoes not at me. "Lisa, I feel awful. I'm depressed, frustrated, and hurt. Will this get better?" She takes several short breaths and her chest shakes with each one.

I lean forward and look at her eyes, but she doesn't make eye contact. She looks away. I lower my voice and say as gently and compassionately as I can, "Bally, I don't know when you will feel better, nor can I guarantee everything will be alright, but I do know the acute grief usually subsides with time. You've been overwhelmed these last few weeks. It's normal to want to put this all behind you and move forward. Unfortunately, grieving doesn't work like that, it takes time." I wasn't sure what else to say. I didn't want to offer her false hope.

Bally nods and looks up briefly. "This won't go away easily, but I hope after we confront my Dad, I will be able to begin contextualizing this family mess."

"Contextualizing?"

"Yeah, I know I sound like you, don't I?"

I ignore her attempt at being funny and stay with the topic. "What do you mean by contextualizing?"

"I'm hoping once all this torrential pain is over, I'll be able to understand how this caused me so become the person I am today. I want to know if I turned out to be a bitch because of my father's actions and my mother's inaction. Once I know why I reacted the way I have all these years, I will be able to bring about some change in my way of relating to others."

"I think you've already begun."

"You think?" She's still looking at her shoes.

I nod. She needs to look up to see I'm nodding, and I catch her eyes. Swollen, tired, red.

"Yeah, me too." She looks away.

"How's it feel?"

"Good, scary at times, but I like myself better each time I make a decision to react differently. One thing bothers me though."

"What's that?"

"I find myself critiquing how other people are acting. Is that normal?"

"Did you do this before?"

"Yes. But, this is different."

"How?"

"Before I was **critical** of others, like 'she shouldn't wear that color', or 'he didn't present that information well'. But now I'm **critiquing** them. I say to myself, 'That was a good response.' or 'I don't think I would have said such-and-such in that way.' Stuff like that."

"Interesting."

"Am I crazy? Or am I watching and learning?"

"What do you think?"

"I feel like I'm watching and learning."

I nod. She smiles a little. She already knows the answer to her questions. She's just looking for confirmation

Bally takes a deep breath and looks me in the eye. "You know Lisa, I want you to know that, when you asked me for my earliest memories, I thought you were crazy and I just accommodated you and gave you a memory flash."

"I remember."

"Well, that little, tiny memory flash caused all these secrets to spill out."

"I guess that's true. It prompted you to call your mother and Carly and request pictures."

"You want to know the really uncanny part of this?"

"Sure."

"That memory was not about Little. It was about her cousin, Annie, who came over from the Philippines to look after me and Carly while Mom was on bed rest during the last two months of her pregnancy. In other words, that memory was wrong. It wasn't Little, it was Annie. Evidently Annie and Little look very much alike. So all this crap was unveiled because of a misidentification by a three year old. The memory was true, but Little wasn't there. If Annie hadn't looked like Little, there's a very good chance I would never have found out about my biomom or my father's rapes. I would have just thought my father was a womanizer, but I would never have thought Toto wasn't my mother. I would never have gone to the pictures in search of truth. Even if I had, I wouldn't have found her there. Life is an f'ing piece of work! All this pain and all these secrets have been revealed because of a three second memory glimpse by a three year old child."

Long silence as this sinks in for both of us.

"Bally, I have a question."

"What's that?"

"When you asked Little about the memory, how did she take it?"

"Not well. She was shaking. I couldn't tell if she was hurt or angry or both. She seemed to be close to this cousin. We were arriving at the airport and I didn't want to push her too hard."

"My hunch is she was enraged at your Dad, and maybe even Annie, for allowing that kind of thing to have been going on in front of you..."

Bally interrupts. "I didn't think about that. I thought she might be feeling more sadness because my father took advantage of Annie, too. According to my memory, Annie was laughing and enjoying his attention. I see what you mean, but I don't know if I will ever find out. Little isn't very forthcoming and I don't want to discuss it with her again."

"That's an incredible story, Bally." Another long silence while both of us try to comprehend this turn of events. "Are you going to be ok, Bally?"

"You mean am I going to drink?"

"Yes, and I need you to promise me you will take care of yourself and not harm yourself or anyone else."

"Yea, I know the drill. No drinking. Call my sponsor. If I feel suicidal, I call you and 911 etc., etc."

"I'll see you next week at the same time, but if you need me or something else happens, feel free to call, ok?"

"Sure. Bye."

Bally is really changing! I think this family revelation and crisis has forced her to make some serious alterations in the way she interacts with herself and others. I just don't like the rapidity of the change and the intensity of the situation. She and Caz have both been forced into warp speed insight and change. Both are still very vulnerable, Caz from the trial and Bally from the accident and the discovery of her biological mother and rapist father. She still has to internalize this information and decide how it affects her and her future. The revelations are coming too fast for her to process the ramifications. I hope and pray she has some time before the confrontation with her father. That could be a difficult experience, devastating maybe.

Noelle's Progress

Noelle and I have been seeing each other for several months. She's made many changes in her way of viewing her world, but I wonder if she's strong enough to manage school, job, a relationship with Gerry, and whatever life will throw her way. She seems to be feeling more confident about her skills. However, life stressors can emerge quickly and create a set back.

In our last session, I noticed she was making an effort to speak clearly. She called me Lisa not Leeza a couple of times, she enunciated more clearly, and she put the 'g' on her 'ing' words more frequently. This is a great metaphor for her. Life has never been clear for Noelle. She has had a difficult time understanding what was happening to her so she never became skilled at making herself understandable either. I think Noelle would say, "I can't understand life and others, no one can understand me, why bother being articulate?" It was easier for her to give one word answers and scowl instead of clarifying her beliefs and embracing life. She's made progress and she's happy with it, but this progress is new to her and I fear she'll become discouraged with the tedious, difficult work ahead. Only time will tell.

Noelle's Father

In the last two months I've seen Lisa four times. I can't believe I am sayin' this, but I miss our weekly sessions. School's not as fun as it was when I was 18, however it's more interesting now that I have some life experience. I'm seeing school as just a means to an end. I need to finish my AA degree and start on my bachelors, so I'm puttin' in my time, taking classes. Some are kinda boring, and I'm taking them just to git the required subjects finished. Others are interesting. I especially like the English courses. I'm learning a bunch about writing and speaking properly.

Gerry's been very supportive. But, I feel guilty 'cause I am not putting in my 40 hours a week. He's still pursuing me. I can't say I feel as strongly about our relationship as he does, but I enjoy his company, and I like the fact he's interested in me. I know he would like a more physical relationship, but I'm not ready.

I did do something I hadn't done in a while, I went to see my father. I hadn't seen him in three years even though we talk on the phone once a week. I was shocked at how he looked. I know he's pushing 70, but he looks much older than he did three years ago. He looked kinda grey and thin. I told Lisa about my visit and she asked me if I told him I'm worried about him, because he doesn't look well. I didn't say anything to him because I didn't want to offend him. Now looking back on it I should have said something to him. Maybe he doesn't know he may be sick. In fact he looked a little like what Dr. Brown looked like before he died. Should I say something to him? I don't know how to approach him. We haven't been close since I was 18 or 19. Lisa went through the pros and cons with me of whether to say somethin' to Dad. I made the decision to call him after the session, but I still haven't done it. I keep puttin' it off. I may not want to find out the answer.

Dad's retired and maybe that's why he's failing. He's not active the way he was three years ago when he was working. I don't know. He seems sad and lonely. He reminds me of...me. I can see myself all alone at 70 with a cat and just lettin' myself go, too. It makes me glad I have Gerry in my life. Dad never remarried after my stepmother left. He just kept sayin' he was through with relationships because they're too hard. I sure understand that. I'm going to call him and stay in touch better than I have been. He's my last connection to my family. Dialing.

"Hello."

"Dad?"

"Hi Noey. You wuz just here a few days ago. Is everythin' ok?"

"Yes, I'm worried though."

"Bout what, Noey?"

"About you."

"I see."

"You look tired, Dad. Are you ok? Have you been to a doctor?"

"I been to lots of doctors."

"And?"

"Noey, I'm dyin'."

"What? Why didn't you tell me when I was there?"

"I didn't want ya to worry. You've had so many deaths in your young life. I didn't wanna add to your burden."

"But, you're my father. It's not a burden if you're sick. What did the doctors say?"

"Ma heart's giving out an' I'm not a candidate for a heart transplant 'cause of my age an' other health issues."

My body's going numb and my head feels dizzy. Why didn't he tell me? Why didn't I ask when I was there? What am I going to do? All the other deaths in my life have been sudden and tragic. Dad's dying will be expected. I'm scared. I've never done this before. I don't know what to say or do. I feel the familiarity of anxiety building inside.

"I don't know what to say or do, Dad. Would you like to come live with me for, until, umm, awhile?"

"Ya mean do I wanna move in wiff you 'til I die? No. I don't wanna burden ya."

"But, you won't be. I have a two bedroom apartment and, and, I don't think you should be alone."

"I've been alone most of my life, Noey. What's different now?"

He's saying things I would have said several months ago if I knew I was dyin'. I would have tenaciously blown off life and others' help. Now, I see things differently, but my dad's still stuck back there in the pain of losin' my mom and brother and all the other deaths we endured. It's funny, but until this moment, I never considered that all the deaths I went through as a child, he also went through. I was too involved in my own grief and I never saw his. I gotta do somethin'. I might be the stronger one now.

"Dad, I insist you move here. I want to take care of you until you ....leave here. I love you and I don't want to get a phone call from some stranger tellin' me you've croaked." Good grief what a horrible choice of words. I still don't have this speaking thing down. However, instead of insultin' Dad, I made him laugh.

"Noey, you're too much. Ok, I'll start packin'. I don't have much stuff left. It won't take long. I'll get out of my lease, sell my furniture, an' pack the car. It'll take a couple of weeks. I'll call when I'm comin'. Ok?

"No."

"No?"

"No. I have a school break comin' up in less than a week. My boyfriend and I are going to drive up there and pack his SUV with all your stuff and drive ya back here. I'll be there in five days. In the meantime, get out of your lease and pack the small easy stuff. Don't over do it! Gerry and I will load the SUV, and then Gerry will drive his SUV and I'll drive your car. Ok?"

Long pause, then a teary reply. "Ok, Noey. We'll do it your way. Thanks." And he hung up.

I can't believe I just volunteered Gerry and his SUV without askin' him. I also took control and told my dad what to do. I **am** stronger. I think I did real good, but I pick up the phone and call Lisa. I need an appointment. I leave a message for her to give me an appointment anytime in the next four days. Then I call Gerry and apologize and tell him how I committed him for a trip to Hagerstown to get my dad. Gerry is, of course, his accommodatin' self. He thinks I did exactly what I should have done. But then, he's my biggest fan.

Noelle's Emergency

Noelle asked for an appointment very soon but left no information as to why. She still has that "to the point" attitude sometimes. She's due in 30 seconds, and here she comes. She's walking with more attitude, more confidence, less scowl. She opens the door and bursts into tears and throws herself in my arms. I catch her, but I almost fall over.

She disengages abruptly and walks right into my office and lands in "her" chair. Noelle is still crying. "My father's dyin'. He has a heart condition and the doctors told him there's no hope. No transplant 'cause of his age and his other medical issues. He's dyin'. Remember when I went to see 'im and he looked awful, very grey, like Dr. Brown did before he died? Well, I thought 'bout what we talked 'bout at our last session and I took the chance and called him. Dad wasn't goin' to tell me! He was goin' to die alone. I could see myself in him at that moment, stubborn, independent, not wantin' to be a burden on others, not wantin' to be hurt by others."

I notice her diction has slipped a bit now that she's facing a crisis. "What are you going to do?"

"I told dad to git out of his lease and sell his furniture, and Gerry and I will drive to Hagerstown, load the SUV, and drive back to Balmer. I told him he's not dyin' alone. He's goin' to live with me."

"That's quite brave of you."

"Brave? You think?"

"You've lived all your life fearing the next death, believing you somehow caused them. Now here you are taking control, bringing your father into your home knowing he's going to die and abandon you to this world. You didn't miss a beat. You acted. What's that like for you?"

"I never thought about it."

"That's the point. Death's always surprised you with its abruptness. Now death's going to be known. Your father will come here and he will die here. You'll have nothing to do with causing that death but everything to do with helping him to be comfortable while he dies."

"I **have** turned a corner, haven't I?" The tears are subsiding as she talks.

"I think so. Do you?"

"Yea, I think the reason this isn't as scary is because it's normal. Dad's not real old, but he's ill and dyin'. Everyone else died suddenly, tragically. Even my Gran didn't die of old age, she died of the flu. Funny, I thought at the time she was old, but you know what? She was only 52, maybe 53. That's young to die so tragically. My mom was only 31 and she developed pneumonia from having the flu. I found out recently she had asthma and that's why she died of the pneumonia. Now it makes sense, but at four years old death looked different than it does now."

"And your dad? Are you ready for the possibility of a long vigil?"

"I think I am. I don't know really what to expect, but I want to take care of him. He took care of me until I went to college. I'm the one who pulled away after the Chase train accident. I think he must have been a little sad that we weren't as close. You know, Lisa. When I was talkin' to him on the phone, I suddenly realized he suffered the same losses I did, and I never thought about it as a kid. I never thought about how all them deaths affected him! So as I pulled away from life, I pulled away from him. And, now I realize in my selfishness to avoid being hurt, I denied him a relationship with me, the last person in our family. I don't want to deny him anythin' anymore. We both need each other."

"Well done."

"Really? I wasn't sure if I was being too bossy or too self-centered or just plain stupid for purposefully starin' death in the face at this time. You think I am doin' right?"

"You're doing what **you** think is right. This won't be easy for either of you, but you both need each other at this moment in your lives. I also think you did a great job of thinking and feeling this through and arriving at a decision."

"Thanks. Will I ever get to the point where I will **know** I'm doing the right thing and don't need to call you for an appointment?"

"Sure. You almost did it this time."

"What do you mean?"

"You made all the decisions and arrangements and then called me, sort of as an after thought."

"Well, not really, I keep you in ma mind a lot and I did what I wanted to do, but I kept hearing your voice coachin' me along."

"Maybe it isn't my voice. Maybe it's your own voice coaching you along."

"Maybe both?" Noelle offers.

"Good enough." I affirm.

Noelle has faced her greatest fear and didn't lose her strength. Instead she found her resolve.

Noelle
Dad's Move

The drive to Hagerstown is a little over an hour, and the time goes quickly with our chit-chat about work. Dad's waiting outside for us and he waves as we pull into the parkin' spot beside his car. I introduce Dad and Gerry, and we load Dad's stuff into Gerry's SUV in an hour and begin the trip back. Dad rides with Gerry and I drive Dad's car. This is it. Dad's leaving the home he's known for the last 15 years. I see him turning to look one last time as we exit the parkin' lot. I wonder what he must be feeling right now. I tear up in empathy for his pain and sadness. I also feel the pangs of guilt for the pain I've caused him by remaining aloof in order to protect myself. I feel mucho guilt (this semester I'm taking Spanish). But, I need to cut myself a break. That was before I realized what I was doing. I'm different now and I'm not pullin' away from Dad an' his impending death. Saying the words 'Dad's death' makes me feel a little panicky in my stomach. I haven't been to a funeral in years. I get jittery, out of breath, and light headed when I go to funerals, so I haven't been. I tried to go to the engineer's funeral, but I got inside the front door of the church and had flashbacks of seein' him die. The anxiety overwhelmed me, and I left before embarrassing myself. Now, I'll be facin' Dad's death and funeral. God, I hope I can do this. I was more certain when I was talking about it in the abstract with Lisa, but now I'm drivin' his car back to my apartment, for the last time. He'll die while he's living with me, and I'll have to make all the arrangements. The anxiety's building.

Gerry pulls into my parking lot, jumps out, "He slept most of the way home." I peek in and see that Dad's still sleeping with his head against the window. Gerry and I begin quietly unloading the cars. We finish quickly. Dad's still asleep. Gerry opens his door gently to wake Dad, but he won't wake up. Gerry looks at me and his eyes are round with fright. We both try to wake him up. He's not responding. I dial 911 on my cell phone. Dad's barely breathing and his eyes flutter, but he isn't coming around. Is he going to die right now, right here? I thought we'd have a little time together to redevelop our father-daughter relationship. No, not now, not just when we're getting to know each other again!

The EMTs work to revive him, but he looks neither revived nor dead. The siren grates on my entire being, down to my toes, as they take Dad to St. Joseph's Hospital. Gerry and I follow in the van. We're both quiet and I'm fighting back the tears. Gerry keeps peeking at me out of the corner of his eye as if he's worried about me. That's comforting.

This is unfair. God, if you're real, please give us just a little time together before he has to leave. I don't know what the paramedics do to Dad during the drive to the hospital, but when they open the door, Dad looks at me and smiles a little. The EMTs rush him into the emergency room and then through the "NO ADMITTANCE" doors. A clerk named Mrs. Snell asks me a lot of questions I can't answer. She wants his Medicare card. I don't know where it is. She wants his social security number, and I don't know it. She asks if I have his power of attorney, but I don't, yet. She seems miffed that I'm unprepared, but she doesn't know the situation. I can't handle this. I stomp my foot, like I used to do when I was five and I couldn't meet others' expectations. I turn my back on her and leave her cubicle to sit in one of the waiting room chairs. The tears are now more frustration than fear that Dad will die tonight. Gerry takes a stab at talking to Ms. Snell. He seems to be able to make her understand the situation, so she's less snippy with him. I have no people skills compared to him.

After an hour a nurse appears through the NO ADMITTANCE door and calls my name. I follow her into Dad's cubicle. He's sleeping quietly, but the machines are monitoring his bodily functions. I look at him and wonder if we will have the time together I want. Dr. Ricca clears his throat to awaken me from my thoughts. He looks somber. "How much do you know about your father's condition?"

"He told me he's dying because his heart's givin' out'. He told me there's no hope, because he's too old and has too many other problems for a heart transplant."

"He's correct. He's dying. He's not a candidate for a heart transplant, but he may have a few weeks left if he follows his medication regime and reduces his risk behaviors. Right now, he's doing neither."

"What do you mean?"

"He's still smoking and drinking. He's not taking his medication every day and he's not eating well or exercising at all. He should try to get up and walk a little each day."

"I don't know what to say. I just learned of his health issues four days ago and when I did, I told him to pack 'cause he was coming to live with me. We had just arrived at my apartment with his stuff when we noticed he was barely breathing."

"You saved his life… for the moment. Your quick action saved him from dying… today. But, you must know something. Your father has no desire to lengthen his life if he can't smoke, drink, and sit around each day and watch television. He also doesn't want to take his medication or use his oxygen. He did not take his medication for the past three days, hoping he would die before he reached your house."

"Why?"

"He doesn't want to burden you."

"Shit. Oh, excuse me. I'm sorry."

Dr. Ricca has a crack in his veneer, and smiles slightly.

"Tell me what to do."

"Convince him you want him around for awhile. Get him to stop smoking and stop drinking. Convince him to eat well, walk a little each day, and get him to take his medication and use the oxygen that was prescribed. If he doesn't do these things then he will be back in here in a week and next time we might not be so lucky. But, you do realize there will come a time when his heart will not be able to work any longer. However, he has a little time left if he takes care of himself.

"I also suggest that, if he desires, he should give you his power of attorney and medical power of attorney and he should consider signing medical directives. And if he and you agree, he can sign a DNR, do not resuscitate, order. Any lawyer who specializes in elderly care or family law should be able to do this for you."

"There's a lot I don't know, isn't there?"

"All this seems new to you. It's a tough way to learn."

"Will he be able to go home?"

"That's up to him and you. He's going to stay here for the night and if he responds to the medication he can go home tomorrow. If he doesn't respond well, then he'll stay a few more days. But there's another alternative, Ms. Kilpatrick and that's hospice care. They're good at working with patients who are dying. I can have someone come by and see him and you tomorrow before he's discharged. Ok?"

I take a deep, deep breath. "Ok. Send the hospice people tomorrow and I'll talk with him about his options. Thanks, Dr. Ricca."

Dad stirs in his bed and calls my name. "I thought I heard your voice. Get ma wallet and take it to the admittin' nurse. It has all ma medical information in it. I don't want you to get this bill."

"Dad, is that all you can think of? You tried to kill yourself by not taking your meds!" I can feel my anger rising. I take several deep breaths. "I'll talk to you tomorrow when I come to visit." I grab his wallet and leave. I feel a little bad that I spoke sternly to him. What if he doesn't make it through the night? Hell, he didn't think of **me** when he did this!

I return to the waiting room and hand the Medicare and social security cards to Mrs. Snell. She's more gracious this time, but I'm still irritated at her and my famous scowl lets her know it. After she finishes her work, I wave to Gerry to follow me and we leave.

"What happened in there?"

"Gerry, I really don't want to talk about it right now. I'm too angry with my father."

"You're angry with HIM?"

"Yes." Ok, I need to download on someone so I told him the story. His only response was "I'll be damned."

"Please drop me off at home. I need to think this through. I brought him here to live with me so we could have some quality time together before he dies and he's trying to off himself so he doesn't have to spend time with me."

"Wait, wait, Sweetie. I don't think he did this so he wouldn't have to spend time with you. He did this so he wouldn't be a burden to you."

"You're right. But, he didn't even give it a chance. Now I have to get him to a lawyer and have all these papers drawn up and signed. I don't have this kind of time. I thought I was doing something good by bringing him home and now there are all these complications and legal issues." I can feel the tears burning my eyelids.

"Tell you what. Let me call the lawyer who drew up my will and power of attorney. She can do this fairly quickly. It's all done on computers now. They just plug in names and batta bing, batta boom and it's done." He smiles hoping to make me laugh.

I shake my head. "You always make me smile. Ok, give her a call. I'll see Dad in the morning and go over what his wishes are and then let him make the decision. You're a really good person, Gerry, thanks for helping me today." The hug I gave him was sincere. I don't know what I would have done with out him. He lifts my chin and kisses me. "I love you Noelle."

"You do?"

"Yes."

"Then I guess I love you too."

"You GUESS?"

"No, I don't guess anymore. I love you."

The next morning it's raining chickens and roosters. Dad used to say that to me when I was a little girl. I would then say, "No Daddy, it supposed to rain cats and dogs, not chickens and roosters." He would then say, "Then don't step in a poodle!" It would send me in to giggles every time and never got old.

Dad's been moved to another floor. He's in some kinda of a step-down unit where he can have visitors any time. He's not sitting up when I go in, but his head's raised a bit more than last night. He's awake and more alert. He also looks chagrined.

"So dad, what's up with that thing yesterday? Is being with me so horrible that ya had to off yourself to keep from havin' to live with me?"

He looks hurt. I don't think he ever considered how his actions would affect me. "Noey, I just don't wanna be an invalid. Did the doctor tell you…no smokin', no drinkin', and takin' medication and usin' oxygen fir the rest of ma life?"

"Yes, Dad, he told me, but I don't get it. What's bad about giving up smoking and drinking?"

"I have nothin' else to enjoy. That and watchin' television's all I have."

"No dad you're wrong." (I feel myself getting angry.) "You now have **me** in your life and I need to count for something here." Am I being too harsh?

He looks like a little boy laying there. "You're right ya do count. I just didn't want to put ya out. You have a life and a very nice guy. You don't need to sit around and watch me die."

I roll my eyes. "Pulleeeeeze! I wouldn't have asked you to come an' live with me if I thought that. Look, Dad last night the doctor laid it out for me and now I need to do the same for you. And you need to make some decisions. Also, we need to get some legal papers signed. So here goes. You up for this?"

"Yes. But, if I fall asleep, let me sleep an hour an' then wake me up an' continue our conversation. Ok?"

"Deal." I take a deep breath and start. "You're dying. We both know that. Whether you like it or not, I'm your next of kin, and I have responsibilities. You need to make those responsibilities easier on me by signin' some forms. A lawyer will draw them up and explain them to you."

"Bring them in. I'll sign anythin' that'll make it easy on you, Noey."

"Ok. But, listen to her first ok?"

"Ok."

"Second. You do not need to prolong your life if you don't want to. If you're ready to go see Mom and Billy, then you can go to hospice. Do you know what that is?"

"Sorta. They help keep you comfortable while you die. Friend of mine used dem."

"That's the gist of it. I looked it up on the internet last night and the website explained that if a person has been given six months to live or less then hospice will help that person finish his life with dignity. Remember I'm paraphrasin' what I read and I can't do it justice. Ok?"

"Ok."

"So if you want to get off your medication and let nature (your heart) take its natural course, then hospice will help ya do that."

"They will?"

"Yep."

"That's not considered suicide?"

"No. It's your right to die with dignity."

"Wow. Do I hafta go to a nursing home?"

"My understanding is you can stay home and sleep and watch television and they will only give you medication for pain. No IVs, no drastic life saving measures, no trips to the ER. Your other option is to do what the doctors are telling you to do, quit drinkin' and smokin', eat healthy, walk a little each day, and try to live as long as you can. We can do every life saving measure in the book. And we can call hospice at any time to take over. This is your life and your choice, but if you think you're ready to die, then, let's do it right and call hospice."

"Could you arrange for me to talk to someone from hospice?"

"They're coming to see you sometime today. No matter what, Dad, you need to sign the lawyer's forms. If you had signed the forms already, one of which is a DNR, Do Not Resuscitate, the doctors would not have brought you back yesterday. If you're unconscious then I give them the DNR and they know what to do."

"Got it. Thanks for lookin' into all dat, Peanut."

He hasn't called me 'Peanut' in years. It makes me smile. "Dad, I gotta go to work for awhile. It's just a couple of miles away. Would you have the Hospice person call me when he or she gets here? Also, if the lawyer comes by today, would you get her to call me and I will come right over. Here are my phone numbers. Gotta run. Love you. Bye."

"Bye. I'll have 'em call ya."

Whew, that went well. I was worried he was going to fight me or something. He seems eager to make this easy on me. I've never experienced a death like this one. All this is making me think differently about death. It's kinda eerie plannin' for someone to die.

I get some work done before the phone rings. Caller ID says it's the hospital. I jump. What if he's died? "Hello?"

"Hi, Ms. Kilpatrick, this is Tina, the hospice representative. I'm on my way to see your father. Would you like to join us?"

"Sure, I'll be right there." How polite and inviting is that? Not at all like most medical professionals.

Dad's sitting up more, and his color is better. Tina has already filled Dad in on some of what I read on the internet. Dad's eager to sign up already. At first, I'm hurt that Dad isn't going to fight for some extra time, but after talkin' with the doctor last night, I realize Dad could die at any moment and he has the right to make the decisions that affect him. This isn't about me at all. It's all about him and what **he** wants. Tina explains everything to my dad, while I listen. Hospice makes a lot of sense. Dad's saying that if he had a chance to recover then he would fight, but he doesn't have any chance, just time. The question is, how does he want to spend the time? After an hour, Dad signs the papers. The nurses come in and take all the machines away, disconnect his IV, and discharge him to hospice. The hospice worker explains that she can find Dad a bed in a hospice facility or he can go home and a hospice worker will stop by each day. Dad looks at me and says, "I'd like ta go home wiff you, Noey, if dat's ok. If I need a hospice bed later on, then I can change my mind then, right?"

Tina says, "That's right."

I'm relieved, but I can feel the scowl returning. I notice it happens when I get intense. I want some time with Dad even if it's only an hour. "I'll pick you up around 4:30, Dad. Love ya. It was nice to meet you Tina." Tina smiles and shakes my hand. Dad's signing all the forms and I excuse myself to go back to work while the transfer from the hospital to hospice takes place. My throat feels like it's filled with Jello. I can't swallow without feeling tears in my eyes. My head is stuffed with cotton. Nothin' feels real.

Gerry's back at the office and I fill him in. His reaction surprises me. "I would feel exactly the way your dad feels if I were in his shoes."

"Really? I guess I'm a fighter. I'd fight for every minute I could get out of life."

"That's why this decision has to be up to each person. No one can make that decision for another. I signed papers stating my wishes years ago."

"Really? Wow! I've spent my entire life trying to avoid talking or thinking about death. Maybe I've had too much close contact with the subject to be objective."

Dad shuffles into my apartment. He tires easily and has to sit down every few minutes. I'm trying to let him make his own decisions. I promise myself I will not nag if he smokes or drinks. If television is his refuge, then that's going to be ok with me. I'm makin' a healthy dinner of salmon and salad. I think Dad believes I'm doing this for him, but this is how I usually eat. Perhaps I need to tell him this. "Uh, Dad, I'm making salmon and a salad for dinner because it's what I like to eat, but I'd like a list of things you'd like to eat too so I can alternate. His face lit up! "What's for dessert?"

"I don't know. I haven't thought about it."

"Can we go git ice cream after dinner, like we used to when you wuz little?"

"Uh, sure."

Dad cleans his plate like a little kid, and then gets up as if we're leaving right away. I follow his lead. We enter the grocery store, but Dad gets 15 feet inside the door and asks me to buy him double chocolate chip and goes back to sit in the car because he feels tired. Next time I need to get him one of them driving carts. I make a mental note to get a handicap tag, too.

In a week, Dad's gotten weaker without his medication, but he has no desire to go back on it. He hasn't smoked or drank either. We've had some good talks, reminisced, played games, walked 50 yards each night. Last night we tried walking further, and I had to go back for the car and pick him up where I left him.

Gerry's been great, too. He took Dad with him to the bowling alley and Dad kept score and drank a beer. Dad slept 13 hours after that outing.

I'm grateful for this time. Each day seems very precious. People should live each day as if they're dying. One by-product of knowing one is dying is boldness. I guess people who are dying decide life is too short to beat around the bush. Last night, Dad asked me when Gerry and I are getting married. I was shocked he had the nerve to ask that of me. "I don't know Dad, I got a lot on my plate right now with work, school, and, and...other things."

"You meant to say "You, Dad."

"Well, that's true, but I'm glad you're here. I like havin' this time with you."

Silence

"Are you an' Gerry going to git married?"

"He hasn't asked me, so I don't know."

"Time's too short ta live in the land of 'I dunno.' "

It's been two weeks and Dad can hardly get out of bed. He's having difficulty taking care of his personal hygiene. Today, he didn't get out of bed all day. When I arrive home, Dad says in a nonchalant way, "It's time fir me ta go ta that hospice place." He says this as if he's saying, "We need a quart of milk."

I call Tina and she arranges for Dad to be transported to the facility that night. We arrive to a welcome that seems more appropriate for a cruise ship. It's kinda weird, but I think these people have the right attitude. Dad settles in and smiles at me, "Thanks fir all you've done. This is it, kid."

I walk out of the hospice facility that night and cry my heart out for the first time since I brought Dad home to live with me. I call Lisa and ask for an appointment.

Noelle
Emergency Appointment

Lisa's with another client when I arrive. When her door opens, a very tall, blond, boyish looking man walks out. He looks at me and then quickly looks away. He looks familiar, but I can't place him. My turn!

"Lisa, do you need a quick break before we start?"

"Thanks, Noelle, I'm fine. How are things going for you and for your dad?"

"This has been a rough journey, but I've learned so much. Dad's making choices faster than I can process 'em. He knows what he wants and he's comfortable with his dying. I guess I just don't understand, and maybe I can't understand until I'm at that point in my life. When I think of arrivin' at death's door I get prickly and panicky. Death has always felt harsh, hurtful, rushed, and angry. With Dad though, it's a slowly meandering stream and he's just floatin' with it. I've had dreams of the Chase engineer who died in an instant meeting Dad who's dying in inches. They seem so different and yet the end result is the same."

"Say more about what you are learning."

"I'm learning we can't change the reality of death, just the how we live our lives until it occurs." Long pause. "Dad wants to be cremated and his ashes scattered on top of a mountain. I can't imagine doing this. Of course, I've agreed, but it seems barbaric."

"More barbaric than entombment?"

"That seems awful too."

"What seems not awful?"

I think for a long time. "Nothing, the whole scene seems barbaric. We have this body to 'get rid of'. That body gave me a life. It worked all those years and provided for me and then it's going to be burned up and scattered? How awful!" Tears are rolling down my face. "I don't want my father to be burned up and thrown to the wind."

"Your father?"

"Yes."

"You equate the body of your father with your father?"

"I never thought about it that way, but yes."

"Noelle, what do you believe in?"

"What do you mean?"

"Well, do you believe this life is all there is? Or do you believe there is more to a person than their body?"

"I've never been a religious person."

"A lot of people misunderstand that question. This isn't about religion. I'm asking you to say what you believe this life is about. Like, who are you? You clearly are a body, a mind, and you have emotions. Do you believe there is a transcendent part of you or do you believe there's nothing to us except the body we live in?"

"I want to believe we are physical and spiritual beings, but I have nothing to base that belief on."

"You say you want to believe. Do you believe every person has a spirit that's released at death or what?"

"When you say it that way, yes, I believe each of us has a soul that leaves the body after death. Where it goes I have no idea."

"What part of the person fathered you in this life? The body of your dad, the mind of your dad, your dad's emotions, or your dad's soul?"

"All of them."

"Ok."

"When your father dies, what do you believe will happen to the rest of him, his mind, his emotions, his soul?"

"I know the correct answer is he will go to heaven, but I'm not sure I believe in heaven, or hell for that matter."

"There's no correct answer here. Only what **you** believe."

"Then I believe he might just go back into the world to be recycled."

"You mean like fertilizer or reincarnation?"

I laugh at the image. "Both."

"So only the body dies and becomes fertilizer and the rest enters into a place where we are reconstituted and then we come back?"

"Yea, sort of."

"Then your father never dies."

"No. But, his body will."

"Right. But, in your belief, he will return as another person."

"Someday. But I won't know him."

"According to some traditions, you might."

"What do you mean, Lisa?"

"Have you ever met someone and just hit it off, finishing each other's statements, enjoying the same things? Or have you ever felt you've lived somewhere before? Things felt familiar, yet you've never been there before, in this lifetime?"

"Yes."

"Well, some people believe that when reincarnation happens, we carry a little bit of us into the next life. It accounts for the child prodigies and innate talents like being able to learn a language."

"I see what you mean. I believe his soul will live on, and I may encounter him again."

"Many people believe that."

"What do you believe, Lisa? I notice you wear a cross sometimes. Is it just jewelry? Or are you a Christian?"

"I'm a Christian, but I don't want you to believe what I believe. You need to come to these decisions by yourself."

"I've always been attracted to Jesus as a person. I believe in him, but I don't like the way some Christians reject others who don't agree with them. It puts me off. It's why I never go to church."

"I understand. But, Noelle, you were born on the same day the Christian Church honors Jesus' birth. Does it mean anything to you?"

"I don't know. I don't think so. It's just a day to give and receive presents."

"Do you know what your name means?"

"No."

"Noelle (slightly different spelling) means Christmas in French.

"It does?"

"Yep."

"Were your parents religious people?"

"They never went to church, that I remember."

"So why did they name you "Christmas"? They could have named you anything that would have been related to the Christmas holiday. Like they could have just used your middle name, Holly, or something else festive."

"I never asked." This is too much to take in. I feel the Jello again. "I better ask my father before he dies. Thanks. I didn't think I would be talking about this kind of stuff in here. I need some time to sort all this out."

Angie

When I leave Lisa's, I drive straight to hospice. Dad's awake, but he's getting weaker. "Hi Dad, can we talk?"

"Sure, Noey. What's up?"

"Why did you name me Noelle?"

"Because you were born on Christmas eve."

"Besides that."

Dad takes a deep breath and he looks like he's dreading telling me this story. "Noelle, many years ago, I wuz a Roman Catholic, and your mom wuz Baptist. We loved each other very much, but both of our churches were demanding us to make decision about how we were going to live our lives together. Her family said I had to give up my Catholic beliefs because Catholics were goin' to hell. My church wuz 'sisting your mom sign a paper sayin' she'd allow me to raise you an' your brother Catholic. We both loved our churches, but we loved God more. We finally decided we needed to break with both our churches an' focus on what both religions had in common. We felt the rest wuz just human trappings, so we developed our own way of worshippin'. We met with a few other people each Sunday night an' read the Bible an' prayed. I guess you could say we had our own little church community an' we loved it. Whenever any of us needed help, all of us were dere."

"I don't remember any of this."

"This wuz before you were born. When your mom found out your due date wuz around Christmas, she wuz thrilled. She kept sayin' this wuz God's plan, him blessin' us with a child wuz confirmation we were right in how we were worshipin'. She wuz a little hysterical about religious stuff, so I let her go when she got wound up." Dad's tired and he's slurring some of his words. "We worked hard at findin' you a proper name an' decided if you were born on Dec. 24th or 25th then we wud honor your birthday by callin' you by the French word for Christmas, Noel. That's pretty much it."

"Why's my name spelled differently?"

Dad shifts in his bed. "That wuz my idea. I wanted you ta be called "Christmas", but I needed to think bigger than only one day so I added "le" to your name. The "le" stands for 'lives eternal'."

"My name means Christmas lives eternal?"

Dad's tired and he leans his head back and smiles.

"Dad, do you believe in God now? Mom died, Billy died. That had to be hard on your faith."

"It wuz, at first. And I turned my back on God. Never prayed or nothin'. But, later, I decided, if I believed in God, then I had to trust God. I heard that somewhere on the radio. So I trusted everythin' would work out for gud. It didn't in a lot of ways, and I lost my way again for awhile. But now, I love God more than ever, an' I'm looking forward to seeing your mother and brother in a few days."

"You believe still, after such a hard disappointing life?"

"Yes, Noelle. I BELIEVE!!!" That last sentence took every bit of strength out of him.

Dad falls asleep. I don't know what to think or feel. I'm numb. I'm inspired. I'm baffled. Who **is** this God who takes away mothers from their children and allows children to grow up with so much death and violence around them? I stroke Dad's hair and kiss his forehead and leave his room. A sign catches my eye: "Chapel". I push the door slowly so as not to disturb anyone in there. The room's empty and I'm glad. I walk to the cross with Jesus hanging there. It's gross, seeing someone hanging and bleeding. Why do people worship that image. Emotions are boiling inside of me as I look at it. I'm lit up inside with anger. "Why the hell did you take away the very people who could have made me healthy and happy? I've wasted most of my life hiding from life and why? You decided, yes, YOU decided my mother and brother and Gran and nanny and everyone I loved were better off with **you** than with **me**. You are a God Damn Greedy, Stingy, Son of a Bitch, and I hate you. I don't know why anyone would love you. You took everything away from me and gave me nothing in return except the air I breathe. How can Dad have faith? HOW CAN DAD HAVE FAITH **IN YOU?** Answer me, damn it. How can Dad have faith?

I collapse to my knees near the altar. My tears are pouring out of me and on the floor and I'm staining my dress with tears. My mascara is running down my face, and I don't care. I can't hold this anger, fear, resentment, and bitterness in any longer. After many minutes I decide there is not going to be an answer because there is no God who cares. I'm done with this selfish God and I sit up and look at the crucifix. There's Jesus still hanging on the cross with blood dripping out of his hands and feet and side. I boil again... "You are such a mean God that you let your own son die. How could you do such a thing? You let everyone I loved, AND NEEDED, die and you even let your son die. I bet he hates you too. I know I'm going to hell for yellin' like this, but YOU sent me there!"

Someone stirs behind me and I gasp. Someone, other than God, heard my words. I'm mortified. I don't turn around, but the hand is on my shoulder. "It's ok, sweetie." The voice says. "It's ok to be angry with God." I turn around and see the sweetest little face I ever saw. She is probably 80 years old and no more than five feet. She's smiling! She takes a tissue out of her pocket and dries my tears and leads me to a pew.

"I'm sorry you had to hear that, ma'am. My father's dyin', and I guess I lost it."

"Never apologize for talkin' to God, honey."

"I wasn't **talking** to God. I was **screeching** at God with all my hatred. Didn't you hear me?"

"I heard your pain and anguish. I heard your questions and frustrations."

"No, I called God an SOB."

"I supposed she's been called worse."

"You don't think I've sinned against God?"

"Some might think that, but I have a different take on it."

"Really? What's your take?" I'm still wiping and blowing.

"We're all children of the one who created and is still creating. We forget that God is a lot like a parent and as parents we expect our children will become enraged at us at times and call us names and think we're unfair, but we still love them. God loves us no matter what. Our job is to love God no matter what."

"Ma'am are you a Christian?"

"I guess you could say that, but I think all religions have something to offer this world and us. And my name is Angie. What's yours?"

"Noelle."

Angie nods like she understands what my name means. "

"Angie, why would God spend so much energy to purposefully hurt his children?"

"I don't think God purposefully hurts us. I also don't know why we have to suffer here on earth. It's one of those questions philosophers have asked for thousands of years. But, I think God must've hurt when he allowed Jesus to die. He didn't interfere or rescue him from the cross even when Jesus called out from the cross, 'My God, my God, why have you forsaken me?" Isn't that what you were asking a few minutes ago?"

"Yea… but, not so eloquently."

Angie laughs. "True. In my times of anguish I've been less than eloquent with God, too."

"But Angie, Why wouldn't God want us to live happy lives? Why didn't he take Jesus down when Jesus called out to him? Why doesn't he answer our pleas for his intervention?"

"I don't know child. I only know that to know God is to know love. God loves so much better than we do, even let his son die for our sins, which you can read in the Bible. But, remember, his son didn't stay dead."

"Are you saying God knows how hurt and injured I have been?"

"I'm sure of it."

"Then why didn't he interfere and help me?"

"Maybe for the same reason he didn't interfere when his son was dying."

"You mean he didn't care?"

"No. He sees the bigger picture. We don't see what God sees. I bet God has been active in your life from your birth, but because of all the horrible things that happened to you, you haven't seen the interaction with God. You only saw the painful things. Look back, when was God there?"

I'm stumped and I feel like I'm back in Lisa's office when she asks me hard questions that make me think. "Maybe, um, probably, well, recently he might have been with me when I needed help and found a counselor who hung in there with me despite my being rude to her."

"Ok."

"I have a great job and my boss is paying for my education and giving me flex time, so can go to college."

"Nice."

"I saw a really horrible accident when I was 18 and I could have been injured by the explosion, but I wasn't. When my mother died, my dad got us a nanny who was wonderful. But, then she died too.

"I decided to reconnect with my father just at a time when he's dying. If I had waited another week or two to call him, I would have missed the opportunity. But, something kept telling me to call him."

"Really? Have you had this something reminding you of things often?"

"Yes, but I thought I was intuitive or somethin'. Now that you mention it, the day of the horrible accident, I kept getting an impression I needed to go to the store, but I kept ignoring it and I finally gave in and left. If I had gone 10 seconds later I might not be here at all. But, that's not God talking to me. Right?"

"Honey, I have no idea. But, you're trying to fit God into a human body. God is so immense and has so many ways to communicate with us that we need to stop worrying where the reminders come from and just trust them."

"Why didn't you admonish me when you heard me yelling foul things at God?"

"It's not my job to admonish you or to judge you. You do more than enough to yourself. I'm just here to let you know you're loved, God is love, and we all should love the way God does and forget about judging others or trying to make other people see the world the way we do."

"So I need ta love God, talk and listen to God, and forgive?"

"That pretty much sums it up."

"I don't think I can do that. I'm too angry."

"Just keep the lines of communication open."

"Angie are you a preacher or a nun or something? Do you work here? Helping others when they come in to scream and curse at God?"

"Lord no. I'm just a visitor. A friend of mine is dying."

"Oh! I'm sorry."

"She heard your pain and sent me here."

"Oh, my, she heard me yelling? Tell her I am sorry."

"She's in a coma."

"So how did she communicate with you?"

"There are other ways to communicate than talking."

"I don't understand."

"I know. It's difficult to explain, but someday you'll understand."

"Thanks Angie.. for...for being here with me. I guess I'll see you around. I'll be here often because my dad's dying and he's a patient here."

Angie nodded.

"I better be going. Thanks again."

Angie nods again and hugs me. For the first time in my life, I feel a sense of peace. Exhaustion doesn't begin to describe how I feel. I'm numb, I'm embarrassed. I'm scared God will hate me and ...I can't begin to think of the awful things God could do to me for my outburst. I can't believe I did that. And to think someone heard me. Cripes! I haven't lost it like that in years. I've prided myself on holding stuff in, but I have to admit I feel better letting God know how I felt, but I hope Angie's right about God lovin' and forgivin' us.

I enter my apartment still in a fog about what just happened. "God forgive me. I didn't mean to harm our relationship. I just don't know what I believe in because I never was taken to church after Mom died. Dad just stopped going, but he still loves you and...and I, I,...I don't know. I'm too tired. I need sleep. I hope that's ok."

Angie/Angela

I never saw Angie again, despite camping out at the hospice center every day for the last four days. I'm disappointed because I wanted to thank her again. Dad's vital signs are getting weaker. He's melting away in front of me. My watch says it's 8 p.m. and Dad's asleep. It's been another long day and I want to go home, but I'm afraid if I do I won't be here when he dies. Betty, the night nurse, gently knocks and enters to check on Dad.

"Hi Noelle, you still here?"

"I'm afraid if I go home, he'll die, and I won't be here with him."

"We'll call you when his heart rate begins to drop. Honey, go home and get some rest."

"Ok." I start for the door and get an idea. "Hey, Betty. You know everyone around here right?"

"Pretty much."

"Well, I met Angie in the chapel. She's visiting a friend of hers who's in a coma. She really helped me when I needed a shoulder to cry on. I want to thank her again. Do you have her number, or do you know a time when she usually comes to visit?"

"So you met Angie! Well, she comes and goes. She seems to appear when someone is dying or is in need. Then we don't hear from her for awhile."

"She's a frequent visitor here?"

"Pretty much. We call her one of our volunteers."

"If you see her, will you tell her I'm looking for her to thank her?"

"Sure, I'll pass the word around to others, too. But, she just seems to arrive and leave, ministering where she can. She's quite a dear. We love having her here."

"She helped me a lot."

"Noelle, **GO HOME!** If there's any change in your dad's condition, we'll call.

"Ok, and if you see Angie, tell her thanks again from Noelle."

"Will do."

Escort Service

It's 8:00 a.m! Oh, crap! I slept 10 hours and I'm now late for work. Thank heavens I know the boss real well. Smile. I call Gerry at the office and leave a message that I'm on my way, but I have to stop by and see my dad first.

The hospice is buzzing with breakfast trays and carts. I dodge several people who are trying to get patients where they need to be. I don't see Dad. His door is closed so I knock. No one answers. I enter. Dad's still in bed and he looks like he's sleeping, but there's something different. It's his breathing. It's shallow and a bit labored. Jillian, one of the nurses, opens his door to peek inside.

"I don't think he's doing well today, Jillian."

"I just left messages at your home and office. I thought he was breathing irregularly. I think we're nearing the end. Why don't you sit with him and talk to him?" She closes the door and it's quiet, like a tomb, I shudder. The staff respect our time with our loved ones.

"Hi Dad. It's Noelle. How are you feeling?" No answer. "I don't know if you can hear me or not, how about raising you finger if you can hear me." No movement. I guess this is what a coma looks like. "After I was here last night and I left (remember we talked about my name?). I went into the chapel and met a lovely lady who was visiting a friend of hers. She and I had a chat about God."

Dad stirs and says "Angela". "Well, close. Her name is Angie. Have you met her?" No answer. Dad stirs again. He says, "Thanks."

I'm not sure what he means so I say, "You're welcome."

Dad moves his arms around and says "Bev." And then he mumbles something I don't get at all. Then he says "Billy." I guess he is dreaming about them. Jillian pokes her head in again.

"Jillian, Dad's not responding to me, but he said, "Angela". I guess he met the lady who visits her friend here. Jillian looks a bit confused. Then he said "Bev". That's my mother's name and then he said, "Billy" that's my brother's name."

Jillian inquires, "Can you get a hold of them and see if they would be able to come here and be with him?"

"Oh, Jillian, I'm sorry, they are both dead."

Jillian walks in and closes the door. "Did he say anything else?"

"No he just mumbled something that sounded like he was having a conversation with them."

"Noelle, that probably means we're close to the end. They may have come to escort him home."

"What? Escort him? What does that mean?"

"Well, loved ones often show up near the end to help the dying person cross over."

"You mean my mother and brother are here in the room?" I say as I look around. "This is all new to me."

"That often happens. Why don't you stay with him, and I'll get a chaplain to drop by." She left the room quietly and respectfully.

Within minutes a tall, thin, red-headed woman opens the door. "Hi, may I come in?"

"Sure. I'm Noelle and this is my dad."

"I'm Chris and I know your dad well. We've had several conversations. He's an interesting person. I'm the chaplain. Jillian thinks we should have a chat."

"She said something about my mother and brother being here to escort my father. This is all new to me. It sounds a bit like voodoo."

Chris smiles and explains that when a person is dying they are often living between two worlds, this one and the next. It's not unusual for them to start talking to those who have already died. It's not hallucinating although some medical personnel believe it is. She says she's been working in hospice for 20 years and she's personally seen some of the escort services. She also says other family members have seen them too. It usually happens in the final stages and the person usually dies within 72 hours. She asks if I would like to talk to someone who has observed this phenomenon. I immediately say "Yes." Chris excuses herself and comes back with a volunteer. I recognize her. Her name is Dee. We've spoken often.

Dee begins, "I will tell you my story of when my brother, Clark, died, but you must promise me you will keep an open mind." I promise and she sits down to tell her story. "My brother was three years older than me and he had cancer and was in the final stages of life. My mother had died suddenly about two years before my brother. About three days before he died, he was beginning to be non-responsive. I wasn't a volunteer then so I didn't know what to expect, just like you. I have two other brothers and between the three of us, one was always with Clark. This one day it was my turn, and I came into the room and saw my mother standing in the corner. At first, it seemed normal. Of course Mom would be there at a time like this, but after a few seconds, I realized 'Hey wait a minute she's dead.' I kept looking at her, then looking away, and then looking at her again. She looked exactly the same as she had when I was younger. She always wore a house dress with a full length apron over it. Both pieces of clothing were always flowered and never matched. We used to laugh about buying her solid colored aprons so she wouldn't clash. Well, there she was in a house dress and an apron and both were flowered and neither matched. She was moving slightly too and smiling. But, not at me, at my brother in the bed. She looked like she was talking to him, but there was no sound, like someone had pushed the mute button. I was sorta like a hologram. My brother was mumbling and I heard him say, "Ma." That's what we called her. I backed out of the room, went to the bathroom, peed, washed my face with cold water and returned to my brother's room. She was still there! I tried to talk to my brother, but he was unresponsive and then she was gone. I didn't see her leave.

"I was in a graduate program in social work at the time, and I had a class that night. I tried to get my insides to stop shaking so I could drive to school. I thought I was going crazy from the stress. I called one of my other brothers on my cell phone as I drove to school. I must have sounded a little hysterical because as I was telling him the story, he kept telling me to calm down and slow down. Finally, I got the story out and he nonchalantly said, "Yes, Dee, I saw her too." Well, you could have knocked me over with a breeze. I was dumbfounded. I thought we were both going crazy. I got to school and I was still shaking and one of the school's secretaries looked at me, saw my tear stained face, and said, 'Oh Dee, did your brother pass away?' I responded, 'No, I just had a weird experience though.' She asked if I would like to share it. I was afraid to share what I saw but I needed to tell someone. I don't know why. I just knew I had to share it. So I told her the story. She listened quietly and nodded and then said, 'That means your brother is about to cross over. It will probably happen in the next couple of days. My father came for my mother.' My brother died 48 hours later, just like she said."

I'm trying to take all this in, but I can't. For someone who has been inundated with death, I don't seem to know much about it. Dee is still waiting for a response. "I don't know what to say. I'm speechless."

Chris has been listening to Dee's story, too. "Be open to your experience and just trust."

"That's interesting. That's what Angie told me yesterday. Dee and Chris look at each other. Dee asks, "You met Angela yesterday?"

"Yes, I was sorta yelling at God in the chapel and she found me."

"Interesting."

"Why is it interesting? She was here visiting a friend of hers who's dying and is in a coma. Someone says she a volunteer and is here frequently."

"True." Both say at the same time.

"What?"

Chris starts, "Angela is an angel. She shows up sometimes when people are almost ready to cross over. She's our little angel of death. People report seeing her three or four times a year. You actually talked with her?"

"It must be a different person. Her name was Angie. She was a real person. We talked for 10 or 15 minutes. She gave me a bunch of tissues to wipe my nose. She sat in the pew with me. We talked about God and religion and how I was being too hard on myself. You see, I had just called God an SOB. I was overwhelmed with feelings, and I lost it and took my stuff out on God."

Chris looks at Dee. "Wow, that's the most she has ever materialized. Most of the time she appears filmy and sometimes she talks to the person in the bed, but she has never handed someone a tissue."

"That's because we are talking about two different people, um entities. This was a real person named Angie. She was about 80 years old..."

Dee chimes in, "4' 10 inches, beautiful face, curly hair?"

"Yes" I say softly. "What's happening to me?" Dee puts her arm around me and we are all silent, lost in our own individual thoughts.

Chris speaks first. "This is an important time for you. Somehow you're being communicated with by the spiritual realm. Sit back and enjoy the ride. You will never be the same again." I just shake my head hoping I'll wake up and find out I'm dreaming.

Before I leave I tell Dad I love him, and he opens his eyes and smiles and whispers. "Almost done, Noey. They're here to take me home." And he closes his eyes and slips back away again.

Connecting With Something Holy

I can't concentrate on work. I'm making too many errors. I just want to go back to the hospice center. I feel something there I don't feel any where else. It's like finding a part of me that's been under-nourished for years and is now being fed. I still don't believe Angela is an angel. How hokey is that? For crying out loud. Either these people are weirdos or all of this is true. I can't decide which. One minute I'm saying "Really?" like I'm the most naïve person on the face of the earth and then next minute I'm doubting everything. I wish I could talk to Lisa or Gerry. They seem to have their feet on the ground. I call Gerry and his cell is off. I call Lisa and get her answering machine. Nobody answers their phones anymore. Crud. I leave messages for both. Let's see who calls first. I start filing and after two hours the phone rings its "outside" ring. "Finance Associates, this is Noelle."

"Hi Noelle, this is Lisa. What can I do for you?"

"I think I need an appointment, any time, I'm desperate."

"Is this an emergency?"

"Dad's hanging on by a thread, but there's some weird shit going on at the hospice. I need to talk."

"Why don't you come by around five o'clock. I have a half hour."

"I'll be there."

My lunch break is a trip to the hospice center. Dad's pretty much the same. I grab some chips and a soda out of the vending machines and settle in for some "lunch" with Dad. He's quiet and his breathing is very shallow. Suddenly he opens his eyes and calls my name.

"Hi, Dad. How are you feeling?" What a stupid question! He's dying. How's he supposed to feel?"

"Ok. Sip of root beer?"

"Sure, Dad. I pour some into the cup and hold the straw for him. He closes his eyes and remarks how good it tastes.

"I was just about ready to get some ice cream. Want some?"

"Sounds great. Chocolate?"

"I'll find out."

I leave the room to look for someone who can find me some ice cream. The nurse at the station looks up and smiles as I approach. Everyone here smiles a lot. This place is a paradox. All the patients are dying and all the people are happy and smiling. "Can I get some chocolate ice cream for my father?"

"He's awake? And he wants ice cream!" I nod. "Sure I'll get some for you. Would you like one for you too?"

"Sure!" I'm smiling too. It's catching.

I return with the ice cream and Dad's sitting up! He reaches for the ice cream with shaking hands manages to hold the cup and spoon some into his mouth. I want to ask him about Mom and Billy, but I don't want to spook him. We're both quiet and he's eating the ice cream, letting it roll down his throat. "Ummmm, **so** good. Noey, this is quite an experience, dyin' I mean, not eatin' ice cream. I've eaten ice cream b'fore, but I never died b'fore. Not dat I know of anyway."

"Yea."

"Your mom and Billy were here. Dey're waiting for me. When it's your turn, I'm comin' back for you. Noey, don't be scared. Nothin' to be afraid of."

"How do you know?"

"Almost been there. Angela's helpin' me." He's weak again and hands me the half eaten ice cream and lays back down with a deep sigh.

"Who?"

"Angela, 'Member, met her in chapel. She said her name was 'Angie'." Dad leans back against his pillow, closes his eyes and he falls asleep.

I kiss him and leave. I take the ice cream with me as if it's a souvenir of our time together.

Lisa's waiting for me when I arrive. I'm a couple minutes late. Not like me. Must be the stress.

"Hi, Lisa. I'm glad you could see me. My life is in turmoil."

"An impending death of someone you love is difficult."

Gosh Lisa just did a therapy trick with me. She just gave me back what I gave her. She must be tired, too. Maybe she needs a vacation.

"It's not the death of my father. It's what's happening around the death of my father." I tell her the whole story. It takes a long time to tell the story. She listens patiently and I feel pressured 'cause I'm running out of time. I've been talking for 20 minutes and I was late to boot. I need to stop and get Lisa's reaction. I look to her to say something. I never thought I would hear from her what she says next.

"So you met Angela?"

"What?"

"She's a legend there. Several people have seen her. There's a sighting at least every three months or so. I've had a couple other clients who reported her visitations. I've never had the privilege."

"You mean, you believe this? They're not pulling my leg. I'm not going crazy?"

"Not that I can tell. You're being asked to consider a different way of viewing the world. Instead of living in your head, you're now living through your heart and in your spirit and that brings some choices. Some people go through these kinds of experiences and ignore them. Others learn from them and begin to look at the possibilities. Which are you going to do?"

"I want to believe my mom and brother are here ready to escort my dad to heaven or wherever. I just need to see it to believe."

"What about Angie. You saw her and you still don't believe."

"I'm not saying I don't believe. I'm saying I need to eliminate all the other possibilities, like for example, there might be an angel who is Angela and a person named Angie. But people there aren't open to the fact I didn't meet an angel, but a real person."

"This is where faith comes in. You need to know what you believe. Do you believe you're experiencing a wonderfully enlightening event or do you believe that everyone is trying to fool you?"

"I don't know. I'm scared that if I say I believe and it isn't real, then I will be a fool."

"And if you say you don't believe and it is real, then what?"

"I've lost an opportunity to connect with something holy."

"Wow, that was profound. Where did that come from?"

"I don't know the words just popped out."

"They did? Well, then remember those words, Noelle. I have a feeling that they may play a part in your decision about which way to go."

"Ok. I usually feel energized and focused when I leave here, but today I feel just as confused as when I walked in."

"That's because you're trying to figure this all out using your head. Try using your intuition, your gut, your heart instead. The answer will come to you if you just remain open."

"Thanks, Lisa." I'm collecting my things and stop. "You know Lisa, you look tired. You need a vacation."

"Thanks Noelle. I'll do that."

Lisa
Reflection on Noelle

Noelle is out of my hands. She is confused and reticent about acknowledging her experiences as real. I'm holding her gently in prayer, but she has to make the decision about whether to believe in what she is encountering or not. She's right though. I do need a vacation. Come to think of it, that's the first time she stopped focusing on herself in here and actually noticed me.

To Believe or Not Believe
That is the question

I turned my phone off while at Lisa's and when I turn it back on, there are six messages. I don't like the sound of this. Message one and four are from Gerry. He wants to meet me at the hospice center at six and then take me to dinner. I text message him back and say 'yes'. The other four are from the hospice center. I call them. I reach a worker named Gigi. She's telling me my father has drifted back into a coma and his heart rate is irregular. I'm on my way. The first person I see tells me the same thing and when I arrive at

Dad's room, the nurse practitioner is there. He says, "This is the end. His heart can't keep this irregular beat up any longer. I don't know if he will leave in a minute or an hour or a day, that's up to him." I thank him and he asks if there's anyone he can call for me. I say 'no thank you.'

Dad looks pale blue. His heart is definitely not keeping the blood flowing. I sit beside his bed, hold his cold hand, and cry. Chris arrives and stands beside me with her hand on my shoulder. "Chris, he ate ice cream just a few hours ago and we talked. What happened?"

"Some patients rally for their loved ones just before they die. Did the ice cream have a special meaning for the two of you?"

"Yes, we liked to treat ourselves. As a kid, he and I would share a bowl at night and talk. We did it recently, too, when he was livin' with me before he came here."

"That's lovely. What a great memory to hold onto!"

Chris begins to pray quietly for my father to have no pain and to pass quietly into the next world. She prays for me and for everyone my dad touched. The silence is so loud! Gerry quietly enters and kisses me on the cheek. I throw my arms around him and tell him Dad's dying and we can't have dinner tonight. I don't know why I'm worried about dinner and hurting Gerry's feelings. The things we think about while under stress! Dad takes a breath and stops. We all turn around and look at him. He takes another breath and stops. I don't know why, but I'm holding my breath, too. A minute goes by, and then he takes one more breath and stops and doesn't breathe again. The nurse listens to his heart and pronounces "He's "gone". I collapse into Gerry's arms and cry. I'm messing up his shirt. Why do I care about that? Dad's face looks "empty". He's not in there anymore. I kiss his cheek and say "Godspeed." As I turn around, I see everyone in the room is crying. These people do this all the time and still find the empathy to cry with those left behind! But, they're not sad, they're smiling through their tears. Chris pats me on the arm. "This has been quite a journey for you, Noelle. You've had an opportunity many don't have when a loved one dies…you've really had the opportunity to connect with the holy." There are the words I just spoke in Lisa's office! Enveloped in Gerry's arms, I've made my decision. I believe.

Gerry and Noelle

Gerry and I get married two weeks later and take a honeymoon to Colorado. We drive up Pike's Peak, and when no one is looking we toss Dad's ashes into the wind. It doesn't feel as disgusting as I thought it would. It actually feels liberating.

I don't see Lisa often, because I'm really too busy to see her. Gerry and I joined a small, intimate, nondenominational church. Gerry hired another office worker so I can concentrate on my education. I'll finish in less than a year. I've been accepted already at the College of Notre Dame in Baltimore. My major is education for now but I might switch later, most students change their minds a couple of times. I chose Notre Dame because they require philosophy and religion classes allowing me the opportunity to read about God and the world.

Dad's death seems to have broken the grip death had on me. Lisa's skillful handling of me seems to have broken the grip of mistrust I had for others. Gerry's love broke the grip of feeling unlovable. Angie helped break the gripe of anger in my heart. It takes a village to raise a person to their potential. I feel vibrant.

Chapter Twelve
Closure and Termination

The goal (of treatment) is for the sexual abuse to become an item in their (the survivors') personal museum of history. Something that happened but that no longer controls their lives
                                          (Caloff, 1993).

Update on Caz

Caz was gone for three months and I saw him four times. He never did ask for a referral, and when he came home, his grandmother moved with him. She's living in a retirement facility only six miles from his home.

During the first of his monthly sessions, I found out about the panic attack during his drive to Chambers. He was proud that he managed it. He also said he was very welcomed by his grandmother and felt loved and supported by her. He was so afraid of "pissing her off" or "making her worry" that he got up every morning at 8 when she did. She went to bed at 10, and he did too. There's something to be said for people with dependency traits. They don't like having people angry with them, so they do whatever it takes to make others like them. Caz was a bit of an exception because he also had passive aggressive traits that wreaked havoc with his relationships, especially with his father and brother. With his grandmother, Caz was all dependency. He wanted very much for her to continue loving him. She provided an appropriate surrogate mothering presence.

Caz said he's never worked so hard as he did at his grandmothers'. The fact she never offered to pay him bothered him somewhat until he realized she was giving him a roof and food plus she indulged him whenever she could. She gave him his grandfather's trains. She bought him clothes. She took him out to eat. She even took him on a vacation to the Grand Canyon and paid for all of it. Interestingly, as the moving days approached, and most of the work was done, her neighbors began to ask if Caz was available to do some work around their houses and Caz was paid well for these tasks. He opened a checking account and had over $2000 in it when he moved back home. Caz stated he liked being self-employed. He liked the flexibility and the ability to turn down jobs if he was emotionally overwhelmed.

When Caz moved back home the atmosphere was very different. Stewart was on his third girlfriend and had no plans to marry. Rom was dating a woman and was thinking of marriage. Caz arrived home with a financial nest egg, and an idea of what he wanted to do with his life.

Caz called me when he had moved back home and asked if he could return to counseling once a month. Caz calls the once-a-month sessions his 'check-ups'.

I agreed. He looked leaner, stronger, and more focused. His first topic of discussion was about his career goals. His idea was to become a handyman for the elderly, but to take on this role he needed his father's help. He felt he could only handle working part time and that meant he could not live on his own. His father would have to continue supporting him by letting him live at home. In exchange for the room and board, Caz agreed to do all the cleaning, shopping, and cooking. Evidently Stewart was pleasantly surprised at Caz' plan. No longer did Caz want a handout. Caz wanted to barter. His father accepted. Rom was buying his own house so Stewart was glad for Caz' company.

Bally
Debate Over Medication

Since the trip to Mom's and the confrontation we did with her I've heard nothing from my family. To be honest I haven't called because I needed a break from this mess. I've had a difficult time concentrating at work, and I think it shows. I also don't have the same fire in my gut about my job. I don't want to be a business woman anymore. I'm confused. Nothing looks or feels the same. The grass doesn't look real, the trees look like cardboard. Even my food tastes blah. Am I depressed? I thought if I had a couple of weeks off from all the family issues, I would get some perspective. Instead, I feel like I have descended into a pit. Lisa has referred me to a psychiatrist, but I don't think I'll take the meds even if the shrink prescribes them. I need to experience these feelings of hopelessness and helplessness. I feel comfortable wallowing. Sleep takes care of a lot of the ill feelings temporarily, but at least I'm not drinking. I keep thinking about Seattle and the peace and quiet out there. I considered picking up my painting hobby again. I loved to paint. Oils, real painting not that pastel watercolor stuff.

Today is bright and sunny and so is Dr. Jamison. Nice enough, but I don't want to be helped out of the abyss. I feel more real down here. When I was a teen, I used to cut my thighs to feel real. Now, I don't need to cut, I can feel the emotional pain that tells me I'm real.

When I was an angry, bossy, know-it-all bitch, I felt phony and walked around waiting for someone to challenge me. Then I could razzle dazzle 'um with my wit and knowledge, and he wouldn't know what hit him. I was the best at the corporate game, but I was a plastic person filled with piss and vinegar. Now, I may be depressed, but I feel like this is ME, and if anyone doesn't like me this way, too bad. My boss hasn't said a word and neither have my co-workers. Do they not notice or do they notice and like the new Bally better? Do they notice and don't care? See, that makes me feel like cutting or drinking. There is one other possibility. Maybe I **feel** different, but I'm **not** all that different. That's a scary thought. All this therapy and painful discoveries and I'm not coming across as different? I don't really care. I just need to be left alone for now. Dr. Jamison prescribes an antidepressant. She says I'm depressed, but it involves the situation I'm in and is not sure medication will help me. However, she prescribes it anyway because I'm an alcoholic and, she says, some alcoholics are depressed and drink to self-medicate. She would rather I take the medication than use alcohol to dull the pain. I take the script, but don't get it filled today. I might in the future if this funk doesn't lift soon. I want to feel the pain for now, but I don't want to stay here for the rest of my life. The prescription can sit in my purse 'til I'm ready.

Bally's Dilemma

Another week goes by and still no calls. If I call Atlee, Little, or Carly, I'm going to stir things up again. Do I want to do this? Or do I still need a break? A shiver goes down my spine. What was that about? Maybe Lisa will know. I have an appointment.

Her door is locked. Did I get the wrong day or time? I pull out my calendar, and check. Nope! I have the date and time written down for now. I try the door again. Cell phones are a technological wonder! I call her number and get the answering machine and leave a message. Returning to my car, I acknowledge that I've changed! Several weeks ago, I would have used this mix up to vent my pent up anger on Lisa. Now, I'm concerned something may have happened to her. I decide to give her 15 minutes, that's what we gave our professors when they were late for class. After 15 minutes of 'no show' we could leave. I close my eyes and then there's a knock on my window. It's Lisa. "I'm sorry, I was at court for another client. Come in."

I don't feel anger or resentment or dismissed or anything. I'm depressed. I don't feel anything! Now I know why I like it down here in depressionville. I don't care as much.

"You know, Lisa, if this had happened weeks ago, I would have been furious. I would have felt you didn't care enough about me to be on time. I would have used this as an excuse to quit therapy. But, today, all I felt was worry that something had happened. Is that depression? Or is that healthy?"

"What do you think it is?"

Crap, I hate when she does that. "If felt....um.... weird but normal."

"Did you say to yourself, 'I don't care if she comes or not.'?"

"No, I cared, but I felt mellow, like either you will show or you won't. I did get a little scared that maybe something had happened to you, but I put it out of my mind."

"That's really a shift for you."

"Yes. I guess it is."

"Did you see Dr. Jamison?"

"Yep and I got the prescription for Lexapro in my purse."

"Will you fill it?"

"Not sure. This mellow feeling is comfortable, for now, but I don't want to feel this way the rest of my life, but for now it's a pleasant change from anger, irritableness, and spitefulness. I do want to ask you a question though."

"Ok."

"I haven't heard from Atlee, Little, or Carly for the last three weeks, going on four really. I'm enjoying the peace and quiet... gives me time to think. But now, I'm getting concerned. I want to call them, but I don't want to stir things up if they don't need stirring."

"That's quite a dilemma."

"Yep. What do you suggest?"

"If you were to call one person only, who would it be?"

"Atlee."

"Why?"

"He calms me down and doesn't over react."

"What keeps you from calling him?"

"I don't know. I just don't want to be the one to light a fire under everyone to confront Dad. I'm tired of feeling like a firecracker all the time. I needed the rest, but now I'm getting concerned."

"And why are you thinking about it now?"

"It's almost been a month. Mom was supposed to confront Dad and then call us. She hasn't. I think she may have chickened out."

"So you feel if you call your mom, then you will be bringing up stuff that maybe the rest of the family has decided to forget?"

"Yea. I just want this over and it's dragging on."

"This is your call, Bally. When you feel ready, you'll call."

"I guess I'm getting ready because I'm worrying about what's happened. I can't get this out of my mind."

"And you want to know, but you don't want to stir things up if they are supposed to lay dormant for now."

"Yes. Any suggestions?"

"If I said, 'Trust yourself' what would you do?"

"Great." The sarcasm came out in a spurt. Lisa smiles.

Silence.

"I need to call Atlee." Without asking permission, I whip out my cell and dial Atlee. It rings a number of times and just as I'm about to hang up, he answers.

"Hi Atlee, Bally here."

"Hey, Bally, how are you."

"I'm good, but hey, I'm wondering if you've talked to Mom since our visit almost a month ago."

"No, I tried calling her several times but no answer. At first I thought she was ignoring me, then I thought she was on the trip to see Dad, but now I'm getting concerned, too I called her landlord and he checked on the condo. He said everything was neat and tidy. No Mom, though."

"Mom is always at home. Are you getting an uneasy feeling?"

"I have been in the last week."

"Me too. Have you called Carly?"

"No. What do you want to do?"

"I'm going to call Carly and see if she's heard from Mom. I have a bad feeling about this, Atlee. But, right now I'm seeing my shrink (I mouth 'I'm sorry" to Lisa for the slur, but she just waves it off and smiles). I'll call Carly when I'm through here and call you back."

"Gotcha, see ya."

Lisa looks puzzled.

"I'm confused too. Mom said she wanted to confront Dad herself and then would get back to us. She never called me or Atlee. I'll call Carly later and then if something doesn't feel right, we'll go into overdrive again. I have a bad feeling about this? Do you believe in premonitions?"

Lisa naturally turns the question to me. "Question is, do you?"

"I never did before, but hey, I'm discovering all kinds of things about myself."

The discussion turns to my discoveries, my feelings, the changes I've implemented, etc.

Walking out of Lisa's office, I get the shivers again. Dialing. "Carly, hi, this is Bally."

"Hi, Bally. Did you hear from Mom?"

Crap. My heart sank. "No. I was hoping you did."

"Oh, no. I've been on pins and needles waiting to hear what's happened in the last couple of weeks. I didn't call because Mom was insistent she would see Dad and then call us with his address and phone and let us take it from there."

"Yea that's what I remember, too."

"Something's not right, Bally."

"Yea, I know. Atlee had her landlord open her condo and look and she's not there, but there is no evidence of anything wrong. I would go, but I can't take any more time off work. You're the closest. Can you go?"

"Sure. I'll go tomorrow."

"Thanks, Carly. Call me when you get to Mom's."

"I will."

I don't like this. Why hasn't she communicated with us? Maybe she called Little or Sassy. I leave a message for Sassy, but Little answers her phone. "Hi Little, this is Bally."

"Hi Bally, have you heard from your Mom?" My heart sank again.

"No, I was hoping you had."

"No, She was going to call Atlee after seeing your dad."

"She hasn't called him, and he's been calling her regularly. He called her condo's landlord and the guy went in to check on her and said everything looks fine. I knew we shouldn't have left her alone to do such an important task, but she was adamant about talking to him by herself first."

"I know. What's the plan?

"Well, Carly's going to check in on her tomorrow."

"Good. Bally, call me with any news ok?"

"I will. Bye."

I can feel the panic rising in my chest. I get the prescription filled. And then I do something I used to do with my first husband and, I haven't done in decades, I go to a Buddhist temple. It's calm there. I'm calm there.

Where's Toto?

After meditating, I call Lisa and ask for another appointment this week. She had a cancellation for two days from now, and I grab it.

Gee! Lisa looks tired. There's a lot going around now, I hope she hasn't caught whatever "it" is. Okay enough about her. I'm ready to confront my fears and I need her input. I have been walking around holding my breath and I need to exhale somewhere safe. This is the place.

"What's going on?"

"Nothing good, Lisa. Remember last time when I said I hadn't heard anything about my Mom confronting my Dad?"

"Yes, and you called Atlee while you were here and he didn't have any contact with her."

"Yes, so I called Carly. She hasn't heard from her either. I then called Little and she hasn't been contacted. I called all of them and none of them know where Mom is. I'm panicking inside. Where the hell is she? Why isn't she home or returning our calls when she's home? Atlee even called the landlord who manages her condo and he went in with a passkey and said she wasn't there and there's no indication something's happened to her. Then, Carly went to Mom's and let herself in. She found nothing except Mom's purse was missing, but most of her clothes (as far as we can tell) are there".

"Has anyone tried to get a hold of your father?"

"No, that's been a blind alley for the last two years. He moved and left none of us a forwarding address. Mom claims she knows where he is. I guess the next thing to do is to really go through Mom's things to see if we can find Dad's address. It feels like we are invading her space though. Also, I think someone should go there and stay there until Mom returns home. That way one of us will corner her and know she's ok.""I bet you're frantic."

"Good word for it."

"Has she ever done anything like this before?"

"No! She's always home and we could always reach her. The best we can figure out is she was last seen when Atlee, Little, Danny, and I were at her place. That was almost four weeks ago. Is she so angry that she won't return our calls? Has something happened to her? When Carly was there she could only stay a few hours and Mom didn't return home while she was there. She didn't go through her things. That's the next step. It just feels so invasive."

"Did Carly check her refrigerator?"

"What for?"

"If she is just avoiding you, then the food will be fresh. If she's disappeared or something has happened then by now the food would be spoiled."

"Wow, you should be a detective!"

Lisa smiles and shakes her head. "

"So someone's going to go back there? Who?"

"Don't know."

"Who's the best choice?" Lisa asks.

"Me."

"Why are you the best choice?"

"No kids or spouse. But, I can't leave work. I've taken too many days off this year. Someone else will have to do it."

"Where do you go from here?"

"I don't know."

"Do you have access to conference calling?"

"I thought about that, but I only have access at work. I would need to get permission to make a personal conference call with that many people and duration. I've been hesitant. Interesting."

"What is?"

"I would have just done it several months ago, but now my job is precarious, so I'm being extra cautious. I'll ask Ron this afternoon. He'll say 'yes' I'm sure. That's a good idea, thanks. Get all of us on the line and hash it out."

"Do you know a good detective?"

"You're just full of good ideas today! And I thought you looked tired!"

I then turn the conversation to a variety of other topics related to finding Mom but really have to do with me. My identity, my lack of brilliant work on my job, and my lack of desire to do the brilliant work. Lisa suggests that I am 'down', but I don't feel that way. I tell her I feel like I am outgrowing the need to be a corporate shark. I just don't like it anymore.

Bally
The Sleuth

Ron says "of course". Great! I can call my family and get their input as to where Mom might be. He only asks that I call after five o'clock when the rates are lower for businesses. I agree and thank him and then email everyone with a list of times I can have the conference room. Now I have to wait for everyone to respond. To my surprise everyone emails me immediately. They'll make any time work, just set it up. Everyone's as concerned as I am.

The conference call is set for tonight at 7:00. I'm a nervous wreck. What started out as concern is now escalating into a feeling of dread and panic. At seven, I start calling. Everyone's sitting by their phones. The connection's good.

"Hi everyone this is Bally." Everyone says 'hi'.

Discussion follows as to whether Atlee and Danny were the last to see or talk to Mom. So now we have the exact date and time when she was last seen by us. Now I turn the discussion to the big question "What's next?"

Mom is missing. Little will contact the landlord again and ask him to find out who in her building saw her last. Then depending on the answer, Atlee may file a missing person's report. Carly is going back to Mom's because she lives the closest and will go through Mom's things, including the refrigerator to see if the food is spoiled. Carly will check to see if the plants have been watered, too. She'll also be looking for names and phone numbers of people Mom might have gone to visit, especially Dad's number. Sassy said she could meet Carly at Mom's condo and help her. Carly loves the idea. Mother-daughter time. We agree to another conference call in 48 hours.

That went very well. Everyone was cordial, concerned, and cooperative. The three 'c's'. Cool! I didn't get a task assigned to me and I feel the need to do something. I call my friend, Mike, a private detective, but I get his answering machine. I leave a cryptic message.

At home, I pace and nibble. Not much appetite. I try to read but can't concentrate. I watch T.V. but can't concentrate. The phone rings and it's Mike. I explain the situation about Mom and Dad without going into the details. However, he asks a lot of questions about both Mom and Dad and I end up spilling the beans. He promises to get back to me, soon. I insist I didn't want to bother him by asking him to do the leg work, but to tell me how to get started looking. He pauses. "Bally, let me do this for you. Let me make the initial contacts that I have in that part of the country. I have computer access to stuff you don't. I'll be back in touch."

Crap! More waiting. I like the 'doing' stuff, not the 'waiting' stuff. Never was patient.

The phone wakes me from a deep sleep. I fell asleep on the couch in front of the television. What time is it? 10:30! Who the hell is calling at...oh, my God! It's about my Mom. "Hello?"

"Hi Bally, this is Mike. I'm sorry to be calling this late, but what I found out is really important."

"Is it about my mother or father?"

"Your father, Bally. He's dead."

I can't catch my breath. I hated the s.o.b. for what he had done but I didn't want him DEAD! At least not until I got my chance to tell him off. Oh my God! "Are you sure? When?"

"He must have died... let's see, about three weeks ago but they found him two weeks ago. Evidently, he was living alone and he died of a heart attack. They found him because the neighbors complained of the ..."

"Stench?"

"Yeah. I didn't want to say it. Were you close?"

"Not at all. But I didn't want him dead." NOT YET!

I dread hearing the answer to my next question. "Any lead on Mom."

"No leads yet, but I requested phone records and airline reservations etc. The police tried finding the next of kin, but they thought he had no family. There were no pictures or addresses or anything to indicate he had a family. The neighbors said he had no visitors except for delivery personnel who brought his food etc. Evidently at the end, he was pretty much a hermit."

"He was blind so he was unable to get out easily."

"Really, that wasn't mentioned in the report. How could they have missed that? Wait, here it is. Yeah, the neighbors said he was blind."

"The police would like to speak to someone from the family, evidently he left a will. He had a couple of paintings around the house and a local gallery agreed to hold them in case family showed up."

"Why?"

"I don't know, Bally."

"Where was he living?"

"In a small town in New Mexico called Archibald. It is near the US and Mexico border."

"Why there?"

"I don't know."

"I'm sorry I know you can't answer that. I was just thinking out loud. Please give me the detective's name."

"Officer Juan Ruiz. Look let me fax you all this."

"Ok, my fax number is 410-555-0134. Can you fax it now? Or will it be tomorrow?"

"I'll fax it now. You don't seem upset, I guess you weren't very close."

"No, he wasn't close to any of us, but he disappeared from our radar a couple of years ago. The only person who knew where he was living was our mother and she's now missing."

"Ok, here goes the fax."

"Mike, thank you so much. This is all confidential right? No one can know this. I like my privacy."

"Of course."

"Hey, let me pay you for your time tonight."

"No. that's what friends are for. I'll keep looking for your mom. Does she go by another name?"

"Not to my knowledge. Thanks, again."

The fax is beginning to print. I'm reading as it comes out of the machine. The question is, do I call everyone tonight or wait until tomorrow. It's late. Oh, oh, I forgot it's not late out west. I finish receiving the fax and take off for the office. I need to have another conference call, even though 48 hours hasn't passed.

The office is eerie late at night. I've worked late before but reentering the building in the middle of the night, gives me the 'willies' when no one is here. The conference room feels larger at night. I begin calling everyone and soon I have everyone on the phone except Carly. How do you tell people that the man who created such pain in their lives was dead? There would be no confrontation. Everyone was stone cold as I related the information. I ended with, "So that ends it for us. There will be no intervention or confrontation. We each will have to arrive at closure on our own."

"Bally, maybe I'm jumping to conclusions, but I wonder if Mom's disappearance is related to Dad's death?"

"What do you mean?" All of us say almost in synch.

"I'm not accusing her of anything, but you have to admit this is a huge coincidence. We confront Mom, she says she will confront Dad, then she'll call us. She never calls and then Dad is found dead and Mom's nowhere to be found?"

"Bally, you must admit this is a strange string of events." Sassy has joined in Atlee's drama.

"I just can't believe Mom's somehow involved in this!"

Little tries to calm me. "I don't think Atlee and Sassy are accusing your mother. I think they're just saying the timing is weird."

I can't think. My ears are ringing, my heart is pounding. Why are they so calm? I feel like I'm out of my body, floating in the corner of the room and watching myself having a conference call. Breathe, Breathe! Damn it!

After a minute or two, I feel my brain taking over, again. "Ok, I'm going to this Archibald, New Mexico place and I'm going to talk with the police, I'll pack up his few belongings and will take them wherever you tell me."

"Do you need someone to go with you?" Sassy asks.

"That's not necessary, but if someone wants to go, I'd welcome the company." There is no response to my statement. What a shame. My father cannot even get his family to gather around him even in his death. "No. I can do this by myself. I want to do this by myself. If I need any of you, I will call."

"Good luck, Bally. We will continue to look for Mom." Atlee offers weakly.

"Let me know if I can do anything else. And Bally, if you need help, I'll fly down to El Paso to help you."

"Ok, Little, thanks."

Sassy offers. "Bye, everyone. I'll call Carly tomorrow, if that's ok with you, Bally."

"Sure, I'll be flying tomorrow. I'll talk to you when and if I find something that's important. How about you all keep looking for Mom? Keep going with our plan." They all agree.

I sit back and wonder about that conversation. It was odd in many ways. No grief, no sadness (or happiness) over Dad's death, no energy around this mystery at all. I had more reaction than anyone else did. But then, I usually have more reaction than most people. I know if Lisa were here, she would ask me how I feel. I feel nothing except a desire to know the truth and regret that I didn't get a chance to tell the s.o.b. what I thought of him. To be honest, I feel relieved. I was dreading the emotional energy I was going to expend to let him know how he hurt me. I knew he wouldn't care and I wondered how far I would have gone to get him to understand. Since I'm the empress of over-reaction, I could see myself losing it and making a fool of myself in his presence and he would smile that smug smile of his as if to say, "Gotcha!"

I leave a note for Ron telling him I had a death in the family and had to fly to New Mexico. I would be gone a couple of days. I don't think bereavement leave counts toward sick leave or vacation time. At least I hope not or I'll owe Ron some days. I get online and look up the closest airport and see that El Paso is the closest airport. Little was right. I make reservations and go home to pack.

The flight's smooth, but my insides feel like they are connected to an electrical current. I rent a car and drive to Archibald and look for the police station. It's easy to find. There's only one stop light in town. The police station is at the end of Main Street. How provincial! I find Officer Ruiz. He looks like he could be my son. Obviously, Hispanic, baby face, a little overweight, and a smile that would make any grandmother pinch his cheeks. Bless his heart. I introduce myself and the first words out of his mouth are "I'm sorry ma'am."

"I'd like to find out what happened and I'm here to collect his effects."

"Sure, let's talk and then I'll take you to his apartment."

Officer Ruiz's office is shared with two to three other officers, and I surmise that's the entire police force except for maybe the border patrol. He offers me a seat and coffee. I accept both. "Officer Ruiz, please tell me what happened."

"When we arrived on the scene, we found your father's body. There was nothing missing and no indication of violence. No one saw anything. He seemed to be somewhat of a hermit. So maybe you could help us."

"I doubt it, but I'll try."

"When was the last time you saw him?"

"We weren't real close. I saw him over two years ago when he lived in Arizona."

"How about other children or relatives?"

"He has, had four other children. I have been in touch with two of them and they haven't seen him in years either. The other two siblings are not close to anyone. None of us have seen them in years. As far as I know, he was quite alone at the end."

"Was there bad blood between him and his children?" His cops' ears sense something.

"He was a difficult man and alienated most everyone he came in contact with."

"His friends seemed to think he was quite a nice man, just isolated because of his blindness."

"I really don't know how he was in the last two years. I only know him as I remember him earlier in his life. He was an angry man. My siblings will back me up on that."

"There is one thing that may help you. My mother was supposed to have visited my father three or four weeks ago."

"Really? No one reported seeing a woman visiting him. At that retirement center they are into each other's business. So if your mother had visited, then the place would have been a buzz with gossip."

"That's what I'm afraid of. She's missing."

"What do you mean, she's missing?"

"She told me and my siblings she was going to visit our father a month ago. After she visited, she was supposed to contact us. But, she never called, and we got concerned after we left many unreturned messages. She hasn't been seen since."

"Do you have a picture of her?"

"Sure." I dig in my purse for my family picture pouch and give him the picture of mom that was taken five years ago. Mom and I are standing together in front of her condo. "May I see his apartment...and his um...things?"

"I'll take you and let you in. The complex would love to have his things removed so they can clean it and rent it."

My father's apartment is a third floor walk up. Why would a blind man take an apartment where he had to walk up three flights of stairs? Unless he decided to not leave his apartment very often. The apartment has one bedroom with a kitchen, bath, and living room. It's non-descript, with no decorations and nothing that matches. I feel sad that a man who was successful and had money and prestige and friends ended up with nothing, no wife, no contact with his kids or his family, and blind. He was an angry, bitter, manipulative man in his youth and when he died, he had no one to care for him. I don't want to end up like this.

As I look around the apartment, nothing seems important, and then I see a painting on the living room wall. It was a beautiful impressionistic picture of the house we lived in growing up. The most unusual thing about the picture is its depth. Dad must have found a way to build up the thickness of the paint so the picture was almost three dimensional. One cannot only see the picture but also feel the picture. Of course! A man who was blind would rely on his sense of touch more than the rest of us. I take it off the wall to examine it.

"I would like to look around and see if there is anything of value."

"I'll leave you alone to go through his things. We have already been through them trying to find names of his closest relatives. Help yourself, but if anything strikes you as odd, please let me know." He notices I'm holding the painting. "We all thought that was a most unusual painting."

"Thanks." was all I could muster.

I feel slightly odd walking through the place where my father died. The man who sired me and raised me is not the person who lived here. I start with the bedroom. There is nothing here that gives any hint Dad had children and grandchildren. No pictures of them or handmade items. But then, he couldn't see them. But then, no one cared enough to send him loving messages and presents. The sadness overwhelms me.

I'm deep in thought when Ruiz appears at the door with the picture of Mom and me in his hand. He looks very serious. "I am afraid I have to ask you some important questions."

"Ok."

"We have to go down to the station."

"Why?"

He takes a deep breath. "Your father's neighbor across the hall said she can identify you as the person who arrived late one night a few weeks ago."

"That's impossible. I live in Maryland, and I've never been here."

"Could you come with me, please?"

I'm trembling. How could that woman identify me? I want to run, but I dutifully follow him. At least he didn't handcuff me! Well, it might have been nice if he weren't married and ½ my age. Stop it! My wicked sense of humor is one of my defenses when times get tough. This time it isn't working for me. Ruiz is now in his serious cop mode. He put me in his cop car and drives me back to the station and asks me to sit in a green room that looks like it was painted 35 years ago. The chairs and table are metal and very uncomfortable. He is followed into the room by his "boss", the head honcho of the police department, small though it may be.

"I am bringing in the neighbor and she is going to look at you and see if she can make an identity."

"Am I under arrest?"

"No m'am."

"Then do I need a lawyer?"

"That's up to you."

"Gentleman, I assure you I've never been here before."

"Then there is nothing to worry about is there?"

Why do I always end up in trouble! Shit.

The woman arrives and looks at me. Puts on her glasses and looks at me again. She asks that I stand up and I do. I hope I'm not making a huge mistake by not having a lawyer.

"How old is she?" the woman asks the officer.

"How old are you?"

"41"

"That's not her. She's too young. Thought she might have had plastic surgery when I saw the scars. The woman I saw was more like 60."

I gasp and catch myself before a sound comes out. Little! For once I kept my mouth shut. "May I go?"

"Yes, we're sorry for the scare, but we thought you had lied to us."

"Thanks for the... um... hospitality? I'm going to finish going through the rest of my father's things." Officer Ruiz gives me back my picture and they part like the Red Sea as I leave the station and get in my car. "Holy crap what the hell happened here?"

I pick up my cell phone and call Little. No service! Of course! I always get in trouble AND stifled. The drive back to Dad's place went very fast because I don't remember it. I was on automatic pilot using my brain to sort through what had happened. The only thing I can come up with that fits is Little came here four weeks ago. But why? And where is Mom? Now that I think about it, I was surprised when I said I was going to Archibald and Little piped up that she would fly down to El Paso to help me. I didn't have any clue what airport Archibald was near. How did she know? She knew because she'd been here before. Crap! I just reconnected with my biological mother and it turns out that instead of having two mothers, I have one missing mother and a liar for the other. Am I jumping to conclusions? Hell yea! I can't figure out why she would have lied about being down here when we were on the phone. Ok, ok, take a deep breath. There has to be another explanation. I can't think of any reason she would have withheld that information unless there is YET ANOTHER major secret.

Outside in the heat, I try my cell phone. Success! I call Carly and thank heavens she answers. "Hi Carly, this is Bally."

"Hey, sis, where are you?"

"In Archibald. I have one of Dad's original paintings!"

"What paintings? He was blind wasn't he?" Carly sounds incredulous.

"Yes, he only saw grey shadows. At least that's what Mom told me. He knew daytime from nighttime, but he couldn't see anything else."

"Then how could he paint?"

"It's hard to explain, but he made the paint really thick and used a palette and molded it onto the canvas. There are a few of them. You want one?"

"Maybe, I have to think about that one. Have you found Mom?"

"No. Do you know any reason why Little would have lied about never having been down here?"

"No? What in the world have you uncovered, Bally?"

"I have no idea, but here is what I know. A woman was down here three or four weeks ago to visit Dad. One of Dad's neighbors saw her and at first thought it was me. The police took me to the station and made her come to the station to identify me. The woman said I'm too young, that the other woman looked just like me but older. I gotta tell you, I was so scared, that I kept looking for a bathroom!"

"Bally, what happened down there?"

"I don't know, but I have a feeling I'm going to be here awhile and may lose my job. I've got three days bereavement leave, and there's no way I'm going to solve this mystery in three days before I run out of time and money."

"Sell a painting!"

"Cute, Carly."

"Ok. Have you heard from Little, Sassy, Atlee?"

"No. I'm at Mom's now and Atlee and the sisters are arriving today. Bally, the stuff in the refrigerator is gross. I have been dumping everything down the disposal. The stench is awful. And her plants are dead. When everyone arrives, we are going through this house with a fine tooth comb over the next 24 hours. I spoke to her neighbors and no one's seen her in weeks and a couple of them cried saying something horrible must have happened to her."

"Well, I'm calling Little now and confronting her."

"I wouldn't do that. We don't know what she's involved with."

"I'm several hundred miles away. What can she do?"

"Fly there and kill you."

"My God! You think that's what happened to Mom?"

"That's one possibility. I've been running scenarios through my head and I can't figure out why she'd be cagey about having been here. One thing though, Mom did say she had contacted Dad and he knew she was coming, right?"

"I don't remember."

"Me either."

"Do you want me to fill in the crew when they arrive or do you want to go on speaker phone?"

"That's a great idea! When all of them have arrived, I'll call back and fill them in on what I've learned including the part about the woman across the hall recognizing me and we can see what Little does with that. Her reaction may give us the answer. When are they going to arrive?"

"Let's see, everyone should be here seven tonight, if all the planes are on time. We're going to order dinner and then get started on the search."

"Ok, I will call around eight."

"Sounds good. This really is a mess isn't it?"

"Yea, Carly. It's a mess and a mystery. Why can't we have normal, dull, average, parents?"

"Good question. And by the way, Bally. You're really handling this well. There was a day when I dreaded sharing anything with you. You would fly off the handle and spout filth and assign blame and you're not doing that. I'm glad you're my sister." She chokes at the end.

"Thanks, Carly." I get choked up, too. "I gotta go. Call you tonight." I hang up quickly before Carly knows I'm crying too. "By God, I'm getting better!" I get in my car and let the emotion pour out all over the rental car's dash, seat, steering wheel. Feels good to cry. The depression log jamb is breaking up.

I head back to my hotel room for a nap. I think I'll need it before the 8 o'clock phone call. I'm drifting off when my cell rings. "Hello?"

"This is Mr. Anders, your father's attorney. The police just called and said you are here to retrieve your father's things.

"Yes I am."

"I am glad you flew down here. Your father had no idea where you were and he didn't have any of your siblings' addresses either. He only had his ex-wife's address. I have been trying to reach your mother over the last couple of weeks."

"I just found out yesterday that my father died. I didn't know where he was living. And my mother was, um, not able to tell me. I called a private investigator who found out about his death. My siblings elected me to come here to make inquiries."

"Your father left a will. Could you come by my office with some identification and we can begin the process?"

"Sure, I'll be there in a few minutes if you'll give me directions."

He does and I'm on my way.

Mr. Anders has a modest office and his secretary is a plump, happy, lady with a strong Texas accent. She calls me a 'sweet thing' and says how sorry she is for my loss.

I hand him my driver's license as identification. "I'm glad Dad had a will. I can't imagine going through all this without a will."

"He left everything to you."

"Me? I'm the black sheep of the family. Why me?"

"He said he loved you very much and he wasn't close to his other children and he wanted you to have everything. It's all in his will. He hands me a copy."

"He didn't leave anything to my mother?"

"No, they were divorced, and he didn't think he owed her anything."

I wanted to say, "If you only knew!"

"I also couldn't contact your siblings about the will. They are not named."

"I see. Where do we go from here?

"Well, I will now probate the will and as soon as the process is over, I will send you a check."

"What about his personal effects?"

"His instructions were that you can have or dispose of anything you like. They are yours."

"Do I have to wait until the will is probated?"

"Not in this state. Because you are the only beneficiary, you only have to wait about 30 days. I have to make sure no one will challenge the will."

"I see. Should I take his effects with me?"

"If you so desire, but the money will come to you after probate."

"Ok, that's easy."

"Ms. Hawthorne, are you aware of your father's wealth?"

"Wealth?"

"Yes, his estate is worth approximately two million dollars."

"What! How could that be? He lived like a pauper. Did you see his apartment?"

"Yes, several times and I encouraged him to move to a better place where he could get some help. He refused. He said he was done with life. To be honest, I think he was depressed."

Wow, depression runs in our family.

"You are a wealthy woman. Or at least you will be as soon as the will is probated."

"I have done alright for myself without his money. I've been married and divorced a couple of times and had nice settlements. In addition I have a good job. I don't think Dad knew me well enough to know how successful I've been."

"You're right. He didn't. He said you couldn't hold onto a man, you changed jobs frequently, and you have an addiction. He also said you were the apple of his eye and he wanted to make life easier for you."

"So, he felt sorry for me."

"Yes, you could say that. But he loved you too."

"Thanks, but I never felt his love."

Tears, more tears. I'm going to be dehydrated before dinner at this rate! He calls his secretary about getting me something to drink. He also handed me the box of tissues on his desk.

"Is there anything else you need from me or to tell me? You have my address, phone, ss#, etc. Anything else?"

"Just two things."

"What's that?"

"First, your father said he hoped you would know what to do with the money."

"What's number two?"

"Will you have dinner with me tonight?"

"I would love to, but I need to take a rain check for two reasons. First I have a conference call at 8:00 and it will take at least an hour. Plus I'm going to be exhausted afterwards."

"What's number two?"

"I find you **way** too attractive right now and I'm **way** too vulnerable. I have a habit of falling for guys and getting involved too fast and then the relationship doesn't last. I'm not ready to fall for a guy right now."

"And by setting these boundaries for me to jump over, you are doing this correctly?" His light brown eyes are dancing while teasing me.

"Yes, I know you don't understand, but I must change the way I do life. My father didn't know me well and he still knew that about me. I have been impulsive, angry, and manipulative. Just like him."

462   *Sharon Hutson Cheston*

"Fair enough, but before you leave town will you call me and let me take you to dinner?"

I want to say "YES!!!!" Instead, I say, "If not this trip then the next. I will be back to finish up my father's affairs." And I exit stage right!

I grab a carry-out of nachos from the local restaurant and head back to my hotel room. The nachos are delicious and the television program is old and stupid. I'm trying to take my mind off of the phone call at 8 o'clock, but my mind can't follow the program. I close my eyes and pray for wisdom. I've meditated but I haven't prayed to God in years. I wonder if God knows who I am anymore. God's gotta be disappointed in me the way everyone else has been. My mind wanders to Bernie.

As I become calmer, more focused, less reactive, other people are noticing. Carly and Atlee have noticed some change. I do feel different. People at work are reacting to me as if I have something to offer, not like I am a pain in the neck and therefore to be feared. Funny, I always wanted everyone else to change so I could be happier, it never occurred to me that I had to change in order to be happier. Maybe with this insight, I can approach God again. "Please help me manage this confrontation with grace, whatever the outcome. I do not want to be like my father, ever again."

Then a flash of insight! "God, Dad was wrong in leaving all his possessions to me. When I was a child, I knew my father was treating me better than Carly and Atlee and I knew that the pampering, praising, and letting me get away with murder was wrong, but I took what he gave me anyway. Today he excluded Carly and Atlee from his will and while I could take all the money, and legally it is rightfully mine, I cannot keep allowing Dad to do the wrong thing. I will do the right thing this time. I will split the estate with Carly and Atlee. Carly may refuse the money because she and her husband Cory are very wealthy. That will be up to her. But, I know Atlee could use the money. As for me? What will I do with 700K? I don't know right now. There are other things I need to decide before the money becomes important. Thanks for listening. Signing off."

Oh my, it's 8:05. I call and Carly picks up. "Hi Carly, did everyone get in on time?"

"Yes, Bally, we are all here."

"Hi everyone. Well, this mystery never stops. There's some really good news and some questions I can't answer. Let me begin with what I have done since we talked. I arrived here very early this morning and went to the police station. I told the police officer I was Dad's daughter and I came to collect his few belongings, which was a little lie because I was there to **go through** his belongings looking for signs Mom had been here. I told them Mom had been on her way to see Dad and has disappeared. As you can imagine they became instantly alert to the possibility of a crime. The police officer asked me if I had a picture of her, and I gave them a picture of mom and me, which was taken a couple years ago. While I was doing a preliminary walk through at Dad's, the police had taken the picture to some of the neighbors focusing on whether anyone had seen Mom recently. Within minutes I was being escorted out of the building, put in a police car, and taken to the police station. They told me a woman in Dad's building had not recognized Mom, but ME!"

Everyone gasped. I wish I could've seen the look on everyone's faces. "They brought the woman in to look at me in person and the woman asked if I had had any plastic surgery done. Guess she saw the scars. When I said 'no', she declared she hadn't seem me, but a woman who looked just like me but older, someone in her 60's."

There is a dreadful silence as this information sinks in. I can imagine at this point, everyone is slowly turning to look at Little.

"The police let me go and I then went back to Dad's to finish looking through his apartment. It appears Dad was an artist and, despite his blindness, he was able to invent a technique in which he thickened the paint to make the picture more three dimensional. The picture I found was of our house, the one we grew up in as kids. I found a few more too."

Atlee breaks in to ask, "Are they any good?"

"Atlee, I can't tell you that. I like them, but I'm not an art critic. Anyone want one?"

No answer. I continue. "The police called Dad's attorney. I never thought to ask how they knew his attorney. His name is Mr. Anders. When he called me, he was relieved that the next of kin was found. He took all my information and declared he can now have Dad's will probated." I stop to see if the issue of Little comes up and it does.

Carly says, "Little, did you go to see Dad around the time our mother went?"

The quiet in the room is uncomfortable. Then a small voice, "Yes."

Atlee breaks the silence. "But why? When we all left here, Mom was adamant that she see Dad and confront him by herself. Why did you go?"

Little's voice is trembling. "Your mom went to Archibald and when she arrived she went to see your father and using the key he had given her years ago, she let herself in and immediately began confronting your Dad. She must have told him everyone knew what he had done over 40 years ago and all of you were on the way to accuse him. He panicked and began begging for mercy. Then he suddenly dropped dead. She must have felt sorry for him because she said she cleaned the place up and went back to the motel. Then, and only then she remembered she'd left her purse back in his apartment and she freaked out. She had her wallet, because she carries it in her pocket, but not her purse. She knew that whoever found him, would suspect her because her purse was there. She always carries a laminated card in her purse with emergency contact information on it. She got that idea from me. She said she couldn't go back there with her dead ex-husband's body sitting there. That's when she called me. She was hysterical. She wouldn't calm down. I told her to call the police, but she wouldn't. I was worried about her, so I flew down there on the next plane. When I arrived almost 8 hours later at her hotel room, she was sick, really sick, throwing up, dehydrated, crying, eyes rolling back in her head. I got her calmed down and then tucked her in bed. I told her we should go to the police to report Cameron's death, and she became hysterical again. I told her I would go get her purse and then come back to the hotel and we would figure something out. So I went and retrieved it. That's when the neighbor must have seen me. When I got back to the motel, Toto was gone and so was her luggage. I thought she had headed back to the airport, so I went after her. When I arrived in El Paso I was told the plane to Phoenix had left so I took the next one back to Seattle thinking she would arrive home and call Atlee like she promised. But I guess she never arrived home.

Little is becoming hysterical and is talking a mile a minute.

"I didn't know what to do…I've been hoping she would show up. Over the month, I called her apartment several times a day…but no answer… I then figured she was with one of you…I jumped every time the phone rang…I was afraid it wasn't her and it was one of you telling me something awful happened to her. After a month when you called Bally, I still didn't know what to do or say, so I said nothing. When Carly came here and went through the house and interviewed the neighbors, I was glad. I thought maybe some news. But, no. Then when we made the decision to meet and go through everything, I was hoping that getting together and searching would turn up some names of people she might have gone to see. I'm sorry. I made things worse. Bally, you're so smart, I thought you would be able to figure out everything in Archibald, find Toto, and bring her home, but it seems things are a mess instead."

Wow, I thought I screwed things. I wanted to scream at her, "Why didn't you start calling her when you arrived in Seattle and then call us?" I don't. I just sit while everyone else sits in silence, except for Little's sobbing.

"Little, I'm glad you told us the truth, because I thought for the last few hours you had killed Dad."

"Oh my Gawd! I would never do such a thing. I've fantasized about it, sure, but I would never do it!"

"Even in his death he is screwing around with this family. It has to stop here, with us! We need to tell the truth no matter how bad it is. Got it! And I'm going to go first. I want you to know, totally unbeknownst to me, Dad left all his possessions to me and only me."

Carly tries to make things ok. "Bally, he only had those paintings and a few things. Look at how you said he lived, in poverty. So take the paintings, sell them, and do whatever you want with the money."

Atlee, Little, and Sassy agree.

"Ok, here is the toughest part of the truth. Dad had over two million dollars."

Now, there is dead (no pun intended) silence and then shifting in their chairs as the amount sinks in.

"Now here is what I'm going to do. I think Dad has favored me all his life and that was purely wrong. He was an opinionated, arrogant, willful, hardheaded, unforgiving s.o.b., and he was wrong most of the time. In his death he made a decision that was also wrong and I'm not going to stand by, like I did as a kid, and reap the reward of his ignorance. I am going to split the money with Atlee and Carly. Period. NO DISCUSSION. We are family and we should be all for one and one for all just like the musketeers. Carly breaks the silence.

"Bally, you know we don't need the money so here is what I want. I want one dollar and one of Dad's paintings as a reminder of how a sick man can waste his life when he had so many gifts. My third is to be split between Sassy, Little, and Mom. NO DISCUSSION."

Everyone is quiet. Atlee speaks next. "Thanks Bally, I can't tell you how much this means to me. I need a college fund for Danny and that's what I will use the money for."

Sassy is next. "I speak for myself and for Little when I say thank you to Bally for your generosity and to Carly for hers. This will give us both a nest egg to fall back on when we are ancient." Everyone laughs. "I too would like a picture. What about you Little?"

"If I can find the right one that will inspire me to be a better person and not remind me of him, then I would like one, a **small one**. Like his dick." More laughter. Peels of gut splitting laughter. "What about you Bally? What will you do with the money?"

"I'm not ready to make that decision yet. As for the pictures, I have the one I want. It's of our house growing up. I will take the rest of the pictures home with me and will photograph them and then send you all the photos and you can fight over them. The rest of the stuff is not worth much. I will give it all to a charity down here and they can use the furniture and stuff to help others."

"Now let's talk about Mom." Carly says.

"Well, why don't you all do what you agreed to do. Leave no mattress unturned, literally, and then call me. Perhaps you will have...Hey, wait a minute. What about Little's other two sons. Where are they? They were the ones who had the most contact with your grandparents. Would they know anything?" Little takes a deep breath and says, "I think I'm the one who should contact them. I have kept abreast of who they are and where they are. It's time to rock two more worlds like ours have been rocked. After we go through Gladys' condo, I will go to their homes and talk with them." Sassy and Atlee offer to go for emotional support and Little says, "Let me think about it."

"Everything seems finished except one thing. Where's Toto?"

No one answers.

And that's the end of the discussion. I feel much better, but I'm depleted. Has it only been 24 hours since I made the plane reservation?

I return to the police station to thank them for their help and ask where my father is buried. They give me the name of the cemetery for all those who have no family to claim the body. I stand in front of a small metal plate with my father's name, birth date, and death date on it. That's all. Seems befitting. Then I return to Bob Ander's office and ask to see him. When he hears it's me, he gets off the phone immediately and greets me warmly. "Bob, I'm going to be leaving this evening so I can't take you up on your offer of dinner, but how about lunch? I'm buying, I'm rich!"

He laughs and agrees. Lunch was wonderful, comfortable, and safe. I like him, but he's over 2000 miles away and I'm just beginning to know who I am. The old Bally would have jumped in the sack with him, married him in Mexico, and then found out he wasn't what she needed and divorced him to run around with someone else. The new me is going to be more realistic, rational, and calm. As I drive to the airport, I hear the song *Somewhere over the Rainbow* on the radio. That's going to be my theme song to myself. I feel lighter and brighter. And I need to quit my job and find out what I really want to do, but not in that order. As I doze off on the plane, I remember that I'll see Lisa tomorrow. Wow, do I have a lot to share. Maybe I'll wear my new colors: Honesty and Integrity. My last thought, before sleep claims my mind is that we still have to find Mom. My money's on the Philippines. When I arrive home, there is a message from Little on my voicemail. "Hi Bally, the mystery is solved. Your mother took off for the Philippines when she left Archibald. She always carries her passport with her as identification because she doesn't drive. That explains how she was able to get on an international flight. We found some old letters with addresses from there and contacted the writers. She's there, I talked with her. She said she was in a daze when she went to the airport and doesn't remember buying a ticket to the Philippines, but the next thing she knew, she was landing in Manila. She says she thinks everyone is better off without her. I assured her we love her and want her to come home. She's going to stay for a couple of months to recover. Thanks for everything you did. Um, ah, I love ya."

Lisa
Reflection on Bally

There's something about Bally today. She's dressed in an indigo blue suit with a yellow blouse. She looks calm and energized all the same time. She unfolds a story that should be a feature film on the Lifetime channel, and when I tell her that it reminds me of one of those stories, she laughs and agrees.

"You know, Lisa, when I came here months ago, I said my family was like a soap opera and I thought that was true and kinda funny. Now I think you're right. The soap opera has become a Lifetime feature film. How is that for a metaphor?"

"What does that mean to you?"

"I knew you were going to ask a question like that. Well, I think I've gotten to know myself as a person of talent, brains, and beauty. I believe over the last months of twists and turns in the family, I've grown and, like the Velveteen Rabbit, I have become real, not the over reactive, screaming, jealous, mean-spirited narcissist that I was. I'm not who I want to be yet, but I'm beginning to think instead of reacting strongly, understand rather than jump to conclusions, love instead of feeling jealous. Somewhere in all this I've grown. I don't know why you hung in there with me or how you made this change take place, but I want to thank you."

"You're welcome, but Bally, you did the hard work and you didn't give up when the work got hard. But, let me see if I have this correct. Sounds like you have decided to stop therapy?"

"No, not really. I want to see you, but can we go every other week for a while. I came really close to drinking last week, and I still feel shaky. I still need to reconnect with Mom when she returns, and I need to find out more about Little's visit with my two brothers, but things are slowing down a bit, so I'd like to see you two times a month for awhile. Can you do that?"

"Can you?"

"Sure. I think I'm ready. I have some decisions to make."

"Like what?"

"'Well, like I'm thinking about leaving my job and going back to school."

"To do what?"

"Well, Not sure. That's one of those things I have to sort through. I'll have plenty of money to support myself when the check comes so now's the time to think about the next 40 years."

"You are very blessed to be in this position, to be free to decide what you want to do with your life and to have the resources to do it."

"Well, I also may have to move if I choose a school that's residential."

"True. We'll work on all that over the next few sessions. But for now, let's just sit and celebrate what you have accomplished."

"Good. Hmm, Well, Well, Well." She shakes her head in disbelief.

"Bally, I notice you use the word 'well' a lot. Does that word have a special meaning for your?"

Long pause while she considers my comment. "Maybe I felt like I was in a "well" most of my life."

"Interesting, and now?"

"I'm beginning to climb out."

We agree to meet in two weeks and she agrees to contact her sponsor and go to AA meetings.

Bally
Reflecting on Life

Three months have flown by, and I have talked with Mom several times. She's living with her cousin and is recovering nicely after her experience of watching Dad die. Mom says she can come home now, to clean out her apartment and move back to Manila. A year ago I would have told her she was being stupid and would've gone on a drunk. Today, I told her I look forward to seeing her and I would visit her in Manila. Who knows, she may hate it and be back in a year. It's her life anyway. The money that's coming from Dad's estate through me and Carly will help her live like a queen in the Philippines. Good for her. She deserves it. Atlee isn't happy about it, but he's able to let go and is making plans to visit her with Danny. Sassy and Little had the strongest reaction. They had been making plans for Mom to move to their neck of the woods so they could all be together again. Well, they'll just have to visit! Little told me my two brothers are not interested at this time in connecting with me, Carly, or Atlee. They are in shock and may be quite angry with my father and grandfather, though Little said they were polite and reserved. I told her to let all this sink in and then contact them again and see what happens.

As for me, I'm still thinking about what I want to do when I grow up. I like the excitement of Mike's work. I kinda got hooked in Archibald while playing detective. But, I'm afraid I'd get bored with domestic type investigating. Mike says that spouse spying is his bread and butter. He loves it when he's called in on a missing person case. Would I be bored? Not sure. I have a knack for the intrigue, but detective work seems too routine 90% of the time.

Then Lisa mentioned I like to paint, like my Dad. Did I have the fire in my belly to paint? It was always my love, but people can't make money at it and when you do, you sell one painting and not another one for months. I think I better let my painting remain a hobby. But, to be a hobby, one has to paint! So, I'm planning on taking classes.

I really want to look into a career that's totally different. Something I've never told anyone about. I love animals and would love to be on the animal rescue patrol. I can't imagine that anyone will think it's a good idea and the pay is lousy. But, if I moved to Washington or Oregon, I could live on a small salary if I invest wisely. When Atlee told me what his house cost, I almost fell off my chair. I could buy some land and put up a house and have no mortgage. It's risky. But, Lisa had a good point. If I didn't do it, how will I feel in 20 years? If I did do it and didn't like it, how will I feel?

The phone rings, awakening me out of my future planning. It's Little with bad news. Mom died of a heart attack while waiting for a friend at a restaurant. They tried CPR, but she didn't respond. Her family is burying her there because trying to get a body back to the U.S. is very complicated. All the ups over the last few months just came crashing down.

Life is not going to let up on me no matter how much I change. I go to the bar and order a sour apple martini. For a month, I don't go to work, get fired, skip my appointments with Lisa, and hate myself. My brother, sister, and Little do an intervention and ship me off to an inpatient setting for 28 days. I gave up all the progress I made to a sour apple martini, well several martinis. All that work, all that pain, and I'm back where I started over three years ago. Now, in an inpatient setting again, I'm sitting in a new shrink's office. She looks like she hates the world and me with it. Crap.

Lisa
Reflecting on Bally

Bally missed her last appointment and when I called her home phone I got a recording that her phone was disconnected. I called her cell and it's turned off. It was a company cell phone, so I assumed she lost her job. Later in the week, I received a release of confidential information from an inpatient facility out in Oregon. Bally's there and they want my notes. I'll send them immediately, but I feel sad for Bally. I hope she comes through this regression into addiction.

Lisa's Solo Journey

My last client just left and I am headed home to finish packing. I haven't had a vacation since Milly, Maggie, and I went to the Caribbean over a year ago. I don't remember taking a day off or even a sick day since then. The stress is oozing out of my body as I drive home. Tomorrow morning we are bound for San Diego. I've been packing for three days and making lists of things to do before I leave for the airport. Almost done with all the items on my "to be done" list. Tonight I sleep on the East Coast and tomorrow I will sleep on the West Coast.

Holy cow! The alarm didn't go off, now I have to rush to finish the final few items and leave for the airport. I'm meeting Milly and Maggie at the gate. My body is halfway out the door when the phone rings. I am tempted to ignore it but it's 7:00 a.m. It has to be Maggie or Milly or an emergency.

It's Maggie. She's in the hospital having just had an emergency appendectomy overnight. She insists Milly and I go ahead…and have fun. I feel sad she's missing our trip. She was the one who suggested we go to San Diego and now she can't go. Her attitude was typical Maggie, though. She laughed and said, "San Diego isn't going anywhere. I'll take in the town later. I'll miss you guys." Darn, Bummer, Disappointment. Now I really have to hurry. The traffic is light, thank God. I could have been in real trouble time-wise if the beltway was backed up. List of things to do: Park the car, check in, check baggage, go through security, and arrive at the gate. Done!

Waiting for Milly. I check my cell phone to see if she called. She did. How did I miss that? Must've rung when I was in the security line. I try to call her back, but the line is busy. I thought she had call waiting! It's only 45 minutes before we take off and Milly still isn't here. I call her again. She answers. I try not to sound too irritated. "Hey, where are you?"

"I am at the Pittsburgh Airport. I got a call from my mother late last night. She had a mild heart attack and is in the hospital. She's fine and she's insisting I leave for vacation. My two sisters are here for the week. I'm at the ticket counter trying to get my ticket changed to go to San Diego from here but later tonight, a red eye. The airline counter people are being very helpful, but it looks like

I won't get into San Diego until tomorrow morning. I'm sorry. I didn't call at three in the morning, because I didn't want to wake you. When Mom insisted I leave, I called your cell to let you know I'll be flying to California from here, but there was no answer."

"Oh, my gosh, you must be frantic. Should we cancel the vacation?"

"No, no, you and Maggie get on the plane and I'll meet you in San Diego tomorrow morning."

"You haven't heard from Maggie?"

"I haven't been home, what happened?'

"Maggie's in the hospital. She had an emergency appendectomy in the middle of the night".

"How awful!"

She's doing fine, but she's obviously not coming with us. This vacation seems to be falling apart."

"Look, Lisa, we can still salvage this vacation. And we both need the rest. Get on the plane and when you arrive pick up our rental car at the airport. You have the reservation number, right? (I indicated I did.) Enjoy your first night at the hotel and I will be arriving in the morning. We'll have a great time."

"Ok. Please let your mom know I will keep her in my prayers."

"I will, now get on that plane. If you don't, I'll never speak to you again."

"Ok. I'll see you tomorrow."

"See you in San Diego."

So here I sit at the gate, without my two friends, and have a nagging, horrible sense of being totally alone. How could this happen? I had a vacation planned with two friends and both are having difficulties. Should I do this alone? Should I really get on a plane, fly across country, rent a car, check in at a luxury resort and take the risk that Milly's mom is ok enough for her to leave Pittsburgh? Why is this happening? The gate attendant just called my row, and I get up just as I am ordered to do and walk to the end of the line. Am I crazy? This is a real leap of faith. I could end up all alone on the other side of the country. As if in a fog, I enter the plane find my seat, stow my gear, and click my seatbelt in place. I utter a prayer that Milly makes it tomorrow. How self-centered is that? I utter a different prayer. I hope Milly's mom's ok and that Maggie heals quickly. I open my book and settle in for a five hour flight. Five hours, a movie, a meal, and 125 pages of my book later, the flight attendant announces we are preparing for landing. I look out the window and see the Pacific Ocean and feel the tingle of excitement. Everything will be fine.

I'm still on automatic pilot with my lists of things to do. Exit the plane when they tell me to, find my luggage, pick up the rental car, ask for a map and directions to the resort. Done.

The car rental lady says it's easy to find. Coronado Island has only one access bridge. San Diego is a beautiful city and I can see why Maggie wanted to vacation here. The Hotel del Coronado (or the 'Del' as the locals call it) looks exactly as it did in the Marilyn Monroe movie "Some Like It Hot". Red roof and white siding with a huge veranda that over looks the Pacific Ocean, a throw back to the 1920s. I check in using my credit card, hoping Milly arrives to split the cost or I'll be broke paying three times as much for the hotel than I planned to. The suite is gorgeous and the view of the ocean takes my breath away. There is something about the eternal rolling of the waves that soothes my head, which has been still spinning with the recent changes in our plans. Everything will be fine. Everything will be fine. If I keep saying it, perhaps it will be true. It's only noon here (3 p.m. Eastern time) and I have no idea what to do with myself. The beach issues a sun and sand invitation and I change into my swimsuit and take my book to the beach. Lovely white sand. People are playing and reading, but no one's swimming. I need to take the plunge. I never swam in the Pacific Ocean before and it looks very calm. Whoa, shock to my entire system. The water is freezing! I almost had a heart attack. No wonder no one was swimming. I should have noticed the kids weren't playing in the water either. I just revealed to everyone on the beach that I am from the East Coast where the Atlantic Ocean is warm in the summer. The others on the beach watched me dive in and are now snickering at my stupidity. (At least that's my fear.) I tried to act real cool like I knew what I was doing, but I don't think I pulled it off. I smiled as I walked back to my beach chair all cool and confident, but inside I'm feeling foolish AND COLD. I should have read the **entire** travel brochure not just the parts that talked about the fun things I could see and do.

As the sun sets spreading beautiful hues across the sky, I finish my book, and contemplate what I'm going to do for dinner. Am I going to the formal dining room and sit alone and eat dinner? I've done it before at professional conferences and have always been a little uncomfortable, but at a conference lots of people are sitting alone in the restaurant. For some reason eating alone where others are doing the same thing doesn't bother me. Tonight will be different. This is not business, this is vacation, and I feel uncomfortable being alone. Perhaps I should order room service. It would be the easy way out of an uncomfortable situation. But is easy always the best answer? One thing for sure, I need another murder mystery to read. I only brought the one book, because I thought the three of us would be chatting so much there would be little time for reading.

The options keep running through my mind as I shower and get dressed. Should I do what is easy and safe (room service) or should I take a chance and do what's uncomfortable and perhaps grow from the experience? When would I have this opportunity again to be alone on vacation and experience the solace (and anxiety) of eating alone in a large restaurant where everyone else is chatting with a companion?

I take a deep breath, finish dressing, and leave to purchase a new book at one of the resorts many shops. I choose a mystery that guarantees to keep me engaged and on the edge of my seat (so promises the back cover). Another deep breath and I leave for the formal dining room. The host greets me and asks how many. I gulp (well I wasn't that obvious…I swallowed) and say "One". He looks a bit surprised, but only for a split second, bows and asks me to follow him. He seats me in the back, near the kitchen door. He asks if this is satisfactory. I can't believe what comes out of my mouth next. "Actually, I feel isolated back here and it's a bit noisy, could I have another table, please"? He instantly smiles and bows slightly and shows me to a table that is nearer the center of the room but still gives privacy. I smile and feel surprised at my tenacious, but appropriate, request. A waiter instantly appears, as if he popped out of the floor next to my table. He asks about my choice of beverages. I order water with a lemon wedge and a red wine. The waiter smiles and says politely, all our water comes with lemon. Should have known, this is a classy restaurant. As I pass through the first stage of discomfort, I sit back and look around instead of immersing myself in my new book. The room is beautifully decorated. Couples and families chat and laugh and I feel the sadness of being alone, but also, in some small way, I feel like a voyeur. An outsider watching others interact. Well, it's how I make a living. This insight makes me feel more comfortable, or at least less obvious as the only one-person-table in an upscale restaurant filled with families, couples, and groups. Then something odd happens, a calmness fills me and a sense of confidence begins to take the place of my initial anxiety. I'm enjoying my own company! My thoughts about the things going on in this room are not being crowded out by the chit-chat that would have occurred if my friends were here. As a therapist, I use silence frequently to clear my mind and observe more closely what's happening. This isn't too different. The difference is this silence isn't in service to others but in service to me. I begin to see the blessing of being totally alone in the sea of humanity were others are engaged in their own conversations. I check out the curtains, the silverware, the glassware etc. And I notice the subtle decorative touches that would have been lost on me had I been with other people. I ordered my favorite meal: filet, salad, asparagus, baked potato. Isn't that what Noelle ordered on her first date with Gerry? I could have tried fancier food, but this is my time. That's what I want and therefore that's what I order. I observe, read, eat, watch others, read more, and finish eating. After an hour, my awareness of my own thoughts and feelings are heightened. I realize how much I have missed **me**. I grew up in a large family, lived with roommates in college and after college, married, and had two children, Then when my daughter died, my marriage ended and my son started traveling, I found myself alone. As a teacher and counselor, I am always with others and the problem, I decide as I sat in a large formal restaurant, is I haven't formed a solid relationship with myself. I have neglected my relationship with the one who will journey through my entire life with me, from womb to tomb. Instead, I have immersed myself in work and friends and my son and daughter-in-law. I was comfortable in my world but not in myself. This experience allows me to look at what I have missed, and I am determined to develop a healthy relationship with myself from this moment on.

Amazing! One night alone and the noise seems to be clearing in my head. I am grateful for this opportunity and look forward to doing this again sometime. But, tomorrow Milly arrives and we will reconstitute our silliness and fun. However, I will not lose this moment, and I make a resolution that I will spend time alone in the future. I will think about the world, God, politics, ethics, etc. I will learn what I believe in, not what others think. As I leave the restaurant, I feel like I am standing a little taller and walking a little more confidently.

The message light on my phone in my room is blinking and I have a presentiment that something's wrong. I try to erase the feeling from my mind as I pick up the message from the front desk. The anxiety's building as I wait for the front desk to give me the message. The message is that Milly called and I should call her. I try her cell phone, but she doesn't pick up. Is she just checking in about her flight tomorrow morning, does she need me to pick her up at the airport, or is there news about her mom?

I try to concentrate on my book, but I begin awfulizing. What if she isn't coming? Could I enjoy an entire week by myself? I doubt it. First, I can't afford to stay at the Del for an entire week by myself. Second, I may have had a wonderful dinner, but I don't think I could I do this for an entire week. No way. I was feeling very cocky and sure of myself when I thought I'd only be alone for a night, but the possibility of facing an entire week alone, frankly scares the bajeebees out of me. I'm such a wuss. I could go home, but that's so sad, after looking forward to this vacation for months. STOP!! I tell my clients not to jump to conclusions before they have all the information and I'm falling into the same trap. My cell phone rings jolting me out of my catastrophizing. It's Milly and she doesn't sound upbeat. "Hi Lisa, my mom has taken a turn for the worse. She had another heart attack and is on a respirator. I have to stay here with her."

"Of course you do."

"I'm sorry. I know you're there all alone. What will you do? Will you come home? Will you stay? If you stay, I'll pay my half of the room. It's the least I can do. I know how expensive the Coronado is."

"Don't be silly, I'll be fine. I'm a big girl, I can handle this. I'll just have to decide what I want to do. You need to focus on your mom."

My mind's swimming. What **am** I going to do? Why is this happening? Poor Milly she must be beside herself with worry.

"Milly, don't worry about me. You're in my prayers. I'll stay in touch, ok?"

"Thanks Lisa, I'm worried about her." Her voice begins to crack and she catches herself from crying. "I'll call back when I have more news."

"Take care, Mil."

"I will, bye for now."

Now, what am I going to do! The tears begin to fall. I'm all alone in a city I don't know, 3,000 miles away from home, in a suite I can't afford, and I'm supposed to be enjoying my vacation. Well, there's nothing I can do tonight, except worry. Tomorrow I will have to make a decision. The salty air makes sleep come fast and I welcome the escape from my dilemma.

The birds' singing rouse me out of a dream that seems significant. I'm standing at a canyon looking across to the other side. On the other side is a deer, a hart, and it is looking at me. I decide I can talk to it, so I yell across the canyon. I tell it how beautiful it is. It's the most beautiful hart I've ever seen. I ask if it can also talk to me and it paws the ground. Its eyes are not deer eyes but human eyes, and it smiles at me. Then it turns its head slightly as if beckoning, but I can't cross the canyon, there's no bridge. I stand there feeling frustrated that I cannot follow the hart as it bounds off. I awake and I don't move, lest the dream fade. The dream tells me what I want to do. The question is whether the Hotel del Coronado will let me out of the week commitment we made. I dress and pack and head for the management offices. Mr. Graham graciously invites me into his office and offers me a chair. He says he hopes the Del has lived up to its reputation and asks if my two friends are enjoying themselves too. Wow, they really know their guests. However, what he doesn't know is my two friends are not with me. I explain my situation, fighting back tears, I don't think he saw them. Even if he did...so what? Mr. Graham is very gracious. He agrees to let me pay for last night only and check out today. He even gives me a complementary breakfast. He also offers to reduce my per night cost by changing me from a suite to a room, if I want to stay for the week. I spent over $700 for the suite and last night's dinner. When your guests are paying an enormous amount per night, you can afford to be gracious when they have an unforeseen event. I feel relief to be out from under the week's commitment. Mr. Graham politely inquires what I intend to do during the rest of my week of vacation. I already knew, but I hadn't given words to my plan yet, so in Mr. Graham's compassionate presence I make a decision that will change my life, I'm following my hart (heart)... "I'm going to keep my rental car and drive to the Grand Canyon and explore the area." Mr. Graham asks (politely of course) if he could offer a few suggestions and he pulls out a map of the area. He recommends I see the San Diego Wild Animal Park on my way to Kingman, Arizona where I will spend the night. He tells me about a Best Western in the town, the only motel in the town, and he promises to make a reservation for me. The next morning, I can drive to the south rim of the Grand Canyon. Then follow the south rim east, stopping at the look outs along the way until I get to the end of the road. I will turn left and drive across the Painted Desert. I began to get tingles up and down my spine thinking about the desert. Then he shows me how to drive to the North Rim in time for sunset. "A must see!" he says. He recommends the Lodge at the North Rim and also will make a reservation for me there. Then he recommends I drive to Lake Powell and take the boat ride and stay the night in the town near Lake Powell. "You must see Monument Valley." He moves his yellow highlighter moves across the map showing me the path to take. Finally, I was to drive back the way I came, and then head west and see Bryce and Zion Canyons, and he shows me where to stay all along the way. From Zion, I have a long trip back the final day to San Diego, but I must see London Bridge and the Sand Dunes.

Looking at the map, I marvel at what I will see in the next six days. More importantly I'm more convinced than ever that this is what I'm meant to do. Alert! Insight! This is the trip I was trying to put together months ago when I decided to go on a vacation. But, I allowed myself to be side-tracked by well-meaning friends who wanted to go on vacation with me. The only glitch (psychologically speaking) to this plan is I will be totally alone for the next six days and I will be driving many miles. Fear, anxiety, trepidation wash over me, yet I also feel energy...and excitement...and anticipation. Looking down at the map with the yellow highlighted lines illustrating the way like a stream of yellow sunshine lighting my path, I heard words (not a voice, thank God) in my head. "You won't be alone. I am going to be with you." Or was it Mr. Graham?

I need to check this out. "What? Mr. Graham did you say something?"

He looks up puzzled and he's on the phone arranging my lodging for each night. (My imagination is running away with me.)

With his contacts and knowledge of the area, he was able to accomplish in 15 minutes what would have taken me all morning to do. It appears everyone knows Mr. Graham.

"Mr. Graham, I cannot tell you how grateful I am for your understanding and your help. You are a gift from God!"

He smiles and says it was his pleasure, asks me to consider returning with my friends to San Diego and staying at the Del in the near future. I agree. Jeeves! How could I not agree! The man is amazing. Everyone ought to perform their jobs with the same kindness and helpfulness Mr. Graham does. What a saint!

I pack the rental car (actually the bell hop packs my car), stop on my way out of San Diego, and buy a cooler with water and other drinks, and begin a trip that might change my life, though I have no idea why I feel this way, just do. Kingman, Arizona is only three or four hours away, and Mr. Graham recommended I stop at the San Diego Wild Animal Park on my way. He said it would put me in the mood to be out in nature. The Animal Park was fabulous, and I spend way too much time there. It's 3:30 and I still have a three plus hour drive. When I left on this personal pilgrimage, I promised myself I would stop before dark.

The drive to Kingman took me into the Wild West in a matter of an hour. The rocks became boulders and the red earth became spires and small canyons. I was in love. I spoke out loud, "We have nothing like this in the East." Words filled my head. "You ain't seen nothin' yet." I didn't look around to see if someone was in the car with me, I'm getting use to hearing myself think, at least I hope it's me. What if it isn't? What if I'm becoming psychotic? Am I hearing voices for the first time in my life? What if I am possessed? Or, what if I have a nasty non-human being hanging around.....WHOA, Lisa. Slow down. Just enjoy the ride and let the trip unfold. Breathe, that's it.

I arrive at the Best Western at 7 p.m. and check in. I ask the lady behind the counter where I can grab a bite to eat and she looks at me as if I have two heads. "Honey, all our eateries are closed by now."

"Oh, no!" I exclaimed. "I'm hungry."

"Well, I know you've come a long way already, but if you think you can drive 20 miles more, there is a saloon in Oatman. It is just down Route 66."

Is she kidding me? Twenty miles = twenty minutes. And how cool is it to drive on the famous Route 66 and eat in a saloon? What else do I have planned? "How do I get there?"

She tells me, and as I'm leaving, she yells with her hand to her mouth "Watch out for the wild burrows. Don't touch 'em and go slow. They sometimes stand in the middle of the road." Burrows? Great! I make the left turn onto Route 66. The first mile was easy and then the hairpin turns start. I can't do 60 miles an hour on Rt. 66. It has twists and turns around huge boulders and hills. And it's two lanes of rural road. I saw a documentary recently about the famous Route 66 and I know it's an old highway that connects Chicago to Los Angeles. It was built in the 1920s, but I never considered that **this** is what they considered a "highway" back then. The sun is getting low, but I figured if I drive it once in the daylight then I would be more knowledgeable about getting back to Kingman in the dark. Beside the road are interesting old gold and silver mines that looked exactly like they did when they were built in the 1880's. One said "Keep well clear." Another said, "Don't even think about it!" There's desert brush and tumbleweed and I love it. I find a station that's playing music from the 1950's and 60s and everything is perfect.

Oatman suddenly appears. It is a town that was built in the late 1880s. It looks exactly the way an old-west town would look back then. This town is not a re-furbished town for tourists. This is the real deal with hitching posts, a post office, hotel, and saloon. And there in the middle of the street is a brown burrow eating something on the main street. The sign says Oatman, Arizona, Elevation 2700 feet. There's no one in sight, but the saloon is open and there's one other car parked out front. The saloon is perfect! Wooden tables, long bar, and only a few people in the place. The bartender nods toward one of the many tables and I sit down. A couple of tables to my right is a family of four, parents and two elementary school kids. To my left is a man who looks like he hasn't shaved in three days and he's passed out on the table. I think of Bally. His friend is downing a beer and flirting with a woman who's wearing a white blouse with fringe hanging from the sleeves and a seriously plunging neckline. She has on very tight, and very skimpy, red jean shorts, fishnet stockings, and four inch platform cowgirl boots highlighted with more fringe. She looks to be in her 50s, 5' 3" and weighs about 160-175 pounds. As I look in their direction, in an attempt not to stare, but to really take in the atmosphere of having stepped back in time, the bartender rounds the bar, approaches my table, and sits down. "What will ya' have, little lady?" I almost laugh at his accent, until I realize he's serious, this is who he is. It isn't an act. The "town drunk" is real, the prostitute is real, and the saloon is real. I'm dreaming, but they are real. "What do you have?" I asked. "Saloon stuff." He answers with a cute wide grin. "Hamburgers, steaks, hotdogs, fries, stuff like that."

When in Rome do as the Romans. When in Oatman eat like the cowboys. I order a hamburger, fries, and a chocolate shake. He nods, writes nothing down and leaves for the kitchen. I lean back in my chair and begin to feel the tears of pure delight sting my eyes. I would have missed all this if I had taken the easy road and took the first plane back to the East Coast. The passage "a road less traveled" comes to mind.

I don't feel lonely or alone. I feel alive, connected with myself and the world and I want more and say so… to myself. Don't want to be seen talking to myself in Oatman, Arizona! The words flow again. "Hang on, its going to be quite a trip." Was I going crazy? Am I hearing things? Or, am I really listening for the first time in my life. The noise of the world blots out any real messages and they can't get through. Instead of worrying about the many things that could go wrong or whether I would find the next place to stay, I just need to let the trip unfold. I need to let go and let God, lead. God. God. Is all this being orchestrated so I can have my heart's desire? Or is it being orchestrated so I can have the opportunity to really connect with the Creator and this guide, whoever He/She is? Maybe it's me! Or maybe it's my daughter? Could I dare to hope? Have I really been far away from my spiritual center, too crowded with life? "YES!" The words again. But, now they are becoming comfortable and even comforting. "Thank you God. Are they yours?" Why does it matter? The hamburger, fries, and shake arrive and I realize how hungry I am. Not just for food, but for the real thing, not the plasticized, artificial food I am used to but the real hamburger, fresh cut fries from real potatoes, and a shake made with real milk, and real ice cream. I close my eyes half way and eat. And I feel held, cuddled, and loved. "Whoever you are, thank you." I pay my bill and leave as the bartender tells me to "be careful out there." I wave back and get in my car, drive around the persistent burrow (who's still eating his or her way through town) and two other burrows that are just entering town. Once out of Oatman, I drive into the pitch black night on Route 66. No street lights for the next 20 miles back to Kingman. The moon is my only light. It's so peaceful and breathtaking. Tears fall down my cheeks all the way back to my small hotel room, but I'm not crying, just leaking. As I'm falling asleep, I laugh. Last night I spent the night at the Hotel del Coronado and had an elegant suite. Tonight I am four steps from the bathroom and the bedspread is worn thin. Which one feels real to me?

The birds woke me up at the Del. Today, the maid's cart rolling past my door is my alarm clock. Yesterday I saw the Pacific Ocean.

Today, I see the Grand Canyon! I turn on the radio and drive. When I'm 25 miles outside of Kingman, my radio dies. At first, I think I've lost the signal because I'm in the middle of wherever, but then a sign indicates it's only 15 miles to Flagstaff. The radio did indeed die. I'm tempted to stop in Flagstaff and buy a radio to keep me company. A conversation with myself ensues about why the radio died and perhaps I need to stop reacting to things that happen with an "I can fix this" attitude and start believing if the radio died, it's ok, and there may be a reason. I might need to listen to something else.

The sheer anticipation of seeing something as grand and well known as the Grand Canyon can set one up for disappointment. But not for me. I stand at the South Rim and have to catch my breath. I keep opening my mouth to say something about its grandeur and beauty, but nothing comes out that befits its magnificence. I cannot wrap my mind around how big it is. The depth and breadth are mind boggling. And the COLORS! Oh my God, the COLORS. How could I have lived this long and not seen this? How could I raise two children and not bring them here? Would they have been as awestruck as I am now? I doubt it. To enjoy the Canyon, you have to put yourself in its spell and sit and smell it, listen to it, drink it in through you pores. Being with others would have usurped my personal relationship with the canyon.

I allow the canyon to **be** with me, but I'm unable to grasp its immenseness. It's simply too big to comprehend. A plane ride around the canyon allows me to get closer and deeper into its center, but still it's simply too big to assimilate. I wish I had the time to take a donkey ride down to the bottom and camp there. Perhaps then I would feel a kinship with this magnificent canyon. Even, then, there is so much more to the canyon. I would have only explored a fraction of it. I drive slowly along the south rim and stop at every overlook. If other people had been with me, I would have been driving them crazy with the frequent stops and my grappling with the words to describe it. No, this is a place I needed to see alone. The Canyon becomes your lover, your friend, your family. Others would have only gotten in the way of the relationship that the canyon is building with me.

At one of the stops, I see kids climbing 20-30 feet down its face while their parents talk and point at different parts of the canyon. A sign says, "Danger! Keep off!" One slip and one of these children would be gone forever. The park ranger says it happens every year. How can they be so cavalier with their precious children? They don't know how painful it is to lose a child? They think it won't happen to them. They're wrong. I want to scream at them to take better care of their kids, but I know this is my "stuff" to work on. The parents of these children will have their lives and calamities to bear. Theirs will simply be different from mine. Let go, let go.

As I drive out of the Canyon Park I come to the road that takes me through the Painted Desert. As directed, I turn left. The scenery changes instantly as if the desert demarcates the eastern end of the canyon. At first the desert's colors look tan and boring but as my eyes begin to adjust and see the subtle hues, the colors emerge as I drive deeper and deeper into its heart. I stop along the side of the road and take a picture of a blue and mauve rock. It's hot, probably 110 degrees, but I don't care. I feel alive in this desert.

I have been in a spiritual desert for many years. The divorce, the deaths of my daughter, my two aunts, my uncle, and my best friend, have all taken their toll. I'm a good therapist, but I'm living a desert life. The living desert is now my teacher. It teaches me to enjoy being alone, to listen to the voice inside me, to hear God's voice. Living in my personal desert has not taught me the wisdom I need to learn so I can live again. Perhaps this desert, the one God painted, will teach me. I listen to the desert fathers and mothers and ask them to help me, protect me, and teach me. I feel a cooler breeze on my face. Each part of the journey holds a specific key that opens another room in my heart. Just as I feel "this is it! I am fully alive", the next turn in the road presents me with more delight.

The desert ends at the Vermillion Cliffs and Marble Canyon and I turn left again to go to the North Rim of The Canyon. I sense the air is getting cooler as the desert fades away and the lush forest takes its place. There are deer, raccoons, and rabbits crossing the road at various intervals, as if to say "welcome"! I barely make it to the lodge, where I will spend the night, in time to see the sun set. Everyone who was inside the lodge is out on the veranda overlooking the North Rim. I can see across to the South Rim where I was standing hours before. The colors are brilliant and they change from blues, to greens, to golds, to pinks as the sun dips further and further into the Canyon. Over a hundred people are standing there witnessing the event of this day, an event that's been occurring for millions of years. No one speaks a word as if we are in church. The silence shows respect and awe for this magnificent event. The spirituality of the moment brings goose bumps that have nothing to do with the chilly air. Then the sun is gone and the Canyon is grey and everyone applauds the magnificent event that seems to have occurred especially for each one of us.

And then the chatter begins. As I turn to leave the veranda-deck, I see the family with the children who were climbing down the Grand Canyon's side where the sign warned of danger. They made it! Why did I become overwhelmed with fear for them?

I miss my daughter every day. I feel the ache of her loss every day. But here at the North Rim, I don't feel the ache and loss. I feel her standing beside me. How many times has she stood beside me, and I couldn't feel her presence because I was too busy, too wordy, too distracted. I need to be quiet, to listen, to hear, to feel. All is as it should be. I have not felt this peace since her death. For me, life has not been what it should be, what I thought it would be, but here, having been virtually silent for over 24 hours, I know everything is as it should be. And I feel the need to cry and laugh all at once. She is ok and I am ok. I can still miss her and regret I will never see her married, nor will I enjoy any grandchildren that she may have given me, but everything feels ok.

The Native Americans believe that this area that I am exploring is a spiritual place and I believe that now. I feel holy just standing here. As a Christian, I have attended church all my life, but I have never felt closer to God than at this minute. "You ain't seen nothin' yet." The voice, again. I laugh out loud and draw attention. I don't like to be inappropriate in public, but it doesn't matter, here. I felt like laughing and I did. Everything is as it should be.

Dinner and sleep. I haven't slept this soundly in years. Is it the air, the spiritual aliveness of this place, the quiet? Who cares? Everything is as it should be. And I feel gratitude.

Today's 'agenda' is to see Glen Canyon and Monument Valley. Glen Canyon is actually a lake. The Native Americans own the land and the U.S. owns the lake. I bet that was an interesting negotiation 100 years ago. The tour guide keeps looking at me as if I'm an alien. He's amazed I'm alone and says this a couple of times. Everyone else on the boat has a family or friend, except me. If this had happened three days ago, I would have shrunk back into a shell, but now I feel that this is where I should be and I don't care whether it fits into others' ways of conceiving how the world is suppose to work. He points out where the Planet of the Apes was filmed etc, etc. I just want to "be" here, and so I block out the jokes and the history and just love the trip. We stop at Rainbow Bridge and as I walk to the bridge, I see a fossil in the rock, but no one stops to notice but me. I see hieroglyphics, but no one notices but me. If I had been with Maggie and Millie I would not have noticed either. I know I'm trained to notice things, but now I see how much I really miss by surrounding myself with noise.

Monument Valley looks like the scenery in every John Wayne cowboy movie ever made. In fact, I read last night as I was preparing for today's sights, that he loved this area and most of his movies were actually shot in Monument Valley. The geologists think the monuments were once huge mountains that have been worn away by the wind, leaving strange looking monoliths sticking straight out of the sand. One looks like a glove, another like a steeple on a church. "God, how amazing your world is. And you did this! You set the elements in place to create this wonderful land. I can feel your power here. Why can't I feel it when I sit with Bally or Noelle? I can feel YOU here. I feel peace here. I feel love. I have to bottle this and take it home. I need to use this experience to become a better mental health professional, a better mother to my son, a better person of God. You're teaching me so much so quickly I cannot take it in. It's as if you are changing me with every mile I drive. 'Thank you' does not seem to say enough, but I know that 'thank you' is all you need to hear from me. No, that's not true, "I love you!"

The drive to Bryce and Zion gives me time to ponder what I have experienced. When I was on the Glen Canyon boat and listened to people talk to each other, or watched parents with their children at the canyon, I realized that you can look at these areas in several ways. One can simply see the sights, sightseeing. Or one can see them as learning experiences and enjoy the intellectual information about the various formations. Or one can romp and play through the canyons, parks, and valleys. Or one can drink them, ingest them, breathe them. If one only sees sights, learns intellectual information, or plays, then, upon arriving back home the words used to describe the sights would be, "It was great! Did you know that...?" We did the greatest thing...". However, if you let this land teach you in the depth of your soul, then you will never be able to explain it to other people. The experiences become transformative as well as unexplainable. But given the choice, I embrace the last option even though I have to be alone to experience it and when I describe my trip to others, they will not be able to "get it". They will nod and say how great it sounds, but they will not be able to understand unless they have had a similar experience. I have to recognize that in order for me to be at this place in my life, experiencing this incredible journey, certain things had to happen, God had to put certain events into place at the right time and I had to be open to staying here and listening. And when I heard the words in my head, I had to embrace them and not be quick to dismiss them. What a gift I have been given. Now, the challenge is to discover how to use the enlightenment. I know I will never be the same again. "Wait, you ain't seen nothin' yet, my love." This time I speak out loud and respond, "I look forward to what you have to teach me."

The entrance to Bryce is like driving into a fairy land. The road becomes magenta and the walls are various colors of red, orange, and pink. Many parking areas make it possible for visitors to climb down and explore the formations, as well as look at the hoodoos. The spires are fascinating and each has a theme or story to tell. Stopping and discovering the shapes is like looking at clouds on a summer day and seeing shapes and animals, only this time, the animals are made of rocks and dirt. Of course I am taking pictures throughout my trip, but I know, when I return, people will flip through them and remark how beautiful they are but will not be able to experience them as I have. Pictures are poor imitations of the real thing; the real energy of this part of our world must be personally experienced. I can almost imagine God, Jesus, the Angels et al. planning this out and laughing as they designed the monuments, the arches, the Grand Canyon, the spires. I can hear them saying, "Oh, what if we put this there and let the wind come through and carve this. Wouldn't that be so neat?" Well, maybe not quite that colloquial, but it feels like God had a lot of fun designing these sculptures where the earth is color of a baby's lips.

Driving out of Bryce Canyon feels sad because my final big "sight" is Zion, and then I will be heading back to San Diego to catch my flight home. However, I feel Zion may be holding a gift for me. I don't know why I believe it, but I do, and if I have learned one thing on this trip, it's to go with my gut.

The entrance into Zion is not for the faint of heart or those with claustrophobia. A mile long dark tunnel through a mountain and then hairpin turns take me down a mountainside a mile high into a valley. The temperature change is a remarkable 20 degrees cooler. The canyon of Zion is a blind canyon. There is one way in and one way out of the canyon. The drive into the park puts with the river on the left and the wall on the right. At the end of the canyon, there is a u-turn and the river is now on the left and the wall of the canyon is on the right. Wild life abounds. I park and get out of my car and stand with my back up against the canyon wall to take a picture of the three patriarchs which are enormous rock formations that guard the canyon.

Aiming my camera high to capture the majesty of the patriarchs, a feeling sweeps over me and I lower my camera. A tingling sensation starts in my head and moves through me to my toes. Soon all my feelings are percolating and the torrent of emotion is threatening to sweep me away like a flash flood through this precious canyon. The tears start slowly and build until I have to sit down. Sitting on the canyon floor with my back against the wall I realize that I'm finally "experiencing" a canyon, the way I could not at the humongous Grand Canyon. This canyon I can touch. I can wade in its water. I can see the deer and fox. Flashes of painful life experiences and joyous occurrences are like a slide show in my mind. Then they stop and all is calm. The insight is imprinted on brain and heart instantaneously and leaves me speechless. God is so great, so immense, like the Grand Canyon, that we cannot "know" God while we are in a human body. The enormity is overwhelming. But, Zion lets me feel and see, taste, and smell a canyon. That's why God sent Jesus, in human form, so we can know God. He was human and touchable and we can have a relationship with God who is in human form. Jesus said, "Know me know my father." This insight grabs my heart and won't let go. I know I'm making a fool of myself, sitting there crying with my camera in my lap, but I don't care. People pass by and look and respect my right to cry. No one says, "Are you alright?" It's as if they too have sensed the holiness of this place, and they know what I'm feeling. Perhaps they thought I was a nut case. So be it. I was brought here for this moment and if I want to cry, I will cry, and I did freely, unabashedly, unapologetically. I feel much love and peace and it overwhelms me. The tears give voice to those feelings. I will never be the same again. And somehow, with this knowledge, my life will change because I am changing. At this moment, I also know that this is the first of many trips that I will take alone. I must continue what has begun this week. I must make a pact with myself and God that I will spend a week every year alone with my best friend, the one that created and is creating this world and me.

After many minutes, how many, I do not know, nor do I care, I feel myself calming and I leave Zion. A small gift shop beckons as I exit the canyon and decide to stop to get a souvenir. The tinkling of the bell announces that the crying lunatic has arrived. I forget to check out what my face looks like since I've been crying and have tears staining my face. The shop owner comes out of the back of the shop, takes one look at me, and says "Just been to Zion?" I wipe the tears away and she continues without my prompting. "People come from all over the world to see The Grand, Bryce, and Zion. They frequently come here with tear tracks. This is a very holy place. That's why when I came here 20 years ago, I stayed."

I must admit I'm tempted to stay. Even people in this holy place must need a therapist! But then, no, this place needs to be special, a place to connect and to be in awe, not a place for me to live and work, lest I take it for granted and it becomes mundane. I never want that to happen. I need Zion and my experiences of her to stay special.

The drive back to San Diego allows me to settle. I drive through Lake Havasu and see the London Bridge (I actually drive across it), and the desert with its enormous sand dunes are very interesting and impressive, but I can feel my body shifting and my spirit is growing. I have a lot more to process, but the cake is in the oven. There is no turning back. I'm hooked on plugging in and connecting with my Creator. This may sound trite, but I have always loved God, but now I am in love with God. Will anyone understand? Is the difference noticeable? This week has been transformative, and what will I be like when I get back to "the real world?" My sense is I will be a more centered, quieter person. That may mean I won't be as much fun. I don't know. But when I'm back in Maryland and I resume my life, this experience must change how I experience my daily life. The trite, trivial, and silly parts of life may bore me. At least, that's what I'm feeling now. Perhaps I'm wrong. But I don't think so. I'm forever changed, and I will take these changes into my work and into my personal life. And if life gets too difficult I have a place to visit in my heart, Zion.

Bally's Message

While I was traveling the canyons, Bally called and left a message on my voicemail. She wanted me to know her mother died in the Philippines and she started drinking. "You know alcoholics, any excuse to fall off the wagon will do!" She says that she's almost ready to be discharged and she feels strong again. She has decided to live in the Portland area, paint, and work at a mindless job for awhile before she starts her career search again. Also, she wanted me to know she's sorry she disappointed me, she learned a lot and will be 'perpetually grateful.'

Returning home, I also found out that Milly's mom was recovering at home and Maggie's feeling great. I was relieved to hear that both were on the mend. No client emergencies had occurred and a couple of referrals had been made to me. The world hadn't stopped during the week I was in the canyons I only felt it had.

Caz
Termination

Caz continues to touch base once a month and pays me out of his earnings. He has a thriving handyman service that allows him to monitor and regulate his energy level by only working 25 hours a week. Caz is amazed at how much he is needed and how much money he's making. He loves working for the elderly. Most of them are grateful for the help. They pay him and they make lunch for him or give him dinner to take home. One lady makes cookies for him every time she sees him in her neighborhood. He has two subdivisions of customers and he always has plenty of work, but he doesn't allow the pressure to overwhelm him. During one session, he decides he should pay his father a little rent but his father refuses, appreciating that the meals Caz brings home more than makes up for any rent Caz would pay.

I notice that Caz is growing up. The 10 year old persona is seldom present. He emerges every now and then when Caz is teasing or complaining, but the now 31 year old man is mostly evident. Caz notices it too. He comments one day that he's taking responsibility for his life.

In another session, Caz brings up his half-brother. I was wondering if he had been in contact with Jake when he was in Chambers. Caz reports his grandmother is keeping in touch with Jake, and I listen as Caz carefully describes his relationship with Jake. Caz is neither overly attaching nor pushing Jake away. He is establishing the relationship slowly and cautiously. Caz says, "I know I was excited to have another brother, but to tell you the truth, I don't know this man. I could glob on to him and play the dependent brother role, but I'm fighting that impulse. Jake seems like a nice person and he and I will continue to do things together, but I'm treating him like a new friend not a brother for the time being." Caz pauses, "When thinking about Jake, I wondered about something that plagued me for awhile: If my Mom had AIDS, then I wondered if Jake does."

"And what did you learn?"

"He didn't contract AIDS from my mom."

"You were cautious about establishing a relationship and then losing him?"

"Yeah, I don't want to appear selfish, but I just couldn't handle another loss right now. I mean, I would support him if he was ill, but I would have to take real good care of myself. Does that make me sound uncaring?"

"What do you think?"

"I gotta take care of me for now. Jake has heard about my past, and he, too, is being cautious. I think he may feel that I could overwhelm him with my neediness."

"Nice processing, Caz."

"You think? Huh. Thanks."

After another few months, Caz dropped to every other month sessions. He was too busy to keep coming every month. Then the biggest change of all occurred when Caz decided to take a vacation by himself. He loved the Grand Canyon and he wanted to see Yellowstone National Park. I couldn't believe what I was hearing. Caz, the dependent who couldn't get out of bed in the morning two years ago, was going to travel almost all the way across the country to Wyoming and spend six days by himself. I certainly could relate, and I smiled inside wondering what his experience would be like.

He came back and spent an entire session telling me every detail of his trip. He fell in love with traveling and said he was going to take a trip like that every year. He was going to see the world, but he was starting with the States.

After another six months, Caz revealed he had decided he was gay after all. He had to work on his theology of homosexuality and Pastor Craig helped him with this. I wasn't privy to the conversations they had, but Caz kept referring to the good book. I thought he was talking about the Bible when he corrected my misperception by telling me that there is a book called *The Good Book* and it helped him to see homosexuality in a different light. I bought the book and read it, and I must admit the author makes a fascinating, well-grounded argument.

Caz doesn't need to be in counseling anymore, but he keeps coming anyway. I think he likes to spend one hour every now and then recapping his progress. The flashbacks are mostly gone, and the anxiety only occurs when too many people are demanding his services. He has had to say 'no' or 'not until' to his clients, and, at first, he was afraid they wouldn't like him anymore. Instead, he found when he says 'not until' to his clients, most of them are grateful he is putting them on his calendar. One day, several weeks ago Caz said, "These elderly people need help. I sometimes feel a little resentful that they are so dependent and needy because they can become demanding."

I wanted to laugh, but then realized he was serious, and he didn't know he was talking about himself a couple of years ago. I failed to share my insight with him at that moment. I didn't want to rain on his parade. A couple of months later Caz came to counseling with a smile. He said he had an insight and shared with me why he was feeling a little resentful of his elderly clients being so needy, dependent, and demanding. With a smile on his face, he told me they reminded him of **himself** two years earlier. I smiled with him and kept my mouth shut.

The last time I saw Caz, he was more than ready to quit counseling. By this time Caz was working 30 hours a week and had hired an assistant. Caz approached his last session as if he were apologizing. He stated he felt strong enough to terminate, but always wanted to have the option of returning. Of course, I agreed and he smiled and said, "Thank you." His father had remarried and his brother had married. Caz had purchased a house of his own and was renovating it himself. He said while he knew he was gay, he had no desire for a partner at this time in his life. He was scared that having homosexual sex would cause the flashbacks to reoccur and he was very comfortable where he was in his life. His family was pushing him to date and find someone, but Caz wanted to maintain his celibacy. I had come to trust his judgment and let him know that if he changes his mind, I was always available for a consultation or a referral to a gay therapist if he felt it would help him.

As Caz was leaving, he began to cry. This time the tears weren't the huge, sobbing tears of the past but tears of celebration and gratitude for how far he had come. As he left my office he handed me a card. In the card were a poem and a single pearl he had picked up in the Philippines.

How do you say "Thank you" to someone who
listened even when she was tired of listening?

How do you say "Thank you" to someone who
pissed you off by nudging you forward when you
didn't want to move?

How do you say "Thank you" to someone who
stood beside you in the worst moments of your
life and said, "You can do it?"

How do you say "Thank you" to someone who
made room in her schedule for an extra 50
minutes when you need it?

How do you say "Thank you" to someone who
hangs in there with you when others want to hang
you?

How to you say "Thank you" to someone who
didn't see you as damaged, but only a mentally
gritty and helped you smooth the edges to become
a pearl?

You don't. You only say, "God bless you, Lisa."

Tears inform me of the power of change as I hold the pearl and
the poem in my hands, and I think back to the Boy/Man who was
so hurt and suffering, who stood up to his abuser, and within a
couple of years was successful and thriving. I think about Noelle
who didn't want to be in counseling and yet used it to make her
dreams change from gray to vibrant colors. And I think about
Bally, who had everything in her grasp, like a halfback who reaches
for a pass and is able to touch it with his fingertips, but can't get a
strong enough grip to bring the ball into his hands, so it tentatively
bounces on his fingertips and then falls to the ground. Bally had

her sobriety and future at the edge of her fingertips and let it all fall away from her with one Green Apple Martini. What a process therapy is! I think back to myself as a 22 year old who was going to be a great elementary school teacher, to my marriage, to my changing careers, to the death of my daughter, to the divorce, and my trip to the canyons. My rainbow is now colored brilliantly and each event helped to shape it. I'm not so different from my clients. Each of us has a journey that can destroy us or can make us wise. It's not about who gets to have a perfect life, but who allows life to perfect us. I hold the pearl, turning it over in my fingers and I inadvertently drop it from my fingertips and watch as it rolls under my sofa. Should I let it go or turn the sofa upside-down to find it? I retrieve the pearl.

Holding it tightly so as not to lose it again, I pick up the phone and make the call that I've been putting off since my daughter died, the PhD that slipped through my fingers. I dial the number of my doctoral program and ask what I need to do in order to complete my dissertation. I'll not let go of this real pearl from Caz, nor the pearl of a PhD that I have always valued and never grasped.

Suggested Readings

American Psychiatric Association. (2000) *Diagnostic and Statistical Manual of Mental Disorders, 4th ed. Text Revision.* Arlington, Virginia: APA.

Bass, E., & Davis, L. (1988). *The courage to heal: A guide for women survivors of child sexual abuse.* New York: Perennial.

Bendiksen, R., & Fulton, R. (1975). Death and the child: An anterospective test of the childhood bereavement and later behavior disorder hypothesis. *Omega, 6,* 45-59.

Bowlby, J. (1998). *A secure base: Clinical implications of attachment theory.* London: Routledge.

Beck, Aaron. (1976). *Cognitive therapy and the emotional disorders.* New York:Meridian.

Brisch, Karl H. (2002). *Treating Attachment Disorders: From theory to therapy.* New York: Guilford Press.

Caloff, D. (1993). Conference speaker, "Advances in treating survivors of sexual abuse: Empowering the healing process II." Reston, VA.

Campbell, Joseph. (ed.) (1971). *The portable Jung.* New York: Penguin Books.

Ellis, Alfred & MacLaren, Catherine. (2005) *Rational emotive behavior therapy: A therapist's guide.* Atascadero, CA: Impact Publisher.

Erikson, E. (1950). *Childhood and society.* New York: Norton.

Herman, Judith. (1997). *Trauma and recovery: The aftermath of violence – from domestic abuse to political terror.* New York: Basic Books.

Holmes, T. H., & Rahe, R. H. (1967). The social readjustment rating scale. *Journal ofPsychosomatic Research, 11(2),* 213-218.

Glasser, W. (1965). *Reality therapy: A new approach to psychiatry.* New York: Harperand Row.

Gomes, Peter, J. (1996). *The good book: Reading the Bible with mind and heart.* SanFrancisco: Harper Collins.

Hood, R. W., Spilka, B., Hunsberger, B., & Gorsuch, R. (1996). *The psychology of religion: An empirical approach.* New York: The Guilford Press.

Janoff-Bulman, R. (1992). *Shattered assumptions: Toward a new psychology of trauma.* New York: The Free Press.

Lew, Michael. (2004). *Victims no longer: The classic guide for men recovering from sexual child abuse.* New York: HarperCollins Publishing Co.

Mc Bride, J. Lebron. (1998). *Spiritual crisis: Surviving trauma to the soul.* New York: Haworth Press Inc.

Meichenbaum, Donald. (1977). *Cognitive-behavioralmodification: An integrative approach.* New York: Plenum Press.

Miller, William, & Rollnick, Stephen. (2002) *Motivational interviewing: Preparing people for change.* New York: The Guilford Press.

Nouwen, H. (1979). *The wounded healer: Ministry in contemporary society.* New York: Doubleday.

Nye, R. D. (1986). *Three psychologies: Perspectives from Freud, Skinner, and Rogers.3rd ed.* New York: Brooks/Cole.

Rogers, Carl. (1942). *Counseling and psychotherapy.* Boston: Houghton Mifflin.

Rando, T. (1984). <u>Grief, Dying, and Death.</u> Champaign, IL: Research Press.

Russell, D. E. H. (1986). *The secret trauma: Incest in the lives of girls and women.* NewYork: Basic Books, Inc.

Scaer, Robert C. (2005). *The trauma spectrum: Hidden wounds and human resiliency.*New York: W.W. Norton & Company, Inc.

Seligman, M. (2004). *Positive psychology in practice.* Hoboken, NJ: John Wiley andSons.

Sweeney, Thomas. (1998). *Adlerian counseling: A practitioner's approach.* Athens,Ohio: Accelerated Press.

van der Kolk, Bessel A., McFarlane, Alexander C., & Weisaeth, Lars. (eds.) (2006).*Traumatic stress: The effects of overwhelming experiences on mind, body, and society.* New York: The Guilford Press.

Printed in the United States
204924BV00001B/1-57/P